SWINGMAN

THE UNFINISHED SONG

A NOVEL BY

JOE EDMONDS

Content Warning
This book contains coarse language and sexual content some readers
may find offensive.
Not recommended for readers under the age of eighteen.

Music "Connection"
A CD of original music was written and produced to complement this book.
Please see Appendix for details.

Wholesale discounts for book orders are available through
Ingram Distributors.

ISBN
978-1-987985-98-6 (softcover)
978-1-987985-97-9 (ebook)

Published in Canada.

First Edition

Part II (Bridge, Last Chorus, and Out)

TABLE OF CONTENTS

Part I (Intro, Verse, Chorus)

Some songs end with heroic splendor; others, with a quivering sigh. And sadly, some remain unfinished, with what *could* have been . . . never to be known.

My son Jason may not have been here to see this book's completion, but his energy and spirit surely helped me find the inspiration to begin, and ultimately, the strength and determination to continue. Although, tragically, his life may be described as an unfinished song, his memory lingers on as a beautiful melody in the hearts of all who were fortunate enough to have known him.

My father was my first music instructor, accompanist, and role model for both stage presence and teaching manner. To this day, I still have people introducing themselves to me after I've performed locally, to ask if my father was Carl Edmonds whom they remembered from their school days: such was his impact on thousands of people in his career as a music teacher and choir director.

This is multi-purpose dedication: to honor my father's memory, and thank him for jumpstarting my life in music; and also, to serve as a form of "disclaimer" that a certain unsavory character in this book not be assumed to represent him. The only ways in which this character resembles my father are in his penchant for joking, and his initial positive musical guidance for his son in the story.

ABOUT THE AUTHOR

*B*orn in London, Ontario, Canada, Joe Edmonds has been a professional musician since 1969, having performed and resided in Toronto, Montreal, Miami, Las Vegas, New York City, and innumerable other locations across North America. His experience has included jazz combos, big bands (including a stint in the world famous Jimmy Dorsey Orchestra), rock bands, "Vegas-style" show bands, and symphony orchestras. During his career he has been privileged to share stages and recording studios with top professionals from around the world as sideman, leader, and producer.

Joe's CD of original music, *Reflection,* has been receiving regular airplay on CBC's Stingray (formerly Galaxie) jazz station since 2007. In 2010 he recorded a CD with multiple-award-winning Skip Prokop, drummer, co-leader, and founder of the legendary jazz/rock band Lighthouse. Out of that recording came the formation of Skip's new band, Smoothside, in which Joe played saxophones, trombone, and flute. In 2012 *Smoothside* won Jazz Album of the Year at the Hamilton Music Awards. Joe's latest recording project, *Swingman,* was produced to coincide with the release of this book. (See Appendix)

When his son Jason was killed in a highly publicized road rage incident in January 2000, Joe decided he had to try to pull something positive from the tragedy. Utilizing his abilities as a public speaker, acquired through years of musical performance, he created a presentation about the dangers of aggressive driving and road rage, which he has presented to over 100,000 listeners at schools and conferences in both Canada and the USA, including the World Health Organization's national and international conferences in 2002.

Joe's flair for writing was evident at age twelve, when he began to bang out poems on his family's ancient Underwood typewriter. By age thirteen, he had completed a collection of short stories, which prompted his teachers to predict a career as an author. As fate would have it, his life plans turned to music, and the book writing dream was replaced by performing and songwriting . . . although throughout his adulthood, he continued to write poetry, and countless articles for magazines and professional association publications.

The latest chapter of Joe's life now has him going back to his earliest artistic ambition, while actually combining the writing of music *and* literature: *Swingman,* the CD . . . and *Swingman,* his first novel. (A second novel, *The Cold Room,* is nearing completion.)

For more information, see Joe's web page: **www.joeedmonds.ca**

ACKNOWLEDGMENTS

MY DEEPEST GRATITUDE TO ALL
WHO HAVE MADE COMPLETION OF THIS BOOK POSSIBLE.

Jim Good,
who took the time to read several early versions of *Swingman* and offered advice and encouragement, which gave me faith in my ability to finish this work. In the later stages of re-writing, editing, and plot development, his suggestions were most valuable. Without doubt, his assistance was instrumental in the completion of this book.

Joan Barfoot,
who took hours of her valuable time to read early versions of my first two novels. Her words about *my* words were truly inspirational and motivating, her comments and suggestions bolstering the belief that I could do this. For a first-time novelist, hearing this from such a highly respected Canadian author was . . . as a jazz musician might say, *most* copacetic.

Cindy Williamson,
who searched tirelessly and relentlessly, multiple times, through the final drafts for spelling, punctuation, grammar, syntax, timeline issues, and historical accuracy: the nuts and bolts of writing. Undaunted by my typical writer's sensitivity to critical suggestions, she could easily be described as my literary Rosie the Riveter.

Anita O'Keefe,
for her professional input and advice on the accuracy and realism of the psychotherapy scenes in the book, and her feedback on characters' responses to emotional trauma and resultant struggles with personality disorders, PTSD, and more.

Gayle Collins,
who helped immeasurably in the early stages of my journey to forging a fictional world: showing, not telling; merciless self-editing; and rewriting, rewriting . . . and more rewriting.

And all the other friends and family who read various drafts and shared their comments as the book approached completion.

PREFACE

Swingman is fiction, woven with threads of reality from a professional musician's life experiences. Although many of the situations in this book were either experienced or witnessed by the author, no individual fictional character or location is based on a real person or place; rather the story is replete with amalgams of actual persons, places, and events.

Several real-life individuals are mentioned in the story, four of whom: Joe Bendzsa*, Lenny Breau, Don Francks, Max Gordon, Buddy Morrow, Buddy Rich, and Margaret Whiting are incorporated into the plot. The historical information is accurate for all; however, the scenes in the story involving Breau and Francks with characters in Swingman are purely fictional, although linked to true historical events. Whiting's and Morrow's scenes are based on actual encounters with the author, while anecdotes involving Buddy Rich are based on stories recounted to the author by former members of Rich's band.

Nightclubs and musical venues depicted in scenes are fictional, with three exceptions: George's Spaghetti House in Toronto, and The Village Vanguard and Roseland Ballroom in New York City.

*A fictionalized segment with my dear friend and band-mate, who passed away a few years ago at age fifty. Joe's tragically shortened life is yet another example of an "unfinished song". How many more years of his brilliant musical gift might we have enjoyed, had he lived longer?

PART I
[INTRO. VERSE. CHORUS]

PRELUDE

FIVE - SOUTH TOWER [1]

*T*he music came from nowhere . . . from everywhere. Floating on breezes stirred by angels' wings, it found its way to the fifth-floor tower of the Broward General Medical Center. Meant not for ears, but for one man's soul, it was not heard, but felt . . . *understood*. Agonizingly unresolved, the sweet melody was sung by ghosts who whispered between the notes, "Join us . . ."

One unfinished song, for another.

♪♪♪

Outside the door to room 510, police officer Stanley Poole glanced at his watch again. "Phew," he sighed, wondering how it could only be five minutes since he'd last checked. Drumming fingers on both arms of his chair, he found it hard to believe this was just the third hour of his second night of guard duty.

While easy exasperation may be a given in a man of his youth, this Ft. Lauderdale cop could have written the book on restlessness—if he could sit still long enough to finish it. This duty was an ordeal for him, not merely because of its inherent boredom, but because it allowed him too much time to reflect on how much he didn't even want to be a cop. Sadly, the book on Stanley Poole was being inked from a well of expectations from his career-cop father.

Officer Poole got up and went across the hall to the visitors' lounge to search once again through the ragged pile of standard hospital waiting room material: *People, National Geographic, Reader's Digest*—nothing new or interesting. As he turned to leave, he noticed the lone occupant of the lounge, a dismal-looking old man, had tossed what he'd been reading onto the chair next to him.

"Mind if I check it out?" Poole asked.

"Go ahead, take it if you want," said the man. "I'm done with it. But you might not want it. Ain't exactly everybody's cup o' tea."

Poole said, "Thank you, sir," and picked up the magazine. "Wow," he said, discovering it was for him a whole *pot* of tea—a treasure—a five-year-old issue of *Guitar Player* magazine.

The young cop was delighted to have found the tattered 1994 musicians' publication. Already beyond bored, with almost a whole night left to sit, he went back to his chair and flipped pages, desperate to find something to activate some brain waves.

Man, only midnight? Wonder if tomorrow night I could sneak my guitar in and practice a bit? Could claim it was music therapy for the patient.

Yeah, right, like I need to get into more shit than I already am. Drawing this duty was bad enough. So I partied hard and didn't make roll call. What was I, a half-hour late? What's next, back to the front desk as glorified receptionist again? Screw that . . . at least I can read here.

If my dad was at this precinct, things would be different. Yeah right, they'd be worse.

Officer Poole thought of returning the magazine to the man in the visitors' lounge, or tossing it back into the periodicals' graveyard. Instead, he gave it another quick look-through.

Missed this issue, I think. Yeah, I don't remember any of these articles. But mostly looks like stuff I already know backwards.

The next page turn made him smile.

Hey, a piece about Lenny Breau? Sweet.

He began to look through the article about the legendary Canadian guitar genius whose celebrity was lamentably enhanced by his untimely demise.

♪♪♪

Lenny Breau was absolutely the best. Man, I didn't realize how young he was when he started playing pro. Still a frigging teenager? And by the time he was twenty, playing big time clubs in Toronto. And just forty-two when he died? Man, only the good, they say. And he crammed in a career to remember, in about the same amount of time that I've been alive.

That sucks. A musician, and his "contract to live" gets terminated so soon. Here I am, a cop, a gig with "danger" in large print, and I'll probably live till I'm like, ninety.

Officer Poole looked at his reflection in the visitors' lounge window and smacked his lips in an impression of his toothless grandfather.

And what a gross end for a great artist like Lenny. They find the poor guy face down in a swimming pool. Damn, I wish I could play my axe right now.

He sighed, picturing that wonderful fifteen minutes in his final year of high school when he'd stolen the show at the annual talent night. Blessed with the ignorance of youth, he had pictured a life replete with such moments—an unwitting validation of Andy Warhol's outlook on fame.

Lenny was so ahead of his time. Did stuff that sounded like three dudes were playing. Maybe I could be as good as him if I had the time to work at it? I gotta quit this job.

Poole began to finger the chords to McCoy Tyner's "Vision", a song Breau had recorded multiple times. As he closed his eyes, the cop drifted into a search for lost dreams. He was yanked back out of Lenny Breau's world by the sound of someone approaching. He pretended to be inspecting his fingernails before looking toward the noise which turned out to be a cleaning cart being pushed by an orderly in green hospital scrubs.

Waving the magazine like a caution flag the cop said, "Hey, hold it there, man. You got clearance?"

"Of course I do," said the orderly without looking up from his cart. "Captain Rosetti said to tell you I'm doing a special cleanup, just the bathroom stuff."

Poole chuckled and said, "But I may have to *use* the can in there, man. Hey, just kidding. Go ahead."

The orderly began to push the cart through the door, clumsily banging the sides as he went. Without turning, he held the door with one hand and said, "Sorry, kinda new at this. I won't be long, thanks. But, you won't be needing in here for real will you? If you mess it up, my boss will think I didn't get it done."

"Don't worry, pal, I'm only jiving you," said the cop, "and hey, if you wanna earn the rookie-orderly-of-the-year award, you better learn to be more quiet."

Officer Poole went back to the Lenny Breau article, quickly forgetting about the awkward orderly. One particular picture of the ill-fated guitar player caught his attention.

Wow, those hands. Looks like he could do brain surgery with those fingers . . . or break your neck. Artistic touch, and strength.

Poole looked at his own hands. *Nah, these mitts are nothing next to his, and I practice every day. I guess you gotta be born with it. Hey, maybe it's my destiny* to record a CD, called "Poole", and dedicate it to Lenny . . . ? Whoa, that makes me shiver.

The cop gripped the magazine in his teeth and stood up to play an air guitar solo, writhing and grimacing to put Jimi Hendrix to shame. Down the hall a nurse walked out of a room and glanced toward Poole's one-man show. He spotted her and dropped into his chair, but not fast enough to avoid a giggle from his one-woman audience. Embarrassment reddened his cheeks and deflated his brief pseudo glory.

What a laugh, that's about all I got in common with Lenny, my last name, and where they found him. Huh, wonder if they're going to say anything more in this rag about what actually happened to him?

His deep sigh turned into a yawn which he only halfheartedly tried to stifle.

Ooh boy, am I tired, and most of my shift still to go. Crap.

Officer Poole yawned again, put down the magazine and stretched. His thoughts drifted to the patient in room 510. As far as he'd been told, there wasn't much chance the guy would be conscious yet.

Wonder what he'll have to say when he wakes up, if he can give a description. Hell, if he even saw who tried to whack him? Anyway, from what I hear it looks like he's going to survive. Better off than poor Lenny. Not fair.

The memory of the orderly's voice and something about his appearance materialized into awareness like headlights looming out of a night fog.

What was it about that guy that seemed "off"? Nervous? Yeah, but there's something else I can't figure out. How he carries himself . . . just, "different". Not a real big guy, but not small either, but "should be"? What the hell? And his voice, kinda soft; not Michael Jackson high, but sure ain't Darth Vader. Weird.

He's not the same one who was here last night. What was that guy's name? Aw shit, I didn't get a good look at this guy's ID badge. Maybe I should go in there and . . .

The thought evaporated as Poole glanced back down at the magazine in his lap. Lenny Breau's picture gripped his attention like ten strong fingers around the neck.

Man, those hands.

♪♪♪

Inside room 510, the orderly closed the door and set aside the cleaning cart. As he stood, staring at the unconscious patient, he wiped his forehead with his sleeve to prevent a second rivulet of sweat from stinging his eye. His lungs were aching; he hadn't breathed since entering the room. Sucking in a chestful of relief, he walked across to the room's solitary bed which was surrounded by medical equipment. There before him lay an unconscious man ensnared in a web of wires, plastic tubing, oxygen line, and mask.

As all strength evaporated from his legs, the orderly collapsed into the chair next to the bed, his mind bobbing amuck in a bubbling cauldron of feelings: fear, sorrow, tension, exhilaration, loathing, and inexplicable fatigue. To accomplish his objective, he knew he had to concentrate on just one of these. He chose loathing.

Motionless, like a stalking lion, he watched the patient in the bed, waiting for signs of impending consciousness. He checked his watch—already one minute gone, and there might be only about ten available. This would be tight.

Feeling a bead of sweat clinging to the tip of his nose like a reluctant suicide, he shook his head, sending the droplet to its splattering demise on his lap. He wondered why the hospital room felt so hot.

It was a long shot, coming here like this, but to be in the room alone at just the right time was crucial. The cop at the door was young and inexperienced—and not by chance—but that didn't ensure he wouldn't do something unexpected. If he came in at the wrong moment, the whole scenario would take on a new, more dangerous tone. Killing a cop wasn't supposed to be part of this. The orderly had no serious grudge against anyone in the world except the man in the bed. But if anyone got in the way now—cop or not—they would suffer the same fate in store for the sleeping son of a bitch in front of him.

The orderly stood and looked down at the patient. Carefully removing the oxygen mask, he inspected the familiar face up close. "Come on, my friend," he said softly as he stroked the patient's forehead with one gentle finger, "you have to hear what I need to say to you."

Was the anticipated moment worth killing for? Worth dying for? Regardless, it had to be *soon*. The first words heard by the patient upon regaining consciousness would also be the last thing he heard.

He so needed the patient to be awake: to know what was going to happen to him, to know fear, to know revenge was about to be unleashed upon him . . . and by whom.

SEGUE

OUT OF TIME

The back of the "open" sign in the front door window doesn't mean the world is closed, but here in the lounge it might seem to be. Unlike *Cheers,* this is a place where *nobody* knows your name, or what thoughts of past or future trouble you most. The hour, the day, and even the year get left at the door. Within these faded walls countless stories abound: various mixtures of truth and myth, joy and sorrow, conquest and collapse—each filled with the songs and dreams which lived and died here.

Stories and songs share two things that dreams may not: a beginning and an ending. What follows is both at once.

♩ ♩ ♪

There are the usual conflicts of sounds and purpose, as gentle jazz struggles through the clinking of glasses, scattered conversation, and occasional laughter from the sparse audience. Surviving this gauntlet of indifference, ragged remnants of melody arrive at the front door and escape into the night—from orchestrated darkness to nature's own. Street noises, seagull squawks, and the moonless sky's infinite solitude swallow up what remains of the notes—born, and gone so soon. There is no time to mourn them; the musicians have moved on. And no one else has noticed they lived at all.

The battered upright piano is "desafinado", slightly out of tune—has been for years—not quite "broke" enough to fix. Equally decrepit and less than upright is the man playing it, his gnarled fingers coaxing notes from yellowed ivory, like a gentle lover trying hard to please. As the drummer brushes cymbals and snare with delicate swishing strokes, the bass player slumps over his instrument, holding its slender neck close to his cheek. He is the spine binding a book from scattered notes and rhythm, pulling simple patterns from the strings, and meaning from the madness.

Like portraits painted in smoke and sickly blue light, the faces of the musicians reveal nothing. The music is their story: new thoughts mixed with old, innovation born of habit—disappearing inexorably into the ether of spent ideas. Wasted on apathetic ears, it weaves an ancient tale of love, fear, ecstasy, and despair into a tapestry: the fabric of their souls.

Barely visible in the shadows to the side of the stage sits a tenor saxophone, collared in its rusty stand like a dog, waiting with infinite patience. The funereal lighting hides the true face of the beast: dents, scant pitted remains of darkened lacquer, discolored mouthpiece, and pads in various degrees of decrepitude. Ugly to most, it might still be beautiful to someone who needs it to be—like a last-chance pickup at closing time, if tired eyes and whiskey's lies can work their magic once again.

From its solitude, you can almost hear the cold silent metal begging for someone to hold it, love it, and let it sing.

CHAPTER 1

LOSERS' LOUNGE

AUGUST 1999 - MIAMI BEACH, FLORIDA

"*T*hat's a saxophone up there, ain't it, honey?" said one of the women at table eight. "We gonna get to hear it, or is it just a planter or somethin'?"

Dixie lowered her order pad and glanced over the top of her reading glasses toward the stage. Through all the years she'd been walking by musicians and their instruments, she'd rarely paid much attention to any of them—except one. She often dreamed of how it might feel to have him caress her the way he did the piano keys. Like her, the instrument was old and weathered, but that didn't seem to discourage him from loving *it*.

Not waiting for an answer, the woman winked and said, "Yeah, a sax. Hmm, that's one sexy instrument all right. Bet it's mighty fine to kiss a guy who plays one o' them, huh?"

Dixie focused back down toward the table and said, "Yeah, whatever. What'll it be ladies?"

♪♪♪

She didn't look as good now as she had from across the room—wasn't that a given? On a busier night the smoke would have been thicker, providing a proper fog to view her through, à la the smudged-up camera lenses on the old *Doris Day Show*. As Al studied the woman from his new vantage point at the bar he wished he had a cigarette, even though he'd never been a smoker. A large puff of camouflage smog would be welcome about now since the sole positive resemblance this woman had to Doris Day—even an *old* Doris— was her blond hair.

She isn't all that bad, said the beer in front of him to the whiskey in his gut. *Don't kid yourself, man. These old eyes, just like the rest of me, aren't too reliable anymore.*

He wondered if the young man standing next to him eyeing the same table would even know who Doris Day was.

What is this guy, twenty-five . . . thirty?

Apparently bar chat bore no boundaries for the man, as he leaned over and said, "Nice tits on that one, huh?"

Al winced. *Christ, no wonder some women say "all men are scum". They hate that word, and so do I. "Tits", yuck. Seems like something small and pointy, but hmm, that's what cows have . . . but spelled different? And those things aren't exactly small. Hey, a mammary quandary.*

Boobs? Better, I guess. Nah, sounds like some damn bouncy, rubbery thing . . . and boob means like, a moron, right? Real erotic word, boob. Could be it describes the beholder, better than the beheld? Huh, lot of other stupid choices too. Rack, hooters, melons, bazooms, gazongas, jugs, knockers, bodacious tah tahs. Hey, what about bust? Sheesh, maybe on a mannequin. Nah, only one actual word that's cool. Breasts, yeah technically, and esthetically.

It was for Al the most sensuous of all words. When he was a kid he only had to see it, even in an ad for chicken breasts, and he'd get an erection. He could still remember the excitement of discovering any passage in a book with "breasts" in it—savoring the very sound of it and the image it conjured, like a starving man imagining the first mouthful of a succulent steak.

Man, they don't write like that anymore . . . "heaving bosoms", "milky white breasts". So corny, but so . . . mmmm.

Holy crap, I sound like Homer Simpson drooling over donuts. What am I, thirteen again? Is this a men-are-scum thing, to still think like that in my late forties? I used to be an incurable romantic, fuelled by hope and hormones. Now I'm just an incurable idiot.

♪♪♪

With the fascination of a wildlife biologist, Al watched the young man reconnoiter, appearing to be calculating the potential for "sexcess". For him, the basic one-night stand criteria were likely to be considered mainly between neck and knees, but would a long-termer have to be at least somewhat attractive?

Observation and analysis concluded: her potential, absolutely short term; the young man's requirement to appeal to her, simply to be male.

Al looked back toward the woman. She had small eyes, bordering on hard-to-find beneath over-thick layers of eye shadow and mascara, and her nose was thin and disproportionately long. No amount of makeup could make this face look good; she reminded him of a giant rat. An anthropo-morphic erotic-dancing rodent came to mind, shimmying and shaking her voluptuous fur-covered cleavage.

Minnie Mouse never wore a shirt. But she was flat as a . . . Damn, why do I think these things?

Perhaps this woman had adapted, mole-like for nightlife, her small eyes perfect for Lou's Lounge. But there wasn't much to see in this tribute to tackiness. The room was big for a jazz club, at over 150 feet from front door to stage, and 50 feet in width. But it *felt* small. The bar took up a large part of the stage-left side, creating a sensation of narrowness. Stretching from halfway down the opposite wall up to the front were wooden banquette-style seats upholstered in dark reddish leather, their high backs effectively covering up most of the window surface, leaving little space for outside light to sneak in. Along the front wall was a shorter version of the same style of bench seat. A liberal assortment of chairs and small tables sat opposite the lengths of the seats, with minimal room for customers to squeeze through.

Exacerbating the almost claustrophobic atmosphere was the overall darkness of the décor. The central section contained a scattering of small tables-for-four, draped in dingy covers the same dried-blood burgundy as the carpet, which was as worn and weary as a washed-up comic's routine. The sparse sections of benchless, windowless walls were covered in red and black wallpaper with part felt-like and part glossy consistency, like a yard-sale Elvis painting. Customers in these areas could easily imagine they'd been trapped in a three-dimensional velvet mural from "art hell".

One could almost hear the groans of distaste coming from the few dusty celebrity photos hung there. Being included as part of this decorating disaster was not something Satchmo, Duke, or Ella would have welcomed. They'd had no say in it; they'd never been here. What sad irony that so many of the great jazz clubs once flourishing here on Miami Beach, and in most other cities, were now long gone; while Lou's Lounge—more commonly referred to as "Losers' Lounge" by most of the regulars and staff—lived on in all its mediocrity.

♪ ♪ ♪

The young man said, "Hey, pal, check it out. Her friend just came back. Which one you want? I'm into the friend, if that's cool with you. Wow, her titties are even bigger than the blonde's and loads of jiggle. I love that. By the way, I'm Curt."

Al bit the side of his tongue, desperate to hide his amusement.

Far-out; his name and description, all-in-one.

Hiding his laugh by pretending to clear his throat, Al said, "Yeah, sure that's cool, and to quote Paul Simon, you can call me Al."

Small Eyes' friend was another rat, almost a twin, but with dark hair. Were they sisters? And her chest *was* even more spectacular, but displaying a lower degree of "stability".

Jiggly, hmm, not a fan of jiggly. What do so many guys see in that? They even used that word to describe those Charlie's Angels chicks, and they were young. It's not an age thing. And not like they have to be firm as rocks or anything.

And what the hell, I'm not exactly firm myself anymore, and in more ways than . . . Damn, don't think about THAT right now. Got enough depressing thoughts already, including why this bonehead Curt thinks I'm just like him. God, don't let him be right.

He began to run backwards down mammary lane, searching for more positive images.

Nora. Even when she was sixty-something, still looked like she could have been the model for the Venus de Milo. Sweet, precious Nora.

Curt grabbed Al's arm and said, "C'mon, buddy, let's move in. Gotta tell ya though, if they smell bad, I'm outa here. From head to foot, I need clean. So they aren't supermodels and . . . they *are* kind of old. No offense. What the hey, I'll still do her. But not if she's hard on the nose . . . 'cause that could mean, hard-on, who knows? Right?" He laughed, spluttering beer onto his jacket sleeve. "Let's go. It's cougar time."

Al sucked back a quick swig of his beer.

No offense? Yeah, right.

He was indeed offended on several levels by this brash young man, but mostly for the age reference: reminders of growing older being plentiful enough, just by being next to him. For Al, a more pertinent issue than Curt's crude concerns about odor, was how breaching the booze barrier could ruin all penile promise.

What was it Shakespeare said about drinking? "It provokes the desire, but it takes away the performance . . ." Ha, or as I'd say it . . . too much to drink, down goes the dink.

Christ, would I have worried about that ten years ago? What a joke. I gotta write a book, The Power of Negative Thinking.

Al looked toward the stage where the three musicians were cooking up a solid groove. As much as he wanted to pay attention to the music, this mini-adventure with Curt and the girls was intriguing, and he was compelled to join in, if only for a minute.

"Sure," said Al, "maybe you can teach me how to meet women. Would ya?"

Al and Curt moved over to the ladies' table where Al sat down beside Small Eyes, while Curt moved in next to the other.

"So, haven't we met somewhere before?" Curt said to the rat sisters. "Guess not. But no better time than right now, huh? I'm Curt and this is . . . Hey, buddy, what was your name again? Paul . . . ?"

"Was, and still is . . . Al."

Crap, has discourteous Curt never heard of Paul Simon? How the hell young IS this cat?

Curt began to chat up the ladies, appearing to comprehend the strategy of always addressing both, to show you were polite; and of course, if you bombed with the first one, you might still have a chance with the other. Al wondered if he had been sucked in through some kind of time vortex into a TV and was part of an old *Saturday Night Live* skit.

Two wild and crazy guys having a swinging time, hitting on the fox-ez with their big American breasts.

He hoped he might at least find some humor in this game, but he didn't mention his thought to Curt who probably wouldn't be familiar with the classic Steve Martin/Dan Aykroyd routine or any other early-years *SNL* bits.

This kid likely wasn't even born yet when I first saw that. Damn, do I feel old.

♪♪♪

Al pondered the situation in silence, waiting for inspiration to participate.

Oh, what the hell, let's see if I still got it.

Nuzzling up to Small Eyes' frozen explosion of starchy blond hair, Al purred and said, "I love that. What *is* that scent?"

"Tabu," she said with the piercing tone of a scratched chalkboard.

Ouch, a voice like a crow with a cold. That, and those yucky tiny eyes might just be over the limit, even for me. Was there really a time I'd go through with this? Was I stupid enough, drunk enough . . . lonely enough?

"You're a pretty big guy," she said, smacking on a wad of gum. "You play football or somethin'?"

He straightened in his chair. "How can you tell, with me sitting down?"

She glanced toward the bar and said, "I saw ya standing there, you know, before you came over here. You're pretty cute, kinda like that actor, um, you know, Peter Brosno, uh, Peace Bronson? Whatever . . . the James Bond guy, only you're bigger, and older, I think."

"Not that much older, honey. And I'm about six-foot-three, two hundred and thirty pounds, with my clothes off. Like me to demonstrate that?"

The laugh didn't come, so he continued, "Not exactly Mr. Universe under this outfit, but a lot closer to him than Mr. Rogers. And no, I'm not a football player, honey lamb, though I wouldn't mind tackling *you* sometime."

"Huh?" she said as her lip twisted upward and her false eyelashes flapped down like twin Venus flytraps. "Oh, I get it. You're into the rough stuff? I ain't down with that. That's for pervs."

Most often, what a woman first noticed about Al, after his initial imposing physical presence, would have been the weary mystery in his Omar Sharif brown eyes, the artistic elegance of his large hands, or the strength of his jaw which was punctuated by an inch-long scar pointing downward from the left side of his lower lip. If asked, he would always make an absurd shaving-accident joke about the scar, preferring not to hear the real story about how traumatic that wound had been. This woman, however, wasn't aware of anything but the superficial aspects of any man. She asked nothing with her heart.

She's SO stupid, although . . . Pierce Brosnan, huh? No way. He's too pretty.

"Nice jacket," said Small Eyes. "That one of them 'Har-*monies*'?"

Al raised an eyebrow. "Armani? Of course it is. I like my clothes the same as I like my women, first class."

First class? That's a laugh. To be with this flooz I should be wearing a dirty tee shirt and torn jeans.

He cringed at the thought. He always wore a sport jacket and dress pants whenever he was out. Even at home, he rarely wore anything but slacks and golf shirts. He didn't even own a pair of jeans; hadn't since he was twelve.

He pushed back the chair. "Got to go, baby. You gonna *be* here?"

"Not goin' anywhere for a while, big man," she said, her gaze fixed just below his belt. "Where *you* off to? Gotta have a whiz?"

Shit, she doesn't know who I am . . . ?

He bent closer, feeling her haystack hair on his cheek as he asked, "Hey, babe, whadaya think of the band?"

Small Eyes scrunched up her rat nose. With the whine level of her voice reaching a new high she said, "That's jazz, ain't it? I hate that stuff, don't you? Not real music to my thinkin'. Can't even tell what song they're playin'. Be nice if they did somethin' *good*. Maybe some old Hank Williams, or Garth Brooks, or even Shania? Whatever. At least somethin' nice to dance to would be better than this junk."

At that moment she didn't know how lucky she was not to be a man as Al pictured the satisfying image of pouring his beer over her head. There should be some kind of law to make it okay to slap someone this dense. She didn't even know he was in the goddamn band—*his* band—the Al Waters Quartet.

With those few words, she had proven she was even more of a twit than first impressions had suggested. His days of being able to ignore such things were long gone, and even in his youth there had been a limit to what he could put up with, no matter how physically attractive a woman might be. While her stupidity alone might not have been an outright turnoff, a critical line had been crossed with her preference of country music over jazz.

The play-along-with-Curt game was over, but with the end of it, a different game had simultaneously self-started. Al's mind drifted, inwardly scanning a list of dance gig tunes, but he stopped himself in the midst of this unsavory impulse.

Shit no! Don't even THINK about playing some damn old Hank Williams song to show her you can play "real" music. Aw, hell, who am I to put down ol' Hank anyway? At least he's written a ton of tunes, and he'll be remembered forever. What have I ever done but cover songs by other people? I will write something someday . . . something good that'll be remembered. Damn it, I will.

Al walked away from the table of rats and headed a little too fast for the stage where the rest of the band was playing the second of a couple of tunes on their own. He hoped Small Eyes would see what was going on and feel embarrassed, but he figured she wouldn't really give a damn anyway. She was too dumb to be humbled by "foot-in-mouth disease".

To hell with her and her jiggly friend. And to hell with Pierce Brosnan, the skinny bastard. Sean Connery could still kick his ass.

♪♪♪

As Al arrived at the stage, he stopped to listen. The guys were sounding good—really good. How could anyone not appreciate this exquisite complex music played with passion and skill by masters of the art? Small Eyes was an idiot.

So, we don't play "real" music? Shit, the sad thing is, her opinion puts her in the majority. And maybe she's right. Maybe all I've ever worked at, and fought for, and loved . . . is crap.

CHAPTER 2

THE VILLAGE VANGUARD
October 1980 - New York City

Al stood for a few minutes staring up at the marquee, ignoring the light rain spattering on his coat and instrument cases. As ice-cold drops began to sneak through his hair and trickle down onto his face, he remembered the first time he'd stood on this same spot, ten years earlier—at the age of twenty—when he predicted he would perform here before turning twenty-five. Now here he was, about to fulfill his goal, albeit nearly five years behind schedule.

The Vanguard. Damn, is this for real? Am I actually going to gig here? Am I ready? Is this a dream . . . or a nightmare?

Dream or nightmare, it was time to wake up, to swallow the fear and head inside. Once he reached the canopy over the door, he didn't have the rain to deal with, but now faced a storm of annoyed looks and comments from the people waiting in line. Al wedged his way amongst those nearest the staircase. Focusing downward to avoid bumping anyone with his instruments—and to avoid angry eyes—he said, "Sorry . . . 'scuse, please. I'm with the band. Sorry, sorry."

With one horn case in front and the other behind, he struggled sideways through the queue, past the iconic red doors and on down the steep fifteen stairs, apologizing the entire way.

Down, down, down through the fiery red tunnel. Never felt like a journey into hell before. Why tonight?

He knew there had to be a better way in for performers. Why hadn't he asked? As the cover charge collector at the door let him through, a subtle smirk betrayed her friendly greeting, telling Al he'd certainly committed his first faux pas of the night by using those stairs. How many more blunders would follow? Surely enough to kill his dream forever, but there was no way out now. Might as well go down swinging.

For a performer, those stairs down into the Vanguard provided delicious irony, since this gig meant you were on the way *up* in your career, or were already at the top. Although Birdland, on Broadway up in Midtown, may have had more widespread name recognition, the Village Vanguard, in the lower part of Manhattan known as Greenwich Village, was still the hallmark of jazz success. This was the "Carnegie Hall" of jazz. The only thing better might be . . . Carnegie Hall.

Al Waters had listened to more musicians than he could remember in this hallowed venue in the basement level of 178 Seventh Avenue South, but tonight was to be his debut in *front* of the audience. As he walked through the room, already packed to its official capacity of 123, he had the unshakeable feeling that the entire experience might turn out to be his imagination on overdrive. Would he suddenly awake to find he was still playing just down the street at The Straw Hat, the sing-along honky-tonk showroom where he'd started his professional career? That was no jazz gig; while the Vanguard was *the* jazz gig. The pictures lining the walls said it all: John Coltrane, Charlie Parker, Sonny Rollins, Dizzy Gillespie, Thelonious Monk, Bill Evans, Coleman Hawkins—a veritable jazz rogues' gallery of the history of the club. The Monday night Big Band—now led solely by Mel Lewis after Thad Jones's sudden departure—still played weekly on this same stage where Al was fumbling to open his cases.

And what was with those crazy old instruments attached to the walls? One, some kind of weird euphonium-tuba-like thing, was on one wall amongst the pictures; on the opposite wall, a multi-dented sousaphone. Had some hapless performers once played those here? Had they been so bad that the audience had ripped the instruments from their hands and banished the disgraced musicians forever? Al contemplated taking down one of the relics and blowing a note or two, to attempt to resurrect the dignity of the old horns. Whoever had once played them, however poorly, it didn't matter—people forge their own fates. But no musical instrument deserved to be shackled up as room décor. How must it feel to be left hanging on a wall for all eternity?

Huh, maybe that's better . . . to be on the wall and ignored. Beats being on the stage and paid attention to. At least there on the wall no one expects anything out of you. No way to fail.

For a moment he considered just scooping up his instruments and running back up those stairs, back into a world where he could hide among the billions of "normal" human beings who had never played here. This was one of those moments in life and career when a first impression was all you got: a good one, and you're made; a mediocre one, and you're gone and forgotten.

It was too late to back out now. In a few minutes the opening set would begin and Al Waters would either become part of the legend—perhaps to join those in the pictures on that wall—or be permanently demoted to audience membership. Or worse, maybe the audience would storm the stage, wrest his instruments from his fingers, and hang them—*and* him—up with those other hunks of musical refuse.

♪♪♪

Al was no stranger to moderate success, and more good things seemed preordained. The thirty-year-old's reputation had been growing steadily for the past few years, as a man who could not only handle the technical end of musicianship, but also had a particularly strong sense of style and expression. And against convention, he was achieving this on two instruments of contrasting physical requirements: trumpet *and* tenor saxophone; although on sax he was "just another good player", while on trumpet he was garnering high praise and was at the top of everyone's must-see list. He was a publicist's dream: with genuine on-stage charisma and physical presence, enhanced by his sturdy six-foot-three frame and Hollywood-handsome face. According to all reports, Al Waters was the whole package. His audience was steadily growing in a business where something different, something with "show biz", can often be what it takes to make it big; at least "big" as it applies to the jazz world. There was room for another Chet Baker—who had selfdestructed long before his time—more than for another Miles Davis who cared nothing for pleasing his audience. Against-the-wind innovation may give an artist a place in history, but seldom does it sell enough tickets in the present . . . especially for an unknown.

♪♪♪

Al chatted briefly with the other musicians, all of whom he knew and had worked with in various combinations; although tonight was the first time they would play together as a unit. The only one he knew really well was piano man Billy Crothers. With all due respect to the bassist and drummer, Al knew that Billy, who was no stranger to the Vanguard stage as evidenced in one of the pictures on the wall, would be the glue for this group. Because of the pianist's reputation for irresponsibility, several people had cautioned against using him for this important gig. But Al had weighed that against the comfort of longtime musical collaboration and friendship. There was no other choice; he would either make it or break it, with Billy behind him.

Al pulled back his jacket sleeve to check his watch; it was time to start. Just as he was turning to take center stage, Billy grabbed his arm and pulled him in close, saying the same old line he'd used for years. "Remember, kid, you play good, or you play bad. They love you, or they hate you. Either way, nobody dies, right?"

Al squeezed Billy's arm and said, "Thanks, man. I'm cool. We're cool. Let's groove."

"Copacetic," said Billy. "And groove, we shall."

This was it. Now, think of a song. Why hadn't he worked out a set? This wasn't just a gig; this was a life-changing moment. Would his instincts let him down? Al picked up his trumpet, since starting with his strength made sense. As he began to scan his list, there it was: "Autumn Leaves", the perfect choice, overdone maybe, but comfortable for the band and recognizable to the audience. If there was anything Al knew about pleasing an audience it was to always give them more of what *they* wanted than what *you* wanted.

Looking outward for the first time, he scanned the room through the glare of stage lights and smoke. The tiny round tables in the center of the room were all fully occupied as were the square ones in front of the banquette-style seating along the walls. From his viewpoint most of the audience's faces were either indiscernible or completely masked in shadow. This was good; silence after a song would be unpleasant enough, but to see disapproval in their eyes? No words could describe that depth of pain.

♪♪♪

For Al Waters, music was life: breath drawn in and expelled as the very energy of existence, with a perfect balance needed to survive. Rhythm was as powerful a need, and as vital to his soul, as was his heart to his body; while melody and harmony were extensions of his thoughts and feelings from as far back as his conscious memories could search. A song was not just a song, but was rather, for the few minutes of its performance—everything. To abandon your fears completely to the dangers of such naked public exploration is always a gamble, playing the thrill of success against the threat of failure. Tonight, all the chips he'd earned in a lifetime of practice and preparation were on the table.

♪ ♪ ♪

While the audience applauded after each musician's solo during the opening song, Al couldn't help but wonder if this was true appreciation, or just the patrons proving they knew when to respond. This was the archetypal New York crowd: there to be seen as much as to listen, for whom erudition equated with being cool. Cannonball Adderley could have just blown the paint off the walls and expected no more than *appropriate* response. Al was fully aware of this, but when "Autumn Leaves" ended and the applause was pleasant but not enthusiastic—and from only two-thirds of the audience— his unavoidable initial feelings were disappointment and annoyance.

Al told the band to begin the intro for "Little Sunflower"—a change of pace from bebop standard, to Freddie Hubbard's modal masterpiece. After waiting an inordinately long time while the rhythm section continued the one-chord vamp, he began to play the head, unafraid of potential accusations of audacity for playing Hubbard's signature tune on this same stage as that trumpet phenom had done so many times.

What the hell, the whole night's a gamble. Might as well live for the moment. One thing about playing the Vanguard . . . you can only bomb once.

Solos were appreciated once again, and at the song's conclusion there was somewhat more response than earlier. Maybe there was hope yet. As Al pondered the next song choice a voice rang out across the room, shattering the mood. "Hey, man, you're no Freddie Hubbard."

Al Waters had been through wars of words and worse in so many bars, so many times, his first instinct was to head for the table from where the voice had come, to deal with the loudmouth boor face to face. But he found the courage to stave off a fight—using artistic offense as emotional defense—by asking the band to give him an introduction to Miles Davis's "Four".

Just before he began to play the melody, Al said into the microphone, "And I'm no Miles either, but here's one of his tunes, played the best Al Waters can play it."

Al wasn't certain whether the subsequent smattering of applause was for his words or from recognition of the song. After a few bars of Billy's piano solo, the heckler's voice called out once again. "Get that has-been off the stage. Hey, maybe stick some reefer in front of him and lead him out to the gutter where he belongs."

Al stopped the band with a quick gesture. As he set down his trumpet, his teeth were gritting so tight he thought they might crack. There was but one thing to do now, and it would surely mean the end of this night, and probably the end of the Vanguard in his life. No one was going to say that about Billy. Only a few people in the room understood what was happening, but the best possible outcome was the least likely.

As if in a warning from another time, another world, Al heard Billy's voice from behind him. "Al, don't do it, man."

Sometimes, whether beckoned or not, angels arrive in time. The room manager was already at the table speaking to the disruptive customer, and within seconds was escorting the man out the door and up the stairs.

♪♪♪

The remainder of the set proved to be as successful as the first songs had been, and with no further disturbances. When Al went to buy a beer, the bartender said, "Hey, man. Nice sound. I dig your style. Swingin', man. You'll be back, no doubt of that."

"But they aren't exactly doling out standing ovations *are* they?" said Al. "You sure I'm doing okay?"

"Hey, man, you must have been in here before. This is how they are. I've seen nights where someone new like you gets up there and the crowd just plain ignores 'em. It isn't pretty. But it happens. Don't worry, my friend. I can tell right now, you're in. Hey, I like how you handled that heckler too. You did exactly the right thing by letting us take care of it. If you'd gotten into it with that guy, the boss would have had you tossed out too. Glad you showed a cool head like that."

Al smiled and rubbed his aching jaw, realizing the pain wasn't from playing, but from the tension he'd allowed to envelope him when the heckler had almost ruined everything—or drawn *him* into ruining it.

♪♪♪

By night's end, Al was drenched in sweat and self-satisfaction. His career, within these few hours, had been cemented into a formidable foundation. While the Vanguard was booked up for several months ahead, a repeat engagement was assured. Another probability was recording the next gig as an album. Countless iconic jazz recordings had been made in this room, starting in 1957, with Sonny Rollins' classic, *A Night at the Village Vanguard*. And since then, the very location virtually guaranteed interest from major record labels and subsequent sales success.

An *absolute* certainty was that if Al didn't want to go home alone this night, his choices were many. At the front of a modest line of autograph seekers was a tall beautiful woman who introduced herself as Rachel. Her fashionista attire and chic coiffure matched her demeanor: Upper East Side professional, inside and out.

"You're one hot jazz man, Al Waters. Great choice of tunes, but I confess I didn't recognize a couple. Were they something you wrote?"

"No, sorry, babe," said Al. "All stuff by the greats. Someday I will be doing my own tunes though. And who knows, maybe other guys will be playing them on their gigs? That's my dream anyway."

"Dream big, Al. You've got something special going. And if you don't mind me saying, it doesn't hurt that you're such a hunk too."

Al laughed and said, "Don't mind at all. Shows you have good taste, right?"

He signed the autograph as *Al Waters, jazz hunk*. As he handed it to her, she slipped him a second piece of paper which had a phone number next to her name. Moving in closer she said, "Don't wait too long to call . . . or should we just go to my place now?"

Al heard the voices of many demons from his past screaming for him to pounce on this opportunity, but he found the strength to shut them off. After drawing in enough breath to play a John Coltrane mega-solo he said, "Sorry, babe, can't do it."

Rachel asked, "You're saying no? Really?"

"Hey, I know this sucks, but I have business to take care of and people to talk to and . . ."

"Just lose that number then, okay? I mean it." She turned and walked away, indignity narrowing her eyes, as she tossed her Al Waters autograph onto the floor.

Wow, what's up with that? I thought the only ego that fragile around here was mine. Huh, I just pissed off a woman I don't even know? Usually takes me at least a week or so. Such an amazing night, in so many ways.

♪ ♪ ♪

Before Al packed up his trumpet and sax, he thanked the band for a great gig, assuring them they would all be on the next one when it happened.

Billy Crothers said, "Al, my man, this is it for you. I think you've done it. Roses, and milk and honey all the way from here on, right? And hey, did you notice? Nobody died."

"Sure, Billy," said Al, "but there is one more level to get to before I actually die. My own tunes, and Carnegie Hall, man. Hey, don't call me crazy. Carnegie Hall. I can smell it. Gonna get there, and soon . . . I just know it."

CHAPTER 3

MERELY PLAYERS

August 1999 - Losers' Lounge

*L*ike a refracted vision of Shakespearian allegory, Al's world was a stage—for now, the one in Lou's Lounge: only an eight-inch elevation, but somehow feeling higher; especially when his energy and his mood were low. Tonight the short climb was but the first hurdle of a long race he didn't want to be in—and couldn't win. He grabbed his tenor saxophone out of the stand, slung the neck strap over his collar, and licked the reed.

Why do I keep licking this stupid synthetic reed?

He snorted at his habit from the days of cane—reeds carved from nature, not some chemist's formula. The sonic qualities of organic reeds—*real* reeds, as traditionalists called them—used to be worth the effort required to prepare and maintain them. When had that changed? Many sax players he knew still went through the bother of selecting the best reeds from a box of new ones, soaking them in water the necessary length of time, trimming and shaving them, then sanding them to perfection with emery paper. For Al, it might seem worth it for the couple of weeks—sometimes only days—of satisfaction this process achieved, but eventually the natural cane reed would cease to function properly, and would have to be discarded. He had always found this inevitable short life span of cane reeds a source of frustration and irritation.

Fibracell synthetic reeds, made from a high-tech Kevlar and rosin formula, could play perfectly right out of the box, last for many weeks—sometimes months—without deterioration of quality, and required no licking to keep them moist during the gig. The sound was *almost* as good as the best cane, as long as the right combination of reed strength and mouthpiece specs were found through trial and error.

Synthetic reeds . . . synthetic soul? Is that me now? Quick, easy, lasts a long time without much maintenance. Guess that's how a relationship should be. Huh, as if I'd know anything about that.

He laughed out loud, ignored by the other musicians. They all had witnessed enough of his inner dialogue moments to know better than to ask.

♪ ♪ ♪

Al started to play mid-tune, right on top of the piano solo, not caring in the least what Billy would think.

So I'm a jerk. Billy's solos suck tonight anyway. Sure, he used to be good, sometimes still is. But most of the time these days he wanders over the keyboard like a drunk trying to pass a sobriety test, too damn careful, still falling on his ass.

He found he was playing too loud and too much, as if he were being paid by the note.

What am I trying to do, make Small Eyes change her mind, and "discover" jazz? Hell, playing like Coltrane on a caffeine rush sure won't do it. Must sound like garbage to her. Shit, sounds like garbage to me.

Al looked over toward table eight for the first time since he'd returned to the stage. There was already another guy there with Curt and the girls, rat-chatting. As he pictured Curt enjoying the jiggle fest with rat number-two, he squelched a laugh, sending an inadvertent honk from his sax.

Small Eyes was nuzzling her new companion, and the Tabu on her neck appeared to be doing its job. Soon nothing would be taboo for that guy.

I bet she still hasn't noticed I'm in the fucking band. Was a time I'd head over there and . . . Aw, screw it, I wasn't even into hustling the babe anyway.

As depression and disappointment began to supersede anger he was tempted to play "Your Cheatin' Heart", and get her to want him, to swoon in his arms. She would moan, "Ooh baby, you turn me on with your music."

In an extraordinary moment for Al, emotion was losing the battle against discretion. Having this woman want him, based on pretence, wouldn't sate the hunger in his heart.

♪ ♪ ♪

The song was over. Without looking up, Al leafed through his gig book and selected a Thelonious Monk tune. Announcing his choice to the band, he began an ultra-quick offbeat finger snap and said, "Okay, guys, let's get a little outside on this one."

She'll hate this . . . Christ, this is fucked up. Used to want everyone to love me.

Now I'm trying for hate? Anyway, she's too fucking stupid to hate me. What the hell, Pierce Brosnan? Damn, I think I look more like Sean Connery, a YOUNG Sean Connery.

Al licked his synthetic reed, bit down on the mouthpiece and began to play. Digging deep into his long-dry well of enthusiasm, he wrenched out turns of phrase beyond his usual lounge jazz restraint, recalling the time in his life when he had always strived for excellence. As notes spilled out of the old saxophone he could almost feel it groaning as if it were surprised and awakened by his energy. Soon it was laughing with joy at the chance to sing freely as it once had.

During the other musicians' solos, he sat back on his stool, fiddled with his reed, ran a dollar bill under a couple of sticking pads, and stared at the floor as he pretended to be into the music. He didn't want to see how the guys at the rat table were doing. He knew if he got involved—got competitive—trouble could result. It wasn't worth it.

But his ego screamed to be listened to.

Come on, Al, you're the best looking guy in the room. If you wanted the broad, you could have her. That twerp making his move has no right to think he could get her, not if you wanted her. Come on, Al, do you? Are you afraid he'd win? Or are you afraid YOU would? Win what? A quickie with a skank piece of trash? You have Kathleen at home in your bed, okay, HER bed. And she's smart and nice looking and . . . Damn it, with a bit of effort you could make it work with her and fix your pathetic life. Think that way, man. What the fuck are you LOOKING for?

♪♪♪

Wesley was coming to the end of his solo, twisting notes and chords out of his bass with true mastery. Al's attention was drawn to the power of the young black man's playing and to his face which was contorted into a passionate grimace. Out of the musical context that expression might have indicated either intense pain or impending sexual climax.

Seems like I get those feelings mixed up all the time too, but not in my music.

Al looked toward Pete to see if he wanted to take a full solo, but the drummer shook his head—in perfect time of course. Al said, "Come on, man, let's trade fours."

When the turnaround into the top of the song approached, Al indicated with his standard nod that he and Pete were going to take off together. Bam— the rest of the band stopped on the downbeat of the last bar of the head, leaving sudden total silence. Al knifed into this sound void with a furious flurry of sixteenth notes, followed by four bars of simple but hot riffs—brief staccato lines mixed with fluid legato notes. He was singing inside his head in scat lingo as the notes poured out his horn: Bee-iddle ee-dat ... bee-iddle ee-dat ... bee-iddle a dee-*dat* ... doo-dut, da *dee* dat ... doodle ee oo *dat.*

Pete followed with four bars of percussion scat in a rhythmically exact replication of Al's phrasing: Bee-iddle ee-dat . . . bee-iddle ee-dat . . . bee-iddle a dee-*dat* ... doo-dut, da *dee* dat ... doodle ee oo *dat.*

Pete's musical response sent a delighted shiver up Al's spine. Every four-bar phrase he presented—ever more complex and daring—was duplicated in essence by the drummer, and then ingeniously expanded upon. This was a moment jazz musicians cherish; this was as good as sex. Without any prompting by either man, they finished the final eight bars of the solo chorus playing together: a spur-of-the-moment duet that could never have been written to paper; a one-time-only creation of two men's spontaneous exploration of one song, one shared inspiration, one unique moment—lost forever, as quickly as it had been created.

This was *better* than sex. Two heterosexual men were, for a few seconds, the most intimate of lovers in a passionate embrace of intertwined artistic expression.

Al began the head of the song in standard form, sticking to the melody as the bass and piano rejoined him and Pete. But as he approached the bridge section he began to stretch out, feeling an urge to not let go of the excitement of having found—however briefly—something to live for.

The chord progression in the bridge didn't normally allow for much adventure, presenting a bit too much movement to get around without careful, methodical thinking. But Al ripped into it with abandon and somehow got through without getting mixed up.

During the last eight bars, he played so far away from the written melody he forgot what song it was, lost in a cloud of emotion and the sensuous impending climax of the music. It was as if he were alone with it, loving it, drawing it with him to heights of passion as only the shared energy between musician and Mother Music can achieve. The rest of the band and the notes they were adding were merely the bed supporting this frenzied fornication.

The guys were used to this from Al, having seen him lost and rambling through many a song. His reasons for this may have been different on this occasion, but the skills needed to accommodate his meandering were well honed. No one but Monk himself would have known how close to a "train wreck" they had come.

After a smooth landing into the end of the song—the band guiding Al like support fighters on the wing tips of a smoking bomber—the sax man let fly a flourish of punctuating notes. He then held a final low D in a diminuendo into nothingness. After several seconds all there was left was the pulsing "fuh-fuh-fuh" of air-only vibrato which seemed desperate to resuscitate the note back to life.

♪♪♪

"Whooee," said Wesley. "That was some cool shit, Al. Sometimes I forget who I'm playin' with. No disrespect, boss, but tonight you validated your reputation. Ain't heard nobody swing like that since . . . hell, can't remember. You ARE swing, man."

Wesley paused a moment, then laughed and said, "Hey, that sounds like some kinda superhero. *Swingman*, to the rescue. He come flyin' in whenever the band don't swing, and he save the day?"

Pete grinned—an outpouring of emotion for the normally reserved drummer—and leaned back against the curtained wall, cradling his sticks against his chest.

To most frequenters of jazz clubs, the stage set-up might have seemed odd, with the old upright piano's back toward the rest of the band, and its player's back to the audience side of the stage. But this was a choice made from space limitations and acoustics. With no microphone on the sound-board, the instrument could be heard better this way by the other musicians, and that outranked the patrons' perspective. It did, however, set the piano player somewhat apart from the group, the visual impression being that of a man outside, looking in. From his face, one could infer this was what he preferred, isolation being for him perhaps more friend than foe.

Al looked across the cigarette-burned, booze-stained piano top. Billy was slumped over, picking at a loosened piece of ivory. Still able to make music, despite its once proud exterior being covered in scrapes, scars, and missing bits, the instrument was still majestic to Billy. For him, he often joked, it was like a mirror. Once, when someone had cruelly disparaged the old upright he'd said, "Look past the outside, man. Listen to its heart."

Every time Al looked at him he was still caught off-guard by the absence of the pianist's signature purple beret. A few weeks earlier he'd shown up bare-headed: so out of character, it was like seeing Indiana Jones without his fedora. But since Billy had said nothing, Al asked nothing. Without the beret, Billy's hair had become at once a central feature: oily and thinning, slightly graying, parted from the left so it flopped over the middle of his head, with the rest dangling down his left ear and cheek. He looked ready to do the old Red Skelton bit wherein a sneeze would produce a wild scattering of hair in every direction. If Al hadn't known Billy Crothers for as long as he had—approaching thirty years—he might have had trouble believing this frail-looking man was only fifty-five. Most would estimate him at least in his late sixties if not several years older. But the real look of age was in his eyes which were sunken, lonely, and permanently half-closed, the right one more than the left, creating an erroneous impression of a sleepy dimwit. The mind behind the haggard face might not often shine with anything near its once legendary brilliance, but even now few could equal Billy's skills.

Christ, Billy, you'll wake up later and think about what we just did, and maybe you'll appreciate it. Damn it, man. In your messed up head you're probably somewhere in New York right now.

♪ ♪ ♪

There was no applause. Not surprising; they were used to it. They had long ago acceded to the idea of live music performance being doomed to extinction. Al glanced over to the "rats' nest" and saw that Big John, the bartender, was cleaning up the abandoned table. Seeing Al's "awakening" from the music, the large man set down his tray of glasses and ashtrays, and paused to towel off the abundant sweat from his forehead, bald pate, and neck. A giant smile flashed from the blackness of his face: a beacon in the darkness of the room and the mood. In a voice ragged from nearly two decades of late nights, smoke, and talking over noise and music, he said, "Hey, boys, knock it off. You're only playin' to me and Dixie now, and she's done sat down, and lookin' 'bout ready to doze off. Go on, get out of here, so's I can lock up."

It was only eleven o'clock. Al looked around the room: no one there, except for one yawning waitress, and Big John who could count as two. Al half-wished he had played "Your Cheatin' Heart", or "Cold, Cold Heart".

That's a laugh. Both those songs kinda describe me better than any jazz tune I can think of. Maybe country music ain't so bad as I always done thunk. Yeehaw.

♪ ♪ ♪

"Well, we outnumber the audience again," he said over his shoulder to the band. "Hey, Big John, we should put a notice in the paper. The Al Waters Quartet: still packing 'em *out* at Lou's Lounge."

The big man muttered, "Ya keep playin' that weird shit, and no familiar stuff. No wonder nobody stays. You oughta know that by now, Al. It's the nineties. Damn, it's almost the new millennium. Sometimes I think you're livin' somewhere way in the past, my pale brotha. Or maybe like on another planet or somethin'."

"At least I don't *look* like a planet, John. Hey, maybe nobody comes in, 'cause you block the view, *and* the sound."

Big John didn't respond. He just went back to cleaning tables and humming "Moon River", wondering why Al wasn't throwing a snide comment about how unnatural it was for an inner city-raised black man to like a Henry Mancini song. Such verbal attacks from Al were taken as a sign of affection by those who knew him; it meant he liked and respected you. If he didn't, he ignored you, no matter how much of a scumbag he considered you to be. The exception to this was if you presented a threat to anyone in an underdog position—especially someone he cared about—then another, far nastier kind of attack could erupt. That was something Big John had witnessed and hoped never to see again.

♪ ♪ ♪

This was getting old fast. How much longer could they keep a gig when this was happening? Sure, it *was* Thursday, second-slowest gig night of the week, but Al feared the suggestion would soon come to be paid only per hour instead of per night, or cut down the band, or worse—no more gig.

Gigs, songs, bands, love, even existence itself. Everything has to come to an end sometime. Maybe all at once?

He set the sax down on its stand, making sure it was firmly cradled. While the timeworn and tarnished 1957 Selmer tenor could have been mistaken for junk by some, Al knew it was far less in need of an overhaul than its owner. He'd likened it many times over the years to the perfect wife: never complaining, and always ready to go whenever he was; although she could act a little cranky at times when he neglected her.

Last song should have been "Round Midnight". If there was any prophetic ironic stuff going on here, we'd have got in another hour anyway.

He looked back down at the music stand where his gig book was still open to their last number. The title of the Monk classic tightened his gut:

"Well You Needn't, It's Over Now".

Shit, guess it was damned prophetic and ironic . . . in more ways than one.

CHAPTER 4

UPSIDE DOWN AND BACKWARDS

*W*hen a lover was kissed goodnight, when songs were over, when sets came to a close, when nights were nearer to morning than midnight . . . Al Waters thought about death. The end of anything—always felt like the end of everything.

♪♪♪

As Wesley zipped up his bass case and Pete draped a sheet over his drums, Billy lingered at the piano, engrossed in a peculiar, perplexing melody. Al was tempted to play along, but the chord progression, though simple, was somewhat unconventional—even for Billy. Whether it was mere musical meandering or a glimpse of the piano man's former ingenious creativity, it was beyond Al's comprehension. He stayed out of it, too tired to concentrate, too reticent to ask, and too proud to risk screwing it up.

It's something I should know, something simple hidden in there. Why can't I get it?

Wesley stood briefly at the door, listening intently before finally shaking his head and waving goodbye. Al nodded a farewell.

Good. At least I'm not the only one who doesn't get it, or did that look mean Wes DOES get it?

Standing next to Al, Pete mumbled something and left the stage, slipping into his jacket as he walked. He smiled back at Billy as he paused at the door before leaving.

Pete knows what Billy's doing. Shit.

Al leaned over the piano top and said, "Hey, man, come on. Let's get outa here."

Billy dropped his hands to his lap, eyes shut tight, as if trying to find words to argue; but as quickly as it had appeared, the dissent drained from his face. After pushing back the piano bench to stand up, he fired off an insincere salute and muttered, "See ya tomorrow, boss."

He went over to Dixie and helped her to her feet. As the two of them shuffled to the door, he said gently, "Come on, old girl, I'll share a cab with ya." He began to sing, "A heart is a wish your dream makes . . ."

"Dang it, Billy," growled Dixie, "you should stick to playin' piano. That's supposed to be, 'a dream is a wish your heart makes'. You can't never get the words straight when you sing. Hell, not even when you talk."

Her own words gave her pause as she wondered, as always, how much of Billy's addled persona was just an act. Was there hidden meaning to any of the nonsense he continually spouted? She thought more about what he had just sung. In a crazy way it made as much sense as the correct words to the song. To be close to his heart *had* long been the foremost wish in all her dreams.

As she walked, assisted by Billy—who was probably not half as strong as she was—she knew the cab ride would be the end of their time together once more, a brief but sweet moment to be cherished. Once home in bed, alone again, her dreams and wishes would come together as they always did, to fill another tomorrow with hope.

♪♪♪

Al picked up his sax, fingered a few meaningless patterns, and then set it back down on the stand without having played a note. Again he heard Big John humming that damned annoying Andy Williams tune.

A sudden beam of recognition pierced through the cloud of melodic mystery. "That's it," said Al, "bloody 'Moon River'."

"Say what?" asked Big John, looking up from the glass he was drying.

"It was 'Moon River' . . . the song that Billy was playing. That's just crazy, man. Didn't even recognize it till now when I heard you humming it again. Christ, you know what he was doing? Playing it upside down and backwards. Damn, that fried brain of his still has some zap to it."

Big John said, "Sounded to me like ol' Billy just tossed some notes in a pot, stirred 'em up, and poured 'em out. Though it was kinda pretty I suppose. Sometimes the best stew does come from bein' throw'd together."

The bartender stopped drying for a moment, inspecting the discolored, smudged old glass which could never again look truly clean. He sighed, looking at the overhead rack of equally worn-out drinkware, and his wistful observation of the general past-its-prime look of the bar reminded him of Al and his saxophone.

"Hey, man," said Big John as Al headed for the front door, "you just gonna leave that horn sittin' there again? Why you do that?"

Al glanced back toward the stage and said, "Don't know, Johnny. Maybe 'cause it feels like the night never quite ends this way? I hate packing it up in that stuffy old case. Reminds me of a coffin. Endings aren't my thing you know."

Big John didn't understand what Al had meant about endings, not in the musical context. But he did know something was wrong. Al was too quiet these days, ever since the New Year's Eve incident—nowhere near his usual insult quota.

"See ya tomorrow night, Al."

Al said, "Nope, before that. We got rehearsal tomorrow, about 12:30 or so. Got to add some new shit to the repertoire. Maybe we'll get 'Moon River' down for ya. Maybe even so you can recognize it?"

♪ ♪ ♪

As Big John locked the door behind, Al turned away quickly, not wanting to see the "open" sign turned over to read "closed". There was too much finality in that. He looked at his watch and thought about where he could go, other than home. Some of the more popular places would still be buzzing. Maybe a walk down to Charlie's Place would be worth it. Maybe not, but it would still be less uncomfortable than going home to Kathleen. She would probably be asleep, but likely to wake up at this early hour, since it would be out of the routine for him to be home so soon.

To the average man it might make sense to head for home in eager anticipation of waking his woman and perhaps making love on a week night, or if for nothing else, just to talk; they seemed to find so little time lately for even that. Al wasn't interested in either activity with Kathleen. The sex, he wasn't sure why not. But the talking? That was easy. If they found time to get beyond chitchat, he might be trapped into revealing what he was feeling. And that could be ugly.

♪ ♪ ♪

It was a short walk to Charlie's Place and Al still knew lots of people there, including staff and most musicians who might be on the bill. Sure, he'd be chided for Lou's closing up early again, but so what? Since he didn't keep up on the scene much anymore, he wasn't even sure who might be gigging there. A surprise might liven up his mood. How bad could it be?

The walk was a healthy shock to Al's system as the night air filled his lungs, replacing the stale, smoke-laden atmosphere of Lou's Lounge with ocean scents. He found himself enjoying the transition from performer to listener, as a medley of seagull squawks and rustling palm branches reminded him of how wonderful the simple, gentle music of nature could be. Al mused on how humankind had taken the inspiration of the music of the universe and cultivated it, making it ever more complex in rhythm and harmony, yet never improving upon its intrinsic purity or unpredictability.

So cool . . . when the birds and wind and waves start jamming, it's different every damn time . . . like snowflakes. Funny, our "Bird" of jazz, Charlie Parker, never played the same solo twice, and yet even with all his creative juices flowing, you could still pretty much predict where each line he played was headed. He had his trademark licks, like real birds' songs. But those, like breezes whispering or waves lapping, never come exactly when you think they might, or from the same direction. It's kind of an ensemble expression, spontaneously mixing the expected with a minute-to-minute element of surprise. People, even geniuses, are pretty darn predictable, while nature is infinitely variable. That's the real genius of whatever the hell the point of everything is.

The sweet moment was shattered from across the street by the harsh cry of rubber ripping against warm pavement, immediately followed by a man's voice blasting epithets which were rudely rebutted by a car horn and the roar of an engine pushed to its maximum. In the settling silence afterward came the nervous giggling of a man and woman.

Can't I have a second of undisturbed musical bliss, even from wind and birds, without some knuckleheads ruining the moment? At the gig I don't even notice it anymore, but out here? Come on.

He soon realized the peaceful moments had been numbered, regardless of that particular disturbance, since with each few steps closer to Charlie's the car and foot traffic increased. As he neared the familiar view of his former house gig, the sounds coming from within gradually overpowered the surround-sound mix of cars, seaside noises, and sidewalk chatter which, against logic, proved to be even *more* musical than the music. With its mix of natural and electronic tones, the artificial *attempt* at jazz chased away any lingering guilt in his mind concerning his use of synthetic reeds. This was the scourge of all musicians who still hoped for a return of the days when live music was necessary for entertainment: the unmistakable tinny sound of sequenced, computerized background tracks being used to enhance the inadequate talents of some turncoat musicians.

Al wanted to burst through the door to confront the quisling perpetrators of this travesty, to smash their synthesizers and see if they could actually play something on their own, without the cowardly use of electronic accompaniment. Instead, knowing he could not defeat the system, he decided to cross the road, to head anywhere but here. The old days were gone. If people were happy with this phony kind of music, let them have it. That was their loss, although they'd never know it.

A new sound stopped him in mid-turn—the addition of a woman's voice to the music. The rest of the sounds coming from Charlie's evaporated, along with street talk and laughter, birds and cars, and even the romantic rush of wind through the trees. All were pushed aside by the incredible beauty of this singing which had begun, in mere seconds, to drown his anger and his pain and even his loneliness. With every note, the voice called out to his heart as if she knew he was there in the street listening to her. She seemed to know him, and accept him for all his darkness, as she stripped away the layers of his resistance to the belief that real passion for anything was possible. The words were unclear, but the texture and sensuality of her voice were all it took to convey volumes of meaning to his soul, while miraculous alchemy transformed the sidewalk from concrete to "cloud nine".

A sharp sting of bitter memory interrupted his joy, as he realized he had felt this way once before: the first time he'd heard Michelle sing. Although few people might believe a man could fall in love with a woman solely from the sound of her voice—for Al, it was not hard to conjecture—just difficult to comprehend that it could be happening for the second time. He was struck with both wonder and fear. How much else about this might turn out to be the same as his experience with Michelle? If similar in any way—other than the effect of the voice—he would rather die, than relive that part of his past.

As the song ended he realized he'd been standing with one foot on the sidewalk, the other on the street. He turned back toward the nightclub, intending to see what this angel-voiced lady looked like, sensing she must be gorgeous, but not caring if she was. If she turned out to be a grizzled old woman with one leg and no teeth, the feelings were there, regardless.

Be nice if the grizzled and old part isn't true. But damn it, I have to find her. She's beautiful, whatever she looks like.

Before he could move, a sound of an entirely different nature caught Al's attention. Somewhere not far away a woman was crying out. The fear in this voice told of a worse danger than falling in love. Someone was being hurt. Al concentrated on the direction from where the distressed voice emanated: an alley two buildings down, back in the direction of Lou's. He strode quickly toward the sounds, trying to determine what was being said, other than just crying. A few words filtered through the sobbing.

"No . . . stop it . . . please . . ."

This was enough to increase Al's pace to more than a jog. As he rounded the corner into the alley, he spotted a small pickup truck halfway down the lane, with the driver-side door open. A man's legs were sticking out, but that was all he could see of those involved. Al walked up to the vehicle. Keeping back about three paces, he said, "What the fuck's going on here?"

A man scrambled to get up from a prone position on the front bench seat of the truck and Al could see a woman emerge from where the man had been on top of her. She said to Al, "Help me, please . . . this ain't what I . . ."

Al said, "Okay, pal, what's up? The lady doesn't seem to want what you're offering here. Let's just leave her alone and everyone can get outa here. Nobody needs to get hurt."

The man stepped out of the truck, revealing an open shirt, tousled hair, and a look of you-messed-with-the-wrong-guy written into his brow. He was taller than Al, and at least ten years younger. The advantage was still Al's; age and size difference overruled by the musician's experience with trouble, and those who like to cause it.

The man said, "This ain't your problem, dickwad, but it can be, real quick."

Al noticed the woman was pulling up the top of her dress, placing it awkwardly back over her exposed breasts. The bottom half was still pushed up, exposing her legs all the way to her panties—a testament to the man's ardent exploratory efforts. Apparently he had been expecting more from his charms, and an over-indulgence of liquor, than she'd been willing to allow. Her makeup was streaked and smeared, both on her face and on the man's shirt. Probably, she had initially been more inclined to participate. As Al speculated on the point whereupon she might have begun to fear her companion's advances, a dark apparition drifted across his conscious, as fleeting as a cloud's shadow darting across a sunlit meadow. He tried to see it for what it was—but it was already gone.

The room with no windows . . . ?

The man moved toward Al and said, "Get the fuck outa here. Or do I have to show you the inside of that dumpster? The lady and I are just havin' a good time, and it's none of your business."

The woman slid over to the open door, and as she stepped out, Al noticed her hair for the first time: a blond blast, sprouting from her head like a mop left to dry in the wind. The sudden recognition almost made him laugh; it was Small Eyes. With her makeup ruined, she looked so different; her horrendous hair had revealed her identity. Could he risk a fight over *her*? Why should he? An answer was soon supplied by his grinning adversary.

"You're the weirdo sax player from that stinkin' Lou's Lounge, *aren't* ya? Ya think yer special or somethin', 'cause yer a fuckin' musician, huh? For all I know ya could be a fuckin' faggot. That what you are, a fag?"

Al looked at Small Eyes and then back at the man. He sighed, knowing there was but one outcome at this point.

She's not worth it. Too bad Mr. Hairy Chest here had to go and say that. Would have been just as easy to let her rot in the pile of shit she got herself into. Then again, she might have ended up with me tonight. Maybe that would have been worse. But hey, I DID sort of get to see her boobs. Too cool.

Al stood waiting for the man to make the inevitable foolish move of stepping closer. As expected, the idiot made an attempt to grab Al by the throat, and before the extending hand was within a foot of its target, Al had it in his grasp. He twisted the man's arm with his left hand, while holding the thumb back in such an unnatural position that it snapped under the stress. Although this was a common result from the maneuver, it never ceased to amaze Al how easy it was, or how quickly even a big man was on his knees and begging. The mercy came as easily as the punishment, but not until Al had slapped his cowering opponent across the face with the back of his right hand. After all, most music is played with both hands—why not this rhapsody of retribution as well?

Small Eyes looked down at her wilted, whimpering, escort-turned-attacker and said to Al, "Oh my God, did you have to do *that*?"

Al said, "You better get outa here, lady. He won't bother you anymore. Watch out who you pick up. There's lots of scum out there. Maybe make your choices better. Won't always be someone around to help you."

"Screw you. Whaddaya want me to say? You're my fuckin' hero or somethin'?"

He wished he had never heard the voice from the alley; had never tried to be Prince Charming to this poor man's princess. Maybe she'd wake up tomorrow and understand what had happened here. It didn't matter, because Al knew, and so did the man on the ground.

"Guess I won't be seeing you in Losers' Lounge again, right, honey? Not exactly your scene?" said Al as he turned to go.

"Lou's?" she said, looking puzzled. "Were you there tonight? Right, that's where I seen you before. The guy who sat down with us and then split."

She still doesn't know who I am. Didn't even remember me at all till just now? Christ, and I care? She's not worth feeling this way over. All the notes I've played: high, low, in between, right, wrong . . . and the spaces between. They all meant something. She doesn't.

As Al watched Small Eyes hurry to the street to hail a cab, he noticed her "friend" had managed to get back into his truck.

Al said, "I guess Broward General's the closest hospital. Want directions?"

The man said nothing as he started the engine and slowly backed out of the alley.

"You're welcome," said Al. "You know I probably saved you from a rape charge. Anyway, have fun driving with one hand."

Shoulda' left it alone, damn it. They both deserved what might have happened, as much as what did.

♪♪♪

Al headed back to Charlie's Place.

Only midnight. They should still be open.

When he arrived at the main door the closed sign was being placed in the window. He asked a couple who were about to get into their car if they had seen who was singing there earlier.

"Didn't see her," said the man. "Heard she was gangbusters though. Somebody said she was just sitting in with the band."

"Did you catch her name?" asked Al.

"No," said the man after helping the lady into the car. "Sorry."

Al peeked through the front window of Charlie's. He saw the *electro*-musicians packing up some small equipment on the stage. He wasn't surprised that he didn't know them.

Probably northerners, new down here, thrilled to work cheap, just to get to be in Florida. Schmucks. I wouldn't lower myself to talk to them, even if it means never finding out who that singer was. What the hell was I thinking anyway? I'm way beyond falling in love ever again. One more time, too many Scotches. Makes me nuts.

♪♪♪

Al walked a few blocks up Collins Avenue, then crossed and went down a side street to the beach where the ocean breeze seemed to whisper secrets amid the arrhythmic wash of breaking waves. Plunking himself down on a bench, he wheezed out the same "oomph" his father used to make whenever he sat. When had this started? Wasn't this one of the surest signs of old-man status?

As he stared at the moon's reflection on the water, Billy's odd rendition of "Moon River" once again floated into his mind.

Probably the only way Billy can get into a song anymore, upside down and backwards. Sounds like my life.

Behind him, something moved amongst the scrub bushes—the buffer between the end of sand and beginning of pavement. Al turned and saw a cat peering at him from the foliage, a mangy, skinny, reddish-orange colored creature with a look in its eyes more forlorn than his own. While tapping his fingers lightly on the back of the bench, Al made a clicking sound with his tongue and cheek to entice the animal to come closer. It ignored him and slunk back into the bushes to continue its pursuit of whatever it was seeking. Al felt a pang of rejection.

"Stupid thing," he said out loud.

Don't know why I bothered. Never have liked cats.

"Hey, cat, if it's geckos you're looking for, you'll have to be slick. The ones that come out at night have extra strong eyes. They'll see you coming way before you see them."

He wished he could be a gecko—a slow blind one—and maybe then both he *and* the cat could get what they wanted.

A tear rolled down his cheek, but he didn't feel it, or what had caused it. As he got up to go, he shivered as the stiffening onshore wind flattened his hair. His eyes tightened against the flying sand and the growing dread of having nowhere to go.

Seventy degrees out, on a Florida beach, and I'm cold. Guess it's true what they say: you can't go home again. True for me anyway.

Canada seemed so far away, it might never have existed.

Hey, Nora, I wonder, is there a statute of limitations on somewhere you've left, still feeling like home?

CHAPTER 5

RED

1959

"Freddy," called his mother from the top of the basement stairs, "come on up for lunch."

"COMIN', in a minute, Mum," yelled the little boy. "Hey, don't call me that anymore, 'member? Supposed to be just 'Al' now. I'm nine and a half . . . *ten* next March. No more 'Freddy', okay?"

He'd been "Freddy" since he was a baby and being called that fuelled the feeling that he still was one. "Junior" was another name he hated. Nobody dared call his father "Senior" did they? His father preferred to be called "Fred" or even the full version, "Alfred". Little Freddy wanted an identity of his own. From now on he wanted to be known as "Al".

He didn't want to go up for lunch. He had a project underway, and he wasn't ready to leave it yet. In front of him, inches from his face, was his new friend, Squeaky. The mouse wasn't a willing participant in the relationship, but since Al had caught him in a brilliant shoebox trap the tiny creature had no choice but to accept his new home in a glass jar. If the mouse knew what sad fates had befallen his recently deceased relatives in the traditional traps Al's dad had set, perhaps it would have been grateful for the captivity. It was a more merciful outcome than the crushed heads or broken backs many of his fellow pantry-raiders had suffered.

If mice weren't too much like people, maybe their friendship might just last. Certainly Al had never held onto a human relationship for any length of time. He had trouble letting other kids get to know him; something about it made him nervous. Casual friendships were okay, but he never had a best buddy, which earned him a reputation as a loner. He was unable to trust anyone enough to get close; although he knew his older sister, Anne, was always there for him if he needed. But how could a guy be *real* friends with a girl? And even worse, she was part of his family, and for Al, family didn't equate with the warmth and security of typical television shows like *Father Knows Best*. For him, familial normalcy was assuming his parents could stop loving him, or even forget he existed when they were angry or tied up in their own big-people problems. The mouse would be different; its love would be dependable, and forever. Squeaky was going to have a life unlike any other mouse, never again having to worry about traps or finding food in the cold wet world outside. He would feel wanted and appreciated. Al would see to it; he and Squeaky would be true friends.

"Al," called his mother again. "Get up here, or I'll call you 'Freddy', or maybe 'Junior' again. And the kitchen window's open, so everyone will hear me."

Stretching as high as he could reach, Al put Squeaky's jar up on a storage shelf. No point taking chances. Red would be around somewhere, even though he hadn't seen him all day. For sure he must be lurking about. Cats do that.

♪♪♪

As he wolfed down his peanut butter and honey sandwich, Al tried to tell his mother about his new friend.

"Guess what I got," he said, smacking rudely as he chewed.

"Hmm, what you . . . *have*?" she asked, ever the teacher. "And please wait to tell me when your mouth isn't full, Alfred."

"A new pet, Mum. Guess what it is . . ."

"Not another snake, is it? You know better than *that*, young man. I hope to goodness!"

"Nah, better than that. It's a mouse! I caught it this morning. Chased it around the whole basement and got him with a shoebox when he came out from under the shelves."

She ran her hand through her short, prematurely silver hair. "Land sakes alive, Alfred Waters Junior, what do you want with a mouse? It's probably diseased. It didn't bite you, did it?"

"Nah, it's a nice mouse. I'm calling it Squeaky. Like it?"

"Very appropriate, I guess," said his mother, as she went back to cleaning up the kitchen counter. "You know your father isn't going to be thrilled, not at all."

♪♪♪

Of medium height and weight, she was a plain woman with a charming, slightly crooked smile she seldom revealed. Her figure was average except for being somewhat buxom—a trait she tried to de-emphasize by wearing loose-fitting tops. Al hadn't paid attention to such things until that past summer during a family trip to the beach, when for the first time, he saw her in a swimsuit with no cover-up. Until that day his mother's general appareling strategy—plus his callow disregard—had kept him pretty much unaware of her bosom. He couldn't resist stealing brief glances. But the venture ended abruptly, when in a moment of true preadolescent horror, his mother turned and caught him in the midst of a peek. As she slowly turned away, attempting to show no reaction, Al ran across the burning sand and jumped headfirst into the lake. For the rest of the day she wore a towel draped over her shoulders and across her front, even though she hadn't once been in the water. Al stayed submerged at least waist-deep long after beginning to shiver—until finally his dad called him in to go home.

♪♪♪

The sound of breaking glass was a guided missile, fired straight up from the basement into Al's heart. "Oh no," he cried as he ran toward the stairway. "Red . . ."

Halfway down the steps, he caught sight of what he least wanted to see. Red had Squeaky and was tossing him up into the air like a catnip toy, playing with his victim before the kill. Hoping to thwart the cat's villainy, Al cleared the last two steps in one jump, landing barefoot directly onto a piece of broken glass. As the shard penetrated deep into his flesh, his scream sent the cat scurrying into the back storage room, its jaws firmly clamped on the mouse.

Al's mother hurried down the stairs. "Freddy, what's . . . ? Oh, dear God, you're bleeding! The glass, it's everywhere. Your father is going to just . . . Come on, we have to get you to the hospital."

♪♪♪

Al's backyard ball hockey career was put on hold by a foot full of sutures. Every day he'd have to tell the neighborhood kids to go ahead and use the yard without him. He could only watch in misery as they ran back and forth, chasing down the ball, slashing their sticks, fighting over who got to be Maurice Richard, Gordie Howe, Jacques Plante, Red Kelly . . .

Red. Damn it!

Anything to remind him of the cat . . . made him *see* red.

The day his stitches were removed, Al began to seek revenge. He'd never been fond of the cat anyway, having suffered many deep scratches and bites from the imported farm animal. If his dad didn't love the feline fiend so much, Al might have taken a baseball bat to its head long before now.

He began a systematic tormenting of the beast: putting salt in its food; locking it in a closet whenever possible; and trapping it behind doors and under tables, where he would pelt it with rolled up socks, and sometimes stones. Red would rear up and hiss, baring fangs, and batting at Al's projectiles with open claws. But in spite of his displays of ferocity, he was no match for the boy's rage.

Al found himself enjoying these episodes with increasing passion for the cruelty, although every time afterward he felt remorse and shame. Sometimes he would even fight back tears when his lust for acts of revenge was sated. As infuriating as the mouse incident had been, there was a much deeper anger inside him—an overflowing toilet bowl of feelings—whenever he attacked the cat.

♪♪♪

One day Al went too far. He'd learned to catch Red with feigned tenderness: offering the cat an assortment of tempting food items, and then stroking it gently. The forgetful creature would often begin to purr.

Al had a neat new idea. While petting the foolishly unsuspecting cat, he risked claws and fangs to whip a hockey sock over its head. He stretched the wool over half the cat's body, before retreating from the slashing back paws, one of which ripped a jagged wound on the back of his hand. Red let loose an earsplitting "Hwaahhhh", so loud that Al's dad heard it from the next room. He came in to see the cat writhing around on the floor, hissing, clawing, and jumping frantically in attempts to free itself from the sock. Smashing his fist onto the kitchen table, he said, "What in bloody hell . . . ?"

Literally caught red-handed, Al didn't know what to do, other than to say, "He killed my friend."

His dad managed to catch the terrified animal and pull off the sock, sustaining a mess of deep scratches before he was done. With blood bubbling from the wounds on his hands, he grabbed his son by the throat. Al didn't struggle. As much as the viselike grip hurt his neck, he said nothing, did nothing. If in this moment he were to die by his father's hand, so be it. Even if he had been physically able to fight back, he wouldn't have. This felt natural somehow, and less painful than the deeper feelings of disgrace oozing from his heart like a squeezed boil.

His only thought was *I deserve it.*

Al's mother prevented potentially lethal injury the one way she could—by crying. It wasn't the first time Junior had heard her cry because of Senior, but it was the first time he could remember being part of it.

Fred Waters released his grip and yelled, "You little brat. Don't ever let me catch you being mean to that cat again. Where the bloody hell do you get off being so cruel? What's WRONG with you?"

As soon as he was let go, Al hobbled out of the house, his still-bandaged foot trailing crimson splotches in the snow from the reopened wound. He hid behind the garage, and without coat or hat, stood shivering in the winter wind.

Alfred Waters Junior seldom cried anymore. Something about it disgusted him. But in a few minutes the tears were uncontrollable when he understood that no one—not even his mother—was coming to see where he was and if he was okay.

♪♪♪

Al's first music lesson with a professional instructor had been scheduled for the next evening. His dad had been his teacher so far, having given him the basics of producing a sound on the trumpet and how to breathe with proper support. Although Alfred Waters Sr. played several instruments, all were self-taught; his knowledge and skill level on most were, at best, slightly better than rudimentary. Long before the mouse-and-cat incident, he had decided his son's musical promise was beyond what could be nurtured at home.

For Al, getting a new teacher couldn't have been timelier. Mr. Fordham proved not merely to be a wonderful musician, but an equally gifted instructor. For motivation he used inspiration instead of intimidation, gentle, humorous cajoling instead of threats, and displayed patience instead of annoyance whenever Al fell short of expectations.

So much more than trumpet mastery was demonstrated in these weekly lessons. After each one, Al wished he could stay forever, with Fordham not only replacing Alfred Waters Senior as his teacher, but as his father too.

CHAPTER 6

FIVE — SOUTH TOWER [2]

Officer Poole checked his watch again. The orderly hadn't been in room 510 for more than a few minutes. What was the correct procedure here? He'd already screwed up by not verifying the name badge, but what did it matter if the guy was in there for—how long was it now? How long was *too* long?

Should he check in now to see what was going on? Or was it better to wait it out and perhaps prove his *own* incompetence? He decided to hold off. A few minutes would be okay. All was cool. Clearly this was just an odd but ordinary orderly. These guys must change shifts all the time. Tomorrow the other guy would be back.

What did it matter anyway? If he screwed up again, maybe they'd fire him off the force. That might not be so bad. Sure, his father would be upset and disappointed, certainly not his mother; she'd never wanted him to do this anyway. If he were to be fired maybe he could go back to school. She'd like that. He could go into music as she'd always hoped.

Poole went back to imagining duets with Lenny Breau. Just a few more tunes with the master—a few more minutes of fantasy—then he would return to the real world to see what the orderly was up to.

♪♪♪

Timing is everything: in music, comedy, sex, car motors . . . and murder.

CHAPTER 7

YOU CAN CALL ME ANYTHING

August 1999

*B*efore today, Al Waters had been to a psychiatrist once, at age sixteen; he'd considered it a total waste of time. In fairness, he was aware that no counselor could really make a difference in three sessions—especially if you didn't talk much, and half of what you did say was untrue. And how ridiculous had it been that a recent family tragedy, with emotional trauma so deep it would haunt the young man forever—was left unmentioned?

He had worried his parents into seeking help for him, ostensibly for his difficulty in mixing with "normal" people, and by choosing solitude over friendship. Teenaged Al didn't see the problem. Strength in numbers? All for one and . . . ? What a crock. The only one you could trust was yourself, and even then, not a hundred percent. Since that time his thinking hadn't changed much.

For most of his adult life Al had found it easy to get along with just about anyone. But get close? Truly close? No. With a man it seemed utterly unnecessary, and even with women true intimacy wasn't likely. They wanted something he couldn't give honestly. Even though it didn't seem "right", Al had spent much of his life living by one credo regarding romance: to make love, you have to *fake* love. He was able to rationalize the process in musical terms, comparing it to playing an A-flat against an F7 chord, which should be "wrong", but works in jazz since it's simply altering, or *embellishing* the chord with a raised ninth. What he wasn't able to grasp about human relationships was that an embellishment of the *truth*—is just a lie.

At least a woman would try to understand what made him tick: his needs as a musician, as an artist. They had something else he needed: not just sex, but a deeper, more meaningful connection that proved to be as elusive as it was essential. But it seemed inevitable that women would end up needing something too—something beyond *reasonable* commitment. He'd tried that and had been soundly kicked to the ground as a result. No more.

Sex was an area where Al considered himself to be an expert—an *artist*—totally in control, patient, understanding of needs: all this for his partner, but unfortunately not for himself. Sexual pleasure for him was almost always entirely in the buildup, not the climax which usually spawned depression. And now, a new complication had arisen around that issue: a true conundrum, named Vickie.

Having officially reached middle age, an expression he hated for its implication of being just plain *old*, nothing much had altered in his approach to friendship, love, sex, or human relationships of any kind. But one concern, simmering in the back of his mind for years, had recently been cranked up to full boil: the issue of finding a reason to stay alive. While Al never talked about suicide to anyone, it was always there—its consideration a constant companion, ready to be called upon, if ever he felt that final curtain had to be self-drawn. While love might have been a source of apprehension, death was not; his primary rationale for hanging in, being the slim chance he might be wrong about how useless life really was. This was not a pleasant mindset to wake up with every day, along with thoughts of having lost Nora, the Vickie situation, diminishing interest in music, the ever-accumulating aches and pains of growing older, and of course Kathleen, and how to manage his relationship with her. Maybe now, with self-destruction's seductive whispers becoming a veritable roar, it made sense to seek help—at least while Nora's health plan still covered the cost. What harm could it do?

♪ ♪ ♪

What a place—the doctor's own home, in Ft. Lauderdale's luxurious Las Olas Isles—a suburban monster home, with a front room set up for seeing clients.

As Al had driven in, he was required to identify himself at a security booth. He wondered if the gate guard knew why unit 286 had so many visitors. Was that a judgmental look on the guard's face as he handed back Al's license?

Smart guy, huh? Can you judge mental cases, buddy?

♪ ♪ ♪

Fireplace, coffee, even a dog named Godzilla, the cutest little schnauzer-like thing you ever saw—except for George. Too bad this fuzzy creature reminded him so much of George and all the other feelings that little dog's memory brought back: Michelle, Las Vegas, his dad's tears.

Al settled into the leather couch.

Here we go. Nice couch, must have cost a bundle. This guy does all right. Look at these digs.

Doctor Davidson sat about six feet away, in a large plush arm chair opposite Al. With the main window curtains drawn tight, the single utilized light source was a tiny lamp on the small end table beside the doctor's chair. This, along with the mainly dark oak décor created a warm, calming atmosphere.

Al had figured he'd end up in an isolated chair facing the doctor across a desk in a Spartan office. There would be coffee, light introductory chat, then a stream of: "Describe your dreams . . . How does that make you feel . . . ? Tell me about your parents . . . blah blah blah . . ."

♪ ♪ ♪

Al knew right away this guy was different from his teenage psychiatric experience, and from most of what he'd seen in movies. Good. This was why Kathleen had recommended Doctor Jason Davidson: psychiatric superstar, albeit "a little full of himself", as she had put it; a character, with his own way, and a reputed credo of "Damn the conventions, let's get healthy."

As a 'psych' nurse—or *psycho* nurse, as Al liked to call her—Kathleen was well up on who was who, and who thought what about whom in the field of mental health. She had hoped Al was into seeking help with his relationship issues: the eventual outcome being therapy as a couple, even though they'd only been together a few months. Too bad she wasn't too up on what was really going on, and why they could be splitting up soon. Oh well. *There* was one thing, besides the Vickie situation, this odd looking shrink could work on: if it was time to break up with Kathleen. And of course, maybe finding a reason to live might just conveniently segue out of those issues.

♪ ♪ ♪

"Well, Alfred," said the doctor, as he leafed through a small notebook, "I hope this early afternoon session is convenient for you. Many people prefer evenings, but I understand you work uh, late hours. A musician? Fascinating."

Looking up, the doctor tugged his glasses down to the tip of his slightly crooked nose. He reminded Al a bit of former Canadian heavyweight boxing champion George Chuvalo: round face, steely deep-set dark eyes, muscular neck, wide shoulders, and broad chest. His thick, dark brown hair was combed straight back against its natural curl which became more evident at his shirt collar where it turned up in all directions with a Beethoven-like wildness. The one average thing about him was his height of about five-foot-nine, and although perhaps not ready for a marathon, he appeared to be in shape for his age, which Al guessed to be early fifties.

"Well, Alfred, can you tell me what prompted you to seek counseling?"

The doctor had a soft voice, with an almost effeminate quality, belying his athletic frame; Al found wondering about the percentage of gay pro football players. And the use of his full name "Alfred" shot a fear-of-heights queasiness into his groin.

Why does that get to me? Because when my mother was mad she called me that? 'Cause it's my dad's name more than mine . . . ? Christ, this guy's got me thinking about my parents already? Could this whole thing be as bad an idea as I thought? Hey, why am I asking myself questions? That's HIS job.

In light of Al's silence, Doctor Davidson decided to rephrase his question. "Sorry, I'll put that another way. What brings you here?"

"My Mercury Cougar," said Al, straight-faced, unable to avoid the ancient joke.

The doctor said nothing as if waiting for more.

Oh no, he doesn't get it?

Al said, "Come on, man. You know, '*brings* me here' . . . ? My car? Sorry, a little humor. Yeah I know, very little. Okay, okay, seriously . . . I guess that's a tough question for anyone, Doctor Davidson."

"No need for formality here, Alfred. Please call me Jason if you like."

Pondering the suggestion briefly, Al said, "I got a thing about names and what they remind me of, and there was this guy I knew named Jason. Used to kick my butt at anything we competed at, especially basketball. Hmm, I got it. Doc Goldberg was a bass player I knew in New York, hell of a nice guy. Used to play with Glenn Miller, but I never held that against him. Anyway, how 'bout I call you *Doc*?"

"Fine with me," said Doctor Davidson, smiling. "You can call me anything. Just don't call me after midnight."

Cool, a comedian shrink. Well, as long as he laughs at my stuff, I'll try to find him amusing too.

"So, Doc, I thought shrinks always answered a question with a question. That's not your style?"

"Would that upset you, if it were my style?" asked the doctor.

A question? I'll show him. I'm good at games, and I don't like to lose.

"Do you mean as in really upset, Doc? Or just a tad pissed off?" He hoped it was a game.

"Do you get pissed off easily, Alfred?" The doctor looked absolutely deadpan.

Uneasiness crept up Al's spine. "Would that be a problem for you . . . JASON?"

Was this an Abbott and Costello routine they'd fallen into, or an intellectual butting of heads? He wanted to like this guy, but if a trained professional couldn't actually tell when he was kidding, and if this was in fact the doctor's approach . . . to do the question-upon-question thing for real?

Let me outa here.

After what seemed an eternity, the doctor said, "Okay, you win. We could go on for days with this bit, and you're probably much better at it than I am."

Al was perplexed. Was the doctor feigning submission?

"Alfred, certainly you knew I was playing along, but I felt something in your voice that I want to know more about. Unless you're a good actor, there appeared to be some real tension developing. Would you describe yourself as a competitive person?"

Al was reminded of occasions where he'd played the bridge section of a song and ended up in a different tune than he'd started.

This guy is good. Kind of scary too. What the hell's with the change of direction?

Had it truly been a game? Or was the doctor testing him, trying to bait him into revealing his nature? Was a shrink supposed to be so open with a serious question . . . so fast?

HEY, that WAS a question after all. Shit, just answer it and let's get going here. Did Doc just win round one?

"Yeah, Doc, I guess you could say I'm competitive. I like to win as much as the next guy. But I don't think I'm obsessive about it or anything."

After writing something in his notes, the doctor asked, "How does it make you feel when you lose?"

"Depends on what I lose at. If it's a game, like basketball or golf, I don't feel all that bad as long as I play up to my standards and the other guy beats me by playing better . . . like that guy Jason who I mentioned. I think that attitude actually makes me not as good at those things as I might have been. Know what I mean? If I don't care so much, maybe I don't try as hard, I guess. But . . ."

Al was looking for a way to say it more clearly, but another thought occurred to him. "By the way, Doc, when you asked about being competitive, that was after you admitted you were joking around. That shouldn't count, you know, as a strict question-following question, because you put a statement in front of it."

The doctor's eyes narrowed as he chewed the tip of his pen. "Oh, you mean when I asked if you were competitive, you think I was trying to slip in a question-answer to *your* last question, which as I recall was 'Does that frighten you?' Correct? No, Alfred, I wouldn't have broken the rules. Basically, I just wanted to move ahead with why you are here.

"Let's set some guidelines. I will not be dishonest with you in any way. I won't use psychobabble techniques, or pressure you into any directions you don't feel comfortable taking. You, in turn, need to assure me you won't purposely keep things back that might help me understand you. It won't do you any good to come here and try to outguess me, or to analyze every question I ask before you answer. Yes, I have developed efficacious ways of helping people to express their feelings. If you are uncomfortable with this at any time, please feel free to talk about it. The main thing is I need to get to know you, what makes you tick. I may be able to help you with your problems, but first, you have to help *me* to understand what they are."

Al again wondered if the doctor calling him "Alfred" meant he was angry with him the way it did with his mother. No matter. This direct approach was fine—a game he could play just as well.

"Okay, Doc . . . I'm here because I am forty-nine years old, in the middle of screwing up yet another major relationship, and my career always seems to be in a state of flux."

Flux? Where did I come up with that word? Is it time to mention Vickie? Nora, what should I say?

Al felt as if someone else were talking—a voice sounding like his—but coming from a different room, a different world. Embracing the liberation of this vocal detachment, he went on. "And I get depressed sometimes, actually a lot lately. Don't get any pleasure from anything anymore, except the occasional tune I play where I manage to say something special. But that's the exception these days. And my whole life, I've wanted to write some tunes of my own, instead of just playing everybody else's shit. But whenever I try, I can never get one done . . . always some lame excuse. Almost like I think maybe it's useless, like, I wouldn't do it any good, so why bother? And yet I have this killer desire to get even *one* song done before I'm gone, maybe like leaving the world with a piece of my life that won't just blow away in the wind like the rest of me . . . ?

"And then there's sex. Almost never worth it. I feel like crap pretty much every time after. I get so depressed, real deep and dark . . . way worse than just feeling blue. Kinda always been this way. It's like one of those bees, or whatever they are, that die after sex? Sometimes I think I must be some kind of reincarnated goddamn bee.

"Seems I've spent most of my life chasing love, then chasing it away when I got it, or having it taken away from me, just when I was ready to believe in it. I'm getting tired of, well, everything . . . even living sometimes."

After a brief silence Doctor Davidson said, "Good start, Alfred." His voice was soft, radiating compassion, and Al felt comfort in the gentle smile and genuine warmth in that one small sentence.

Leaning forward, the doctor added, "One thing though: if *ever* you are in a state where suicide feels like a serious option, you must call me . . . at *any* time."

Where's the not-after-midnight line? Must be serious.

"Alfred, I must tell you, I have lost two patients to suicide, and in each case I believe it was entirely avoidable. If you seriously think you are that close to the edge, please be truthful and tell me now. I know this is a professional relationship we are entering, but as time goes on it will become increasingly layered. No, we won't be 'friends', as in meeting for a beer or watching the game together. That can't happen. But, because of the intimacy of what we may talk about, and my sincere concern for you as a patient and as a human being, I will care about you. I am not a machine. In order for me to help you, please be forthcoming about any suicidal feelings. Can you do this?"

Al paused, absorbing the magnitude of what the doctor had just said. It had certainly seemed genuine.

"Hey, Doc, you said if I'm in a state that'll make me feel suicidal. Which *state* is that? Maybe Nevada? Sorry, I'll be serious. Okay, I promise I won't off myself before I give you a chance to save my butt. Cool?"

Wonder if he'll ever discover what a good liar I am. I know these guys can read body language and stuff. Can they see inside your head?

"Yes, cool, Alfred. I'm glad you can say that. I'm looking forward to working with you, because I feel you are here for good reasons, and you're certainly intelligent and able to express yourself well, although you do perhaps tend to hide from some issues behind that offbeat wit of yours. Together we will explore some of the motivation behind this as well as those difficulties you've mentioned thus far. We may need to dig into painful times and experiences. I'm hopeful you're willing to take some risks."

"You got a deal, Doc. What's life without risk? I can handle it. Hey, more than once I've shown up at black-suit gigs, wearing brown socks."

CHAPTER 8

REHEARSAL

August 1999

*B*illy was late. Of course he was—and the last time Al checked, the pope was still Catholic. One o'clock in the afternoon was okay for everyone else, but Billy was probably not out of bed yet. Maybe he hadn't even been to bed yet.

"I'm going to try him again," said Al.

Pete looked up from his drums at Wesley and shook his head slowly, lips pursed and eyebrows arched in mock optimism. The young bass player responded with a similar look and then turned to Al and said, "Yeah, cool, boss. Ring him again, and again, and—"

"Come on, guys," said Al. "Ease up. So he hasn't answered twice now, because he's either on the way, in the shower, or still sleeping." A fourth possibility crossed his mind, but he chased it away, choosing not to conclude the worst—not yet.

Big John said, "You guys are gonna be here a while, right? I'm headin' out for a bit. Al, if ya do hafta split, don't forget to use your damn key and lock up, huh? If I run into Billy, I'll kick his butt for ya."

Standing up from his stool, Al grabbed his cell phone and hit redial. He heard three rings, followed by the expected piano music and Billy's too-familiar message: "Sorry, Billy Crothers ain't here, and us mice are having too much fun to talk to ya while he's away. Leave a message and the world's greatest piano cat will call ya back. *Cat . . . ?* Did somebody say *cat*? Run for your lives, boys!"

At the beep, Al yelled into the phone, "Come ON, Billy." He punched the cell phone's "end" button as violently as he could, wishing someone would invent a way to hang up a cell, so it slammed. Once, Al had literally slammed his cell phone, full force down onto a bar top. The satisfaction had quickly given way to regret as he looked at the shattered electronics soaking in his spilled beer. Being stood up had cost him more than a bruised ego that night.

Al said, "Let's wait a bit longer. He could be stuck in traffic."

"Not likely, man," offered Wesley. "You know Billy don't drive. Maybe could've missed the bus again?"

Al loved the sound of this young man's voice. It had a Lou Rawls burnt umber rattle. This couldn't be the voice of a twenty-three-year-old, but then this was a twenty-three-year-old who had been playing bass in bars for several years. Maybe you "grew" a voice like that?

Can't be, 'cause I don't sound like Lou Rawls, damn it, and I've been living in bars a whole heck of a lot longer than Wesley. Seems black people just have better voices than white people. Would Wes or Big John think I'm racist for that? Nah, they probably think the same thing.

"Yeah I know, Wes," said Al. "Guess I meant like geriatric sidewalk traffic, or maybe he got caught in the stampede of hookers heading home after work."

Wesley smiled briefly and went back to cleaning the neck of his Fender bass. Fastidiousness was his way, not only in how he looked after his equipment, but even more so in his musicianship, *and* personal appearance. His narrow precision-trimmed goatee and mustache suited the hip look he was after, as did his tight-knit cornrowed hair, and the tiny-framed dark glasses he wore even at night. If there were a country named "Cool", Wesley would have to be its ambassador.

As Al watched Wesley polishing his electric bass, he couldn't help but think how times were always changing, and mostly not for the better.

Wish he'd bring the "real" bass to the gig, but I guess it's not worth the bother of lugging it anymore. Love that big sound, comes from the belly of all that wood. And damn it, for jazz, acoustic bass doesn't just sound better; it looks cooler too.

The nightclub always appeared so different in the daytime: smaller, dirtier, lonelier. Through the small bits of exposed window surface along the south wall, a few shards of light pierced the gloom, rudely revealing slow-dancing dust particles, and cruelly exposing the losing battle the carpet and furniture waged against the ravages of time. Most tabletops were crowned with upside-down chairs, placed there to make way for a snaking, room-length, multi-patched vacuum cleaner cord. Oddly, the stink of cigarette smoke seemed even more conspicuous now—when no one was smoking.

As Al drew in a long, slow lungful of the room's acrid ambience, he had to fight back a cough.

That'll be my luck. Cigarettes will kill me, and I've never smoked one.

Sunlight crept through the lone full-sized window up front, barely illuminating half the room—an earnest, but bland substitute for the flashing blue neon of the Lou's Lounge sign at nighttime.

Lou Farina—there was a thorn without a rose. The cheap bastard hardly ever showed his greasy face around the joint anymore, especially on pay night. Big John would have to rummage around for something to sign as a receipt and try to scrape enough cash out of the till.

Big John Lima was one of those rare truly nice guys. Too bad he had to work for such a worm. A real pro, he knew the regulars' preferences, and made newcomers welcome; working the room with skill and charm, utilizing years of experience, a big heart, and the listening skills of a therapist. He probably felt no one else would hire him because of his age and weight—and sadly, even in these times, maybe because of his race—but most likely because he could have qualified as the poster boy for heart disease. Never in Al's life had he seen someone sweat as much as Big John.

Lou could probably make the place look a lot better for a few bucks, but that answered that. If anything was about to change, it was most likely the band. More than one source had reported seeing Lou visiting other clubs, talking to band members and singers. Someone had said they'd seen him in the company of one particularly gorgeous young lady. Lou had talked at length with her after she had sung with the band at Charlie's Place. Apparently, other club owners were already after her—she was that good.

Lou would love to get rid of me, especially if he could get a chick to work this room.

They were getting stale, and Al knew it. Something had to give, probably sooner rather than later. As he mused on the interior of the bar, it reminded him of Billy Crothers—weary, worn, tattered. Bits of a once-successful past were in evidence, but like an old soldier stuffed into his uniform, the pride was tinged with sadness.

Even more than Al, Billy, and Big John, the pictures on the walls showed their tiredness and age—fading memories of musical legends. Most of those jazz greats would never have heard of Lou's Lounge, although Lou claimed Louis Armstrong had actually sat in back in the '60s. Other "stars" had been there, but none of the actual giant figures of jazz—other than Armstrong, if that sit-in story was true. Lou's had opened well after the heyday of the genre and mainly faded heroes or up-and-comers had worked here. Al often wondered which of the two he was considered to be—he preferred the latter. In spite of his age and experience, he still thought of himself as a rookie, since the sax was his "new" instrument.

It was sacrilege having Ellington, Armstrong, and Fitzgerald up there amongst the also-rans, even though these legends had surely performed in worse places in the down periods of their careers. So had Al. And like them, he'd played in far *better* surroundings.

He looked at his saxophone in its lonely corner of the stage, blending into the scenery like a tarnished trophy. He hardly ever took it home anymore, or even packed it in its case—it was far too ugly to tempt a thief. Al sometimes wondered if he subconsciously wished someone *would* steal it.

Al loved the place in the afternoon—hated it at night, when there were people there to ruin it. People ruined most everything he loved: movies, beaches, golf, and most of all, music. If he could play alone on a beach or a deserted street corner—anywhere alone—and get paid for it, he would be happier. Even better yet, would be to play for free. Money for music, in spite of its practical necessity, had always seemed "wrong".

What a dump. Huh, feels more like home here than at Kathleen's. Guess that makes sense. Your heart has to know it belongs in a place, for it to be a home.

♪ ♪ ♪

Pete began noodling around on his toms and snare, using brushes to create neat little swirls of sound. He was one of the best brush players Al had ever heard: true command of the style, and love for it showing every time he sat down at his kit. This smallish, scholarly man could use his hands and feet to set free the most complex rhythmic patterns, while at the same time keeping a solid, driving beat. When Pete Logan was on the gig he invalidated all the old jokes about drummers not being "real" musicians.

Wesley was drawn into Pete's mood and began to play a complementary bass pattern, a simple, but interesting use of walking lines and syncopation in a minor mode. What had been raindrops of sound had transformed into a river of music. Al was torn between listening and joining in. In one of those moments a jazz musician lives for, Al grabbed his tenor and let a melody grow from his soul. He didn't think about what key they were in, or what style they might call it, or if he'd ever played these same notes before. He knew he must have, from the comfortable feeling of familiarity about them. It didn't matter—there are only so many notes in the universe, and so many ways to string them together. He resisted analysis and just sang through his horn. Words to this tune were unnecessary. If anyone were there to listen, they would have been carried off to the same uncharted exotic world. Maybe, at last, this could be a song of his own, that he'd finally finish. It had such organic embryonic promise, how could it fail?

Magic happens.

♪ ♪ ♪

The piano slipped into the mix so subtly, so perfectly, Al didn't even notice at first. He was caught up in a particularly satisfying phrase, and as he repeated it, he was startled to have his sax riff joined in unison by a piano voice, supported harmonically by exquisite chording. The anger he wanted to have for Billy was washed away with one wave of those warm, soothing notes.

The blend shared by these four men was special, and each in his own way brought out the best in the others. There would be a time to chew out Billy for being late, but not now. This was too good to ruin.

This tune had developed from the prenatal gestation of drums and bass, and then sax, into a true musical love child. Billy had tenderly joined in and become an adoptive parent, nurturing their creation as his own.

♪ ♪ ♪

Magic happens—sometimes. Other times, something less than lovely emerges—and in this case, a pot full.

As quickly as the ecstasy had begun—it was over. Without warning, Billy killed their child. He began to sing an ersatz version of a Ted Weems hit from 1923—unbefitting the time, key, or gentle nature of the music they had been playing.

"Somebody stole my gal," he croaked. "She could've been my pal . . . yeah, she'd be my pal, till she met Al . . ." He stopped singing and began to yell. "Yeah, Al, who steals everything . . . hearts, women, time . . . and songs. Thinks he can write music, and all he does is fucking steal from them who really can."

Billy hadn't yet realized that his nonsensical singing and ranting was now the only sound in the room. Wesley propped his bass up against the amp and walked to the back door. Leaning back against his stool, Al jammed the mouthpiece cover onto his sax. Annoyance turned to concern as he checked to see if he'd wrecked his reed, but his attention was quickly diverted from possible equipment issues as he looked over at Pete.

The drummer was staring at Billy in simmering silence, with a look of sheer rage behind his little round specs. Al had never seen Pete like this.

Oh man, he's going to kill him.

Al moved over to a point between the piano and drums.

"Where'd everybody go?" said Billy. "Is the reherpal, I mean rehershal . . . SHIT . . . you know what I mean . . . We done practicin'? We were cookin' . . . most copacetically, weren't we, Al? Reminded me of when we used to play up on . . . uh, you know that street we used to play on, 43rd . . . 34th, whatever. No wait, I know what it was like . . . it's like the time we worked the Vanguard. Yeah, that was so far-fucking-out, weren't it? Only thing missing is your trumpet, and a few more of my teeth. How come you don't ever play the trumpet no more, Al? Tell me again—I always forget."

The scene now reminded Al more of the hotels in the Catskills and backing up Foster Brooks than it did of the old days in the jazz clubs of New York City. But Brooks was funny: his famous drunk act exactly that—an act.

Pete was approaching Billy, not saying a word. Al could see what was coming. He said, "Get a grip, Pete. We've been through this before. No need to push it. Come on, just calm down. Let's talk about some new material."

Al could see it wasn't working. All the drummer saw was a buzzed out piano player who had ruined something special. Those moments didn't happen much anymore, especially at Losers' Lounge, and Pete was already starting to feel like he fit in here too well, with "loser" stamped clearly on his forehead. Something in him had just snapped.

"You are a fucking MORON," Pete screamed at Billy. "First, you're late. Then you get here hopped-up on something, and now you destroy everything we had going."

He lunged at the startled piano man so quickly Al couldn't grab hold of enough of him to stop the attack. Billy and Pete toppled off the piano bench and rolled on the floor.

Al moved in as fast as he could, with Wesley close behind, saying, "What's up with this shit, man?"

Al blocked Wesley's way and said, "I'll handle this. Go to the door and don't let anybody in here for a few minutes. Okay . . . ? DO it."

As Wesley retreated without further question, Al reached down and grabbed Pete around the waist and hoisted him up like a sack of squirming farm cats, holding him in a bear hug until the struggling stopped. There was no need to worry about Billy taking advantage of Pete's inability to move— he would have enough trouble just getting to his feet.

"Okay, OKAY," Pete pleaded in trembling whispers. "Just let me down, and I'll be cool. I promise. Please."

Al hadn't meant to hurt him, but he figured he must have, with the force it took to lift him off Billy. Though he had developed a pretty good grip on most of his emotions, anger management was an ongoing struggle. Pete was lucky this wasn't the Al Waters from "back in the day". Al gently lowered the drummer and was glad to see he could stand.

"Go sit down over there," said Al in a fatherly tone. "I'll see how Billy's doing."

Feelings, and foggy faces, and places from the past seeped into his thoughts.

Alfred Waters Senior, Stupid Stewart Carter, Montreal, the room with no windows.

"You all right, Pete, for sure? Sorry if I hurt you, man. Was just trying to stop either one of you from getting busted up. I need both you scumbags okay to play tonight."

Pete wasn't laughing at this feeble attempt to lighten the mood. He sat quietly, inspecting his glasses for damage. Anyone even remotely familiar with Al's history knew he might have snapped Pete's neck if he'd really hurt Billy, even if he *had* deserved it. Friendship through so many years supersedes everything, including logic and moral justice.

Billy lay curled up under the bench, blubbering in a child's voice—pitiful sobs from a fifty-five-year-old man who had just had his ass kicked in a schoolyard brawl. Al looked down at his old friend, and for the millionth time hated that he loved him.

♪♪♪

Al sent Wesley out for some subs and coffee. By the time he returned, Big John was back, making a pot of coffee—the real stuff, as he called it. Appropriately, you had to be made of the *right stuff* to force down a cup—it might well have been mistaken for rocket fuel. The guys had once debated whether the walnut woodwork in the place had actually been finished with John's brew. It was either good for that, or paint remover, or maybe chemical warfare—terrorist groups would probably pay big bucks for the formula. But it hadn't killed anyone yet as far as they knew. After his first sip, Wesley agreed the warnings had been warranted, but suggested John's "lava java" was such a powerful eye-opener, it might not in fact be deadly—but would more likely, *wake* the dead.

One of Al's earliest tasteless jokes had been to suggest that Big John was actually a white man, but years of drinking his coffee had given him the dark-roasted look—stained from within?

John had laughed and said, "Al, I bet you wish somethin' could turn *you* black. Don't matter anyhow. Still wouldn't give you no soul."

♪♪♪

Big John could see the mood was pretty grim, and he knew enough to stay out of it. He began to clean up the tables, and then stacked chairs, preparing to vacuum the dreary carpet. To no one's surprise he soon asked, "Any of them subs goin' to waste, boys?"

At Al's insistence, Wesley always bought a couple of extras. The young man grinned at Big John and said, "Got yo fave, my bald nigga. Meatball and gravy. Mmm these succas lookin' *good*. Maybe I might just eat these here extra ones myself. That okay, Al? You paid for 'em."

Big John forced a smile, in spite of his displeasure in being called "nigger". He had grown up in an era when that was unacceptable, even from a fellow Afro-American. And although he knew Wesley's generation embraced the N-word as his own peers had with "brother" or "bro", it still bothered him. He remembered too well a time when he wouldn't even have been allowed in many bars like where he now worked—a time when the word "nigger" was never used casually, but implied disdain, anger, or hate—often all three.

Big John knew Wesley was kidding. He accepted the bag of subs and began *hoovering* the first one as he expressed his gratitude. "Fankths guyths . . . oophs thorry, scooth me . . ." He was trying to eat and talk—etiquette giving way to enthusiasm, as usual.

The big man was not uncomfortable with his appearance and weight—almost one hundred and fifty pounds heavier than the two-fifty or so he carried in his professional boxing days. As he put it himself, he was born to be strong, not fast. He was six-foot-five, and in his youth, extraordinarily muscular. With a little more speed to go with his power, he might have been a serious heavyweight contender. A more easy-going or gentler man you'd never meet—another reason he'd never made it to the top in the boxing world. If you were a friend, you could call him "Big John", or "Big Man", or "Big Guy"—as long as the adjective was "big", or a proper synonym. Anything to do with "fat", though, was unacceptable and would have you facing a large cold shoulder—only fifty percent figuratively.

Al remembered the first time he and Big John had met, during his first gig negotiations with Lou Farina. It was difficult to fathom it had really been almost five years since that day.

♪♪♪

"Hey, Al, dis is Johnny Lima, my number one man here," said Lou Farina in a voice brimming with Brooklyn. He laughed, slapping his paw on John's massive back. "Don't worry, he wouldn't hurt a fly. Too bad, too. I lost a bundle on him when he was in da ring. Couldn't believe anyone dat big could lose. Anyways, he's 'Big John' to his friends, and since he's da bartender, I'm sure you'll be calling him dat, real soon."

Al took to Big John right away—not so, to the shiny-suited, slick-haired Lou, whose good-fella-wanna-be act had stirred an instant revulsion.

"Good to meet you, John," Al said as they shook hands.

"Please, my friend, it's 'Big John'," laughed the bartender. "What you see is what you get. And what do you see? *Big*, right? Tell it like it is, I always say."

"Well, let's see," ventured Al, "do you have any single malt Scotch in that cabinet? That'll make you *my* friend."

"I do, indeedy do," said Big John. He proceeded to unlock a sliding door at the back of the liquor cabinet behind the bar brands where he revealed a selection of premium Scotch whiskeys, a couple of which Al had never seen before.

"Wow," said Al. "Big John, you just met your *best* friend."

♪♪♪

Five years—a record for Al in both longevity and stability—during which Al and Big John had seen staff and band members come and go. Even Billy had once "disappeared" for a couple of months, until Al tracked him down and saved him from himself one more time. The only other constants had been Dixie who had been there since the sixties, and was now almost in *her* sixties—and of course, Lou.

Al and Big John both wished Lou Farina had been one of the "goes", but they were stuck with him. He owned the joint, and the longtime employees shared the mind-set that he pretty much owned *them* too.

♪♪♪

"Can we get past this and get on with some new tunes now?" Al asked the band. They were sitting at three different tables—not good vibes. "Wesley, you cool, man?" asked Al.

"I'm here to work, boss; let's do it," answered the kid in a lower-than-usual tone.

Al nodded and turned to Pete. "Hey, man, let me deal with Billy. It's my job to sort this out. Trust me on this one, okay?"

Pete didn't answer, but simply walked to his drum kit and sat, ready to play. Al turned back to Billy.

I know what I should say . . . what every other band leader in the world would say. Billy's crossed the line again, and about as bad as he ever has. Why can't I do it?

Sitting down next to Billy, Al asked quietly, "Hey, man, are the shakes gone? Can you play?"

Billy appeared to be on the verge of collapse, no longer shaking on the outside, but still pretty messed up. His intense thirst was clear—but for what?

Al said, "Get your butt back to the piano. I'll go grab you a soda."

What's your pleasure, Billy, for real? Coke, smoke, uppers, downers . . . a little smack? Won't learn EVER, will you . . . not till you're in the ground. Christ, man, you'll probably find a way to smoke the weeds that grow through your fucking coffin walls.

"Boss," said Billy, pulling Al's face down next to his so no one else could hear. "Sorry I fucked up, but you know, you really did steal that tune you were just playing."

"Like hell I did, Billy. It was a spur of the moment thing that just came to me."

"No, Al, you stole it, and I know you don't got any fucking idea from who, *do* you?"

"Billy, you're full of crap. Now come on, we gotta get back to work here."

"Yeah, boss. Sure. Just forget it, huh?"

Billy rose slowly, falling back onto the chair once before making it to his feet. As he headed unsteadily toward the piano, Al watched, flinching with each stagger and stumble from his old friend. This was not a time to help him; loyalty to the ensemble had to rule the moment.

Wesley picked up his bass while Pete sat wearily at his kit. As Al returned with Billy's drink, he thought about the music they had created for those brief minutes, the special little song with no name. He knew—they all knew—they would never find it again.

It's lost, like that first time you love somebody . . . until they screw you around. You can never find that kind of joy again either.

A single tear struggled for freedom until Al's involuntary blink sent it trickling. He pictured the drop as the beginning of a river of blood being released from his wrist—a bathtub full of swirling crimson relief.

Jesus Christ, what the fuck is wrong with me? No way I'm letting this get to me. Come on, man. Grow up.

Setting Billy's glass of soda on the piano top, he wiped the tear away and said, "Damn bug in my eye . . ."

He grabbed his saxophone, and just the feeling of it in his hands gave him a musical idea.

"Let's try a new version of 'The Girl With Emphysema'. Get this—in three-four. An up-tempo Latin waltz? The dimwits will recognize it, but we'll be the only ones who know what's different about it."

Billy smiled and said, "It's been done before, Al, but you're right, it'll be kinda like putting one over on 'em, won't it."

"Yeah, Billy, you got it. Let's go . . . Unn, two, three. Two, two, three . . ."

Yeah, here we go . . . fools fooling the other fools as usual. Where does it end? Miles knew; he knew everything. I wonder if he wanted to die young.

CHAPTER 9

FIVE - SOUTH TOWER [3]

*T*he patient's breathing appeared to be lighter and more rapid—a possible sign he might be close to waking? The orderly leaned forward in the bedside chair. He wished he could light up a cigarette, but smoking would be a definite giveaway. Hospital staff certainly wouldn't do that, not in a patient's room. More than for a smoke, he yearned for a shot: wine, whisky, rum, vodka, even beer—anything alcoholic. The couple of drinks he'd had before coming to the hospital were now ancient history, their confidence-bolstering powers miserably faded.

"Hey, my friend," he whispered, "let's wakey wakey, huh? I need to be sure that you know I'm here. It's kind of important that you know, before I do what I came for. Shit, I hate you so much. I try to anyway . . . but, I'm so fucking confused.

"How long have I known you anyway? Crazy, it's not really very long at all when you think about it . . . but it seems like all my life, at least the part of it that sucks the most. Might as well be a million years, with my anger growing every minute of those years. I don't think you really knew what you were doing when you hurt me . . . but it's too late now. Done is done. And you're *done*.

"But damn, it still pisses me off that this had to happen. All your damn fucking fault. I just know we could have had something, you and me. Could have . . . if you could've accepted me somehow. But you had to fuck that up, *didn't* you. Now, I'm gonna fuck *you* up real good. Kinda funny, huh? Funny, and so sad, all at once."

CHAPTER 10

A GIRL NAMED SUE
1966

*A*l waited until 7 p.m., the agreed-upon time he was to call. The phone sat there, looking all black and businesslike. It didn't look like a device for calling Sue. How could the voice of the prettiest girl in the entire world be transported through this ugly upside-down Mickey Mouse Club hat?

Five after seven. He'd looked up the number in the phone book, just in case he'd written it down wrong when she gave it to him. There was her name, at least her last name, with her father's first initial—it looked so real in print. It shouldn't have been so easy to find. Princesses, and even girls as perfect as princesses should be protected by castles, and moats, and knights on horses—their royal phone numbers unlisted. He was glad it wasn't so, as if seeing the name in the directory proved he hadn't only dreamed she existed.

Courage was even harder to find after seven o'clock had arrived, especially since Al was certain her father would answer. Would she be allowed to pick up the phone, a mere teenager—a child?

Ten after. Damn it! His hands were sweating. He'd dialed the number over twenty times now without lifting the receiver, holding his finger in each number hole as the dial whirred all the way back around.

Eleven after. He had to do it. He lifted the phone—the whole phone. When did it get so heavy? He held it in his lap as he sat cross-legged on the floor. As carefully as he dialed—pulling numbers around as slowly as he could and releasing each one after a few seconds pause—it was finished far too fast. Burbling through the earpiece came one ring . . . two rings . . . three—

"Hello," rumbled a voice so deep it was how God might have sounded if you were to call heaven.

After a dry gulp, Al said, "I'm, uh, I mean, is Sue home please, sir?"

He waited for the line to go dead. Mr. MacDonald's car would surely roar into the driveway seconds later, and the enraged father would have a shotgun in hand as he broke down the front door.

The voice of God returned. "Well yes, but . . . oh, is this Al Waters? Sue said you'd be calling."

"Yes, sir," said Al, his voice quavering with adolescence and terror. "Hello, sir, I mean, Mr. MacDonald. How are you doing tonight, sir?"

"Just fine, thanks, Al. Hold on please, I'll fetch Susan."

Al now knew what Einstein had meant. Time does funny things relative to what you're waiting for—and even more so, according to how scared you are. It was about a hundred years before Sue came on the line.

"Hi, Al, I was hoping that was you. Whatcha doing?"

This was so easy for a girl. Al figured she must have been doing this for years already. He knew she'd be on to him—it had to be so obvious this was his first time. She'd laugh at him, and tomorrow everyone at school would hear about how he'd messed up, and what a loser he was.

"Hi, Sue. Not much . . . Was just doing some homework. You know, that stupid history assignment Mr. Lawson gave us . . . and I remembered it was time to call. I did say seven, didn't I?"

Of course I did; we both did. I'm saying idiot things.

"So, Sue, how are you? Hey, a poem. Told you I was a poet."

God, that was dense.

"Um, got your homework done, Sue?"

Agghhh . . . what a dumb, damn, stupid question!

"No, Al," said Sue, "I was waiting for you to call first."

Holy jumpin'. Did she really just say that?

Al said, "Uh, that's nice. Umm, sorry. I didn't mean to, uh, say that homework was more important than us talking . . . I just—"

"Al, I've been hoping all year to get you to call me. Do you think I dropped my books right in front of you in the hall today, by accident? You're cute *and* cool. Everyone thinks so. Come on, you know that, don't you? We all figured you had a best girl at another school or something since you never went out with anyone at Central."

"Gee, Sue, I never thought about it much."

I figured they all thought I was a square.

"But if you say so, then I'll take your word for it. Thanks."

Al took three slow deep breaths, the phone and the silence becoming heavier with each one. He drew in a fourth, even more slowly, vowing to use it for . . . the *question*. After what felt like an hour, the words leapt from his throat—far too quickly for a guy who was supposed to be so cool. "Does that mean you'll maybe go to the dance this weekend, like, you know, with me . . . ?"

"Oh my God, Al, I'd love to. Do you know how neat that'll be? The last time you like, played your trumpet at school, all the girls were like, wow what a dreamboat. Like Herb Alpert from the Tijuana Brass."

Herb Alpert? Yuck.

Al said, "Friday then? Pick you up at seven-thirty?"

"This is so cool, Al. Can't wait. See you at school. Bye."

As Al hung up he wondered how he had managed to sound so composed. His hands were soaked and his insides squirmed like a bucket of live worms.

Three days till Friday. Please, God, don't let me get any monster zits before then, not on my face, please?

♪♪♪

Sue MacDonald. He was going out with Sue MacDonald!

The first time Al had ever danced with a girl it had been Sue, way back in grade seven—a slow dance of course. She'd come all the way across the gym to ask him on a ladies' choice, and all the guys sharing the wall with him had laughed and made lewd comments. As the music started, he'd held her clumsily, about as far away as his gangly arms could keep her. But she said, "No, silly, like this," as she pulled him closer.

She had breasts already—the first girl in their class to need a bra. As her budding womanhood squished against his chest—Sue being as tall as Al was at the time—he felt awkward, not so much for himself, but for her. What must it feel like to have breasts? It must be so weird to have this visible *thing* about you—your sexuality just sticking out there—and then, to have them touch a guy while you danced? How embarrassing must that be? For a girl, a developing chest must be like an erection for a guy—a permanent one, that you couldn't hide with books, or untucked shirts, or sweaters stretched to the max. He prayed he wouldn't get one right then—every boy's nightmare, a boner in *public*. This wasn't the same thing at all as hugging your mother or aunt. They had breasts, and bigger too. But they didn't make you feel that *way*, that incredible way that Sue's breasts were now making him feel.

Al had first noticed his sister, Anne, beginning to develop when she was twelve—he was ten. As any normal little brother must do, he kidded her about it; he just thought it was silly seeing her with *bumps*. But a couple of years later, almost overnight, those bumps were appealing, even if she *was* his sister. He sometimes tried to catch her getting dressed, but she would scream and then tell on him. His dad had raised the roof over that, so he quit trying. One time he'd seen her through the slightly ajar bathroom door, as she got out of the shower. He nervously enjoyed a long peek before scrambling away when he heard his dad's ominous footsteps on the stairs.

He'd dreamed about that moment more than once and often masturbated thinking about Anne's breasts. But afterwards, always came guilt and disgust for thinking of her in a sexual way. Another feeling bubbled beneath the surface as well, and directly because of it, he stopped using thoughts of Anne for self-gratification. One night, the specter of his father's face had drifted in like a total eclipse across Al's sexual imaginations of his sister, extinguishing his excitement and blocking out all pleasure from the moment. From the shadows of this image grew a deep, confusing, illogical, gut-knotting anger.

♪♪♪

When, in grade seven, Al had been fretting about going to his first mixed party, Anne had tried to teach him to dance. She'd held him back at arm's length, trying to describe where each foot should go and when, but instead of a waltz or fox trot it resembled the toy soldier strut. The stumbling sibling team appeared as uncomfortable as two human beings could get, as Al repeatedly moved left instead of right, or forward instead of back. Since he was a musician, everyone—himself included—assumed he should have been a natural at dancing. But this first attempt, and many more throughout his life, proved the two activities were not symbiotic motor skills.

Finally, it was party night and here he was with Sue MacDonald, having the first-ever non-family breasts yielding tenderly to his skinny, going-on-thirteen-year-old front, and then, the ultimate "uh-oh"—his pants stretching ever tighter beneath the fly. He was positive everyone in the room would notice the bulge. As Elvis's "Love Me Tender" came to an end, he said, "Thanks," without looking at Sue's face, and hurried away to get behind the nearest table to hide his inopportune erection. When he turned, he was relieved to see that Sue had rejoined her friends on the girls' wall. Once he managed to "settle down" his lower region, he'd be able to approach her again.

Al's relief was short-lived. His heart belly-flopped into a pool of fear as he saw Richie Peters, the tallest guy in grade seven, on the prowl. "Big Dick" they called him in gym class. No fair. He'd failed a grade; he was a year older. Al hated when Richie would strut around the locker room at the YMCA, proudly naked, for much longer than should have been necessary. Since the big goof was the first of the guys Al knew, to have developed pubic hair, he figured Richie was showing it off—his major life accomplishment.

As Sue began to dance with Richie, she glanced over at Al and smiled. But he refused to be distracted from the food table's array of mini sandwiches, soft drinks, and pastries. His feigned interest in food was a feeble attempt to mask the pain of seeing the prettiest girl in the world cradled in Richie's arms.

For the rest of the night Al was too shy to ask her to dance, especially with Big Dick all over her. He might have tried harder at the next dance, but after that night Richie and Sue had started going together—end of dream.

♪♪♪

Now, three years later, he was about to go to a dance *with* Sue as his date. Life was amazing.

When Al told Anne about Sue and their impending first date, she asked him if he wanted to try the dance lessons one more time. He said no, but maybe a bit of advice about girls in general might be invaluable.

"Okay, Annie, when we're dancing slow songs what's the rules about how close I get? Is it too forward to kind of hug her close enough to touch, uh, you know, our 'fronts'? And do I hold her hand up high, pulled in up to my face? And my other hand . . . should it stay way up high on her back, or slip down a bit towards her bum? And how do I know if she wants me to hold her hand or not, like when we're walking home and stuff?"

"Wow, Al," said Anne, "you're really into this, aren't you? You're using preparation and planning like you were working on a trumpet piece or something. Hey, you can't just assume anything about this kind of thing. As far as the dancing, I'd let her guide you. If she thinks you're too far away, she'll find a way to get you closer; same with where your top hand is. Trust me, girls know how to do this stuff instinctively. And keep your other hand off her *bum*. That's not for a first date, and for sure not at your age, you perv. Now, as for handholding: if it was me, and I really liked the guy, I'd want him to hold my hand even before the dance, and on the way home, for sure."

"Geezes, but how do I know if she likes me enough?"

"Look, Al, from what you told me already, she pretty much asked *you* to take her to this dance. Don't worry, she likes you enough all right."

"Okay, what about, um, okay, if she likes me so darned much, is she going to want me to kiss her?"

"Alfred Waters," said Anne, with southern belle shock, "I do declare you are such a rogue. This young lady will want no part of you if you try that on your first date. A true gentleman would never be so bold."

"Good," said Al. "I'll be lucky if I don't run home halfway through the dance and throw up anyway, just from worrying about the handholding stuff."

Anne's voice grew softer. "Little brother, you're going to be just fine. Use common sense and your heart. You'll know what to do. You won't make any mistakes, and even if you did make a little one or two, if she's someone you'd want to keep seeing, she'll ignore those. But don't . . . *don't* touch her bum when you're dancing."

Al laughed along with Anne. He said, "Thanks, Sis. You're the best. I'll do you proud. Mmm, can't wait to grab that cute little bum."

As Al ran from the room, Anne got up to chase him, yelling, "You little bugger. I'm gonna kick *your* bum! C'mere, you brat."

♪♪♪

For Al, the sock hop was, for the first time, *not* boring. He and Sue had danced to most of the slow songs—his favorite part of the night—holding her close, curling up her hand in his, and pressing her head to his chest. Anne had been right; from Sue's body language he could tell exactly when to try these things.

Fast dances like the "monkey" and the "swim" were a bit hard to master right away, but fun nonetheless. Al especially liked the "twist", because it was so easy; but when muscle cramps shot up his torso Sue giggled at his pained look and protestations of agony, which quickly turned into his own laughter, mixed with yelps whenever he twisted to the left.

Breathless from dancing *and* laughing, they sat for a few minutes, before Al grabbed Sue's hand and said, "Come on, let's dance, I need some more torture."

♪♪♪

After the dance as they walked toward Sue's house Al's hand brushed hers a couple of times. The third time, she grabbed his wrist and slid her hand down into his. The cool skin of her tiny fingers sent electric waves through his body: simple Morse code-like messages, received in his heart as melody, and in his groin as throbbing primal rhythm. He wondered if anything could be both as wonderful *and* as frightening as these sensations.

The route home took them by the city park and Al suggested they cut through. It wasn't really a shortcut, but a romantic strategy he'd dreamed of all week. Stopping by a majestic old elm tree, he held both her hands and pulled her close. She gave no indication of resisting, so he began to stroke her face.

"Sue, this has been the best night ever. You're so pretty. Would you, um, ever want to go out with me again?"

She closed her eyes, saying nothing, and moved her face upward, closer to his.

Did this mean what he thought it did? What if he tried to kiss her, and it wasn't what she meant?

Christ, if Anne was here she'd clobber me. I am a creep.

He had to take the chance. Starting by nuzzling the side of her neck, he slowly inched upward until his cheek touched hers. Then he brushed his lips across her tiny ear before moving his mouth slowly down to hers. While their outward breaths pulsed as one, the minimal contact between them was still more a mingling of air than flesh. The fire of passion in his body and mind was rapidly kindled, and he wished desperately to press his lips more firmly against hers, but the choice was taken from him.

Sue moaned and kissed him back ferociously. This *couldn't* be her first time. Her tongue darted between his lips, finding his tongue, and lighting it on fire. Biblical tales of snakes came to mind and developed instant validity as the growing serpent stirred in his pants.

She gripped his left hand and guided it down to her breast. His first thought was, *Oh God, don't let me do it wrong.* This was far beyond what he and Anne had discussed. Even through the sweater, her body felt so much better than he'd ever imagined. A breast was so soft and yet firm to the touch at the same time. He marveled at the resiliency of this wondrous part of womanhood which no man can relate to with any part of his own body.

Sue whispered, "No, not like that." Without warning, grabbed his hand away from her breast. Convinced he'd done something terribly wrong, Al felt a noose of fear crushing his throat and his brief-lived joy.

Damn, I've blown it. Oh crap, will she forgive me?

But instead of pulling his hand away from her body altogether, she directed him to the bottom of her sweater and drew his hand up underneath to the silky-smooth skin of her torso. Moving upward cautiously, his fingers found the edge of her bra. He ran his hand over the yielding delicacy of the bra's thin material, until his fingers tripped against a delightful swelling protrusion in the center.

So that's why they call it a "titty hard-on". Wow.

She whispered, "Take it off."

Oh God oh God oh God. What am I supposed to do?

Al didn't know what she meant—the bra or the sweater. Before he could figure out how to ask, she reached behind her back with both hands and said, "There."

Al's hand was shaking as he slipped it back up under the sweater. Then came the moment he'd dreamed of so many times. As her flesh yielded to his fingers in a way only a woman's breast can, her skin felt cool, almost cold. Or was his own skin hot? As he ran his fingers back and forth between her waist and breasts, he was fascinated by the different feel of both. Her firm nipples were an intriguing contrast to the surrounding softness as he repeatedly brushed his hand over them. He was captivated and excited by how they sprang back to upright after each finger glided across them.

Al said, "I'm not hurting you, am I?"

"Oh, Al, you won't hurt me," said Sue. "Let me help."

She took his hands and guided him through the way she wanted to be fondled, squeezing his grip tighter than he'd been doing. She then pulled the sweater up over her head, the undone bra going with it. As abrupt and unforeseen as this moment was, it felt like slow motion, as Al gasped in complete awe of what he beheld. The only bare breasts he'd seen were the posed perfection of magazine images—and Sue's were even *more* perfect.

"Sue, what if someone comes along? Aren't you afraid?"

"Shut up, and c'mere," she giggled as she lowered herself to the grass, pulling Al on top of her. This was too much, too fast, too hot, too crazy. Letting the moment run on its own fuel, he arched his back, supporting himself at full arm's length, moving his pelvis up and down against her. This felt so good; could actual sex be any better? Unfortunately, his sense of coital timing was yet to be trained—as he comprehended what was happening, far too late to stop it. His orgasm was both dizzying and painful inside his pants as he kept moving much too long after ejaculation. Finally, slumping to his elbows, he touched his lips to her ear and cheek. Did she know what had happened?

Geezes, I hope it won't soak through, past my underwear. Thank God it's night. Maybe it won't show.

"We better get going, Sue," said Al. "It's really late."

Sue laughed. "Getting a little chilly too," she said, slipping back into her bra. He turned away, with an inexplicable feeling that it wasn't "right" to watch. When she fumbled with her sweater she said, "Al, help me out here."

Together they straightened it out and once she got it back on, he held her in a long, tight hug.

"Sue, I hope I wasn't too forward here. Wasn't sure how far you wanted me to—"

"Shhh, Al, you were wonderful. You could have done anything you wanted with me. I'm not afraid with you. You just showed me something wonderful by stopping on your own, instead of making me decide. I can't even guess how hard that must be for a guy to stop like that when you're all worked up. I love you."

Could have done anything? Loves me? Doesn't know I came off in my pants? LOVES ME . . . ?

"I guess I . . . I mean . . . sure, I love you too, Sue. I've had a crush on you since like, forever."

"You mean since that dance in grade seven?"

"Actually no, even before that. I was always too shy to talk to you."

"Oh, Al, why do you men have to be so bad at understanding us? I've always thought you were, well, special, so different from the other boys. All they can think about is sports and spitting and dumb stuff. You're deep. You remind me of Jimmy Stewart, or Ben Casey . . . no, Richard Burton! *That's* who you're like: rugged, but sensitive and gentle. It'll all work out, Al. I can see our future. I've got names picked out for our kids. We'll be together, forever and ever."

Al took a deep, slow, shuddery breath. "Uh, kids? Isn't that a little bit ahead of schedule? I've got a career to think about, you know, making it as a trumpet player and writing music? There'll be lots of travelling and . . . Don't *you* want to go to college?"

She kissed his cheek. "Everything will be perfect as long as we're together. We'll figure it out."

♩♩♩

For Al, the remaining walk to Sue's house was incredibly uncomfortable, both because of his wet underwear, and the fear under each streetlight that she might notice the growing wet spot next to his fly. He prayed no one would be up when he got home.

♩♩♩

It seemed as if Sue's prophecy was not pure fantasy. For several weeks they walked to and from school together, had lunch in the cafeteria every day, and talked on the phone for hours each night. Al wrote her more than a dozen poems which he read to her in the park near *their* tree.

Sue's parents were never home from work before 6 p.m. After school, she and Al would go to her place where they would make out: the first time, innocently, on the couch; the time after that, more intimately, upstairs in her room. The third time, she said he could remove all her clothes, as long as he kept his underwear on. This worked out satisfactorily for less than a minute. While moving against her, his shorts slipped down, just enough to expose his tumescent splendor.

He tried to cover himself, but Sue pulled his hand away and said, "Al, you can try to put it in if you're careful, you know, about . . ."

Al was shaking as he slowly began to push himself inside her. His fears were twofold: to not hurt Sue, and to not have an orgasm. The latter was determined quickly by the former.

Sue cried out, "Oh, ow . . . oh my God, Al, please stop. It's hurting too much."

Al immediately rolled off to the side and held her as she cried. Kissing her gently on the cheek, he said, "I'm so sorry, Sue. The last thing I want, *ever*, is to hurt you. We don't have to do that, not yet. We've got the rest of our lives, right?"

♪♪♪

Two weeks passed before their next opportunity to be naked together—naked, except for Al's underwear, which he checked regularly for proper placement.

As he lay on top of her, moving in the way that comes so naturally, his groin began to ache with sensual urgency, recalling that first night by the tree when he'd lost control so quickly. For fear of another underwear accident, he rolled over and asked if he could remove his shorts—just for a minute. Although his intentions had been sincere, the forces of nature overruled caution—and without thinking about it, he was back on top of her. He said he wouldn't try to put it in—only rub himself against her, until he was almost there—then she could finish him with her hand.

Al said, "Don't worry, Sue. No way I'd hurt you again. I can hold back."

It was a promise she wouldn't allow him to keep, as she grabbed his penis and pulled him downward, like a sweating, panting, 170-pound pull toy. She rubbed him against herself, right where all that warmth and wetness was.

"Yes, Al, please . . . yes," she whispered, as she began to guide him inside her.

Surprisingly it didn't appear to hurt her at all, but she practically broke *him* in her zeal. Sweet, shy Sue had become Mata Hari.

He was in. This time, a different duo of fears fought for the spotlight: climaxing too quickly, and actually climaxing in there at all. Getting a girl in trouble, especially at their age, was a truly horrifying prospect.

He tried to enter deeper, in tiny slow-motion increments. Einstein be damned; time was not cooperating here. This felt so good. Motivated by insuppressible biological forces, he found himself making a sudden aggressive thrust, as far in as he could go. Sue gasped—then smiled up at him, as if wanting more of the same.

Al's urge to thrust proved not to be his only relevant control issue.

Oh God . . . oh no . . . already?

He had planned to pull out well before any chance of an *accident*, but inexperience trumped good intention. If he'd known how intense the sensations were going to be inside her, he might have stopped, or at least moved slower or not so deep to prevent this—but a hand this was *not*. He'd been overpowered by the newness of the feelings, his lust defeating all restraint.

Ecstasy, fear, joy, dizziness, and shame flooded through his body and mind all at once. This mixture of feelings was not at all what he'd dreamed of. When masturbating, he had command of where his hand touched. But inside of her, it was out of his power, the sensations so intense, they'd almost caused him to cry out in a combination of pleasure and panic.

The thought raced from his pounding heart to his melting brain: *Does she know?* He decided to pretend nothing had happened, so he remained inside her, his erection still almost at full strength. After a few moments he began thrusting once more—this time, like a maniac.

What the hell. Nothing to lose now. If she's gonna get pregnant, it's too late to worry about that. Damage done. Might as well try and enjoy the rest of this, and hope she doesn't figure out what happened.

Finally, with his passion past its peak, he slowed and then collapsed on spaghetti arms. He sighed and said, "Better quit now."

Sue said, "Thanks for stopping, Al. I know how tough it must be, but you mustn't climax inside of me, not without a rubber, not while I'm not safe."

Thank you, God. She didn't feel it.

"Shhhh, I know, Sue. It's okay. Let's just lie here for a bit, all right?"

She's so wet anyway. Will she notice my stuff's in there now too?

"Oh, Al," said Sue, "I'm different now. You just made me a woman. Love me forever?"

One of the benefits of being a teenage boy is being able to have an orgasm and be ready again in minutes—unless you're trying too hard. Al conjured every sexy thought he could muster, fondled Sue's breasts, and began to move inside her again. It was working—not as intense as before—but still more than pleasant. When he was again fully erect, he pulled out of her, and began furiously stroking himself.

Sue asked, "Don't you want me to do that for you?"

"Just trying something different," said Al. "Let me do it on you. That'll be so hot."

God, I can smell the jizz. Will she know what that smell is?

He thought he was going to rub his skin completely off, but with the visual excitement of her beautiful body stretched out beneath him, the effort finally succeeded. As his ejaculation splattered onto her chest and stomach, all joy drained along with it—both from his body and from his heart.

Something wrong here . . . something wrong with me? This isn't how I thought it was supposed to feel.

Al watched the rivulets of semen begin to slip down her torso, sneaking away as if to hide, ostrich-like in the bed sheets.

"Geez, let me get some Kleenex," he said, rolling off her and reaching for the box beside the bed.

Sue said, "Oh, Al, no rush. I love it on me. It's part of you. That was wonderful. I'm so glad you like my body."

In spite of her enthusiasm and loving attitude, he couldn't fight off a deep shame and embarrassment as he fumbled with tissues to clean up the aftermath. He tried to appear as content as Sue, as he lay next to her, holding her hand against his chest, and singing to her until it was time to get dressed. She couldn't possibly understand how he really felt. How could she—when even he didn't?

♪♪♪

A month later, they had to talk.

"Al, I don't know how to say this, but, I think we have a problem. My period is late, by about four days. What if . . . ?"

Al wondered if his heart would ever start up again. Somehow he managed to sound calm. "Sue, we'll work it out if worse comes to worse. Don't worry, I'll be here for you."

God no, not now. My life is messed up enough without this. My dad will

KILL me.

As tears filled her eyes, she said, "Al, there's, uh, a complication I have to talk to you about . . . You won't like it."

"Sue, what could be more complicated than you maybe being pregnant?"

Sobs came as stabs of punctuation between her words. "I . . . I don't know for sure . . . if it's . . . yours or not."

The last time he'd had the wind knocked out of him was in a pickup football game. This was worse; this was being hit by the entire Toronto Argonauts team—*and* their bus.

"What does that mean, Sue? How could it *not* be mine?"

"Please don't hate me, Al."

"I promise I won't," said Al. The lie came easily. "Just tell me what you're trying to say."

If it's what I think, I'll hate you forever.

"Al, remember I told you about that guy I used to see . . . before you and I—"

"Yeah, yeah, Graham, right? That college guy. What is he, like, nineteen . . . *twenty*? You saw him for a bit last summer."

Her eyes scanned the floor, and then the walls and ceiling—anywhere but Al's face. After a deep breath, she said, "Well, he's been coming home the past few weekends. He called me, and we got together a couple of times. I thought it would be okay. I told him I was seeing you now, and he didn't seem to care. He said he and I could be friends, and he wouldn't push me for more. But he had beer with him the second time, and we kissed a little bit. Remember, I *had* been sort of in love with him last year . . . I was so mixed up.

"Then it went too far. It was the week before you and I did it. I was actually going to tell him I didn't want to see him anymore, but I had too much beer; yes I *know* that's not a good reason. But he kept kissing me, and more. And then, before I could think straight, we were doing it . . ."

"You mean, you went all the way, with *him*? After I'd been so patient, and careful, so I wouldn't hurt you? Is that why it was finally okay with you? 'Cause you'd already done it with him?"

"Al, I didn't know how to tell you. I didn't really think you had to know . . . until this 'problem'. Graham didn't care that it hurt me. But *you* did. You're always so sweet and gentle with me."

Al's pain burned far deeper than his anger, because he did believe Sue really loved him. But the cruelest form of betrayal is from someone who's earned your trust and built a nest in your soul. He wondered if he could ever again look into a woman's eyes and not see Sue's—not see lies.

He told Sue to call Graham and let *him* worry about the "problem". She cried and said she didn't really care who the father was because she wanted to work it out with Al. She promised never to see Graham again, no matter what.

♪♪♪

Two days later, it didn't matter about any of it—when Sue discovered she wasn't pregnant. When she told Al, he said, "Too bad. Maybe you should ask Graham to try again."

He never spoke with her again—except in dreams.

CHAPTER 11

STUPID STEWART CARTER

"Alfred," said Doctor Davidson, "so far today you seem a little less talkative than in our first session. Please don't forget; anything you're feeling, good or bad, is certainly worth talking about. Are you perhaps not well, physically?"

"Nah, I'm cool, Doc. Maybe a little tired. Extra late night, last night . . . past couple of nights actually. Sorry, I don't think I'm all here."

"I understand, Alfred. You've been very open and communicative, considering the fatigue you mention. I have noticed though in our chats, you haven't yet said much about your family, other than a few short remarks about your father."

"Hey, I can do that," said Al. "Always great to relive those happy childhood memories."

The doctor turned to a blank page in his notebook. "Sarcasm again. Correct, Alfred?"

"Of course, Doc. Always beats facing the cold hard truth, right?"

"Hmm, now sarcasm in your response about sarcasm. Or do you sincerely feel it is better to avoid truth in this instance?"

"Sorry, Doc. Am I a tough case or what? I'll try to be more serious."

"In your own time and your own way, Alfred . . . I know you will. Okay then, your family. Where would you like to begin?"

"My parents were thrown together, Doc, in a time when people didn't have the luxury of finding out enough about each other before they got hitched. My mother was a smart person without a lot of self-confidence. If she'd had the chance to go further in school she could have done a lot with her life."

"So by that, Alfred, do you think she wasn't happy in her role as wife and mother?"

"Well, Doc, I know she always sort of resented us—I mean my sister, Anne, and me. Annie told me that our mother once said that she might have left Dad if she hadn't got pregnant so soon after her first child, Annie, that is . . . I was the youngest, the last born. Guess it was too late for her to *escape* after I came along. Makes sense too, being as Mum used to cry all the time, up in their room usually, where she probably thought we couldn't hear; though sometimes just out of the blue almost anywhere, like at the dinner table. *That* was scary. Dad would tell her not to be so silly, that there were people all over the world who had it a lot worse than her. She should be glad she had a comfortable home. One time I remember him going ballistic and yelling about how none of us had ever seen real trouble . . . had never seen our friends *die* in front of us. He was talking about the war. He did that sometimes when he drank too much . . . but never any details, just gloomy muttered references to seeing guys die.

"Mum told me once how she wished she could have been an English teacher. She read all the time, well at least when Dad wasn't home, hardly ever when he was there. It was great when she'd read us stories and tell us how there was this big world of wonderful things out there. But most times she'd ruin it by getting all teary and saying stuff like how we'd never see those things because, like her, we didn't deserve to. Funny, she never talked about any of that stuff when *he* was around. Guess it made him mad although sometimes he'd laugh at her,which was worse I think."

"Alfred, you mentioned this in our first session, how it bothered you that your father made jokes out of everything. You seem to paint him as a tough, mean person, but then there's this picture you portray of his joker side. Can you explain?"

"I think his comedian side was the meanest part of him, Doc. He used his humor to belittle us, me and my mother anyway, not so much Anne. But it was at its worst when he was into the sauce."

"Would you consider him an alcoholic?"

"Don't really know, Doc. He had a few beer every night. Oops, sorry . . . *beers*. There's that small-town Canada thing again, *eh*? But when he'd get into the Scotch, that was the scary time. You rarely actually *saw* him drink it, like maybe he didn't think we'd know? But you could smell it on him like cologne. That's when he was at his meanest, with the put-down jokes and all."

"And your sister, she wasn't subjected to those jokes?"

"Annie . . . ?" said Al, louder than he'd meant to. "She was immune, or off-limits for some reason. She was his perfect little angel, always pleasing him, always bringing pride to the family."

"In what way did she bring pride, Alfred?"

"She sang. Won all kinds of music festivals and talent contests, even a beauty pageant once. She did great at school. Never got in trouble. Perfect she was, Doc. Dad used to play piano for her when she sang. He was so proud. His face just lit up when people would clap for her. Can't blame him, really. She was good."

Doc looked up from his writing and said, "Sounds like you're proud of her too. What is the age difference?"

"Two years older, Doc. I mean *she* was."

The doctor set aside his notes, leaned forward and asked, "*Was*, Alfred?"

"Well, Doc, back then I always felt I'd let my dad down my whole life, not living up to his standards and so forth? Well, she let him down real good."

"Please don't be ambiguous here, Alfred. What does that mean?"

Al stiffened, sinking into the couch cushion as far as he could and said, "She died."

After a brief pause, the doctor asked, "Can you tell me about it?"

"My memory's not so hot about a lot of stuff back then, but . . . it was exactly one day before her nineteenth birthday. She was driving Dad's big old '59 Buick. Funny, he let her use his car all the time, but when I got my license, he said he wasn't going to let me. Anyway, she lost control, ran off the road, hit a tree dead on. No air bags or even seat belts in that beast, Doc. She went right through the . . .

"Let's just say, it was a mess. They wouldn't let him see her in the morgue. Guess they figured he'd go off his rocker. I think he did anyway. At the funeral they had her picture up on the casket and they played a tape of her singing Schubert's "Ave Maria". Christ, it was a horrible place, everybody crying, lots who I didn't even recognize. My dad was stone-faced, but we all knew how much he hurt. The veins in his head looked like they were going to burst. When he got up to do his eulogy, he couldn't speak, just froze. *Nearly* cried, I think. You could almost see the knot in his throat. He went over to her coffin and bent over to hug it and started kissing her picture and whispering stuff. I only picked out a few words, but I'll never forget those, '. . . So sorry, sweet Annie. Did you hate me that much?' Stuff like that.

"I got up and spoke after he sat down, and I said some things off the top of my head about how much she was loved by everybody who knew her. Then

I sort of heard myself saying she was my best friend; then finished with 'I'm sad you died, but happier you lived.' Corny I know, but it came to me, and it made sense at the time."

The doctor said, "Makes a lot of sense, Alfred."

"Huh? Yeah sure, Doc. Everyone kept telling me how strong I was to do that, but I told them I had her strength in me now, that she was sort of 'in' me and giving me some kind of guidance. Dumb, I know, Doc, but it felt right at the time. I really did love her."

"It's clear that you did, Alfred. And I'd never call any words like that dumb or corny, not when they're sincere. Your parents must have been proud of you: to see you, in spite of your grief, speak of your sister with such eloquence and passion."

Al dropped his chin into his hand. "I wanted to play a trumpet solo for her, but Dad said no. He said I'd screw it up and ruin Annie's day."

"Why do you think he wouldn't allow that, Alfred?"

"Not sure, Doc. Maybe he wished it was me who was dead? I don't know. Just 'cause *he* didn't play something, I still think he should have let me. I bet he would have let Annie sing, if it was my funeral, and he'd have accompanied her, for sure. Funny thing, when he passed away, I brought my trumpet to his funeral and played his favorite piece, Handel's Largo. I nailed it, Doc, not one cack or even a slightly off note."

"Excuse me, Alfred . . . *'cack'*?"

"Sorry, Doc, that's an expression us brass players call missed or 'split' notes. Funny thing, now it's come to mean like, when somebody dies, they 'cacked'."

"Thank you, Alfred. Please go on. So, you played well, under what must have been difficult circumstances."

"Yeah, Doc, and pretty amazing since I hadn't played trumpet seriously at that point in years. Not since this . . ."

Al rubbed the scar near his lower lip.

"What caused that injury, Alfred?"

"Nothing important, Doc. Call it a little New York souvenir. Anyway, back to the Largo. At first I didn't think I'd get through it; too much emotion. And my chops were so rusty. But when I started, I turned towards his coffin just for a second and he looked so . . . *harmless*? I was filled with some crazy sense of, I don't know, relief maybe? It was like I was free from him, or he couldn't stop me from ever doing or feeling anything again, or something. You know it's weird, but I felt Annie was right there with me at that moment, thinking the same thing."

"Alfred, before you continue . . . the expression, 'chops'? I assume that refers to your lip, or, your embouchure, I believe it's called?"

"Yeah, Doc, with a horn player it's pretty much about your face, or used to be anyway. These days it's sort of come to mean almost anything to do with your technique or ability on an instrument. Guitar players refer to their chops when it comes to their fingering and hot licks and stuff."

"Thank you, Alfred. Please go on."

"Okay, Doc. Anyway, I played that Largo great, my lip as strong as a steel-belted radial. Hell, I was tempted to launch into some jazz licks, but it would have upset my mother. Strange, huh, Doc?"

"Alfred, you indicate he had substantial influence in your emotional development. But do you think it was more than his disciplinary approach that induced your strong feelings of resentment toward him?"

"No one should have that much power over another person, Doc . . . not even your father."

"Here's what occurs to me, Alfred. When he prevented you from performing at Anne's service, I wonder if his reluctance was based not so much on questioning your ability, but from a fear it might have been too much for him to handle? Perhaps it might have made him cry? From what you've told me so far, he needed to be in control, of himself and those around him. What do you think?"

Al slumped into the couch, feeling small, reliving the torture of his first visit to the school principal's office.

"Could be, Doc. Never thought of it that way. I just figured he didn't want me to embarrass him, but he had to know I was good enough to pull it off. Geez yeah, he could have been trying to be mad at me, to avoid being as *sad* as he really felt. Man, does that make sense?"

"Did your father ever accompany you on the piano, as he did your sister?"

"Before the funeral he did, at least up until the music I was playing got too tough for him. It was a long time after that before he suggested we play together again, and I said no."

"Why, Alfred?"

"I was too mad at him for the funeral incident and something else that happened right around the same time."

"Please tell me about that, Alfred."

"I was a tall kid in my middle teens, but kinda skinny. Got picked on a lot by the jocks . . . over my music usually. Everybody knew me at school as the trumpet guy. I played solos at all the band concerts and a lot of school assemblies. There was this one kid, Stupid Stewart Carter, had some real thing against me. He'd taunt me when I walked home from school and sometimes he'd try to get my trumpet away from me. He was older and bigger, and I didn't know how to fight back, so I'd laugh and pretend not to care while he danced around playing keep-away till he got bored.

"One time, about two weeks after Anne's funeral, I was on the way home from school and Stewart confronted me. He was a sick-in-the-head idiot; started saying how my sister's accident wasn't really an accident. He said she'd killed herself, and was a rumor going around that she was pregnant, and the father must be a teacher or pastor or something, 'cause she didn't have a boyfriend.

"That made me so mad. I asked him what the hell he meant by all that dumb stuff and he laughed at me, like I was the only one in the world who didn't know what he was talking about. I lost it, Doc, and I jumped him. But he was too strong for me. He smacked me around pretty good; grabbed my trumpet and took off. When I got home my dad saw me all dirtied up and asked what was going on. When I told him . . . should have left out the part about Anne; he turned so red I thought he was going to explode. He pulled my arm nearly off, dragging me to the car. It was another Buick, same year, same color. Never got why he did that. We went looking for Stewart, and halfway down the next block, there he was.

"We got out of the car. Don't know why the stupid kid didn't run; *too* stupid I guess. Dad dragged me over to him. 'Give me the trumpet,' he barked at Stewart. The goof did, but he smirked, and I knew that was his biggest piece of stupidity yet. Dad said to me, 'Teach him a lesson, Al. No one can talk about your sister that way.' Man, I was shaking, literally shaking. I couldn't fight, not back then; had already showed that. Stewart laughed and pushed me down. That was it. Dad backhanded him so hard you could hear the smack echo down the street. He grabbed the moron's throat . . . looked like his neck actually stretched . . . and pulled him up to his toes. Much as I hated Carter, I was sorry for him right then. Been there, felt that.

"With his face an inch from Stewart's, Dad said, 'I look out for my family. You ever say anything about any of them, or come near my son again, I'll break you in half, I swear it.'

"The way I saw it, Stewart got off easy. He didn't have to go home with Mr. Waters. No, my dad didn't hit me, but something in his eyes, and the way he said nothing to me for a couple of days, hurt worse than a bust in the mouth. It told me he probably had more respect for Stupid Stewart Carter . . . than for me."

♪♪♪

Doctor Davidson asked, "Did this Carter fellow continue to bother you after that?"

"Well, Doc, notice how I keep calling him '*Stupid* Stewart Carter'? We all called him that, or 'Stupid Stewey'. Not to his face of course because of what a bully he was. But later, he earned that title even more, big time. After that day when my dad clobbered him, the dumb-ass still didn't let up. He'd come and push me around and say how he wasn't afraid of my dad, that *his* dad would kill my whole family if I went and ratted on him again. You know, stupid childish threats, Doc."

"Yes, his words were certainly ill-considered, Alfred, but did it truly frighten you?"

"It did, but something else happened. When he made it sound like it was more than me in danger, something just changed inside me. I started working out. Yeah, you know, like those old ads where the guy gets sand kicked in his face: the Charles Atlas thing? I used anything I could find at home that I could lift at least once, and made myself increase the reps as fast as I could. Did push-ups too, and I got stronger really fast. I was also in a growth spurt, and within a few months I grew almost to the height I am now, Doc: from smaller than Stewart, to taller. I wondered if for once God was on my side, and I was getting stronger and bigger just to get even with Stupid Stewart Carter. Of course, I know now it was just Mother Nature's convenient timing, but I can even remember thinking maybe Annie was there coaching me along, as she would have, if she'd been alive.

"I read books on self-defense; learned a few tricks about how easy it is to bring somebody down using their own energy and mass against them and so forth. Anyway, you can see where this is going, can't you? One day Stupid Stewart was waiting for me after school again. He started to push me in the chest. Right out of the blue, not even thinking about it, I grabbed his hand and held his thumb back, like in the books. He went down on his knees so quick, I almost laughed. I took his arm and pulled it around behind him in a half nelson, like wrestlers do; told him I was going to break it. Doc, he started to cry, 'I give, I give...'

"You know, I actually felt sorry for him, again. He was so pathetic. Inside I was kicking myself for not trying to fight back way sooner. Could have saved me a lot of aggravation, and maybe my dad might have looked at me different.

Funny, I actually looked around, just in case Dad might actually be coming, but no such luck. So I kicked Stewart's behind and sent him running home crying. Guess what? He never bothered me again. I know, easy to predict, right? But hey, guess what else? I never even told my dad about it: kicking Stewart's ass like that."

"Interesting, Alfred. One might have thought you'd want your father to hear about you defending yourself, especially with that particular bully. Any thoughts on why you chose not to tell him?"

"I don't know, Doc. Two things sort of come to mind. I was sick of trying to please him. That never seemed to work anyhow. Maybe I just didn't want him to have the pleasure of ignoring another one of my accomplishments? That makes sense to me. But another thought I had didn't add up at all, but I still wondered about it."

"What was that, Alfred?"

"I can remember thinking if I told him, he might have felt that I didn't need him to protect me anymore. Maybe even that I didn't need him at all anymore? Like I said, Doc, couldn't have been that. Doesn't make any sense . . ."

CHAPTER 12

FIVE – SOUTH TOWER [4]

I *need a smoke so bad. Maybe if I duck into the can for a quick one. Only take a second to light up and get a few drags in. God, I need it.*

The orderly got up and shuffled into the bathroom where he began to rummage through the pockets of his uniform.

Nothing. Shit, left everything in my clothes when I changed into these goddamn scrubs.

As he glanced into the mirror, the face looking back startled him.

Crap, forgot for a second who I am today. I'll never get used to this . . . never.

He went back to the bedside chair. As he stared at the injured man, he fumed inside, shaking with frustration. A little luck was necessary to pull off this evil endeavor—which was iffy to begin with—and for it to work, everything had to be perfect. Forgetting his cigarettes was not part of the plan.

♪♪♪

Officer Poole dropped the magazine to his lap and turned toward 501. He had to go in. This was too much stress, to sit there and wonder if he'd messed up by letting the new orderly in. All it would take would be a quick look to make sure things were okay. No excuse needed, just part of his job.

What's the big deal?

As he stood up, he saw a nurse coming down the hall, the same one who had witnessed his air guitar solo. She was *hot*.

"Hello," he said as she walked by. "Nice night for nursing isn't it."

Oh man, I'm a fool . . . stupid damned fool.

She stopped and turned to answer. "Well, Officer, I suppose it is, and an equally good night for copping?" Her smile relaxed him somewhat after his miserable attempt at wit.

Poole said, "This isn't exactly what I do all the time. I drew this duty because I was a bad boy."

Raising one eyebrow, she said, "Oh, now that sounds intriguing. How bad were you? Did you give the mayor a ticket?"

"That's a good one, ma'am. You know I wish I could sometime. I'm sure Jim Naugle's a crook, like all Republicans."

"Hmm," said the nurse, "last time I checked, Mr. Naugle was a Democrat. Done any reading on local politics? And if so, are you sure your eyes are good enough for your job?"

Oh man, of course I know the mayor is a Democrat. Just watched him on the news this morning, yakking on about his ultra-conservative crap. I think the jerk's a damned donkey in elephant's clothing. No wonder I got his politics backwards.

Poole's attempt at saving face was as feeble as his opening line. "Well, ma'am, these eyes have no trouble seeing that you're a most fine and foxy lady."

Her smile slackened noticeably. "Well, your social skills are about as great as your knowledge of local government. 'Fine and foxy'? Give me a break. But, calling me *ma'am* got you serious negative points. And you did it twice."

"Sorry, nurse."

"Good night, cop."

As she walked briskly down the hall, Poole sat back down and picked up his magazine once again, momentarily forgetting about his concern with the newbie orderly in 510. All he could think of was how *not* cool he had just proven himself to be.

CHAPTER 13

OUTSIDE LOOKING IN

"Alfred," said Doctor Davidson, "I'd like to ask you about something you said about your father, and the situation with the car."

"Sure, Doc," said Al.

"You said he wouldn't let you drive the car, which was exactly like the one your sister died in, correct?"

"Yeah, Doc, some kind of weird, huh?"

"What do you believe your father's reasoning for that might have been, Alfred?"

"That's an easy one. Because he didn't trust me. He thought I was a total useless fuckup."

"Alfred, if that is the most negative possible answer to that question, what would be the most positive way of thinking about it? In other words, with a more optimistic outlook toward the circumstances, what might be another reason that he would not permit you to drive the car?"

"Well, I suppose if I was to magically make things better back then, I'd say maybe he was afraid I'd end up like Anne? And he didn't want to lose me too . . . ? Ha, now that's a hoot. As if he cared. Maybe he bought the second Buick just so I *would* be wiped out in it, just like she was? But maybe, 'cause the insurance company would have balked or something, he chickened out?"

"Alfred, for a moment you allowed yourself to let your inner voice be positive, but then instantly pushed that aside and let the negative voice take over again. That's called cognitive distortion, and I'm afraid you seem to be quite prone to it. We need to find a way for you to control those negative feelings with more positive thinking. Your inner voices *can* change. I am an ardent proponent of cognitive behavioral therapy. I'm convinced that's the direction we must go for you to develop a healthier and happier outlook on your life."

"So, I'm a distorted thinker am I, Doc? C'mon, guitar players use distortion. Why shouldn't a sax player? Okay, sorry, I actually can see what you're saying pretty much does describe me. Okay, let's get to work. Damned if I want to be mistaken for some kind of guitar player. Unless it was Lenny Breau, huh?"

The doctor paused to write, then looked up and smiled. "Thank you, Alfred. Okay, if I may, I'd like to get a picture of your teenage development years. Let's look at aspects of your social life, such as partying, friends . . . girlfriends?"

"Wasn't much of a party guy, Doc. I had one girlfriend, named Sue, before Annie died. Nothing serious there. Just a teen crush that ended about as fast as it began."

"As young as you must have been, and as brief as that relationship sounds, was there any sexual intimacy, Alfred?"

"Doc, if ever there was a time to say 'don't go there' . . . please, just don't go there."

"Of course, Alfred. In your own time and on your terms, perhaps we'll address that situation later. Was there anyone with whom you could talk about things, someone to confide in, since it appears you couldn't do that with your parents?"

"Just Annie, Doc. Just Annie."

"Alfred, her death must have been so difficult for you in many ways. The incident with the Carter boy too . . . what he said about her, and then how your father reacted. Do you understand what was going on there?"

"No, Doc, I don't. After Stupid Stewart's transformation from bully to wimp, I might have been able to get it out of him, by force, if not with friendly persuasion. But that chance got taken away by his damned stupidity and a bit of ill fate. The fool signed up for the U.S. Army. Here there were all these American guys running up to Canada to get away from military duty, and *he*, a Canadian, totally safe from the draft, signs up? And wouldn't ya know it, gets killed on his first day of duty in Vietnam. A friggin' helicopter accident, Doc. Fell out of it and broke his stupid neck. Least he could have done was get himself off'd by the enemy. Friggin' idiot. At one point I actually wondered if he had signed up maybe because of what had happened with *me*, but I decided not to blame myself in any way for his being stupid."

"That was wise thinking, Alfred. No need to place such guilt upon yourself. Mr. Carter made his choices completely for reasons of his own, I'm sure. But let's back up a bit. It would seem you describe the loss of your sister as basically losing your best friend and confidante. Were there any other friends in your life at all?"

"Not too many, Doc, other than the kids in the band, and they looked at me mostly as an outsider. I was into sports a bit, mainly basketball after I got bigger. But that made the music kids even more wary of me, since I began to hang out with the jocks. But the jocks thought of me as a music pansy, so basically I was never *in* with either faction. The worst of both worlds, Doc. There I was, outside looking in . . . from two directions at once.

"It got worse, when I got fired off the basketball team for missing too many practices 'cause of band rehearsal. Then, the band director gets mad at me 'cause I wanted to try saxophone, since the school band music was getting really boring for me. My private lessons, and I guess a bit of above-normal talent, had put me way ahead of the average high school trumpet player. One day I see the basketball coach and band director talking in the hall. As I walk by, the coach says, 'Thanks for letting me down, Al', and the band guy says, 'Yeah, he's good at that . . .' Great lesson in maturity from those guys, ya think, Doc?

"So I never went back to band. Waited to see if he'd call me in, but nah, too much pride I guess. Well, he did ask me in 1967, 'cause the band was going to Expo 67, and he needed my trumpet skills. But I said no, just to prove a point. I guess since I was a kid, I had a more legitimate excuse to be immature, right?"

"What was the reaction at home, Alfred?"

"When I told my dad that I was off the team *and* out of band, he said he knew it would happen 'cause I couldn't stick at anything. He said, 'basketball, no big deal, but the band? Why couldn't you work that out? Oh, when you take out the garbage tonight, think about getting used to having those bags in your hands. You'll likely end up doing that for a living some day.' Nice, huh, Doc?"

"Well, Alfred, 'nice' is not the word I'd really choose, nor would you in seriousness. Without sarcasm this time, think how you'd really describe what it made you feel."

"Okay, Doc. That's easy. Made me feel like garbage."

Al sipped on his coffee. The doctor wasn't commenting, so he continued. "There ya go, Doc, no sarcasm for a change. Anyway, after that, for the next few months I practiced my trumpet for as many hours a day as I could find: scales, arpeggios, lip drills, playing along to jazz records I got at the library. Dad didn't like jazz very much, maybe because he didn't get it. He had no swing in him. By eighteen I was playing in local dance bands and started my own jazz combo too. I learned about Lenny Breau and wanted to be like him. You know anything about him, Doc?"

"Of course, Alfred. I have several of his recordings. He was possibly the most innovative guitarist in the second half of the century."

"Yeah, Doc, and he was Canadian, and playing in famous places when he was still a teenager. I wanted to be just like him. Man, he had everything going for him: movie star looks, talent, fame. Guess I never got my wish to be that much like him, but at least I'm *alive*, right? Too bad for the world to get stuck with me and lose *him*. If I could, I think I'd do it. You know, trade places with him? Might be best for everyone."

"That worries me, Alfred, to hear you talk this way. Remember your promise to me. And besides, your being dead couldn't bring back Lenny Breau, nor would it solve the problems he had when he was still alive."

Al closed his eyes and said, "Maybe if I died I could jam with him, wherever we'd be. Probably be darned warm I'm guessing."

The doctor couldn't help but smile at Al's way of turning a suicidal reference into a joke. He said, "Do you think you might have been friends with Lenny Breau, if you'd had the chance?"

"Almost had that chance, Doc, since I did meet him in 1978. But that's another story. Hey, you asked me about friends, didn't you? Nah, didn't have time for 'em. Music was my best buddy once I realized how much I loved it. Girls? Didn't need them either, not between when I was about sixteen and nineteen. Ha, kinda been making up for that ever since though, haven't I?"

Al laughed. The doctor scribbled notes without comment. When he looked up, he asked, "Nowadays, would you say you had anyone you'd call a close friend, maybe even best friend?"

Al said, "Well, yeah, I guess Billy would be the closest thing to that."

"Yes, Alfred, you've mentioned him, the piano player you've worked with for . . . how long did you say?"

CHAPTER 14

BILLY
1969 - New York City

*T*he world was changed forever in the summer of 1969 when Neil Armstrong set foot on the moon. Only weeks later Al Waters took a giant leap of his own, landing his first-ever gig in the U.S. It was almost more than the nineteen-year-old could fathom: the prospect of playing in a house band in fabled Greenwich Village.

New York City . . . me . . . wow.

It seemed nothing short of a miracle that a small ad in the International Musician magazine could have led to this: flying to New York; auditioning by joining in for a set at The Straw Hat, billed as the world's second-busiest nightclub; being offered the gig, and to start the next night; diving in headfirst as a full-time professional entertainer in this wild, raucous sing-along atmosphere.

Since the club was so shamelessly modeled after the nearby Your Father's Mustache—flagship location of a worldwide chain—The Straw Hat was stuck in the same rankings rut as Avis Rent a Car. The only way to compete effectively from a second-place position was to try harder.

Al Waters needed to expand his personal resources beyond musical talent; he had to learn how to "sell", as the manager, Ira Goldman, called it. This was show business, not art. Designed to peak and ebb in such a way as to promote participation *and* ample drinking time, each set was a strategically precise operation. The servers at this good-time parlor had to perform almost as much as the band, constantly doing ensemble cancan dances and joining in with the old-time songs to get the audience going. Most of the staff, including Ira, were young energetic types, many of whom were aspiring actors and dancers. Conspicuous among them was a gawky older man, appearing to be at least mid-forties. As he lurched from table to table, out of breath and drenched in sweat, his ignominy was as obvious as his physical discomfort. Al felt sorry for this man dressed up in the club's required uniform of plastic skimmer style straw hat, striped shirt and suspenders, and piano key-patterned garters on both arms: his self-respect buried beneath the buffoonery.

One night at closing, as Al was punching his time card—one more of the aspects of this gig copied from the Mustache—he noticed the out-of-place waiter was sitting in front of the stage, staring at the piano. Before heading to the door, he stopped near this apparent misfit, instinctively keeping a table and some chairs between them. One of his earliest lessons in life had been that such sadness in someone's eyes could be the calm before many types of storm.

"Hey, man," said Al, "you thinking it'd be cool to be in a band?"

The waiter said, "Huh?" and spun around, sending his fake straw hat tumbling to the table. As he fumbled to replace the hat he said, "Sorry, man. I was just waiting for my check and I was thinking about, uh . . . Hey, be cool, man, and just back off, okay? I'll go wait by the bar."

"Whoa, hold on," said Al. "I just wondered, you know, the way you were looking at the stage. You look maybe like you wished you were up there or something? I'm confused, 'cause I've noticed when you're working, how you don't seem to like being in front of all those people in the audience and all. Hard to picture you up there on stage with the musicians. Wouldn't that be even worse for you?"

The man's eyes narrowed to slits as he said, "You jive ass *mother*. Who are *you* to tell me what it's like to be on a stage? You and those other hacks should be so lucky as to have me up there."

Al was glad he'd stayed behind a table, as he gripped the chair next to him, ready to swing it if needed. He didn't allow his breathing to resume until the waiter straightened his hat, jammed it on, and got up to walk away. Against better judgment, but compelled to know more, Al said, "Hey, guy, I didn't mean to get in your face. Wait up. That should be easy, eh? 'Cause that's what you *do*, isn't it?"

The man turned, with trembling fists clenched at his side and said, "What the *fuck* are you talking about?"

Al said, "You're a waiter, aren't you? So *wait* for me. Get it?"

"Man, is that supposed to be funny?" asked the waiter. A smile slowly curled up from his thin lips. "Oh shit, I dig. Guess it sort of is. My name's Billy Crothers". As he held out his hand in a palm-up, thumb-grab position, his smile widened, revealing crooked stained teeth, with one missing from lower center.

"I'm Al Waters, Billy. Nice to meet you, man. Hey, how come you got so uptight about me talking about you being in a band?"

Looking downward, Billy rubbed his forehead and said, "Sorry I jumped on you, man. You see, I *am* a musician; well, used to be anyway."

He was medium height, slim to the point of emaciation, and sported a thin wispy mustache. His thick black hair was greasy and matted, displaying flecks of dandruff and random streaks of white hair cream. With his gaunt pasty face, dark circles under his eyes—discernible even through the tinted glasses—he looked like something out of a cheap zombie movie.

Al had only been in the city for a couple of weeks and already had met more guys than he could count who claimed to be former or temporarily retired musicians. In subway stations, if he had his horn case with him, he'd often encounter a derelict telling how he used to play with the Duke, or Count Basie, or the like.

One of them had once asked, "Got a tenor sax in that case, right?"

This was a giveaway; any real musician should know a trumpet case from a tenor case. On another occasion he had wished he'd *had* a sax case, or at least something bigger than the trumpet, when a seedy looking man had come up and said, "Gimme dat horn." Al's reaction had been to ram his case into the guy's groin and then run without looking back for at least four blocks. From then on, he followed the advice of native New Yorker Tommy, the club's bandleader/banjo player, who on the first night had said, "Always look like *you're* looking for trouble. Mess up your hair, turn up your collar; try to look like a wack job. Then the real nut bars or the punks won't mess with you. If you're on the subway in the middle of the night, this could save your life, man."

More than once it probably had.

♪♪♪

"You got a nice sound, man," said Billy. "You should be playing real music, not the crap they do in here."

Al couldn't help but wonder if Billy was just being nice. "Thanks, man. How about you, Billy . . . what do you play?"

"I'm great on the eighty-eights. Comp till you stomp. You dig? I tinkle on the ivories . . ." Billy paused and smiled. "Ha, sounded like I meant I pissed on the keys, man. Guess I only tinkle now since I got no keys to play on . . . *or* piss on. Just urinate cuz it's my fate, *not* to be great, not anymore. Sorry, man, I'm a little tired. The *medicine* does some weird shit to the mind."

"Believe it or not," said Al, "I get it. You're a piano player. But what does that mean about the medicine? You sick or something?"

Billy scrunched his eyebrows and said, "You've heard of methadone haven't ya, kid?" He could tell by Al's blank look that he hadn't. "I have to take the meth so I can't hit up. Hey, I'm a fuckin' junkie, man. Heroin? Don't tell me you never heard of that. They tell me you're from Canada, *eh*? Don't you have *candy* up there? What do you and the goddamn Eskimos do to get high, man? Say, what key is your national anthem in? 'A' . . . ? Got to be, right?"

Oddly, Al was more offended by Billy's mocking use of "eh" than anything else.

Canadians don't say that all the time. How prejudiced can you get? Does he think our cops are all Mounties, and it's winter all year?

"Of course I know about it, man," said Al. "I've been high lots of times, but not heroin. Grass, mescaline, a little THC. I never heard of methadone though. What is it exactly?"

Billy found himself liking this kid from Canada, whose unabashed frankness was not a common trait in his present circle. "I'll be straight with you, man. Ha, that's a hoot. Lots of people might find that a funny word to associate with *me*. Yeah, Billy Crothers *straight*? As if."

"You mean, you're gay?" said Al, daring to joke again.

"Yeah right, kid. Shit, maybe I might as well be, with the way things have worked out for me with women. Hey, lemme be serious here. Methadone is a synthetic opiate drug that shuts off the withdrawal symptoms from the junk you've been doing, and takes away your cravings. And if you did take some dope, your buzz is blocked by the methadone, so why bother, right? Could kill you if you took too much, or you combined drugs. Even alcohol, man. I can get away with a *little* smoke and booze, but really I'm pretty much supposed to lay off everything.

"You pick up your ration from the City; I'm at the two-week level now. And they won't give you any more until you're due. If you mess up and take too much too soon, or sell it, like some guys do, you go into withdrawal, or you'd have to score some smack, or suffer like you wouldn't believe."

"Are you on this stuff for the rest of your life?" asked Al, knowing he might as well have "rube" tattooed on his forehead.

"Hopefully not, man. Then again, depends on how long you got to live, I suppose. Could be months or even years. I know a couple guys been on the medicine for fuckin' *ever*, but the way it's supposed to work is you cool down over time. You know, taper off, and end up clean. Doesn't always work. It's hard, man to stick to it, you dig? Lots of 'repeat offenders' in the program. Some of us are lucky, and we get job placement assistance, and employers take a chance on us, like Ira here. He's a cool dude, and he knows how tough it can be. Cuts me slack sometimes."

Al was fascinated, not just by the insider's view of the drug world, but by Billy himself. "How long you been on it?" he asked, hoping he wasn't being too pushy.

"About a year or so," Billy said, taking off his silly hat, exposing more greasy hair which was noticeably thinning on top. "Since I was . . . twenty-five? Yeah, 'bout a year."

Al was silent, trying not to react openly to the revelation of Billy's age—*twenty-six?* Those sunken eyes and sloped shoulders had to have suffered the burdens of many more years than that.

Al changed the subject. "You play piano, eh?"

Shit, did I really say "eh"?

Billy went to his locker where he hung up his suspenders and garters. Tossing his fake straw hat to the locker floor, he winked as he replaced it with a faded purple beret. This one small sartorial touch instantly changed his entire demeanor. "Yeah, man," he said, with less fatigue in his voice, "I was pretty good before I got the damned monkey on my back. Played with a lot of heavies. You'd know 'em. I could show you pictures and stuff. Come on home with me after we get paid and I'll show you who I was."

♪ ♪ ♪

Al tried to look cool as they walked down the dingy side streets toward Billy's place. Few street lights were functioning, and of those that were, several blinked sleepily on and off.

Damn lights, please don't conk out on me now.

From several alleys they passed by, Al thought he heard furtive voices, but he resisted looking back, trying to display the looking-for-trouble attitude he'd been taught. He swore to himself, if he survived this, he'd never drink on the gig again.

"Here we are," announced Billy, turning to descend a dark stairwell. "Next stop, paradise!" He laughed, with an odd constricted throat noise—almost a cough, closer to a cackle—not like a chicken, but more the way you'd anticipate how a vulture might laugh: "Hack, a-hack, a-hack."

Billy opened the door to "paradise", flicked a switch, and a single cover-less ceiling lamp weakly illuminated the room. Glowing pitifully through the dirty paint-smudged bulb, the light revealed a scene straight out of *Midnight Cowboy*: the first sight of Ratso Rizzo's abysmal abode in a condemned building. Billy's apartment was below street level, and it wasn't difficult to surmise there was a sewer just on the other side of the wall. You could hear *and* feel the frantic retreat of a million tiny beasts under the carpet and behind the plaster. Bloated stalactite sections of the too-low ceiling drooped from above; a rush of bats would not have seemed out of place. In the far corner, next to a rust-stained sink was a yellowish round-shouldered refrig-erator, the handle bent sideways. Beside that was a stove with a folded-down element cover. What evil vermin lurked under *there*? The furnishings were minimal: a couch with non-matching cushions, a green kitchen table with one chair, and an old dresser-like cabinet. Among all the sensory effects, what stood out the most was the smell—desiccated and dank at the same time. It brought back memories of an abandoned 1940 Ford Al had played in as a kid.

Billy shouted, "I'm HOME . . ." Noticing Al's raised brow, he assumed a stuffy British accent and said, "Just thought I'd alert the rats. You know, so the shy little buggers could make themselves decent."

As Billy cackled, Al crossed his fingers that this was in fact a joke—even a small percentage of truth being a stomach-turning prospect.

Bringing to mind a Monty Python routine, Billy asked, "Would you like a coffee, old chap? Sorry, there's no beer. Some tea, perhaps?"

"Um, no thanks," said Al. "Can't stay long."

Ugh. How do you take your tea, sir? One roach or two?

"Gotta show you something," said Billy as he began fumbling through the cabinet across from the couch. Al ignored him, now worrying about how to find his way home.

Billy stood up with an armful of musty photo albums and sat on the couch. Beckoning Al to join him, he said, "Check it out, man. Nothing's in much of an order here. Umm, here's me and Lionel Hampton. I was seventeen, man; youngest cat who ever played with him. Far-fucking-out, huh? And, oh yeah, this is me and Maynard, 'bout a year later. I still get headaches when I think of him. That mother was LOUD, man. Hey, a Canuck 'trumpetiste' like you. You must know him, EH?" He cackled loudly.

"Sorry, no," said Al. "I've never met Maynard Ferguson. He's from Montreal. That's like another country to where I'm from, in more ways than one. What's he, around forty-something now? Getting old, eh? Still the best screech player in the world. Love that dude, man; one of my heroes."

Billy turned another page. "Look, look, here's 'King Shit' himself, Buddy Rich. Motherfucker made everyone in the band watch him while he played his solos, like we were in awe of him or something; which most of us kind of were, actually."

He let out a weak version of one of his cackle laughs which Al noticed was a little different from the others; this time it seemed tinged with sadness.

Billy went on. "If he caught you looking away, you were in deep shit. He loved me, man. Said he hated to let me go; tried to help me. But the *monkey* was too strong.

"Shit, when he was pissed off he used to rant and rave in intermissions; get right up on a table in the dressing room and yell at us like he was Vince Lombardi or something. He was the prick of all pricks sometimes. Once in Singapore, his drums got stuck in customs or whatever, and a local kid offered for Buddy to use his drums. When Buddy got on stage and tried them, he kicked the whole kit right off the stage, yelling, 'I can't play on this shit . . .' The kid looked at his busted up set and started to cry. That was the one time I really truly hated the motherfucker.

"He *was* great though. One time, he was playing like all get out, crazy fast even for *him*. Cut his hand on a cymbal as he played, and blood was flying everywhere; he didn't even notice. The drums *and* him looked like they'd been in a war. He was the best, man, and he did give me more than one chance. Too bad I had to fuck that up. Ran outa lines to cross."

♪ ♪ ♪

For the next hour Al was given the tour of Billy's career: a few years of a man's life, pressed between those fading pages like a saved leaf, a crisp colorful reminder of something once beautiful, once alive. Now crumbling around the edges, it seemed too far from the forest to have ever been real.

From the age of seventeen through nineteen, Billy Crothers had played or sat in with almost all the top bands in New York City. The jazz prodigy rose to first-on-the-list when anyone needed a piano man. Maynard Ferguson, Woody Herman, Stan Getz—all these guys wanted "Billy the Kid", as he was tagged. Buddy Rich offered him a gig-for-life—before the drug issues peaked. Along the way, Billy recorded with many of these artists and made two albums of his own with legendary heavies in his ensemble.

For a rookie on the road with veterans, the problems were as inevitable as his nickname: first, the booze; then, from the jive jungle around him the *monkey* jumped on his back—heroin, in all its ugly glory. For a couple of years, youthful energy and talent enabled him to pull it off, his genius always finding its way through the drug-induced fog. But not blessed with a strong constitution to begin with, he was trapped in the fast lane to disaster, which rapidly aged him in general health and appearance. Before long, the joy ride ended up in the ditch. Still in his early twenties, Billy was already a has-been, not only strung out—but out of the circle—from too many missed rehearsals, forgotten club dates, and incidences of falling asleep on stage. With this growing negative reputation, no one would touch him. He could still play, and sometimes still with unbelievable proficiency. But you never knew which Billy Crothers would show up—the kid who could blow you away—or the addict who could blow your gig.

♪♪♪

So, Billy Crothers *was* a musician. Al now felt humbled by the company he was in. This grubby Ratso Rizzo clone had been, but a few years ago, a handsome young rising star playing with legends. Now here he was, living in a hole, working as a waiter in a schlock nightclub. Regardless of current circumstances, Al was mortified that he'd been patronizing toward a man who was probably *still* a better musician than *he* would ever be.

"Billy, you hear me play every night. Do you think I might ever get good enough to, you know, make it? I think I should take some lessons with somebody really good, now that I'm in the Big Apple. Any recommendations?"

In a matter-of-fact tone Billy said, "Hey, man, you can't play jazz worth crap, and you screw up half the melodies you're supposed to have learned. And those are shit tunes at that. I'd hate to hear you slaughter something by Bird or Monk."

The words seared directly into Al's heart, dissolving it into a stream of melted hope, draining downward into a puddle of despair.

I knew it . . . I stink.

Billy said, "Hey, man, don't look at me like that. That's the bad news, but there's mucho copacetic stuff too. Like when you play one of those old Harry James style ballads. Man, you make me listen. Yeah, kid, you got this fat, warm sound, almost like Chet Baker, or maybe more like Maynard when he plays down low. Not his high shit; nobody can touch that. But yeah, you got a sound that shows me your heart, and it gets into mine. Something else you do that shows me you could be real good is how you got a natural sense of the silence. By that, I'm saying you make the spaces between the notes count. Any cat, any true swingman, knows how important the silent spaces are, small as they might be. You could just call it phrasing I guess, but it's more than that. Ain't no real words for it. For fuck sakes, you swing like Zoot Sims, man, and I've jammed with him. Yeah sure, he's a sax guy, but you blow that trumpet kinda like you *were* playing a sax sometimes. Can you dig what the hell I'm trying to say here? It's cool, trust me, far-fucking-out cool."

Billy released a gentle muted cackle and then continued. "It's something special, placed into your heart by the gods of music. I don't think it can be taught. It's a gift, boy."

Somehow this twenty-six-year-old calling him "boy" felt right to Al. It seemed Billy had lived a thousand lifetimes compared to him. Too bad they hadn't met before the drugs had wrecked him, but they probably wouldn't have crossed paths otherwise. Al wasn't really sure what Billy was saying about the spaces being so important, but he definitely liked the comparison to Zoot Sims. Although he had listened to a gamut of great jazz artists during his formative years, he'd never been aware of how much he'd been influenced by the phrasing and patterns associated with saxophonists.

Billy's life story seemed to be temporarily on hold, so Al grabbed the opportunity. "As far as guys who play different axes than trumpet, I really dig Lenny Breau. You ever get to hear him, Billy?"

Billy sat without talking, lost in the pictures he was shuffling through. His brow furrowed as he searched more intensely. Then he cackled loudly and said, "Check this out, man."

Al looked down at a small curled photo of a very young Billy Crothers at the piano—next to Lenny Breau. "Holy shit, man," said Al. "You played with Lenny?"

"Wasn't actually on that gig," said Billy. "Lenny was playing at George's Spaghetti House in Toronto, '62, I think it was. He had a trio with a guy named Don Francks, a TV actor, but actually a damned decent singer too. I was working a club down the street. We finished up earlier there; it was more of a high-class, rich-guy hangout. I went to hear Lenny after hours, hoping he'd still be on, and the manager there recognized me and asked Francks and Lenny if I could jam with them. Lenny said he'd absolutely dig on that, and we worked out for a whole set, man. Francks didn't sing; just sat down and listened, with a big grin on his yap. It was a gas."

Al couldn't think of anything to say. Billy had shared a set with Lenny Breau? It was as if he'd been brushed by a piece of his hero's soul by meeting and talking to this strange man who had walked as an equal among giants. Here they were, Al Waters and Billy Crothers, sitting next to one another, as friends?

Once again, Billy had gone silent, appearing to be struggling to say something he wasn't sure he was ready to say. Then his face burst from pensive to a jack-o'-lantern smile as he said, "Tomorrow, I'm going down to Roseland, to the musicians' union gathering of the needy and the greedy. Want to come? You will most definitely dig it. I'll introduce you to some guys. And yeah, I'll help you score a teacher. I don't think *everyone* hates me yet."

Billy's smile creaked open to its fullest yet, revealing more spaces between teeth, and a rapidly closing gap between two souls. "Al, my swinging brother, it'll be a gas for you, man, of the most copacetic dimensions."

Al laughed and said, "Far-out. Far-fucking-out."

And Billy's cackle filled the room.

CHAPTER 15

IF I CAN MAKE IT THERE

*R*oseland Ballroom's three stories of fading grandeur at 239 West 52nd Street stood as a sentry against modernity, as a mob of musicians milled about on the sidewalk in front. The former roller skating mecca—just around the corner from another icon of entertainment history, the Ed Sullivan Theater—was a proper backdrop for another sadly non-self-aware anachronism: Billy Crothers.

Al hardly recognized Billy at first, since he'd only ever seen him in his Straw Hat garb, but the purple beret stood out in the crowd. He was dressed in black jacket and pants—a "B-flat suit", to those in the business—which hung on his thin frame like an under-stuffed scarecrow's Sunday *worst*. Any elegance these sorry threads may have once born, had been long ago eroded by time and ill care. Fittingly, his tie—a dark yellow triumph of tackiness— had a grease spot smack in the middle of it. Al figured it had once been part of a band uniform, and he wondered if someone like Buddy Rich or Woody Herman had witnessed the origin of the stain.

As they worked their way through the sizeable gathering at the entrance, Al was introduced to several "cats". He was both amused and perplexed, as Billy would say, "This is Al," at each meeting, but seldom mentioned the name of the person he was introducing him to. Was this behavior based on a presumption that Al would recognize these people—or just forgetful- ness? Fortunately for all concerned, most of them seemed to know Billy well enough to offer their identity before the pause had a chance to become awkward. Some were friendly, some obviously anxious to get on to someone more useful. Clearly, Billy *was* recognized by all, but useful to few.

Once inside, they began to navigate through the crowd on the dance floor. Al asked, "So this is it, the famous exchange floor run by the AFM Local 802 guys. The offices are right here? Man, so cool. Biggest musicians' union local in America, right? Or is L.A.'s bigger?"

The scene was dizzying: hundreds of musicians jostling for engagements, schmoozing, bragging, complaining about bandleaders; basically chitchatting about all things related to the music business. A bank of payphones lined one wall and a switchboard operator paged musicians from the center of it all. This was right next to a booth where both black and white bow ties were sold.

Over by the stage, someone announced there was a call for musicians for a road band, in big band format. Billy said to Al, "See, see . . . ? That's the way it works, man. You go over there and tell him your name, what your axe is, who you've been with and everything. That's one way how you could get a gig. And hey, who knows? Might even be a name band."

"Don't forget, Billy, I've got a gig," said Al.

"Actually I did forget, man . . . 'cause did you notice how *everyone* we talk to has a gig? Most of that is lies. Nobody wants to admit they're not working. Makes you look, uh, unsuccessful. To *get* a gig, it helps if you look like you don't need one."

Billy recognized a passing man and turned to grab him by the arm, saying, "Hey, Buddy. Meet my man here, Al, from Canada."

Holy shit . . . Buddy Morrow . . . trombone giant. "Night Train".

"Hey, Al-from-Canada, what's happening?" said Morrow. "Billy, what you up to? Haven't seen you around in a while, man."

"Hey, you know, this and that. It's all copacetic. Right now I'm at a club down in the Village. What about you, man?"

Al wondered if Billy had considered whether anyone he said this to might call him on it and find out where he meant, and then perhaps show up there and see he was waiting tables.

Buddy Morrow waved hello to a group passing by, then turned his attention back to Billy and Al. "I'm playing a show, Broadway shit, just for fun you know, and the bread's not bad. Good way to keep the chops up anyway. Might get another road band together after the run if there's any agents who'll book a tour for me these days. Been a long time since 'Night Train' got me to number twenty-seven in the charts, my million-seller. Yeah, 1952; *long* time, man."

"Great seeing you, Buddy," said Billy, shaking his hand. "Good luck on the tour thing if it happens. Don't forget me if you need a piano man. And hey, I'll make sure I say hi to that *other* Buddy if I see him."

Billy cackled as he held on too long to Buddy Morrow's hand. The trombone player's weak smile betrayed the lie behind his response. "Yeah, yeah, sure, Billy. I'll call you first . . . straight up, man. Hey, I gotta split. There's Jimmy 'M' over there . . . gotta catch up with him. Later guys. Nice meeting you . . . uh, Al, right?"

As soon as Morrow was out of earshot, Billy said to Al, "Wow, Buddy Morrow working a Broadway show? What next, huh?"

"What's wrong with that?" asked Al. "I'd kill for a gig in a show."

"Hey, kid, once you been up as high as him: his own band, couple of hit songs, pretty famous guy, on TV and stuff; doing a pit band gig is like backing up a step, a *lot* of steps actually. Like he said, pay's not too bad, but it's a musical hell, playin' the same crap the same way every night, eight friggin' shows a week, you dig? For a jazz cat, man, it's painful. Guess he's got bills to pay, like anybody."

Al wondered how many steps lay ahead of him before he even caught up to where Buddy Morrow had slipped back to.

At least he's not waiting tables. And he won't be calling you, Billy.

Billy said, "Okay, you've seen one aspect of the scene here today, but the best, most normal way you get a gig with heavies like Woody or Maynard is to be known by all the guys who play in the rehearsal bands in town. A lot of the top guys like to sit in with these kinds of bands. Shit, man, some of those are better than the actual road bands. You could look around and there's Jimmy Maxwell from the Tonight Show band, who we just saw Buddy go over to rap with . . . or maybe Lew Soloff from Blood, Sweat & Tears. And these cats are blowin' their asses off just for fun. You get to know these guys, and if you can *play*, they'll remember you. Then one day Buddy, or the Elgarts, or whoever. They need a cat, and one of those guys you sat in with says, 'Hey, there's this guy. I got his number . . .' Next thing you know you're gettin' a call, and you're in. Of course, if you can't cut the gig, you're out just as fast, and your name is mud for fucking *ever*. Got to be ready, man. Got one chance to make that first impression; it better be a good one."

♪♪♪

Al and Billy made their way back outside and began to walk down 52nd Street. From behind them came a resonant, almost regal voice. "William Crothers, reports of your death *have* been exaggerated. Or *are* you dead? You look rather . . . a little under the weather."

Talking to Billy was a small, smartly dressed man who had emerged from the mass of musicians at the front of Roseland. Al had never seen someone in person who truly fit the word "dapper", but here he was. Although only five feet, six inches tall, he acted bigger—with the resonant voice of a stage actor, and broad gestures with arms and hands for almost every word. He wore a tweed suit with matching vest, and an ascot perfectly in tune with the rest of the outfit. Topping it off was a derby, cocked at just the right jaunty tilt.

His face was small-featured and angular, with thin lips, receding jaw, and a sliver of a nose impossibly supporting his frameless spectacles. Behind the lenses were tiny black eyes, twinkling with the joy of knowing more than you did, no matter who you were.

The newcomer pulled his spectacles slightly downward and scanned Al from top to bottom. Turning to Billy, he said, "William, who is your young friend? He certainly presents a refreshing change from all the dreary has-beens in this horrid place."

Billy hesitated in the way that indicated he was having trouble with a name. To break the awkwardness, Al spoke up. "Hi, I'm Al Waters."

Billy quickly added, "Al, yeah. This is my *man*, Ed Wilson. Nobody better on Broadway for first-call rehearsal pianist; big-time theater, man. I'm talkin' top shows, with Rodgers and Hammerstein, Adolph Green and Betty Comden . . . you know, all the heavies."

"William Crothers," said Wilson, "you embarrass me. I shall most surely faint. Will you catch me, Al?"

To the best of his knowledge, Al had never met a homosexual; he was pretty certain Ed Wilson was his first. It seemed incredible to meet someone and instantly think that—especially since Ed was older—around fifty? The concept of gay people growing old had never occurred to Al, as if perhaps they ceased to exist past sexually active years. Could someone actually still be considered homosexual . . . if *non*sexual?

"Excuse me," said Al, "I'm kinda new to this scene. What's a rehearsal pianist?"

"Allow me," said Wilson. "A rehearsal pianist is hired during the construction period of a musical, to play for the singers and dancers while they learn their material. I'm a convenient cheap substitute for having the musical director and full orchestra in attendance for the nuts and bolts part of building a show. My boy, you are apparently in need of some *Education*; I could teach you *so* much."

Billy appeared to be trying to wipe something disgusting from the soles of his shoes, alternately scraping and shifting from side to side. "Leave him alone, Ed. He's not your type, not that I've seen any sign of. We're here for business."

"Oh, William, you aren't jealous are you? You could have me if you wanted. You know that, don't you, my sweet, oh so tired-looking boy? Look at those hands. I'm going to cry. What have you done to yourself? Those fingers are precious. Al, I'm angry with you. How could you let William abuse himself like this? Such a crime. Has this affected his playing?"

Al shifted his eyes toward Billy and said, "Actually, I've never heard him."

"I beg your pardon?" said Wilson. "That makes me utterly furious. Aren't you a musician? How could you not have heard this magnificent creature play, not ever? A crime, I say."

"Sorry," said Al, trying not to smile, "I'm new in town."

Wilson glared at Al. "So what instrument do you purport to play then?"

"Trumpet," said Al, ready to make up something different if that answer was unacceptable.

Wilson's small black eyes seemed to double in size. "Ah, the noblest of all instruments. I'll wager you have the most marvelous strong lips. Oh, I *am* going to faint."

Joining Billy in the let-me-outa-here shuffle, Al said, "I understand Billy's really good. I do want to hear him sometime."

"Good? GOOD . . . ?" said Wilson. "You insult him with such a pedestrian word. This emaciated hobo next to us is the finest piano player I have ever heard. The first time I witnessed his artistry, I entered a soiled little piano bar in the Village—that's *Greenwich* Village, my young virgin New Yorker—whereupon I thought for sure I'd lost my directions, and gone in circles, since I had just come from listening to Bill Evans. Surely you've heard of *him,* haven't you, my lad? And there I was, hearing the same level of sheer genius and, dare I say it . . . even better? Evans was backed by bass and drums whereas William Crothers was alone, and I swore I was listening to a symphony. The angels were no longer *a cappella*—"

"Come on, man," said Billy, "you're full of crap. Nobody cuts Bill Evans. His bass man, Eddie Gomez, did say I was kind of a cross between him and Dave Brubeck. I dug that, but not what the Village Voice reviewer once said: that I was the 'next' Bill Evans. I never wanted to be the *next* anybody."

Al had been feeling small. Now he thought he might slip through the cracks in the sidewalk down into *Nobody Land* where he belonged, far from the lofty company he had fallen in with.

"Tell me, Mr. Crothers," said Wilson, "or, Billy the Kid as they call you, where are you performing? Anywhere I'd know of? How silly of me, I know of *everywhere*." He grabbed Billy's wrist. "This is a tragedy. These splendid, perfect hands are being ruined."

Al said, "Billy's at The Straw Hat."

Kicking Al's foot, Billy quickly added, "Not a place you'd want to see me, Ed. Just a bunch of old-time sing-along crap. Embarrassing, man."

Wilson winked at Billy and said, "I love it when you call me 'man'. I feel like John Wayne. Not too often I get associated with manliness. Strange, but then, did you know that John Wayne's real name is Marion Morrison?"

Billy stiffened and replied, "I call everyone 'man', *man*. Hey, we got to go. Been a gas seein' you, Ed."

When they were far enough away, Billy looked at Al with rattlesnake eyes and said, "You fucking idiot. Why'd ya have to mention the Hat? I'm enough of a joke now. As if I need it getting out about what I'm doing."

"Sorry, Billy, guess I blew it."

Billy's frown turned into a smirk, and then a huge grin. He said, "Hey, kid, don't ever say *that* around Ed Wilson. Blowing is his life, and don't try to tell me you didn't notice he's a fag. Or don't they have those up in Canada?" His cackle reverberated amongst the buildings as he and Al walked off toward the subway station at 50th and Broadway.

♪♪♪

The gig was going reasonably well for Al—boring, but okay. No small challenge was the task of memorizing hundreds of old songs—those ones you think you know, until you're on stage in front of a roomful of people who do. The list seemed endless: "If You Knew Susie", "By the Light of the Silvery Moon", "Side by Side", "You Made Me Love You", et al. There were medleys of Irish, Italian, and Jewish songs, and even old rock 'n' roll; every night the same basic sets. The words were projected on a screen behind the band so the audience could sing along.

Al often wished the songs' notes could be displayed on a screen in front, for *him*. Sometimes he'd forget what tune they were playing right in the middle—the "bridge", as he learned to call it—and come out into a different song. The band would sometimes follow him, but often Tommy would take over the melody, playing his banjo loudly over Al's erroneous rendition. This always embarrassed the young trumpet player. He could play jazz songs with complex chord patterns and almost always know where he was, yet here he was messing up simple old standards. He figured it must have something to do with attention and interest, neither of which came easily for him with this hokey music. It was a paycheck—period.

Breaks went slowly. The constantly repeated silent movies with accompanying ragtime piano background became tedious after the first week as did the nightly beer-chugging contest. Early in his second week, Al had been lured into it, making it to the finals. He never knew who won though he later dreamed it might have been him. One goal he hadn't achieved that night was being able to get on his feet for the last set. To no one's surprise he was banned from further involvement in the contest.

♪♪♪

On a rare slow night at the Hat, Billy said to Al, "Hey, man, we'll be done early for sure. But don't split like Speedy Gonzales. I need to rap with you about something."

"Sure," said Al. "Your place or mine? And don't take that wrong, man."

"Hey, man," said Billy, "I've seen your taste in sexual prey and I am clearly not in danger. Anyway, we can hang out here. Ira won't be leaving for a couple hours after closing. It's Tuesday, and he does the books or something. He'll let us stay."

"Okay, Billy, what's on your mind?"

"Let's just say, Al . . . that I'm going to introduce you to your new teacher of the jazz arts. He'll be here in a bit."

"Far-out. That is cooler than cool, Billy. Who? No hints?"

"No, Al, but I guarantee it will be most copacetic. Hey, here comes Ira. Let's see if we're knocking off now."

♪♪♪

Ira told the band to punch their time cards, and the staff to start cleaning up. When Billy and Al asked him about staying around he paused, lips pursed in disapproval, then muttered, "Okay, but only till I'm done my paperwork."

While waiting for Billy and his mystery guest, Al sat on the edge of the stage, messing around on a blues riff, using a cup mute to keep his trumpet quiet for the guys still working. When the room's appearance met Ira's requirements, Billy went to his locker and removed his Straw Hat garb, and then walked back over to Al and sat down next to him.

Al said, "Okay, man, where's this teacher? Or did you make that up?"

"No, Al, he's about to appear . . . right . . . now." Billy whipped out his purple beret from behind his back and slapped it on his head. "Ta-dah," he sang. "Here he IS . . ."

Al laughed and said, "You mean . . . *you?* You're going to be my teacher, Billy? That's as far-out, as *out* gets."

Billy climbed up onto the stage and sat at the piano. After stretching back his bony fingers, one by one, he began to play a medium-tempo chord progression. "Okay, Al, what's this I'm playing right now?"

"Well," said Al, "you're doing a twelve-bar blues pattern. Sounds like it would fit most any blues song there is."

"That's right, man, totally right. Now, how did you know that's what it was?"

"Was easy, man. I recognized the type of chords, and how many bars each got. You know, it's a blues. It's just . . . the *blues.* Simple as that."

"Yeah, man. But *how* did you know? Did you look at my fingers? Did you read my mind?"

"Nah, Billy, I listened and—"

"That's it, Al. Don't make it complicated. You listened, and you heard what it was. That's so important, man. No matter what you *know,* you have to be able to *hear* what's going on and what's coming. I can teach you all you need to know about chords and scales and where they fit together and stuff. But no matter how much of that you have down, you aren't going to create anything but mechanical crap, if you don't learn to *hear* the music as you play, from inside your own head."

"I get it, Billy. I think I do. I know a certain amount about what scales fit with what chords and all, but I wonder if I'll ever get to where I can just forget all that and just play what I hear in my head."

"That's cool to hear you say that, Al. That's basically it. You learn all the rules so well you know them in your sleep; then you kinda dream the music right out into the world, without worrying about the technicalities anymore. You won't be thinking about scales at all, or the notes in the chords . . . just the melodies you create with them. Dizzy Gillespie once said something cool about how he thought up rhythms in his head, and just let the notes 'happen' from his horn to fit into those rhythms.

"Okay, kid, best thing is to show, not tell, right? What would you do to solo over what I'm doing right here?"

Al picked up his horn and began to play a basic blues riff, modifying it only slightly as he and Billy continued.

Billy stopped playing, leaving Al hanging in mid-phrase. "Hey, man, I thought you understood. What was *that*? Al, was that your heart playing, or your head? I told you we need both. All I heard was six notes of blues scale tedium."

"Come on, man," said Al. "Gimme a break. The blues scale is such a nice simple way to make anything sound good in a blues tune. How can that be wrong?"

"Because it's *too* right, Al. Too easy, and no need to think or feel. If you want to always be a half-assed jazzer, then go ahead and play your fucking blues scale anytime and *every* time. Hell, you can play it in Cole Porter songs if you want, and half the time it'll work there too. If you want to be really good, and if you want me to help you, then open up your mind, and your heart. Be straight with me, man, did you hear those notes before you played them, or did you just let your fingers and lips go to familiar places, so it would sound *right*?"

"Let's try it again," said Al. "Don't give up on me already. I do enough of that to myself."

Billy started to play again, this time altering the chords with more complexity. Al was about to join him when Billy said, "Wait, man, don't use the horn. Take the mouthpiece out and play on *it* for a couple of choruses. Come on. You'll be amazed what you can do."

Al smiled and decided it was worth the risk. No one was there now, except Ira in the back. He started a few lines buzzing on the mouthpiece, at first resembling the unsubtle belches of a drunken duck. But after a few more tries, Al was able to get his mind's melodies working in sync with his lips. Other than the abrasive kazoo-like tone, his riffs began to sound quite good. And he was actually playing things he had never produced on the trumpet. Some notes from the blues scale fit, and made musical sense, while others came from elsewhere, needing no explanation.

Billy shushed Al with a finger to his lips and took a solo chorus. Within the twelve bars there was not a note that didn't say something, not one which was "wrong" or "too right". It was simple, and yet melodious beyond words.

"Wow," said Al, "I'll never play that good."

"Yes you will," said Billy. "You just did. Didn't you dig that most of what I just played was what you played for me on that last chorus on your mouthpiece?"

Al said, "Billy, I'm glad you found me a teacher. He's pretty damn good. A bit hard to look at, but good."

Billy cackled. "Well, there's lots and lots of work to do, my friend. But you'll get it. Hey, let's talk a bit about what happens here." He played an altered version of the five chord of the progression. "Tell me what I'm doing now."

"Umm, flat nine?" asked Al.

"Yeah, man. Okay, now your ol' blues scale, based on the key we're in can work. But it won't do much there, that takes advantage of the possibilities, will it? There's diminished chords and scales, and bebop scales, and on and on. And guess what, every time you get to a spot like this, you can throw in a flat nine as part of your note choices, even if it's a plain ol' dominant seventh. Listen to Bird and Dizzy, man. If you want to sound like you know how to play bop, you'll learn a bunch of their licks; and man, did *they* use flat nines, sharp nines, flat fives, and sharp fives. Here, I'll show you. Parker would do something like this on a C7 chord . . ."

Billy played a medium fast, one-bar lick, typical of saxophone legend Parker. "Okay, now let's look at what he played over the chord. There's E, D, C, A, going down and back up to G, back down again . . . E-flat, C, and G-sharp. Now, how many of those notes are 'right', according to what you'd think would fit a C7 chord? Yeah, just three of 'em, if you wanted to be anal. But he added the ninth, sixth, flat third, or actually that could be a raised ninth . . . and a sharp five. All that in four beats. And that's just one of his simple licks. But trust me, he wasn't thinking about doing that at the time. Poor bastard was only half there, or *less* than half, most of the time, 'cause he was almost always high. Don't tell me he was analyzing chords and substitutions as he played. Sometimes he was lucky to be standing up. He played all those blazing fast runs with lots of notes that if you did analyze 'em by the chords, wouldn't be 'right'. A lot of what he did of course, was filling in chromatic approach notes too. *Chromaticism*, man, not mysticism."

Billy paused, realizing it had been far too long since he'd taken a breath. "Shit, man, let's not get ahead of ourselves. Back to the blues, and stick with just the mouthpiece for now, kid. Man, this is gonna be fun."

After this first session, Al and Billy got together several times a week, whenever they could get some uninterrupted piano time. It was fun for both of them and was the beginning of a new chapter in Al's musical life. And although neither of them fully recognized it yet, it had awakened a long-dormant passion in Billy's soul as well.

♪♪♪

The following weeks and months of learning, practicing, and working passed by in a blur. One night, while on break, Al was standing by the front door, keeping away from the hubbub as much as possible, when he heard an instantly recognizable voice calling, "Oh, Al ... Al ... over here ..."

It was Ed Wilson, stretching on tiptoe to be seen over the line of people waiting to get in. Al indicated to the doorman to let him through, prompting angry looks and grumbling from several others in line.

"Hey, Ed, what's happening, man? Been waiting long?" Al looked around for Billy, hoping to ward him off.

Shit, can't let Ed see him in his waiter's getup.

Observing the noisy standing-room-only crowd, peanut-shell-covered floor, and smoke thick enough to eat with a fork, Ed stretched up onto his toes to speak into Al's ear. "Let's go outside. I'd like to talk with you, and we can't in here."

Al nodded, glad to get away from the noise and Ed's impending discovery of Billy's true reason for being there.

He hasn't asked where Billy is. Shit, where IS he?

After a sigh befitting an overzealous Shakespearean actor, Ed said, "You can tell William that I won't be back in. He can stop hiding." A tear clung to his cheek, begging to be dabbed. Both men ignored it.

"You saw him, eh?" said Al.

"How delightful. I thought you might be Canadian," exclaimed Ed. "It's *aboot* time you came *oot*. Love Canadians."

I don't say "oot" and "aboot". Why do Americans accuse us of that?

"Oh, yes," said Wilson, "I saw the poor lad just as you were assisting me through the queue. I pretended not to as he scurried away, clearly having noticed me too."

Scanning the surroundings, Ed scowled. "This . . . *establishment* is so upsetting, a travesty. And Billy Crothers, a waiter? You, my young friend, are you working here too among these cretins?"

"Yeah, I am, Ed, but I actually am in the band here."

"Oh my," said Wilson, "then you are wasted here in this despicable place. You must let me help you find more appropriate employment."

Another tear slipped down, chasing the first. As Ed flicked away the evidence of emotion with his baby finger, his anguish seemed to disappear simultaneously.

"Oh . . . but, Al, here is some good news. I'm playing tonight, just around the corner. I'm on a break right now. You must promise to come over to see me after you're done. I play until three. Disgusting hours I know, but it's a delightful establishment. When do you get off?"

Get off . . . ? Never with your involvement, my friend.

Al waited for a wink or a nudge, but Ed displayed neither. His word choice may have been innocent, but if intended as double entendre to gauge Al's reaction, ignoring it seemed prudent.

"Probably around one-thirty," said Al. "Crowd's thinning early tonight, and we never go past that profit margin line."

"Wonderful," said Wilson. "It's called Emile's. You can practically see it from here. I doubt William will accompany you. Please don't say that I saw him. Promise? We'll let him believe I came here hoping to find you."

♪♪♪

Emile's was cozy and dark. Al was jealous. *This* was the right atmosphere for jazz. At the door he was greeted with the sounds of piano and laughter. Ed Wilson was one of those musician/showmen who could concurrently play and banter, with incredible skill at both. After a brilliant flurry of arpeggios, he would suddenly play softer and slower as he began an anecdote or a joke, then play louder and faster between vocal pauses. Music and chat were choreographed seamlessly, each as punctuation for the other.

Ed spotted Al, and with unfettered glee introduced him to the small group around the piano. With eyebrows arched in anticipation, he said, "Margaret, you must sing again, and we'll get this lovely young man to join us, if he will do us the honor."

Everyone seemed relaxed and jovial, sharing the role of friend more than audience member. A blond woman arose from her chair, picked up a microphone from beside Ed, and beckoned to Al. As he tried to insert his mouthpiece into his trumpet, his hands were shaking. Something about this elegant middle-aged woman's appearance and bearing subtly implied she was *someone.* She was striking, possessing an air of grace, and something else Al construed as . . . power?

My chops are busted after the gig. Hope I can play. Can hardly feel my lip.

The woman introduced herself to Al. "Hello, I'm Margaret Whiting. Ed told us you might be coming. Can't wait to hear you play."

Margaret Whiting? My God, she's like . . . a STAR, from big bands, the hit parade, and everything. Didn't I see her on the Ed Sullivan Show?

Ed, already rambling through a series of intro chords said, "Let's do 'I'll Walk Alone'. You *own* that song, my lovely."

Al couldn't avoid the thought of the song's joke-title, "I'll Whack Alone", which he now swore he'd never use again.

Damn, I hope she can't read minds.

As she sang, Al's trumpet fills came naturally and with ease from a place unknown—beyond all previous experience—as if from another plane of existence. Pieces of musical history of which she had been a part, seemed to flow into him, spurring his embryonic creativity. He was a jockey, riding her voice, becoming both controller and the controlled. She *was* powerful, not only in ability and technique, but equally in raw musical energy. And Al was not just going along for the ride, for the notes he proudly played led *her* to new feelings and expression. Her smile showed him much more than approval; she had sincerely enjoyed his efforts. When the time for a solo arrived, he was as ready as a racehorse at the gate.

Lord, don't let me mess this up. Keep it simple.

Miraculously, most of his notes were acceptable—no cacks. He was basically pleased with what he'd played. With nothing too high, too fast, or too "outside", he'd kept it plain and sweet, faithfully staying with the basics Billy had been teaching him.

Man, it was over before I could worry.

Margaret applauded along with her friends, gesturing that it all should be for Al. She turned to Ed and said with a smile, "Reminds me a bit of . . . Bobby Hackett? Lovely sound, and so melodic."

Ed flourished through a half chorus, and set up the ending with a complex modulation, guiding their way to a simple logical tag. Whiting twice repeated the last iconic line about walking alone until reunited with her lover. As she sang the final line, she smiled and glanced toward a man at her table.

Ed winked at Al, who tried to accept it as either a compliment about his playing, or an acknowledgment of Whiting's gesture toward her companion. An unavoidable, less palatable third consideration was champing at the bit in his subconscious.

Please don't be flirting with me, Ed.

Requests flew from around the room and the impromptu ensemble performed several more songs, including the quintessential favorite, "Stardust", with just trumpet and piano. Al had but one thought, as the after-hours session spilled too quickly from late night to early morning: this experience, albeit fleeting, had produced the most enjoyable, successful, and satisfying moments of his life. At 3:30 the Whiting party bid farewell, leaving Ed and Al with a sincere wish to meet again. But if Al could really have had a wish, it would have been for time itself to stop; or better, that it would rewind, and replay the night over and over again from the first notes of "I'll Walk Alone".

Something about endings had bothered Al Waters for as long as he remembered, and this experience quickly descended from ecstasy into depression. It was impossible to believe things could ever be that good again, that he could feel so happy and self-confident. It had taken only seconds for the memory of the night to be clouded with self-doubt.

Happiness and success were for other people. Any achievements Al had managed must have come from luck or deceit. The people who had just left were probably faking having liked him, or at best were too drunk to know he didn't fit in. Or at worst, they were laughing at him as they drove away in their luxurious cars to their luxurious homes and their luxurious lives.

♪ ♪ ♪

Ed and Al walked from the welcoming, warm cool of Emile's into the literal coolness of the West Village streets, the late-night air permeated with an entirely different array of noises, aromas, excitement, and dangers.

"Allen," said Ed, "I have a proposition for you . . . No, no, don't run away. I'll behave, I know you're straight. I have need of another person to share my home. Now, I said don't run away. Let me explain. I have the most lovely and commodious apartment, on the Upper West Side, 71st Street and Broadway. Been there since the fifties, and I'm not moving till they carry me out in a coffin. Rent control, you know. It's made moving out impossible to consider, since I've been there so long. You wouldn't believe what I am paying. If someone were to take it over, their rent would be astronomically higher. But even so, I am frugal and I feel a large portion of the space is going to waste. I do have one renter now, an older gentleman; rarely see him. Like him, you could have your own bathroom, bedroom with a TV, and use of my kitchen: seventy dollars a month. How does that sound?"

Al said, "Sounds like a nice chunk less than I'm paying now at the Hotel Albert on West 10th Street. Not the classiest pad, man, but it's walking distance from work. But I'm sharing with two other dudes who are, to put it politely, kind of freaky. Be nice to get out of there. I'll have a look at your place, Ed. But remember, don't get any ideas that you can . . . *convert* me. By the way, 'Al' is short for 'Alfred', not 'Allen.'"

"Apologies, my dear, *Alfred*. And I'd never change a thing about you, my handsome lad. You are perfect."

"You know what I mean, Ed."

"That I do . . . sadly, I do. But I can deal with it. For heaven's sake, I'm sure *you* can have a female friend, and not feel compelled to seduce her. It's quite the same for me with a young man."

Al hoped that was truer for Ed than for himself. "Name a day, Ed, and I'll have a look."

♪ ♪ ♪

Ed might not have been able to seduce Al, but the apartment did. Incredibly large and ornate, it confirmed Ed's statement about rent control and how it would cost a fortune to rent at the 1970s market value. Luxury oozed out of every corner: a nine-foot grand piano, more antique furniture than a small dealership, original paintings—even one by an artist Al had heard of.

Al gave a month's notice at the Albert, and even before his time there was up, he moved in to Ed's. His room there was as spacious and comfortable as an expensive older hotel, with his own bathroom right across the hall. Unfortunately, Ed's bedroom was also only a few feet away to the right of Al's door, and this was more than mildly disconcerting, both for its proximity, and for the resulting clothing restrictions necessary to access the bathroom. Slipping across the hall naked, or even in his briefs, would be a non-option— for fear of stimulating Ed's appetite for more than a platonic relationship.

The benefits of the move were somewhat offset by the inconvenience of getting to and from work, as The Straw Hat was more than sixty blocks away, requiring expensive taxis, or a public transit thrill ride on buses whose drivers appeared to be frustrated NASCAR racers, or the faster and always fascinating Lexington Ave. Express. Subway trips were always an adventure, but at two or three o'clock in the morning a different mood pre-vailed. Tommy's advice about looking mean and disheveled helped: nobody seemed too interested in bothering a six-foot-three scruffy man, with collar up, enjoying an animated self-conversation. Al added his own touch, a beat-up old suitcase for his trumpet, in place of its pristine case which he realized was like a sign saying: *Look, a nice expensive musical instrument . . . come and get it.* At first, it was troublesome to feign insanity; but he soon learned to enjoy the process, realizing it was like being an actor, with the freedom to be anything or anyone he imagined. He felt sorry for anyone he saw who appeared nervous or withdrawn. This was tantamount to a proclamation of vulnerability to the predators—vaguely analogous to Al's approach to seeking female companionship.

♪♪♪

Al had not risked a serious relationship since Sue MacDonald in high school. Since that time, a few inconsequential dates had sufficed, with music being his life's singular focus. This dedication showed in his steadily increasing musicianship. With Billy's help, and through listening to legendary players at great clubs such as the Village Vanguard, he had reached a new cloud from which to shout to the world that he was working full-time as a musician. He was ready for anything—maybe even love, or something similar.

With music, he'd had good teachers and role models from early on, but with love, he was on his own. A man who defends himself in court could be said to have a fool for a lawyer. Al, self-taught in affairs of the heart, had settled for an inept instructor.

He approached the *hunt* as he did late-night subway rides, his confidence drawn from playing a role, instead of just being himself. Whenever Al met a woman, he'd immediately sniff out her emotional liabilities, especially regarding men. He had an intrinsic ability to zero in on a need for something he could supply. If it was strength, he had plenty; if it was sensitivity, he could be as sweet as a spring breeze. When he sensed a wounded soul, he swam, shark-like around her, energized by the smell of apprehension—the attack eventually coming with his most formidable weapon, a natural empathy for any victim of emotional subjugation. Deep in his heart, Al had normal needs for intimacy and commitment, but insatiable urges pushed those aside for the opportunistic immediacy of a veritable sexual buffet, set before him by the environment of his gig.

Meeting girls was not the challenge; however, sifting through myriad choices on a particular night often *was*. Sometimes on a break, he would sit with someone who appeared interested, and by next break he'd already have spotted another quarry. "Two-in-the-bush syndrome" was how Billy saw it, and he would laugh at Al's typical plight: alternating from table to table, mixing styles of charm for different women. He was a chef, simultaneously preparing two different meals in separate kitchens. More often than not, both the soufflé fell, *and* the steak burned. On these occasions Billy would cackle and tease with lines like, "Well, ya coulda had one, but ya hadda try for two. Now ya only got me . . . are ya feelin' blue?"

Al's prowl practice was naturally destined for disaster, eventually creating a classic triple whammy awkward moment.

♪♪♪

Al was beginning to think of himself as the king of conquest—Casanova reincarnate. What the self-appointed lord of love didn't know was how to throttle back; until one night the hunter became the hunted.

Her name was Patsy, an *un*pleasantly plump young woman who, within minutes of meeting Al, had suggested heading to his place after the gig. Although he had never had much concern about a woman "having a little meat on her bones", as his dad had put it, Patsy was more than mildly over-weight—more accurately describable as morbidly obese. With too many beers and shooters having dulled his already questionable discrimination, he was able to ignore the negatives: her face was not in the least attractive; she spoke with the abrasiveness of a TV used car salesman; and she pos-sessed the intelligence of a brick.

The sex had been mutually satisfying, albeit quick; but when he rolled over to sleep off both the booze *and* her, she'd cajoled him into a repeat per-formance, and then again—and yet *again*. By the time he'd convinced her to leave him alone and take a cab home, he thought he might never be able to have sex again—or even walk, without difficulty.

For the next three nights, when she showed up at the Hat, he avoided her at closing time by hiding in the stockroom, begging the waiters to tell her he had gone out the back way. There *was* no back way or he would have made it the truth. Until the fourth night when she finally failed to appear, Al began to wonder if he might have to take up permanent residence in the stockroom.

♪♪♪

Wendy was the first girl Al met at The Straw Hat who hadn't latched onto him like a Velcro-pawed puppy. It wasn't that she didn't appear to be attracted to him as he sat next to her on the band's first break, but instead of idle chitchat or any flirtatious innuendo, she began asking about his musical aspirations. Caught off guard, Al started in about what jazz meant to him, thinking after the first few words that she would be bored enough to bolt. She not only didn't run, she listened intently and asked intelligent, sincere questions about what he had said.

"Wow," said Al, "you are something. I wish I could play something special for you when we go back up, but what we do here isn't jazz at all."

Wendy laughed and said, "Play 'Five Foot Two', since that's me. Maybe throw in a few jazzy notes for me, or would that get you fired?"

Al noticed the band was back on stage and said, "Oops, got to get back to work, but I'll do something just for you. Um, how about 'Ain't She Sweet'? That's you too."

♪♪♪

After two weeks of phone talks and lunch dates, Al and Wendy were getting to a point he hadn't thought possible for him. Handholding and kisses of slowly magnifying intensity had been the extent of their physical intimacy, but each loved being in one another's company. As they grew to know and care for each other, a bond was developing beyond anything Al had experienced as an adult. Sexual intimacy seemed a natural next step for them, but Al wasn't sure how to get to that stage with someone he cared about.

On a Wednesday lunch date, Wendy said, "Al, I'm going to come to The Straw Hat Saturday night, if you want me to. I know we can't spend much quality time there, since it's so noisy, and of course, you're working. But maybe after, we can just walk and talk, and figure out a bit more about all this between us. Whatcha think?"

"Sounds like a plan," said Al. "I wish it was Saturday right now."

♪♪♪

Friday night was typically crazy busy as the audience was packed with tourists from all over the world. It looked like a United Nations New Year's Eve party. Against Tommy's wishes, and the club's new policy of not allowing band members to compete in the beer chugging contest, Al talked Ira into letting him enter for the first time since he'd inspired the policy change. The necessity of the "Al rule" was proven again, and for the final time, as the trumpet player's skills and behavior degraded exponentially with each downed draft.

A young woman sitting directly in front of the stage had practically burned a hole in Al's pants with her stare throughout the first set, and he figured he at least owed her the opportunity of chatting with him, however briefly.

Her name was Mary Lou, and she was most receptive to his visit. As she talked of exchanging phone numbers and hinted at possible get-togethers, Al went along with it out of pure habit. She was attractive enough, and clearly interested in more than chat, but he was confident he'd found someone special in Wendy. This situation was merely a plumage display, partially to provoke a look of exasperation from Billy; Al's beer-fueled reasoning was that soon he'd be back on stage, and he'd file Mary Lou under the also-rans and never-weres of his New York life.

He felt a tap on the shoulder. It was Wendy, happily announcing she'd been unable to wait for Saturday. As there was one empty chair to his right, Al pulled it out for her, dodging what was an obvious attempt on her part to lean in for a kiss. This was uncharted social territory. Should he have made a bigger deal of welcoming her? What was the protocol for having a girlfriend show up unannounced? Al didn't know the rules—if there were any—and his instincts in this area were woefully inadequate.

He was now perched on a wobbly chair between two women: one whom he'd already dated, and to whom he was supposed to be *attached*, and the other, whom he had just met. The ensuing dialogue in the noisy room proved a true test of Al's skills at managing a dual conversation, as he tried to come up with a way to separate them before the next set without offending or hurting anyone. But an illogical guilt was creeping up his spine, eroding his equanimity. He hadn't really been doing anything *wrong*—or had he?

Al thought he had a handle on this complicated game. By faking a bad stomach from all the beer chugging, he'd convinced Wendy to go home and to return on Saturday as first planned. But fate had decided to raise the ante beyond even *his* prodigious improvisation skills.

Tommy began to head back to the stage, calling the other band members to follow. It now seemed too late to prevent Wendy and Mary Lou from sitting next to one another for the next hour—or at least for however long it took them to determine their mutual interest in one sweating trumpet player. If this wasn't stressful enough, Al then spotted someone else headed for the table. Worse timing could not have been possible.

"Hi, lover boy," said Patsy, planting a lusty wet kiss on Al's inadvertently open mouth. "Tonight we go for five times, okay? Unless you think you could manage even more . . . ?"

She was as ambitious as she was obnoxious. And worse—equally as loud.

♪♪♪

Until this moment, Wendy had been feeling pretty much in love with Al, captivated by his charm and sensitivity. He did have a strong attraction for her too, although he wasn't ready to define it. This terrible scene reeked of yet another ending—an instant incineration of all potential joy, hope, and belief. Within seconds of Patsy's words, Wendy got up and ran to the front door, saying nothing as she went.

Mary Lou sneered at Al and said, "Looks like you've got more than enough woman to handle already, you prick. Piss off."

"What's that supposed to mean?" said Patsy. "You think he's interested in a beanpole like you?"

While the two women glared at each other, Al searched for something to say to Patsy or Mary Lou. But words were as impossible to find as any real concern for either of them. Wendy was the one hurt by this, and without question meant something to him. He ran to the door and down the street, and within two blocks he caught up with her.

Grabbing her hand from behind, he pleaded, "Hey, come on, let me explain, baby. You shouldn't be out here by yourself anyway. It's dangerous in these streets."

She pulled her hand free from his and rubbed the tears from her face. "God, I'm stupid," she yelled. "I wondered why you didn't hug me or kiss me when I came in. I might have known you were a lying son of a bitch. Leave me alone, or I'll call a cop. I thought you were a decent guy. Serves me right. I'm a damn fool for trusting you."

Glancing toward The Straw Hat, Al said, "I gotta get back there, but I can explain if you give me a chance, please?"

He touched his fingers to her cheek. From this gentle gesture he then drew his hand back and twice slapped his own forehead with frightening force. Seeing the dread in her eyes he said, "Hey, I'm mad at me, not you. I'd never *ever* hurt you."

Wendy said, "Wouldn't *hurt* me? No? What do you think you just did? That girl you were next to when I came in; it looked like you were pretty into her. And that other one, who was *she*? You told me I was the first girl you'd cared about since you came to New York."

"Hey, come *on*, that girl at the table was . . . nothing. I just sat down next to her there for a minute. Was only messing around and stuff. I guess I screwed up. But when you came in, I still felt like I got . . . *caught*? But I hadn't done anything to get caught *at*. Stupid, eh?

"As for Patsy, yeah, I was with that pig once. But damn, I was piss drunk that night. I was outa my head. And anyway, that was before I met you. Please believe me, we can get through this."

Al sank to one knee and held both her hands. "Baby, I promise I won't do anything like this ever again. One more chance is all I ask. Neither of those bimbos means anything. But you . . . you're special to me."

His words and his eyes radiated real pain and remorse—it *had* to be true. She turned toward the street, fighting back a smile she neither understood nor wanted him to see.

"Okay, Al, call me tomorrow. We'll talk some more. Right now I'm going to get a cab home. There's one now. Call me; we'll work it out. I think I could love you, Al. I wish to hell it wasn't so, but . . ."

As he gently placed his fingers across her lips, he wanted to say "me too", but the words became entangled in the root structure of his tree of self-doubt which had grown from sapling to giant redwood since his earliest childhood. He was reminded once again of the old Groucho Marx line: "I wouldn't want to be part of any club that would have *me* as a member."

She can't really love me. And how could I love anyone who's so dumb that she thinks I should be loved?

Al handed Wendy his last twenty as she entered the cab. As the vehicle disappeared into the mostly yellow 7th Avenue traffic, he watched, and wondered just how many ways were there to mess up a chance for love?

♪ ♪ ♪

As Al turned to head back to The Straw Hat, a thought struck him as hard as one of his father's cuffs to the back of the head.

Christ, break must be over. Is the band already playing without me?

He set out running at full tilt. In almost any other city in America, he might have drawn stares, with piano key garters on both arms, red suspenders, and plastic straw hat which he held with one hand to prevent it from flying off. Here in Greenwich Village, not a soul took heed for his entire sprint back to the club.

Sure enough, he could hear the band from a half block away. Reaching the front door, he scrambled past the lineup and then pushed and shoved his way through the congested bar, slowing when he caught sight of the table where the trouble had begun. Mary Lou was gone, and so it seemed was Patsy. Stumbling onto the stage he grabbed his trumpet, trying to avoid Tommy's eyes as he joined in with "The Old Gray Mare". Acting as if nothing was out of the ordinary, Al hammed it up with several "ripped" high notes and a comical half-valve horse whinny sound at the end of the song. The audience cheered, as Tommy rolled his eyes, playing it up as if all part of the act. Over the mike he said, "Welcome back, to our Pony Express trumpet player."

He was off the hook with the band—not so with Patsy. There she was, back sitting in front in her favorite spot, staring hungrily at Al. By the end of the evening he'd consumed enough beer to remember why he'd taken her home the first time, and more than enough to forget everything dissuasive of a repeat performance. His only reason for backing out this time would have been his promise to Wendy. But booze, and a heart bereft of trust, provided the easy rationale that she'd brought this on herself by showing up unannounced—and by loving him so soon.

♪ ♪ ♪

In the following days, Al thought a great deal about Wendy, *almost* calling her several times. But finally he took the crumpled piece of napkin with her number, tore it up, and flushed away the temptation forever. He had decided she was too good for him. While there would be many more like Patsy and Mary Lou during his stint at the Hat, Wendy was the only girl he met who affected him in such a way. After what happened with her, he avoided involvement with anyone to whom he might get close enough to hurt—and give a damn that he had.

♪ ♪ ♪

Ed was becoming a pest. Increasingly, he ignored his promise not to be flirtatious, and each time Al rebuffed him, he responded by being extra picky about domestic issues, such as kitchen mess, bathroom cleanliness, and late-night noise. Al had all the annoyance of a bitchy nagging wife, without any of the benefits of marriage—at least none he was willing to be involved with.

One night, in the second month of living with Ed, Al was in his room smoking a joint, assuming it was safe since the *nag* would be asleep. There was a Marx Brothers movie on and he'd always wanted to experience Groucho while stoned.

The tapping on his door sounded like a wrecking ball in double time.

God, no . . . he's awake?

Ed hadn't declared any rules about smoking dope, but Al knew he would most likely disapprove.

Oh man. Gotta just stay quiet.

"Alfred," came the familiar voice through the door, "are you alone?"

Al held his breath, until his lungs felt close to re-enacting the Hindenburg disaster.

Oh, the humanity . . . or should I say, the hoMO-nity? Maybe he'll just go away.

Ed cracked open the door and peeked in, whispering, "Sorry to bother you, Alfred . . . you *are* awake, aren't you?"

Al had long suspected that while he was out, Ed would come into his room, so he'd set up traps, such as carefully placed threads over the dresser drawers. Busted—three times now, but Al had said nothing, not wanting to raise a fuss; although it did creep him out knowing that Ed had violated his supposedly private space.

He's got the balls to come in here NOW, with me home? Shit yeah, he's got balls. And he'd just love me to see 'em.

"Ed," said Al, "I'm in bed, man. What the hell do you want?"

Ed pushed the door open wider. "I recognize that odor, my young friend. Smoking marijuana are we? Are you okay? Depressed perhaps?"

"I'm watching TV, Ed."

I don't like this. Is he going to make a move? Damn, don't know if I CAN move.

Ed had slipped quietly all the way into the room, and he sat on the corner of the bed at Al's feet. "So, Alfred, what are you watching? Oh goodness, my favorites. I knew Groucho. Did you know that? Such a sweet man *and* a true genius. I was *involved* with one of the musicians in his television band."

Al wanted to kick Ed away—to shove him out the door. But he was naked beneath the bed sheets, and getting up might convey the wrong idea, even if he was forceful—and he wasn't entirely sure he could be.

This weed is some heavy shit.

"Alfred," said Ed, "we must do this more often: watch TV together, and we should go out more often as well. The friends I've introduced you to all think you're a wonderful young man." He was touching Al's feet and began to massage them through the sheets. To Al's stoned and stressed brain, the cloth felt as thin as tissue.

"You know, Alfred . . . they all think you're my lover. Does that bother you?"

It did, on many levels, but Al said, "Not really, Ed. Sometimes though, with some of the girls you've introduced me to I've felt like screaming, 'Hey, I'm not gay'."

"Alfred, that could be a song: 'Hey, I'm *not* gay, hey, I'm *not* gay', in fast four-four time of course. Hmm, how would it sound in five-four? 'Hey, I'm not gay, man. Hey, I'm not gay, man'. Delightful!"

Ed's high-pitched laugh made Al picture the wicked witch from Oz, but neither that, nor the clever musical joke could provoke even the slightest smile in turn. There was real-life wickedness to deal with: Ed's foot massage had traversed to Al's knees. He felt numb, unable to move, stuck like a gnat in a giant flytrap.

Don't want to hit him. I do like him, just not the way he wants. God, don't let me get a hard-on. Why would I . . . ? Damn, these sheets are thin.

"I brought you something, Alfred," said Ed, pulling a rumpled magazine from under his sweater. "Thought you might enjoy it. It's an old one, but quite interesting . . . like mine, I mean, *me*. Oh goodness, the heat on my cheeks; I'm surely blushing."

Ed leafed through pages until a particular picture caught his attention. As Al's irrepressible curiosity pushed aside his apprehension, he looked toward the page. To his surprise, it was not men, but two naked women, apparently engaged in an intense mutual breast examination.

A Cancer Society brochure? Yeah, right.

Ed held the magazine in his right hand while his left resumed its upward trek from Al's knee. "You have such athletic legs, Alfred. You could have been a dancer."

The fondling had become firmer and had now gone well beyond the invisible line of acceptability.

Why didn't I say no when he touched my feet? This is bad.

Al grabbed the magazine and threw it on the floor. "Ed, I know what you're trying to do. Come on . . . not *fair*."

Squeezing Al's thigh with both hands, Ed paused and said, "You're right, Alfred, *this* would be better for both of us." In one nimble move he rose up on his knees and tumbled across Al's body, snuggling up next to him.

Holy shit, he's the dancer.

Al tried to remain calm, lying still as a corpse and feeling just as cold. "Ed, I'm not cool with this. Please get up and get outa here."

Ed didn't move. He said, "Just tell me you hated my hands on you, and I'll leave."

Al said, "Come on, this is crap. If you were a girl . . ."

"How do you know I'm not?" asked Ed, tugging Al's hand to his abdomen and trying to force it downward.

Al pulled out of Ed's grip with more effort than he'd anticipated needing against the older man. "Ed, I'm gonna tell you one more time. Get OUT. I don't want to hurt you."

"Oh, Alfred, that means you love me, doesn't it? How do you know I don't *want* you to hurt me?" With the speed of a cobra, Ed shot one hand over to Al's crotch. "Ah," he purred, "don't tell me you aren't a bit more than curious. This glorious bulge seems *quite* happy to meet me . . ."

It was only seconds before Al could push away the intrusive fingers, but even that small delay sent a frightening mixed message to his brain from his fully erect penis. "Ed, if I wasn't stoned, I'd have smacked you for that. I trusted you, and you try to take advantage of me? Get outa here . . . *now,* damn it."

Ed was still on the bed, hands now to himself. "Alfred, I'm sorry. I only thought maybe if I got close to you, you might discover the feelings I dream you could have for me. Confess, you didn't fight that hard to stop me . . . *did* you?"

"I liked you, Ed; wanted to be your friend, but you've fucked it up. How can I look at you, now that you've done this?"

Ed turned over, speaking now with his back to Al. "There's no chance you'd let me touch you? I know ways to please you . . . you can't imagine. Why couldn't you pretend I'm a woman? Close your eyes and picture the girls in the magazine . . . ? Alfred, you have no idea what you're missing."

Al tried to drive the impossibly intriguing image out of his head. Would it be *that* different—that wrong? Maybe he *could* pretend?

What am I doing even thinking about it? I'm sick. Ed can get me farther in this town than I could ever get on my own. If I do what he wants, it could be a good career move. What would that make me . . . a prostitute? Another aspiring musician willing to sacrifice anything for my art . . . or just a whore?

Al was disgusted with himself; his heart was racing and he knew it was only partially from fear. Worst of all, his penis was still fully erect. "Can't do it, Ed. Sorry, but I've had it. You better leave now. I mean it."

"Al," whispered Ed, "please, just let me touch you, just a little. No one need know, except you and me. Our little secret, forever?"

Al sucked in a long, slow, deep breath, trying to find even stronger words to rebuff Ed. Surmising this silent pause to be consideration of his proposition, Ed snatched back the bed sheet without warning. His hope was heightened instantly, upon seeing Al's body in fully engorged denial of his professed lack of interest.

"Oh, Alfred, you are wonderful," gasped Ed. "Please let me touch it. I must have that beautiful cock in my mouth."

As Ed reached downward, Al lay still and watched, mired in disbelief and confusion as to why he'd not yet stopped what was happening. Then the words came from somewhere inside, somewhere deep: dim echoes of another time, another existence.

Slowly and softly, but with the foreboding of a lit fuse, Al said, "Ed, if you do it, I will crush you. I will kill you with my hands. I swear on my sister's grave . . . I mean it."

Ed said nothing as he slunk out of the bed and disappeared out the door without looking back. Any man—even of half Ed's intelligence and savvy—

should have known how close to death he had just come.

Shortly afterward, they each found temporary peace in solitary satisfaction: Ed thinking of Al; and Al, looking at the porn magazine pictures—forcing himself to think of anything *but* Ed.

It was these fucking pictures. The women . . . THEY turned me on.

As much as he tried to convince himself that there had been no hint of temptation to give in to Ed, the thought continued to nag him throughout the night—a doubt, as inextricable as that one piece of popcorn husk you can't get with your tongue. In some elusive and incomprehensible way, it would stay with him forever.

♪ ♪ ♪

Al moved back into a two-bedroom suite at the Hotel Albert, sharing it with the tuba player from The Straw Hat. Since the bedroom incident, it had become much too uncomfortable being around Ed. Afterward, they ran into each other a few times, and Al even sat in once with Ed at a piano bar similar to Emile's. From the day they'd met, and all the time they'd lived under the same roof, Ed had treated Al with warmth and charm. Now that Al had moved out, there was a superficial, businesslike atmosphere between them—nothing more.

He's tossed me aside because he didn't get what he was after. Is that all I'm worth? No sex, so no friendship? Wonder if it bothers him at all . . . or is he able to just throw away his feelings right along with me?

Al tasted a bitter irony: the perspective for once of *being* the object of failed seduction and consequent rejection. For many men it might have changed their attitude about how women should be treated—but not Al. An ego built on shame and guilt cannot sustain true morality.

Inexplicably, he sensed it wasn't the first time he'd experienced the Pandora's box of emotions Ed had evoked, but he refused to even try to understand. He shoved the incident deep down into that same tangle of roots imprisoning his feelings for Wendy—the latest cellmates alongside the longtime denizens of his repression. He rarely smoked pot again after that night since it almost guaranteed a "bad trip" straight into those roots which writhed angrily toward his neck whenever he dared confront them. And yet, inconceivably, a worse betrayal of trust lay just ahead.

♪ ♪ ♪

One Tuesday night, nearly a year into Al's stint at The Straw Hat, Billy didn't show up for work, and Ira said if he didn't hear from him by the next night, that would be it—no more chances. Al wasn't surprised by Billy's failure to appear again; he'd checked his apartment and found it vacant, with a prospective tenant already being shown around. Even though Billy talked frequently about how much he hated being a waiter, it still came as a shock the way he'd handled things.

While Ira was angry, he was relieved to be free of his commitment to his least efficient employee. Al's feelings involved much more than anger; he'd lost his mentor *and* best friend. The connection with Billy Crothers had provided a high unlike any previous human relationship in Al's life. Withdrawal pains were instant and close to debilitating, sending the young man into a nose dive to depths he'd never imagined. Over the next several weeks he practiced his trumpet obsessively while spending every moment away from music on a fervent quest for sexual satiation. His thirst was of course unquenchable in either endeavor—since what he truly needed was woefully misperceived.

♪♪♪

On a typical bustling night at The Straw Hat in mid-September of 1970, Ira answered a phone call in his office. Putting the caller on hold, he tracked down Al, who was on break, schmoozing at a table of young women. He said, "Hey, Al, a call for you. Not sure who it is, but they said it was urgent. You better come see . . ."

The caller was Billy Crothers. He had a music gig, with a newly formed jazz ensemble, *and* there was a spot for a trumpet player. They'd been breaking in the group up in the Catskill Mountains in a few small lounges, preparing for some one-nighters in Buffalo, with some club dates lined up in Canada after that. The band's trumpet player had split after too many arguments with the leader, and Billy had told them they had to get this kid he knew back in the City.

"Al, man, remember this is how I told you it works? This is a good little group, and we get to play jazz! Far-fucking-out, huh? You dig? No more crappy sing-along shit for you, Al baby. Say yes, man."

As excited as he was by the idea, Al was not going to screw the people at The Straw Hat. "Billy, for sure I'd be into that, but I'd have to get someone to take over the gig at the Hat."

"Hold on, Al. Here, talk to Mike. It's his gig."

"Hey, Al . . . Mike Zabic here," said a new voice on the line. "Billy says you're a *player*, man. It's your gig 'cause of that recommendation."

"Mike, I just can't walk out on the Straw Hat gig without getting a sub. I'd love to come work with you guys, but I can't leave 'em hanging."

"Cool, I can dig that, man. Shows you got honor or loyalty or something. Proves you wouldn't do it to *me* either. Tell you what, I'll give you a couple days to find yourself a sub, okay?"

It took Al over twenty phone calls to track down a suitable replacement. The musician he found was overqualified and priced accordingly, but he was available when no one else was—no one at least who was willing to work for the Hat's low pay which Al agreed to top up with a hundred dollars of his own money to secure the deal.

The Straw Hat had lost its Canuck trumpet player, and the world had gained a brand new jazz cat. For Al, the downside of the deal was having to leave New York City—at least for a while. The up side far outshone any negatives; if he'd made it *there*, he could make it *anywhere*—or so the song promises.

CHAPTER 16

FIVE - SOUTH TOWER [5]

*M*oaning softly, the man in the hospital bed stirred. It had only been a few minutes since the visitor in green had entered room 510, but time was desperately limited—and the patient's return to consciousness at this moment would be perfect. If only there were such a thing as "perfect". The universe began from what must not have been perfection, or why would whatever it was, become what it is . . . or rather, what it continues to become? Is it chaos? Is it a plan? Could those two words describe one thing at once: one *moment* . . . like this one?

"Come on, my friend," whispered the sweating orderly, "that's it. Let's have a little talk and I can get down to business. If I know you can hear me, then I can do what I have to do, and you won't ever have to worry about anything ever again. Isn't that nice of me? Think of it as me putting you out of your misery. Or more like putting you out of *my* misery . . . and everyone else whose life you've screwed up."

Frustration and fear were quickly mixing with the hatred already in his heart. This had to end soon. If not, he'd have to go without completing his scheme to the letter, and there might never be another chance as convenient as this—surely not one where the man in the bed would be so vulnerable. It was disquieting to be so close to him, even in his weakened condition. The orderly couldn't shake the notion that his bedridden prey might only be feigning helplessness; might be about to awaken, fully aware, and in command of his normally formidable strength. One encounter with that was enough—the pain lingered still.

CHAPTER 17

THE SOUNDS OF SILENCE

*D*octor Davidson stood up and walked toward the wall to Al's left. "I'm quite a jazz fan myself, Alfred. My collection is extensive, as you can see," he said, shuffling through CDs in the wall rack which also held cassette tapes. Beneath these was a shelf containing hundreds of vinyl records.

"Beats mine, Doc, by a mile and a half."

"That surprises me, Alfred. I'd have thought you'd have an extensive collection. You say mine is bigger?"

"Don't get too excited, Doc. Size doesn't matter, right?"

"Alfred, I believe I see a pattern here, and I suspect it is not just with me, but a part of your everyday behavior. Do you always find a way to turn any discussion into something of a sexual nature?"

"Well, maybe I do . . . unless of course, we were *already* talking about sex."

The doctor tapped his pencil against his temple. "Ah, you mean because if we were actually discussing sex seriously, perhaps as it pertains to you *personally*, then you'd change the subject? By the way, this is an area we haven't yet talked much about . . . other than your innuendos and jokes. And early on in our first session, you mentioned how sex can bring on depression. If I may be so blunt, you seem to have had rather an active romantic life. If you're ready, I would like to discuss, for lack of a more clinical term, your 'sex life' and the difficulties to which you've alluded."

Al picked at his nails and cuticles, clearing imperceptible bits of debris with his thumb and forefinger. "Doc, my collection of music of any kind hardly amounts to anything. Hey, but when I was a kid, I had a bunch of records, including lots of classical stuff. I used to play one favorite all the time, Borodin's Prince Igor Overture. There was this French horn solo in it that made me cry, it was so beautiful, by this guy named Lucien Thévet. He used vibrato, which most French horn cats don't, or at least didn't back then.

Sounded a bit like Dorsey on trombone, or more like one of those English brass band guys: sweet, sweet sound and so much emotion.

"The first jazz I ever listened to was big band stuff and Dixieland, then blues. Not rock blues, but the jazz combo kind, with real singers like Ella Fitzgerald and Satchmo, or Joe Williams. Later I got into Miles, Bird, Coltrane, and Lenny Breau of course. But you know, I confess I never totally dug the really far-out stuff they did. I learned to mimic the style, but I really always more enjoyed the guys like Chet Baker and Paul Desmond . . . yeah, and my favorite on tenor was Dexter Gordon. On alto, no question, Cannonball Adderley. What a sound he had, man. So much feeling came through that horn, and he had chops to burn too. But his sound was the ultimate: huge, and pretty at the same time.

"Cannonball played on an American sax, a King; not like the majority of jazz guys, including me, who swear by the French saxes; and of course he played alto, and I'm a tenor guy. Mine's a '57 Selmer Mark VI, a warm, dark sounding horn; great axe, especially the ones made in the fifties and early sixties. Legend has it they were built out of brass from melted-down World War II shell casings. Who knows? Cool story anyway.

"There's some guys who think the old Kings, Conns, Bueschers, and even Martins sound better than a Selmer. I gotta say though, when I first tried my VI, I fell in *love*. Totally cool tone, and way better ergonomics than anything else ever made. Feels like it wasn't *built*, but was born with you, right in your hands. Man, if I ever lost this one I'd be sunk; hard to find a good one anymore that doesn't cost two arms and a leg, from all the mystique around them."

"Goodness," said the doctor, "as I recall, I was attempting to delve into sexual matters wasn't I? Next time I want a history lesson on jazz music and instruments, I guess I should ask you again about your love life."

"Can I ask you about *yours*, Doc? Just kidding."

"Alfred, you've indicated you were rather a 'tomcat' when you were in New York; only once during that time did you even get close to a solid relationship. Well, not close at all I suppose from what you say. Wendy was her name? And in high school, there was only the one girl . . . Sue? Maybe you can share more detail with me about what happened there as I sense there's substantial discomfort in that memory. Perhaps you could explain a little more about her and how you two broke up?"

"Well, Doc. I'd have to say my favorite solo trumpet player for ballads was Chet Baker. Simple, sweet, gorgeous playing. No real high stuff, but you didn't miss it; his emotion came through the phrasing. He'd tell you such a story with that horn, just like his singing. It was like he'd *lived* every moment of all those sad songs. In the long run, his own story was sadder than most of the lyrics of just about any song ever written. I never saw him perform live, but I've watched old movie clips, and no matter who he was playing with on stage, it was like he was completely, desolately alone."

"Okay, Alfred, I get it. You did just tell me a lot, and I'll wager not entirely unintentionally either. As I'm getting to know you, I'm realizing how much you say sometimes, in what you leave *out*."

"Right, Doc. That's swing, if you could define it, it's got a lot to do with *feel*, not just the notes. The silences, even the littlest ones, have a way of making the sounds *say* something. I think you're the kind of guy who gets that."

"Talk about *saying* something, Alfred. Are you aware of how much you just told me . . . in your description of the way you play your music?"

"Never been too good with words, Doc, but with a horn in my hand I get the message across pretty good I think."

"You need to listen to the spaces, Alfred . . . the ones between your words, and those even *bigger* spaces, between your times of well-being. For you to be able to relate to other people in an intimate way, you must open up your heart as you do when you play music. Sometimes the words you say are like, I suppose, unnecessary notes, the kind you say an overly technical jazz musician plays.

"Alfred, could it be that music is the only language with which you feel comfortable relating to others openly and completely?"

"Could be, Doc. It's a whole lot easier to let out feelings through a horn, since the language doesn't get in the way so much. And the risks are less . . . personal?"

"Yes," said the doctor, "and don't forget about the importance of the spaces you've described in musical communication. I believe there may be too many *protective* silences guarding thoughts and memories within you. Perhaps you could learn to replace those with conscious thoughts and words . . . not only to me and others, but also to yourself. Do you think you could ever be completely intimate with a woman until you can be honest with yourself about who you are, as opposed to what you seem to feel you are *supposed* to be?"

"I don't know, Doc. What should I try first, to make that happen?"

"First of all, let's abandon the word 'should'. We have choices to make about everything in life. We must not say 'I should', but rather, 'I choose to', or 'choose not to', or 'I shall try to'. But never . . . 'I should'."

"Yeah, Doc, I know I should . . . Oops, I mean I know I *must* work on that. Makes a lot of sense but, man, it's not easy."

"I understand, Alfred. Let's talk a bit more about your music. It's fascinating to hear some of the things you've done and places you've been. We don't have to spend the whole session digging up demons."

"Digging up my demons doesn't require a shovel, Doc. They're real close to the surface, and plenty crowded at that."

"Crowded, Alfred, I'd agree, but close to the surface? I'm not so sure about that. In time we shall see. And please believe this, there are times when I am glad to be wrong."

"What do you want to know, Doc? Where did we leave off when we last talked about my sordid past?"

The doctor leafed through his notes and said, "Let's see, uh . . . after New York, you and Billy were in a band, right? Would you like to tell me more about that experience?"

CHAPTER 18

ROLLING THUNDER
1970 - Montreal

*M*ontreal, Québec, 1970: the year of the "October Crisis". In Canadian history, on home soil, nothing matches this period for drama and turmoil; likewise for Al Waters. The young man from Ontario who'd already left behind his family, his home country, his teens, and any vestiges of innocence was now headed toward yet another new world full of life-changing events—for which not even his experiences in New York City could have prepared him.

♪♪♪

Jazz was hot in Montreal, and many American musicians were lured to this "European" city just north of the border from Vermont. A fan could easily enjoy several great performances, in many styles—from big bands and small combos, to solo artists—each night for a week straight, and still not catch them all.

Al and Billy were part of a thrown-together ensemble called Minus Milt. The name had come about because the original group had featured a vibraphonist whose idol was Milt Jackson of The Modern Jazz Quartet. He'd wanted to call the band The Milt Jackson Quartet-Minus Milt; but that being too long, confusing, and misleading, they'd decided on simply Minus Milt. This name proved in the long run to be just as confusing, but at least it was short; as was the tenure of the vibraphonist who turned out to be inconsistent, unreliable, and irresponsible. Billy was his replacement—definitely an ironic choice considering *his* reputation.

They were a New York band, so they *had* to be good—at least according to the booking agents. No one would—or should—know that two of them were actually Canadians, one of whom was living illegally in the States. Al had bused it from New York City all the way up to Buffalo, and across the Peace Bridge over the Niagara River to Fort Erie, Ontario where the band was waiting for him. Going through Canada Customs into his own country was unsettling; as if coming home were a clandestine operation because of his connection to an American band.

Mike, the band's official leader—purely because someone had to be, and he was the oldest—spotted Al sitting on the curb, surrounded by pretty much everything he owned: a suitcase, two over-stuffed garment bags, and his trumpet case.

"Hey, kid, it's me, Mike Zabic . . . Come on, it's nearly two hours to the top end of Toronto from here, right? Hey, maybe you got better directions than the agent sent me."

Al scrambled to his feet and said, "Pretty simple, man; just take the Q.E.W. right from here all the way, unless your car floats. Could buzz right across the lake then, eh?"

"Real funny, kid . . . Q.E.W? Oh yeah, the Queen Elizabeth Way. That *is* what I was told." As he helped Al pick up his stuff, he added, "Hey, man, you never been on the road before, *have* ya? That horn case is way too clean."

Al wobbled, arms full, over to the rack-top Ford LTD station wagon and U-Haul trailer, accompanied by the laughter of Nate, Elliot, and Billy, whose familiar cackle rose above all. The sound of it was a bit like coming home for Al. He'd missed that quirky laugh.

After grabbing Billy and squeezing the wind out of him with a hug, Al said, "Hey, Mike, there's a reason my case looks new: self-preservation tactics, New York style. I *never* used the good case there. Hey, you old pros oughta know all about that, right?"

Billy said, "Hey boys, don't let the long hair fool you. The kid can *play*. I taught him everything he knows." He cackled even louder.

"You didn't teach him *everything*, did you?" asked Mike with a frown. "Music, sure. Recreational *habits* . . . ? Hope not."

As the only one in the group who had worked with Billy Crothers at the peak of his "Billy the Kid" days, Mike Zabic had personally witnessed the legend's fall into the pit of alcohol and drug ruination. In the awkward moment after the comment, Al wondered if anyone would say anything about how malevolent those words had been. Should he himself? Would that end his gig before it even started?

Nate broke the silence by asking, "Why we going to Toronto? Isn't the gig in Montreal?"

Mike glared at him. "Want to work without drums, shithead? We're picking up our second Canuck, Joe Bendzsa, in Scarborough, the top end of Toronto. The agent says he's supposed to be one of the best young drummers in the country . . . and his gig ends tonight, remember? And it's sorta, kinda on the way." He turned to Billy and asked, "Are all bass players so spaced, man?"

Billy pushed back the tip of his beret and said, "He's a *spaceman*? Far-fucking-astronautically *out*."

Mike ignored the comment. Doing his best to mimic Billy's cackle he said, "Hacka, hacka, hack . . . Hey, guys, this is Al Waters. You heard what Billy said. He's supposed to be good."

After each band member shook hands and self-introduced, Al began loading his possessions into the trailer. Elliot settled into the back seat of the car, pulled his hat over his face and said, "The kid better be good. It's a long walk back to New York from Montreal. Now shadap, all of you. Gotta get some shut-eye before we hit Toronto."

♪♪♪

Al felt a sense of irony, as a Canadian, being the only one in the group who had never been to Montreal. At twenty, he was five to seven years younger than Nate, Elliot, or Billy. And then there was Mike who looked about forty—but after the night he'd first met Billy Crothers, Al had lost faith in his initial impressions of age.

Joe Bendzsa, as it turned out, was even younger than Al—not even eighteen by Mike's guess—a true jazz prodigy. His Sunday gig in Scarborough was officially over around midnight. By the time all the catching up, and some after-hours jamming, and loading the Joe's baggage and drums into the trailer were done, the trip to Québec didn't get underway until the early morning hours. After driving a few hours, resting for a breakfast stop, and then more driving until a lunch break, they arrived at the club in downtown Montreal on Saint Catherine Street West, or rue Sainte-Catherine, as Francophones called it. It was early Monday afternoon as they unloaded the equipment and prepared to set up.

The place seemed unusually large for a jazz club, with a twenty by thirty-foot dance floor directly in front of an expansive bandstand. Billy and Mike stood at the edge of the stage, talking quietly, with anger on their faces.

Confused and curious, Al walked over to them and said, "What's the deal, guys?"

Billy whispered, "The name of this joint had me worried anyway. Rolling Thunder? Check out this fucking dance floor. I'm real nervous about what this place is about. And dig the stuff on the wall, man: car parts; sports pictures, including some of pro wrestlers? This is a *jazz* club? No way, not copacetic at all. We're in trouble. I can feel it . . ."

Al had never seen a bar like this one. The main floor was covered in a filthy short-pile carpet, with more cigarette burns per square foot than a drunk's coffee table. Above the dance floor was a large mirror-ball light fixture, dormant and offering little hope of brightening up the almost-black stained hardwood below. Gallons of beer had no doubt seeped into that wood, no doubt along with the odd bucket or two of blood. The tables and chairs were a haphazard combination of styles and materials, some wooden, some metal. Of the few tablecloths in evidence, most were a hodgepodge of colors and sizes, mostly checkered in blue and white—"white" being relative, these lighter tones being more akin to the teeth of an old hound. Several pool tables were visible in the far right corner of the establishment, each beneath an antique light fixture, some of which dangled crookedly and precariously from shoddily repaired chain suspensions.

The bar extended almost the entire width of the back of the room, its dark wood highlighted at the base by a brass foot rail which was dented and bent from years of heavy-booted use. Filling the air was a mélange of smoke, beer, and wet carpet smells, joined in the vicinity of the restrooms by the unmistakable odor of seldom-cleaned urinals.

Next to the bar's far end a door opened, and from it emerged a giant of a man—close to seven feet tall—sporting a white-guy Afro hairdo which was as over-puffed as the muscles straining, Hulk-like, against the fabric of his tee shirt. Al tried not to catch Billy's eye, thinking he'd either laugh or run screaming. Whichever the choice, he knew he'd likely join him.

"Hey, you guys must be the band, eh?" said the giant in a rumbling basso profundo voice.

Mike introduced himself, and the two men disappeared into the room beside the bar. When he returned alone, the bandleader called everyone together. "Boys . . . we got a dilemma. The boss, Danny, is a good guy. Thank God . . . did you see the *size* of him? He ain't no fool. When he saw us come in he had the same thought me and Billy did . . . fucking *agents*.

"Rolling Thunder is not exactly what we were led to believe. We can play if we want to try, but the clientele is, shall we say, a little on the *rough* side. They usually have rock or blues here, and the last time an agent sent in a wrong style of band; I think he said it was a Vegas type act, the place got kinda busted up. So did the band."

Elliot spoke up first. "What are we supposed to do, man, go back to New York? I gave up a gig in a dance band for this; a shit gig, but it was good bread, man. But I hooked up with this combo 'cause we were going to play jazz."

Of everyone, Joe was frowning and pacing the most. "I turned down a month at the El Mocambo. This is SHIT. What fucking agent did this? Jules, again?"

Mike's raised eyebrow answered that question as he said, "Look, we were supposed to have two weeks here. Then we got six weeks booked up after that, and those places *are* cool. I know them. Maybe we should try one night here. If we can get by, it means a few bucks anyway."

The only one who wasn't looking at the floor and shaking his head was Al. After a few minutes a consensus was reached. Strictly because of economics, it was decided to give it a try. How bad could it be?

♪ ♪ ♪

Accommodations were next on the agenda: Elliot and Mike were crashing with friends; Nate and Joe booked into a place up on Sherbrooke Street; while Billy said he knew of some cheap digs on MacKay Street, only a ten-minute walk. As he and Al headed west on Ste Catherine, Billy pointed out how it was officially called "rue MacKay" but you could say "MacKay Street" and anyone would know what you meant. Most would just refer to it simply as "MacKay"—no "street", no "rue". He also pointed out how the street wasn't pronounced "Mac-*hay*" by locals, but "Mac-*high*".

Al laughed and said, "Mac-*high*? Seriously, Billy? Is that 'cause *you've* stayed there? Sorry, man. Sorry, just kidding."

As Billy punched his arm in mock anger, Al wondered how many street names and expressions he'd have to learn to pronounce before he could go unnoticed amidst Montrealers.

Pierre Trudeau could walk into a restaurant in Toronto and order a meal, gab with the waitress, and I guess if he had on a fake beard or something to hide who he was, he could pass for someone from Ontario. But damn it, Alfred Waters, you're no Pierre Trudeau.

♪ ♪ ♪

When they entered the cramped mini lobby of the rue MacKay rooming house, Al felt homesick for his hotel-apartment in Greenwich Village which was also small and dingy, but at least had character. This place on MacKay was an old home, rebuilt haphazardly into commercial accommodations.

There was no one at the desk, so they rang a bell next to the guest book.

"Tabarnak," came a gravelly voice from behind a partially open door behind the desk. A short, thickset bald man in a sleeveless tee shirt appeared, followed by the biggest German Shepherd Al had ever seen. The dog growled . . . prompting the bald man to yell, "Ostie, câlisse mon de tabar-nak. ASSIS."

The dog sat, tongue hanging, tail wagging.

"Great dog," said Billy. "I bet you sleep well."

The man's French Canadian accent was thick. "Eh, no one will mess wit me. You are right mon ami, not wit La Gueule at my back." His chest shook with a hearty Long John Silver laugh.

"La 'Girl'?" inquired Billy.

"No, no . . . like la gueule du loup," said the man. "Jaws of de wolf."

"Perfect name for him," Al laughed.

"I 'ave a name, apropos myself," said the man. "Dey call me 'Baldy'."

Billy looked confused. "French is weird, man. You got this beast here, and you call him, what sounds like you're sayin' . . . 'girl'?"

Baldy smiled and said, "A wolf by any udder name would bite as 'ard. If you ever run into 'im when I am not around, just say 'Gueule' real loud, and ee'll not bodder you. Ee's not so tough, really." His pirate laugh echoed through the room once again, joined by Billy's nervous cackle.

Al whispered into Billy's ear, "Yeah, I bet he's just one big puppy . . ."

♪ ♪ ♪

Their rooms were up a single flight of creaking stairs which lead to a narrow hallway to the left.

"Two-O-six for you, monsieur," said Baldy as he handed Billy his key, "and you are de lucky one," he said, turning to Al. "Two-O-two, just h'across from de bat' room. And remember, dat's for de whole floor, mes amis, so don't 'og de time in dere, eh?"

The luxury didn't end with the bathroom's proximity. Al's room was furnished with a small wooden chair, a single bed, and a dresser with only half the mirror still intact. In the middle of the popcorn-stucco ceiling was a single light fixture, a brownish half globe with a large knob in the center. Al's first inevitable thought was how it looked like a breast—a utilitarian one with a string switch dangling to slightly more than two feet above the bed.

This seemed particularly appropriate to him. *Cool. Breasts are a turn-on; now I get to turn one on.*

There were no windows; the room was in the middle of the building, probably at some point in history part of another bigger room. With a small toaster oven and bar fridge in the corner, the value of the place was in line with the twelve dollars a week it cost. It wasn't pretty; wasn't fancy; it was what he could afford.

♪♪♪

When Al and Billy arrived at the entrance to Rolling Thunder at 8:30 p.m. all the band members, except their leader, were waiting at the door.

Al said, "Hey, are we 'Minus Mike' now?"

Billy cracked a smile, but it faded quickly once he saw that no one else had found the remark amusing. Nate said, "Mike's inside guys. Let's get this over with."

Minus Milt was about to make their grand debut in Montreal. Since no one appeared too anxious to lead the way, Al went in first, and finding the room almost empty, smiled and waved for the rest of the troops to follow him into the battle zone.

At the bar were a few men, and two couples occupied a table near the stage. Al said, "Hi," as he passed the table. One of the men, a Neanderthal in a black leather jacket and no shirt said to him, "Hey, boy, maybe you should grow a beard. That might make you half a man. Yeah, a beard for sure, and maybe some balls?" Then, turning to the other man at the table he laughed and said, "Whatdaya think, Wheelie?"

"Hey, Snake," said Wheelie, "I think he's one o' them hippies, don't you?" His smile slackened as he turned toward Al, and with narrowed eyes he said, "You a hippie? Or a *girl* maybe. That long hair's real pretty."

Al focused on what not to say, remaining calm—at least on the surface.

Be cool, be cool, be cool. Don't say it; don't even think it. I'm in way over my head here.

Wheelie had a full, thick, dark beard and sagebrush eyebrows which appeared to have been over-fertilized. Under his blue denim vest he wore a tee shirt with the sleeves rolled up to his shoulders, revealing impossibly large arms with so many colorful tattoos, there appeared to be no room for more.

Snake sported what might have been a three-day growth of dirty blond facial foliage—three days' worth for a normal man. Al suspected this might be just one day's crop for this guy. The rolled-back sleeves of his leather jacket revealed herculean forearms, with a large tattoo on each: one, an eagle perched atop a crucifix; the other, an artistic depiction of a motorcycle in flames. On the mid-left side of his chest was a jagged six-inch long scar, clearly never sutured professionally—more likely a do-it-yourself effort for a slash from a knife or broken bottle. And adorning the left side of his tree-trunk neck was a smaller tattoo of a sword encircled by two cobras. Both men had bandanas tied around their foreheads, exposing most of their brush cut hairdos.

Al cleared the fear from his throat and said, "Boys, come on. You calling me a *girl*? I think I'm man enough to take on *both* you scumbags. But I, um, wouldn't want to upset your lovely companions here."

Yuck, scrag city.

As the two men rose, the full extent of their dimensions became abundantly clear: Wheelie was Al's height, with a bulldog build; while Snake stood at least six-foot-seven, and was even more muscular than his friend. In a bear-like growl, Snake said, "Wheelie, I think we're gonna have to have a *talk* with our hippie friend here."

Al set his horn case down beside him and grinned. "I guess 'man-enough' doesn't cut it right now does it? But I *am* smart enough to know I couldn't take either one of you with both your arms tied behind your back. Can I buy ya's a couple o' beer instead?"

The cave people laughed—all except Snake. Wheelie slapped a meaty hand on his friend's shoulder, pushing him back down into his chair. "Snake," he laughed, "let it go. The kid's only joshin' us. Good one, eh?"

As Snake's face softened, the craggy creases around his mouth deepened into smile lines; the one on the left blending into two large scars on his cheek, which now fashioned a roadmap through the stubble forest from mustache to temple. As his crooked teeth appeared, a gold cap glistened among them. Over by the stage, Nate and Elliot eased their grips on the microphone stands they'd had at the ready.

One of the women asked, "What kinda music you boys goin' ta play for us tonight?"

"What would you like to hear?" said Al.

"Somethin' *good*," said Snake, straight-faced.

Al said, "Aw, sorry. We only play shitty songs . . . too bad, eh?" He felt one leg trembling.

Damn it, leg, stop it. Can anyone see that? Too late to change directions now.

Gotta go with this. Dad would have expected me to back down.

"Hardy har har," laughed Wheelie. "Kid, you is funny, ain't ya? You guys are probably crap, but we'll stay for a couple o' tunes and see. Leave 'im alone, Snake. I like this kid. I ain't seen nobody stand up to you like that, and not be kissin' floor by now, so you must like him too."

"Sure, Wheelie," grumbled Snake. "He does have balls, and maybe he *will* grow a beard someday."

♪♪♪

By the time the first set was due to begin, there were close to thirty people scattered about the room, most of them resembling Al's new "friends" in dress and grooming, if not in dimensions. Mike had decided they couldn't go too far wrong with some blues. Jazz was out for sure. Al suggested "Kansas City", since he knew the words and a vocal might be a good idea.

"Cool," said Mike. "Didn't know you sang."

"Had to at The Straw Hat," said Al. "Don't know if I'm any good or not, 'cause there you could never hear yourself over the crowd. We'll find out I guess. How about B-flat, guys?"

Billy joked, "As long as you don't *be* flat, Al."

"Thanks for the vote of confidence, Billy. Any other wise words to ease my nerves?"

"Hey, kid, just a gig. Nobody is gonna die, right? Hmm, but maybe after seeing this place, I can't be so sure . . ."

"Right, Billy, thanks a lot. I feel *so* much better now."

Mike said, "Okay, boys, gimme the last four bars as an intro." Snapping his fingers on the offbeat, he counted in the standard medium shuffle tempo for the song.

Al was a little shaky in the first verse, but by the second, he settled down and surprised everyone—especially himself. Although he had often joined in with the staff at the Hat, the only place he'd ever sung solo was when he was alone in a car, far from critical ears. As Mike on sax and Elliot on trombone added impromptu horn riffs, Al felt great. He wasn't any threat to B.B. King or Joe Williams, but he pulled it off convincingly enough to please the rest of the band who, one by one, gave each other a smile or wink that said "He ain't bad". Al found himself fantasizing about having his own band one day.

I can do this.

At the end of the song, Rolling Thunder seemed becalmed in the eye of a hurricane—the menacing quiet emphasized by slow-drifting smoke which masked most of the patrons' expressions. Only those in front could easily be scrutinized, but as yet there was no discernible response on their faces. Al took the mike out of the stand and stepped down off the stage.

"Hey, Wheelie, Snake . . . was that any good?"

The pair eyed each other and laughed. "Yeah, hippie boy," said Wheelie. "Weren't too bad, not too stinkin' bad at all. I still agree with Snake though; ya do need a beard, to hide yer ugly face."

Snake slapped his friend's back and roared, "Yeah, that's why *you've* got one, ain't it, Wheelie?"

Both men and their dates began to clap in a steady, slowly increasing rhythm. A few other tables joined in, especially when Snake and Wheelie turned to see who was or wasn't agreeing. In short order, everyone in the room was applauding. Al asked for an intro to "Georgia", and Billy began on his own, his fingers drawing pure beauty from a palette of chords unfamiliar to the old piano. As Al began to sing, there was a smattering of applause from the first words of the familiar tune. Someone at the bar called out, "Ray Charles, yeah, fuckin' 'A' for Ray."

The band followed after a few bars, blending sweetly into the mood, and the young man sang better than he ever knew he could, finding new exciting ways to phrase almost every line. Everyone soloed for a chorus, and in the final vocal verse Al held nothing back. On the last word he soared to a falsetto high B-flat and sustained the note, milking every second of the moment, pretending to be fainting, looking at his watch, staggering—holding the note so long, the polite applause which had already started, turned into a standing ovation.

Al was a natural—Al was in deep shit.

♪♪♪

"You little prick," said Mike, away from the microphone. It struck Al as funny, being called "little" by a man who was at least three inches shorter. "How fuckin' *dare* you take over like that? This is *my* band and I decide what we play and who sings, *and* who talks. Get it?"

Caught off guard by Mike's attitude, Al said, "They're digging this, man. What does it matter who calls the tunes?"

Someday he would know first-hand as a leader why it mattered, but the exhilaration of wowing the hostile crowd had filled him with a sense of power. Total control over a situation or another person was something rare to him—but over a *roomful* of people? This was a high he'd never experienced.

Turning away, Al said, "Sorry if I stepped on your toes, Mike, but back off, man."

Mike spoke again, inches from Al's face. "Talk to me on the break. I'll fuckin' teach you how to behave on the stand."

Billy had been observing the exchange and although he hadn't heard the words, he knew something was up—something bad. For all the time he'd known Al, this was the first time he'd seen that look in the kid's eyes. He thought of La Gueule.

♪♪♪

When the set was completed, Joe, Nate, and Elliot headed for the bar, while Al, Mike, and Billy went to the dressing room which was a combination staff toilet and storage space. Mike slammed the door behind them. "You think you want to lead the band? Do ya?" he said, with his face so close, Al had to wipe flying spit from his cheek. "You fuckhead, I'm in this business over twenty years. I got underwear older than you. You know *zilch* about the business."

Billy forced his way between them and pleaded, "Come on, man. He did good out there. Saved our butts; I think you owe him that."

Mike threw Billy aside, knocking him hard against the wall, then continued his rant. "I decide what we play and when. That's the way it is, period."

Al didn't hear the words; all he saw was his friend being pushed. Grabbing Billy by the shoulders, he guided him out the door and locked it. He turned and faced Mike. "Okay, man, you're the boss. I apologize, okay? I just thought . . . whatever. But, man you didn't have to shove Billy. He's only trying to help."

Inside Al Waters, something frightening was churning, bubbling to the surface. If Mike hadn't been blinded by his own bruised ego, he might have left while he could. Instead, he went too far, *much* too far. He yelled, "Fuck that has-been piece of shit. He got you this gig, but he can't keep it for you."

Al hadn't hit anyone since he was sixteen, and years of ass-kissing and holding back were released with one punch. Snake and Wheelie would have been proud of their beardless hippie friend. As Al looked down at the bandleader, he could hardly remember having swung. Mike had hit the floor like a bag of fish.

Christ, is he dead . . . ?

♩♩♩

The cops were used to house calls at the Thunder, but this was something new—a guy in the band gets punched out, by another guy in the band? In his twenty years on the force, Sergeant Gérard Lalonde had seen bloodied faces, cracked skulls, sliced guts, broken bones—many caused by the old familiars, Snake and Wheelie—and here were those two, laughing and calmly watching the proceedings as cops and musicians discussed the incident.

"Hey, Lalonde, nice to see you," said Snake. "Wouldn't you just love to pin this one on us? But we ain't got nothin' to do with it. Fuckin' Wheelie's too drunk to hurt nobody no how."

Lalonde smiled and replied, "Well, nobody's dead, so I believe you." The sergeant still had a couple of sore knuckles from the last time he'd taken them in, and he was glad they weren't involved this time. "Maybe you two saw what happened, eh, mes amis? Sounds funny, me asking for *your* help, but someday maybe it might be, uh, worth your while?"

"The kid over there," said Snake, "the one with the hippie hair; he was the one. Think he had a problem with his boss and he handled it, pretty good if ya ask me."

Lalonde walked over to Al who was with another officer. He introduced himself and then said, "So tell me, why did you do this? You busted his nose by the looks of it. He must have made you real mad, eh?"

Al stared at the floor. The other cop reported to Lalonde how this was the kid's total response so far—nothing.

"I think we better take him in, Sergeant. Nobody will say what happened. This guy, Waters, and the other guy, Mr. Zabic, were alone in the room, so no one saw it."

"Let me talk to the other guy," said Lalonde. "You said his name is Zabic?"

The sergeant approached Mike, who was sitting alone, holding a wet towel over his face. Lalonde, pulling gently at the edge of the towel said, "Let's see that nose, my friend . . . Ooh boy, you got clobbered pretty good. What happened here, Mr. Zabic?"

Mike spoke slowly through the pain, "It's between me and him. You didn't need to come. I can handle this."

"You aren't going to press charges?" asked Lalonde. "I can do it myself if I think it's for your own good, or his."

"Nothing happened 'cept I slipped and hit my face, that's all. Waters was there, but he didn't do it."

This didn't surprise Lalonde, but it worried him. Something in Mike's tone tickled at his cop's instincts; he'd witnessed how an unquenchable thirst for revenge could drive a normally reasonable man to acts of insanity.

"You're able to play your instrument like that? I think we better get you to a hospital, don't you?"

"I'll play," grumbled Mike, "if it fucking kills me. It was my own fault. I'll be okay."

In a voice, lowered so only Mike could hear, Lalonde said, "We're done here, for now. I don't know what happened, but I have a pretty good idea. I don't want to have to come back later and scrape either one of you off the floor. Whoever's at fault, I won't go easy on him. Comprends? Understood?"

Mike nodded, covering his face once again with the towel.

♪♪♪

With Mike back in charge, the rest of the night went relatively smoothly, although for him it was pure torture. He would close his eyes and hesitate as he drew his sax toward his mouth before sucking in the courage to play. The very air hurt with each inward breath; every riff he blew felt almost as bad as another punch to the face.

Nate and Elliot each sang a couple of tunes, and they managed to come up with enough ideas to keep the small crowd content. Tapping into their years of experience at club dates and dance band gigs, they knew enough blues, rock, rhythm 'n' blues, and country songs to fill three more sets. Al played his trumpet where it fit—but said nothing to anyone.

At the end of the night a meeting was called between the bandleader and the owner, Danny—better known as "Thunder" in his days of professional wrestling. He had a proposal quite different from what the musicians had expected.

Danny said, "Life's a bowl of surprises, eh, guys? You didn't do all that bad, but I got an idea. I'll keep you on for the two weeks, but we has to add a little pizzazz. I'm goin' to call and get a dancer to work some of your sets. By the way, no more cops, okay? Still don't know who the hell called 'em. Haven't had 'em here for over a month, and now they come 'cause of *you* guys? Shit, what next, eh?"

♪♪♪

Mike hadn't spoken directly to Al since the incident, but after his discussion with Danny, he said, "Hey, kid, come here."

Being wary didn't occur to Al as he walked over and stood within an easy sucker punch of the man he'd assaulted. As he picked at the loosened label on his beer bottle, he asked, "What's up?"

Mike whispered, "Tonight, in the parking lot: I might be waiting for you; might not. Tomorrow . . . ? Same thing. I don't know when yet, or who I might have with me, but I *will* get you for this."

Al grabbed the nearest chair and swigged his beer as he sat down, still avoiding direct eye contact.

"Hey, Waters," added Mike, heading for the door, "enjoy the walk home."

Al turned around, smiled and said, "Night, Mike."

As he began to pack up his trumpet, he noticed that out of all the band members, only he and Mike had lingered. Billy had gone with Nate and Joe to catch a late set at the jazz club where Minus Milt was booked next, and no one had thought Al would be into going. Now Mike's warning crawled up Al's spine as he looked around the almost empty bar, hoping to spot Snake and Wheelie.

Damn, four hours ago, who'd have thought I'd miss those guys? Looks like I'm on my own. Going to be a real enjoyable walk all right.

As Al left Rolling Thunder a light rain began as if on cue. He tried to move at his normal pace but Mike's words followed him through the dark wet streets, echoing from each unlit alley he passed.

Guess I should have gone with Billy. I am so stupid.

Pride gave way to instinct, and he began to run, his pant legs becoming more and more soaked from each puddle-splattering stride. When he rounded the corner onto rue MacKay he was too caught up in his fear to look around; he was ten years old again, scrambling up the cellar stairs after the light was off. The run-down rooming house was a dream castle of warmth and welcome, as its flickering no-vacancy sign guided him home.

Al cursed the key as he unsuccessfully tried it twice, both directions, before realizing he was using the wrong one. As long as his back was to the street, he couldn't feel safe. He was certain Mike had only been messing with his head, but damn him, it had worked.

There, at last . . . now, up the stairs, and I'm—

A growl came from behind as Al reached the bottom stair.

Shit . . . the fucking DOG. Say his name . . . the name. Oh shit, what was that name?

Al bounded up the stairs with the beast right behind. At the top stair he tripped and did a summersault toward 202, landing hard on his rear end, with his back against the door.

Key . . . where's the fucking KEY?

As Al scrambled to his feet, the dog lunged at him, the snapping jaws within inches of his crotch. Al could feel the animal's hot wet breath on his pants. He knew he was a dead man, or worse—an emasculated one.

The bite never came. La Gueule was on a chain which ended, ever so thankfully, just at the right length. Al had defensively slapped his hand over himself so hard it hurt like a kick in the groin. As the dog strained mightily at the chain, Al began to laugh. "You ugly mutt . . . 'Gueule', la gueule du loup, the wolf's jaws. That's it. NOW, I remember. Fuck YOU, GUEULE."

La Gueule sat back on his haunches, his dangling tongue dripping slobber on Al's shoe.

From a room farther down the hall came an angry voice. "What's goin' ON? SHUT the fuck UP."

Al found his keys; he had been sitting on them. As he opened the door to 202, he whispered, "Good night, Grampa, 'night, John Boy. 'Night, 'La Fruit Loops', you stinky mutt." He looked once more at the panting dog still sitting near the top of the stairs.

Shit, what if my room was 201 . . . ? The chain actually reaches that far. Holy Christ.

♪♪♪

The next night, when Billy and Al arrived at the club, they stopped to check out the modified poster in the front window display. Taped under the Minus Milt name was a picture of the new featured guest performer, Busty Brigitte. She was attractive, in an artificial, airbrushed way, in her practical three-piece outfit: two pasties and a G-string.

Musing out loud, Al said, "I wonder if you say it like Bridgitte Bardot or 'Bridg*eet*'? The 'Busty' part of the name is certainly well-thought-out. Apropos, eh, mon ami?"

Indeed, if the photo was unenhanced, the lady was *extremely* well-endowed. Al wondered if the light fixture on the ceiling of his room had been molded from one of her breasts.

Maybe I could get her to autograph it sometime. Hey, this gig might not turn out so bad after all.

Mike Zabic was waiting just inside the door with the rest of the band members. His face was blue-black from cheek to brow and his nose resembled an overripe pomegranate. As he spoke, his mouth barely moved. "You guys get anything you need out of the dressing room now. The chick will need the room in a minute, and then it's off-limits to you."

As Al passed Mike, there were no words or even eye contact between them. The salutation in Al's head was less subtle. *Fine, how are YOU, asshole? Any more wise-old-bandleader advice for me?*

Billy cackled and said, "Yeah, we wouldn't want to embarrass the lady, and see her *nekked*, would we now?"

"Fuck off, Billy," snapped Mike, glancing at Al as he spoke. "She gets the room at a quarter of nine. Stay away from her, all of ya. Okay?"

"Glad to stay real far away from her," said Billy. "I've heard them little crab critters can jump like more than three feet."

♪♪♪

To warm up for the gig, Al got his trumpet and went to a dark, back corner of the room. He put in a cup mute, and facing the wall for an acoustic "bounce-back" effect, worked his way through a few lip slurs and long low tones, a routine he'd maintained since his first year of playing.

I could do these better than my dad in six months. Damn, I'm not doing them as well right now as when I was twelve. Got to find some time to work on my chops.

Immediately forgetting thoughts of technique practice, he drifted into a melody, sifting through licks until something cool was hatched. This was the kind of playing he enjoyed above all: no tempo restrictions, key signatures, bar lines, or song form rules for how to start or how to end—just Al and his horn, having fun creating music.

"Belle musique," said someone from behind, during a moment between Al's phrases.

Although he was annoyed, something in the voice softened him. He turned and said, "Thanks, I was just making it up," before the full visual impact of the interloper had hit.

No more words came easily as he stared at a woman unlike any he'd ever seen outside a porn magazine. Her height had to be close to six feet without her stiletto-heeled shoes, since *with* them she was almost as tall as six-foot-three-inch Al. From the top of her head, several inches of glossy black coiffure sprang forth like a fireworks display, with scattered shards of hair suspended in stiff, curved spark-trails which triggered an impulse in Al to shield his eyes from falling debris.

Al felt small. Nothing much was small about her. From her centipede lashes to her rouged cheeks and full, pale, glossy pink lips, everything on her face seemed unreal. Straining to escape the deep V-neck top of her gold satin dressing gown were two mountains of mammary—a breast man's dream— or nightmare. Al imagined wedging his face in between them, smothering in the mothering.

The woman walked closer to Al and said, "Bonsoir, mon jeune ami, je m'appelle Brigitte . . . et tu?"

Al attempted to reply. "Uh, je suis Al, comment c'a va? Brigitte . . . ?"

"Oui, Brigitte Dubois; 'Busty Brigitte', for, uh, de stage. Comprends?"

"Je comprends, yes, I get it. Your stage name is 'Busty Brigitte'. You're the dancer. I thought it was like, Bridg-*ette,* but you pronounce it more like, 'Briszh-*it*'? Is that it? I'm sorry, my French sucks, and what we got in school was *France* French, not Québec French. Hey, can you speak English?"

"Not so good too much . . . So, you play trompette, um, nice." She giggled and added, "Nice, yes, and you are look nice too, mmm."

"So, it was very cool to meet you, Brigitte, but I have to go. Time to play. Good luck tonight. Uh, bonne chance."

"See you at de stage, bon homme. See you h'after, maybe?"

Doffing an imaginary cap, Al sauntered to the stage with all the cool he could muster from the fluster—he knew she was watching.

♪♪♪

The room had filled appreciatively since 8:30, most of the crowd being male. They were indifferent to the band's first song and halfway through the second, began calling out for Busty. Mike announced that she would be out in a moment.

"Hey, what happened to *you*, buddy?" someone called out. "You look like a boxer who just lost."

Joe played an overloud rim shot, drawing laughs from most of the crowd. Al saw an opening. "Hey," he said into the microphone, "I used to be a boxer, and I was so bad . . . I sold advertising space on the bottom of my shoes."

Another rim shot. No laughs. Billy groaned and asked Al, "You been reading Henny Youngman joke books again?"

As Mike glared at both of them, Al smiled and said, "Sorry, boss, won't happen again."

Not till I come up with better jokes anyway.

Mike directed his attention back out front. "Ladies and gentlemen—"

Al cut him off. "Hey, don't leave out Snake and Wheelie," this time getting a laugh, the biggest coming from the two targets of his insult.

Mike ignored Al and went on. "Let's have a big hand for the stunning, sexy seductress of Saint Catherine Street . . . BUSTY BRIGITTE."

As the band launched into "The Stripper", Busty strode into view from stage right, her gold satin robe giving her a Cleopatra-like majesty. Al, being on her side of the stage, stopped playing and reached out his hand to help her up beside him. Though his space was now somewhat constricted, he had no objection to this arrangement.

As the applause died, Mike called "Route 66", with a rock beat. The song began and Busty removed her robe: no striptease, no seductive buildup; just tossed it aside and started directly into an awkward "go-go" dance.

There was a sprinkling of jeers amid the cheering, but the crowd generally seemed to appreciate her "act". Except for her shoes, gold sparkly pasties covering her nipples, and matching G-string, Brigitte was nude—looking remarkably similar to the picture in the window—but with a few years of added "character". The structure of her body was essentially unchanged, but time and gravity had wielded their inexorable powers in a subtle redistribution of the fleshy wealth. It was no wonder she didn't move with much enthusiasm; pain might well have been the result. Accordingly, her dancing consisted of slow, graceless back and forth sidesteps with semi-rhythmic torso turns to either side, which seemed to be solely to facilitate the view.

Al was too close to be objective. Even for a confirmed breast man, this was not the most flattering of vantage points, especially as she moved. The aging topography was uncomfortably evident, from the stretch marks on her chest and belly, to her dimpled butt cheeks. She had to look better from out front—a theory bolstered by the mostly cheering mob, with the odd "boo" from those with not enough beer in them.

Al found the whole experience oddly sad. At first he wasn't sure who was the most pathetic: Brigitte, or the drooling patrons, or himself.

She's the one getting paid for showing us something we've all seen. She doesn't love or hate the watchers; probably doesn't even see them. She's in control. It's us who are pitiful, not her.

Another more disturbing thought sent a sudden stabbing ache through his heart.

Like I should judge. It's me who's repulsive. I'm supposed to be playing music, exploring my art. But like a cheap stripper who once dreamed of being a ballerina, I've exposed myself; not my flesh, but my soul and the emptiness it contains. Funny,

Brigitte may be the only one in this room with any dignity at all.

Busty Brigitte danced for three songs, then reached for her robe and slipped it on. As she left the stage, she glanced at Al and said, "Merci."

He smiled, hoping no one had noticed their exchange. The band continued, accompanied by the crowd's diminishing hooting: "Hey Busty, come back,"... "More tits, less music,"... "Where'd she go? I'm in LOVE..."

Danny and his staff kept a watchful eye on the proceedings. Two of them were his brothers, also ex-wrestlers and abnormally large men. Each had a blackjack in his back pocket. Never having seen one of these tiny leather-covered clubs in use, Al wondered how effective such a small device could be.

♪ ♪ ♪

Busty returned to close out the set, again removing her robe as she climbed up to the stage. With a laugh, she tossed the garment at Al, who caught it clumsily, smiling as he freed his trumpet from beneath it. She began her understated dance which was an invitation to admire her form, not her movements. In spite of Al's reticence to join the crowd in their lustful enthusiasm, he couldn't avoid watching her.

Somewhere in the middle of the song, a couple of plaid-shirted behemoths rose from their chairs and began to heckle Busty. "Hey, can I touch 'em?" one yelled. The other followed with, "I wanna stuff my face in those tits, ooh, baby!"

Snake called out from across the room, "Sit down, you cocksuckers, or I'll *sit* you down."

The hecklers started for the stage and Al anxiously scanned the room for the brothers-three. They were not far away. Danny moved in behind trouble-maker number-one, grabbed him in a half nelson, and with a quick one-leg undercut, the man was dropped to the floor. The other two brothers moved in with panther-like stealth on heckler number-two. With one swift thump of a blackjack to the back of his head he was laid out for a nap. The offending parties were escorted, feet dragging, out the door so fast most people in the bar didn't even notice what happened. Al was impressed with this perfectly executed operation. By the looks on Snake's and Wheelie's faces they'd seen this before—probably from up close. They'd chosen to admire the action from their chairs, offering a salute as the men were hauled by.

"Good time for a break," announced Mike. "We'll be back in twenty minutes for the next set. Let's hear it for the beautiful, bountiful BUSTY

BRIGITTE . . . and us, we're Minus Milt."

♪♪♪

Al sat by himself in his favorite dark corner, nursing his third Labatt's Blue: a delight after the watery American beer he'd settled for in New York. Billy was out in the alley with Elliot and Nate; Al knew it wasn't to drink beer. It seemed none of them could get through a night without smoking up at least once.

He didn't blame them, wondering if maybe he'd end up doing likewise before this gig was over. But for now he preferred to sit in seclusion, his beer being all the mind alteration and company he needed.

Everyone just leave me alone, and I'll be fine.

♪♪♪

He noticed her when she was halfway across the room, heading straight for where he was sitting. She was young—late teens?—wearing wire-rimmed, John Lennon style glasses, and no makeup. Her long, straight, blond hair was held in place with a tie-dyed headband. Everything about her screamed that she didn't belong in this sort of bar.

She walked up to Al, and with no hesitation said, "Hi, hope I'm not bothering you, but can I ask you something?"

Setting down his beer, he smiled and said, "What would you like to know?"

"My friend thinks you're cute; well, so do I, but I'm here with my boyfriend. Anyway, she's over there and she wonders why you sit all alone?"

"Why don't I tell her myself?" said Al. "Where is she?"

"Come with me. We are sitting over by the door, and by the way, my name is Alice." She had only a slight accent, more of a tendency for over-careful pronunciation, which suggested she was French Canadian—a Québécoise.

Must be how I sound to them when I speak French.

"Hi, Alice. Funny, Al 'iss' my name too. Al . . . *is* . . . ?"

She stared blankly, not understanding Al's pun. "Your name is Alice?" she asked. "But that is a girl's name only."

"Sorry, just being silly. My name is Al, just Al."

Must be the language gap. I thought it was sort of funny.

Alice laughed and said, "Okay, Al-just-Al, come and meet my friend. Her name is Charlotte."

CHAPTER 19

CHARLOTTE'S SONG

*C*harlotte Benoit and her friends Alice and Rèmi were obvious misfits—flower children in a biker bar—definitely *not* regulars at Rolling Thunder. But of the three, only Rèmi appeared nervous. He seemed grateful to have Al join them as he said, "Assis toi, prend une chaise, uh, pardon. Anglais? Here, sit with us." Perhaps he hoped being joined by another guy with long hair was a narrowing of the odds. Now instead of one, it was *two* against a hundred—feeble consolation which wasn't even completely correct.

Al did have long hair, but he resented being classified a hippie and this trio was evidence of why: bell-bottom jeans, tie-dyed headbands, a flowery shirt, turtle neck sweaters. To his thinking, all these made a guy look effeminate, and the girls he'd encountered from this culture were usually airheads. Al had long hair because he liked *not* getting it cut—no political or social statements involved. If it weren't for concern that he'd appear even more hippie-like he might have grown a beard by now, although Snake's initial mocking suggestion may have complicated that consideration forever. At this very moment thoughts of Snake and his ilk gave Al pause to reconsider whether he should even be seen at this table of "peaceniks". But this cute friend of Alice made the risk seem worth it.

Cool, a far-out, happening, Québec babe.

Introductions done, Alice and Rèmi quickly became embroiled in a deep dialogue about the true in-depth meaning of Bob Dylan's "Blowin' in the Wind", while Charlotte sat quietly, looking away from everyone.

Dylan, crap, the answer is blowin' in the wind for sure, right out of Bob's butt. If that's the shit these guys are into, then no way this chick will like what we're playing.

Al decided to attempt a conversation. "Charlotte, do you like the music, you know, my band?" He startled himself with the use of "my band", but he liked how it felt.

She talked into her coffee. "Well, I don't know much about it, really; and that lady, the one with no clothes, she kind of *distracts.* Sorry, I hope I don't offend you."

With her last couple of words she finally looked up at him. He was for the first time fully able to behold the face he would never forget—deep brown eyes, a startling Snow White complexion, and natural ruby red lips—the fragile, impossible beauty you only saw in Disney movies, children's story-books, and magazine ads. Her thick brown hair, even darker than her eyes, was a magnificent mixture of all three of those images as it flowed back, Pocahontas style, so long down her back she might have to pay heed not to sit on it.

Al realized he was staring; hadn't answered; hadn't moved; hadn't breathed. It was as if he'd become a stone monument to all the woefully inar-ticulate men ever confronted by such perfection. As the silence grew ever more uncomfortable, he conceded that his normally formidable wit, charm, and eloquence were no-shows. All he could come up with was: "Offend me? Uh, yeah, I'm afraid you've deeply wounded me, but you can make up for it if you let me buy you a drink. What can I get for you?"

"What kind of beer is that?" she asked with a childlike laugh. "May I try a taste?"

Al handed over his glass with a warning. "Sure, but this is actually an ale, Labatt's 50, a bit on the *mean* side of the beer family."

She took a tiny, tentative sip. "Oh, that is *very* strong. Maybe, um, I will have some wine."

Al said, "The wine list is a little on the short side here. You should stick to the suds; not a 50 though . . . a lager, maybe a draft Molson Canadian or Labatt's Blue? I think they water it down a bit, so it should be a little milder for you."

Charlotte's attention returned to her coffee cup for a moment, then she looked back up and said, "Okay, sure. You choose one for me and I'll pretend to like it."

Al hurried to the bar and ordered another Labatt's 50 for himself and a draft Blue for Charlotte. When he returned to the table, his moment of hap-piness was sucker-punched by the sound of Snake's unmistakable bark. "Hey, Al, who's your *three* girlfriends? Two of 'em are kinda cute. Other one's ugly; looks *kinda* like a guy, but dresses like a chick."

As Rèmi rolled his eyes, Al leaned over to him and said, "Let it go, man. These guys will be cool if you go along with it. Just laugh."

Snake got up, approached the table and stood directly behind Rèmi where he said, "Does your head hurt, little girl?"

Rèmi froze, with eyes shut, and his beer halfway to his mouth, as he tried to shrink down into his black turtleneck sweater.

"It should hurt," said Snake, "since I'm standin' on yer HAIR."

A deadly silence hung in the air, until Al dispersed it with a laugh. He stood and sidled over to Snake, put his arm over the man's enormous shoulder, and said, "In the men's room I stood next to Snake, and he goes, 'OW' . . . 'cause I was standing on his DICK."

Laughter erupted amongst those near the table—until Snake raised his fist, bringing a hush to the room once again. But the hooting began anew when the big man smiled broadly and slowly brushed Al's cheek with a mock punch. He then strutted back to his table—his territory duly marked.

Rèmi could take no more. "Alice, let's go," he whispered, "now, please. Your little joke is over. This is NOT a cool place. Merci, for risking our lives."

With arched eyebrows, Alice looked at Charlotte and said, "We have to go, if Rèmi is not to shit his pants. Are you coming?"

After an icy glare at Alice, Charlotte turned to Al and said, "It was so nice to meet you. Maybe sometime we could . . . get together?"

"Come on, Charlotte," said Al, "do you have to go? If you stay, I could make sure you get home okay."

The more agitated Alice became, the more evident was her Québécoise side, as she said, "Come on, we are leaving. Don't be crazy. Dis place, c'est trop dangereux." She looked at Al and said, "Sorry, but we don't know you. Maybe you are not like all de animal in here, but we do not know dat."

Charlotte was half-standing, half-sitting, holding onto Alice's arm with one hand and Al's with the other. "Al," she asked, "do you think it will be okay if I stay? Do you promise to walk me home when you are done playing? I don't live far, not really."

"Merde, NO," said Alice. "Come with us. Sacrament, please?" She again looked at Al to engage his support.

Al, looking only at Charlotte, said, "Don't go. It'll be all right. You're safe with me."

Much to Alice's surprise and chagrin, Charlotte smiled and gave Al a nod. The San Francisco flower child from Montreal was going to defy the danger and stay with the New York jazz musician from Ontario.

♪♪♪

Snake and Wheelie happily volunteered to watch over Charlotte during the band's next set, although their lady friends were less receptive to the company—but they had no say in it. As Al headed for the stage, Wheelie said, "Don't worry, my friend, your little girl is safe with us. Anybody looks at her, and we'll kick the crap out of 'em, okay?"

Charlotte couldn't have felt more out of place, but she knew she'd done the right thing. If anything was for sure, it was that she could trust Al. How could this gentle, adorable guy hurt anyone?

♪♪♪

The next sets flew by without incident, with the crowd tolerating the band, even occasionally dancing to a song. Topless dancers were normally as hot as it got in venues other than true hard-core strip clubs, so Busty's repetitious routine was appreciated with only slightly dimming enthusiasm. Although she continued to flirt with Al on stage she seemed quite occupied during breaks. Clad in her satin robe, she visited almost every table, however briefly—and her prime targets appeared to be those tables occupied only by men. Quelle surprise.

When the evening crawled to a close at last, Brigitte slipped into her gold robe and blew Al another kiss. "À demain, mon ami . . . see you?" she said with a wink.

Al smiled back and said, "Bonsoir, Busty, uh, Brigitte. See you tomorrow." As he packed up his horn, he beckoned to Billy and said, "Hey, man, did you see the girl I met? Come on over with me."

Billy narrowed his eyes to look across the room through the smoke. "You mean the chick with your biker pals? How old is she, man, like *twelve*?"

♪♪♪

"Charlotte, this is my friend Billy Crothers. He's really why I'm in Montreal, because he got me in the band."

"Merci, Monsieur Crothers, for making it possible for me to meet Al. I understand you are from New York? Here, join us, please."

Billy removed his beret and sat next to her, avoiding the chair next to Snake. Despite Al's comfort with this gang, Billy was still uneasy with them. He didn't know how Al did it; it was as if he'd been hanging with these guys all his life.

"I'm from Mars," said Billy. "Really. Don't tell anyone. It's a secret."

"You are a space alien?" she asked, poker-faced. "Why did you come to

Earth . . . to conquer us?"

The flower child was no child; Billy could see that now. And her face so perfect, it could only be described as angelic. It never ceased to floor him how Al so often ended up with these "nice" girls. He continued with his spaceman routine. "My mission is to capture all the Earth women and make them my slaves. I particularly like long brown hair and dark eyes, like yours, my dear," he said with an evil cackle, while wiggling his fingers like antennae over his head.

Al grabbed a chair and pushed in between Charlotte and Billy. "Don't laugh, Charlotte, Billy isn't kidding. Hey, don't you think it's time we left? Get out into some cleaner air?"

"See you, Mr. Martian," laughed Charlotte as she and Al got up to leave.

"See you, sweetheart," said Billy, "and I ain't referring to *you*, Waters."

As Al and Charlotte walked out into the night, Billy watched and sighed. Once again his young friend had found someone so easily. Most times it didn't matter to him, as Al's prey generally was never of any interest to him. This time it was different; this time Billy was seriously envious; this time— it hurt.

♪♪♪

It was *not* a short walk to Charlotte's, and was virtually in the opposite direction from rue MacKay—to the northeast, on rue Saint-Urbain near avenue Duluth. But Al didn't mind the half hour it took. She was adorable in ways that defied words, defied belief. And incomprehensibly, she seemed as instantly smitten with him as he was with her. As they walked, she talked more and more freely.

She was eighteen, a library science student. She loved books above anything and had never had a steady boyfriend. With school and part-time work filling her life since age thirteen, there'd been no time for serious romance. There was a boy whom she had dated a couple of times—Carl White, a classmate—but though he was crazy about her, she didn't feel the same way about him.

With her bilingual skills, she would have her pick of jobs after graduation, especially good-paying government work. Her voice had a tuneful quality, but she professed no musical talent. "I love music," she sighed, "but I sing like a *cat*."

"I knew you were *purr*-fect," said Al with a little growl. They groaned in unison.

"Thank you for avoiding the *pussy* jokes, Al," said Charlotte.

Wow, with this little book-girl, there's a lot of pages between the covers.

♪ ♪ ♪

Bad news: she lived with her parents. Good news: they were away for the week.

In Charlotte's kitchen, she and Al finished a bottle and a half of white wine while they talked about books, politics, war, movies, and music.

"Al, you don't seem like the kind of guy who should be playing for those roughnecks at the Rolling Thunder. That isn't the kind of music you prefer to do, is it?"

"Geez no, Charlotte, I play jazz mainly. We got booked in there by mistake, and we're just getting by, doing blues and old rock stuff we know enough of to cover the night."

"Jazz?" said Charlotte, "I don't know a lot about it. Any I've heard has been, well, sort of *strange*? Sorry, but I guess I don't get it. I was raised with classical music. Do you like that?"

"I love classical music too. It's the first music I played."

"Why don't you try to get in a symphony, Al? Wouldn't that be a better lifestyle than being in bars and smoky places where everybody drinks so much?"

Al finished off a third of a glass of wine in one swig and poured another full one. "Charlotte, like the altar boy said to the bishop, 'that's a hard one'. Sorry, that's gotta be the wine talking."

"Don't worry about it, Al, *my* wine tells me to laugh at your dreadful jokes."

"Okay, Charlotte, we'll debate religious sex another time. Hey, don't look at me like that. Sex . . . *sects* . . . ? Get it?"

"Oh, Al, even the wine can't make *that* one any good."

"Sorry, sorry, sorry. Okay, back to the discussion of classical music. I guess I couldn't stand the restrictions, you know, playing the music the same way every time? It drove me nuts. Don't get me wrong, I respect those guys who do it. Getting into a symphony is really difficult. You have to audition, with sometimes hundreds of others for one spot, and the pressure is on you to play perfectly, from that audition process, right through *every* time you perform.

"Jazz has a freedom about it; allows a musician to express himself . . . how he feels at the moment. You never play a song the same way. I'm not saying there's no discipline to it. Good jazz guys have to practice and learn how to utilize scales and chords so their expression conforms to . . . *form*. But the tempos and nuances are up to your mood each time. And in the basic song . . . the 'head' we call it, lots of the melody notes can be different in each performance and the song is still recognizable. And then there's the *blowing*, the jazz choruses. You're free to go almost anywhere you want within the chords, and any chord has tons of variables possible. You could sort of say there *aren't* any wrong notes. I think it was Miles Davis who said, 'It's not any note you play that's a *wrong* note; it's the note you play afterwards that makes it right or wrong.' I love that.

"Here's my take on it. Jazz means never having to say you're sorry. Ha, *love* should be so simple, eh?"

Charlotte was spellbound. She wanted to understand, but much of what Al was saying was a foreign language to her. She asked, "So jazz is *easier* than classical?"

"Hey, whoa there, my beauteous book babe. Personally, I think it's harder, but then a symphony player would argue that I get away with stuff he couldn't, since I can make a mistake and have it turn into something cool. They do have a point, in that with jazz there is less pressure to be perfect. You know in the old days, great composers like Bach and Handel, I think even Mozart . . . were avid, skillful improvisers. They wrote down what they thought was the best of what they came up with. Some say the advent of modern music scoring destroyed the abilities of the musicians after those times to improvise, because having everything on paper meant they didn't have to memorize everything, and it was always played exactly the same.

"Those early baroque and classical guys were improvising all the time and kind of playing 'jazz' in a way. If I played classical, I'd likely be into it that way. People do expect certain conventions in their music no matter what genre they like. To be accepted as a 'real' jazz player, we have to stick to accepted styles within loose but finite boundaries; unless you get off on a free form tangent, with no rhythm or chord structure at all. But that's another whole story in itself. Those free form guys are weird. I need to feel the 'swing'."

"What is 'swing', Al? I've heard that word, but I never understood exactly what it meant. Is it like the old big bands, um, you know, like Glenn Miller?"

"Wow, it's tough to define. Yeah, Glenn Miller's stuff is based on the swing rhythm per se, but in a way that's more for that older era of swing dancing. Jazz swing has a difference, but let's get at what basic 'swing' is . . . Hmm, technically it's partly the way you string notes together, especially eighth notes. Let's say you have a series of four eighth notes, followed by a quarter note. The classical, or 'legit' way to play it would be, da da da da dah, exactly on the down beats and up beats, with each eighth the same length. To *swing* those same notes, you'd go doo *dah* doo *dah* dut, when the notes are all the same, and doo *ah*, doo *ah* dut with a moving pattern. Hear the difference from the legit way? It's not easy to put in words, except to sing it like that, or play it. On paper, the notes would actually look the same but be interpreted totally differently by classical and jazz players. Sometimes arrangers and modern composers who try to write music for symphonies to play in a swing style, will attempt to write an approximation of swing in six-eight or twelve-eight time. Close, but not quite it. Am I making any sense?"

"Sounds like fun, Al. Let me see if I can do it. Da da da da dut . . . Like that?"

"Almost, Charlotte. If you were playing a horn it would be easier to show you how the notes need to be tongued or slurred to make them sound right. There's a way you should articulate that makes it better, basically tonguing the upbeats and slurring into most of the downbeats. But that's getting pretty technical."

Charlotte laughed. "Maybe sometime you can give me a trumpet lesson?"

"No way, sweetheart. You're so damned smart, you'll likely get good real fast and steal my gig."

"No way, Al. I love music but I don't think I could ever be a performer, not like you. Tell me more about swing music and how you play it. I love this."

"Okay, sure . . . Another important factor, even harder to describe, is the *spaces* between the notes. They have a life of their own. It's like, without them being just right, the notes have no meaning. And notes aren't just notes, crazy as that sounds. Somebody once said about Sonny Rollins, that every note he plays tells a story. I guess you'd get that, since you're a book person, right?"

"Well, Al, I hate to argue with you but I don't think a *note* can tell a story, not even a series of notes. Maybe they can make someone feel something that reminds them of a story, or something that happened in their life? But not a story, really. We studied that in a class about music and narrative. 'Program' music tries to convey a story of some kind but usually is accompanied by some kind of text. And 'absolute' music is lyrical, but essentially with no story at all, except those feelings the listener has for it. Please don't be mad, but that's how I think of it."

"Yeah, smart girl, you're sort of right. I guess those feelings are what the notes bring out, and each listener can kind of make up their own narrative to go with them, eh? But a song with lyrics, that's another story, no pun intended."

"Hmm, I still disagree, Al. Most songs, even with words are just expressing feelings and moments of joy or sadness or other emotions. Not a story."

"Okay, Charlotte, here's a story, okay? There's this guy who's in love with a beautiful girl, and every day he sees her as she walks by . . . and like all the other guys around, he tries to catch her attention . . . but she ignores them all as they just sigh. She is so lovely and graceful she looks like she's dancing a samba just by the way she walks, with a gentle sway in her hips. This guy continues to watch her every day and asks only how can he tell her he loves her . . . He'd gladly give her his heart, if only she'd let him. But each day as she walks to the sea she looks straight ahead, as usual, not even seeing him. Sad story, eh? And guess what, that's a song, called 'The Girl From Ipanema'. What do you say to that?"

"Romantic and sad, yes, Al. And *very* short. More of a description of a scene than a story. You haven't convinced me. Sorry."

"Okay, okay. I get what you're saying, but we have to continue the debate another time. I bet I can come up with better examples. Right now maybe I'll just look at you and sigh, like the guy in the song. Will you ignore me if I do?"

"Al, I'm afraid ignoring you has been impossible since you first sat down at our table in the bar."

"Wow, Charlotte, that is so cool. I'll have to write a song about that."

"Okay, Al, and I'll write a story about it."

"Touché," said Al. He smiled and sipped at his drink, savoring it and the moment, and Charlotte's face with equal delight.

"Al," said Charlotte, "you seem to know so much about music. How did you learn all this?"

"Billy sort of taught me a lot of it, but really, what he showed me I was pretty much doing already, the swing rhythm anyway. Note choices, that's another story, and Billy has helped me a ton there. I'm not sure how anyone can learn swing other than by listening to great jazz players and absorbing the sound and feel of the way it works. Some cats play all the right notes, and lots of 'em. But without the spaces being right, to quote the Duke, 'It don't mean a thing'."

Charlotte was smiling, enthralled by the enthusiasm with which Al talked about something he so obviously loved.

"Al, the way you describe these spaces, it's something like in the way a writer describes something that is, say . . . beautiful? You don't want to have every detail pointed out in words. The pictures come into the reader's mind as much from what the writer leaves to the imagination, as by what words he or she actually uses. Basically I think music is like any art. It has to be loved by the artist to be loved by the listener, or looker, or reader: whoever is there to enjoy the art. Do I make any sense?"

"You make so much sense, I can't stand it. And *you're* something beautiful. No writer's words would be enough to describe you."

"Al, would you play something for me?"

Al took out his trumpet and put in his cup mute. "Here, a song just for you, Charlotte."

When he had played the lush, poignant melody—just one chorus—he put down the horn and sighed. It was a perfect moment, one of so few in his life he wished could have lasted forever.

Charlotte said, "Al, that was so wonderful. Thank you. Is it a song you wrote?"

"No, don't I wish? It's an old tune you made me think of, called 'Angel Eyes'. I do want to write my own songs though. Maybe someday as good as that one, but right now I'm just learning."

"Have you finished anything enough to play for me now?"

"Damn, I wish I had. Well, actually, there is this little tune I've had rattling around in my head for a little while. I'll show you, but be gentle, okay?"

Al took his trumpet and began a slow simple melody, based on a single minor chord. After only a few notes he abruptly stopped and said, "Man, I told you; not ready yet."

Charlotte wiped a tear from her cheek. "Al, it was so wonderful; as good as 'Angel Eyes'. What is it called?"

"Oh heck, doesn't have a name. Well, okay now it does. I'm gonna call it 'Charlotte's Song'."

"I know you will finish it someday, Al. And it will be fantastic."

♪♪♪

At 4 a.m. Charlotte suggested they go upstairs, adding quickly, "Please don't be mad, Al. I want you to stay, but we cannot make love, if that is what you are thinking. I am not on the pill, but more than that, it's not something I take lightly."

"Never crossed my mind, Charlotte. Well okay, maybe for just a second or two. But you're right, it's too soon."

It was the closest thing to a lie he had yet told her.

"Al, we can sleep together; I mean *sleep*, in the same bed, if you promise . . ."

"Of course, Char. You can trust me."

For Al—on this night, at this moment—there was complete sincerity in these words.

"I know I can trust you, Al. I knew from the start. I think you are a wonderful man."

"And I think so too. I mean, I *am* pretty wonderful, aren't I?"

Charlotte laughed. "And so *not* modest. I exercise my woman's right to change my mind. You are horrible."

Al blew a loud Bronx cheer. Jumping to his feet, he said, "Wanna race, Miss Mind-changer?"

She pushed Al back into his chair and ran for the stairs, giggling. As he followed her up the steps, grabbing at her heels in an ersatz attempt to catch her, he thought, *I am wonderful. She's wonderful. Everything is wonderful.*

♪♪♪

On Charlotte's parents' queen-size bed, they pillow fought, wrestled, debated the best and worst jokes from Marx Brothers' movies, and then finally gave in to exhaustion.

Al said, "Charlotte, you said you trust me, right?"

"Yes, Al. I do, with all my heart."

"Then please keep that in mind as I ask . . . may I kiss you, just once?"

"Yes, Al. I want you to, but . . ."

"No worries, my beautiful girl. One kiss, I promise."

She closed her eyes and waited as Al touched his fingers to her face and moved closer. As he brushed his lips against hers, a river of raw energy flowed between them, growing more powerful with each second of contact. A simple, inevitable embrace exploded beyond platonic as the intensity of the kiss mounted, their libidos and souls competing for dominance of the moment.

But the surge of passion building in Al's entire being was uncharacteristically restrained by a dam of self-control and respect. He pulled away, knowing for the first time in many years how it felt to love and trust—and to be loved and trusted. They fell back onto the bed and cuddled, fully clothed. Within minutes they were asleep.

♪♪♪

The morning is a fickle friend: the sunlight loved her face; hated his.

"Ooh, don't get too close to me," said Al, slowly unsticking his lips and his eyes. "My mouth tastes like the inside of a decomposing camel carcass."

She had been awake for a while but hadn't stirred, content just to look at him and let him sleep. When she heard him awaken, she said, "You look like a painting I once saw, of Jesus, especially with that beard starting to come in."

"Well, au contraire, ma chére, I feel like the *Devil*. Got any coffee?"

"Guess I'll have to make you a heavenly breakfast, Al . . . or brunch I guess. It is after ten, you know. What would you like?"

♪♪♪

For Al, the meal was a feast: bacon, scrambled eggs, toast, and hash browns made from day-old mashed potatoes. For Charlotte, it was a smorgasbord of emotions: infatuation, unease, happiness, and shame—marinated and slow-cooked in a Catholic girl's leftover guilt.

As they ate, the conversation drifted from music to Canadian history, to astrology: he was Pisces; she was Taurus. Al said he knew she had to be that—because she was full of *bull*, and Charlotte countered with how she knew something was *fishy* about him. They vowed to never bring up the subject again, unless the jokes got better.

As the morning slipped ever closer to afternoon, Al told her he had to get going, since he didn't know how long it would take him to walk home, and there was a band meeting scheduled for one o'clock.

"See you tonight?" he asked as he leaped down the front steps to the sidewalk.

"Wait a minute," she called after him. He sprang back up, three stairs per stride and they shared their second kiss. As he pushed back her wind-tossed hair from over her forehead and eyes, Al looked into the past, into his one brief memory of innocent, pure, simple love. He vowed to make this good, make it real, make it last. He promised himself to think only of the future, not of what had *been*. Saying goodbye to her wasn't an ending—but a beginning.

"Charlotte, I want to see you again; *need* to. Please come to the club tonight?"

They kissed again, this time lingering in a sweet crescendo of passion as Al slowly moved his hands up and down her body. Placing his fingers on her forehead, he traced a gentle pathway over her eyes, her cheeks, her lips, her chin and neck, brushing carefully down the middle of her chest, and back up the side of one breast. She sighed and pulled him closer.

"I'll be there, Al," she whispered in his ear, as they melted into each other's embrace.

♪♪♪

Al's walk/run from rue Saint-Urbain to rue MacKay took over half an hour. By the time he washed and changed, it was almost 1 p.m. No way to get to the club on time. Running the full distance, he made it by 1:05. No one else was there yet.

Shit, when will I learn?

Danny's brother Phillipe, or as he preferred, "Phil", was at the bar cleaning glasses. "Hey, trumpet man, have a coffee. Man, you're sweatin'. Cops after ya?" He grinned, showing the scattered remains of teeth.

"Thanks, big guy, I will," said Al. "You seen any of the band? Supposed to meet here at two o'clock."

"Nope . . . well, yep. Here comes two of 'em now."

Nate and Joe sauntered up to the bar, their New York style *cool* leaving a wake in the roadhouse atmosphere. Both were wearing sport jackets over tee shirts and wore Wellington boots which were only occasionally visible under their bell-bottomed pant legs. Nate's jeans were tie-dyed, while Joe's were fashionably faded.

"Just you here, kid?" asked Joe.

"Yeah, man," said Al. "Where is everybody? I don't want to waste the whole stinking day here. Feels like my life is nothing but this damned place. No offense, Phil."

Phil chuckled. "Hey, I feel the same way, kid. Sometimes I sure miss wrastlin': shorter hours, more pay, higher class of company. But here, at least I get to hit guys for real."

As the four men laughed at Phil's philosophy, Mike walked in and a shroud of silence immediately enveloped the room. Only seconds after him came Elliot. Mike decided not to bother waiting for Billy and said, "Guys, here's where it's at. I got an offer to go on the road with Woody Herman. Pay isn't so hot, but it's been a while since I worked with a name band. Gotta take it. I go next week. Only hope my fuckin' chops are okay by then."

Al knew where that last remark was directed, but he refused to give Mike the satisfaction of reacting to it.

Nate spoke first. "Where does that leave us, man? What about the gigs we got booked after here?"

"It's cool," said Mike. "We're booked as a unit, with no fuckin' *star*. Heh, except of course Mr. Showbiz here . . ." There was no need for a glance toward Al as he continued, "All you have to do is get another tenor man. I know a guy right here in Montreal. He's a *monster*. I already called him and he can do all but the first week of the third gig, and he promised he'd have a good sub for that. Anyway, it's done. See ya all tonight."

An ensemble "cool" was mumbled by Joe, Nate, and Elliot as Mike headed for the door. Since the tension between Mike and Al had been producing only negative vibes in the band, no one would miss their departing leader/sax player. A change would be good.

As soon as Mike was gone the conversation spun around choices of repertoire and division of responsibilities. It seemed all had forgotten the group was at this moment short *two* members. Phil called attention to that when he asked, "Where's the piano guy?"

♪ ♪ ♪

Ten minutes before show time—and no one had heard from Billy all day. He had been good lately, keeping clean from the hard stuff, but he was never far from the edge.

Al saw Billy first, or rather heard him, as the weaving, wobbling piano man loudly announced his arrival. "How-dee-doo . . . cock-a-doodle-doo. Hey, didn't Busty say that? Nah, she'd say, 'any cock'll do.'"

His eyes were hardly open and the first chair he reached became an emergency mooring post. Al caught Billy by the shoulders just as his knees buckled, but keeping him from falling was not the primary concern.

"Geezes, man, you gonna be able to play?" asked Al. With the ambivalence of the mother of a lost child who had just been found, he was both thankful to see him, *and* furious.

Billy carried on in his absurd banter. "Nobody plays like me . . . deedle dee . . . ooh, got to pee. Where's the can? A can o' pee? Hey, one's great, but a couple of 'em could make you too tense. Come on, guys, you know, canopies . . . ? You dig? *Two tents*? Ha, that's me all right . . . too dense . . . Ho boy."

As he dragged Billy to the men's room and helped him stand while he relieved himself, Al thought it might be the worst he'd ever seen him. Through a special arrangement, a methadone clinic in Montreal would keep him supplied. But Al suspected Billy was cheating. It must have been more than just booze tonight, but that didn't matter right now. Whatever the poison, this was going to be a rough night just keeping him from getting killed, if he were to talk this way to the wrong person at the Thunder.

♪ ♪ ♪

The first set went by without any musical disasters, as years of experience and the dregs of genius still allowed Billy to play remarkably well during these moments; and Al just kept shushing him whenever he'd get too talkative. By the second set, Al's mind was elsewhere; Charlotte had not appeared.

During break, Busty approached Al, who was sitting by himself on a stool at the far end of the bar, rapidly finishing off his sixth beer of the night.

"Si beau, mais seul, encore. Pourquoi? Why lonely?" she said, as she stroked his hair.

Al said, "I'm waiting for someone. Here, grab a seat."

"Your amie, from de night ago?" Her English was worse than his French.

"She was supposed to meet me. I thought she liked me. L'amour, eh?"

"Femme stupide, I would not be making you wait." She ran her hand up his thigh. "Ooh, un *bander*."

Al hadn't learned that word in French class, but it was easy to interpret, from where her hand was—and from what was happening there in his pants.

"Hey, come on," he said, "this isn't the place." He pushed her hand back down to his knee, glancing around to see if anyone had seen.

"Oh, je comprends . . . I see. You are liking *men*? Quel dommage . . . too bad." Her pink lower lip slid into an exaggerated pout.

"No, no way," proclaimed Al. "I like women, a LOT." Then, lowering his voice he added, "Geez, don't say I'm a homo. In this place? I won't get out the door alive."

"You must prove dat to me, mon chèr, ce soir . . . tonight?"

Looks like Charlotte isn't coming. Might have known she wasn't for real. Who could turn down a private showing from Busty? Ooh la la.

Al slugged back the remainder of his beer and slammed the mug down like an angry judge. Phil looked over and said, "Another one, my friend?"

Al motioned for two more drafts: one now, and one for the stage. No doubt he was in for an interesting night, and lots of beer seemed the thing to do.

Phil brought the mugs and said, "You sure you can play with this much beer in you? Never seen you have more than a couple or three."

"I'll be fine, my muscle-bound friend. I need stamina tonight . . . lots of it."

Phil looked at Busty's hand—still on Al's thigh—and raised an eyebrow of understanding. "Yes, trumpet man," he said, smiling. "That you will; *that you will.*"

♪♪♪

Charlotte arrived at midnight, during the third set.

Oh boy . . . oh no.

Snake saw her and waved her over to his table. "Hi, girly. Hardly recognized ya. Ya look different. Yeah, you ain't wearin' that hippie stuff. Sweater looks good on ya, shorts too. Ain't it a bit chilly for them? Hey, can I get ya a beer? Come on, I'm lonely here. Wheelie's outa town a couple days."

Charlotte settled into the safety next to Snake, and waved to Al, who was squinting through the stage lights in disbelief that it was really her. Having watched her walk from the door to Snake's table, he was intrigued by the difference in her appearance, mainly from the altered emphasis brought about by changing clothing styles. She had a perfect figure, with slim waist, medium bust—appearing much more prominent in this shape-accentuating sweater than in her hippie clothes—firm athletic legs, and a cute *caboose*, as Billy would have called it. Al usually paid most attention to a woman's chest, not her rear end, but these *were* times of great change.

He couldn't remember his first physical impression of her, other than her pretty face.

I spent a whole night with her, lay next to her, even kissed her . . . and this is the first I've noticed what a great shape she's got? What's going on here?

During the remainder of the set, Al couldn't take his eyes off her, albeit staring through a fog of confusion. The day-late first impression, combined with too much beer, was blurring his vision and his judgment. Busty was dancing directly beside him, and despite her blatant presence—she was now invisible to him.

♪ ♪ ♪

As the set ended, Busty disappeared into the dressing room.

Good.

Billy was about to disappear off the edge of the stage.

Yikes.

He jumped down and caught Billy just as he teetered into a fall. "Come on," said Al, "let's get you to a chair. Only one short set to go. Think you'll make it?"

"I could play all night," muttered Billy. "What time is it? Did we start yet? Hey, I'm only kidding. I'll make it, man. All is copacetic. Help me to a chair, Al. A chair, a chair; my kingdom for a *chair*."

Al got Billy seated safely next to Charlotte. Snake, looking disgusted, bid a fond adieu and headed for the door. Charlotte whispered, "What's wrong with Billy? Is he sick?"

"He's sick in the head, he is. Just a little too much of a lot of things. He should be okay if he stays away from everyone. Hey, how are *you*? I was beginning to think you stood me up."

Tonight she was wearing makeup, just enough to set off her already stunning features. "I had to do a few things, Al and . . . I hope you're not mad, but I couldn't reach you. You don't have a phone, remember? I didn't want to come here too early because this place . . ." She touched his hand and leaned in close to say, "This place has only one thing I am interested in."

Billy was staring at her like a dog begging at the dinner table. "You are simply perfect," he sighed. "Will you marry me?"

Charlotte laughed. "Maybe I *should* marry you, Billy. Are you Catholic?"

"Oh shit," said Billy, "I knew there'd be a catch. I love you anyway."

Al wondered why there was no familiar cackle as Billy closed his eyes and slumped back in his chair.

♪♪♪

Charlotte's appearance had much written beneath it. Even the most naive of men could have read the message in her attire and makeup: a subtle invitation, needing minimal interpretation, unlike Busty's approach which required no interpretation, translation, or intuition at all.

"Al," said Charlotte, "I want to see you after work, but I can't stay here now. This place is too creepy, and Snake was the only thing between me and the rest of the men in here while you're playing."

"Yeah, I get it, Charlotte, but where will you go?"

"Please don't think I'm terrible," she said, again moving close so Billy wouldn't hear, "but I have an idea. Tell me how to get to your place, and I'll meet you there."

"Sure, I guess so, but what about your place?"

"That's part of why I was late. My parents came home early; thank God not a day sooner. I'm sure you understand, we cannot go there now."

"Okay, here's my keys," whispered Al. "Hey, if you see the dog, you have to yell 'Gueule', and he'll leave you alone."

"*Gueule?*" asked Charlotte. "That is just a bit intimidating, Al. Do you live in a zoo?"

"Long story, sweet girl. Just remember to say 'Gueule', and it'll be fine. He won't bite, but I can't make that same guarantee for Baldy."

"Baldy . . . who *bites*? Al, I am beginning to wonder if where you live is scarier than where you work."

Al struggled to sound sober. "Hey, I'm kidding, not about the dog though. Seriously, just say 'Gueule'. Anyway, it's so cool that you're doing this. But I may be a bit late. I gotta get Billy home safe."

"That's okay, Al. I have all night. My parents think I'm at Alice's."

Al's heart quickened a few beats per minute at yet another hint about her intentions. As he walked her to the door, he said, "Here's some money for a cab. It's not that far, but I don't want you walking these streets alone."

"Silly," she laughed, "I have my own money. Maybe you should use yours to take a cab yourself . . . to get home to me faster? And please don't have too much more to drink, Al. I don't want you to fall asleep, not right away."

It was too dark to see, but her trembling voice tattled that she was blushing. As worldly as she was trying to act, her innocence shone through the sultry surface in the most endearing way. It made her all the more appealing—and frightening.

Just before entering the cab, she turned and kissed him, and a subtle but unambiguous flash of her tongue made one more strong statement about what she had in mind for later. Al watched the cab merging into the Saint Catherine Street traffic. For the first time in months he thought of Wendy and the last time he'd seen her.

♪♪♪

Minus Milt's final set was underway for only twenty minutes, when Phil waved for them to quit since no one was left to play to. This was not bad news for any of them, especially Al. As he assisted Billy to the front door—more carrying, than dragging him—Busty caught up with them.

"I have to help Billy get home, Brigitte. He couldn't walk ten feet on his own. We'll grab a cab."

"I can help?" she asked. "Maybe . . . ?"

♪♪♪

Yaphet, the cabbie, had a new story for his collection: "a tall hippie and a stripper, or hooker . . . whatever . . . with *humongous* knockers . . . bring this drunk guy in a beret out of Rolling Thunder . . . They want to go to rue MacKay . . . and then the drunk guy starts singing and yelling wild stuff . . . that he's an alien, like from Mars or something . . . Meanwhile, the stripper is all over the hippie and he keeps trying to fight her off, but he's too busy holding back the drunk from jumping out the door . . . Drunk guy says,

'Take me to the president!' As the stripper swallows the hippie's face, he says, 'Canada doesn't have a president . . .' *She* don't speak English, so she's no help . . . *She's* the one looks like a friggin' Martian . . . Hippie pays the fare . . . They all spill out at that cheap rooming house, the middle of MacKay, little ways down from Ste. Catherine, you know, Baldy's joint . . . Hippie says to me, 'Martians are really nice people; don't judge 'em by this guy'."

♪ ♪ ♪

After fishing in Billy's pockets for his keys, Al and Busty dragged him up to room 206, unimpeded by neither man nor beast; La Gueule must have been dozing. As they got him undressed, he was like an unstrung puppet, his head, arms, and legs awkwardly flopping about. He slurred into Al's ear, "Hey, is that Busty with us? Are we gettin' laid, man?"

Al said, "Hey, man, you already did her. You showed her a *good* time, man."

Billy practically snored out the words. "Far-fucking-out . . ." as he slipped into unconsciousness, still sitting up. Al let him go, and his head, beret still in place, thudded down onto the pillow.

Al whispered to Brigitte, "Wait here, I'll be right back."

He wasn't sure what he was going to tell Charlotte; maybe stall her for a few minutes only. He could say Billy was sick or something; at least that was partly true. Having Busty Brigitte pawing at him was more than his fragile morality could handle. Here was a chance for a few minutes alone with her; a sleeping Billy didn't count. What harm would that be? Just to mess around a bit—just a little bit.

Al headed for the door, but Busty grabbed his shoulder and spun him around. In an instant she had unbuttoned her blouse and unsnapped the front-hook bra. "Ici, pour toi . . . for *you*, mes boules. No pastie now. You like?"

Her mushroom stem nipples stood out like dual microphones at the ready for the ring announcer to introduce the big fight, featuring wrong versus right. The odds clearly called for a knockout punch: the winner, in the near corner, soon to be wearing no trunks—"Kid Wrong".

As she moved closer he was mired in quicksand which began to suck him downward to his deepest pit of self-loathing. She put her hands around the back of his neck and drew his face closer, until her soft, slippery pink lips pressed against his mouth with such force, he thought his teeth would crack along with his resolve.

Brigitte shared no such dental danger. "Attends, mon chèr," she whispered, turning toward the dresser. She reached into her mouth and removed a full set of dentures which she set down on the dresser top. She pulled off her panty hose and dropped to her knees in front of him. "Ici, mon home, let me see," she whispered as she undid his belt. In seconds she'd pulled his pants and underwear down around his knees.

"No, Brigitte . . . don't," said Al. "I need to go. I have to—"

She cut him off at the intended pass, saying, "You 'ave one ting to do, only . . . Be 'appy, 'cause I do dis . . ."

Before Al could even consider pushing her away, her lips and tongue began to work their magic. He wanted to make some kind of pun about "tricks", but in a rare moment, words both serious and sarcastic, escaped him as he became lost in a dizzying whirlwind of physical feelings and emotions.

It didn't take long, since the novelty of the situation was hyper stimulating, and she was experienced and efficient. When it was over she sighed and sat back on the floor in front of him, with a grotesque smile revealing the darkness of her toothless mouth.

For most men this would be a moment of bliss and complete satisfaction. For Al Waters, it spelled instantaneous anxiety and depression, a sexual result he was familiar with, but never with this severity. The strongest ingredient however, mixing into his emotional cocktail, was anger: at his inability to enjoy what should have been a simple pleasure; at her, for seducing him; and at himself, for not being with Charlotte.

"Mmm," Brigitte moaned, as she ran her tongue over what remained of her lipstick and the last few drops of Al's spent passion. She reached up and pulled his face down to meet hers. As she kissed him, the smell and taste on her mouth brought fear and disgust up from the depths of many nightmares. But the angst he wanted to scream out wouldn't come, blocked by overpowering inner forces of self-protection. As his stomach churned, he fought desperately against impending vomit and buried truths.

Al pushed her face away from his and he tried to move away, but his pants around his knees made escape too awkward. As she grabbed at his cuff to stop him, she saw he was fully erect once more.

"Si vite? So . . . fast? Mais tu es . . . so young, mmm. Encore?"

He'd been afraid she'd ask that. As he pulled back, finally free of her grasp, he tried to steady his wobbly legs and said, "I really have to go now. This wasn't supposed to happen."

"Oui, it was, mon cher," she said as she gripped his hand and dragged him down next to her on the shag carpet. With surprising strength, she then pushed him down onto his back and straddled his chest. From this angle the view of her body recalled all the wildest fantasies, straight out of an adolescent's centerfold-induced dreams. As he began to grope at her impossibly voluptuous body, his wall of resistance had the strength of a sand castle in a tsunami, sucked away by a single overwhelming wave of lust. She arched her back and cried out, "Take me. Je t'aime. Love me, please . . . *now*."

♪♪♪

If to be raped means having no choice, then Al Waters was about to be violated: by temptation, by weakness, and by demons from within. He did have a choice: down the hall, in room 202 where sensibility and self-respect awaited—with Charlotte.

In room 206, there were three addicts, each having made wrong choices too many times to go back: Billy, wasted on booze and drugs; Brigitte, wasting no time in seeking simple passion; and Al, wasting yet another possibility to love for real.

Oh, Charlotte . . . yes, I am a worthless piece of crap. Please just don't know it yet.

♪♪♪

Once again, the beast ruled over the spirit, virtually a no-contest situation for Al. He shoved Brigitte to the floor, climbed on top of her and entered her so violently she gasped, "Tabarnak, you are 'urt me . . . Oh, mon Dieu, not so 'ard."

He held her arms back over her head and continued even more aggressively. Her resistance ebbed quickly, and she began to enjoy his brutality, spurring him on like a wild bronco gone berserk in a reversal of the roles of rider and ridden. Neither she nor Al understood—he was making *hate*, not love. What he *was* most conscious of during the next few minutes was feeling excruciatingly alone.

♪♪♪

As Al opened the door to 202, the light was off; only the pure darkness of the windowless room awaited.

Oh please, God, let her be asleep.

The door squeaked; he waited—nothing. Stealthily entering the room, he felt his way along, with the trembling trepidation of a man who hated heights, on a tenth-story ledge. If he could only just *slide* into bed.

Like an anaconda easing into a river, he lowered his body down onto the nearest edge.

Please Charlotte, be asleep . . . Okay, head onto pillow, easy now . . . one foot still on floor, good enough . . . Don't even breathe.

♪♪♪

When Al woke up, it took a moment to figure out where he was, when it was, *who* he was. A room with no windows tells you nothing. Reversing his entry procedure, he sat up far enough to pull the string switch, planning to snap the light back off if Charlotte was still asleep.

She wasn't. She wasn't *there.* He squinted at his watch—three o'clock.

What . . . ? Wasn't it after three when I GOT here?

He struggled to his feet and opened the door, and his question was answered by the sunlight from the window at the end of the hall. It was three in the *afternoon.*

CHAPTER 20

FIVE - SOUTH TOWER (6)

*T*he orderly thought he saw a movement from the injured man's right hand. He was thankful his own heart wasn't hooked up to any monitors; alarms would have been screaming.

"You thinking of waking up now?" he whispered. "It won't be a long night for you when you do. I have to do what I came for and get out of here, real soon. I'm not sure how I'm even gonna do it. I do have my gun. Could put a pillow over the barrel and blow your brains all over this nice white room. No, too quick and easy, not to mention too much commotion, with that cop out there. You . . . you scum, need something special, and as slow as I can manage."

♪ ♪ ♪

Officer Poole, hands behind his back, was pacing in short circles in front of room 510. He had known the worst part of this duty would be boredom, but the Lenny Breau article served to exacerbate that. Too much time to think: to ponder career options, motivation, inspiration, and fate. The patient in 510 had little say in *his* own future. That lay in the hands of the medical people. But what about him, Stanley Poole, cop by choice? Or manipulated by a single-minded father: a man who was good at what he did, but couldn't see that his son was good at something else. Was it too late? He was only twenty-five. Maybe with hard work he could get his guitar playing skills together enough to make a go of it—maybe a couple of years?

I wonder what it's like to be on the road, playing in a band, living the music, living the life. That's gotta be so sweet.

♪

CHAPTER 21

SHUT THE DOOR SOFTLY

Al showered, hating the across-the-hall facility more with every minute he spent in it. Since other tenants had to have access, there was no privacy. Baldy had disabled the latch, so no one could monopolize the facility; which might force someone to vomit, or worse, in the hallway. Because of that, the only way to ensure not being walked in on while sitting on the toilet, was to stretch out your foot against the door. Even this small protection from sudden interruption wasn't an option when you were in the shower.

Pleased to have finished washing undisturbed, he hurried back into his room and started to get dressed. It was only 3:30, five hours or so before work. Might as well go for a walk—anything was better than being cooped up in this hole. As he tugged a comb through his matted hair, a knock sounded at the door.

"Billy . . . ? That you? Just a minute."

Al opened the door to find Charlotte standing in the hallway, trembling, staring at the floor, with her arms folded rigidly across her chest. In an almost inaudible whisper she said, "I . . . I need to talk to you. Are you . . . alone?"

He was frozen in place, speechless, as he held the door in one hand. After a moment Charlotte said, "Al . . . ?"

Awakened from his momentary paralysis, he said, "Yeah, yeah, sorry. Come in. Here, there's only the one chair. You take it."

He sat on the bed. Since *she* was now saying nothing, he figured he should start. "Charlotte, I'm real sorry about last night. I was so late. I don't blame you for leaving."

As Charlotte sat down in the chair, he saw she was wearing the same clothes from the night before. Her hair was tangled and one cheek was smudged with black. Had she actually gone home at all? Why wouldn't she look at him?

She said, "I didn't leave soon enough."

"What does that mean?" asked Al, hoping he was guessing wrong.

Her voice had been quivering, but now grew stronger, as she began to say the words she'd been practicing over and over in her head. "I heard you and Billy, and *her* in the hall. I opened the door to greet you, and I saw you go into Billy's room."

"Hey, Char, Billy was—"

"Shhh, Al . . . I know what happened. I was stupid enough to go and stand in the hall near Billy's door to wait; stupid enough to listen to everything."

She finally looked up into his face. In her eyes was a perplexing meld of containment and contempt as she said, "Today I am not so stupid anymore. I am much smarter about many things, thanks to you."

♪♪♪

For the moment, time and space were out of sync. Al was eight years old, standing in a basement corner; his mother was scolding him for stealing a dollar from her purse. In spite of her annoyance with his misdeed, she had talked gently, cajoling him into being honest about it, rather than making him out to be a bad person. Then, with no warning, came the tears he had seen so many times in his young life, ruining the beauty in her face. Momentarily unable to speak, she pulled a tissue from her apron pocket and wiped her cheeks with fragile grace. She saw the distress in his eyes, but when she reached out to touch him, he flinched—though it had been years since the only time she'd ever struck him.

She seemed to understand his reaction, even if *he* didn't. She gripped his shoulders with both hands, sending lightning bolts of pain through his body. After drawing in a long, quivering breath she said, "Your father will be so disappointed in you, Freddy. I know how that feels. I was never good enough. Why did I think *you* could be?"

His mother let him go and ran up the basement stairs, with her face buried in her hands. He sat down on the floor and stayed there until suppertime—nearly an hour later.

Why won't she come back down?

He could hear her crying from all the way up in the master bedroom until she went down to the kitchen to cook. Then, paradoxically, she began to sing her familiar "La dee da dee da" made-up song she always did when in the kitchen or doing housework.

She changes so fast, so easy. I wish I could do that. How come one minute the dollar means everything and then, nothing? It was only a dollar. What if I'd taken ten?

He was too young to know: it could have been a million dollars, or only a penny. The theft was forgotten. There was no way he could comprehend that her tears were from her inability to protect her children from a special kind of harm only a family can inflict: the potent poisonous merger of betrayal, abuse, and denial. His little heart did understand one thing: no amount of money could buy back what she had just stolen from him with her words.

She's right. Look what I did, and she cried again, and because of me. I'm not good.

♪♪♪

Charlotte got up to leave. Al wanted to scream something. He didn't know what—maybe just scream. Admitting guilt was repugnant to him, but he knew she was worth suffering for. Was there any hope that she could ever forgive him? Wasn't anything supposed to be possible if you wanted it badly enough? He slapped himself back into reality with the unspoken part of the ancient adage: wanting something, combined with making a sincere effort toward that goal, can indeed make dreams come true. But just *wanting*, doesn't cut it.

How could I mess this up so bad? Can't let her go.

"Charlotte, please, don't go yet. Listen to me, I was drunk, I'm a pig, but I can change."

Standing in the open doorway, she looked at him resolutely and said, "You're not worth a second chance, Al. Yes, handsome, charming, brilliant in more ways than you know. But you're right about one thing; you *are* a pig."

She backed out into the hallway and shut the door softly, leaving him alone in the room with no windows.

♪♪♪

Al sat back down on the end of the bed and looked into the half-mirror on the dresser.

Are you proud of yourself, Mr. Waters? There goes the best thing that might ever happen to you, and you're too damn stupid to know what to do. Al baby, you're the original born loser.

He pulled the string switch, and fell back on the bed into a deeper darkness than a simple lack of light, wishing he could live the last two days over again from the start. But he knew too well that wishing, like wanting—is never enough.

♪♪♪

Billy was coming out of the bathroom and nearly bumped into Charlotte who was leaning against the wall next to room 202.

"Hey, honey, what are you doing here?" he said, just before noticing the room number over her shoulder. "Oh man, stupid question. Sorry, sorry, none of my business anyway."

Having kept calm long enough to get through the door, Charlotte's resources for cool had run dry—not so, her tear supply.

"Hey, hey, what's up, kid?" said Billy. He reached into the bathroom to grab a wad of toilet paper which he then awkwardly dabbed at her streaked face.

"I'm okay," she said, as another sob escaped.

"I don't believe it for a second, honey. That old stool pigeon, mascara, has given you up. The truth's right here . . ." He blotted her cheek once more. "Tell me what happened, kid. Is that Al up to his tricks? He's not too cool sometimes in matters with the ladies, but he doesn't mean to be mean. Just can't help himself. I know he wants to be loved, and to love back, but I think he just plain doesn't know how. Trust me, Charlotte, if he's gone and hurt you, he's hurting too, real bad."

Charlotte found herself cradled in Billy's arms, her cheek against his chest. He patted her shoulder and said, "Aww, hey come on, little girl, Doctor Crothers can help. My prescription? Coffee, let's go."

♪♪♪

Billy Crothers was unlike anyone Charlotte had ever met. His unkempt maladroit exterior was a veneer she saw through easily. Behind the sad clown demeanor was a man of complexity, humor, and passion. It was not easy for him to expose his serious side, but in her company he found security in the knowledge that he could trust her. She knew he'd been crazy about her from the beginning, but instead of fearing him she felt a peaceful acceptance. Al had been a glittering treasure with a curse attached, while Billy was coal, refueling the depleted warmth of her spirit.

♪♪♪

A full week passed, and the extent of their physical intimacy had been handholding. Then, on a Sunday afternoon during a sightseeing walk, they entered one of the great cathedrals. Billy asked about the rows of burning candles. When Charlotte explained how they had been lit for departed loved ones, he noticed one had gone out.

With tears welling up, he asked, "Should I light it again? Would that be wrong? Don't even know who it was for or anything."

"God would know, Billy, and so would the departed soul it's for. And I know a little more about you, for wanting to do it."

She moved closer, and as her shoulder touched his, he slipped his arm around her. As he lit the candle, she held her hand on top of his. This simple touch became an instant conduit of love, as a mighty force surged through them—from the tiny flickering glow they'd ignited, and from a joyful radiance erasing shadows in their hearts.

♪ ♪ ♪

They stopped for lunch at an outdoor café. While waiting for their drink orders, Charlotte said, "Billy, you know so much about me already and I know so little of you, other than your musical life. Tell me about yourself: where you went to school; brothers and sisters? What about your parents? What are they like? Sorry, if they are still alive? They must be so proud of you."

Billy turned toward the street and began a running commentary of the passing traffic. "One black car, two green, a fucking red one . . . 'nother black, a truck . . . *another* fucking truck. Damn bicycle. Shit, more of 'em . . . too many fucking bicycles—"

"Billy," said Charlotte, "did I say something wrong? Why are you upset?"

He turned back toward Charlotte, with only a sizzling of spit sneaking from the corner of his pursed lips in place of words. Before Charlotte could say anything else, the waiter returned, gaily singing as he placed their glasses onto the table. "Here you go," he said, "de best cocktail in town, serve by de best server in all Montréal."

The young man's laughter was short-lived as Billy stood up and snarled, "Just shut the hell up, you jive-ass freak. Go get our fucking food orders before I chuck Montreal's best cocktail right at your fat head."

As the waiter gasped and scurried away, Charlotte whispered, "Billy, please sit down. Just take a deep breath or something and try to calm down. Or I will have to leave."

Billy complied, his face as white as the tablecloth, as he placed both hands over his face as if to block any further outbursts. Charlotte had no idea what to say next as the pain of the moment hung in the air like a foul odor.

At last, Billy spoke. "Oh God, Charlotte I am so sorry. Your questions caught me off guard. I haven't thought about that stuff for so long, and that's no accident."

"Explain, if you want to, Billy."

"All I can say, sweet girl, is that I was an only child, and I think my parents would have preferred one less kid than they had. Can we drop it for now, please?"

"You will talk about it only when you are ready. Thank you for saying that much anyway."

A different waiter arrived with their orders. His smile was strained as he asked if there would be anything else.

Charlotte said, "Merci, but we will be leaving soon."

They ate and drank, with no conversation at all for the next few minutes. As the awkwardness began to fall away, Charlotte asked about how things were going with the band, and Billy answered freely and ever more enthusiastically with stories of gigs past and present. The moment of angst had all but disappeared, when a new one dropped on them with the joy-dampening clout of the first splat of rain from an unexpected storm cloud.

♪♪♪

Al ran up to the table, grabbed a chair, and exclaimed as he sat down, "Hey, look who's here. I wondered what you'd been doing with your days, Billy. Hi, Charlotte. Okay if I join you guys?"

Charlotte looked at Billy, and when he nodded, she turned back to Al and said, "I guess it's okay."

Al knew they'd been seeing each other. Billy had told him at the gig about going for coffee with Charlotte after she'd left Al's room on that unfortunate day. There were no apparent hard feelings on anybody's part. Billy was happy. Charlotte seemed to have forgotten all about Al. And Al was living it up with one-night stands: an oxymoronic expression, as Al had always thought, for an activity usually requiring the participants to lie down.

Oddly, the more Al's search for sexual gratification escalated, the less it seemed to equate with pleasure. His lust would be sated, but it seemed love must be a necessary element to make sex a happy experience. This was his theory, based on his limited experience with that combination of factors.

He'd had the chance with Charlotte, but she wasn't his type; she was too good for him. Worked for Billy; worked for Al. Charlotte let them believe what they chose to.

♪ ♪ ♪

Al made it clear he was not there for idle chat. In a voice much too loud for public places he spewed out his words as quickly as a child with a new toy. "You guys heard about what's going on downtown? Cops everywhere, not just like, *some* cops, man; there's armies of 'em, and *real* army too. Yeah, man, soldiers, with guns and clubs and stuff."

Charlotte was well aware of the recent historic events around the strike by police and firefighters, which had been forced to an end by the government. The nation was then shocked by the kidnappings of British Trade Commissioner James Cross and Minister of Labour Pierre Laporte by the Front de libération du Québec—the "FLQ". When asked what he would do in response to what had been dubbed the "October Crisis", Prime Minister Trudeau's response was his famous, "Just watch me," followed by the unprecedented move of invoking the War Measures Act, essentially placing the country into a state of "apprehended insurrection". The result was a Montreal full of police and armed troops who had the authority to make arrests and detentions without charge.

♪ ♪ ♪

Al was almost giddy with enthusiasm. "Come on," he said, "let's go watch the action. Just a couple streets over. You won't believe it!"

Billy and Charlotte paid their café bill and followed Al to boulevard Dorchester where the view was something none of them would ever forget. One side of the street was choked with onlookers, while the opposite side was empty, except for an advancing phalanx of troops. Al was high on the fumes of apprehension from the crowd. Was this real, or a newsreel of 1940s Paris?

Al ran up to the nearest corner to cross the street, and with it, the invisible line between innocent adventure and insanity. The crowd's collective murmur changed to cheers, as he walked recklessly down the sidewalk directly at the oncoming forces. He did a bow to his fans just before the soldiers reached him, whereupon he hopped nimbly onto the bordering lawn. None of the helmeted men in the twenty rows seemed to notice him, and this spurred him on to one-step-too-far.

As the last few lines passed by, Al extended his right hand, with first two fingers forming a "V", and said, "Peace, brother."

The last trooper in line smacked him on the arm with the butt of his rifle, adding under his breath the verbal clout, "Try it again, asshole . . . come on, see what happens."

The unexpected personalization of the scene by the trooper's vocal and physical assault, instantly changed Al's bravado to dread. This was no game. His puerile attempt to walk a fence for the girls across the road had turned abruptly adult. Trying to preserve a modicum of poise, he waited until the troops were a few paces further away. Then, to the boisterous appreciation of the gallery, he directed a middle-finger salute at the goon who'd hit him. Several people on the far side of the street now began to edge out past the curb as if considering joining Al on the *forbidden* side.

What have I done? This could turn into a riot.

Fortunately, no one there was as foolish or cavalier as Al. There was plenty of serious protest to be performed; but not here, not now, under the direction of a buffoon. He turned away from the scene, and ran for several blocks, finally collapsing in exhaustion on the steps of a church.

Shit . . . what happened to Billy and Charlotte? I guess I'll find them later.

♪♪♪

Al heard a commotion and looked up to see a group of young men running down the street toward him. Carrying handmade signs, they were yelling in French; and though only part of it discernible to him, he could feel the urgency in their voices. He got up as they went by, and ran along, merging unnoticed among them. Turning the corner onto Bleury, off Ste. Catherine, Al noticed the group had quickly grown into a mob—at least fifty people now. One of them, appearing to be a leader, stopped in the middle of the road. He barked a short command. "Ici . . . ici. Arrête."

Everyone obeyed, and in seconds all were blending in among the innocent passersby, or standing along the building fronts, with their placards behind their backs. A rumbling noise came from the east with an earthquake's energy, sending eerie shock waves from the ground up through feet, legs, and torsos; while heart rates climbed as the vibrations and decibels grew. The first police motorcycle turned the corner, followed by at least twenty others, most with sidecars. The cops slowed to a crawl, scanning the bystanders for suspects.

Al realized he was standing shoulder-to-shoulder with the mob leader, and with each passing cop's Gestapo glare, he felt the ice behind the dark glasses. The man next to him whispered, "Ne dites rien."

Say nothing? Yeah, right, like I'm about to make a speech. How about "Hear ye, hear ye. I stand among the protesters, ignorant of what they protest. Arrest me for my criminal stupidity. Put me in jail with them, and oh yeah, don't forget to tell them I'm from Ontario!"

Crap, what if these guys are FLQ? They kill people. Don't worry, mon ami . . . no way I'm saying a word.

♪ ♪ ♪

Only ten paces away, two demonstrators were recognized, and were grabbed by the cops. They foolishly resisted and were badly roughed up while Al's wall-mate watched, mumbling curses, straining at the reins of reason. As the man turned and said something in French beyond Al's rudimentary vocabulary, he responded with a guttural "Oui", figuring his odds were fifty-fifty to be right. The man nodded and turned back toward the scene of brutality as the veins in his neck swelled into rivers of rage.

He wants so much to dive in and help, like I would want to. How can he do nothing? I guess only pure logic tells him he has to get away; has to be free, to be useful to the cause, not to his friends. I don't even know for sure what this guy's beef is with the government or whatever, but his self-control is freaky.

♪ ♪ ♪

With the noise of the disappearing cop cycles lingering like pins and needles in their chests, the protesters bolted back up Ste. Catherine. Al decided not to follow. Instead, he walked slowly through streets he'd never seen before, wondering why these people were so angry. He resolved to read about it, to learn about these fellow countrymen whose mysterious enmity toward other Canadians drove them to such lengths.

♪ ♪ ♪

Al eventually found himself in the middle of a deserted Place des Arts, the expansive public square where only days before, he'd been part of an immense living wave of 40,000 screaming fans at a concert by the band, Chicago. Today the emptiness of the barren expanse of pavement was a black, silent ocean, swallowing him up like a grain of sand. He thought about how he had missed a chance to perform here three years earlier, during Expo 67.

His high school band had been selected to play, but Al wasn't a part of it anymore. When the band director asked him to rejoin to play principal trumpet and a featured solo, Al laughed in his face and walked away. As good as it felt to spurn the invitation with a not-so-subtle "fuck you" in his eyes, it pained him deeply to have missed the opportunity.

There was an ethereal sense of universal balance for him to be standing here alone; it was *his* turn now. He wished he had his trumpet with him so he could join in a duet with the breeze which was playfully chasing bits of paper around his feet.

A distant drone slipped into his consciousness. Was it subliminal conjured memories of the throngs of concertgoers from last week? Perhaps echoes of all the crowds in history to have filled this space? In moments, the sound was as loud as a squadron of B-29 bombers.

The motorcycles.

Before he could think about running, he was surrounded by five cops on full-sized Harleys. They were yelling at him in French. All he could understand seemed to imply something to do with clubs—and his head.

One cop dismounted and approached Al. Through his dark visor he said, "I've seen you on the streets today more than once, and you are in the wrong place at the very wrong time, my friend. But you are lucky. I know you don't belong, and I will tell you once only. Go home now. If I put you in jail with the real protesters they will discover you and rip you apart. Go on, go home!"

"Yes, sir," said Al. "I'm outa here." As he ran off, he dared a quick glance back, and saw that the officer who had spared him was removing his helmet. He now understood how incredibly lucky he had been.

Sergeant Lalonde said to his men, "That one has enough problems without getting mixed up in this. He follows trouble like a rat to the piper."

♪♪♪

After running most of the way home to rue MacKay, Al more resembled a rat that had followed a sinking ship to its grave. He found enough energy to take two steps at a time and once in his room, fell onto the bed, making donkey sounds with each breath he sucked in. When his breathing finally slowed, he sat up and removed his sweat-drenched clothes, tossing them one by one onto the chair. He lay back down as he threw his second sock, which hit the light string, sending it swinging. As he watched it slow into a pit-and-pendulum-like dance, it reminded him of the night he'd messed up with Charlotte. This place was getting to him. So many bad memories—so soon.

Sex—with Busty Brigitte or any of his other conquests—was arousing but never satisfying, always leaving the feeling a weight had descended upon his heart when it was over. If he had gone to Charlotte that night instead of giving in to Brigitte, he was certain it would have been ultimately as disappointing with her, and probably less exciting while it lasted. She was an amateur, a *nice* girl—the kind you should make love with, not just screw. Even so, the pain would have followed—the pain which grew from guilt and shame. If any enduring benefit could come from the coupling of man and woman, he'd yet to find it. Yet the lust was always there to drive him on to try one more time.

Each time Al had sex his libido was proven to be a liar, a seller of lemons, dealing from its lot which was stocked with shiny used promises.

When will I stop believing the lies? Why can't I just stop asking for something that can't happen?

Al didn't understand that simple lust was not the engine of his need, but merely the transmission. In his heart lay the answer, but he'd slammed shut the door on it years before; and now, locked it up tight and thrown away the key—along with Charlotte.

♪♪♪

For Minus Milt—now minus Mike—the gigs after Rolling Thunder in real jazz clubs were another world, especially the second of these, a restaurant called Le Mirage. It was essentially a fine-dining establishment with entertainment as an appetizer; and sadly, although the patrons appeared to listen, many of them regarded the musicians as being on the same social stratum as the servers and bus staff. Their applause was always polite although never completely masking an underlying scent of scorn. But at least they weren't outwardly dangerous. Al never thought he would miss the Thunder, but Le Mirage was *too* tame, downright *sterile*: no Snake, Wheelie, or Busty Brigitte; no big Danny quelling trouble; no Phil behind the bar—no true *character* at all.

The band was really cooking with Mike's replacement, Marcel Lebeau: a "local giant", as a newspaper columnist had dubbed him. Lebeau loved to quote this press reference, reveling in its backhanded irony as an intended accolade. Every night was an adventure in musicality, especially for Al. It was during this time he decided he wanted to get more into playing saxophone again, so Marcel helped Al find a cheap used tenor sax in a pawn shop. Bonds of both mentorship and friendship grew quickly between them, as Al was in awe of Lebeau's playing, and the older man saw tremendous natural ability in this rebellious, sarcastic young musician.

"You have a *sound*," said Lebeau, the first time he'd worked with Al. "It comes from somewhere most of us can only dream of, my friend. Reminds me a bit of Libert Subirana, my biggest sax 'rival' in Montreal . . . but the fact that the trumpet has been your main instrument boggles the mind. I've seen players who have dedicated many years of their life to only the sax, and their tone quality is not as rich as yours. I believe there are some of us who are born with it: a sound not acquired as much from practice as from somewhere deep within us. Never question your gift; never abandon it. But no matter how wonderful is what you've been given by nature, you must still strive to learn the instrument and its idiosyncrasies, and all the technical aspects of playing. Work always to improve, and in that journey will you find your true voice."

Lebeau began to work with Al during afternoons at Le Mirage. Although impressed with his student's progress after such a short time, he declared, "Al, don't waste my time. If you are going to be as good as I know you can be, you must choose. Trumpet or saxophone . . . the tuba, for God's sake! It doesn't matter what you decide to play, you'll be great, but only one. You must dedicate yourself to an instrument."

"But, Marcel," Al protested, "*you* play sax and clarinet and flute. Isn't that just as bad?"

"Al, you don't compare woodwinds to brass, or mix them; that's musical suicide. I've only seen a couple of guys who could do that: Murray McEachern, a super Canadian trombonist who also plays fine alto sax, and of course there's Ira Sullivan in Miami, who doubles on jazz trumpet and sax; and he cuts *you* on either one. I do still think he'd be even greater though, if he stuck to one horn."

Al had never heard of McEachern or Sullivan, but contrary to what Marcel had intended, he was encouraged rather than discouraged by this information.

I can do it too.

"Monsieur Lebeau, let's just work on what you can teach me about the sax. I'll worry about doubling on trumpet or not. There's lots of time to figure that out."

Marcel gave a halfhearted nod, knowing far better than his enthusiastic and naive student that time never negotiates with reality regarding the dreams of young men. He also knew Al was going to do what he wanted, so he let it drop.

♪♪♪

Billy and Charlotte were together almost every day; still, their relationship grew at a Victorian pace. Though she trusted Billy completely, she wasn't ready to be hurt again, and he was too in love to push her. Unlike Al, he believed that sex was secondary to true intimacy.

At first they avoided Al, but he *was* Billy's best friend, and after a while they began to invite him along on certain outings—with whomever of his lady friends he chose to bring, except for Busty. That was a non-issue anyway, since the stripper had drifted away from Al, favoring her more *professional* relationships.

Al seemed relatively at ease during their double dates, but conversations inevitably left out his companion du jour, since generally only he and Billy and Charlotte ever understood what they were talking about. Eventually he stopped accepting suggestions to join the party and disappeared back into his own little world-within-a-world.

♪♪♪

On rare days when Al and Billy spent time together, they'd end up discussing only music: personal matters being mutually agreed upon to stay away from. On one such occasion, Al mentioned to Billy that he had been trying to write an original song, and asked for advice.

"Okay," said Al, as he picked up his trumpet, "goes like this."

After the eight bars of the basic theme Al had played, Billy indicated for him to put the horn down. "Sorry, man, but I know you want honesty, but that's garbage. Not the notes, so much as the fact that it's so much like a couple of other tunes. I don't think it's original enough. Sounds like you just stole the gist of it from 'Angel Eyes'. Just my two cents, man. Don't go ballistic on me now."

"Shit, Billy, what are you now, my fucking father? I think what I wrote is plenty original, and not that much like any other tune I've heard. Hell, if you're reminded of 'Angel Eyes', then I should take that as a compliment. It's not even finished anyway. Damn it, I knew I shouldn't have done this."

"Come on, Al, I hear you play cool innovative stuff every time you do a jazz chorus. Try to think that way when you write something down, the same way you do when you improvise on stage. Maybe start with something easier, like 'rhythm changes'. You know, 'I Got Rhythm'. Everybody and their cousin writes at least one song based on that. Hell, Bird wrote more tunes on those same basic chords than all the rest of his stuff put together. I'll even start you off with a title, 'Thingamajig?' No, I know , 'Rhythmajig'! Cool, huh? Maybe too close to Monk's 'Rhythm-a-Ning', but—"

"Keep your crap titles, and your suggestions. Fuck songwriting anyway. I'll stick to what I do best: blow my horn and chase chicks. Later, man. I'm outa here. See you tonight at the gig."

With the slam of the door still ringing in his head, Billy slapped himself over how unfair he had been. The first time he'd heard those same notes had been only hours before, when Charlotte had hummed them to him, and told him Al had written the tune, giving it the title of "Charlotte's Song". The melody was in fact enchanting, and although somewhat reminiscent of "Angel Eyes", it did possess its own identity and a definite charm: a potentially exquisite piece of music. But Billy had refused to let Al know his true opinion—his remorse for being unsupportive, only short-lived— soon overrun by a rare feeling of victory, however hollow it felt, based on dishonesty.

♪♪♪

On an unseasonably warm mid-November day, Charlotte and Billy's care-free carousel world ground to an abrupt halt when Al changed all of their lives forever.

They were sitting on the edge of a park fountain when Al rounded the corner at a full run, stumbling to a stop just shy of falling into the water. Between gasps for breath he said, "Billy, remember that guy who was so nuts about us the other night? That American cat, said he *knew* people? Well, he left me a message at the club today. He's for real, man. And he wants me to front a band in New York. Next month, man, my own band, back in the *Apple*."

Charlotte watched quietly as the two men jumped around as if they'd just won the big game. As they leapt into the fountain, they became two clumsy Gene Kelly wannabes, splashing each other and Charlotte, taking turns singing disjointed bits of songs and nonsense. "We're going to the Apple again. Birdland is ours for the taking, rum pum pum, here we come. We'll take Manhattan, *and* the boroughs and the burbs. Start spreading the news; the boys are coming home."

After they wore themselves out, they sat down on the fountain's edge, laughing like children on the last day of school. Billy noticed Charlotte was not celebrating with Al and him, but was sitting quietly, looking away from them. He walked over to hug her and said, "Aw, hey, Char, we can work this out. We both *knew* I wasn't in Montreal for long. I mean, what if . . . ? Hey, you can come *with* us."

She pulled free from his arms and began to walk away, saying only, "I need to go now."

As Billy ran after her, Al sat quietly on the pool's edge, knowing he need not interfere.

Billy will be with me, no matter what. For him, music has more power than any woman could ever have.

♪♪♪

Two weeks later, to the day, Charlotte watched Billy and Al board the train. As she looked down beneath the wheels, the gleaming tracks became two swords, aimed directly at her heart.

The night before, in Billy's room, she had given herself to him. He hadn't expected it, and he was even more surprised at how much she cried afterward; he figured it must have had something to do with it being her first time. As he held her, kissing away her tears, he thought to himself how important this was for a woman. He'd been a virgin of a different sort—he'd never loved anyone before.

As he stuck his head out the train window, Billy's cackling just barely rose above the din of the rail station. He waved and yelled, "I love you. Au revoir. Remember, I'm only going to New York, not home to Mars. I *will* be back . . . soon as I can."

Al, sitting across from Billy in the opposite seat, remained silent, expressionless, never taking his eyes off Charlotte, even as the train shuddered into motion and slipped away from the platform.

Understanding too well what each man was saying, she whispered, "Goodbye."

CHAPTER 22

THE DOCTOR IS OUT

"My friend Billy is pretty messed up again, Doc. Anything you can suggest?"

"Seeing your friend this way must be very difficult for you, Alfred. You told me he's been an addict for as long as you've known him. That would be close to thirty years? I can make a call to a friend of mine who is a specialist in that area. It's going to be up to Billy though, to follow through with appointments and prescriptions."

"Thanks, Doc. Right now anything is worth trying. I think he's on the way out, fast. Actually, I don't know how he's stayed alive this long. He had 'toast' written on his forehead before he was twenty-five."

"My friend is highly regarded, Alfred. Maybe he can help Billy." Doctor Davidson looked down at his notebook. "Now, where have you gone with what we talked about last time? Your relationship with Kathleen; have you talked with her about your feelings?"

Al reversed his crossed legs, rearranged pillows, and scratched Godzilla's chin. "Not really. I tried the other night, but you know what her hours are like. Mine are nutty too. She's gone before I get up in the morning, and when I get home, *she's* asleep."

"What about when she gets home from work, Alfred? That would be around late afternoon? I'm assuming you don't go to your gig until later in the evening. Don't you two have dinner together at least some of the time?"

"I've been real busy lately, Doc. I'm gone usually every day by noon, even earlier if I play golf." Al braced himself to be grilled about that.

"Alfred, you don't rehearse every day, actually from what you'd said, not often at all. And golf? Isn't that quite expensive by the way?"

Doctor Davidson had never yet appeared angry with him, and Al assumed he'd hide it if he was. But right now his voice had an unusual edge.

"Hey, Doc, golf is usually free for me. Customers at Losers' and other places I've worked are always taking me to their private clubs. Okay, man, I know where this is going. It's not about golf, or what I'm doing, but why I feel the need to stay away so much, right? It's the honesty thing. Come on, Doc, confrontation is not my thing. I friggin' hate it. I don't want to hurt her. Did I say I loved her? I really do care about her, but I'm not sure how to define it. It hasn't been that long after all."

"Alfred, have you considered that your silence *and* your distancing yourself could be hurtful to her?"

"Well, I suppose, yeah," said Al.

"Do you think she deserves to be aware of your feelings? Is it fair *not* to share that with her?"

"I know she'll be upset, Doc. She already is for that matter. I'm not sure what'll happen when I get into it. If only I could just disappear into the night. That's what I'd do if I could. Does that make me a coward?"

"Alfred, of what might you be afraid?"

"I don't know, Doc, maybe the finality of the situation?"

"What situation, Alfred?"

"If I tell her how I feel, she'll ask me to leave, to get out. I know she will. I don't know where I'd go. Money isn't exactly pouring in right now."

This is fucked up; this isn't what I'm here for. This is embarrassing.

"So, Alfred, you're afraid of being on your own; of not having a roof over your head?"

"Easy for *you* to say," Al shot back. "You've got shitloads of money coming in from schmucks like me."

"I'm sorry," said the doctor. "I phrased that question poorly. Is there something you're avoiding? Could it be your feelings about ending the relationship as opposed to the details of relocating?"

What is he getting at? What does it fucking matter? I was as well-off as him, when I had Nora.

Al leaned forward, entwining his fingers as if in angry prayer. "What if that *is* all I'm afraid of? A simple matter of economics? Does everything have to have some goddamn hidden meaning? I thought you weren't a Freudian, Doc. Am I supposed to start talking about my bloody *parents* now, for Christ's sake?"

"Would you like to talk about them, Alfred?" The doctor's voice was a calm contrast to Al's, as he spoke with his eyes closed, in the exasperating almost-asleep mode he sometimes drifted into.

Al was normally annoyed at the doctor's habit of sleep-talking during sessions, but this moment particularly incensed him.

We'll just see if his eyes stay closed now . . .

"Yeah, my mother never wanted me, and my dad was a child abuser! Yeah, a perverted parent if there ever was one."

With eyes now wide open, the doctor said, "He abused you? Can you be specific?"

"Come on, Doc, lighten up. I'm kidding. Can't you tell by now?"

I wonder if meanness and unfaithfulness to your wife count as child abuse on your kids.

"No, Alfred, I can't always distinguish your serious side from your joker side. You are extremely good at camouflaging your discomfort with humor. Sometimes I wonder if even *you* know the difference."

The doctor leafed through his notebook. "Your father was always making a joke out of everything, right? You also said . . . yes, here it is: that it made you feel like you didn't really know him?"

Al smiled and said, "He had to make everyone laugh. He needed it I guess. There was a dark side to him, like I've mentioned, and his funny-man routine must have been some kind of compensation? I don't know. As he got older the jokes got pretty sad, and mostly they were just the same old ones he'd been telling for years, but told like he'd just made them up. Some of the time, when I was little, I have to admit I thought he was pretty cool because everyone he worked with, or in stores and stuff, thought he was so funny. I wanted to be just like him. Huh, I guess in a lotta ways I got my wish, right, Doc?"

"You mean because you joke a lot, Alfred, or because of your infidelities?"

"Let's make a list, Doc. Let's not. My dad had lots of different jobs in his life. Mostly I remember him doing sales. I think he hated it, but his humor helped him to be decent at it. A lot of jobs he quit because he couldn't stand being told what to do by someone he didn't respect, or being criticized over anything. He was in the army during World War Two, and believe me, it was tough on him being in the military. Orders, and Fred Waters? Not a good mix, Doc. He was in the Normandy invasion. Never talked much about that though. I did get the impression it was a source of a lot of his anger. Sometimes he'd drink a lot and get going about things that didn't make a lot of sense to me as a kid; like how he was *dead*, even though he survived?"

"I have seen many cases of postwar trauma, Alfred. It can be a devastating affliction."

"Yeah, Doc, I've known a few Nam vets, and some of them are really messed up. Anyway, back to my dad. He was a self-taught musician, piano mostly, but he could play almost anything. He was my first trumpet teacher, but it only took me a few months to get better than him on it. But you know, even when I got to where I was playing professionally, something *he* never did, I felt inferior somehow. Funny, he could always bring me down with one tiny criticism. The first time I tried to show him a song I tried to write, he laughed and said it was just something I'd heard on the radio, nothing but a rip-off. 'Learn how to play what the real composers have written,' he said more than once. Son of a bitch did the same kind of thing to my mother her whole life."

"Is your mother still living, Alfred?"

"Yeah, in fact I just felt her over my shoulder, disapproving of all this."

A sudden oppressive shame enveloped Al. The words had come from a place he hadn't visited for a long time. He wasn't sure why it troubled him so much to talk about this. Was he betraying his deceased father?

How is this supposed to help me? So far, every visit, I feel worse than before I came. This is worse than jamming with a drummer who slows down. This is worse than sex.

Al continued. "My father was unfaithful to my mother for most of their marriage."

He looked for a response, but the doctor said nothing, and his eyes were closed again. This was part of the routine. Once in a while Al suspected the doctor actually dozed off, but if he tried to trick him by asking a question, he'd always respond, often with eyes still shut.

He must be relishing this: me saying something heavy about my father. I bet this shit makes his day. Why haven't I told him more about Nora? Christ, what would he think if I told him about Vickie? Damn, I have to, and soon, or something in me is fucking going to explode.

"Yeah, my dad had a steady stream of affairs. Mostly out of town, but some right in our neighborhood. I guess my mother knew all about it, but learned to *accept* it. It was my sister, Anne, who told me all this. I guess because some husband of one of Dad's affairs was on the warpath, they were worried the guy might come to our house or something, so they had a talk with her one night when she was eighteen. Gee, is that the legal age for learning your dad is an asshole? It kind of hurt that my parents didn't include me in that talk with Anne. I was sixteen, old enough to be treated like an adult. She told me about it 'cause there was no one else she could talk to. And there was something else to it, something really creepy. I could see it in her eyes, like a combination of sadness and fear. She did say it was weird how our dad actually cried after the talk, but our mother didn't. Now there's a role reversal if ever there was one, huh? Man, like seeing Groucho play the harp, while Harpo rattles off puns? But she wouldn't say any more about it, except for how our dad was the philanderer king of Canada. Ironically, it was just a week or so before she died in that car accident.

"My mother once did say some stuff about him to me. I remember her saying he was 'oversexed'. Gee, do you suppose that could be a genetic trait, Doc? I think my mother worried it might be. Hell, as far as she was concerned, I think 'over-sexed' could have meant just wanting it *at all.*

"As you've heard already, I've hardly been faithful to anyone for long. A few years ago . . . well, *quite* a few, I had sex with five different women in a seven-day span. That's once at home and four *trysts.* Whatever. Not in Wilt Chamberlain's league. What was his claim, twenty thousand women? Amazing. But I did pretty good none-the-less. Too bad there isn't an Olympic event for that, huh? Hey, I *do* know that's a bad thing. You must be used to my shtick by now.

"Funny thing though, the one at home, sex with my wife I mean, at the end of that crazy week was probably the best it had been for a long time. Maybe I was so worn out I was too numb to let it be bad. Speaking of worn out though, that'll never happen again. Just don't have the drive to chase after that anymore. Not sure if it's more mental than physical. I am getting kinda long in the tooth now. Ha, that's a hoot. That's what my dad used to call old people.

"But you know, it wasn't really about sex, not the physical part most of the time, as much as it was a quest for being wanted, a need to prove over and over that I was desirable. I guess I've been kind of addicted to that. Like anyone, more than most I suppose, I hate rejection. A lotta times, especially when I was young, I'd try to avoid it by seeking out women who were flawed in some way, usually emotionally; but sometimes even physically, like maybe overweight, or not so good-looking and stuff. Was almost guaranteed success because I became an expert at the hunt. I figure the old expression 'wolf' fit me pretty good, Doc. Like one of those, I preyed on the weak or wounded. Guess it's better now. Can't worry about rejection if you don't try, right?"

Al settled back into the couch and sighed, feeling satisfied with his frank self-assessment. After a brief pause he asked, "Doc, does it sound like I'm proud of being a scumbag?"

There was still no response. Al looked at the doctor and decided to wait. It did appear he was sleeping. Was this the biggest irony yet? Finally, you spill your guts out about some real deep shit, and he says . . . nothing?

Doctor Davidson remained in the same position, eyes still closed. Al decided to wait it out.

What if I don't say a word for a few minutes? I want to know.

He couldn't stand it any longer. In a low voice Al said, "Last night I had sex with a chicken, and then I ate it alive, and then the couch blew up."

Still . . . no response.

How long is long enough?

The next few seconds felt like a thousand—ending mercifully when the clock sounded the hour. The doctor's eyes opened before the end of the second chime and he said, "Alfred, I have to tell you I am appreciative of how much you've told me today. It took courage for you to take this risk, and I thank you. Unfortunately, our time is up for today. Might I ask that you continue with some of these thoughts next time?"

Damn, still don't know how much he was awake for. Would have been a great time to bring up Vickie. That's more nuts than the chicken story.

Wonder what he'd think if I told him I've killed someone . . .

CHAPTER 23

MICHELLE AND GEORGE

*A*l stretched his arms behind, then in front, as he hustled up Doctor Davidson's front walkway. As he reached out to hit the buzzer, the door opened.

"Good morning, Alfred. I hope I didn't startle you, but I saw you coming," said the doctor as he moved aside to let Al through into the session room. "You must be feeling a little disoriented at this early hour. Please, let me get you a coffee."

"It's okay, Doc, I can handle it," said Al, feigning a yawn which turned into a real one. "And 'disoriented' isn't a strong enough word. 'Brain dead' might be closer. Sorry if I'm a couple of minutes late."

Man, definitely too early for a night person.

When Al had asked for the appointment change, he'd been obliged to take this time slot or miss for the week.

♪♪♪

Al sipped his coffee while the doctor shuffled through his notebook. He couldn't help but wonder if this morning session would make it easier for the shrink to stay awake. For himself, Al figured it might be *his* turn to snooze.

"Doc, last time you said you wanted me to continue on with where I left off."

"Yes, Alfred, that would be excellent."

"Well, I do have to say I was kind of pissed off actually, at the last part of the session."

"What caused you to be upset, Alfred?"

"Well, I said some serious things, and then some ridiculous things when I suspected you were dozing off while I was talking."

"Alfred, do you mean about the chicken you had sex with and then ate? Well, I suppose if you *devoured* all your lovers after sex, you'd certainly accomplish your goal of avoiding commitment. Oh, and did you buy a new couch yet? I hear there's a sale on explosion-proof furniture at Walmart."

Al laughed and said, "Doc, I think *you* need a shrink; no, *definitely.*"

"I apologize for what you perceived as my inattention, Alfred. Perhaps early on I should have explained certain of my mannerisms or quirks. I realize clients may misinterpret some of them. One is that I do tend to close my eyes when I'm listening. It aids in concentration, but I can see how it might be misconstrued. Thank you for bringing it up. In some ways that could be a good thing since you were comfortable enough to confront me about it today. What do you think your reaction may have been if this had happened during our first session?"

"Good point, Doc. Honestly? I'd likely have just said 'fuck you' and headed for the door."

"Hmm, just what I thought. So we have made progress. Well then, not to be flippant, but may we back up just a bit, for clarity? I'd like to make sure I have your relationships in proper sequence in my notes. There have been, well, quite a few."

"I can't blame you, Doc. Can't keep 'em straight myself sometimes."

"Okay now, let's see: you're currently living with Kathleen, only for about two months? Where and when did you meet her?"

"Well, Doc, it was just this year in the late spring, I guess. I put in another of my ads in the Bargain Hunter. Out of the bunch, she was the best."

"Interesting how you put that, Alfred. Would you go so far as to describe this as almost a form of *audition*?"

"Well," said Al, "what would you call it?"

"So I take it Kathleen struck your fancy right away?"

"Yeah, that's it, Doc, 'struck my fancy'. Good way to put it. Now she's kind of 'striking out' I guess."

"Puns aside, could you describe your feelings for her, Alfred?"

"You know, Doc, I'm not sure how to describe it. She's smart and educated and funny. Gets all my jokes *and* makes a bunch of her own, a real punster, as bad as me. Hey, she and I figured out something about puns. You know how most people don't actually laugh at a pun, but groan or make a comment about them being 'bad'? We came up with the idea that puns aren't actually supposed to be 'funny'. They're supposed to be 'fun'. Groan or laugh, any reaction is a success. Cool concept, huh?

"She's not a knockout, you know, in the traditional sense; more what you'd maybe call a 'handsome woman'? I know that sometimes means not so good-looking, but in her case it means what it's supposed to. Tall and nicely built, kind of like Sigourney Weaver almost? Not someone you'd fall out of your chair over, but still pretty darned attractive. Great eyes, warm and dark, and they always tell exactly what she's feeling. When we first met, we'd talk and talk and talk, about most everything. And we were comfortable with silence too. We could sit and read in the same room and enjoy each other without a word. But lately that's not so true. There's silence, sure, but not comfortable at all. There's tension in it now. My fault, I know. Guess she's finally caught on to what a jerk I really am."

"In what way are you a jerk, Alfred?"

"The old story, Doc. I've tried like hell to be a good guy, to not cheat on her, you know? And I was doing pretty well until just a little while ago. Not catting around, not like the old Al. There's been just one really. And uh, another 'thing' that happened, but that's a long story. Can we get off this for now?"

"Alfred, it sounds like Kathleen is a wonderful woman and a good partner for you. You say you were faithful to her 'at first'. What do you think you'd need to do in order *not* to be adulterous, with her or anyone you might be involved with?"

"Well, like I said before, I'm kind of addicted to it I guess. Is that possible?"

"Quite possible, Alfred. There are many kinds of addiction, including emotional ones. There are forms of sexual addiction, but I do not think that describes you. Your needs, or compulsion, seem more of a search for emotional fulfillment or 'connection', something you most likely learned as a coping mechanism when you were quite young."

"Wow, is there a pill for that?"

"No, Alfred. The 'pill' for you will be when we discover what makes you feel this need. Controlling it must come from within, from understanding."

"Suppose so, Doc. So my problems go back to when I was a kid, huh? Do we need a time machine or something? We can't 'fix' the past. So my parents, and how I related to them, are part of why I can't make a proper go of it with a woman now? How the hell do I fix *how* I am, with *who* I am now? Man, this relationship shit is friggin' complicated."

"Of course it is, Alfred. I would suggest all human relationships are complicated to some extent: man and woman, parent and child, friendships; never easy. Have you ever experienced anything contrary to that?"

"Not really. Seems like something is always messed up. You know, I think the more you're 'in love' the more complicated it *is*. Is that crazy, Doc?"

"I believe I understand what you're saying, Alfred. If you don't mind, how would you define being 'in love'?"

"Come on, Doc, you know: those crazy feelings so many songs tell about. You're walking on air, flying high, daydreaming about her, heart racing, your breathing feels like you're on top of a mountain, all that wonderful stuff. It becomes the most important thing, maybe the *only* thing in your life you even think about. Being 'crazy' in love is a good way to put it, right?"

"Yes, I suppose it is, Alfred. But, you haven't had these feelings for Kathleen?"

"Actually, I don't think either of us is 'in love', Doc. Maybe we're . . . in *like*. Make sense?"

"Yes it does, Alfred. Do you think being 'in like' is enough?"

"Should be, Doc. Damn it, I wish it was. Being in love has never worked out too good for me has it?"

"From what you've shared with me so far, I'd have to say you haven't had the best of luck with romantic love. But are you truly convinced it can never happen again for you?"

"Likely best if it doesn't, Doc. My love record doesn't have a hit on it. The first time I ever fell was for a girl named Sue, when I was a kid. And that was a disaster. Then, maybe Wendy in New York, but I didn't give that much of a chance at all. After that, Charlotte in Montreal. And man did I mess *that* up. Talk about being a fuckup. Only other time that really counts would have to be Michelle. And she and I were both fuckups I guess."

"Alfred, 'disaster', 'messed up', 'fuckup'. Such negative words to describe what you've said were the greatest loves of your life. We must explore each of these relationships in depth when you are ready. It's not my place to prioritize. Perhaps you could begin where you feel most comfortable?"

"Sue, Wendy, and Charlotte were so long ago, they don't matter, do they? Wouldn't more recent stuff make more sense to talk about?"

"Anything you think and feel makes sense to talk about here, Alfred. You once mentioned someone named Nora, and I detect significance in that name for you. Would you tell me about her?"

Al said nothing.

The doctor said, "Okay, I can tell when you aren't ready to discuss something. We'll get back to her, and Kathleen another time. You've alluded to some problems in your marriage with Michelle, but you've never elaborated.

Is there more you would like to say about her, and that time in your life?"

♪♪♪

"Funny enough, I met Michelle right here in Florida, not far from where I work now, late 1973? Yeah, it had to be that. Billy and I had decided to get out of New York and head south for a while, and we'd only been here for a few weeks.

"She was singing in a small club; I forget the name, and it's long gone. I didn't meet her that way though. She was off early one night and stopped in with some friends to see what was happening in Café Cool where I was working. My band was on break when she came in, and I was at the bar. She and her gang were noisy, laughing and making a real scene. I hear this chick say, 'Hey, Tiffany, you said this is where the action is. Okay, where's the action?' I went over, crouched down behind her chair and said in a deep voice, 'Hello, I'm Action Man, to the rescue.'

"A lot of people don't *get* the wacky side of me right away, but she was different. She said, 'Pull up a chair, Action Man, and tell me about your super powers.' I acted like I couldn't lift the chair and said, 'My powers are more mental than physical.' And she said, 'Too bad, Action Man. If you can't lift a chair, then how do you expect to pick *me* up?' I said, 'I can make love to a woman from across the room . . .' and she came back with, 'So like, you mean with mental powers, or that's how long your dick is?'

"We hit it off right away, even though she was an 'older' woman; twenty-nine she was. That's such a hoot. I was only twenty-three, and twenty-nine sounded so friggin' old. Man, pushing *thirty*. Wow, seems like yesterday, and yet I could have a kid that age now. Yikes. Anyway, five minutes after hearing how old she was, I forgot all about it. Man, she was such a *doll*.

"We only gabbed for a few minutes 'cause I had to go back and play, and she and her friends left. But on the way out, she stuck a folded paper in the bell of my sax and blew me a kiss. Her note invited me to meet her the next day at a rehearsal she was going to be at.

"So of course I went. I snuck in and sat in the back so she wouldn't notice me and be distracted. Some musicians are really sensitive about being listened to when they're working on new stuff. I know I am. I fell in love with her after five notes. What a singer: a combination of Eydie Gormé, Barbra Streisand, and Ella Fitzgerald. Not many vocalists weave all the words, notes, and emotions of a song together into a performance the way she did. And this was in rehearsal; no audience. With a crowd, she was spellbinding. Had 'em in the palm of her hand from start to finish of every song and every set. Me too, Doc, mesmerized, every time.

"She spotted me when the band took a break, and she came over to me right away to ask what I'd thought. I told her it wasn't bad for a first take. With a little work, it might fly. She laughed so hard she spit coffee on my shirt. Guess she wasn't used to my kind of sarcasm, or someone not just saying how great she was. She asked about the arrangement, and if I thought it was the right style for the song. I told her it was a little fast, and how she'd coax more meaning out of the lyrics if they took a little edge off it. I was bracing myself in case she wasn't serious about asking for advice, like maybe she just wanted me to say it was wonderful? Well, anyway, it turned out she agreed totally and had already argued with the bandleader about the same thing. She went to him and told him what I had said.

"Ooh boy, it might have made her like me and respect my honesty, but that guy wasn't too thrilled, especially since he recognized me and had heard of some of my New York 'issues'; obviously believed the negative side of my reputation. He came over and asked me to leave, 'cause I was a distraction to the band and my opinions weren't welcome. If Michelle wasn't standing right next to him, I might have really got into it, Doc. I just said that I understood, and I left, but not before I made a date with Michelle for later. It worked out great, because instead of her seeing what I did as 'backing down', she was impressed that I hadn't gotten angry. Guess she had asked about me and knew my reputation for dealing with disputes with something less than tact. I guess she appreciated that I handled the situation calmly, out of respect for her."

Doctor Davidson interjected, "I think you're right about that, Alfred. She saw a softer side of you, contrary to what she might have heard. And from what *I've* seen, the stories about you were not so much factual, but perhaps legendary to the point of hyperbole, true?"

"Well, yeah, pretty much true, if that means, 'reports of my deadly temper were greatly exaggerated'. I've been in a few, um, altercations in my time, but never usually over stuff to do with me; more often it's because somebody else needed some backup? Whatever, I don't really know why she went for me, Doc. Every guy on the strip was crazy for her. Guess I seemed different somehow."

"Alfred," said the doctor, "I would assume most people would consider you an attractive man. Do you not see that? Or could that be a touch of false modesty?"

"Yeah, yeah, a real pretty boy I am. Hey, are you making a pass at me, Doc?"

"You're not my type, Alfred; maybe with one more X chromosome."

"Glad to hear it, Doc. Speaking of sex, I remember when Michelle and I went to my place and we were going to, you know, get it on for the first time. I went to the bathroom to wash 'the boys', if you get my drift. She was so impressed with that. Made her think I was cool, 'cause most guys she'd known wouldn't usually have bothered. Me, I've always been sensitive about smell. I know how gross it is if the woman isn't clean. So I wanted to be, you know, not offensive.

"Anyway, it was quite a night. Man, feels weird to be talking to you about this, but well, she was really good at oral sex, and sort of made me learn to do it back. I've never really liked that too much; doing it I mean. But she had to have it; could rarely get off any other way. I guess in the long run I got good at it, but I resented it, maybe 'cause it was like, required? Like a friggin' rule or something."

"Alfred," said the doctor, "if it occurs to you, say it. Nothing is going to offend, embarrass, or shock me, if that's what you're concerned about."

"Okay, Doc, but it does feel kind of odd talking about sexual details with a man, even if you are a professional. I'll do my best to just let it all hang out. And please don't take *that* the wrong way."

"Not a chance, Alfred. A figurative reference, I'm sure."

"Okay . . . well, after a few weeks we ended up on the road together in a show band. I had dumped my own band and gig, which Billy took over. He was fairly healthy at that time, and he sure didn't want to be in a group doing the commercial razzmatazz stuff Michelle and I were going to be doing. He and I had been together quite a while, and it seemed like time for a change anyway.

"This new band was an established longtime group, and the leader was opposed to having couples in the same band. Found out later how right he was, but at the time we just thought he was an asshole. We had so much fun, Doc. We had nothing, but we had everything. Reminds me of that Wayne Newton song, 'The Hungry Years', where the two people were happiest when they were poor and struggling.

"Our first Christmas together, we were in a long run at an old Atlantic City hotel; this was the pre-gambling, pre-resurrection Atlantic City. I went out on Christmas Eve to buy her a gift, with the last nineteen dollars I had to my name. In the window of a little shop I saw a watch I knew she'd love, 'cause it had Mickey and Minnie Mouse holding hands; that was who we used to say we were, Mickey and Minnie. So I went in, and it was twenty-two dollars. I had my nineteen bucks out and was digging for change, thinking about actually asking someone for a handout, and the store clerk who had watched me count my money said, 'This is for someone special, *isn't* it . . . ?' I said, 'It sure is'. She said, 'Well, the price just went on *special*, only nineteen dollars.'

"When I got home to our hotel room I couldn't wait to give it to Michelle. And she had something for me too. She'd bought one of those cheap plastic toy organs for me, 'cause I was always bitching that I had nothing to arrange music with, you know, trying different chord progressions and voicings and stuff; maybe even finally get around to writing some original tunes. The thing was ugly and sounded like a dying harmonica, but to me it was a Steinway concert grand. I said 'I love you Minnie', and she said, 'You too, Mickey'. Neither of us had ever had a better Christmas. Even way later, when Michelle was doing well in her career she always wore that watch, even with fancy gowns and all. She didn't care what people might have thought.

"For a couple of years or so we travelled all over: northern and southeastern states, Florida, the Midwest, then finally, Vegas. We decided to stay there and get rich. Yeah, but it didn't *quite* work out."

"What didn't work out, Alfred, the relationship or the career move?"

"Well, I meant the move, and the getting rich part; but the relationship too, because of the money and so forth. We got married there, one of those little chapel deals, and we were pretty happy at first, you know, the struggling young couple, 'Mickey and Minnie', us-against-the-world type of thing.

"We got a puppy: George, a little black fuzz ball cross of schnauzer, poodle, and Scottie. He was the perfect dog for us; was born in a motel. No lie, Doc. The little bugger was a yappy pain, but there've been times I thought he was the closest thing to a real friend I ever had. Michelle loved him and all, like *kissy kissy* and *smoochy woochy* and that kind of garbage, but I trained him and looked after him most of the time. He was my little buddy. Maybe I would have been a good father, Doc. You think? Potential was there anyway."

"Alfred, do *you* think you'd be a good father?"

"Don't know, Doc. I'm a good musician mainly because I had some great teachers and some talented guys to work with. You learn a lot about how to play by being in quality company. As far as my parental influences, I don't think my 'teachers' were quite so good."

"It's the toughest job there is, Alfred. I don't care how many books get written, there's really no comprehensive instruction manual for parenthood.

Unfortunately, you're right in thinking that most of our training comes from observing how *we* are raised. If it's done poorly, we have an uphill struggle to be better than what we had. It's far from impossible, but a lot of work. Did you ever consider having children with one of the women you've been with?"

"Never really been in a position to have kids, or to even think about it; but I had George, and I think I was a pretty good 'dad' to him. I don't know how I knew how to train him since I'd never had a dog before. I taught him commands and tricks, like sitting, lying down, and shaking a paw . . . all the standard stuff. He was so bright, he even learned how to obey hand signs. I'd hold up my hand like a traffic cop, and he'd stop on a dime. Hold it the other way around, and he'd come running. A snap of my fingers also meant to come, and he'd do it every time. The funniest thing was to say, 'talk', and he'd try so hard to do it. I swear he was really trying to speak to me, making all these growly bizarre 'whuh, whooww, whua, whuaah whowwww' sounds. Sometimes you'd swear you heard real words coming out."

Al looked at Godzilla lying beside him on the couch and felt a pang of nostalgia. It was uncanny how much the little dog reminded him of George.

"The crazy goofball got himself into trouble once. One of our neighbors had a Doberman named Killer, that he used to keep tied up in front of his apartment. One day this beast got loose, and when I opened my front door to get the paper, George darted out 'cause he'd seen Killer through the window. I shoulda known he was barking and going nuts more than normal, but I just assumed it was at the paperboy or mailman: the usual suspects.

"I spotted Killer trotting across our pool patio and my heart just pounded as I got what George was doing: heading full steam right at the Dobe. Lucky for George he was so fast. Killer never noticed him coming until the little mutt roared up and started jumping at his throat, snapping and growling like a demon. I got out the door and over to them before Killer could even react. He'd kind of fallen back in a silly-looking sitting position, staring down at this yappy fuzzy critter, one-third his size. I grabbed George by the scruff of the neck and yanked him up in the air as fast as I could, away from the Doberman who was quite capable of ripping us both to shreds. Reminded me of La Geule de Loup back in Montreal, except he *would* have killed us. For some reason Killer just walked away as if nothing had happened. Divine intervention, Doc? Or would that be 'canine' intervention?"

"Sounds like you were fortunate, Alfred, to have saved your dog from certain injury or death, and at great risk to yourself. You *were* a good 'father' to George, wouldn't you agree?"

"Sure, Doc; I wonder if my dad would have done that for me? I was so mad at George, I carried him by the neck scruff all the way back to the apartment. I threw him down on the floor too hard. It must have hurt his leg, 'cause he yelped and slunk away behind the couch to hide . . . from *me*, Doc, the one who loved him more than anything. It hurt so much to see him fear me. I sat on the couch and cried. Stupid, right?"

"Alfred, nothing of what you've just told me is stupid. George went after the Doberman out of instinct, with no logic, no rationality, simply animal reaction to a perceived threat, perhaps partially motivated by love and/or loyalty. He may have seen the other dog as a threat to you. All parents are prone to anger for their children's mistakes, and sometimes we demonstrate that anger in unhealthy ways. A child has difficulty in comprehending that we sometimes lose our cool because we care so much. We don't want to hurt them, but in trying to protect them we occasionally have to be tough. They don't really need to have that explained. It's not the logic therein that has to be understood, but the reality that your love is powerful and protective has to be *felt*. And sometimes, yes, it hurts."

"So, Doc, why did I feel so bad, if I saved George because I loved him, and I knew I didn't mean to hurt him? What was making me so sad?"

"Alfred, you were on the right track when you mentioned your father; and wondering if he would do the same for you as you did for George. We need to explore your relationship with him in depth. When you saved George, risking yourself and then hurting him, you touched a nerve regarding your own upbringing. I'm convinced of it. Somewhere, sometime, you lost faith in the very existence of unconditional love, even though with George you demonstrated it exists within you. Why do you think your father wouldn't have done for you, what you did for George?"

"Time for a music history lesson, Doc . . . ?"

"I won't push you, Alfred, but I would certainly like to come back to this issue sometime soon, when you feel ready. Right now, can we get back to Michelle? Interesting that you digressed from her, to George. Is there some reason you'd want to cease talking about her?"

"Could be, Doc, I suppose. There's stuff I haven't shared about her with anyone before."

"You said things with her were okay, at first?"

"The trouble began when Michelle started getting work, and I didn't. There was a real market for good-looking chick singers, while trumpet players were a dime a dozen. I tried singing. Wasn't too bad actually, but I didn't have enough confidence and I guess it showed. She was getting to be known as a rising star, and it felt like I was getting lost in the trail of smoke behind her."

"Are you saying you had difficulty with her success, Alfred?"

"It wasn't so much that she was doing well, and I wasn't. But she began to change, Doc, almost overnight. She began to act like she was some big hotshot star and she treated me like a nobody. If we were out together and met someone she knew, or some fans recognized her and wanted to talk, she'd leave me standing there, not introducing me or even seeming to remember I was there. Once I got so mad I just left, and later she called me rude for that. She just didn't get it. For a while we still had some good times, especially when she wasn't gigging steady. We'd go for trips down to L.A. or San Diego to get away for a couple of days or so, and everything was pretty good . . . even felt like we still had something special going. But even those infrequent moments got less common the more she got written up in the entertainment columns, and got to sing in the bigger lounges, and made bigger paychecks.

"I remember a dream I used to have, Doc, where I was on this gigantic Las Vegas stage, naked in front of thousands of people. They all look like kids from my high school; even my sister, Anne, is there. I'm trying to sing, but nothing comes out and everyone starts laughing. I pretend to be doing it on purpose and I laugh too, like it was all part of the act. And then out of nowhere I have this gun at my head, like I'm going to kill myself in front of them all. Then, Michelle is standing next to me and I think she's there to save me, but then she starts singing and the audience cheers as her finger joins mine on the trigger. I remember feeling more embarrassed than should be possible. And you know, I could never tell whether that embarrassment was from dying in front of those people . . . or because I was naked."

"Alfred, it's believed that anxiety dreams can often reveal much about our fears and worries in the real world. What do you think that dream was telling you?"

"Well, a lot of it is pretty clear, Doc. The naked-in-front-of-a-crowd part is real common I guess. Insecurity is a wonderful thing, huh? And Michelle's part had to be about 'helping' with my professional demise, and the feelings I had about her success and how she didn't really care anymore about me."

"As good an analysis as anyone's I suppose, Alfred. There are certainly no exact interpretations of any dream, only conjecture. Yes, anxiety and insecurity are signature elements in what you describe, but what do you think about the idea of suicide in front of the high school crowd? Why do you think those people would be the witnesses your subconscious chose?"

"Doc, something about the dream just struck me as I've been going over it in my head. All the kids are couples, and holding hands, and even kissing each other and stuff. All except Anne. She's alone . . ."

CHAPTER 24

FIVE - SOUTH TOWER [7]

*O*utside room 510, Officer Poole looked at his watch again.

What the hell is that guy doing in there? Is he the most thorough custodial engineer in the world? I really should see what he's up to.

Captain Rosetti said he might be stopping by tonight. That'd be good, although I've heard he can be anal sometimes. Maybe I better double-check on this cleaning guy. What if Rosetti comes here and sees the guy and it turns out I screwed up? Christ, what's next for me, a suspension? My dad would shoot me. He's already pissed off about this assignment and why it happened.

He knows what it's like to actually shoot someone too. I wish he'd talk about it. They say he was in the right, that the guy he fired on flashed a piece. Those rumors sure hurt him bad though, the ones that say there really was no weapon found on the dead guy . . . that they planted one to save Dad and the department from all that bad press. Makes me wonder though, what I'd do if I ever had to make that decision to shoot or not.

Poole looked at the door to 510 and decided to get up and determine just what was going on in there. Whether he would ever quit this job, or be fired and have the chance to be a professional musician, were secondary to the immediate matter of his cop responsibilities. Like it or not, he had to be concerned with *now*.

As he rose, he dropped the *Guitar Player* magazine onto the chair and a page flipped open which he hadn't seen yet.

Whoa, a Lenny Breau fingering diagram. Cool . . . gotta dig on this.

CHAPTER 25

GO WEST OLD MAN

*A*l sipped at the dregs of his coffee; it was lukewarm, almost cold. But he didn't let on, not wishing to risk the implication that the doctor was a negligent host.

"It was a tough time, Doc. I couldn't find work, while Michelle was so busy she was turning it down. The musicians' union was really strict about working steady until after you'd been there long enough and transferred into the local and all. On top of that, nobody I sat in with seemed ready to accept a new guy; the town was pretty closed then. Only the old-boys-club would work with each other. So I had an idea, but I didn't tell Michelle."

"Let me guess, Alfred. You called Billy?"

"Wow, Doc, you *are* getting to know me. Yeah, that's exactly what I did, and after a lot of convincing, he hopped a bus to Vegas. I sprung it on Michelle the day he was to arrive. She wasn't thrilled. All she seemed concerned about was where he would stay. She made it real clear it couldn't be our place."

"Was that where you had planned he would stay?"

"Yeah, Doc, I guess it wasn't too cool of me, but I was pretty certain she'd say no. I put her on the spot for sure, and she said he could stay for maybe a few days or a week, but then he'd have to get his own digs. I said that was cool, but I figured we could stretch it out."

"So how did it go when Billy arrived?"

"Well, not so hot. He was in pretty bad shape again. Without me around he's always tended to get into all kinds of shit. This time was no exception, but I figured the weather might help. Anyway, we went around to a ton of places, and finally we found a club in North Las Vegas, which by the way, is a separate town, Doc. Geography trivia, no charge. Anyway, they were willing to book Billy and me as a jazz duo for an open-ended gig. Pay was crap since it was non-union, but we took the chance, and didn't use our real names. It went okay for a couple of weeks; the job did. But at home, not so cool."

"So I take it, Alfred, you went past Michelle's deadline?"

"Yeah, Doc, things got pretty tense. Billy wasn't the world's most desirable houseguest at the best of times; not the neat type, shall we say. One night we came home after work and Michelle was there with some people she'd invited from her gig: two of the musicians and a couple of customers. All guys too, Doc, and I wasn't too cool with that. Billy and I had both been drinking pretty heavy, and boy, was that a recipe for trouble. First thing Billy does is trip on one guy's foot and go ass over tea kettle. When Michelle and her guests laughed, I could see it was *at* him, not with him, and it maybe even hadn't been an accident. I lost it, big time. I told them all to get the fuck out.

"Michelle came back at me like Rocky Balboa off the ropes. She screamed how it was her apartment, since she paid the rent, and I couldn't order anybody out. Then she said to those guys they'd be better off going some-where that didn't stink of booze and failure, and she was going with them. She turned to me as they went out and snarled at me that when she got home Billy had to be gone."

"And she did go with them, Alfred? Were you uncomfortable with that?"

"Uncomfortable doesn't describe it, Doc. I was so mad it's amazing I didn't hurt someone bad right then. But somehow I kept my cool, at least for a while. I helped Billy pack up his stuff and we went right out and got him a room at a motel-apartment downtown. I crashed there on the couch instead of going home."

"Michelle must have been worried. Did you call her?"

"No, I went home the next morning; was nearly noon and guess what? She was just getting in too. Neither of us said a word the whole day. She didn't give a damn where I'd been, and I pretended not to care where she was all that time. There was a look in her eyes that told me more than I wanted to know."

"Do you think she had been unfaithful?"

"Yeah, and it wasn't the first time, just the first time she didn't seem to give a damn if I knew."

"And had you been faithful to Michelle up till then?"

"Well, that's the damnedest thing of all; I actually *had* been. Sure, I'd been tempted here and there when I'd been drinking, but I always fought off the urge. There's some irony, huh, Doc?"

"Irony, Alfred? Perhaps so, in that it shows you indeed *can* be faithful, while you seem to be convinced otherwise. Have there been other times you've managed not to stray while in a relationship?"

"Yes and no. Well, more no than yes, I suppose. And don't try to tell me it's because after Michelle I couldn't trust anyone, so I might as well be bad. That'd be too easy, right? Make it her fault I'm a jerk?"

"Alfred, we've seen that your history has been filled with loss of trust in those whom you should most believe in. I wouldn't *blame* Michelle for how you have dealt with your issues of infidelity, nor would I seek to blame anyone, especially yourself. We are seeking answers, yes, to why you appear to have abandoned hope of a happy relationship. But we are not looking for someone to 'pin the rap on', if I may be so direct."

"So, Doc, how do I know if it could have worked out with Michelle if she hadn't turned on me? Maybe after a while I would have cheated on her anyway."

"We *don't* know, Alfred. What we have discovered is that you know what 'wrong' is when you do it, and you feel bad as a result. If you were a sociopath, that wouldn't be true, and you'd have little hope of changing. Alfred, you *can* find a way to have a healthy relationship, and find happiness in other areas of your life too. I truly believe that."

"Well, Doc, you're the pro. I hope you're right."

"So, please tell me, Alfred, what happened to Billy after this incident with Michelle?"

"We lost our gig right after that, and nothing else seemed to be on the horizon, so he used his last few bucks, and a few of mine, and headed back to New York. It was tempting to go with him, man. But I thought maybe I could still make it in Vegas."

"And how did things go for you?"

"It wasn't a good time for me to be trying to make it, anywhere. I'd lost my self-confidence. I don't know how much of that had to do with Michelle's messing around. We stayed together, but the tension was like constantly living in the last minute of a tied hockey game, and we'd both pulled our goalies.

"Once I commented on the way she was singing a tune she was working on at home. She was phrasing it wrong, so I thought anyway. She snapped at me, 'Lots better musicians than *you* think my phrasing is just fine.' I laughed at her, but it hurt real bad; I didn't know till that moment I'd stopped being her music 'hero.'"

"You felt she'd lost respect for you, Alfred?"

"Yeah, but the kicker was that I knew how she'd got some of her breaks; yeah, not just with her musical talents, Doc. She was screwing her way into some of those gigs . . . and she lost respect for *me?* At least I never did that. I may have become a musical whore by playing show band schlock music. But hell, she did that too. She could have been a great jazz singer, but all she wanted was money and publicity. She was a double whore."

"So, Alfred, when she said, 'lots better musicians than you', it must have bothered you particularly harshly, since you felt you had lowered your standards just to fit in with her aspirations in the first place. And then she berated your very talent. How did that make you feel?"

"I let her think it didn't bother me, Doc. I couldn't hit her, not a woman. That just isn't right, no matter how much you want to. I went out to the car and opened the door; not sure where I thought I was going. Then it hit me, I was already right where I was meant to be: nowhere. I slammed the door shut, then opened it and slammed it again; then again, over and over until I couldn't move my friggin' arms anymore. Then I turned and kicked it so hard I left a big dent. Lost my balance and fell on my ass, and just sat there up against the door, gulping air. A dust cloud settled over me like a dry fog, sticking to my sweat. I remember wishing it was poison gas."

CHAPTER 26

HAVEN'T THE VEGAS

*A*l scratched Godzilla's fuzzy head and smiled as the little dog closed his eyes in ecstasy.

Doctor Davidson asked, "After Billy went back east, what happened with you and Michelle?"

"We decided to try to stay together, but with a special understanding that we never discussed what we did on our own, like seeing other people. In spite of the tension we even worked together a bit here and there. We did some show gigs with a comedian, and played some fairly important lounges where the money was decent. That helped with some of the stress at home.

"I was playing saxophone more and more, and it was good for me, although it took some time before I felt okay working with Vegas guys who were top pros. Eventually I started to get known as a tenor player who could cut most gigs."

"Excuse my naiveté," said the doctor, "but how much difference is there in the techniques of brass and woodwinds?"

"Well, with brass, you're making the sound happen with your lips buzzing into a cup-shaped mouthpiece, all from control and strength of a whole bunch of small muscles around the mouth. With a sax, you make a reed do the vibrating, with most of the control coming from your lower lip. Although most of the same muscles you use for the brass get involved, but with emphasis on different ones."

"Fascinating, Alfred. I have to admit, I've never seriously thought about the technical aspects of these wonderful instruments. Which would you say is more difficult?"

Al laughed and said, "The one you don't practice as much. Okay seriously, if you want my totally honest opinion, it would be that brass is harder. Your lip can change from day to day, and you have to practice all the time. With a reed, you sort of know what you got every time, and it's up to your muscles to make it sound. Sure, reeds can be finicky too, but not as bad as relying on your lip tissue to respond every time. Bad reed? Grab a new one. But you can't go buy a new lip. I think the stress on a brass player is higher than any reed man. Endurance is also tougher with brass. You wear out on trumpet, and man, the notes can just plain disappear. With a reed you can play way longer, and even though you might have to cheat a bit with where your lip goes on the reed, or using too much 'bite', you can still get a sound.

"There's a lot of physical stress with trumpet that I don't feel with the sax. I mean you have to work so much to get range and endurance and tone. Not that it's a piece of cake with reeds, but those skills are definitely easier to acquire, with less work anyway. Trumpet players have this thing they call 'trumpet fever': going after a projecting, room-filling sound that's impossible to describe. When you hear it from a great player you know that's it, and then you spend years, maybe your whole life trying to get it. Remember that Kirk Douglas movie, *Young Man with a Horn* where he just can't get that one note he's after, and it drives him nuts, and he smashes his horn all to bits on a chair? He had the *fever*, and it almost killed him. Man, with the pressure your airway system goes through when you play high and loud, it can be dangerous. I actually once saw a guy blow a vein in his head that way."

Al set his lips and delivered a high, piercing buzz as if playing a trumpet. Godzilla's ears shot upward and he jumped to the floor, and then turned and stared at Al with his head cocked to one side.

"Yes, I see," said the doctor. "Just doing that made your face turn a bit red. The effort you describe is quite intense."

Al said, "Tell me about it. Trumpets and trombones, they're a lot more physically demanding than reeds. If you lay off practicing, you lose everything so fast. With sax it doesn't matter near as much. I can take off a week and still play about the same as if I'd never stopped. If I'd tried that when trumpet was my main axe, I'd have been in serious trouble; couldn't have played half a set without my lip crapping out totally. As I got older it seemed like a good excuse anyway."

Godzilla put his chin on the edge of the couch, looking up at Al as if waiting for assurance there'd be no more disturbing noises. Al patted the dog's head and coaxed him back up on the couch and onto his lap. He said, "Sorry, little mutt. Won't do it again."

Doctor Davidson smiled at the interchange between Al and Godzilla and then asked, "So do you only play the saxophone now?"

"I did pick up the trumpet now and again, like at my dad's funeral. But a few months ago I laid *it* to rest. In the past, when I'd had a break from trumpet for a while, it might take me a few days, but the chops would come back enough to play not too bad. The old lip would never hold up if I tried it at the gig though. I'd have to work out for a couple of weeks to try that; but like I said, that part of me is dead and gone. No more trumpet for me."

"Thanks for another music lesson, Alfred. Can you tell me what happened a few months ago to make you stop playing the trumpet altogether?"

"Actually, Doc, could we get to that another time?"

"Certainly, Alfred. Shall we get back to Michelle?"

"Sorry, Doc. I do that, don't I . . . get going about stuff that doesn't matter when I should be talking about important things?"

"Alfred, remember we don't use the word 'should' here. Anything you feel like saying is important, or it wouldn't have occurred to you. Sometime soon I'd love to hear more details of such a vital part of your life, as music certainly is, and about what made you quit the trumpet. But right now I'd like to know more about Michelle and your marriage 'arrangement', and how that may have worked out."

"Sure, Doc. I might have to start charging you for *my* time if I keep teaching you all this stuff. Okay, so things had been kind of in limbo for a few months. Yeah, we thought of it as an 'open marriage', but what a stupid expression, huh? I think all it does is *close* a marriage.

"Once, I met this Mexican girl in a bar and made a date with her, and I told Michelle about it. Well, of all the crazy things, she wished me well on my way out, and asked me all about it when I got home. Bizarre, right? The girl spoke very little English, and our date consisted of us basically going for a drive, having sex in the car, and then taking her home. At her house she wanted me to come in and meet her parents and her little boy, like now I was her boyfriend? I made excuses and took off as fast as I could. Damn, it was so sad. I've been a rat lots of times I guess, and I usually do feel bad about it, but this time was worse somehow. I pulled over a few blocks away and sat there shaking. I was so depressed; felt like a dump truck had parked on my chest."

As the doctor wrote in his notebook, Al said, "The Mexican girl called me a couple of times from work. She was a maid at the MGM Grand and she could see my apartment from the top floors. Hey, she was a nice person, and not bad looking, Doc. But how can you have a relationship with someone you can hardly have a conversation with? She stopped trying, and the only time I thought of her again was when they had the big fire there. Never knew if she was hurt or not."

"Alfred," said the doctor, "I can't ever recall seeing an instance where this concept of open marriage worked. It is fraught with complication."

"Damn straight, Doc, but in our case I wasn't as good at it as Michelle seemed to be. One time I picked up the phone, and she was on the extension gabbing with a friend, describing a blow job she gave a guy the night before. It was bad enough hearing how matter-of-fact she was about it. But worse, I knew the guy. Damn it, man, I'd been golfing with him a couple of days before as his guest. Now think about it, the dirt bag takes me golfing, then has sex with my wife, and guess what? He wants to go golfing again two days later, like nothing is out of the ordinary. Huh, and I *did* . . . golf with him, I mean. Was he like, the most amoral asshole in the world? Or was I?"

"Al," said the doctor, "as for you, I wonder if it was less a question of morality, than one of self-respect?"

"What the hell, Doc, I've never seemed to have a shitload of either. Hey, didn't you tell me you were writing a new book? Bet I'll be in it, right?"

"Well, if I made it into a work of fiction it might be a bestseller, Alfred. Please go on."

"Well, I got a job out of knowing that guy anyway, at his buddy's golf course. Guess that makes me a friggin' hypocrite doesn't it. I worked the driving range and they let me do lessons once they caught on how good I was. I got bitten big-time by the golf bug for a while. Thought I could turn pro. I played a lot with pros and UNLV golf team guys, and I could hold my own with any of them when it came to the physical part of the game. But when it came down to beating them for money, I bombed out. Couldn't stand the heat. When the cash was on the line, I went from Jerry Pate, to Jerry Lewis. So how could I ever expect to play in tournaments? The only really good thing was that I got smart and went back to playing my horns. Packed up the sticks, my 'clubs' again, for a long time. One more dream, like a grouse: takes flight . . . shot down."

"Your marriage, Alfred, was it basically over at that time?"

"Michelle was getting a lot of work; even had a record deal on the go. You probably heard one of her songs, 'Can't Wait to See You'. Yeah, that was her. A couple of others made her a few bucks too, but her style was pretty much dated and she didn't fit what the market was looking for in the seventies. She's been a lounge act most of the last few years, as far as I've heard anyway.

"She moved out in '78, after we got one of those quickie one-week Las Vegas divorces. We saw the lawyer's TV ad. Yeah, you can divorce that fast if you've lived there for more than six months. How cool is that? It was a riot. We went together and sat in the guy's office filling out the forms, joking around and basically agreeing on everything, and looking like best pals. The lawyer actually said, 'Why are you two splitting up? You get along better than most of the couples I know.' We laughed it off, but it struck me later how right he was. Damn shame really, that we were both such dopes.

"Well, it was done, and I didn't even have time to celebrate, 'cause right after that, I got fired at the golf course for getting into a scrap with a customer."

"A fight at the golf course, Alfred? Tell me about that."

"Long story, Doc. Man, do I have any *short* ones? This guy was there with his buddies to hit some balls; that same guy who got me the golf gig and had been with Michelle. When they got out the door he started laughing, and talking to his pals about this chick singer he'd been with the night before, as he glanced back toward me, kind of nudge, nudge, wink, wink? Guess he didn't realize I could hear him. Yeah, you can see where this is going already, can't you? Anyway, I called him back in to the shop, and told him he shouldn't be talking about her like that. It was nobody's business but his and hers. Well, he told me to butt out, 'cause if he wanted to tell the whole world about the great blow job the whore gave him, he'd go right ahead."

"Alfred, that must have been a difficult moment, to say the least. What did you—"

"Couldn't hold back, Doc. I knocked him across the driving range shop, his clubs and all. Buckets of balls went flying. The room looked like a science class demonstration of nuclear fission or fusion or whatever. Ha, the big bang theory, literally? Even though he wasn't hurt that bad, he was real upset. When he got up, he didn't come at me; just went straight to the pro shop. Security came in minutes to boot me off the property. Guess I was lucky he didn't press charges.

"If I'd kept that job, maybe I'd still be in the golf business. No big loss to the music world. This old temper of mine has certainly ruined a few things for me."

"I understand how you could feel that way," said the doctor. "Your temper is something we must explore in depth."

"I read something Jack Nicklaus said, that 'you don't *get* golf'. I guess he meant no one can ever be perfect at it, not even him. And guess what, Doc. I have this thing about perfection. I don't believe in it, but I still need it. Stupid? I tend to give up on things I don't think I'm going to *get*. I know, don't say it . . . like in relationships?"

"Alfred, you may have hit on something important here. I'm pleased to see you're engaging in this process, better perhaps than you thought you might?"

"But I'll never get it down perfect, right, Doc?"

Doctor Davidson smiled and said, "No, I guess one doesn't *get* therapy either. We just keep chipping away until you feel you understand certain things within yourself, and can make changes which can make your life better. Never perfect; nothing can be . . . But let's back up again. After you were fired from the golf course what did you do?"

"Oh yeah, right. Well, I needed to earn some cash somehow, so I worked as a security guard at a Motel Six; ridiculously big joint, Doc, over six hundred rooms. Wore a uniform and looked just like a cop. That's funny, huh? But the worst part was that we didn't have guns. A couple of times I was *this close* to getting blown away, 'cause someone thought I had one, and *they* did.

"So I lasted about a month at that job and then there I was, broke, no job prospects, just me and George. One night I found I was out of dog food and all I had in the kitchen was a box of Kraft Dinner, you know, Mac and Cheese. I cooked it up and we shared it. Actually I gave most of it to him, poor little bugger. Wasn't his fault we had no food. He didn't feel any guilt about eating more than I did. Only thing he knew how to feel was love. We could learn a lot from these little guys, eh, Godzilla?"

As Al scratched behind Godzilla's ear, the dog turned over on his back and stretched out full length, releasing a long slow sigh of delight.

"All I could think of was to hightail it back to Canada. Hadn't been home in years. I knew my folks would be happy to put me up. This is nuts, but I thought about moving back into my old room and staying forever, I felt so fed up. Maybe I could try and be a kid again and get it right this time? They wired me some money to get home, no questions asked.

"I remember driving up the mountain towards Boulder City and looking back at Las Vegas, the last spot you can see it from. I pulled over to take it in, and started to cry. Christ, I didn't know why; it just felt so sad seeing all the lights below, flickering away, like they were laughing at a joke I didn't get. Maybe it was more like I was the joke, Doc? George climbed up on my chest and licked at my face, whining like a ninny. I guess he was crying too, but he probably understood why, a lot better than I did.

"Why would I be so upset over some stupid city, Doc? It's not like it was my hometown, or anything special to me."

"Have you seen or heard from Michelle since then, Alfred?"

"I didn't hear a thing for about two years; then one day when I was living back in New York, I got a package in the mail from Vegas."

"And it was from Michelle?"

"I was as happy as I was surprised. As I tore at the wrapping, all kinds of thoughts went through my head, like maybe she wanted to see me again, possibly to see if we could make another go of it, or even do some music together or something, maybe even just try to be friends? I couldn't believe how much effect she could have on me after that long, or how excited those possibilities were making me."

Al stopped talking, looked down at Godzilla, and began to scratch the dog's bearded chin.

"Alfred," said the doctor after a few moments, "what was in the package?"

Still petting Godzilla, Al said, "There was no note, just a tiny cardboard box . . . with her Mickey and Minnie watch in it."

CHAPTER 27

UP AND COMING

1978-81

A few weeks in small-town Ontario in 1978 was more than enough to remind Al Waters how much he missed life in big-city USA, and in particular, New York; so he headed back there, hoping to rekindle the flames of his once-promising career. As good as it felt to return to his professional music "birthplace", there *were* noticeable changes: streets dirtier, crowds ruder, traffic noisier, music scene meaner. As disappointing and depressing as this was, the Big Apple was still better than anywhere for someone who wanted to play jazz, and not apologize for it.

After finding Billy near-dead from drugs and booze, Al spent months attempting to reconstruct both their lives and reputations. First, he went through the torture of getting Billy clean, and then the almost-as-difficult job of finding work for them in the overcrowded jazz market. Within the past few years it seemed the number of musicians in town had increased in direct proportion to the decrease in available work. Billy's notoriety for being unreliable was only slightly offset by his legendary ability; while the word on Al was that he was talented, but difficult to get along with. At one point, after a third straight no-deal to a gig proposal, Al suggested they perform in the street as a duo, and call themselves the Depression Twins.

The average pay for gigs had diminished because of the glut of aspiring players; union scale had no meaning anymore, except in mainstream gigs such as Broadway musicals, major studio recording sessions, and high class establishments like The Rainbow Room.

With competition comes weakness in the business end of art. Al was forced to play for low fees, or lose gigs to those who were willing to work cheap. In some venues musicians were working for "the door". If only ten people showed up to pay the cover charge, that money was the total take for the band that night.

Some musicians were even willing to work for free, to break into the circuit. For them, it was a chance to be seen, with subsequent paid-for gigs promised only if they were successful in drawing a crowd. Al refused to do this, although he often did work under false contracts, and agreed to pay kickbacks to agents and club managers.

In spite of the financial hard times, it was a joyful and satisfying musical experience for a couple of years, as Al gradually became a regular on the scene. He was playing both trumpet and sax, but featuring the trumpet more often than he had in his Vegas days. His chops were getting stronger with each gig—as was his reputation.

Success, recognition, and even fame were on the horizon: his 1980 debut at the Village Vanguard being practically a guarantee of a bright future. Blowing this potential realization of a lifelong dream would require being either a complete fool, or an emotionally unstable person. At various times Al Waters was a bit of either, and early in 1981, he managed to combine the two.

♪♪♪

The Upper East Side was known for yuppie-class nightclubs. The patrons may have been more interested in being seen than being entertained, but they spent loads of money, and the steady profits benefitted both club owners and the musicians who scored those gigs. If a band or individual performer was considered "in", the potential for earnings exploded—not only in cash, but also in spin-offs such as private parties and financial backing for recording.

Al, on trumpet and tenor sax, was fronting a quintet with piano, bass, drums, and trombone, for a one-month booking at a Mexican-Italian restaurant called Qué Pasta, on East 51st Street, near Third Avenue. One night near the close of the third set, while trombonist Hank Shaw was soloing, Billy motioned for Al to come over.

"Hey, Al," Billy whispered, "take a gander at the third booth down the right wall, but be cool about it, man."

Al glanced toward where he'd been directed. He saw three people in the booth, an older man and two attractive young women. Though this threesome was engaged in animated conversation, it seemed one of the women was more interested in the music. She was leaning slightly outward from the edge of the bench seat, resting her chin on the back of her fist. With her other hand she was pulling at strands of ridiculously long blond hair, twisting them around her fingers next to her cheek. Her stiletto nails were Ferrari-red, the same color as her lips, and her eyes were as blue as a B.B. King guitar solo. Al forgot all about trying not to notice her, and she returned his stare, as a warm, coy smile lifted a corner of her perfect mouth.

"Do we know her?" asked Al, bending close to Billy's ear.

"Al, you don't know? Seriously? And I thought it was only me who was losing it around here."

"Quit messing around, Billy. Where should I know her from?"

"That's Lisa Ducharme; does a column called *Beat Street* in the *Times* every week. Entertainment section, man. She was at last week's gig on 53rd Street . . . the room manager pointed her out to me. Guess I forgot to mention it?"

"No shit? How did I miss *her*?" said Al. "That pic in the paper doesn't do her justice, man. She's a fox. Hey, did she write us up?"

"I haven't see nothin'," said Billy, "but who knows how far ahead she writes her stuff before it gets printed?"

Al sensed Hank was concluding his solo, so he moved back to the mike.

"Hank Shaw, ladies and gentlemen. Nice blowin' Hank," said Al before he began his own solo. He noticed Lisa was one of those who not only clapped, but had begun before he said anything.

Well, she knows good playing, and at least she has the jazz etiquette thing down.

Al didn't even debate about which horn to pick up. Playing trumpet was being home again, and he was anxious, and ready to *burn*. As he began to play, he saw Ms. Ducharme lean more forward into her supporting hand, as if to shut out her companions and concentrate solely on Al. The gesture was exciting; it felt as if they were alone in the room, and he was playing only for her pleasure. As she clasped both hands together under her chin, she closed her eyes, and a strange sensual delight filled Al. He could feel a life-changing night coming on stronger with each note.

♪♪♪

When the set ended, Al put his trumpet on its stand and headed directly to the table where Lisa and her friends sat. Press relations protocol may have dictated a different, less aggressive approach, but Al Waters wasn't exactly a protocol kind of guy.

"Hi, I'm Al Waters. Mind if I join you?"

"Hello, Al," said Lisa. "This is Sammy Kaplan and his fiancée, Frances Goldberg. And I'm Lisa . . . Lisa Ducharme. By all means, have a seat. I was actually going to ask you over."

Al said, "Thanks," and shook hands with Sammy and Frances, and finally Lisa, as he sat down across from her.

"Excuse me," said Al, "but don't you guys usually keep a low profile when you're reviewing an act? I don't ever remember someone from the press being so, obvious."

She'd be obvious in a stadium full of gorgeous babes.

"Oh, I'm sorry," said Lisa, "you're quite right actually. I have to confess I'm not here for that. Frances and Sammy wanted to meet to discuss wedding plans and such, and I suggested here. I caught your band last week, and I've already written a column that includes a long piece about you. It'll be in this weekend's *Times*."

"Oops," said Al, "that's why I never saw you the other time. You were incognito, right? What do you do, wear a trench coat, dark glasses, maybe a fake beard?"

"Something like that, Al. Can't give away my secret identity now, can I?"

Sammy Kaplan laughed and said, "Hey, if you were as good last week as you are tonight, Al, it'll be a good review. You guys are great. My buddy, Max Gordon, who owns the Village Vanguard, told me to check you out. I gotta thank him, 'cause I have a deal for you. Interested?"

"I'm definitely interested," said Al. He sneaked a peek back at Lisa, wondering if she could sense his double meaning. Her mischievous smile told him even more than he'd counted on.

"Sammy, tell Al what you have in mind," said Lisa.

Al looked at Sammy for the response, but his mind was on Lisa.

Ooh, baby, if you only knew what I had in mind. Maybe you do. Damn, I hope you do.

"Al," said Sammy, "I want you to play for our wedding reception. It's an afternoon, four weeks from this Saturday. I hope you aren't booked, but if you are, I'll top whatever you're getting. Just name your price."

Kaplan turned to Frances, a woman at least twenty-five years younger than his apparent fifty-some years, and kissed her sweetly on the cheek. As she cooed and returned the kiss, her ample cleavage strained to escape the meager confines of her black sequined dress.

"Oh, Sammy," she said, "you'd do anything to make me happy,

wouldn't you?"

Al discreetly scrutinized the bride-to-be. She had the body shape of a Barbie doll, and a head to match: empty plastic.

He'll buy anything for you, honey. Looks like he bought YOU for himself.

"Al," said Lisa, "this wouldn't be just another gig. Sammy's a silent partner in a record company, a major one. They signed some big name guys away from their longtime companies last year, and they're looking for more artists to make them the biggest jazz label there is. There's going to be a lot of big record industry people at the wedding too. Could be they'll be fighting over you for a contract after this. Hey, and if you've got original material, they'd be more than thrilled to sign you up for publishing too. All the more money to be shared that way . . . for them and you. Are you signed with anyone now?"

Al said, "Wow, I'd love to finally finish up some tunes I've been writing; and to get to record them too? Super cool. And no, I'm not signed with anyone. Free as a bird, sweetheart, in every way you could want. I'm getting the idea that your review on me is a good one."

"Can't say, honey," said Lisa. "Ethics, you know. But come with us for a late drink after you're done tonight, will you? I promise I won't review you for that although I have a feeling it would be a most favorable one."

Sammy Kaplan hadn't been paying much attention to the banter between Al and Lisa, concentrating rather on his bride-to-be and her wedding plan chat. Noticing an opportune moment when Al and Lisa were sipping their drinks, he placed his fingers to Frances's lips, stopping her in mid-sentence. He leaned toward Al and said, "There's one thing though; I gotta make a request about the, uh, make-up of the band." The only sound at the table now was Sammy tapping the table with his swizzle stick.

Al hoped the "uh-oh" running up his back didn't show on his face.

Oh crap, don't let that mean what I think it does.

"What is it, Sammy? You need the group bigger, smaller? Whatever you want . . ."

"No, Al, it's the right size. I mean it sounds great, well, except the piano guy. He's not really up to the level of the rest of you boys is he? Why do you have him with you? Were the good ones all booked this week? But what I'm really getting at is that he's not exactly the right *type* of person I'd like to have at my home. You know what I mean . . . ?"

Sammy and Frances laughed; while Al and Lisa sat quietly, both knowing this was a much more awkward moment than Sammy could comprehend. Lisa knew something of the history of Billy Crothers, being familiar with his recordings and his celebrated ability; though she hadn't been around long enough to have seen him in his prime.

She spoke first, hoping to ward off what she guessed might be Al's initial reaction to Sammy's suggestion. "Sammy, don't put Al on the spot about that right now. We can chat later about all the details. Right now let's let him get back to making wonderful music."

Lisa Ducharme was the most stunning woman Al had encountered in many years. His protective nature and allegiance to Billy were being put to the ultimate test, and they were failing.

Al said, "Good idea, Lisa. You and I and the Kaplans will talk some more later. I'm sure we can work it out so we're all happy."

Damn it, why shouldn't I sell my soul? It's been devalued so many times . . . who needs it anymore?

♪♪♪

The easiest way for Al to deal with any bad news was, as usual, to avoid it. He made the decision to take the Kaplan wedding gig with an entirely different group. It was easy to round up a stellar ensemble in New York, especially for a Saturday afternoon. As the weeks before the gig passed, he avoided any mention of it to Billy.

The *Times* review by Lisa Ducharme was not only good; it was a rave. So was the personal one whispered into Al's ear for their personal get-together. She and Al became close immediately after that first night—technically, during it. To avoid accusations of conflict of interest, they publically kept the relationship low key, although they knew it would be impossible to keep secret for very long, since they knew too many of the same people.

Soon enough, things would be good for everyone. Al was riding a high unlike any he'd been on since his first adventures in the Big Apple and Montreal. He'd find a way to make it up to Billy for dropping him off the speeding train of success, one stop short of the destination. Once the luxury of a record deal was in Al's hands, there would be ample opportunity for helping his friend. Now nearly thirty-one—old for not having "made it" yet—Al figured future chances could be scarce if this brass ring was fumbled. Loyalty and friendship weren't going to get in the way—not this time. Billy would have to understand.

♪♪♪

On the day of the Kaplan wedding, Al was flying high. He'd finally managed to get his tuxedo shirt done up with the button holes in line and studs inserted, and now he was starting to curse louder each time he failed to get his bow tie properly adjusted and hooked.

Lisa put down her makeup brush and came over to help. "Here, Mr. Fussbudget, let me do that."

As she tugged and twisted Al's tie into a more recognizable form, he calmed down enough to notice she was dazzling in a long black and white dress, cut low in back and front. Her hair was done up in a gorgeous pile which threatened to tumble down at the slightest breeze as curly wisps of blond clung to her cheeks and adorned her long slender neck.

"Thanks, doll," said Al. "I feel like a total klutz today. Look at you. What are you doing with *me* as your guy? You should be with a prince or a king or something."

"I am," she said, with a wink. As she reached up to fix a few wayward hairs on his forehead, she sighed and said, "You're the king of whatever world you want to be in. Or maybe you're my Prince Charming, in a klutzy kind of way."

"Lisa, I can't wait to tell the world, the whole damned frigging world that you and I are, you know, together."

She gave up on his unruly hair and looked into his eyes. "I love you, klutz. Kiss me and then shut up. We have to get going. Oh crap, look at the clock, we gotta boogie for sure."

♪♪♪

Al and Lisa attended both the ceremony and the reception which were held at the palatial Kaplan estate in East Hampton, Long Island; the backyard having been turned into a fantasyland of tents and flowers. The main attraction for the festivities was a nineteen-piece big band, The Sounds of Sophistication. Al's group was to fill in the ambiance gap between dance band sets: a form of entertainment referred to by those who performed it, as "wallpaper music".

"S.O.S."—as Al nicknamed the large group—began their set with the Glenn Miller standard, "Moonlight Serenade". Lisa grabbed Al's hand and dragged him to the dance floor. He said, "Man, if they play 'In the Mood' I'm outa here."

"You don't like that song?" asked Lisa. "Or does that mean you are *not*, in the *mood*?"

"No musician that I know likes it," said Al, "so friggin' corny and boring, but hey, I'm not the one has to play it, am I. The 'Sophisticated Suckers' can blow it out their sell-out butts all night if they want. I know half those guys up there, and some of 'em are pretty decent jazz players. I bet they make a ton more money doing this crap though. To each his own, I guess. Hey, I got an idea; I'll down a Scotch for every Miller tune they play."

Lisa squeezed his hand a little tighter and said, "You have to go on in about forty minutes, Al. Maybe you should go easy on the booze for now?"

"Yes ma'am. I'll be a good boy. Trust me. Let's hope this crowd is ready for some cool sounds. No old bullshit dance tunes out of us."

♪♪♪

The first number Al selected was Miles Davis's "Tune Up". As the group dug into an energetic hard bop groove, Al reveled in pride for the all-star ensemble he'd assembled for the occasion. He wished one of the record execs supposedly in attendance had brought some recording gear. This was going to be one perfect and productive gig.

At the end of the song there was a smattering of warm applause, mainly from people near the stage. Al wasn't perturbed about there not being more of this polite response. His job was not to do a "show", as much as it was to create an atmosphere of hipness for the event. Most people weren't used to this style of music at a wedding reception, but the high quality of the band was unmistakable to all but a few less-than-with-it slobs. Unfortunately, it was just one of those who was the first to approach the stage. He motioned for Al to bend down to talk.

"Hey, buddy," said the man, "play 'In the Mood' for us."

Al took in a long slow breath and said, "Sorry, we don't do that song."

The man finished off his half glass of champagne in one gulp, dribbling part of it down his shirt. "Come on, pal," he slurred, "you guys are supposed to be something real good, so Sammy says anyway. And you're tellin' me you don't know 'In the Mood'?"

"Didn't say we don't *know* it, my friend," said Al. "I said we don't *do* it."

"Are you jiving with me? Who the hell do you think you are? I asked you nicely to play a song. Now just play the fucking song, okay?"

Lisa, who had overheard most of the interaction, arrived to bring Al a drink. She touched the offensive man on the arm and said, "Excuse me, sir, aren't you Ronald Blackmoor?"

"Yes I am, sweetheart," said the man, "and I do believe I've met you, have I not?"

"I'm Lisa Ducharme, Mr. Blackmoor . . . with the *Times*?"

"Why yes, of course, the columnist—"

"Correct, Ronald. And, if I'm not mistaken, your company is in the middle of negotiations with us for a rather large advertising contract?"

"Yes, right on. My boss, Jackson Brownell is about to do some big business with your paper."

"Well, Ronald," said Lisa, "I suggest you don't hassle Mr. Waters over a silly song. My boss, or yours, wouldn't want to hear about you causing my friend any grief, especially one who's a friend of Sammy Kaplan, now would he?"

"Yeah, no big deal, Miss Ducharme. No problem at all. Hey, sorry, Mr. Waters. You just forget about it. Play anything you want."

As Blackmoor walked away, Lisa looked up toward Al for approval of her successful peace negotiation, but he turned away to talk to the band. After counting off an intro to the next song, he faced the audience, looking over Lisa's head as if she wasn't there.

The song began—an impossibly fast version of "In the Mood" in B-flat. As it progressed, it quickly developed into something new, through an absurd number of variations, including quotes from blues tunes by Charlie Parker and Thelonious Monk. Each soloist blew several choruses, leading the rhythm section into ever-deeper complexity.

Many of the musicians from the Sounds of Sophistication band gathered near the stage to listen, nodding their heads and snapping fingers. To them, it was a performance to remember. To Al, it was pure spite.

After the song was completely chewed up, swallowed, and digested, he finished the final chorus by slowing down the band into half-time, oozing out the original "In the Mood" melody in the sappiest old-fashioned, vibrato-heavy tone he could squeeze from his horn. The dance band musicians laughed while the general audience began to clap—having finally recognized the tune. Al played the standard fanfare-like Glenn Miller trumpet ending up to the traditional impressive-sounding high D, and then took a breath and soared up another sixth to high B-flat—for trumpet, the historic hallmark of screech notes, known as "double C".

It was a definitive "Al moment", with unbridled energy, a little daring, a little innovation—and much more than a little sarcasm—all blended into one musical statement. As Al set his trumpet on its stand and stepped down from the stage the wedding party, guests, members of the S.O.S. band, and even Al's own combo joined in a round of aggressive applause and cheering.

♪♪♪

Lisa was standing near a giant oak tree, with arms crossed, and one hand fisted in front of her mouth. When Al had worked his way through the gauntlet of handshakes, pats on the back, and high fives, he smiled as he approached her. "Hey, baby," he said, "why the frown? What's up?"

"Al, that was like a slap in the face. I did you a favor by getting that boor off your back, and then you go and make me look . . . like a fool?"

"I didn't ask for the favor, Lisa. I can take care of myself."

"Well, I'd say that describes your sex life too, for the next few days, Al," she said as she turned and walked away.

♪♪♪

The next two hours went by smoothly from a professional standpoint, as the less sophisticated among the crowd enjoyed the dance band, and the few "hip" people in attendance grooved to the jazz. On a personal level, things were uncomfortable for both Al and Lisa, as they basically avoided each other, each awaiting an apology. He knew she'd come around. She hoped he would.

"Al," said a soft female voice, "I want to talk with you."

He'd heard it from off to his side, and as he turned, ready to accept Lisa's capitulation, he was surprised to be facing the newly wed Mrs. Frances Kaplan. Not having seen her since the ceremony, he hardly recognized her in her change of clothes. She was now sporting a frilly, pink and white flower-patterned blouse, and a mid-length skirt of bright red which matched her lips and nails. Her hair was down, and longer than he had imagined it would be—even longer than Lisa's. In fact, she slightly resembled Lisa, although neither in personality nor intelligence; a more fitting comparison to Frances in those two qualities might have been a poodle.

Al said, "Well, hello, Mrs. Kaplan. Wow, you look beguiling in that outfit."

"And you're pretty hot in that tux, big guy. Hey, how much are you supposed to play? Aren't you done by now?"

"One more set. Then it's party time for Al."

"Have you been paid yet? Sammy made a check for you. Pretty sure I saw it on his desk."

"No, babe, not yet. Maybe you could get it for me?"

"Sure, Al. Come with me."

"Cool. I got a few minutes yet before we play, and I don't mind getting out of earshot of all this Miller music anyhow. I'm about to barf."

♪♪♪

Frances led Al through the back patio doors which opened into a large study, with a fireplace taking up an entire wall.

"Shit, you could burn a whole tree in there," said Al.

"That's the only place in this house you'll find any hot, solid *wood*," sighed Frances. "Come on, up this way."

The magnificent house made Al think of movies and movie stars, and comparisons to *Citizen Kane* in more ways than the opulence, with the part of tycoon-marrying bimbo played to perfection by Frances—albeit with more beauty, and less talent. As she turned and began prancing up the grandiose winding staircase, Al was uneasy in the direction she was heading, appearing not to have business purposes in mind at all.

"Where are you taking me, honey? Your husband's office isn't upstairs is it?"

"Don't ask too many questions, sweetie. It's dangerous. You know what curiosity did to the cat."

Al was a cat familiar with many kinds of danger, and what he saw above him on the staircase presented exactly that—she wasn't wearing underwear. As she turned to beckon him to hurry, she caught him looking up her skirt, and she smiled. She reached the top of the stairs and pranced to a door directly across the hall.

"In here," she said.

Al followed her into the room, and the first thing he saw was a king-size bed. Before he could say anything, or think of an excuse not to be an idiot, she shut the door and grabbed his arm and pulled him toward the bed.

"Frances," said Al, "hold on. I've got to get back for the last set in a minute; besides, this is sick. You just got married a couple of hours ago."

"No, baby . . . *this* is sick," she said, pointing to her crotch, "sick of waiting. Wanna kiss and make better? And, you want a set . . . ? Here's a *set*."

She undid her blouse and pulled it open, revealing her bursting red bra. Stunned by the sight, and the surrealism of the moment, Al was the literal proverbial pushover, as she shoved him down onto the bed.

As she stood over him, she began a slow, writhing, erotic dance, demonstrating all too clearly what she had to offer. Al said, "Come on, Frances, I can't do this. I'm no saint, but I'm not enough of a slimeball to—"

"How about now?" she asked, as she grabbed the top of her strapless bra and pulled it down around her waist, thrusting her chest toward Al's face. "Can you do it now? You know you want to, baby. You want to feel these don't you?"

He did want to—so much it hurt, from head to toe, and especially in between. But in spite of his booze-impaired scruples, and the sight of her perfect body, and her pouting come-hither look, he wasn't going to give in. Not this time.

Lisa was too important to him to mess it all up for any cheap quickie. Not this time. He would fight this temptation. He'd been weak so many times in his life and hurt someone he cared for. Not this time.

He was going to get up and walk out of the room and go back downstairs as if nothing had happened. For once, he was going to do the right thing. As for Frances, she was certainly destined to ruin her marriage to Sammy, and she'd be discovered for the tramp she really was. But not today, not with Al Waters.

Here was Frances, as beguiling as Busty Brigitte, asking him to once again abandon sensibility and self-respect—to ruin everything with Lisa.

Not this time.

Al said, "Not gonna happen, sweetie. I'm outa here."

Frances yelled, "You son of a bitch. Who do you think you are? Turn me down will you? Let's see how you get out of this . . ."

She screamed, "No . . . no, don't . . . Oh no, PLEASE STOP."

The chilling cries destroyed Al's last remaining ability to think, and he slapped his hand over her mouth and pulled her down on the bed beside him. The sound of her now-muffled voice was momentarily drowned out by a voice at the door.

"Franny, what's . . . ? Oh my God, what's going on?" cried Sammy Kaplan as he stood frozen, incredulous—holding the door in one hand and his face in the other.

Al jumped up from the bed as Frances pulled her bra back into place and struggled to her feet. She ran to her husband, crying, "Oh, Sammy, he followed me up here and tried to . . . tried to . . ."

"Hey, for God's sake," pleaded Al, "this isn't what it looks like . . . Nothing happened."

"You fucking bastard," said Sammy. "This is my *wife*. You are going to die for this."

The older man lunged for Al, knocking him off balance. As he tried to regain his stance, Sammy pummeled at him with both fists. Al did little to resist, allowing the old man to wear himself out, as most of his punches missed the mark or hit him in the chest. One shot did eventually catch Al square on the mouth, but a much more devastating blow came from the doorway.

Lisa said, "Don't kill him, Sammy. Save some for me."

Al wiped blood from the corner of his mouth and said, "Lisa, please don't believe her. I didn't—"

"You lying son of a bitch," yelled Sammy. "Lisa, get Franny out of here. Make sure she's okay."

Al caught Sammy's arms in his hands and stopped him from further blows. He pushed him down to the bed and said, "Man, I'm sorry, but this is all crap. She's lying, man. Damned whore came on to me. Sorry, man, but you need to know."

Sammy lay on the bed, saying nothing. He was breathing so heavily Al was afraid he might have a seizure or a heart attack. Lisa said, "Sammy, I'll look after Frances. Al, if she tried to seduce you, did she drag you up the stairs all by herself? I think we all know what happened here, you piece of shit."

"Lisa, please. I was trying to . . . I only wanted to do the right thing for a change. I tried . . . really, I tried."

Lisa left with Frances, neither of them looking back. As Sammy lay on the bed, Al knew from the sadness in the old man's eyes, he did know the truth—but it was never going to be okay to accept it.

♪♪♪

The following week, Lisa Ducharme's column noted a sad incident in which "up-and-coming" jazz man, Al Waters became "down-and-gone", as he was too intoxicated to continue a gig at a private function. In addition, it was noted by those in attendance how his playing had slipped more than a notch. Perhaps the hype about this supposed new star had been prematurely optimistic. All the record industry execs contacted about his prospects for a deal had similar opinions: "Al Waters? Doesn't have it . . ." "Lots of better, younger talent out there . . ." "Past his prime . . . if he ever really had one."

Behind the scenes, the most damaging of repercussions came from one short phone call from Sammy Kaplan to Max Gordon; Al Waters would not be booked again at the Village Vanguard, or any other club subject to Kaplan's or Gordon's influence—ever.

♪♪♪

When Billy read the Ducharme article, the first thing he did was call Al.

"Hey, man, how come I wasn't on that gig? Not good enough for you anymore? I'm so pissed at you, man, but there's nothin' new about that, *is* there? And I'm not so much pissed that you didn't see fit to use me on the gig, but that you blew it again, and this time so damned bad. Did you stop to think that maybe if I'd been there with you, I mighta kept you in line? Anyway, I guess you messed up real good this time, my friend."

Al knew he could never tell Billy the real reason he'd left him out of the gig: Kaplan's direct request to keep a drug-using, skid row candidate away from his home.

"Billy," said Al, "you're right. I had a different group for that gig because Lisa had these guys she wanted me to be seen with. I'll never do it again; won't screw you around, I mean. You and I were meant for each other, right?"

"Well, man," said Billy, "you might not be a junkie, but birds of a feather we are. That's for damn sure. You got some weird addictions, man, like you need to walk the edge, even though you always fall. You need all these women, and yet you're always on a downer because of 'em. It's like . . . like you're addicted to *need* itself. But it's all copacetic, man. Used to think all the cats who kept it together and made good careers out of their talent were better than me or something. But at least with you around, Al, there's always someone more likely to fuck up than me. Thanks, pal."

Al said, "Yeah, remember 'Minus Milt'? I promise you one thing, my friend. I'll never take another gig, minus Billy, okay? Hey, we still haven't nailed that Carnegie Hall booking. Won't be long . . . I can feel it."

Al felt worse about "cheating" on his friend than he did about what happened at the Kaplans'. He was sure no one there had been hurt as much as he knew Billy was. And yet here he was, calling and kibitzing—and still his friend. Al had to agree with the birds-of-a-feather reference; he had always seen Billy Crothers as an unresolved chord progression, one which left all questions unanswered. If he'd kept straight, what heights might the piano genius have attained? Al knew the unresolved feeling too well from his never-completed attempts to write songs; and now, as a musician it seemed he had finally joined Billy in the what-might-have-been club.

CHAPTER 28

FIVE - SOUTH TOWER [8]

*T*he orderly stood up and walked to the side of the bed. He inspected the injured man's face and bent over close, to speak softly next to his ear. "Not looking too good there, my dear. Most people would have died from what you got hit with. But you're the type of guy who'd stay alive like this just to piss me off, *aren't* you? I bet there's at least ten other people would love to be here with me, and have the chance to make this happen.

"You got to wake up here. There's something important I have to do besides finish this, and you need to hear what I have to say. You've just got to. It's . . . priceless."

♪♪♪

Officer Poole studied the Lenny Breau fingering chart with zeal. He'd seen this one before, but he could never get enough. As he read through the tablature and notation, he marveled yet again at the sheer brilliance of his hero's work. It was both exciting and depressing. He knew he didn't possess the genius required to be so inventive, nor could he ever attain the technical ability to even adequately copy Breau's style—not as long as he was stuck being a beat cop.

Lenny was one of a kind. I can't let that hold me back from trying. I could still be a pretty damn good musician . . . Shit, who am I kidding? I'll never be any good. Might as well get used to being a cop for twenty or thirty years like my dad. Whoopee, what a life.

It must be so sweet to do what you really want: to play music all the time, go to cool places, be respected for your talent.

CHAPTER 29

PROMISES

1983 - 90

*F*rom Florida, to Nevada, to Ontario, to New York, and back to Florida . . .
Al Waters lived a ten-year, no-expenses-paid trip to nowhere. In 1983 he
was back in the Sunshine State for the first time since he and Michelle had
been there together. Billy had come along, and they worked together on as
many jazz gigs as they could dig up. But soon it became evident that club
dates, weddings, bar mitzvahs, and parties provided the most employment
opportunities. For Billy, it was easier, since piano players with experience
and a large repertoire were in demand—not so for horn men. The brass
craze of the seventies had passed, with synthesizers having replaced the
horn sections in most pop bands. Al told Billy not to worry about accepting work on his own, or with groups who didn't need a horn player. Billy
reluctantly agreed, although he tried unsuccessfully to convince Al to learn
bass or guitar, and improve his pop singing chops, so there'd be more chance
to work.

In his heart, Al wanted no part of pop music anyway, wanting desperately
to stick to jazz, even if it had to be "commercial" jazz. He'd rather play half-
decent music for low pay than do crap for more cash—the downside of
this philosophy being that the lifestyle to which he'd become accustomed
was getting out of reach. From 1983 to '85, life and work were a series of
low-paying gigs, low-rent apartments, and lower-than-low self-esteem.
Eventually, adjustment was required to make ends meet, and it was a three-
week stint on a cruise ship which changed things for the better—all but for
the self-esteem.

While playing in a four-piece combo on the Blue Empress, he met Nora
Madison. The rules for the gig included a non-patronizing-with-guests
stipulation, but Al had never been too good with rules. He was fired when

he was reported being seen several times in the company of a certain woman passenger. In the long run, it turned out to be a positive result. Through exchanged phone numbers—after two weeks she called him—the illicit shipmates met up again in Miami. In three more weeks they were living together in Nora's opulent house in Boca Raton.

She was both surprised and flattered that thirty-five-year-old Al had not only shown such interest in her, but had so readily roosted in her home, and her heart. For her, it was simple; she was crazy about him, from the first time she'd seen him and heard his music. Fiftyish—it was only a guess, for she'd never tell him her age—she was attractive in an elegant, mature way, reminding him of when he'd met Margaret Whiting. But while Whiting was music business royalty, Nora was the epitome of erudition, having more formal education than anyone Al had ever known. She'd been married twice, once to a real estate broker, and more recently to a high-level banking executive—no children with either. Both husbands had died relatively young, and Al quipped she must be killing her men with love—a theory not easily verifiable by her simplistic approach to lovemaking. For a twice-married woman of her age and worldliness, she displayed surprising naiveté regarding sexual creativity. He found it hard to believe she'd never experienced some of his erotic suggestions. But the tentative, shy way she'd go about attempting these became a turn-on in itself. He sometimes felt he was in bed with a middle-aged teenager.

A love grew between them unlike either had known before. For Nora, it was completely romantic, her nurturing side induced into rebirth with this wounded, enigmatic, sensitive, and handsome young man. It was easy to say "I love you" from the beginning.

For Al, it was not so much romantic, as it was having found a true friend who could provide not only the physical comforts of a beautiful home, but companionship, understanding, and support for his few remaining dreams. He thought it odd, but in many ways their relationship reminded him of how it had been with his sister, Anne. This may have been why he could say "I love you" to Nora with an atypical supplement of sincerity.

She was wealthy, partially from the death benefits from two successful husbands, but more by inheritance from her multi-millionaire father. Living on investment income, she'd never had to work for a living in her entire adult life; so her days were spent being involved with charities, local arts groups, and her country club activities—the least frequent of which was golf. She did play on occasion, but not well, usually just for the social aspects or for entertaining potential business contacts.

On the other hand, Al practically *lived* at the golf course and driving range, taking full advantage of the membership Nora had provided. His game had always been solid, but with this concentrated effort he quickly developed into a scratch player, holding his own in matches with even the local pros. In 1986 he won the club championship in both medal and match play. It was, however, a bittersweet success, in that he was looked upon as an outsider: his association with Nora, rumored to be only a relationship of convenience.

The word "gigolo" came up in many conversations regarding Al—once, regrettably, in the locker room while he was just around the corner from the men who were discussing him. At first, he held his temper, even after a reference to his status as a bought-and-paid-for companion. He was about to head home when one of the men referred to Nora as a patron of the arts, sharing her wealthy lifestyle with some lousy sax player in trade for probably once-a-month sexual servicing. Al had learned to live in his own skin, and dispassionately accepted that most people couldn't abide his ways. But now, they were insulting Nora; this was a line not to be crossed.

Al threw his towel against the wall, moved out from the end of the line of lockers, and approached the two gossip mongers.

"Once a month, huh? FYI, it's at least once a day boys." It was a lie, but he had to say it. "And by the way, I wouldn't call myself a *lousy* sax player."

He recognized the older of the pair as one of his most easily dispatched opponents in the club match play championships. "Kenneth, it's nice to see you again," said Al. "Hey, guess what? I'm way better at sax than golf, so that must make me a *worse*-than-lousy golfer, huh? And I smoked you five-and-four. So what does that say about how incredibly lousy you must be?"

The men were saying nothing—a wise choice which would have been fine, had it lasted. But the second man, to whom Al hadn't spoken, made a mocking sneer toward his companion, followed by a puerile giggle: a far-from-wise choice he would soon regret.

"So this is funny is it, boys?" said Al. "Well, here's something this lousy sax player and lousier golfer is real good at."

With that, Al picked up the end of the bench the men were on, sending them tumbling onto the floor.

"If you get up, you'll both go down again so hard you won't know what day it is. Stay put like good little boys until I'm outa here, or I'll stuff you into your lockers and take your fucking clothes. You think the membership will get a kick out of me telling them how I found you two naked in here, fondly embracing . . . ? Now there's a nice rumor to spread. Maybe then, everyone will leave me and Nora out of their stinking gossip for a few days."

While Al packed up his gear, the pair on the floor said nothing, not moving an inch until he was gone. The next day, Al's membership was revoked. When Nora told him, he was enraged and began to plan all manner of revenge. But as he stalked about the living room ranting about all the people he was going to tell off, and how everyone at the club would regret the way they'd treated him and Nora, she sat him down and said, "Al, my darling, this could be for the best."

"Come on, Nora, how does that possibly make any sense?" asked Al.

"Well," she said, "you *have* been spending most of your time practicing golf or playing it. What's happened to your music? I haven't heard you play either your sax or trumpet for weeks. Maybe it's time to get back to your true calling."

"But, sweetheart," said Al, "I've wasted half my life doing music and where has it got me? I think if I concentrate completely on golf for a while, I can make it as a pro."

"If that's what you truly want, my love, then that is what you'll have. I know you can do anything you set your mind on. And the club pro once said you showed tremendous promise at the game. Go for it, Al. How can I help?"

♪♪♪

Al began to play the southern mini tours with modest success, once even close to a win, when he had a superlative week and came one stroke short of getting into a playoff. Most of the time, after expenses it was a struggle just to break even, but with Nora bankrolling him, he kept trying. In the second autumn of his new career they flew overseas to try to qualify for some European Tour events, but at this level Al was unable to compete realistically. He had the physical skills for the most part, but not the concentration and composure of world-class champions.

During the entire flight home to America Al said nothing; just stared out the window. From this point of view the world seemed so small, as sea and sky merged at the horizon. All he could think was: if the earth was just a tiny, insignificant pebble in the universe—what was *he*?

♪♪♪

One day, after nearly two years of beating balls and missing more cuts than he made in mini tour events, he came home after a two-week road trip to

Alabama and Georgia. He dropped his golf bag down in the foyer, trudged into the living room, and collapsed onto the couch. Nora, who had been in the library, came in and sat next to him, saying nothing as she gave him a big kiss and snuggled.

Al said, "Honey, remember what you said a while back, about my true calling?"

"Yes, of course I do," she said, as she arose and went to the liquor cabinet. "Scotch . . . ?"

"Yeah, hon . . . if I drink more Scotch, maybe my game will improve. Makes sense, right? The Scotch invented golf, didn't they?"

"Well, actually they prefer to be called 'Scottish', my dear. But in any regard, the only thing a drink will help with right now, may be to get you talking."

"Is my saxophone still in the bedroom closet? Or did you throw it away?"

"It's in the studio, along with your trumpet."

Al said, "Studio . . . ?"

"Yes, Al, your new music studio, on the main floor where the blue guest-room used to be."

"I don't believe this. Let me see," said Al as he jumped up from the couch and grabbed Nora's hand. They ran laughing to the new room she'd had designed and constructed for him.

"You had a studio built when I was away? How did you know I was going to talk to you about getting out of golf and back to music?"

"When a woman truly loves her man, she knows what he's thinking, Al."

"Well, Nora, I sure love *you*, but I'll be damned if I'll ever have a clue what you're thinking."

♪♪♪

Al's new studio was built by recording industry professionals. It wasn't overly large, at about thirty feet by twenty, but it was a veritable musician's play-ground, with a Fender Rhodes electric piano, Gibson Les Paul guitar, Fender Precision bass guitar and amp, compact P.A. system, an array of micro-phones and stands, bookshelves, work desk, and leather office chair. At the heart of it all was a TEAC 3340 four-channel reel-to-reel tape recorder, a Soundcraft eight-channel mixing board with a Crown power amp, a rack of various effects units, and Yamaha NS-10M studio monitor speakers.

When Al saw the room and its treasures, he picked up Nora in his arms and danced with joy. It was a Christmas morning from his childhood—without the guilt behind the gifts.

Nora said, "Al, your 'job' is here. I want you to practice, and write the songs you've always wanted to do, and record every day. Don't worry about money. When you feel ready, you can look for playing engagements. Or if you want, you can write me a symphony and I'll pay to have it performed. Just do what you need to be happy. That will make *me* the happiest woman in the world."

"A musician's dream," said Al. "Is this real? Are *you* real, Nora? Can someone love me this much?"

"Yes . . . someone can," said Nora.

♪ ♪ ♪

For the next two years, Al immersed himself in practicing his horns, and learning piano and bass well enough to lay down accompaniment tracks. He worked diligently to learn the tricks of the trade with four-track overdubbing, and soon was producing decent quality recordings of an all-Al quartet, for the most part, sticking to standard jazz repertoire. While his occasional attempts to create his own original music always started with enthusiasm, they inevitably fizzled as mere snippets of songs, quickly discarded—those tapes destined for erasure and re-use. He wasn't overly concerned, convinced that someday soon enough, he'd get into the right head space for writing, and the floodgates would open on his composing career.

Al eventually accepted that his recording results were not as high quality as he'd like, not for potential commercial purposes. With Nora's always enthusiastic financial help, he started going to a local full-size recording studio called Sound Art, where he had professional drum tracks added into the mix by one of the studio owners. In no time, these men saw great potential in Al's abilities, not only as a horn player of immense skill and versatility, but in his innate sense of arranging parts and recording them expertly. Soon he was asked to participate in professional projects, first as instrumentalist, and subsequently, as recording engineer in an improvised apprentice role.

At first, Al and the studio owners had worked on a barter system wherein he'd do studio work for a certain number of hours, and receive recording time and drum track assistance in return. Soon the balance shifted to where it was only fair that he was paid for his time. He was eventually spending twelve to sixteen hours a day at Sound Art, much of this time being past midnight and into early morning, when many bands liked to record.

Nora didn't complain. She saw Al working hard and loving every minute, so the time they did have together was better than ever; especially since he was earning an income and feeling less beholden to her.

She asked little of Al, other than that he share her life as much as he could amidst his music workload. With her guidance, he learned to appreciate art and its many forms and history, and they often debated the merit of some modern works he claimed could have been done by a five-year-old, or even a monkey on meth. Even in the midst of disagreeing with such crass assessments, she enjoyed every moment, since for at least a part of each day he was all hers.

Another new experience she introduced him to was enjoying fine wine, another instance of his protestations being more flippant than serious. He claimed that after two glasses, no one could tell a four-dollar bottle of red off the convenience store shelf, from a bottle of highfalutin French Bordeaux. To this, she exclaimed that his taste buds must have been ruined by too much exposure to cheap booze and brass instruments. She vowed to resuscitate his discrimination for good wine and food, by exposing him to only the finest of each.

Al began to learn more about a world he'd only seen from the other side of the tracks, and with Nora's Henry Higgins-like direction, he was slowly beginning to feel at ease, both at home and in social gatherings.

♪ ♪ ♪

One day just before he was about to head off to work, Nora said she needed to talk with Al about something important. He felt a cold wind against his heart as he waited for the words which he was certain were about to sweep away everything good in his life.

"Al, it's time we discussed our *arrangement*. I feel there is need of some change."

"Nora, are you unhappy? Am I working too much? Staying out too late . . . ? I can drop some projects. Whatever you need . . ."

"No, no, no, don't think that way, my precious silly man. What I'm trying to say is . . . Will you marry me?"

Al looked at the ceiling and sighed. He said, "Damn it, woman, you've ruined everything."

Nora's smile disappeared, and she said, "Al, what do you mean? I don't—"

He touched a finger to her lips and said, "What *I'm* trying to say is . . . you always do that; always when I'm about to say something, you either say it first, or something like it, and usually put it better."

"Al, I don't think I . . . Do you mean . . . ?"

"Yeah, you precious, silly woman. I was going to ask *you* to marry *me*. Now who the hell gets to say yes?"

They looked at each other without a word for several seconds. Then both began to laugh. They held hands as if to begin a dance, and then together dropped to one knee. Al said, "Okay, together now. After a three-count . . . ?"

With a nod, they began in perfect unison. "One . . . two . . . Yes!"

And their dance began, with a shared promise to make each other's life better than either of them had ever known.

♪♪♪

In 1989, the owners of Sound Art had an announcement to make; they were selling the business. When Al told Nora about it, he thought she might burst into tears, as *he* almost had. She turned around for a moment, cupping her chin in her fingers, then turned back to Al and said, "Find out how much."

"Nora, are you saying you'd buy the studio? For me?"

"Not *for* you, Al, but with you. I'll be the majority partner until you can work yourself into full ownership. Deal?"

It was the deal of a lifetime for Al. With full control over artistic direction and promotion, he saw only bright lights in his future. His marriage was working; his energy was bubbling; his music was blossoming; original songwriting was a natural next step; and his adulterous urges were fading into distant memory.

A memory of another sort had been bothering Al for some time; he hadn't heard from Billy Crothers for months. The last he'd known, his unpredictable friend had been playing piano bar cocktail gigs in various south Florida locations, drifting from job to job. The last time they'd talked was when Al tracked him down and offered some studio work. Billy had said, "Al, you got a lot of good in your life right now. I'm only a reminder of what used to be, so maybe you should stay away from me, huh?"

Al had been so tied up in his work and his happiness with Nora, he hadn't thought much about his old life or the people in it. In fact, he sometimes had to think hard to remember how difficult things had been not so long ago. He decided to take the time to locate Billy and perhaps share a bit of his good fortune of today, with the only person he cared about from back in the day.

♪♪♪

Al walked into the lobby of the art deco Schooner Hotel in south Miami Beach. The door to the lounge was immediately to the left, and from within came the sounds of a badly out-of-tune piano. As he entered the room, he was hit with the odors of stale smoke and dank mildewed carpet, and a palpable air of loneliness and lost hope.

At the piano sat Billy Crothers: his back to the audience of three, slumped in his familiar way, playing quietly, as if it might help the awful instrument sound more musical. Al sat down near the piano, and when the song ended he applauded and said, "Nice hat. I used to know a guy who wore a purple beret like that. I heard he was dead."

"Most of him is, Al, " said Billy, without turning. "At least it smells that way."

Al came up behind Billy, put his arms around him and whispered, "I think you're not quite dead yet, my friend. But you don't look so good. Are you being a bad boy again?"

Billy didn't answer. He was asleep. As Al held him from falling, a man came up and said, "Is that bum *out* again? Christ, I've had it. Last night he passed out right onto a table of customers. He's through. Just get him the hell out of here, will ya?"

Al picked Billy up in his arms—an easy task, since he now must have weighed less than 120 pounds—and carried him out to his car. Once there, Al lowered his friend into the back seat. Billy, now semiconscious, said, "Al, where are we? Are we going to see Charlotte? I wanna see Charlotte. I'm going to marry that girl."

As Billy sank back into oblivion, Al drove homeward. He had to take care of him. Nora would be okay with it—she wasn't Michelle.

♪♪♪

This was about as déjà vu as Yogi Berra had put it, "all over again"—multiple multiples, redundant repetition. In a not-so-instant replay of times past, Al was saving Billy from himself, yet again. Nora set up the main guest room by removing all the furniture except the bed, and Al added a bolt lock on the outside. He sealed the windows with wooden slats as if preparing for a hurricane. From within the room, a tempest of anguish was indeed looming.

The first sign of trouble was the sweat. It had flooded Billy's face and thoroughly soaked his clothes; his shirt stuck to his bony torso like a chamois cloth on a freshly washed 1950 Buick grill. Al tore off everything Billy was wearing and threw it into a pile across the room. He helped him into an old thick sweatshirt and jogging pants before easing him into bed and under the covers.

"Hey, man," said Billy, "I'm gonna ruin these sheets. I can't stop sweating.

But I'm so cold."

"It's only going to get worse, Billy. But let me worry about what gets ruined around here. I can get fresh sheets and clothes anytime. But where could I get another you?"

"Hey, one of m . . . my favorite . . . tu . . . tunes," said Billy, stuttering through shivers.

Al said, "As in, 'There'll Never Be Another You'? Yeah, but man I always screw up the changes near the end, man. You gotta help me with that sometime, okay?"

"Don't take th . . . this personally, Al . . . it's got noth . . . nothing to do wi . . . with you mentioning your playing, but, shh . . . shit, man . . . I'm gonna barf—"

It was only the first of innumerable times Billy would retch over the next sixty-some hours. There was nothing in his stomach except the small amounts of water Al kept trying to force down him, and the heaving never once relieved the nausea. A few times at the peak of this horrific episode there were traces of blood in the vomit.

While Billy was still able to talk even semi-coherently through the shakes, he joked that he must be pregnant. Al denied responsibility since he hadn't seen him for so long. Billy began to cry and said, "Al, you only fucked me th . . . that one time . . . wh . . . when you took me away fr . . . from Charlotte. You knew I'd never go ba . . . back, and you damn well let me lea . . . leave her . . . *made* me leave her. Sh . . . shit, I hate you."

Al didn't sleep for the first twenty-four hours of the ordeal. He sat on the edge of the bed, ready to collect Billy's puke in a pan, or stop him from falling to the floor when he began to writhe in agony. Nora brought food, but Al couldn't eat.

Into the third day, Billy looked near death; the violent shivering had subsided, but his pallor was worse, and his eyes vacant. When Nora saw him that morning she wanted to call an ambulance. Al said, "No way. If he dies, he's better off here with me. If he lives, it has to be this way. We're going to make it, right, Billy?"

Billy was in a state of near psychosis, and whenever his words had been clear enough to understand, many hateful things had come out. Once, he looked at Al and Nora and said, "Hey, what's your mother doing here, Al?" He grabbed at Al's arms with kitten-weak hands and sobbed, "Let me die, Al. Do us all a favor. Fucking kill me; make it quick. I can't fucking stand this anymore. If you were my friend, you'd do it . . ."

Al held him in his arms and said, "Billy, I can't let you die. Who would I have to blame all my screw-ups on anymore? No other piano player I know could put up with me, so you have to stay around. GOT it . . . ?"

"Al, you bastard. I hate you . . . I've hated you since you kept me alive back in New York. I never asked for help then, and I'm not asking *now*."

Nora wiped back tears as she said, "Al, I think you're wrong. He needs professional help. I can't bear this anymore."

As she left the room, Al said, "Now look what you did, Billy. You sent her running. You sure have a way with the ladies."

"You should talk, Al," said Billy a little more quietly. "If you played a note for every woman you've chased away in your life, it'd sound like a Charlie Parker solo. Now *there's* a guy who chased things, man: first, the dream to play faster and better than anyone in the whole world, which he did; but then he went and chased away any chance to even stay alive. I don't wanna be like him, Al. Don't let me be like him anymore . . . please?"

"Billy, you're gonna make it. I know it now for sure. Your level of lunacy is almost back to its normal heights."

♪ ♪ ♪

It was a week before Billy was well enough to leave the room and go outside. That first day in the morning sun, when Nora brought him breakfast, he said to her, "Hey, I'm so sorry if I said bad stuff in there. I don't remember much, but I'm sure I must have been pretty much of a pain in the . . . I mean, I'm sure I was pretty un-copacetic to be around."

"Don't worry about it, Billy," she said. "I understand."

Within a few more days Billy was on his feet and looking much healthier since he was now eating regularly and staying off the drugs. Al took him to his first appointment at the methadone clinic, and on the way home asked him if he would like to stay with him and Nora for a while. Billy was reluctant at first, but eventually agreed to give it a try.

Billy's space was to be the guest room—the "recovery room" as he called it—with the furniture back in place. It was the best accommodations he'd had since his teen years, and he treated Nora and her home with deep respect. During the first few weeks he would disappear daily into Al's studio for hours at a time, playing piano, alone. Al was happy to see this as he was now back at work at the Sound Art studios. So the small studio Nora had built for him saw little use other than by Billy.

Al suggested Billy should come to the big studio and do some work with him, but he shrugged and said, "The way I play these days isn't worth putting on record."

♪♪♪

After several months, things were running fairly smoothly; although Nora was less content than Al, as Billy appeared more and more to be a permanent houseguest. From the beginning, she had thought Billy would eventually get back on his feet and find his own place to live.

Al knew Billy needed to do more than play alone in the small studio, so he began to search for an appropriate gig. One day, early in 1990 a call came from a club owner named Charlie Smythe, who was interested in booking Billy. There was a catch. He would only hire Billy if Al would put a band together and lead it. Charlie knew both sides of Billy Crothers' reputation and Al's history with him. He figured if Al was in charge, it would be worth taking a chance.

♪♪♪

"Hey, Billy," said Al as he came into the room, "stop playing for a minute and listen up . . . I got a gig."

Billy dropped his hands to his side, looked up and said, "You say, you gotta *big*? Cut back on the pasta, my friend."

"Knock it off, man, I'm serious. You know that little lounge down on the main strip, Charlie's Place . . . ?"

"Yeah, but the owner's name escapes me though. Hmm, Franky? Johnny? Um . . ."

"Come on, man. Quit that. Charlie called today and we can start next week. Three nights, and it's *jazz!* The bread is next to zilch, but who cares?"

"Wait a minute, lemme clarify here. You said 'we' . . . ? This gig involves *me* too?"

"Yeah, man, of course it does. Isn't that the coolest?"

Billy cackled and said, "Far-out, man. Far, *fucking* out."

♪♪♪

The task of throwing together an ensemble was simply a matter of a few calls, and a bass player and drummer were soon on board. A few rehearsals were scheduled at Sound Art during off hours. It was going to be one hell of a week, with Al's schedule already being full. It was time to talk to Nora about all this.

For her, it was good news that Billy would be working again, but she was already concerned with Al's work schedule at the studio. And now he'd be doing three nights a week in a jazz club?

When they had a moment alone she said, "Al, are you sure you can handle this? You're burning the candle at both ends already. Isn't this like trying to light the middle? I hardly ever see you *now*. Does that matter to you?"

"I hope that's not a serious question," said Al. "You know how important it is for Billy to get back to work, and at this point I think he still needs me to keep him in line."

"Al, it's been a few years since you worked regularly in the atmosphere of bars. How's that going to be for you, now that you're a business owner, *and* a married man?"

"I'm sure I'll get back on the bicycle as if I'd never fallen off."

"Well, that's partly what scares me. You've been frank with me about some of your old habits, especially when you drink and you have temptations right in your face. Don't forget, it was under somewhat similar circumstances that you and I met. You may not have been 'attached' at the time, but you did break your employer's rules to be with me. You could say that was a form of deceit, or unfaithfulness, couldn't you?"

"Hey," said Al, "Billy's the one who can't seem to change. You know I'm a new man, and I wouldn't do anything to hurt us, no matter how many sleazy Sirens of seduction lurk amidst the darkness of Charlie's Place. Man, can you just hear Sylvester the Cat trying to say that? 'The thleethee thyrenths of tha-*duc*-theeun' . . .'"

"Al, it's not a joking matter. I can't deny you the right to do this, but please promise you'll try to keep yourself balanced."

"Damn right I will, sweetheart. If I fell off the bike again I'd never get back up, and you are my wheels, babe. Don't you know that by now?"

♪♪♪

Three months had gone by at Charlie's Place, and Billy was still clean. The band was swinging like a trapeze artist's dream, and audiences were building steadily. Charlie Smythe offered Al an increase in pay-per-night and added Wednesday, to make it a four-night week—provided he sign a six-month extension to the contract. The catch was, as before, Al had to remain as leader. Al was happy for the guys, genuinely flattered and deservedly proud; but unknown to Charlie, for several weeks he had been planning to quit the band.

"Charlie," said Al, "the offer is a great one, but I have to talk with my wife about this. I've been neglecting things at my studio and at home lately. I really should cut back, not *add* to the load, man."

"So talk with her, Al. But keep in mind if you leave, I have to replace the whole band. I want you, or none of these guys. Yeah, they're good, but without you, I don't want 'em."

The next morning Al got up "early"—10 a.m.—and went looking for Nora. He found her on the back patio having coffee.

"Wow," said Nora, "look who's up. What's that, six hours of sleep? Will you be okay today? Or are you planning on going to the studio today at all? Did I tell you Mr. Montgomery called? He's wondering when you're going to get that last project finished? He's getting kind of worried since it's now over two weeks past what you promised."

Al said, "Hey, I'll handle Montgomery. We need to talk about something else."

"Oh, you mean like, when is Billy going to get his own place?" said Nora.

"Hey, come on, I know it's long overdue. But at least we've kept him straight. He's doing better than he has in years. But anyway, you're right, I'll talk to him today."

"What is it you did want to talk about, Al?"

"So, uh, Charlie offered us a raise last night and—"

"Al, you said you'd only work there a short time. It's been three months already. Raise or no raise, you need to tell him you're quitting."

"Sure, Nora. I'll talk to him tonight."

"Is that it, Al? You look as if there's more on your mind. Let me in on it? Or am I asking too much to be included in your life anymore?"

Nora rose and strode into the kitchen. Al hoped she was going to get another coffee, or to get one for him, but she didn't return. Well, this was better anyway. It gave him time to think about how he could bring up the other details of Charlie's offer about adding a night, and the six-month contract extension.

For the first time since they'd been together, he felt she was telling him what to do, and not in the fun manner of wine tasting or how to appreciate Picasso. This was entering his world and taking hold of things she had no part in. This was getting in between him and Billy. This was—control?

Al had convinced himself that he was content in his life, but autonomy was becoming obvious by its absence. Was it *his* life anymore? Was Nora a source of satisfaction and joy, or a foreign port, so far from his true origins that the homeland of his heart was forgotten? As rough as the seas of his life's journey had been before her, was it time to set sail?

If this ultimately turned out to be launching a ship of fools, at least he would be the captain.

♪♪♪

The first set at Charlie's was typical: medium-tempo tunes, and ballads, and one barnburner to close. Al had begun the night with a double Scotch, and during the set he'd downed another two. On the break, Charlie beckoned him to his office.

"Al, grab a chair. Here, I got you another double Scotch. Let's talk about that contract. By the way, I won't put it on paper . . . but if you sign, I'll keep you and the boys happy at the bar too; no charge for anything, anytime. But you have to keep an eye on that piano player. He still makes me nervous."

Al took the drink and swallowed most of it in a gulp. "It could be me you have to worry about, Charlie. I can put a dent in your bar profits with this stuff." He slugged back the rest of the Scotch and slammed the glass down as if expecting a refill. "Let me see that contract. I think I'm ready to commit. Shall we drink to it?"

Charlie poured them both a generous refill from a bottle he pulled from his desk. "Don't count on this being the Scotch you get normally, Waters. This is my personal stash. Here's the paperwork. Hurry up and sign it, before you forget your name."

Al grabbed the contract and scrawled his signature, slightly tearing the paper as the last letter of his name was scratched onto the promissory page— officially ending his run of kept promises to Nora.

CHAPTER 30

THE SIRENS' ENCORE
1992

*T*he woman at the end of the bar had walked in at midnight, and had remained alone, except for the predictable couple of male admirers who had briefly sat down next to her. Either she was waiting for someone, or she preferred to be on her own, or—as the rejected men probably speculated—she was a lesbian? Motivated purely by curiosity, Al decided to find out for himself.

♪♪♪

"So tell me," he asked, "you like the band?"

He noticed one of the two who had failed with her was still at a nearby table, watching Al's moves, waiting intently for the response. As Al sat down on the stool next to the woman he fully expected to join the crash-and-burn club.

She said, "I *love* it, and especially you. The way you blow that horn gives me goose bumps."

"Hey, thanks, babe," said Al. "Guess I gotta buy you a drink for that review, eh?"

He looked over to the man she had most recently spurned, and winked at the victim of her rejection, who was now getting up to leave. This in itself made Al's efforts worthwhile.

"Well, stick me on a coin and call me a beaver; you're a Canuck," she exclaimed.

"Oh crap, I guess I still sound like Bob and Doug McKenzie after a few beer, *eh*?" Al laughed. "So tell me, do you like Canadians?"

She said, "Well, I do know who the McKenzie brothers are, and the rest of the *SCTV* gang, so guess what that makes me . . . *eh*?"

Al gave the woman a bear hug and hailed the waitress. "Hey, AJ, another round over here, for me and my Canuckette friend."

There's that snarl AJ gives me whenever I chat up some woman. Seems to think she should show her disapproval, just 'cause I'm married. Man, why should AJ give a shit? She doesn't even know Nora. Besides, I'm only fooling around here. Nothing's gonna happen from this little game.

"Thank you, Mr. Sax-man," said the woman, smiling. "So how long have you been in Florida?"

"Long enough to miss Canadian women," said Al. "Everyone knows the northern climate makes them the best lovers in the world. Gotta stay warm somehow, right?"

"Wow, you're giving me ideas, big guy. But it's not very cold right here though, is it? How about we go to my hotel room and turn the air conditioner up to full?"

Uh-oh, as aggressive as a Tony Williams drum solo. What have I got myself into here?

She was a reasonably attractive full-figured woman—late thirties?—with a touch of been-there, done-that tiredness in her face. As if ready for a tennis match, she was dressed in matching light blue shorts and blouse with the three top buttons open, suggesting games other than tennis were on her mind. As her ample cleavage implored him to look down, Al strained to keep his eyes on her face. He volleyed with a line designed to lose the game. "Sorry, can't do that, babe. I'm a married man."

"Hey," she said, "I'm not out to steal anybody's husband. Matter of fact, I have one of my own back in Calgary. Sorry I scared you with the air conditioner line. If you want to come and have a drink with me, great. If not, then I'm cool with that. You know, I could get laid five times a night hanging out in places like this. That's not what I'm after. You seem like a nice guy, not like the pretentious losers I've met so far on my trip."

Christ almighty, is she like, a female version of me? So, she thinks I'm scared? I guess I am. Okay, what the hell.

"We're done for the night," said Al, glancing toward the other musicians packing up gear on the stage. "Let's go. I've got a bottle of wine in my car we can grab. Which hotel are you at?"

♪♪♪

As they walked out into the warmth of the South Florida night, Al heard the moan of a stiffening wind in the palms, and an uncontrollable tremor crept down his spine.

Sounds like some kind of sad, lonely song. Is it those damned Sirens calling my name?

The walk to her hotel was only a block. When they entered the room, Al felt tingles of times past. He hadn't been unfaithful to Nora since they'd met, but he was always mindful of being forever a "recovering" philanderer—the same as Billy with drugs—never actually cured, no matter how long he'd stayed on the wagon.

The woman brought two plain drinking glasses from the bathroom. With a corkscrew she fished out her purse, she opened the wine bottle and filled the glasses to the brim.

"Cheers, sax man," she said, gulping down half her wine at once.

"Here's to . . . Canada," said Al.

"Yeah, about that," she said, moving toward the bed. "I promised you I'd keep you warm. Are you feeling maybe, a little chilly?"

She tugged at Al's arm as she sat down on the end of the mattress, but he pulled away and said, "I think I should sit over here, if that's okay?" He went to the chair by the window.

"So I see you're a *happily* married man," she said, guzzling the rest of her wine. She lay back on the bed, propping on one elbow, with her chin held in one cupped hand. "Good for you. I wish my husband could say the same. He's an asshole. Maybe I am too. But I don't think *you* are. How come you're here with me?"

"I don't know," said Al. "I guess I shouldn't be. You *are* hard to resist, I've got to admit. Maybe I just thought I might have a good time talking with you or something. Have to say though, with you lying there on the bed like that, it's kind of awkward."

"Here, fill me up," she said, holding up her glass. "And of course you know, I only mean more wine."

As she languished, now fully stretched out on her back, Al got the bottle from the dresser. She held the glass up high over her head while he poured. When she tried to bring it down to drink, she spilled some of it on her face and shirt. Laughing and spluttering wine, she said, "Oh damn, look what I've done now."

There was no apology in her tone, nor was there much hope left in Al for surviving this moment, as she undid her blouse, slipped out of it, and tossed it on the floor. "Damn, soaked right through to my bra. Do you mind if I take it off too? Hope that doesn't offend you. Wanna get me a towel please?"

Al was trying to make himself see the humor, not the danger. He laughed and went to get a towel; when he returned, his smile vanished. She was lying back on the bed again, with no attempt to cover her bare chest, which Al could not ignore. This was a splendid instance of cleavage's implications being validated: her bosom, as beautiful as it was bountiful, as perfect as any his adolescent or adult imagination had ever conjured.

"Here you go," he said, as he tossed her the towel, staying back a few feet from the bed. "Um, you've got wine on you. Better wipe it up."

"Come on, don't you want to help?" she said. "Maybe don't use the towel? How about your tongue?"

"That would be nice," said Al, "but I don't dare. You're too damn hot to ignore if I get any closer."

"Then don't ignore me, *or* what you know you want, you dumbbell. Come on, don't pretend you didn't come here for this. Shut off that happily-married-guy act and get over here."

Al moved to the edge of the bed, drawn by forces Billy would have understood too well. As he sat, she reached for his neck and pulled him down. He began to kiss her and run his hands up and down her torso, but she quickly tired of his hesitance and pulled his hand up to her breast. As Al's heart raced with excitement, it felt more like a fist from within, pounding with protestations of his imminent failure to protect Nora from the demons of his past.

The thought of Nora provided just enough strength to pull away. He stood up from the bed and said, "Hey, Canuckette, I gotta go. I may be crazy, but I can't do this."

"You know, sax man," she said without looking up, "that reminds me, I don't think you know my name, do you. I saw yours on the sign at the bar, and you know what? I forget what it said."

"I think it's better that way," said Al. "If I cared who you were, that could mean I like you. And if I liked you, I might have given in."

With that, he left the room. Once outside, he ran to his car back at Charlie's, and sped from the parking lot, with sand flying in the air and a cloud of remorse enveloping his soul.

♪♪♪

Halfway home, he pulled over into a secluded parking lot. He pulled his pants down enough to reach his still-firm erection and stroked himself to orgasm within seconds. The feeling was more of relief than pleasure, numbed by booze, fatigue, and even more by shame. Within seconds he began to cry, trembling like a child, with volcanic sobs bursting from his aching throat. He gained control in a few moments, but a terror climbed out of the inexplicable sadness like a slow-moving, deadly lizard bent on finding and tearing apart his very will to live.

Somewhere deep inside, a thread had snapped, letting go its tenuous hold on something: a hope, a wish, a child's view of God? Whatever it had been, it was now gone forever; and in its place, a hole filled with unfathomable blackness. It was familiar, this place of no light and no purpose, and he knew he'd been here before—just never this deep.

It made him think about the time he'd been fishing with his dad, and the line had broken when he'd hooked a big one. His father had been so angry, accusing him of not trying hard enough. He forced him to spend the rest of the hot summer afternoon alone in the car—the Buick—the one Anne later died in on that same dusty country road. Al had felt loneliness many times, but never again quite like that day—until this moment.

♪♪♪

After cleaning himself up the best he could, Al started to drive, feeling worse with each block closer to home. He knew he couldn't share anything of the incident with Nora, regardless of the fact that he hadn't actually had sex with the woman. He'd been alone with her in her hotel, and shouldn't have been. He did wish he could talk to Nora about his feelings of desolation, but as he pulled into the driveway he decided not to wake her. Maybe tomorrow they could talk.

He slipped in the side door, poured a tumbler full of Scotch, took off his shoes and plunked himself down on the living room couch.

♪♪♪

The next morning, Nora found Al asleep on the couch. Beside him was an empty glass and an equally empty Scotch bottle. She got a blanket to cover him, and slipped an end cushion under his head. After she dressed, she went out for breakfast so not to disturb him, knowing he'd sleep until at least noon. There were errands she could take care of.

Her first guess was that he'd been out with the guys, and to avoid waking her, hadn't come to bed. Her second theory was one that she'd not yet had reason to consider seriously, nor would she this time. She longed for the day when she could fully trust him, but the bottle beside him frightened her. Throughout most of their relationship, his drinking had seldom been to excess, but lately this seemed to be changing. From what she knew of his past, it wasn't his return to heavy drinking that should worry her, but the more complicated addiction he'd once succumbed to—the one where he'd hear the Sirens' song, and start to dance with the demons again.

CHAPTER 31

FIVE - SOUTH TOWER [9]

The orderly put his hands on the patient's face and squeezed firmly, moving the man's head back and forth like a life-sized rag doll.

"Talk to me, you bastard. I gotta get done and get out of here. This can't be complete unless I get you to listen to what I have to say."

The injured man groaned and appeared to be attempting to open his eyes.

"That's it, come on now."

The room door bumped into the cleaning cart, and Officer Poole's voice leaked through the now semi-open entrance. "Hey, buddy, you almost done in there?"

Before Poole could fully enter, the orderly scrambled back to the cart and grabbed a mop, just as the cop was getting the door open enough to see in.

"Bit of a problem, Officer. I almost got it."

The door opened fully, and Poole saw the man in green swooshing the mop across the floor in front of the bathroom door.

"What happened?" said Poole.

"Shit, man, don't tell anyone, huh? I spilled some cleaning stuff and I'm trying to swab it up as quick as I can. Still gotta get the bathroom done too. You don't need to use it do you?" His face was wet enough to need mopping itself.

"Christ, buddy," said Poole, "are you on some union-stipulated maximum sweat quota or something? Cool it a bit. I'm in no rush, and no, I don't have to use the can."

Officer Poole laughed and shut the door. As the orderly leaned on the mop and wiped his forehead with his sleeve, the cop's face appeared once again. "You know," he said, "I shouldn't have let you in here anyway, not so easy as I did anyway. But hey, it's no matter. Guess who's going to be here sometime soon . . . your *pal*, Captain Rosetti. Maybe you'll be able to say hello to him if you aren't done in here yet."

As the cop closed the door, the orderly slumped into the chair to catch his breath. He looked at the still unconscious patient and muttered, "Why did you get me into this? Why couldn't you have just been what I needed you to be . . . what I know *you* needed to be?"

CHAPTER 32

UNSHUFFLED

*D*octor David son had been writing in his notebook for longer than usual. This bothered Al; it felt as if he was being ignored.

"Doc, come on. Can't you write your best seller after I'm gone? The meter is running here, man."

"Sorry, Alfred, but I'm organizing some thoughts about some of the things you've told me. I could do it later. I normally do most of my journaling after my appointments are finished for the day. But sometimes I need to get essential elements of our discussions *unshuffled,* so to speak, so I know best how to move forward in our sessions."

"Unshuffled?" said Al. "So how I've talked about stuff when I was a kid, and stuff when I was in Vegas, and stuff from yesterday and so forth . . . is 'shuffled', as in all mixed up, out of *sequence*? And you want to get it organized, to be able to make sense out of my life? Fat chance, Doc."

"I prefer to think not, Alfred. You're here for a reason: to seek help in sorting out difficulties in your life, correct? If you thought that was not possible, would you be here?"

"Just helping you write that best seller, Doc. Where did we leave off in the epic of Al Waters?"

"Well, Alfred, we've talked about your marriage with Michelle, and certain other major relationships of varying consequence. You've indicated a recurring problem in remaining faithful. Were these always what you'd call one-night stands; or were any of them more long-term, or 'serious'?"

"Depends on how far back we go, Doc. In my early twenties I messed around quite a bit, no matter who I was seeing. With Michelle I was okay until the open marriage deal, and that wouldn't count as cheating, would it? Between her, and when I met Nora, I was pretty much a Casanova clone. But once I married Nora, I was a good boy, pretty much anyway, until . . ."

"Alfred?" said the doctor, "excuse me for interrupting, but you've only vaguely referred to Nora before now. She was your second wife?"

"Can we do a music history lesson now, Doc? Or would you like another description of instrumental techniques?"

"Contrary to your practice of deflection, would you be willing to talk about Nora now?"

"Gee, a *historic* therapy moment for me; maybe *instrumental* in my journey to self-discovery?"

"Possibly, Alfred, but I can't comment about something, until you tell me about it."

"Okay, Doc, for once I won't change the subject. I met Nora in 1985 and in '88 we got married. She was kind of older than me by quite a bit, but it didn't matter to her so I didn't let it bother me either. She was sort of well-to-do . . . okay, *real* well-to-do, and she helped me get my career back on track and stuff. I won't bore you with all that right now.

"With *her*, I was on the straight and narrow for a long time. I guess it was when I started working at a bar called Charlie's Place that I sort of got deflected back into old, uh, *habits*? Not right away, mind you. Mostly it was like teasing myself with flirting and being Mr. Charm, with no intent to follow through. I suppose if you were to compare me to an alcoholic, it'd be like I was going to a bar and watching people drink all night, and believing I could handle that, no problem. Eventually, I did end up going with a woman to her hotel, but I managed to escape without going too far. It rocked me to have come that close. Shook up my belief that I could handle the temptations. And I did stuff like that a few more times, still never going so far as to have sex with anybody. A dangerous game, Doc . . . I know.

"Then, totally away from that scene where you think I'd be okay, someone kinda came along, and I . . . You ever played pool, Doc? It was like when you do a hard break. WHACK; scattered me across the table. Sank everything, including her. Game on, game over . . . all at once."

CHAPTER 33

GINNY
1993

*I*n mid-1993, Sound Art studio was doing well, with a steady business, mainly in demos and advertising jingles. Al and Nora's marriage was equally sound, at least on the surface, while the stress of the late-night gigs continued to chip away at the foundation of her trust. Although she believed he had remained faithful, she knew too well the dangers of the position he put himself in on a nightly basis. His assurances of absolute dependability were impossible to accept for long in the ruthless realm of bars, booze, and babes; it seemed inevitable he'd blunder into a trap, likely of his own making.

♪♪♪

Al was often approached by communication arts programs from high schools and colleges to host tours of the studio facility. During one such occasion, he noticed one of the students was paying more attention to the tour guide than to the tour. More than once he'd caught her looking at him instead of a particular piece of equipment he was demonstrating. She had quickly averted her eyes the first couple of times, but near the end of the session she grew bolder and smiled whenever he looked in her direction. When the scheduled time was completed and the group was filing out the exit, she came up to Al and said, "Thanks, Mr. Waters. This has been awesome."

Al suspected it wasn't by chance she'd found herself last at the door, as she lingered, waiting for a response.

"You're welcome, young lady," said Al. "But hey, you better get going. They'll be waiting on you out there."

Instead of going out, she let the door shut and said, "I'd love to see more of everything, Mr. Waters."

"Hey, call me 'Al', okay?"

"Okay, sure . . . and I'm Ginny Gerard. I love the music business, Mister Wa— Oops, I mean, *Al.* I'd so love to get into it in some way, someday . . . seriously."

Her smile vanished as her prof poked his head back in through the door and said, "Hey, Miss Gerard . . . Virginia, come on. Our ride is waiting."

"Sorry, Mr. Pendleton," said Ginny, "I'm coming." Turning back toward her host, she said, "So, Al . . . later, huh?"

Pendleton shooed her out the door and turned to Al. "Thanks again, Mr. Waters."

Something in the way Ginny had called their host "Al" removed all question that she intended to see the musician again. He made a mental note to have a chat with her later. From his own experience with his brilliant young student, he knew she was shrewd, persistent, and not averse to employing subtle flirtation as a negotiation tool. With him she had been safe since he maintained healthy personal boundaries at all times. However, Mr. Pendleton's instincts warned him of the inherent danger for any of his female students becoming involved in any way with a man like Al Waters: a jazz musician, likely with boundaries even less stringent than the forty-ninth parallel between the United States and Western Canada.

Al's instincts told him he'd just been flirted with by a teenager.

Man, she can't be more than eighteen. Funny, I can remember when Anne turned eighteen, and how old that seemed to me then. Eighteen was so worldly and grownup. This girl looks like a child . . . IS a child. Huh, is that prejudice or perspective? Anyway, she's not my type at all, even if she wasn't a kid. Too "thick"; no shape I can see; a tomboy if ever there was one. And what's with that baggy sweatshirt? Doesn't she want anyone to know she's a girl?

Damn, I hope she doesn't come back here. Haven't been tested in a while. Don't know why I think it, but this one could be trouble.

Although most women found Al attractive, his face wasn't what anyone would call *pretty*; he had more of a rugged, tired look. His soft deep voice, complemented by an easy smile and playful wit, evinced a gentle, genuine warmth. His charm was natural and effortless; he found no reason to inhibit it, unless the situation warranted more caution than consideration.

Okay, if I was available, and I'm not . . . Flirt with a teenager? Unacceptable. Definitely . . . I think.

♪♪♪

Over the following week, Ginny Gerard showed up at several places Al frequented: music store, convenience store, and post office. Each time, she expressed surprise at running into him, as they exchanged brief hellos and pleasantries. One afternoon, about two weeks after their initial meeting, Al walked into his favorite lunch spot, and there was Ginny sitting alone in a booth near the front window.

"Hi there, Virginia," said Al. "What's up? Did you move into the neighborhood or something? We keep crossing paths; not that I'm complaining."

"Hey, it's 'Ginny', remember? Actually, I live out in the burbs, but I was just down this way doing some, uh, shopping. Is this where you usually come for lunch? That's a blast." Her voice was trembling, on the verge of cracking. "You wanna join me, Al?"

He sat down across from her and said, "Thanks, Ginny. Yeah, this is my midday haunt. The food's good and it's cheap, and only a block from the studio. Can't beat it."

As nervous as Ginny was, it didn't take long for her to relax, Al being a master at easing the mood. He joked and gabbed and soon had her talking freely about anything and everything, mostly music-related.

"Al . . . ?" said Ginny, "You suppose I could come to your studio sometime? I mean if I was down this way, you know, just to watch? I wouldn't get in the way or anything. Maybe I could even help somehow."

"Sure, kid," said Al, "you wouldn't be in the way at all. You seem to know a lot about the recording business already, but you'd stand to learn a lot by being there. And maybe there could be ways you could help. The place is always a mess. You any good at cleaning?"

"Sure, I can clean. Awesome, yeah, absolutely. Anything, Al."

Al laughed. "Hey, to be honest, I was kidding, but then maybe that could be an idea if you're cool with it. I could teach you stuff, in trade for your services."

"Hmm," said Ginny, "in 'trade', huh? Your teaching would be strictly music and recording-related, right?"

She had a too-mature, sly look on her face which caught Al off guard. In pausing to study her expression for meaning, he began to more fully observe her features. Her huge, dark brown eyes were full of warmth and a subtle suggestion of sensuality, unbefitting her youth.

Uh-oh, did she really mean that the way it sounded? Is this kid hitting on me . . . ? Christ no. Cool it, you old pervert.

Al said, "I was of course talking music, little girl. What, you think I'm a letch? How old are you anyway, if I may ask?"

Her demeanor returned to shy innocence as she said, "FYI, what I think you are . . . is a very nice man. And a totally outrageous musician. And I was just trying to be cute, Al. Sorry, I'm not too good at that. Oh yeah, and I'm eighteen."

"Cool," said Al. "I guess we have to get used to each other's sense of humor. Hey, when have you heard me play?"

With a look of do-you-really-have-to-ask on her face, she said, "Last weekend at Charlie's Place."

"You were there? I didn't see you. Why didn't you come and say hi?"

She looked out the window for a moment, before saying, "I didn't want to bug you. And I was kind of scared you'd have forgotten who I was and maybe ignore me or something."

"Hey, come on already, the day Al Waters could ignore a lovely young woman is the day he shoots himself. Even if she is only eighteen. Next time, say something, okay? By the way, I'm flattered you think I'm good."

"Al, can I confess something?"

"Sure, Ginny, but I'm no priest. I can't absolve you of anything. I can only listen."

"Al, when you asked me how old I am, I was going to say something bogus, like twenty-two."

Yikes, is that about qualifying for the studio stuff . . . or about me?

Al said, "Well, I have to confess something too. I'm glad you were honest. No point in starting a business relationship *or* friendship based on a lie, is there?"

Not that I haven't done that a million times before.

"Tell ya what, kiddo, let's not waste any time. Wanna come back to the studio with me today? Or do you have plans?"

♪♪♪

Al and Ginny were a pair whose personae were cast from the same unlikely mold. Both were insecure, but outwardly bold—loners, who had learned to connect with others through necessity. This commonality made their bond both instant and strong.

Al was exploring new territory with his approach to both the friendship and their professional relationship as he obeyed a self-imposed no-flirting rule. On Ginny's part, she was less hesitant to display the growing affection she had for Al. He knew from their first meeting that she'd had a crush on him, but he wasn't concerned about reciprocation. While their age differ-ence added an unusual but fascinating element to friendship, it essentially eliminated any realistic options of more intimate involvement. He figured she'd eventually grow out of it, and they could remain friends and profes-sional associates thereafter.

Al enjoyed Ginny's company more than anyone he'd met in years. She was intelligent and quick-witted, possessing knowledge of music and movie trivia uncommon for someone of her generation. As for physical attrac-tion, she'd never have been chosen for a police lineup of potential romance targets for Al. Her dark brown hair was cut tomboy short, and she always dressed in sloppy sweatshirts and jeans. She was tall, just under five-foot-ten, and somewhat heavy, although "fat" wasn't the right word; she was too solid. Whenever she laughed Al felt young, as her expressive, fawn-like eyes radi-ated an innocent joy directly into his heart.

♪ ♪ ♪

Over the next few weeks, Ginny managed to continue her studies and work part-time at Sound Art, declaring she was learning more with Al than she was at school. She handled the phones whenever she was there, and often stayed late to help out with recording session preparations and "go-fer" duties: go for this, go for that. It wasn't long before Al offered her a small stipend for her work since he felt her contributions were above what he'd first thought of for her. She accepted the pay, but insisted on working even more because of it.

She joked, "Okay, I guess this means I have to call you 'boss' now, right?"

If Al had never paid her a cent, she would have done the same; she simply wanted to be there.

♪ ♪ ♪

One night, after an evening session at the studio, Ginny was helping clean up ashtrays, soft drink cans, and assorted debris from the day's activities, when Al realized they were the only two people left in the building.

"Hey, looks like we chased everyone away," said Al.

"Is that a bad thing?" said Ginny.

Al decided to ignore the probable innuendo in her question. "Not tonight it isn't. I'm tired, beyond beat. And speaking of beats, wasn't it a bugger the way that drummer couldn't keep the groove in that last song? Man, he made me think of every bad-drummer joke I ever heard."

Ginny smiled and said, "You mean like, how do you know it's a drummer at your door . . . ?"

"Yeah," said Al, "because the knocking speeds up and slows down. Right, like that. Hey, did I tell you that one?"

"Yes you did, boss," she said with a little salute.

"So, kiddo, do you need a ride home again tonight?" asked Al.

She usually traveled by bus, but the service was unavailable at this late hour. Al never asked her to stay beyond reasonable hours, but she frequently did so, and he suspected it wasn't by accident she'd end up needing a lift. To this point, their rides together had been friendly, full of conversation about music and philosophical ideas. Nothing had happened between them in any physical way, but he could feel her growing affection in the way she looked at him; he often caught her staring at him when he was working. He presumed she didn't expect him to notice, but because it happened so often, he began to wonder.

"Sure, boss," said Ginny, "that'd be great. D'ya feel like grabbing something to eat on the way, or get a drink maybe?"

"You mean, like a beer or something?" he said, laughing. "Not exactly legal for you, little girl."

"Hey, Al, you need to get your eyes checked. I guess you haven't noticed, I'm not a 'little' girl."

Al was caught between two possible meanings for the statement. Did she mean "not little" as in age, or size? He opted for what he thought was the least dangerous response.

"Uh, Ginny, I may be an old man, but I'm not blind. Absolutely I've noticed you're a very attractive, 'fully growed' young woman. Maybe I kid around about it so much, partly because you are?"

"Huh?" said Ginny. "No, no, I actually meant I wasn't 'little' . . . like in those skinny cheerleader types I hate? But hey, thanks for the accidentally coerced compliment."

"Okay," said Al, "let's back up a bit. We can't exactly go for a *drink* drink; not at a bar, 'cause you're a couple of years away from being legal."

"FYI, boss, you know part of why I thought it would be nice, is because my birthday is tomorrow. Tonight at midnight I'll be nineteen. Still not legal in Florida for two years, not to drink anyway. And hey, that really blows. Since I'm eighteen I can legally drive, and vote, and go to war and kill people, and have sex with adults. But I couldn't celebrate any of those things with a drink if I wanted to. Wack law, huh?"

Al said, "Well, we'll have to do something for your birthday. Gee, if you're with me we can declare you legal because I'm from Ontario, and up there it's legal for you at nineteen. Do you drink wine?"

"You mean red wine, like the bottle I saw in the studio fridge?"

"Sure, let's crack it open and celebrate your birthday. Hey, look at the clock. In ten minutes you're legal in Ontario."

♪ ♪ ♪

By thirty minutes after midnight, Al and Ginny had consumed most of the wine. After listening for a while to some of the tracks from the day's recording, Al suggested something more appealing and dug out a Stan Getz tape. He slouched back on the reception room couch while Ginny sat cross-legged on the floor near his feet.

"A toast, to the newest *honorary* Ontario legal drinker," said Al, raising his plastic cup. "Hey, you need a refill, little girl? I mean, big girl. Shit, I mean, *lady*?"

"Fill 'er up, sir . . . best you can anyway," said Ginny, pouting at the small amount of remaining wine. "You should buy bigger bottles of wine, boss."

"I didn't even buy this. It was a gift from a client."

Ginny drank back the final half cupful and threw the empty container on the floor. Raising one hand in a pompous, dismissive gesture, she laughed and said, "Let the cleaning lady get that. Oh, right, that's me."

Al said, "Don't worry about it. I just gave you the rest of the day off 'cause of your birthday."

For a few minutes they sat quietly, swept up in Getz's inimitable tenor saxophone style.

Al said, "John Coltrane was once asked what he thought of Stan Getz's tone. His answer was, 'We'd all sound like that if we could.' What a tribute, eh?"

Ginny said, "That's cute how you say 'eh' every once in a while. Guess the Canadian in you isn't quite all washed away by 'Yankee-speak.'"

Al laughed. "Ya know, I never consciously tried to stop using 'Canadianisms', but over the years most of them have faded. I think if I'm distracted or tired or drunk they come back full force."

Ginny's smile was short-lived. She took in a deep breath and said, "Al, I need to tell you something."

Struggling to sit up straighter, Al said, "What? You're not quitting are you? I've gotten to need you around here. Maybe I can pay you more, or—"

"No, no, are you mental? Not what I was getting at. Not even close. And hey, don't sit up," she said, putting her hand on his leg. "I'll move a little closer."

She gripped his knee to pull herself over to the edge of the couch and leaned against his thigh. Once settled, she didn't remove her hand. Soon she was moving it up and down, massaging firmly, first his calf, then upward to his thigh.

Al reached down and touched her hand with his and said, "Maybe you better not do that?"

She said, "If you really want me to stop . . . I will."

"Wanting, may not be the way to look at it," he said. "What I want, and what I *should* want aren't always easy to sort out. I just know it feels real nice. But I also know it's real wrong."

Ginny wrapped both her arms around Al's thighs and laid her cheek on his lap. She whispered, "Al, is this so wrong . . . if I love you?"

"Ginny," said Al, "I've known for a long time how you feel. At least I've wondered, but it seems so unreal, so . . . weird even? Mostly I guess, 'cause you're so young."

"Al, you're not old. You're hardly out of your thirties really. And I'm almost twenty, sort of . . . you know, relatively speaking. Would you say a guy who's thirty is too old for a twenty-year-old? What's age anyway; just a number, right?"

"Ginny, it's interesting how your math is kind of prejudiced. I'm midforties and you just turned nineteen. We're about twenty-five years apart, my girl. And you make it sound like it's only ten? Nice try."

"Al, I don't care what people think. Is that what you're afraid of?"

"Not really, sweetheart. A much bigger deal is . . . I'm married."

"Your wife doesn't know what she's got. I can tell you're not happy with her. You would be, with me. And by the way, didn't you tell me she's quite a bit older than you? Isn't it a double standard you're showing here?"

"Nora isn't twenty-five years older than me, not even close. But I have to confess we haven't been as happy lately as we once were. My fault, no doubt."

Ginny moved one hand up onto Al's right thigh and stroked back and forth with just the tips of her fingers. Where her head was resting made it impossible to ignore what was happening beneath the fabric.

"Oh my God," she said, "I think I've awakened something . . . something nice."

Al groaned and said, "Oh man, no conscience below the waist. I'm sorry, but you better stop that, and get your head off me before . . ."

"Before what, Al? I said to tell me to stop if you don't like it, not to ask, but to tell me. Go on, tell me you hate this. Your body tells me you like it . . . a lot."

Hearing no response, she moved her hand to where biological urges were responding, and she gripped his swelling desire, the delicacy gone from her fingers.

"This must be so uncomfortable," she said, undoing his fly. "Let's set him free."

In a voice bereft of resolve or sincerity, Al said, "That is definitely not safe. If you—"

"*If* I get my hand in here?" she said with a laugh. "*If* I get this monster out of his cage? What'll happen? Will it hurt me? Oh my God, it's beautiful."

As she caressed him, she asked, "Al, does this feel good?"

He reached down to try to stop her, but she batted his hand away and began to stroke more aggressively. Al reached down again, undid his belt, and pulled down his pants and underwear to give her more room to operate. "Oh baby, that is crazy good. Don't stop."

Hardly able to talk between gasps for breath, she said, "I . . . am not . . . stopping. I want you . . . to . . . get off . . . quick as—"

"Babe," he said, "that's it. You rest now . . . Let *me* rest."

She fell back onto the couch beside him and cuddled up against his chest. She looked at the wetness on her hand and wrist, and on his shirt. "That's as awesome as I imagined it," she said. "Just like in those videos my friend Janey has, but so, *not* gross, since it's yours. I love you, Al Waters . . . so much. You just don't know."

"I think I'm starting to," said Al. "I do think I'm starting to."

Ginny sighed and luxuriated in the moment, feeling she'd changed her life forever. Her tears became a warm, gentle wave of joy, washing away any doubt she may have had about becoming this intimate with Al.

For him, the feelings were comprised of sexual release, embarrassment, fear, and the old pleasure-crushing team of depression and self-hatred.

♪ ♪ ♪

When Al drove Ginny home, she snuggled close to him. They said little the whole way. Before she got out of the car she said goodbye and kissed his cheek. He said, "See ya soon, kiddo."

She said, "Night, boss," and headed up the walk to her home. Al wondered if they *would* ever see each other again.

♪♪♪

Two nights later, Al was alone in the studio, working on mixing sax overdubs into a project. When the phone rang he almost didn't pick up, but on the last ring before the answering machine kicked in, he grabbed it.

"Hey, boss, it's me," said Ginny. "I'm around the corner. Can I come up?"

"Sure, I'll buzz you in when you ring," said Al.

When she arrived she had a tote sack strapped over her shoulder, and she set it down with a loud clank.

"What the heck you got there?" asked Al.

"In a minute . . ." she said, as she ran up to give him an enthusiastic hug, and a kiss on the mouth. "That's freaky, huh, boss? We didn't kiss like that the other night. Are we like, total dorks, or what?"

Al looked in the bag and found two bottles of the same red wine they'd shared before. "What have we here? Are you going to try to party me up again? It isn't your birthday again is it?" He wasn't smiling, and Ginny knew that *look* too well, from times he'd chastised musicians who weren't cutting a part as fast as he'd expected.

"Al, come on. Don't be mean. I knew you were going to be alone, and I thought we could—"

"No, *you* come on, little girl. I think what happened the other night was something that shouldn't have happened. I don't want that to be a habit or whatever. We have to get back to a professional approach here."

He could almost hear her heart breaking as her eyes widened and her lip trembled. "Al, I love you. Don't you believe that?"

"Ginny, I believe that you think you do. But trust me, those feelings can be misleading, and loving somebody can be painful. Don't get hurt by something you might be a fool about."

"I'm a fool already, Al . . . for thinking maybe you might feel that way about me." She began to cry and started for the door.

"Ginny wait. You know I care about you. And if I didn't, I'd throw you on the couch right now and let you love me as much as you wanted. But I do care, and the last thing you need is to be involved with me."

She turned, and through sobs managed to say, "Well, it . . . it's not my birthday anymore . . . but can you . . . can you love me, just a bit? Can we share this wine, and just laugh and talk and play, like we always have?"

He hugged her, with her head against his chest. "Sure, honey, we can go back to square one, or two, or whatever the hell square it was before the other night, okay?"

"Okay, Al," she said between sniffles, "let's get that wine open. I need it bad."

♪♪♪

Al didn't put on the Stan Getz tape, in case it was too much of a mood reminder. Instead, he found a Thelonious Monk album, the least romantic selection he could think of. Over the next hour they listened to the music and chatted about many things, with no mention of what had happened on her birthday. The second bottle was well beyond what Ginny normally would consume, and it became evident in her choice of topic.

"My dad was a motherfucker, Al."

"Well, I guess he kind of had to be, girl . . . or you wouldn't uh, exist . . . ?"

"Ha ha, cut it out. I knew you'd say that as soon as I got the word out. Just shut up, and let me tell you about the motherf— uh, the jerk."

"Okay, fine. Tell me about him. What did he do, smack you around?"

"Nah, worse than that. He loved me to bits. We were peas in a pod for the first ten years of my life, Al. He took me fishing; taught me to play ball and soccer; and I helped him all the time with jobs around the house and stuff. I was like, Velcroed to his ass, so to speak. And I don't mean his actual ass, you ass."

"So why the hell you call him such nasty names, girl?"

"Simple . . . 'cause all of a sudden he decides he's not living with us anymore. He gets a divorce from us. And even though he promised me things would be great 'cause he'd come and see me all the time, and I'd go be with him lots, it didn't happen, Al. In about two months he's pretty much gone. I got cards and money and stuff for birthdays and Christmas, but he was . . . gone. He never really loved me . . . is what I think. He was just lying all those years."

"Hey, kiddo, don't cry again. Makes ya look all red and wet and yucky. Hey, come on, not on my sleeve. Aw, Christ, you did it again. Here, wipe your damn nose on this cleaning rag."

Wavering between laughter and sobs, she managed to say, "Well, we're sort of even then, 'cause the other night you got your 'stuff' on my sleeve. But ya know, old boss of mine, I'm not complaining. I liked that."

Al held her in his arms and stroked her forehead. "It'll be okay, girl. Hey, don't quote me, but I do sort of love you, whether I say it or not."

"You do, Al? You do . . . ?"

"Yeah," he said, "but just a wee little bit."

"That's enough, Al, enough for me. Kiss me, Al, please, just once?"

Al's wine consumption wasn't enough to make him drunk, but combined with Ginny's tears and the anger he now felt for her father, it had him once again teetering along that same old precipice on the edge of poor judgment. The predictable slip down into the abyss came quickly. Not even stopping to complain about the wetness of her nose and cheeks, he kissed her luscious full lips once, as she'd asked, and then again—this time his body doing the asking—and then again, and again.

It was too late for love to get in the way of lust. This was a freight train with no engineer and no brakes. With voracious abandon, they tore at each other's clothes, tossing shirts and pants and underwear in every direction. In seconds they lay together naked, and she said, "Please, Al. Please make love to me?"

He was already on top of her, and as she moved her legs further apart, he began to attempt to enter her. When he saw her wince, he pulled away, but she pleaded, "No, Al, don't stop."

He said, "But I don't want to hurt you."

"It's all right, baby. Please do it. You know it's my first time, don't you?"

"Yeah, Ginny, I figured that. You sure it's okay?"

"Please don't stop, Al. The last thing I want is for you to stop. Don't be Daddy. Don't quit on me. Please don't run away, ever?"

Familiar shadows passed through his thoughts: foggy, dark impressions of words, smells, and feelings—and a place.

The string switch . . . whiskey in the carpet, like a puddle of spilled innocence . . . the room with no windows . . .

♪♪♪

When it was over, she was crying. Al asked if he'd hurt her too much and she said, "No, silly. I'm crying 'cause I'm happy. Men don't get that, *do* they?"

He held her for several minutes and then hesitantly suggested they should get going. There was much to do to clean up, and tomorrow was a busy day. Over the next half-hour as they straightened up the studio, and later as he drove her home, Al began to feel increasingly upset with himself. He knew he shouldn't have bought into this moment of weakness, but this wasn't exactly a return item. Consequences were inevitable, both in his relationship with Ginny, and at home. As normal as depression was for him after sex, this had a tinge of something worse, something different, and yet vaguely familiar.

When he finally fell asleep that night he dreamed of his sister, Anne, for the first time in years. Once he woke up and thought she was really there at the bedside, holding his hand, telling him he was going to be okay—that he wasn't *bad*. As he slowly accepted the cold reality that she wasn't there at all, he began to fall back to sleep, tears began trickling down his cheek over his nose and onto the pillow.

Tears . . . crap. Like that damned whiskey, soaking into the carpet fibers in the room with no windows again. What a waste. Annie, wherever you are, I love you. I'll try not to let you down again.

He held little faith this promise could be kept. But Anne would forgive him. Would Ginny? Would Nora . . . ?

♪♪♪

Al and Ginny continued to be intimate for several months afterwards, and Nora's suspicions grew in direct proportion to her husband's diminishing interest in *her*. Escalating inevitability loomed, with Al sliding down a fast run to the bottom of a steeper slope than he'd ever been on. He could only foresee an outcome like that pathetic crashing ski jumper on the Wide World of Sports opening sequence: the poor agony-of-defeat guy. Soon, Al was spending progressively more after-work time at Charlie's, not just flirting with women, but taking them for intimate car rides and hotel visits. He was fully aware of the irony of his double infidelity, but it was too late.

Ginny caught him before Nora did. One night, after closing time at Charlie's, she waited outside, and spotted Al, arm in arm with a woman. When she confronted them, she said, "Al, what the hell? You'd rather be with this old bitch instead of me?"

The woman with Al said, "Well, honey, it's the second time I'll have been with him, so I guess he sees something in me, huh? Why don't you just run along? I think I hear your mommy calling."

Al whispered to the woman and sent her on her way. "Ginny," he said, "I'm really sorry. I slipped up . . . but it won't happen again. I promise."

He walked off with Ginny and spent the next half-hour calming her down. Once she was convinced of his sincerity, he took her home and kissed her goodnight. As he drove away, she thought to herself. *He's just a man. I love him . . . What can you do?*

Al was headed directly to meet the woman he'd been with at Charlie's. As he fingered the hotel key she'd slipped him, he tried not to worry about Ginny.

Damn it, she's just a girl. She thinks she loves me . . . What can you do?

♪ ♪ ♪

Nora was slower to catch Al in his new old ways. But she was unhappy with their marriage in general, since he was never home, never had anything to say, and appeared to be drinking every night *and* day. He'd taken to sleeping on the couch more often than not. The smell of other women was on his skin, in his hair and his clothes—and even without hard evidence, she knew it was time.

One day, just before noon, she knelt next to the couch and woke him with a few nudges to the shoulder. When he had finally grumbled, "Good morning," she said, "Al, I know you were with someone last night . . . another woman. I can smell it. I can feel it. I can see it, even in your half-open eyes. Is it true . . . ?"

Al's momentary hesitation was all the answer she needed. Before he could attempt any excuses or verbal escape routes, she got up, went outside to the pool deck, and waited. Moments later, when she heard his car start up, she immediately called her lawyer.

The next day she told him he was out. And so was she—from the studio and from the marriage. She filed for divorce, and at the same time withdrew her investment from the business, leaving him on his own. Without her backing, especially since he had let the studio business go basically unattended for some time, he had to sell it all just to cover the debt. He was doing all right with steady work at Charlie's and occasional weddings and party gigs, so he wouldn't starve. But it was a shock to his system to take up residence in a small apartment, and downgrade his transportation from a Mercedes to an old Mercury Cougar. After Nora, the irony crossed his mind with each woman he was with—each "Mercury", as he began to think of them.

He refused to allow himself to miss Nora. There had been a time with her when he'd had it all—not just the pleasure of her home and money—but the peace of knowing he had unmitigated love, and was wanted and needed for who he was, not what he looked like, or the musicians' mystique factor. Too bad she hadn't known sooner who he *really* was. She'd allowed false hopes to convince her that the nice-guy Al was the real one. At least now she had been shown the truth.

He felt as if he'd lost her long before. He was honestly happy for her since she could now try to find some joy elsewhere. For Al, the only way to look at it in a positive light, was to try to enjoy the total freedom he could now experience.

Free to be the real Al . . . Yeay . . . Whoopee . . . Shit.

CHAPTER 34

METHADONE FOR THE HEART
1994 - 98

*W*ithout the built-in stability of being with Nora, Al went from being a one-woman man to an any-woman man: seeking love in all the wrong places, all the right ones, and everywhere in between. His Charlie's Place gig was always a reliable source of female companionship of a temporary nature, since many of the clientele were tourists. When pickings were slim there, he'd usually settle for Ginny who was always ready to come and stay the night in his tiny studio apartment. If she wasn't available, or if he wanted fresh inspiration, he'd go to other bars after work or on off nights. This lifestyle was tiring, but his energy was high from being out of his day job and only working four nights a week. He had to burn off his boredom somehow, and he couldn't be happy unless he was on the prowl, relishing the reward of each conquest, which served as a temporary elixir to quench his thirst for being desired.

Al knew this pursuit was destined—like Billy's lust for chemical highs— for the always hopeful climb, to the inevitable crash and burn. Coming down was quicker and more intense after each excursion d'amour. While a drug addict's eventual tragic outcome would be internal organ deterioration, loss of mental acuity, or lethal overdose; Al's ruination was equally guaranteed, in the form of emotional implosion. He wondered if he could ever find something like "methadone for the heart" to quell the ache for female attention.

Ginny was immersed in such a heavy workload at school, she didn't have time to consider herself in jeopardy; although she was as hooked on her own needs as Billy or Al were on theirs. But unlike them, she was living under a rose-colored bubble of naiveté, unaware of the dangers. She loved being with Al whenever she could, entirely convinced she'd be with him permanently when she graduated and found work.

♪♪♪

Al decided to try a new source of social opportunity by placing a singles ad in the local Bargain Hunter magazine. His hope was to meet someone who could fulfill all his needs and keep him from craving the impossible—she'd be his "methadone gal".

Male Seeking Female

Mid-forties male: humorous, charming, tall, good-looking, intelligent (modest?), golf nut, music nut (generally a nut?). Seeks someone of similar attributes (except the male part). Let's meet for coffee and see if we stir up something special. All the bad jokes you can stand—no charge.

♪♪♪

The response to Al's ad was overwhelming, the first week alone bringing in forty replies. Of those, at least thirty were interesting enough to follow up on. He began the process by phoning each promising candidate. The conversations were, for the most part, enjoyable and fun; with some ending quickly when the wit and charm of the respondent's letter wasn't born out in chat. Within a few days, Al had set up fifteen coffee meetings. It was going to be a challenging week; there were more letters arriving each day.

Over several weeks he met many fascinating women, and while some of them were the type he hoped for, some were of the category he was attempting to stay away from. He had sex with a few of those, but only once with each. There was only so much time in a day, and only so much Al to go around. He was almost relieved he wasn't still twenty-one, with this much opportunity.

Essentially, it was impossible to choose one beauty from the bevy, partially because so many were so "right". This was a problem for which he hadn't prepared: all these decent, respectable women anxious to start a relationship. But would they be content with the Al he had shown them so far, or with the *real* Al? He was fairly certain of the answer, so his solution was to not pursue any of them beyond the first couple of dates. As an efficient manner of sating physical lust, his plan was working, but wasn't giving him what he truly needed. To be an effective habit eraser, a methadone gal had to know what he was.

He was careful to hide the stack of letters, so Ginny wouldn't see them when she visited. But for a man whose life revolved around sound, it was fitting that betrayal wouldn't come from written words—but from spoken ones.

♪ ♪ ♪

One night, several months after Al's coffee date campaign began, Ginny had stayed over. In the morning, with no school scheduled and Al still asleep, she decided to make breakfast for both of them. Dressed only in one of Al's tee shirts, she hummed contentedly as she gathered the necessary ingredients.

The pan was just starting to sizzle as the coffee maker sputtered its final drops of brew. She had begun cracking eggs one by one into the bubbling butter, when the sound of the phone startled her, causing her to drop an egg directly onto her bare foot.

"Shit," she said, trying to grab the phone with one hand, while trying to wipe up the mess with a dishrag. The answering machine clicked on, with Al's greeting: "Hey, I'm out . . . leave a message at the beep."

A woman's voice crackled through the speakers. "Hi . . . Al . . . ? This is Sandra Brooks. Remember me? We met a few weeks ago after I answered your personal ad . . . ? Anyway, I saw another ad this week where a man said he'd met someone from his ad, and they'd had coffee at Denny's and had a great time, and he'd lost her number. Uhh, was that you? If so, did you mean me? If not, just forget I called, but if so . . . here's my number again, 954-555-5002. Hope to hear back from you. Byeee."

The click of the closing phone connection served as the perfect punctuation—a large exclamation point dagger, driven through Ginny's heart.

She turned to look at Al, who hadn't stirred; his back was still toward her. In a rack on the table, next to her left hand was a ten-inch carving knife. She was trembling as she reached for it. As her fingers wrapped around the handle her entire body began to shake. With each step toward the bed her legs seemed to double in weight as if she were slogging through quick-set cement. But determination born of anger and pain sustained her resolve to continue forward where she would end her torment—by ending him.

A rap at the door knocked her back into rational thought, and she stopped just short of the bed where Al rolled over and lifted his head, he too awakened by the noise, which now included a voice from outside. "Hey, Al, come on, open up. It's fucking nearly eleven o'clock."

Al said, "Ginny, it's Billy. Let him in, if you're decent. I can't see yet."

She spun around and stumbled back to the counter like a drunken soldier trying to keep up with the quick-time pounding of her heart. Drawing in a sudden gasp of air, she realized she hadn't breathed since the first step of her homicidal trek toward Al. She tried to set the knife down, but it had been welded to her hand, first by rage, now by fear. Prying her fingers loose, she placed the weapon on the counter and went to open the door.

When Billy came in he said, "Sorry, honey. Ginny, right? I didn't know Al wasn't alone. He knew I was coming by this morning. The bum shoulda told you."

She said nothing as she gathered up her clothes and went into the bathroom while Billy grabbed the coffee pot and poured himself a full mug.

Al said, "Hey, come on, Ginny. I need to go real bad. Hurry up in there or I'll piss myself. And hey, did I hear the phone ring before, or was I dreaming?"

She emerged from the bathroom, fully dressed, and headed straight for the door, still saying nothing.

Al said, "What's up, Ginny? What did I do this time?"

Over her shoulder she said, "Check your messages—" as the door slammed shut on her words.

♩♩♩

If Al hadn't had to relieve himself so badly, he may have chased after Ginny, but once he heard the message from Sandra Brooks, he was glad he hadn't. He glanced at the knife sitting on the counter.

Why'd she need that for eggs and bacon? Holy crap . . . no way she's THAT pissed off, is there . . . ?

Billy poured Al a coffee and sat down with his own. "So what's up with that girl, Al? I've seen her hanging out with you since back when you still had the studio. And now she's what, shacking up with you? Shit, man, she's just a kid. What in damn hell are you thinking?"

"It's a long story," said Al. "Don't go there right now, okay? And don't look at me that way. I got hunted down, stuffed and mounted real good by that . . . *kid.*"

"Well, Al, the way I've seen you catting around, night after night lately, I feel like it's 1970 all over again. I got enough trouble with flashbacks and shit, without you confusing my poor old brain any more than it does to itself. What's up with that? You give up on the 'good boy' life? Is Nora history . . . for permanent?"

"I messed that up real bad," said Al. "She was good for me, and I don't mean just her ritzy digs and cars and stuff. She's a pretty cool lady; needed something that wasn't in me to give."

Billy cackled. "Like what, Al? You got problems in the sack?"

"What? Well, maybe, but not like you mean, you dope. Nah, it's more like I can't accept that someone loves me, unless there's something wrong with them. And if there *is*, then I can't really love them because they're messed up, right? Well, Nora loved me and the only thing wrong with her is that she's dumb enough to want me. There's *her* flaw, isn't it? Damn it, Billy, I don't know what the hell I'm trying to say. All I know is my fucking head hurts. Just shut up, okay?"

"So, Al, was it a drag being with someone, excuse the term, *old* like that? She's like, in her sixties, isn't she?"

"Never found out her age, Billy, but it doesn't matter now anyway. One good thing is I'm still covered by her health insurance plan. I don't know if she did that on purpose or just forgot to cancel me, but I'm afraid to mention it, just in case. Health care for a sax player. Cool, eh? Almost like being in Canada."

"Yeah, in more ways than that, Al. Your mama's Canadian I assume. Or did you ever really have one? Wouldn't surprise me if you just crawled out from under a rock somewhere."

"Billy, you don't want to go down that path. Believe me, Nora's not my mother; doesn't want to be. Although now that you mention it, I kind of wish she could have been. At least I could always trust Nora to love me, yeah, even when she's mad. She can't just switch love off, like my mother could."

"Will she take you back, do ya think . . . ever?"

"I wouldn't ask, Billy. I care too much about her to fail her again. Stupid me, right?"

"That's the Al I like. Yeah, stupid sometimes, but your heart is a lot better than you think it is. I wish I could help you, like you've done for me, man. But I don't know how. I think your problem is, maybe worse than mine."

"Ha, you mean I'm a love-junkie? Well, it doesn't cost as much as drugs anyway, right?"

"Maybe not in cash, Al, but what about the hurt debt you're building up? It's not just yourself being messed up here. You think that girl Ginny is *okay*? No way, man. You may think she's tough and can handle the crap you hand her, like it isn't a big deal for her? But you're way off on that one. I'm no shrink, but I can see a bad scene brewing in somebody's eyes. She's not okay . . . not even close."

♪♪♪

This was clinic day and Al regularly went with Billy since the time he'd "forgotten" to go. First they'd head to the nearby restaurant for brunch. Usually they'd gab about music and musicians, and occasionally, personal issues.

As they headed out the door, Billy said, "So hey, man, the phone message from that chick sounded like she's hot for you. Ya gonna follow up?"

"Sandra Brooks. Huh, I don't really remember her much. But her voice has kind of a nice ring to it. Maybe I'll give her a call later. Hey, let's not talk anymore about my women problems, okay, man?"

"Cool," said Billy. "Let's talk about the drummer situation some more. It is most *un*-copacetic. We gotta make a change. You gotta be fed up with Neil, right?"

"Damn straight, Billy. He's got all the chops in the world, but when I zig, he zags, and well, you know better than I do, I think the only time he's getting into it is when he solos. He's not a team player *is* he?"

"I totally agree, Al. He gets up on stage with us, looks like he's part of us; but inside, he's somewhere far away."

Al nodded. "It's like he doesn't even need us there, except to supply purpose to a soul that doesn't know it's lonely."

Billy looked at Al and smiled. "Hey, man, I thought we weren't supposed to talk anymore about your women problems."

Al gave Billy a gentle punch to the arm and said, "Touché, mon ami. Now let's just go eat, and figure out who we'll get on drums. Hey, I know . . . we'll get a new gig, and just leave Neil behind on his own at Charlie's. He can play all by himself, happily ever after. He might not even notice we're gone."

Billy cackled again. "Hey, playing alone? Maybe that's your answer to the women problems too, you dumb Canuck. Yeah, yeah, I'll shut up about it. But you're buying brunch."

♪♪♪

Ginny watched from behind a tree as Billy and Al left for the restaurant. She had to do something. If she didn't love him so much she could write him off—or "off" him. But neither option would solve how she felt. The third option she came up with was the only one to consider realistically. That same day, she dropped out of school and moved into a small apartment a few miles away in Fort Lauderdale. Within weeks she enrolled in a journalism course at another college, to begin her new life, sans Al Waters.

♪♪♪

Early in 1995, the Al Waters Quartet was signed to play at Lou's Lounge, having been stolen away from their longtime gig at nearby Charlie's Place. The money was not much better, but change is often a good thing for a band. From the original group, Al kept only Billy Crothers, and hired drummer Pete Logan. A handful of adequate but uninspiring bass players went through the turnstiles for several months, until the serendipitous discovery of Wesley Woodward, an extraordinary young talent who'd recently moved to the area.

Settling into the new surroundings renewed Al's focus on music for the first time in a long while. It was a satisfying experience to work with the revised-edition quartet, and even Billy showed signs of not only playing better, but also behaving himself. For both him and Al, life once again had some interest and positive energy. Their old self-description as "the depression twins" began to fade from relevance.

For over two years Al and the group kept a steady stream of business coming in to Lou's. They were a draw to locals as well as tourists, reputed to be the best jazz in South Florida.

Even with the added bonuses of increased status and popularity, Al was unhappy with his life in general. Regular sexual encounters with a variety of women continually bolstered his theory that he needed one special person with whom he could be stable. He decided to give the Bargain Hunter another try. With his first ad, he'd met several possibilities, but had soon determined he wasn't ready. Maybe now he was.

As before, the replies poured in. He'd worded the ad similarly to the first, since it had been so long ago. At this point he figured anyone who had answered the other time must have met someone by now; or if not, they must be pretty undesirable to still be in the market. He knew this technically meant *he* was one of those old-stock items, but what the heck—he was like a fine Scotch, better with age, and therefore worth more than the new stuff. At least it was one way to look at it, without feeling stale-dated right out of the game.

♪♪♪

The year 1997 brought little contentment to Al other than the music which was, as always, the friend and lover who wouldn't let him down. It had no flaws other than what he might inject with interpretation or technique, but the art form in itself was pure. All it asked was that you try to climb as high as

your own limits, and your emotional and spiritual rewards would be bountiful, with no risk of retraction.

One Saturday night during the second set, a rare gift of second chance
was delivered to Al. Dixie handed him a folded piece of paper. Inside was a
hundred-dollar bill, and a handwritten note:

This hundred is for you if you play Blue Spanish Eyes. But you have
to play it as written, Al Martino style. No jazzing it up. If you improvise at all, I get the money back and you owe me another hundred on top.

As Al tried to block out the stage light with his hand, he strained to see
through the darkness of the lounge. It was a fairly busy evening compared
to the norm of late—perhaps twenty-five people. No one looked familiar,
other than regulars whom he knew to be too cheap to part with a hundred
dollar bill for a song, or for a joke.

"Hey, Dixie," said Al to the waitress as she passed by again. "Who gave
you this?"

"Well, Al, old pal," she said, holding up a twenty-dollar bill, "they gave me
this, so's I wouldn't tell you."

"Well, was it a man or a woman?" asked Al.

"Sorry, Al, not supposed to say, and for twenty bucks I can keep my old
mouth shut real tight." With that, she maneuvered back amongst the tables.

Al couldn't see clearly up to the front of the club, so he went back to
playing, deciding on a thorough room search at break time. After two more
songs he said to the band, "This is gonna sound strange, but we're gonna do
'Spanish Eyes', and just like we were on a wedding gig. NO jazz. Got it? Play
it so straight, we'll make Robert Goulet sound hip. Key of F, boys. Let 'er rip."

Billy said, "Far-fucking-out," as he began a rumba style intro. Wesley and
Pete joined in and Al began the melody, fully confident in his ability to play
with total restraint; which he did, until the eighth measure when he accidentally played a sharp five, heading to the natural fifth. In the next few bars
the flood gates burst. Sixteenth note runs began to escape as wildly as mice
scurrying when the cat comes home. Billy cackled, and added altered chords
in growing complexity, followed by Wesley's addition of Jaco Pastorius-
inspired bass figures, and Pete's polyrhythmic homage to Max Roach.

It was the most fun they'd had all night, until Al remembered it had cost
him a hundred dollars; *two* hundred, if he took the note seriously. He told
the guys to take a break, and he set his horn down. Just as he stepped off the

stage, Dixie came up and handed him another piece of paper. "Supposed to give you this now," she said.

The note read: May I collect my two hundred now?

Al said to Dixie, "When did you get this second note?"

"Same time as the first one," she said. "Just had to wait till I got the signal to give it to you. Why?"

"Someone out there knows me too well," said Al. "Yeah, and I got no doubt at all who it is."

He strode through the lounge, eyeing each patron, until he came to the table nearest the front door where he sat down next to the lone woman occupying the bench seat.

"Well," she said, "you owe me two hundred dollars, and you still showed up? I'm impressed."

"It's worth it just to see you, Nora. You look fantastic! Man, I've missed you. How have you been?"

"Do you mean that, Al? Or is it only Mr. Charm doing his thing?"

Al kissed her on the cheek and said, "Here's the hundred. Can you wait for the rest till we get paid tonight?"

"Al, I'll forgive the debt if you talk with me for a while, and if you promise you'll be completely honest."

"So now you want to pay me to tell you the truth? Maybe you should have tried that years ago."

"If you mean 'buy your love', then no. I used to wonder if that's what I had always done. It hurt deeply to think that you didn't love me for me, but for the life I could give you. Was that really it, Al?"

"Nora, I think at first it probably was. But after I lost you it finally dawned on me, I'd come to need you for way more than material crap. I've really missed you. Well, and the Mercedes, but don't tell my Mercury that."

She smiled and touched his hand. "One more question to get you off the hook for that cash. When you cheated on me . . . did you love her?"

"Are you serious, Nora? If there's anything I could say one hundred percent for sure about the crap I put you through, was that love had nothing to do with any of it. And I haven't loved anyone since I was with you, not even close."

"Al, I so want to believe that. A sexual affair is a horrible thing to do to your partner, but if you'd been in love with someone else, that would have been so much worse."

Al held her hand and smiled. "Nora, do you know what methadone is?"

"Of course I do, Al. Don't forget what being around Billy has taught me."

"You wanna be my methadone gal, Nora? Just say yes. I'll explain later."

♪ ♪ ♪

Al moved back in with Nora late in 1997, and this time things were going to be different. She told him she might consider marrying him again, but not for at least a year, because she needed absolute trust in his ability to keep away from trouble. In his heart, he knew it was fair and wise for her to think this way. She kept him on her health insurance plan which she'd never changed even after the divorce; any other fringe benefits would only include a roof over his head and occasional use of the Mercedes. He kept his 1988 Mercury Cougar for daily use, often saying how crappy it looked in her driveway. She only laughed and said, "Clothes don't really make the man, nor does a car make the home."

Al laughed. "Don't you think it's ironic," he asked, "about the Cougar I mean, and you being, you know, a touch older than me? Won't the jokes just be flying?"

"Al," she sighed, "if you were twenty-five maybe. But you're not. You're *so* not, and I think I have to remind you of that much too often."

♪ ♪ ♪

Al's wish for a methadone gal was coming true. With Nora in his life again, he was able to push away his promiscuous urges. He found a way of talking to himself in which he would actually pay attention. If a woman at the bar appeared to be interested in him he would be friendly, but allow only a brief conversation to ensue. He called it his one-minute rule. Big John was the designated timer if Al appeared to lose track. He'd keep an eye on all chat activities, and if the one-minute barrier was breached, he'd beckon to Al with some "important" message, or a fake phone call. With John's help, and sometimes Billy's, the system was running smoothly.

The most dangerous times were when Al would get too heavily into the Scotch. As much as Big John would attempt to "advise" Al on his limits, it was not always possible for him to keep up, especially on extra busy nights. One such night in the fall of 1998 proved to be a test of the most fragile part of the system, Al's alcohol-weakened inner alarm.

♪ ♪ ♪

She was sitting with a man at table three, near Al's side of the stage. With her long blond hair, milky white porcelain skin, and delightful double-D cleavage beckoning from her low-cut black dress, she was a walking, talking, wine-swilling Barbie doll. Al shivered as he was reminded of Frances Kaplan from so many years ago.

During the early songs of the band's last set, the woman had been demonstrating conspicuous unbridled attention toward Al. This was clear to anyone, not the least of whom was her companion, a thickset man dressed in sport coat and open-collared shirt, revealing a dangling expanse of gold amid a forest of black chest hair. By the midpoint of the set, "gold-chain boy" had apparently had enough of his date's behavior, as he stood up and grabbed her arm, indicating they were leaving. The woman struggled to pull free and lost her balance, tumbling to the floor with a thump of her head against the tabletop as she fell.

Al set down his sax and hopped off the stage front to help the woman get back to her feet. Her companion had released her arm and was standing over her, yelling, "You fucking whore. You like the musician do ya? Well, here he is, babe. He's all yours."

As Al extended his hand to help the woman to her feet, her "friend" said to Al, "Keep your mitts off her, or you'll join her on the floor."

Al continued helping the woman up, and said to the man, "That sounds like a threat. *Is* that a threat?"

"It's whatever you want it to be, asshole," said the man. "You don't wanna mess with me. You don't know who you're dealing with. Don't make me show you."

Al wasn't concerned with whom he was dealing, and he certainly didn't care about the woman who had flirted with him. With more than the usual amount of liquor in him this night, he didn't really give a damn about anyone or anything—not a good time to challenge Al Waters.

"I believe you just called me an asshole," said Al. "Would you like to take that back, or would you like to find your head up your own actual asshole?"

The man removed his jacket and tossed it on the chair. "Let's see what ya got, music man. I hope you don't count on havin' teeth to play that saxophone."

Al stood his ground, thinking as fast as his late-night, booze-boggled brain could manage. In his experience, anyone who took off a jacket or coat as a first move, and didn't right away try to throw a first punch—was dangerous. This guy was either a habitual rumble-meister, or a hockey player. He was only of medium height, but with a burly physique now on display with the jacket gone.

"Why don't you try and hit me?" said Al. "Go ahead. I'm old and slow and half drunk. Get it over with why don't you?" Al knew his only chance was to use the man's own strength against him, but that couldn't work if gold-chain boy didn't make a move.

The man circled Al in a slow shuffle, observing his opponent's stance and reactions. "I think you're a chicken shit piece of crap," said the man. "You don't know what to do here, *do* ya? Are you wishing you'd stayed outa this now, huh?"

The woman tottered over to Al and said, "Come on, baby. Let it go. You and I can have some fun, and Bernie can go beat up somebody else."

As she tried to latch onto Al's arm, she tripped, and Al reached out to catch her. This was the opening Bernie had been waiting for. He strode in to throw a right, but when he pulled back his arm, it was caught and held in a vice-like grip from behind.

"Bernie, my lad," said Big John, "what you be doin', fightin' with amateurs? Don't you think you should take on another pro?"

Bernie tried to conceal the pain from Big John's massive hand on his wrist. He laughed and said, "Hey, come on, big man. I was just messin' with this guy. No harm meant."

Al started toward Bernie, but Big John waved him back. "No, Al," said John. "Me and Bernie here are gonna go to the front door, since he's about to leave, peaceable now, right, Bernie boy?"

"Yeah, Big John," said Bernie. "No trouble. I'm goin'." With that, he picked up his jacket and headed for the front door, with Big John behind until it was fully a done deal.

"Al," said Big John when he returned, "that was Bernie Malloy, former middleweight contender. He woulda killed you, man, and me too if he'd taken a second to see how old and outa shape I am. Pick your fights using your brain for once, and not your dick."

♪ ♪ ♪

The woman, whose name was Pam, bought Al a Scotch and had another wine while they sat making small talk, which Al endured only to make sure she was okay after her fall. After a few minutes she said, "Suppose you could give me a lift, Al? I could take a cab, but I'd like to ride with you, maybe more ways than one?"

Al looked at her and saw everything impossible to resist. In all the ways he liked, she was *hot*—and she wanted him. She was saying yes, without the question even being thought. She was a full syringe of seducement, with the needle tip dripping, drop by luscious drop, a promise of pure pleasure into his lap.

Billy came over to the table, pulled up a chair between Al and Pam, and said, "S'up, guys? You okay, darlin'? You took quite a crack on the head when that schmuck knocked ya down."

Al said, "She's fine, Billy. This is Pam. She's a dancer; going to Broadway someday soon. For now she's making ends meet, so to speak, working at Tootsie's Hot House, over in Hallandale."

"Yeah," said Billy, "I know that place. Reminds me of way back when . . . Remember old Busty Brigitte? Think we should call her up and get her a gig there?"

Al laughed. "I think Busty would be a little past her prime for that kind of work now, Billy. But I get your point, believe me I do."

Pam said, "What're you two talking about? You making fun of me?"

Al said, "No, honey, we'd never do that. We're in no position to laugh at anybody's life choices, right, Billy? But I just made one little choice you'll be proud of, old pal."

He turned back to Pam and said, "Call yourself a cab, sweetheart."

♪ ♪ ♪

Close to half a decade had slipped by at Lou's Lounge, and the years, especially once Nora was back in Al's life, were like Dave Brubeck's "Take Five"— smooth and simple, yet laden with opportunities to get off track. This was no four-four swing standard in Al's life, but a chorus of constant discipline from which he never strayed. Nora was Al's perfect methadone gal, as her love and trust grew proportionately with his resolve to reject temptation. With his renewed passion for music and honest love for Nora, the Sirens' songs had become only a dim, distant, empty echo.

♪ ♪ ♪

Nora came along to the gig on New Year's Eve, 1998 where she joined the band members at their table, along with Wesley's girlfriend, Ciara, and Pete's wife, Diane. Dinner was buffet style, far below the standard Nora might have enjoyed if she'd accepted any of her friends' invitations to their homes or classy restaurants; but there'd been no decision to make. Al had to work, and they wanted to be together. On the first break, Al stood up at the table and said he had an announcement to make. He called Big John and Dixie over, so they too could hear what he had to say.

"Everybody, I want you guys to be the first to know. Nora and I have some news."

Billy said, "You're gonna have a baby? Way to go, Al."

When the laughter died out, Al said, "No, but we are thinking of getting a dog. Hey, Billy, want a job walking it?"

"Nah," said Billy. "I can always go for a walk with Dixie if I want to hang out with a—"

Dixie punched Billy's arm so hard he almost dropped his drink.

"Settle down, kiddies," said Al. "Okay here it is . . . well, there's actually two things. I found out about a new jazz festival concert series called 'Legends of the Big Apple' that a guy in New York is organizing. It's going to be a collection of big name jazz groups, and one of the venues is Carnegie Hall. Yeah, and I know what you're thinking. What's that got to do with us losers? Well, one of the ideas this guy has is to include a sort of 'what-ever-happened-to-them' part of the lineup. Billy's name came up in that discussion and I guess somehow mine did too.

"The bad news is that there are hundreds of guys like us out there who would die for this gig as opening acts for the main attractions. Well, the *good* news is that we found out whose palm could be greased to get us on that gig, and my wonderful Nora here is going to take care of that. Is that not the coolest damned thing you ever heard?"

"Whoa, man, major head rush alert," said Billy. "We get to play the Apple again . . . and at Carnegie Hall? Far-*fucking*-out. Man, you been waiting for that, like for your whole life, Al. Think you're ready yet? Hey, we taking these guys with us, or do we get somebody good?" His cackle was drowned out by a chorus of boos and jeers from the entire table.

"It's gonna happen guys, this spring. With Nora's connections, the wheels are in motion already. But, I have other news, and it's actually better than the 'Legends' concert thing. Nora and I, we're going to get hitched again. It'll be sometime in the spring I guess, right before we take off for the jazz concert series. You're all invited."

Billy cackled loudly and said, "So, she *is* pregnant!"

"Yeah, you got it, Billy," said Al. "Why the hell else would anyone marry me? And hey, we'll hire a polka band. Cool, eh?"

"Will that be for the reception or for the ceremony, Al?" asked Billy. "Hey, save some money. I always wanted to learn the accordion. Get me one and I'll do the gig. Copa-fuckin-cetic, man."

"And guys," said Al, "Nora doesn't know this yet, but I've made a promise to myself, and now to her and to all of you. I'm going to finally get into writing some new tunes. Yeah, Al Waters originals to have ready by that Carnegie gig. If we're real lucky, and real good, someone might want to record us. That'd be a win-win-win . . . for me, you all, and Nora."

Al kissed Nora and looked around the table at his friends, musical associates . . . family.

For once I can say, I really feel it . . . Happiness does exist.

♪♪♪

By 3:00 a.m. the gig was over and the party was fizzling, so Nora suggested they head home. Al agreed and pulled out his keys. Nora said, "Al, I should drive. I haven't had more than a couple of wines all night and you . . . well, you've had a lot."

Al said, "Come on, Nora, I'm okay. We don't have that far to go, and once we hit the outside air I'll fee bine . . . uh, be fine. See? I self-correctified . . . If I was drunk I wouldn't hadda noticed what I said, eh?"

Nora said, "Well, you just go slow, okay? No proving your manhood out there. I'll send in a testimonial to the papers, attesting to your virility."

Al said, "Will that be a letter to the ebitor, or a full page ebitorial?"

They got out of the parking lot without incident and onto Collins Avenue heading north. At the first intersection the light was red where one vehicle, an older minivan, was waiting. Al pulled up behind and the light changed almost immediately, but the minivan didn't move. After a few seconds Al pumped the horn several times, but to no avail. The driver ahead looked out his window and flashed a middle finger salute. Al yelled out his window, "Come on, asshole. Move it already. What's your problem?"

The man yelled back, "Fuck you."

Several more seconds passed, and Nora, seeing Al's growing agitation said, "Honey, let it go. Just pass him and keep going."

Al said, "Aww, lookit, the goddamn light is gonna change and we're still here. Fuck this idiot." He rammed his foot to the floor and passed the van, right through the red light. The van driver accelerated too, but had no chance to catch up with a Mercedes E-Class sedan. But instead of leaving the situation "fixed", Al slowed down to allow the van to catch up. "I'll give the asshole some of his own medicine," said Al.

Nora said, "Al, please just go on and get away from him. There's no point in showing him up. You're both acting like fools now."

Al said, "Hey, what's the harm? Look, he's trying to pass me now. What a jackass, eh?"

As the van driver came alongside Al and Nora, he yelled through his passenger-side window, "You jerk-off. I oughta run you off the road."

Al accelerated enough to pull ahead and swerved in front of the van in the left lane. He slowed down even more, forcing the van driver to brake hard. "That'll show the son of a bitch," said Al.

The sound of a horn was joined by a sudden jolt as the Mercedes was struck from behind. Realizing they'd been rammed, Al fought the wheel to control the car, managing to avoid swerving to the right. But he over-steered, and the car veered out of control to the left, hitting the median and bouncing semi-airborne across it. They skidded, passenger side first, directly into the southbound lanes where they were hit broadside by a 1995 Cadillac Fleetwood.

♪♪♪

Sitting in the stillness of the crumpled car, Al was semiconscious, his head spinning from pain and confusion from having struck the driver's side window at impact. He wasn't sure how long it had been since the collision. Had it been only seconds? Or had hours gone by? He heard voices from outside: "The lady is out . . . Looks bad . . . But the guy is moving. We gotta get these doors pried open fast."

♪♪♪

The next thing Al knew, he was waking to bright lights, surrounded by people in white and green clothing. Someone said to him, "Mr. Waters, you're going to be okay. You suffered a mild concussion and you may have a cracked rib or two, but you appear to have no internal injuries. You're a lucky man."

"Nora," said Al. "Where's Nora? I gotta get to her. Is she . . . ?"

The voice said, "Nora Madison, is she your wife? We did everything we could . . . I'm afraid she didn't make it, Mr. Waters. There was severe head trauma, and massive internal organ damage . . . I'm very sorry."

♪♪♪

When Al went home from the hospital five days later, he was met at the door by Nora's sister, Beth, and her husband, Arnie. The exchanged hugs were painful, more for the absence of true feeling than because of Al's sore ribs. The couple had flown in from Cleveland, not just for the funeral, but for other arrangements of a business nature. After the service that afternoon, they sat down with Al to go over the details of Nora's estate, with Beth serving as executor. The news was not good; Al had been removed from Nora's will after their divorce. He knew it had been her intention to reinstate him as soon as they were remarried, but as it was, he might as well never have existed in the eyes of the law. He hadn't been officially living at her address long enough for common-law rules to apply. Al didn't mention Nora's health plan, figuring they'd eventually find out about it on their own—he'd use it as long as he could.

As awkward as Beth and Arnie claimed to feel about it, they asked Al if he would move out all his belongings within a week, so they could market the house properly.

♪♪♪

The second week of January 1999 found Al Waters alone, aching outside and in, homeless and hopeless. As he searched ads for affordable apartments, he wondered if maybe a trip into the everglades with a hose and an exhaust pipe attachment might be a better plan. For two nights he slept in his car—not a healthy approach to recuperating from his injuries. But he didn't feel he deserved anything but to suffer endlessly for what he had done. The police had decided from witness accounts that the crash had been caused solely by the rear-end collision by the van driver who was awaiting trial. With Nora gone, no one could ever know exactly what had happened. But Al knew he could never forgive himself: for losing his temper; losing Nora; losing almost all joy in living—in one moment of irrationality. Any pain he experienced, physical or mental, could never be enough justice for him.

One day he drove out to a secluded beach area and blew his trumpet until the searing pain from his chest injuries sent him to his knees in submission. Struggling back to his feet, he continued once again to blow the horn almost to the point of losing consciousness—into a realm of such detachment, he almost began to enjoy the burning agony.

With tears streaming down his cheeks, Al said toward the sky, "Nora, my love, none of this hurts as much as losing you." He began to play her favorite song, "I Can't Get Started", but halfway through, he collapsed onto the hood of the car, gasping with physical and emotional exhaustion. When he found the strength to stand again, he set down the trumpet and went to the trunk and pulled out his saxophone case.

"This won't be near as hard as the trumpet, Nora. I'm going to play this damn thing until I drop, and I promise you something. Might make you mad, but I have to say it . . . I won't play that trumpet again until I know it won't hurt. I don't mean my ribs and stuff . . . but until I know I don't miss you anymore."

Somehow, as he packed away the old Bach "Strad" trumpet he'd owned since he was fourteen, he knew it would stay in the case forever, along with his dream of Carnegie Hall—and his methadone-for-the-heart prescription.

PART II

[BRIDGE, LAST CHORUS, AND OUT]

CHAPTER 35

STEPHANIE
September 1999

Saturday night, and Lou was there. Uh-oh, this could be it—Lou was never there on pay night. Something must be up, something bad. Who was that sitting with the old fart? Through the gloomy lighting and smoke, she looked darned good: dark shoulder-length hair, striking features, nicely proportioned shape. She couldn't be Lou's *date*; it had to be a business thing.

As Al finished his solo, the woman turned and caught him staring. She air-clapped—a silent gesture of appreciation.

She understands . . . it's better that no one claps, than just one. She's in the business.

During the rest of the song she frequently looked up at Al, even when he wasn't playing. This made him feel a bit uneasy. When he began the final chorus his one concern was to not screw up. Naturally, he did—another of his infamous crash landings—but only the band, who'd compensated admirably, would know.

Al said, "Take a break guys. Good set."

♪♪♪

"Hey, Lou, what's up?" asked Al, as he pulled up a chair between the boss and his female companion.

She's gorgeous. Younger than I thought, can't be more than twenty-five or so.
The woman reached out her hand and said, "Hi, I'm Stephanie."

She was wearing a thin-striped, blue and white blouse, tucked into tan cropped cargo pants. Al's attention was divided between glimpses of the snug pull of the cotton against her chest, and a hint of cleavage where the top two buttons were undone. Using well-honed stealthy reconnaissance skills, Al determined her breasts were neither large nor small—they were perfect.

Her flawless, almost Nordic-white complexion was a giveaway that she was no Florida native, and her incredible red lips brought to mind the old Jimmie Rodgers hit "Kisses Sweeter Than Wine". Against logic, he was certain she wasn't wearing lipstick. Something about her was eerily familiar, yet there was no one she exactly reminded him of. Was she essentially a composite of all the movie stars he'd ever had crushes on?

Sounding, as usual, like a gargling bullfrog, Lou said, "Oh yeah. Sorry, sweet cheeks. I forgot you two ain't met. Al, dis is Stephanie Leblanc. Steph baby, meet Al Waters."

Stephanie said, "I'm really glad to meet you, Al. I've heard about you from lots of people, and they were right. You're one sweet-sounding sax player. Hey, interesting tag on that last tune. Sounded like the band got a little lost? Great how you held it all together."

She IS in the business, and she knows when to lie.

"Thanks," said Al, "but actually it was me who screwed up. You knew that too. Most people wouldn't have known anything was wrong. You must be a musician."

She had incredible dark brown eyes like Natalie Wood's, and Elizabeth Taylor's perfectly sculpted nose and jaw line.

"I'm a singer, Al. Does that count?"

"Well, let's see," said Al. "There have been times when I blow something really good, people say, 'Man, you sing through that horn . . .' If that's the case, and my best playing is like singing, then a singer must be a musician."

Stephanie laughed. "Hey, more than once someone has said to me, 'Baby, you sing just like you were playing a horn.' So which is it, Al? Are you singing when you play, and I'm 'blowing a horn' when I sing? Sort of a chicken and egg thing isn't it."

Yeah, right, honey. So few singers can really scat as good as a horn player. Ella, of course, and Clark Terry, but that's no fair, 'cause he is a horn player. Some singers think all they gotta do is make up some funny words and doodle around the melody. What a bunch of crap. Well, anyway, you sure are gorgeous, Miss Leblanc . . . if maybe a bit deluded about jazz singing.

Lou said, "Hey, you two. I'm startin' ta get lonely here. But dat's cool ta see ya's gettin' along so good. Al, I got a proposition for ya."

"Don't say another word, Lou," said Al. "Stephanie is more than welcome to sit in with us next set. If she sings as good as she looks, we'll talk."

Hell, maybe even if she sucks.

Though his mental word play was inadvertent, it presented an inescapable double entendre.

Damn, why am I such a pig?

Several times recently, Lou had brought up the idea of adding a girl singer to the band. Al preferred not to, but it would be better than losing the gig. If anything could boost the business in Losers', everyone would come out ahead. The Al Waters Quartet wasn't exactly drawing a crowd lately.

Al turned to Stephanie and asked, "What would you like to sing? We can play most anything except the newer pop stuff. Just name a few, and what keys you'd like." He hoped she'd know the keys for her repertoire. Nothing spells "amateur" like a singer who isn't prepared in that way.

Stephanie thought for a moment, and then said, "Okay, how about 'Here's That Rainy Day' in G, 'Georgia' in C, maybe, uh, 'Route 66' for a blues in F, or G, if you prefer . . . or no, let's do it in F and modulate up to G for the last chorus, with an up-tempo Louis Prima shuffle on that okay? And, if this isn't too pushy, one more?"

"Be absolutely my pleasure," said Al.

"Great. Then how about 'Peel Me a Grape'? No, wait, make it 'Well You Needn't' in E-flat . . . Miles' version for the bridge."

Al was impressed beyond words. She sure talked a good game. Without question, this could still turn out to be one of those ya-gotta-let-my-friend-sit-in fiascos, with her voice so caustic it could curdle a cup of Big John's coffee. There didn't seem much chance of that, as there was something extraordinary about this girl, from her looks, to her sparkling laugh, to her unmistakably prodigious musical savvy. Somehow it only seemed reasonable she'd be a good singer too.

♪♪♪

Stephanie Leblanc *wasn't* good. She was great.

From the first difficult phrase of "Rainy Day", her rich voice flowed from note to delicious note like an oil fire on a slow moving river. The familiar lyrics suddenly had new meaning. Only Sinatra had ever made Al listen so intently to what a song had to say. He couldn't shake the feeling he'd heard this fabulous voice before, but her very excellence was distracting him from a clear recollection.

"Georgia" was a place of pure love—a homeland, its beauty sorely missed. And when she began "Route 66", for the first time in a long time, the patrons of Lou's Lounge were not only listening, they were clapping, snapping fingers, grooving.

She kidnaps the crowd, like Michelle used to, but more hip, more chops. Wow.

Stephanie took solo choruses with scat singing prowess Ella Fitzgerald herself would have been proud to trade fours with, especially in "Well You Needn't", which seemed to revive Billy from lackluster lounge cat, to born-again bebopper. All the guys in the band were having fun with this; even Al, who didn't get lost once in any of the songs.

There was joy in Billy's eyes, that Al hadn't seen in years. And Pete, was that a smile sneaking out of the corner of his mouth? When was the last time he'd looked anywhere but down at his drums while he played? Wesley's demeanor remained characteristically cool, but you could hear his enthusiasm as he weaved his phrasing into Stephanie's style.

I think the girl's got herself a gig.

When the applause settled down—not a bad noise level for twenty people—Stephanie told the audience she wanted to thank the band, and especially Al, for allowing her to perform. She had "talk chops" too. When she spoke, the background noises disappeared as if the room itself wanted to listen.

As she left the stage, Al said over his mike, "Anybody here object to the idea of having her back next set?"

Laughter and applause were loud and immediate.

"Anybody here think we should have this lovely and talented young lady join the band?"

The applause grew.

Big John called out, "Maybe she should replace *you*, Al."

More laughter came from both the audience and the band.

"Good idea," cackled Billy. "She sings great, and she's got way better ankles than you, Al."

Al shot back, "I was thinking the same thing. Going to have to start practicing. Anybody here got a book of saxophone scales?" After a loud rim shot from Pete, more laughter followed and Al added, "Nothing I can do about my ankles though. I promise not to roll up my cuffs, okay?"

♪ ♪ ♪

The rest of the set felt better than most nights of late, with a heightened sense of what *could* be, if you cared. Nevertheless, it paled somewhat compared to how it had been with Stephanie. In her brief time on stage she had set a standard they could not match on their own. Al wound things down with an ultra slow vocal rendition of "Angel Eyes", a longtime favorite of his. Tonight, the melody and lyrics he'd known for so long felt brand new, as he found himself adding subtle nuances inspired from another time, another place, another plane of existence?

Am I singing different, even playing my horn different, now that I've heard her?

Al knew she would be familiar with this song, and with delight, he noticed she wasn't singing along. She was cool. Jazz musicians and singers hate when someone, good or not, joins in when you're trying to perform a song. This is your moment and you should be left to it: your interpretation respected, and hopefully appreciated.

Thank you . . . I like you.

♪♪♪

When Al called an end to the set, he went straight to Stephanie and Lou's table. Before he could say anything, she said, "Thank you so much, Al. That was sweet of you to let me sing. I hope I was okay. I know you've worked with some pretty big names."

She knows she's good. But I think the modesty is for real.

The other band members were on Al's heels. "Hey, girl, you got some chops," said Wesley with atypical cheer.

Pete reached out to shake her hand and said, "Beautiful, just beautiful . . ." and walked away.

Billy was on the verge of tears and said, "Aww, that was far-fucking . . . Oops, sorry, darlin'. Didn't mean . . . Well, yeah, you *are* far-out, but I shouldn't have, uh . . . oh damn." The sudden color in his cheeks validated his embarrassment. "I hope you'll be working with us," he said. "You're so . . . farging hip." Turning to Lou and Al, he said, "You two schmucks, get her in the band." As Billy joined the others at the bar, he sang, "We'll be the best band in the land."

Al heard the old familiar cackle, and it made him smile; there hadn't been much of that lately. While Stephanie had seemed at ease meeting the guys, Al noticed something peculiar when Billy had spoken to her. Her expression had changed just the slightest, away from exuberance toward something more like—melancholy?

There's a word you don't hear too often, 'cept when some pseudo aficionado requests "Melancholy Baby". Yeah, but it's the right word. I wonder what's up with that?

♪♪♪

Lou was glowing, and not only from the double bourbons, another of which was just being deposited on the table by Dixie. He said, "Hey, Al baby, I think we got somethin' here. Let's not let this gal get away." He was fumbling with some loose papers. "I figure Stephanie here can make a turnaround for dis joint, big time. She's gonna get plenty of offers other places, so let's make her a sweet deal so she'll stick around for a while, okay?"

Al was not excited about what kind of deal was incubating amidst the scribbled mess of numbers on Lou's papers.

Lou said, "Steph darlin', would you mind leavin' us gents for a couple o' minutes so we can do business here? No offense, but I guess you not bein' in da band yet, you shouldn't really oughta be in on dis. Cool, babe?"

Lou's bluntness neither offended nor surprised her. "Not at all, Mr. Farina. I'll go talk to the boys about what tunes we could do for the next set, if that's okay with you, Al."

"Good idea, Stephanie," said Al. "See you in a bit." As he stood up to help with her chair, she gave him a tiny wink.

I hope that means "Good luck in the business deal" . . . No I don't.

As she turned to go, she said, "By the way, thanks for 'Angel Eyes'. That's one of the first songs I ever learned. My mother used to play it for me when I was little. It's almost like you knew . . ."

There's the melancholy look again. Wild, it does feel like I knew. Is there some kind of déjà vu thing going on here?

♪♪♪

Lou pulled his chair closer to Al and leaned in to whisper. "You're payin' dem guys what for da week, Al?"

Al said, "Pete and Wesley get two-fifty and I pay Billy three hundred."

Lou scribbled quickly and looked up. "Dat only leaves you four hundred, Al. You nuts? You're da main man for fuck's sake. Why you payin' dem punks so much? You cut each guy by a few bucks and you'd be makin' more like *five* bills."

"You're the fuck nuts, Lou . . . who's only paying twelve hundred dollars for four nights. I wouldn't insult the guys with less than they're already settling for. Two years ago I *was* making five bills, but the band was due for a raise that you wouldn't give, so I gave each guy more, out of my pocket. I can see where this is headed. Is that how you intend to afford Stephanie, by cutting into our pay?"

"Come on, Al," said Lou. "Nah . . . well, it did sort of cross my mind, maybe, but what I thought next was, we could cut one guy out altogether. Maybe da drummer? Dat guy's spooky anyway, and lots o' bands these days go without no drums, ain't dat right?"

Al was simmering, waiting for something even more stupid to come out of Lou's mouth. It didn't take long.

"Or maybe, could Billy play da bass part with one hand? There goes da black kid. Just a thought." It worried him how Al hadn't commented on anything yet. "Hey, dis group down at Charlie's, dey got all these electric gizmos, even computers I think. Sounds great too. Just two goddamn guys. Very impressive."

Al had reached countdown to face smashing. "Why don't you hire those guys then, Lou? I can see the headlines now, 'HOLIDAY INN COMES TO LOU'S LOUNGE.' Yeah, you can have jazz karaoke. Fuck that, you bonehead. You want real jazz? You have to have *real* musicians!"

Charlie's . . . the electronic shit band . . . the voice, damn it, that voice. That's why she sounds so familiar. It's her! Without the stupid fake-band backup, and with the street sounds out of the mix, she sounds . . . man, even better.

♪ ♪ ♪

The talk throughout the bar quieted to a murmur, and those who knew Al were getting ready to duck. At the first hint of a raised voice, Billy had disappeared.

Lou slid his chair further back and said, "Al, calm down; untie your nuts, big fella. Let's not get everybody nervous here. Was just feelin' you out on an idea. Didn't figure you'd go for it. Man, don't blow a gasket. I don't wanna have the cops on you again."

Al was too busy thinking, to stay angry over the ignominy of Lou's suggestions. Maybe life *could* get better: the mystery voice had shown up on his doorstep; the prospects of working with, and getting to know Stephanie were beyond belief; certainly the band would undergo dramatic positive changes. He downed the rest of his drink in one gulp and said, "Offer her at least four hundred, Lou, or she'll walk. If she brings in the business that we both know she will, you'll be way ahead in a couple of weeks."

Lou studied his papers, his courage renewed by the fact that he had made Al angry, and yet was still in one piece. "I'll pay da band, with Stephanie in it, fourteen hundred for three nights; we cut out Wednesdays. You decide who gets what outa dat." Lou looked back down, pretending to be going over figures. After a long deep breath he said, "It's dat, or I get another whole new group to back her up. Dat's it, no more discussion."

Lou got up, fully expecting the answer might be a chair over his head.

CHAPTER 36

FIVE - SOUTH TOWER (10)

The sweating orderly knew that time was his primary enemy. The man in the bed was stirring, but if he didn't begin to respond *right now,* it would be too late to do things in the most satisfactory way.

If Rosetti were to show up while he was still here, it could be a mess. Knowing him did have its benefits, but any public evidence of their relationship would be something quickly and firmly denied. More important, a murder was about to be committed in this room—not an event a police captain would want to be associated with.

Murder . . . is that what I'm really doing? Or am I a rat exterminator? Committing murder . . . Huh, that's funny; that's what I should be . . . "committed", for even thinking of doing this.

He stood at the end of the injured man's bed, his lust for revenge suddenly overshadowed by regret. Moving close to the patient's face again, he said quietly, "What a waste. You are beautiful, damn you; if only you didn't know it. I bet you've been loved by everyone you ever met. Your parents probably gave you everything. Everything you wanted, you got . . . every*one* too. A spoiled brat is what you are. Spoiled as a kid, spoiled as a man: Mr. Perfect-life.

"Well, you could have had me too. And I guess you did, and still do. That's one of the reasons I have to do this."

CHAPTER 37

A WALK ON THE MILD SIDE

*I*t was another one of those nights Kathleen couldn't sleep: tossing, turning, scrunching the pillow, more turning and tossing, drinking herbal tea. She even tried counting sheep, but she'd only ended up angry and even more wide awake as she imagined shooting down the stupid jumping beasts, one by one into a bloody, woolly heap on the far side of the fence. Without her normal reasons for discomfort: bedtime spicy snack foods, thoughts of work the next morning, an overindulgence of sherry—she was left with blaming Al. He had been saying less, but revealing more these days about how he really felt about them as a couple. The evidence was simple but vivid: coming home hours after his gig was done, smelling of booze and perfume, sleeping on the couch, displaying a defensive attitude when confronted about these behaviors, and worst of all, offering only icy indifference to her attempts at intimacy.

For the fifth time since 11 p.m. she looked at the bedside clock—it was 11:04. Damn, nothing to do but get up and watch TV, or better, go for a walk. It was an ideal autumn night, about seventy degrees and not as humid as it had been lately. Might as well take advantage of nice weather and a neighborhood which was safe—at least compared to the Detroit suburb she'd lived in most of her life before moving to Florida. Here in this area of moderate to upper-income family homes, there was a sense of peace and well-being at all times, even in the middle of the night.

She threw on a jogging suit, and at 11:10 headed out the door. Directly above, in the cloud-free sky, the features of the man in the moon stood out clearly as the lunar topography they really were, framed by a spectacular fresco of stars. To the south, the celestial blanket of lights merged into the glow of the strip: Hollywood and Miami Beach, living the lie that they were as active as the old days. As she strode briskly through the Ft. Lauderdale suburb, she found her thoughts turning once again to Al, who was down there somewhere amid those lights—he too, living in the past.

When was the last time I saw him play? He doesn't like me to go because it distracts him . . . so he says.

Her long legs carried her ever faster until she was jogging more than walking. For a woman who had "graduated" from her thirties, she considered herself in great shape, especially compared to her "couch cob" friends as she called them, since all they did was watch *corny* crap on TV. It seemed the one person who might even hint at dissatisfaction with her body was Al, but he was the only one who saw her nude. Was that it? Sometimes she'd look at her naked form in the mirror and think, *Damn, pretty good for an old broad. The boobs are still way above my waist, and my legs are quite wonderful, thank you very much.*

She still couldn't help but wonder what Al would have thought, had he known her when she was twenty. But in reality, they'd met just a few months earlier, just after her fortieth birthday. The reality of how soon it had been before she'd allowed him to move in with her collided head-on with her normal standards of timing in a relationship. Since her 1996 divorce from her husband of twenty years, she had dated a few men, but had not come close to the level of intimacy reached at warp speed with Al. None had even been invited to her home; and then she met Al, after answering his personal ad on an uncharacteristic whim. Was it only that recently? Everything about him had been different: her previous male interests all having been involved in some form of medical practice; not one musician in the lot, let alone a professional jazz saxophonist. If nothing else, it was an adventure including obvious risks which Kathleen uncharacteristically decided to ignore.

With only a few weeks of dating gone by, Al had suggested they could make things better for both of them by having him move in. It could of course be temporary since he understood her reasonable reservations to the idea. He even brought up the old gag which asks what you call a musician without a wife or girlfriend: the answer being, homeless. As she chuckled at the joke, she couldn't help but wonder what percentage of the humor was based on fact. And for Al, was it a joke at all?

Now, after a couple of months of cohabitation, her apprehension of risk in this adventure was being validated. It felt more and more as if she'd made a mistake. Somehow she had to figure it out, or learn to live with suspicion, lack of genuine intimacy, and sleep deprivation.

Damn him, she thought, slowing down to a walk. *It's because of that son* of a bitch I can't sleep. Why do I let him mess with my head when he's not even around? God, let me relax and just "be" for a while.

♪ ♪ ♪

The streets were deserted, with only an occasional passing car breaking the stillness. Then—was that a person on the other side of the street? Kathleen's breathing quickened, as fear began to make the tiny drops of sweat on her neck feel like ice.

Don't panic; probably a neighbor out with the dog or whatever.

She ignored her own advice as her stomach and heart jostled like unruly children toward the shrinking space in her throat.

She was certain it was a person, a figure standing still in the area between two street lamps where the light from neither quite reached. Was some creep watching her from this point of darkness? It seemed Kathleen's only recourse was to keep walking. Coming up quick was a better-lit area at the corner where maybe someone would be working at the gas bar.

Is it an all-night station? Damn it, can't remember.

Once she was beyond the part of the street where the dark figure was visible, she refused to look back, although every part of her ached to spin around and see if she was being followed.

Is that the sound of footsteps now? Behind me . . . on THIS side?

As she approached a parked van, she noticed up ahead the lights in the gas bar kiosk were dim.

Oh God, no, it's closed?

Disheartened by the sight, she knew some kind of plan B was needed. As she passed the van, something to her left appeared to move, and she spun so fast she almost fell.

"Aack," she squawked at the sight of someone standing directly in front of her.

"Shit, damn, hell," she said out loud, realizing she was looking at her own reflection in the passenger side window of the van. She stood for a moment in the defensive posture she'd learned from years of dealing with psychiatric patients. As her alarm turned to embarrassment, she glanced around to see if anyone had witnessed her moment of panic.

Someone was standing next to a small, black or blue car across the street. As the dark figure began to open the driver door, Kathleen called out, "Hey, I hope I didn't scare you as much as I just did myself over here." The person paused, car door still in hand, as Kathleen laughed and waited for a response.

But there was no reply. The door slammed, and the car drove off with tires shuddering against the dusty pavement.

Odd, thought Kathleen, *guess I did scare him. Her? These street lights suck.*

Front porch lights came on at three houses almost at once, and from the home closest to her someone said, "What's going on out there?"

Kathleen turned and ran back down the street. By the time she reached her front door, each desperate, inadequate gulp for air felt like a knife piercing her chest. She was still fumbling for her keys when a dark-colored car rounded the corner.

Is it the same car?

The vehicle moved slowly, until just in front of Kathleen's house, and then abruptly accelerated. She followed it with her eyes until it was beyond view, not realizing until then that she hadn't breathed since the car had appeared on her street.

Hell, it's just someone looking for an address. That's all it means. Don't be such a ninny . . . Sheesh.

♪♪♪

It was now nearly midnight, and Kathleen was even less able to sleep than before her walk. Grabbing the sherry decanter and pouring herself a generous glassful, she noticed the clock and said to herself, "Huh, like that song Al plays called 'Round Midnight'. 'There but for an apostrophe go I,' he likes to say when he introduces it. I wonder if that really means anything, or if it's just Al being nebulous? It could mean he's the missing 'A' left out of 'around'? Maybe he's saying he's like the space where the 'A' or an apostrophe is supposed to be? Just a hole? Well, he is kind of an 'A'-hole. Ha . . . I must tell him that one."

Sipping her sherry, Kathleen went to the room where Al kept his music gear. She had been after him to clean up the area for several weeks, but so far it appeared to have been untouched. Maybe a little push-start to the project might be warranted.

Under some manuscript paper and music books she discovered an instrument case. It had a dark, tan-colored leather exterior and was smaller than the one for his saxophone. After a moment of guilt-driven hesitation, her curiosity won out, and she unlatched the case. Inside, was a trumpet.

What the heck is he doing with a trumpet? What other secrets might I find, the deeper I look into this man's life?

Perusing the manuscript sheets, she found little more than what appeared to be random notes and chords, mostly scratched out. One sheet though, had a more completed appearance; at the top of this page was penciled "Nora", with a date of December 1998 written beneath.

Kathleen knew from the beginning that there was mystery to the man. For one thing, he had never told her any details about his previous major relationships, including what she suspected was the most recent, with a woman named Nora. This name had come up by accident one night when Al had been heavy into the Scotch, and having turned morose, called Kathleen "Nora" more than once. When she asked him who that was, all he said before storming out of the room was a puzzling reference to Nora being "methadone", and Kathleen being just another "hit of the old high". This felt too much like work to the psychiatric nurse, so she left it alone, adding it to the list as only one more loose thread in the rapidly unraveling fabric of their relationship. With more evidence building each day, she now suspected Al had been seeing other women—perhaps as far back as when they began to date.

It was time to talk.

♪ ♪ ♪

Outside Kathleen's house the same dark car passed by—for the third time. The driver stared at the house and made a promise to return.

Of course he's not there. It's a gig night. I really need to tell her . . . but I think he should be here when I do.

CHAPTER 38

LAST SET

*L*ou was gone, and the atmosphere of tension had followed in his wake, almost audibly, like air seeping from a punctured tire. It was as if the room had sighed with relief. For a moment Al sat alone, staring into his empty glass. No one had the nerve to disturb him after the meeting, but then he waved and said, "Hey, guys, get over here. You too, Stephanie. Wesley, you mind tracking down Billy?"

"Tracking" . . . ? Bad choice of words.

Al hoped Billy wasn't in the alley with his old enemy, the sinister simian, digging its bony fingers into his spine again.

Pete and Stephanie sat down as Big John placed a tray of drinks on the table, saying, "There ya go. Don't nobody faint, but these are on Lou."

Stephanie noticed the broad smiles all around and asked, "What's the big deal, boys?"

Al laughed and said, "Pete, when was the last time Lou bought a round for the whole band?"

Pete scratched his head. "I think it had to be way back when we started the gig. Or, wait a sec, did he do it again the night Wesley joined?"

"No," said Al, relieved to see Wesley arrive with Billy, "I don't think Lou ever realized we changed bass players."

Billy said, "Hey, who bought the round? No, wait, I bet Lou did, huh? And that can only mean one thing. Stephanie is in, right?"

Wesley added, "Lou never bought drinks when I joined."

Stephanie said, "Maybe this round *is* for you, Wes, because Lou just noticed you?"

Everyone at the table laughed as they raised their glasses or bottles for a toast. In a rare moment, Al's smile was the broadest.

Yeah, girl, I like you . . . a lot.

"Here's the deal," said Al, "you know Stephanie is with us now. And as of next week, if that's cool with you, Steph?" Al saw she was smiling and nodding.

"There's more," he continued. "We're going down to three nights, but hold on, before you get pissed off. Get this. No pay cut. That works out to a pretty good raise if you think about it."

Al bent over and whispered to Billy, "I'll talk with you later, 'cause your case is a bit different. Don't worry, it'll be copacetic."

Al turned back to Stephanie. "Steph, we'll talk here while the boys play a couple of tunes on their own, okay? Hey, guys, get to work. For now you're the Al Waters Quartet, Plus One . . . minus two."

♪♪♪

As the trio kicked in with "The Best is Yet to Come", Al refused to look at Billy, denying him the satisfaction of a reaction to the title of the tune he'd chosen as acting bandleader.

The smart-ass, I know what he's saying. He's probably right too.

Al brought two more drinks to the table—Scotch for him, cola for her.

"Tell me, young lady, why haven't you brought up the subject of pay? I assume you have a fair idea of what you need, and what if I can't match it?"

"First of all, you don't need to call me 'young lady'. Please, I'll be twenty-eight the end of this month, and if you feel old compared to that, you must be heavily made up. What are you, about thirty-eight, thirty-nine?"

If someone could wink with a smile—she was doing it.

Damn it, girl, I keep liking you more and more.

Al said, "Thanks, liar, but let's just say I'm old enough to be your . . . uncle? Anyway, let's get this settled, 'old woman'. I've been given a tight budget, and about the best I can offer you is two-fifty for the three nights."

Still gives me three-fifty, and I can give Billy his three hundred. Please say yes.

"Ooh, Al, I can't go for that, sorry. Lou gave me the idea I'd get at least four-fifty. Now that was originally based on four nights, so I guess I could go down to an even four hundred for three nights." Her voice sounded firm, but her eyes betrayed her fear that this might blow the deal.

Christ, if she gets four, and I already told Wes and Pete they'd get two-fifty . . . Billy gets three, so that leaves me with . . . ? Shit, only two hundred? Billy will have to accept a cut. Haven't really told him anything yet. Still that would put me at two-fifty . . . a hundred and fifty dollar pay cut. Yikes, won't Kathleen be impressed.

"How about you start at three bills, Stephanie? And I promise you a raise if business picks up?"

"Al, I'll tell you straight. I love the band and I want to work with you, but I already have a few offers, all higher than yours. I wish I didn't even have to consider the money, but I blew most of my savings relocating down here, and I really need the bucks. I have to tell you, there is one other group I've seriously considered, and they want an answer right away."

Al's face would have made a hound dog look ecstatic as he said, "Baby, whoever they are, they aren't us. Is money all that matters?"

"Okay, Mr. Waters," said Stephanie after a long pause, "three-fifty to start, with a guarantee of four at the end of one month. If business doesn't get better, I'll go elsewhere."

Al reached out to shake her hand and said, "If business doesn't get better, sweetheart, none of us will be here. Deal."

As her fingers disappeared into Al's hand, the warmth of her skin reminded him of the coldness in his heart. How sweet it would be to have her touch his face, his lips, his chest—everywhere—with those tiny, perfect, smooth fingers. As he sipped his Scotch, the hard cool glass was a harsh contrast with what his other hand held, and the expected soothing burn of whiskey on his tongue was oddly disappointing.

You are one tough act to follow, Miss Stephanie Leblanc.

"I'll go do one song," said Al, "then you come on up. See you in a bit." He let go of her hand, downed the rest of his drink, and went to the stage.

Wonder what she'd think if she knew I'd just cut my own throat. Fact is, I'd have been out of work real soon anyway if I didn't take this deal. Damn, what am I going to tell Kathleen?

♪♪♪

Feeling it was the perfect time for a blazing fast bebop tune, Al suggested they start with John Coltrane's "Mr. P.C.". He pictured what might have happened if Lou had pulled a stunt like tonight's business deal on "Trane" or worse, Miles. It would have turned real ugly, real fast.

As the song ended, someone called out, "Bring back the chick."

Stephanie, having been waved up by Al, approached the stage. When she got there she turned to the crowd and said, "Ladies and gents, I want you to know how happy I am to be singing with this great band. I'm looking forward to a long run here, so everybody tell all your friends about this place. Let's have another hand for Al Waters."

As the audience responded, she winked at Al and came over close to him. Keeping away from the mike, she whispered, "I'll make sure these people appreciate how good you are."

"Thanks, baby," said Al. "You can be my manager. Now go on, show 'em how good *you* are."

She sang eight songs over the next hour, building a show as only a true performer can. A few bar hoppers and after-hours stragglers had wandered into the lounge as the set continued on past 2 a.m. They all stayed until Al announced the night had to come to an end.

"Don't forget. Next week, we'll be here from Thursday through Saturday, nine-thirty till two . . . featuring the incredible Stephanie Leblanc. See you all next week."

Who cares if it's her they're coming to see? As long as they come.

♪♪♪

"Got time for one more drink, Angel Eyes?" Al asked Stephanie as they left the stage.

"Sure, Al. I'm too wound up to go home yet. I'll have a Scotch, unless they only serve blends here? For me it's single malt or nothing."

Al said, "Try this," as he handed her the glass Dixie had just delivered.

Stephanie sipped and said, "Mmm, yes. Tasty. That's either Glen Livet or . . . no, it's Aberlour isn't it."

As she returned his glass, Al grinned and told Dixie to bring another of the same.

I like you . . . too much.

♪♪♪

Falling in love is an illogical, unscientific, and unpredictable process. Sometimes, you see someone new and rockets go off in your heart: the proverbial love at first sight. But, just as with real fireworks, this kind of superficial attraction often fizzles into a quick oblivion. Sometimes, new love is born during a long conversation, maybe over dinner, or walking in a park, or perhaps the first accidental touch of hand on hand. You rarely know exactly when.

The first time Al had heard Stephanie's voice he'd felt it, but the similarity to the time he'd met Michelle brought too much distrust. Now, without question he knew: as soon as Stephanie had sipped his Scotch, even before she guessed the brand; the way she held the glass; the glisten of the drink on her lips; the look of joy as she savored the taste. He longed for her to touch her lips to his—to taste *him*—and have that same reaction.

♩ ♩ ♩

From the end of the bench seat, at the far end of the room next to the entrance, Kathleen watched the scene unfold, feeling equal doses of pain and anger from how Al looked at his new singer. Even on stage, the chemistry had been powerful, and not just the music. There was something in his eyes she had never seen before, not even in the beginning of their relationship.

The last set at Losers' was finished—as were she and Al.

♩ ♩ ♩

"Hey, sweetums, you alone?" asked the drunk at the table next to Kathleen's. "I think ya missed last call. Want some of my drink, babe?"

"Yes, I am alone, and no thanks," said Kathleen without looking at the man. *Guess I'd better get used to being alone again.*

"Fuckin' bitch," growled the man, sliding over next to her. "What's your problem, too good for me? Or are you a lesbian or somethin'?"

Turning to face him, she said, "Cretins like you make me wonder if that's an option worth considering."

His breath reeked of gin and garlic, and the stench of cigar smoke was draped over him like a cloak of "dis-stink-tion". In spite of the looming presence of the disgusting slob, she felt a strange calm; maybe nothing mattered right now. This idiot took up a relatively small space in an ever more meaningless universe.

The drunk wouldn't quit. "If you're a fuckin' dyke, that makes you a useless piece of shit then doesn't it." He was practically drooling on her, he'd gotten so close. "You got nice tits, babe. What a waste. Lemme see if they're real, huh."

Dixie had arrived at the table in time to hear part of the drunk's comments. She said, "Come on, ya jackass, leave the lady alone."

The man turned and said, "Oh, you must be the dyke's girlfriend, are ya? Aren't you kinda old for her? Them old boobies o' yours still perky?"

He tried to grope Dixie, but she easily moved out of his reach. As he turned back toward Kathleen, a new voice from the side made him pause.

"Leave both these ladies alone, pal," said Billy.

"It's okay, Billy," said Kathleen. "Nothing I can't manage."

She could in fact have handled this by herself without any real trouble.

Al had explained to her the time-tested bar rule, that it's always better if a woman deals with a drunk, since they're more likely to back down than if another man gets involved. And this guy was not nearly as scary as some of the patients she had to work with every day.

The drunk stood up, towering over his older, skinnier challenger. "Now what do we have here, the dyke's 'boyfriend'? What's that make you, some kind of queer?" Without warning, he shoved Billy in the chest, knocking him sideways against the table and onto the floor. It had been a tough week for him: first the short fall off the wagon, then Pete's attack—and now this.

As Dixie turned to look for help from Big John, Kathleen slid out and around her table toward Billy, worried the drunken fool had killed him. The man grabbed her by the hair and snapped her head back so hard she almost passed out. As he raised his other hand to hit her he had no idea it would be the last time, for a long time, that he would be able to do anything with that arm.

When Al had seen what was happening, it was too late to keep Billy from being laid out. Leaving a wake of knocked-over tables and chairs in a mad scramble across the room, he arrived just in time to block the attempt to hit Kathleen. He caught hold of the drunk's arm and pulled the man face-first across the table.

"You motherfucker," Al snarled through clenched teeth. He gripped the man's head so forcibly he later found clumps of hair in his fingernails. With his other hand he held the drunk's arm behind his back as he smashed his face against the tabletop.

As he slammed him again, Al said, "Like to pick on women, do you, pal? Old men too, huh? Then you should enjoy this . . ."

Another slam.

"Yeah, 'cause I'm kind of old myself."

SLAM

"Having fun yet, cocksucker?"

The drunk's face had begun to resemble a stepped-on ketchup sandwich.

As Al's face contorted into a map of madness, he wrapped his hands around the man's throat. "You had to hurt her, *didn't* you? Annie didn't deserve any of it, not like you deserve *this* . . ." His grip grew ever tighter as each rapid breath he drew in seemed to bolster his blind rage.

"Al . . . NO," yelled Kathleen, pulling herself off the floor. "He's had enough."

Al's face slackened once more into a look of simple anger. "Maybe he should ask nicely?" he said, as he held the moaning man's head up like a chicken for the slaughter. "Maybe I won't totally fuck you up, buddy, if you're nice now. Say sorry to my friends, you piece of SHIT."

He yanked back the man's arm with such fury, everyone within a few feet heard the dull pop of snapping bone. The defeated drunk slumped into unconsciousness, and Al let him slide back across the table and onto the floor.

♪♪♪

Big John hadn't been able to reach the scene in time to prevent the human demolition display. As he wrapped his python arms around Al and pulled him away from the man on the floor, he said, "Cops are on the way. Ya gotta chill out now, man. Al, you know I had to call 'em. The guy could be hurt bad; this has to go 'official.'"

Al said, "Make sure you tell them what you saw. Everybody. This fucker deserved this, right?"

Al was coming down now, his rage sucking inward like a spent wave retreating from the shore. A variety of emotions now trickled into his gut, diluting anger with doubt, fear, shame, and guilt. Big John could feel the change and released him.

"Didn't see nothin'," muttered Wesley, heading for the door, with Pete right behind, nodding in agreement.

In less than five minutes there were only seven souls left in Lou's Lounge. Considering the appearance of the mangled drunk, one might have said six and a *half*. Al went to Kathleen who was sitting, still dazed, in a chair next to Billy, who was still on the floor, attempting to sit up while talking in half-cackles and curses. Dixie had crouched next to him. As she held his hand and stroked his hair, she said, "Aw, Crothers, you old fool, why'd you have to get mixed up in this?" Her eyes appeared ready to overflow at any second.

Al asked, "Kath, are you okay? Shit, what happened? Why did you guys get into it with this asshole?"

With help from Big John and Dixie, Billy crawled up onto the nearest chair. Looking at the crumpled man on the floor, he said in a shaky voice, "Hey, did I do that?"

Al was worried by the glazed look in his friend's eyes; it resembled the lonely, vacuous stare of an old prize fighter who hadn't known when to quit. He said to Billy, "Yeah, man, you clocked him real good."

Stephanie, who had been hovering in the background, came over and stood beside Billy. She was crying, not holding back as Kathleen seemed to be. "Oh my God, look at you," she said to Billy, smoothing back his hair as she held his head to her chest.

Half smothered in her bosom, Billy looked up at her and smiled. "Hey, getting the shit kicked out of you can have its advantages." His weak, aborted cackle was worrisome to all, in particular to Al, who had never seen his friend look so fragile.

As Al bent over Billy to attempt a layman's check for damage, his attention was momentarily drawn to how gently and lovingly Stephanie was cradling his friend.

Kathleen stood up and pushed Al aside. "Let me in here," she snapped. "I'm okay now. Let me see if I can help." She gripped Billy's head in both hands, putting her face up close to inspect his eyes. "Hey, old man, you saved my ass. I owe you one," she said, kissing him on the cheek.

Snuggling back into Stephanie's chest, Billy looked up at Kathleen. "You mean if a big drunk guy makes a pass at me, you'll clobber him?"

"You got it, pal, anytime." She was as concerned as Al with the dullness in Billy's eyes.

♪♪♪

Someone was pounding on the front door. Big John said, "Shit, I forgot I locked it after Pete and Wesley split." He lumbered to the door where he was confronted by two uniformed cops, the first one about mid-forties, and the second, twenty-something. The pair pushed their way past the bartender, reconnoitering the room as they walked; they'd ask him later why he'd locked the door.

"Ambulance on the way?" asked the older, bigger cop, whose experience told him the injuries were serious but probably not life-threatening. After a quick check of the victim's pulse and eyes, he stood up to further scan the scene. He rubbed his graying mustache, giving each person in the room an instant psychological profile. It was easy with Al; he was no stranger. Satisfied with his perfunctory assessment, he retrieved a notebook from his chest pocket. His partner's composure was at best, marginal, his hand hovering close to his holstered gun as he glanced nervously at each of those present, and beyond; as if anticipating a skulking suspect might come bolting from the lounge's shadowed depths.

"So, what's the story here?" said the senior cop, after introducing himself as Officer Brachman. "Who did what to who? And yeah, I'm sure I know who *didn't* start it. Couldn't have been you, could it, Mr. Waters? Never is, huh? Can we get this done officially, so we can all get outa here?"

Al sat next to Kathleen, saying nothing. He knew Brachman would ask him his version of the story—for the record.

Billy spoke up first. "That guy deserved it," he croaked. "The fuck-nuts assaulted the ladies here, and I tried to help, and then he hits me like a Buddy Rich snare shot. I guess I got a lucky punch in somehow; defending myself, ya know. My name is William Crothers, Officers. I'm guilty. Take me away."

The younger cop blurted out, "You're saying . . . *you* did that to him, sir?"

Officer Brachman turned and shut up his partner with a glare. He said, "Is that the story all around? Can we wrap this up? What about you, Waters? That the way you saw it happen?"

Al looked Brachman in the eye for the first time and said, "Yes, sir, that's correct, sir. I witnessed it all."

A moment later, two paramedics rushed into the room and scooped up the injured man who was beginning to groan mostly incoherent epithets from the floor.

"I know this guy," said Brachman. "Name's Frank Latanza. You messed with more than one guy this time, Al. Oh yeah, I mean, Mr. Crothers. You see, this character is part of a rather large, uh, 'family'. There may be some nasty repercussions."

Brachman wrote more in his notebook and spoke further with everyone in the room except Al. He seemed satisfied with the witnesses' description of the events.

"Mr. Crothers," said Brachman, "do you think you need medical attention? You're not driving, are you?"

"Nahh," said Billy, "I'm just hunky dory. Tough guy like me can handle a little fisticuffs and walk away just fine."

One of the ambulance attendants returned to the bar to tell the cops they were about to go. He said, "The worst injuries are mainly to his arm. Looks like at least one fracture. Got some facial lacerations and contusions. Could be a concussion, but they'll determine that downtown. Anyone else here need to get checked out?"

Brachman said, "No, you scram outa here. We'll finish up and be down to get a statement from Mr. Latanza when he's ready. Thanks, guys." He turned once more to Kathleen, Dixie, Stephanie, and Billy. "So, nobody here plans to file any charges on Mr. Latanza for the assaults you say he committed . . . ?" As only awkward silence followed, he glanced toward Al and said, "Didn't think so."

♪♪♪

After the cops had completed their report and left the premises, Big John cleared up the mess, while Dixie called a cab to take Billy home with her. Everyone agreed he shouldn't be alone overnight. Stephanie could see that Dixie was in her glory, feeling needed, and Al was sitting alone with Kathleen—neither of them talking. The new star of Losers' Lounge left on her own, saying goodnight only to Big John.

♪♪♪

After Al and Kathleen had stared at the table in silence for several minutes, he finally spoke. "You haven't been down here in weeks, Kathleen. Why tonight?"

She said nothing; didn't even look up.

He waited a moment and repeated the question, still to no response. Her silence was screaming that something big was up. She was angry and sad, and it was his fault. He wanted to be open with her, perhaps suggest they separate for a while, to see how it went after a break. After such a stressful event as they'd just been through, this would be rotten timing, callous, even for the master of quick breakups. How would she handle it?

I know she's had trouble sleeping lately. Is that why she's out so late? Or was she trying to "catch" me?

He decided to put off his decision until a better time and said, "Guess we should go home?"

"Yes, we should, Al," she said, finally looking into his eyes. "I know where that is for me. Where will *you* go?"

CHAPTER 39

NOT JUST ANY PORT

Kathleen settled into the driver's seat and tossed her purse onto the passenger side while Al held the door for her. As she fastened her seat belt, Al tried to think of something *right* to say. "I'll get most of my stuff tomorrow, okay? Thanks for letting me keep the key. I'll leave it in the mailbox."

Without looking at him, she wrenched the door free of his grip, closed it, and pulled out onto the main road where the traffic was as scarce as hope and happiness.

Strong woman, thought Al, as he watched her go. *Seems like she's okay.*

After turning onto a side street, Kathleen pulled over and began to cry. She drove on in a few moments, still sobbing so hard she could barely see. "I don't know who Annie is, but she can fucking have him. She and all the others can have him. All of you . . . Annie, Stephanie . . . *anyone* but me. Fuck him, fuck him . . . FUCK HIM!"

When she got home, she had a cool shower and went to bed. Despite the hollowness in her chest and the pain in her eyes, she fell asleep in seconds.

♪♪♪

Al went back into Losers' for a last drink.

Now what?

After two last drinks—and then another, he gave in to Big John's pleas and left for home. But since home technically wasn't Kathleen's place now, he wasn't sure what to do. He drove there and circled the block twice. The lights were all off.

She must be asleep. Any chance I should go in and try to fix things? No, it's over, no question. What am I going to do?

He hadn't told Big John what had happened with Kathleen; he didn't have to. The whole scene had been embarrassing, especially so with Stephanie, having only just met her. In spite of all the unsavory happenings on this ridiculous night, he couldn't get her face or her voice out of his mind. He wished he'd had a chance to talk with her before she'd left.

Al drove around the block once more before finally pulling over to the curb just down from Kathleen's house.

What the hell is wrong with me? Shouldn't I be feeling like shit? Maybe I do, but, does "been down so long it looks like up" apply here? Guess I feel bad for Kathleen. She's not the bad guy here. But hey, it isn't all my fault though.

Maybe I am a first class lowlife, but she didn't try all that hard to see my side of it. Fucking money's all she cares about. Huh, I didn't even get to tell her how little of it I'm going to have soon. Maybe I should call her. That news might make her smile.

To the east, a thin blue-gray strip of low cloud was basking in the dull glow of impending sunrise.

Man, I have to get some sleep.

Al grabbed his cell and hit speed dial number two. After several rings he was sent to voice mail. Hitting the "end" button, he immediately pushed redial, and this time it was answered after one ring. He said, "Hi, it's me. You up . . . ? Sorry, that's dumb, it's so late . . . uh, early, whatever. Can I come over? Yes, I know . . . I'll tell you when I get there. No, it's a long story. I'm so tired. Okay, see you in a few. Bye."

♪♪♪

As he drove up to the familiar apartment building, he found it amusing how close it was to Kathleen's house.

There's a silver lining. I won't have far to go to get my stuff tomorrow.

He found his key, let himself in, and headed up to the seventh floor.

Huh, this'll be the first time I've come here, that I won't be checking my watch every five minutes.

♪♪♪

She was waiting at the door for him. After kissing him, she said, "So you're staying over? Uh-huh, tell me about it in the morning, baby. I'll make you a good breakfast. I won't even make you have sex with me, okay?" She helped him get his jacket off and tossed it on a chair.

Al hugged her so tightly, her lower back felt ready to snap from his powerful arms. She ignored the pain. It was worth it to have him here.

"Thanks," said Al. "Um, you know I'm not always good with words, but . . . thanks."

As she led him to the bedroom, she thought to herself, *I guess I won't be doing anymore late-night drive-bys of Kathleen's house. Maybe she can start driving by MY place.*

CHAPTER 40

FIVE - SOUTH TOWER [11]

*O*fficer Poole couldn't stop thinking about the sweat on the orderly's face; it was as if the man had just stepped out of the shower.

That guy better damn well be authorized by Rosetti. All I need is to get in shit 'cause I didn't check him out. Guess I should keep a closer eye on that screw-up.

As if on cue, Captain Rosetti appeared down the hall, striding briskly toward Poole.

"Captain . . . good evening," said Poole, standing up quickly as he tossed the magazine on the floor behind the chair.

"Hi, kid, how's it going?" asked Rosetti. "Nothing out of the ordinary so far, huh?"

"No, sir," said Poole. Starting with a lie to a thirty-year law enforcement veteran could never be considered wise, but the young cop was worried he'd made the wrong decision about the orderly in 510. Captain Rosetti was a huge man, at least six-foot-six, with the shoulders of a linebacker. His mustache was as black as any Poole had seen. And his face was a map of many experiences—some, obviously rough. As a smile deepened the already prominent crow's feet around his eyes, he put his hand on the younger man's shoulder and asked, "You Glen Poole's kid?"

"Yes, sir. I hope you don't hold that against me."

"Far from it, kid. Your dad's a good guy and a good cop. I've met him a couple of times and I got the right vibes. You gonna make him proud, are you?"

"Well, I hope so, sir."

"So there hasn't been anything unusual happen here tonight? No one suspicious come around?"

"No, sir. Well . . . there *is* an orderly cleaning the room. Bit of an oddball, but no problem there that I can see."

"Good. We don't have anything solid yet on who we're looking for in this case. Seems there might be more than a few suspects."

"He was shot, right?"

"Yes he was, Poole. And lucky for him, not by anyone who knew how. It was from pretty close range and they fired at least five times, and only hit him twice."

Something about Rosetti—a softness beneath the steely exterior—gave Poole the feeling he could ease up a bit. "So I guess, Captain, we're on the lookout for a half-blind guy with a shaky hand?"

Rosetti put his hand on Poole's shoulder again and squeezed firmly, affectionately. His face became an accordion of lines and creases, revealing perfect teeth which contradicted the otherwise rough-hewn look of the man.

"That's right, kid," he said with a grin. "Maybe we should be questioning Ray Charles on this one?"

Poole laughed, masking his discomfort with the captain's joke, and his own—partially for the insensitivity about blindness, but more for the irreverence toward such a great musical artist.

"I'll take a peek in, if it's okay with you, young man?" asked Rosetti.

He pushed open the door, knowing more about both men inside than Poole could ever comprehend.

CHAPTER 41

DOCTOR DO LITTLE

"Well, Doc, you won't have to listen to me bellyache about Kathleen anymore."

"Why is that, Alfred?"

"She's gonski, outa my hair. My new theme song should be 'The Man That Got Away', from the away-getter's perspective."

Godzilla was sleeping upside down in the doctor's lap.

"Please tell me what happened, Alfred."

"We had a talk. Ooh, that word every man hates to hear; worse than 'you're still away' in golf. Actually, she did all the talking, and there wasn't too much of it." Al forced a laugh.

"She asked you to leave?"

"In her inimitable style, yes. Chucked me out like last week's newspapers."

"When did this happen? And how are you dealing with it?"

"Last Saturday night. She's a strong person, she'll be okay."

"Alfred, I asked how *you* were dealing with it."

"I'm fine. It took a load off. I can concentrate on getting my life back together now, my music and stuff."

"So you will need to find accommodations. Or have you managed to already?"

"Doc, can we get off the Kathleen thing for now, okay? Yeah, I've got a place to crash, and that's all I feel like saying about it . . . Cool?"

"Certainly, Alfred," said the doctor as he leafed through pages. Without looking up, he added, "I'm glad you are taking a positive from this, as you mention 'getting your life together'. Anything new and interesting happening with your music?"

"Actually, something pretty darn good, Doc. Hired a girl to sing with us. She's amazing."

"Is the bar's business on an upturn lately, that you're able to add to the band?"

"No, but it will be with her. She'll bring in a whole new crowd, guaranteed."

The doctor scratched Godzilla's tummy and the little dog squeaked out a long satisfied yawn.

"Is everyone in the band getting along these days? How's Billy? I don't believe my colleague has heard from him yet. Has he stayed clean for a while?"

"Billy's not feeling too hot, not since the other night."

"What do you mean, Alfred?"

"There was this, uh, incident. Billy kinda walked into a fist."

"More trouble in the band?"

"No, this was a customer . . . Doesn't matter. He'll be okay. He always is."

Don't go there, Doc, please.

"Sounds like Saturday was one heck of a day for you. Sent packing by your lover after watching an assault on your best friend—"

"Hey, come on, I didn't just *watch*. I got there as soon as I saw what was going down. Holy crap, man, I wouldn't let anyone hurt him."

"So you were involved in the situation, I mean, where Billy was punched?"

"Are you a cop now, for Christ's sake? Billy's okay. Let's just drop it."

"I'm sorry this seems to be causing you so much distress, Alfred. I only ask you things to try to understand you better. If I accomplish that, then maybe I'll be able to help you to better understand yourself."

"Shit, I almost KILLED the bastard, Doc! I fucking lost it. He was grabbing Kathleen, and he knocked Billy on his ass. They said he called him a fag. That's a laugh. Billy, gay? He might be lonely, Doc, but he'd never . . . Besides, that's no reason to hurt someone anyway, is it? What the fuck was I supposed to do? I guess I don't know how to get mad, and not hurt somebody."

Oh God, Nora, you found that out . . . Damn, did you find that out.

♩ ♩ ♩

The doctor closed his eyes, giving Al some space to continue. Godzilla had scurried from the room. Each second of silence felt like an hour. Finally, the doctor opened his eyes.

"Alfred, I believe you just told me something very important. What do you think?"

"You mean about getting mad and hurting someone, Doc?"

"Your exact words were 'I guess I don't know how to get mad and not hurt somebody'. Correct?"

"Is that what I said? Interesting. I'm sorry, by the way, for blowing my top. Heh, that's something my dad used to say, 'blow my top'. Ever find yourself saying things and wondering where you picked them up?"

"Yes, Alfred, my father used to say 'Blast it all' when he was mad. I heard one of my kids say that one day, and they never knew him. I realized I too say that sometimes. Wasn't even aware of it. I guess it's something like keeping a little mental snapshot of someone we love." The doctor touched his finger to his temple, and then his heart. "Up here . . . and here."

"Hard to picture you as a kid, Doc. I guess I figured you were born a psychiatrist."

"I had to grow up, Alfred, be a child, go to school, make mistakes, before I could be a man."

"My dad didn't like mistakes, Doc. I think he made too many himself, so he couldn't tolerate them in me. I know I disappointed him, but not as much as he disappointed himself. I think he felt like he'd let his life slip away without doing the things he was meant to do, and when it looked like I'd turn out like him, he hated me for that."

"Do you really think it was hate, or was he afraid to see so much of himself in you? On the one hand, your father wants you to be a better man than he, but like most boys, you emulate him; you think he's the greatest. Can you see how that frustration may have influenced his attitude toward you? Perhaps he feared and hated not *you*, but the idea that you might turn out like him. Do you think your anger problem could be rooted in your relation-ship with your father?"

"This is too heavy, Doc. I don't think it has to be that complicated. I just don't like myself when I lose my temper. I scare myself, you know, with what I might do if I get out of control."

"Alfred, what does 'control' mean to you? Everyone gets angry. It's part of being a human being. Is it something your father did that makes you feel this way?"

"Sometimes, when we were out in the country, going fishing, he would get real quiet and start driving too fast. It scared the shit out of me, barreling down those gravel roads sometimes close to spinning out. But if I showed him I was afraid, he'd laugh at me, and drive even faster."

Al's fingers made a loud scrunching sound as they slipped on the couch arm, revealing how tightly he'd been gripping it.

"I don't mean to make him seem like such a bad guy, Doc. Christ, he did take me fishing and stuff, not that I wanted to go really. I thought fishing was boring, but he loved it and wanted me to like it too, so I pretended. Actually, I shouldn't make it sound so bad. Sometimes we had fun, like when we went to catch the minnows to use for bait. We had to use these tiny hooks with no barbs on 'em so the minnies wouldn't get hurt. They had to be alive and kicking to be good bait for bass or pike."

Al demonstrated a fish mouth with one hand and the attack motion of a pike against a minnow.

The doctor said, "I get the point. Go on, please."

"*Point* . . . ? Bad one, Doc. But I won't make any 'barbs' about it. Anyway, in the long run, after catching a bucketful of bait, the rest of the day was no fun for me. Fishing with bobbers and standing on this old bridge all day was no way for a kid like me to waste a summer. After I got into music I had a good excuse not to go with him anymore. I had to practice, and he couldn't very well argue that it wasn't more important than fishing."

"Alfred, do you suppose he might have thought it became more important than being with him?"

"Whoa, Doc, that's un-cool. He knew what music was about, and just 'cause he never worked at it enough to get really good, he had to understand what it took, right? Holy shit, was he trying to hold me back because he was jealous of my desire to go somewhere with music, and *he* hadn't? Is that what you're saying?"

"I'm not saying it, Alfred, but I think you just might have. You were into golf and basketball too as you got older. What was his reaction to those?"

"He never showed any interest in them, except that they were one more excuse to not go fishing, to *not* be with him? Shit. Maybe that *was* what I was doing. Wait a minute. Damn, nobody spends every bloody minute with their dad. Wasn't like I was some ungrateful kid. I needed to have interests on my own, away from the things that he did, or we did together. I needed . . ."

"Self-determination, Alfred? Some . . . control?"

"One thing we did on our fishing trips I did like, was him letting me drive the car. First time I did that, I was only about ten. Could hardly see over the wheel. Yeah, it was only out on the country roads, not once we got back into town. We had a Volkswagen Beetle then, four-speed stick shift, naturally. I think all kids should learn that way. Hey, isn't it nuts how we still call a stick 'standard', when most cars are automatic?

"After I quit going fishing with him regularly, he stopped showing any interest in my driving. When I got my license, I did it on my own. I already knew how to drive from that experience out on the country roads. As soon as I got a car of my own I drove like a maniac every chance I got. Still do sometimes, if I've been drinking."

"Your memories of that time seem vivid, Alfred. And in talking about it you seem to express anger, anxiety, even pain. What do you think generates those feelings?"

"Why do you ask, Doc? All I've talked about here is pretty much simple stuff about fishing and things, and starting to play music seriously. Does everything have to mean something . . . something deep?"

"You say you drive, 'like a maniac'?"

"Yeah, sometimes."

"But you didn't like it when your father did."

"What are you getting at, Doc? That was different. I don't do it to hurt anyone. I'm not trying to prove to anybody how much I'm in charge. I don't need to prove anything to anybody."

"So, Alfred, do you think your father was trying to prove something?"

"Give me a break, Doc. He was always trying to make up for not being a big man. I don't mean being big in the height department, so much as in what he did with his life. He was only five-foot-nine, and I was as tall as him by the age of thirteen. Christ, my mother was almost as tall as him. But where he really felt small, was in being a failure. He thought he should have done more with his life, and I grew up being made to feel that I was going to be the same. You think maybe he wanted me to be like him? Shouldn't having a son who made something of himself be kind of an accomplishment . . . something to be proud of?"

"I would think, Alfred, that most men would love to have a son who was successful. Maybe your achievements were a problem for him because he didn't feel part of them. Sport was something he had no influence on, and in music you surpassed him so quickly, he must have felt disempowered from your development, especially after you began study with the professional teacher. Even your physical stature could have been a problem if his self-esteem was low, and it sounds like it was. No wonder he had a need to control you and to criticize you unfairly. He may well have been envious of you, Alfred, and if so, I'm afraid that was pretty unhealthy, for both of you."

"Doc, I think my earliest sense of him is one of fear. I don't remember why. Isn't that strange?"

"Did he ever hit you?"

"Oh, just the old belt across the backside. Most of the time if I was bad my mother would say, 'wait until your father gets home . . .' Then when he did, he'd start sliding out that belt, loop by ominous loop; but then he'd laugh and say, 'I think you've had your licking, just waiting for this.' Worst of it was, I just never knew which version of him would come through the door, the hitter or the laugher. Funny, I'm not sure which one hurt the most."

Al scratched his forehead and then raised both eyebrows and said, "Hey, I just remembered something!" He spoke with the eager voice of a child who had just figured out the answer to the teacher's question.

"Makes me think of this one time, when my friend Dougie and I had played a trick on the neighbors' little girl. We were only ten. She was probably about six. We got her to pull her pants down; offered her a dime or something, and she had to promise not to tell. Think that cost us another dime. Christ, we were only little boys, doing a stupid kid thing. I didn't even know what we were doing really. I'd never seen a girl's crotch before, not even in a picture. I remember thinking, 'What's the big deal?' Just looked funny, her having this sort of half-peach where a guy's junk would have been. I knew girls weren't supposed to have penises, but I couldn't help feeling sort of sad that it was true . . . like maybe girls were cheated or deprived or something. Weird, huh?"

"Reverse penis-envy? Alfred, you do have an interesting mind. Go on please. What happened?"

"My dad found out about it the next day, after the kid told her mother. Guess we got taken for that second dime, huh? Wasn't anything funny about it to him. Holy shit, he went ballistic."

"The belt?"

"No. Not the laugh either. We were in the back yard, and he grabbed a baseball bat. I thought he was going to clobber me, but he started hitting the porch steps over and over, until the bat finally just splintered and fell apart in his hands. All this time he kept saying, 'Damn it, damn it, damn it.' He wasn't even yelling. Just said the words in a low, quiet voice. It was scarier than yelling. When he finally turned and looked at me, I wished he'd hit me with the bat instead of what he said."

"What did he say, Alfred?"

"He said I had let him down, I disappointed him . . . that he was ashamed of me. The words were bad enough, but it hurt twice as much, the way he looked at me."

"What did you see in the way he looked at you?"

"It was just like the time once, when he'd left the bathroom door open a bit, and I saw him in there with that exact same look he had given me, as he was staring at himself in the mirror."

♪ ♪ ♪

The doctor's eyes had been closed during Al's last few words. Godzilla had trotted back in and hopped up on Al's lap.

Just like George used to. He knows how I'm feeling.

"Next time, Alfred, I would like you to tell me more about your father . . . if you would."

"Not much to tell, Doc. He died in 1995. Huh, seems like longer. It was old age, and a heart that started breaking fifty years earlier, and finally crumbled."

"I want to hear more of your feelings about him, and how they may still affect you, even though he's gone. A couple of things strike me as I look through my notes . . .

"You mentioned driving fast as something you 'like to do' . . . and you imply that your father did the same thing, with his motivation being to hurt you, or at best, be in control of you. Also, um . . . ah, here it is. In the middle of recalling a rather important incident where you essentially molested a young girl, you were flippant about what you did, joking about her price, and your father's reaction. In both these statements, do you see something significant, perhaps anomalous?"

"Sort of looks like I'm more a chip off the old blockhead than I'd like to be, huh?"

"I'm not sure exactly what to think. It does seem that you have some of his attributes, especially the joking. You've told me how that hurt you. Whom might you be hurting by driving fast, by too much kidding around at inappropriate times? Who's getting hurt by your being like him . . . ?"

"I think I get it, Doc. You mean I'm hurting . . . *myself*? I'm carrying on where he left off? Getting in my own way, 'cause I'm trying to be him? I can see some logic to it, but I'll be damned if I can figure why I, or anyone, would do that. Heavy stuff.

"You know, Doc, I've never been turned on, or even interested in the appearance of women's genitalia. Breasts, yeah, big time. But in all honesty, I don't even like to look at her crotch. You think that has to do with how my dad reacted to what Dougie and I did?"

"Alfred, our earliest associations with our parents affect our personalities deeply, and can last a lifetime. In many cases this can be a good thing, such as learning proper values and social skills, and even how to love and trust.

Unfortunately, some not-so-healthy behavioral patterns can also result from these childhood experiences. There's no doubt in my mind that your relationship with your father has had lasting ramifications in your life in many ways. We need to go further with this, don't you think?"

"Doc, there's a problem I haven't talked about much. It's hard to, but it's a big part of why I came here in the first place."

"Tell me, please."

"I've mentioned a bit about how I get depressed after sex most times. Sometimes it's so bad I actually feel like dying. It would be a bad idea for me to have a gun near my bed. I might have blown my head off long ago. That would be the ultimate 'blow job', right, Doc?"

"How would you compare this after-sex depression to other times you've felt depressed?"

"Well, I'd say it's worse, and by quite a bit, especially if I've got too much booze in me. It feels like I'm in the middle of this great, nice-feeling, exciting experience, always hoping it'll be finally as good as it should be, and just at its peak, boom, my pleasure is snuffed out. It's like having Peggy Lee singing 'Is That All There Is' right in my ear as I lie there."

"Is it like this every time, Alfred?"

"I could count on my hands and feet, and have a couple of digits left over, the number of times it hasn't been. Once, for sure was the first time with Michelle, same with Ginny the first time she, uh, 'did me', and a few one-nighter situations . . . and with Nora early on, and again a few times just after we hooked up again. That would give her the record, Doc."

"So it does seem, if there is a pattern, it's that the first time, or early in a relationship with someone new, that you have your most pleasurable sexual experiences?"

"Yeah, I've thought about that. So maybe the secret is to never do it more than a couple of times with any one woman. Just keep screwing somebody new, forever?"

"As much as I know you're joking, Alfred, maybe that is what you subconsciously desire. And your sexual discomfort or disappointment is reflective of that unrealistic, basically unattainable goal? One woman won't do, so once you've been with a lover for any length of time, something inside you creates dissatisfaction, as an *excuse* to seek gratification elsewhere."

"Hey, you promised not to psychobabble me, Doc. But it makes sense, I guess. Could be another thing I got from my dad too. He was pretty fucked up that way. No woman, no job, no hobby, nothing . . . could keep him happy. He played around a lot. Must have been hell for my mother."

"What about your mother, Alfred? What kind of sexual 'attitude' did she display?"

"I think she hated sex. She and Dad were not affectionate at all. My bet is they hadn't had sex since I was little, maybe even never again after I was born. Just a hunch. Only saw them kiss once, and that was a peck on the cheek on a New Year's Eve. She kind of taught me that sex was dirty, that it was only a function necessary for making children. I did feel shame about my penis when I was little. If I touched myself, she freaked and made it seem like I was a disgusting animal. Anytime we'd see people kissing, or heaven forbid, getting sexy in a movie or on TV, she'd turn away as if it was immoral to see that stuff. When I was around thirteen, she found a Playboy magazine I'd hidden under my mattress, and we had to have a 'talk'. She was calm and nice about it, but the way she described those 'urges' a boy gets, had an undertone of disgust. I know she was just trying to be a good parent, but she was giving me pretty strong messages that only bad people really like sex."

"Alfred, as long as I've been doing this, it still troubles me to hear about a parent's negative influence on a child. Undoubtedly, your mother was taught this attitude early in her own life, and she was naturally, if unfortunately, passing it on to you. And this could easily be seen as part of why you have difficulty with the enjoyment of sex. I'm sure you've thought about that possibility. It would be nice if it were all that simple, but . . . let's go back. When did you first discover the problem you describe with sexual disappointment?"

"The first time I ever masturbated. We used to call it 'whacking off' back then. Heh, I remember my dad used to refer to mowing the lawn as 'whacking off some grass'. It was so hard not to laugh, but it was embarrassing too, hearing him use that expression like he didn't know it meant something else dirty. What did they call it when *he* was a kid?"

"Goodness, Alfred, I can't quite recall; even though I did major in the history of Canadian masturbation nomenclature."

"Doc, good one. But seriously, right in the middle of thinking how embarrassing and funny it was the first time he said that, it made me kind of mad too. Funny, huh, Doc? Guess I'm whacked in the head, right? Or, just plain wacky?"

"Good thing you're seeing me then, Alfred. My minor in school was the study of wackiness in the North American musician."

"Doc, you're freaking me out. This is starting to sound like a stand-up routine."

"I apologize, Alfred. Your sense of humor does tend to rub off. Oh, for heaven's sake, 'rub off'? Now I assure you, *that* one was unintentional. Please, let's be serious again . . ."

"So, Alfred, when you masturbated, it wasn't pleasurable?"

"It was so scary that first time. I didn't know what was happening as I played with myself. Then, like out of nowhere, the sensations got so strong . . . felt like my brain and entire body were shut down except for my penis. I even stopped moving my hand 'cause it was so scary, and then boom, it just came out of me: a river, pulsing and spurting. It felt great, and bad all at once. It was like biting into a wonderful mouth-watering piece of steak and then having it turn into shit as you chew. I don't know. It's so damned hard to explain."

"And this has been ongoing for your entire sexual life, Alfred?"

"Yes and no, Doc. Masturbation has the best potential for working out, and that might be easy to figure. The old *control* issue? Nobody to ruin my timing, or to disappoint, other than me, right? As far as with a partner, there have been times when oral sex has worked, and even vaginal sex, but strangely, like you said, usually when it's with someone new. Maybe like the first time and/or second, and then it turns bad. Like a cruel joke by the sex gods, Doc? And if I've been drinking quite a bit, it's worse, especially with Scotch. Dumb . . . makes no sense that one kind of booze makes a difference more than another, does it?"

"I think there may be something to explore there, Alfred, but unfortunately we must finish our session now. I feel we're getting into some important issues. We'll continue next time. This is good work you've done here today."

"I guess so, Doc. You sure have made me think about some shit. I wonder why it makes me feel, you know, so uncomfortable talking about my father, and especially with how much I seem to be like him . . . the last thing you'd think I would want to be. And here it turns out I may be more like my mother than I ever thought too. Wow. Anyway, I think you earned your fee today. Thanks."

The doctor closed his notebook and set it on the side table. He said, "I didn't really do too much, Alfred. I didn't have to. Remember, those voices from inside may seem small and from the distant past, but you must listen to them. They, not I, will tell you what's going on in your heart."

Al wondered if he'd ever have the guts to talk about Vickie. *There* was one big voice from within that wouldn't shut up.

Nora, help me tell him . . . and for God's sake, why haven't I told him what happened to YOU?

CHAPTER 42

FIRST SET

*F*or the first time in five years, there was a new sign in the window.

THE AL WATERS QUARTET
FEATURING THE SONG STYLINGS OF
STEPHANIE LEBLANC

Rehearsals had gone so well all week, they hadn't even bothered with one that afternoon. It felt strange to have Wednesday night off, but no one was complaining. Lou had suggested they rehearse on their off night during business hours, but Al wasn't falling for that. Sure, free entertainment. Not with the deal they were getting. This was something no club owner would have tried in the old days, when the American Federation of Musicians was strong.

Five years before, when Al's gig at Charlie's was coming to an end, Lou Farina suggested the band play one night at his club for free, "to see how it went". Lou had promised, "I'll have you back the next night, for pay, if I like what I see."

Al responded with, "Sure, and how about you let all your first-time customers have free food and booze . . . just to see how they like it?"

Lou agreed to pay.

On opening night at Lou's Lounge a small loyal group of regulars from Charlie's had followed the band to the new gig. Performing to mostly familiar faces, Al almost forgot he was in a different club. Once he slipped and said, "Welcome back to the third set here at Charlie's. Oops, I mean Lou's Lounge. Sorry, Lou."

It was sometime during that first night he officially rechristened the place. "Hey everybody, I just thought, now that we're all gonna hang at Lou's . . . does that make us a bunch of *losers*?"

It stuck. And sadly, it didn't entirely feel like a joke to everyone, especially Al.

♪♪♪

Another "opening night" at Lou's Lounge was about to begin, and the band was ready for something special. Pete was smiling so much more than usual, Al wondered if it was really him, and Wesley had brought his acoustic bass for the first time in months. Billy was as clean and sober as Al could ever remember seeing him.

Stephanie, who normally wore little makeup, looked incredible. For Al, there was something almost intimidating about her stage-face: glossy lipstick; longer lashes; dark blue eyeliner; "bigger" hair; and a formfitting white dress covered in sequins, which sparkled almost as much as her eyes. It reminded him too much of Michelle. He had theorized his first wife's stage persona was worn like a bulletproof vest. That, and a couple of brandies always gave her an edge he found disturbing. Under the lights, she became someone he didn't like, other than her singing.

Is Steph going to be like that?

There were about fifty people in the lounge.

Fifty? On a Thursday?

Lou had actually spent a few bucks on some advertising and word was out on the strip; this new chick at Lou's Lounge was hot. Stephanie's picture, added prominently to the front window display had been a good idea.

She's SO gorgeous.

Lou had sprung for a better lighting system, a multicolored array to replace the old pale blue glow. Strangely, Al missed the blue, so he made a point to learn how to adjust the settings to get the same effect the original lights had produced, to regain the past ambiance if and when he felt like it. Lou thought he was nuts.

When Stephanie stepped into the radiance of the new lights, Al forgot all about the blue. He almost forgot to introduce her.

"Hello, everyone," she said softly, looking at Al instead of the audience.

He stared at her, for a moment unaware of anything in the universe other than her eyes. He was beamed back to Earth by Billy's words. "Al, they're waitin', man."

Al turned to the mike. "Ladies and gentlemen, you're in for a treat. If you haven't heard this lady sing, you ain't heard nothin'. With 'Love Walked In', here is Miss Stephanie Leblanc!"

♪♪♪

The hour-long set was a smash. When, after Stephanie's insistence, Al sang "As Time Goes By", the audience was almost as receptive as they'd been for her.

When was the last time they actually listened to me?

His sax solos were expressive and technically strong; his fingers and his mind seemed to have less tension than usual, even with Stephanie watching him as he played. Against logic, it seemed to calm him.

Michelle did that too . . . at first.

Al tried not to look at her too much, for fear anyone else might notice what was going on between them; it was as if the air between them was filled with sparks. This was more than show business. This was real, and what an ironic circumstance to be experiencing it in front of an audience.

He knew Stephanie was feeling it too. But she didn't seem to care if anyone noticed. A single drop of sweat trickled down the bridge of Al's nose.

Feels like a steam room in here. Must be those new lights.

During "Almost Like Being in Love", Stephanie had turned and looked directly at Al each time she sang the title line. Coincidence, or calculated? Her eyes shone with sincerity. But singers are actors, using music and lyrics, and a performance has to be experienced as an imaginary scene where, for those few minutes, reality *is* the song. Her face told a story that couldn't possibly be what it appeared: what he *wanted* it to mean.

This wasn't the phony stage-look Michelle used to put on. She and Al had both become experts at it; even after one of their regular backstage disagreements they could walk out into the lights, with all the tension masked behind their smiles. Their audiences must have thought, "They're so good together, so much in love."

Once it had been true.

♪♪♪

Billy was playing like the old days, the good old days, when he was Billy the Kid, fearlessly riding the range of jazz exploration. Stephanie sometimes sat on the edge of the piano bench, watching him solo. Occasionally a slick riff or altered chord would catch her off guard, and she'd look up at Al, her eyes saying, "Wow". But mostly, she stared at Billy's hands and face as he masterfully coaxed a rainbow of glimmering notes from the piano's black and whites.

Watching her next to Billy, Al thought he saw that melancholy look again, but there was something else there too, something disconcerting—some form of *affection*? He hadn't thought of Billy as a rival.

She's only twenty-eight. What would she want with an old guy like him? But geezes, I'm not that much younger than Billy.

If there was something happening there, Al didn't get it. She'd shown all the signs of being interested in him. And now, Billy too? Maybe she was just an extraordinarily friendly lady.

"Friendly"? Like Michelle? God damn it, get that thought outa your stupid head right now.

Could it be he'd been jumping to conclusions all along? Was the attraction one-sided? In the past, Al had hurt Billy with his selfishness in matters of the heart, and he'd vowed not to do it again. He had to find out where this was going, and right away. After the set Al and Stephanie squeezed between chairs and tables to get to the bar, stopping at every table to accept compliments.

"Steph," Al whispered in her ear, "do you have to take off right away after the gig? I'd like to buy you a drink, to celebrate."

"Celebrate what, Al?" she whispered back, "Lou's success, or ours?" Her hand brushed his.

Was that on purpose?

"Ours, of course," he said, holding out his glass in a toast to the idea.

Damn . . . did "ours" mean just us, or the whole band?

♪ ♪ ♪

After the second set, Al went to the bar while Stephanie circulated amongst the tables, asking for requests and chatting up the customers. Billy joined Al at the bar.

Big John set down two draft beers and said, "My friends, these are on Lou, although he don't know about it."

Al laughed and patted Billy on the back. "Man, could this night get any better? Let's drink to something."

"Here's to everything," said Billy, holding his mug up to Al's.

"To what, Billy, the new sound with Steph?"

"Yeah, that's part of it, but partly too the way we're getting into the music again, more like we used to, when we really cared."

"Was there a time like that, Billy? I mean did we ever really care about the music as much as we thought we did?"

"I did, Al, and I think you did too. For me it was mostly before we met, but there've been some pretty good times working with you too. You gotta know that."

"Billy, I've been low and I've been high, but thinking back, the most highs have been with you."

Billy's cackle was inevitable, followed instantly by Al's laughter at the irony of his words.

"No, Al, it's me that's been 'high' . . . way too much, and you've been there to pull me in like a kite, man."

"Don't go getting all sentimental on me, ya old coot. I only keep you around because no one else will work as cheap."

"And I only work cheap 'cause no one else will hire me, and . . . 'cause you're my best friend."

The words barely squeezed out of Billy's throat as he turned away, trying to hide his sudden tears. Al barely managed to hold back his own.

"Christ, Billy. I told you not to get mushy."

Billy and Al raised their beers and clinked a wordless toast to the moment. There was more meaning involved than Al wanted to admit; but he had to smile as he looked at Billy, who was sitting less slouched than usual, more animated than he'd been in a long time.

"Billy, here's a stupid question. Do you have any regrets? Hold it, that's even more stupid than I thought. Try this. What would you say is your biggest regret?"

Billy looked into the beer foam and twirled his finger in it, then licked it off slowly. "Al, if I had to pick one thing, I guess it would have to be leaving Montreal the way we did."

Al almost choked on his beer. He'd expected something about missed career opportunities or ruined gigs from drug use—at least something to do specifically with music.

"Billy, we went from there to New York, man. What would make you miss staying in Montreal?" He knew the answer even before all the words had slipped out. But it was too late to suck them back in.

"Al, you know what I meant. Nobody else but *you* could."

Al smiled. "Billy, maybe we'll go back there someday. Why not?"

"My man, that's about as likely as you turnin' smart overnight."

"Yeah, I get your drift."

"About as likely as you staying with one woman for more than five minutes; as likely as you not getting into a fight over some stupid damn thing for more than a week; as likely as—"

"Okay, I get it. I get it, Billy. You're busting my chops here. Let's get back to why we're toasting the night."

"Al, ya know's I love's ya. I should hate you. But I guess I'm as mixed up as you when it comes to love and hate, and everything in between."

Slugging back the rest of his beer, Al turned to Billy and said, "You're not gonna kiss me now, are you?"

"Hell, man, I just might, 'cause you got Stephanie in the band. I'd rather kiss her though. Ain't she a cutie? Looks as good as she sings too. By the way, Al, does she remind you of anyone?"

"You mean Michelle? Yeah, but there isn't that same edge that she had. Michelle looked sweet on the outside, but man, don't you remember what a viper she could be too? Steph is nothing like Michelle when it comes to her heart."

Billy shook his head. "Nah, not her. But hey, you think you know Stephanie so well already, big guy?"

"Well, funny enough, yeah, sort of. There's something about her that makes me just know she's a one-off. Can't say what it is, but you know what, Billy? I don't plan to mess this up. She's in the band, and we need her bad. No matter what I do, I won't take any chances. Know what I mean? No falling for this one. Trust me."

Billy, still sipping on his beer looked over the edge of his mug at Al and crossed his eyes at the absurdity. Trust Al Waters? With a beautiful girl around? He set the mug down, cackled, and said, "Let's get back to work."

♪♪♪

The rest of the night moved in slow motion. The music was great, and Al even sang an off-the-cuff duet with Stephanie on "Baby It's Cold Outside", a purposely ironic selection for a Florida nightclub in August.

"Hey," yelled Billy, "it's Steve Lawrence and Eydie Gormé."

More like Fred Astaire and Ginger Rogers, Al thought, as he and his partner spun around the tune in pirouettes of spontaneously choreographed notes and words. He'd never thought of himself as a true singer, but tonight he was Tony Bennett, Nat King Cole, Mel Tormé: one man with a thousand voices, and a single thought. For once he wanted the night to be over, but the song to never end.

♪♪♪

When they were finally able to shake off the well-wishers, drink-buyers, and hangers-on, Al and Stephanie slipped out the back door.

Al said, "Hey, how about un paseo en la playa?"

"Mmm, just what I was thinking too," said Stephanie. "By the way, nice touch, the Spanish. What more hidden talents might you reveal? Come on, I can hear the sand calling my feet." She smiled and tossed back her hair as they headed across the main road toward the ocean.

As she looked up toward the night sky she said, "Hey, where's the moon?"

"Over Miami?" asked Al.

They both groaned at Al's joke and then Stephanie said, "Hey, it is over Miami. The forest of condos was hiding it." Her laugh was as musical as her singing.

They didn't say much during the short walk to the beach. At the edge of the paved parking area Al spotted the bench where he sometimes sat to contemplate nights finished too early, and those songs which seemed destined to remain forever unfinished: the unrealized dreams of his life.

He wondered if the red cat might make an appearance. *Damned thing might even catch a gecko tonight. This feels like a night where the impossible . . . isn't.*

"Here we are. Want me to hold your shoes?" Al asked, as he sat on the bench and took off his Italian leather wingtips and socks.

Giggling like a school girl, she said, "Ooh, warm sand squishing between the toes. Feels good, doesn't it?"

"Yes it does," Al answered, with sand and toes not in mind at all.

They strolled along the water's edge, talking a little, sighing a lot. As Al carried their shoes in one hand, he flung his jacket over his shoulder with the other.

All I need is a fedora, and a lamppost to lean on and I could be Frank Sinatra.

He managed to get a finger hooked on the jacket while gripping the two pairs of shoes in the same hand, just in case he needed the other for anything—maybe handholding?

As she walked, Stephanie began to hum a sweet, simple, yet intriguing melody. Al couldn't help feeling it was something he knew, but he couldn't place it.

"Steph, what's that from?"

"Just a little thing my mother used to hum to me sometimes at bedtime. Nothing to it really, but it comes into my head once in a while when I'm feeling really uh, content, I guess."

"Man," said Al, "could swear I've heard it before, but it's not from any song I know, and it's not really a complete tune though, is it."

"No, Al. But it makes me happy to hum it and remember those cozy feelings of when I was a kid. Cool, huh?"

"Very cool indeed, sweet girl. Tell me more about back then. I want to know all about you."

"Lots of time for that, Al. Right now, let's just love the moment we have, right here, right now, okay? Hey, I want to run; get my feet wet. But this damned tight dress was not designed as beachwear. If I run I might fall on my butt!"

"Hey, Steph, I got to say you are something."

"Why? 'Cause I can actually walk in this stupid dress?"

"Nah, I mean how great you are, your voice, the way you look. You're special."

"Special"? Christ, that's all I can think of?

Stumbling in the sand, she laughed and said, "So much for being able to walk."

"I'll catch you if you faint, Miss Scarlett."

"Why, Rhett, you devil. I do declare you would like that, wouldn't you? Know what? I've got an idea, if your southern gentleman sensibilities aren't going to be terribly offended. Gonna get out of this dress."

"Stephanie, I mean, uh, Scarlett, is that wise? We hardly know one another, and ahem, blushing does not become a gentleman who's desperately trying to remain one."

"Yeah, right, like you've never seen a woman in underwear. I'm going to do it," she said as she turned around. "Here, help me with the zipper."

Al set the shoes down carefully and draped his jacket over his head. Stephanie laughed and said, "Who are you, Lawrence of Arabia, or the Sheik of Araby?"

He was sixteen again. "Yikes, this is . . . Ooh, there . . . wow."

Stephanie handed Al her dress and said, "There, I feel like Victoria's Secret, swimsuit edition. Here I go."

She ran to the edge of the surf and took a timid step. "Yow, brrr. Isn't it supposed to be warm?"

"Not really, not at this time of year, my northern belle. Something to do with changing currents or whatever. Try mid-July." He was trying to play along, to keep it all an innocent game, but his self-imposed rules were impossible to obey.

He snuck peeks at her breasts as she splashed her hands in the sea. Her bra was cut low to suit the dress. And her panties—so small.

What is there about her that seems so familiar? Not just her face. Her whole being cries out that I've known her before. Huh, when was the last time I used that line on someone? "I feel like I've known you all my life, maybe even in a former life. Your eyes are the windows to my own soul . . ."

Can't believe I've actually used that kind of pseudo spiritualistic bullshit. That's a kicker, if that should actually be happening for real now, I'd have to make up stuff that's not as romantic as I really feel, so I don't sound like a fool. Crazy. It's so much harder to talk to a woman when the truth is actually better than a lie.

♪♪♪

Stephanie danced around for a few minutes, then called out, "Come on in, Sheik, the water's fine."

"Liar, you already said it's cold. *You* come on. I don't need you catching a cold, or pneumonia, or anything. If you didn't show up for work, they'd lynch me."

She splashed her way back to him. "Okay, Mr. Stick-in-the-mud, I'm done. Maybe we'll come back here again and you can come in with me."

Leave out the "with" and you got it. Christ, why do I always have to be such a PIG?

"Yeah, yeah, sure," said Al. "Let's get outa here. How the heck are you going to get this stuff back on? You're soaked."

With arms folded tight across her chest, she shivered and said, "I'm all 'wet'? Is that what you're trying to tell me?"

"Come on Steph, let's just get to the car. Maybe if we run, you'll dry off." As he collected shoes and juggled jacket and dress, he was personally less concerned with drying off, than with *cooling* off his stoked libido.

♪♪♪

Al drove Stephanie home at 4 a.m. and parked in the front circular drive of her apartment building. "Holy jumpin'," said Al, "what time is it? I better go."

"Yeah, Al. I guess so. I'd ask you up, but . . ."

"Steph, don't say anything. I'd love to, but hey, we've got lots of time to work on this."

Sometimes I amaze myself.

Something amazing *was* going on, and his usual approach had to be benched: with patience, honesty, and integrity pinch-hitting for caprice, deceit, and debauchery.

"I know you just broke up with your lady, Al. The guys were talking. That was her the other night, wasn't it, when the fight happened? Were you two together a long time?"

"No, Steph, only a short time really. Kathleen's a great person. Wish we could stay friends. You'd like her."

"We can talk more tomorrow, Al. Lunch?"

"Great, I'll pick you up at noon, okay?"

"Excuse me if I'm nosy, but where are you staying, Al? Nobody seems to know."

"At a friend's. See you tomorrow. Thanks, for . . ."

"Shhh. G'night, Sandy."

"Sandy . . . ? Oh, right. Me, *and* the car. No more beach-walking in our gig clothes. New band rule. Goodnight, Angel Eyes."

He watched as she went through the main doors, and then the inner doors, until she disappeared beyond the lobby; all the while wondering if she might turn around and beckon him to follow.

Wonder if she wanted me to kiss her? Damn I'm stupid.

CHAPTER 43

FIVE - SOUTH TOWER [12]

*A*s the orderly wiped his brow with his left sleeve, a drop of sweat splashed onto the barrel of the gun in his right hand. He rubbed the 9mm Glock on his pant leg, and then pointed it at the man in the bed, now clamping both hands around the handle. In spite of the tautness of his grip—or perhaps because of it—he was unable to stabilize the weapon, and the barrel waved like a stalk of prairie grass in the breeze.

Fuck, I can't do this. Wish I could just blow him away right now like this, but that cop would be in here like Rambo. If I can't aim steady at a guy in a fucking bed, then I wouldn't have much chance against a cop busting in here, now would I.

"That's not a good idea," said someone from behind him. The orderly froze in mid-impulse to spin around and fire.

No, not the cop, not now. Fuck, I'm dead.

More words came from behind, wrapped in a strange blanket of calm. "Turn around, slowly. And drop that piece on the bed."

The man in green turned and dropped the weapon as requested. At first, he saw only a black pistol barrel directed at his face. Was this death looking him in the eye? But the flash that followed—was one of recognition.

"Rosetti," he whispered, "what the hell are you doing?"

CHAPTER 44

SCARED WAY TO SEVEN

*D*amned *elevator doors get slower every bloody time!*

Al pushed the number seven twice again, twice as hard.

Stupid. Why do we think bashing it makes a difference? Guess it just makes you feel better.

♪ ♪ ♪

The hallway on the seventh floor smelled of marijuana, especially next to 705. As he walked nearer to the door, the muted sounds of laughter ceased.

Yeah, everybody shush now. Bet you wish you could shut off the smoke as easily as your yaps, huh? I must sound like a whole herd of cops.

He stopped briefly, just long enough to savor the power of knowing they had heard his footsteps cease directly in front of the apartment door.

Poor bastards must be shitting their pants. Should I pound on the door? Nah, leave 'em alone. Already ruined their high.

♪ ♪ ♪

At apartment 714, Al slid in the key, carefully turned the handle, and eased the door open without a sound.

Good, lights are off.

As he padded through the living room, shoes in hand, he could hear gentle snoring from the open door of the next room.

Yes. This is good.

He went to the kitchen and grabbed a quick drink of orange juice before leaving a trail of clothes from there to the bedroom.

Just have to climb into bed, ever so carefully. Made it . . . YES.

Trying not to breathe, he pulled the sheets up to his neck. She stirred, only for a second.

Whew.

A few more minutes and he would be asleep, no explanations needed.

God, I'm good at this.

The snoring stopped.

♪♪♪

"I assume that's you, Al," mumbled Ginny. "If not, at least introduce yourself. Man, what the hell time is it?"

Shit.

"Hi, baby," said Al. "Hey, it's late. Go back to sleep."

"How did the gig go tonight?" She snuggled up, nuzzling the back of his head. Next, she reached over and started to stroke his penis. "Ooh, I missed *you* tonight, my little friend."

"Come on, I need to sleep. Tomorrow you can do that. Hey! Whatcha mean 'little'?"

"Don't have a bird, Al. You know you're just fine. Any bigger, and you'd set off my gag reflex all the way from down there when you screwed me, right?"

"Okay, you don't have to exaggerate. But remember that movie we watched with that guy who had that monster dick? Holy salami, Batman, that was inhuman."

"No woman really wants one that big, but now you mention it, hmm. Hey, what is that? You smell like . . . I know, it's that new singer isn't it? Hah, I caught ya. Just don't forget what you've got to come home to, Al. She can't rev your rocks like I can. Nobody can."

"I'm gonna spend a bunch of time with her, Ginny. So don't be surprised if I smell like her a lotta times. Can't help it."

"Interesting. You never smell like Billy."

"Well, thank God for that. Okay, I'm madly in love with her and I screwed her five times after the gig. Now go back to sleep. Come *on*."

"Only five times? You're getting old, Al." She tossed back to her side of the bed. "What else do you smell like? I know . . . it's the beach. You smell like the beach."

"What is this, an episode of Seinfeld now? I'm wearing Kramer's cologne? I work fifty yards from the goddamn beach. What would you friggin' expect?"

"Night, geezer," she said with a laugh.

"Good night, shithead," said Al, relieved the repartee was over.

♪♪♪

As tired as he was, Al couldn't get to sleep right away. He'd managed to get away with it again, just as he had so many times with Kathleen, as he had with most anyone he'd ever lived with. Sure, this time he hadn't done anything really bad, but he surprised himself sometimes, with how easy it was to lie. Ginny had opened up her home to him without question or hesitation, and here he was thinking only of someone else.

Wonder if my dad was as good at this as I am. Did he feel guilty?

♪♪♪

When he did get to sleep, Al dreamed about Stephanie. Part of the time he was semi-awake, and he thought she was lying next to him. Once he'd even touched Ginny's back and said, "Steph?" Luckily, she hadn't woken.

It was impossible not to envision Stephanie's incredible face. It made him as anxious as a child waiting for Christmas morning: the first time in far too long he could remember looking forward to a tomorrow.

Tomorrow, I get to see her. Tomorrow will be so great. Tomorrow ...

Was now.

"Breakfast is ready, Al."

"Uh, what? Breakfast, yeah ... I'll be right there. What the hell time is it anyway?"

"Eleven-thirty, sweetums. Come on. I've got coffee, fried eggs, bacon, toast and jam, all the stuff that's going to kill you."

"Eleven ... thirty," said Al. "ELEVEN THIRTY? Damn, shit, DAMN!"

He scrambled out of bed and crashed into the bathroom where he turned on the shower and climbed in, not waiting for the water to heat up.

"Eee-yikes," he gasped. The few seconds of cold were horrible but effective. "Damn, this would wake up a dead guy."

He urinated as he washed his hair, as Ginny called through the door, "You're not peeing in there are you? I didn't hear any flush. Hurry up. Breakfast will be colder than that shower."

♪♪♪

Al came to the table but didn't sit. As he ran his fingers through his wet hair he said, "I have to go downtown for a bit. I forgot to tell you last night. Sorry. Here, I'll just guzzle some coffee and some juice. Boy, that looks good. I'll make you dinner tonight, or maybe we could go somewhere?"

Ginny stood in the kitchen doorway and watched him race around the apartment, digging through drawers, grabbing socks and underwear, tripping into his pants.

"I washed your shirts, Al. They're in the main closet. Your shoes are by the door."

"Oh, thanks, doll. You're the best. Gotta run. See ya in a couple hours, I promise." He ran down the hall, fumbling with shirt buttons all the way to the elevator.

Ginny sat back down to her cold breakfast. She'd taken the morning off, for this? She looked up the number for Lou's Lounge.

"Hello . . . yes, I'm trying to remember the name of the singer . . . the new girl, yes, I've heard she's great . . . Stephanie? Leblanc . . . ? Small 'B' . . . ? Thank you."

As she hung up the phone she wondered if there was sand all over Stephanie's place too.

CHAPTER 45

LUNCH

*I*t was 12:10 p.m. as Al "approached for landing" at Stephanie's apartment building. With a dust cloud on his tail—like Wile E. Coyote in mad pursuit—he screeched around the circular drive up to the main entrance. She was standing by the curb, in case Al might have forgotten which building was hers, and she jumped back in mock terror as the car slid to a stop in front of her.

"Good morning, Mario Andretti," she said, laughing as she leaned in through the passenger side window. "Am I supposed to fuel you up and change the tires now?"

"Sorry, sorry, sorry. I'm never late. Come on, get in and we'll go somewhere nice."

"I'm somewhere nice right now," she said, sliding over and kissing him on the cheek. "Ooh, caveman no shave today."

God, she's pretty.

Last night she had been gorgeous; today, pretty. Al thought maybe he preferred pretty—both were wonderful—but the made-up, gorgeous look still presented the intimidation factor.

Michelle was always glamorous at night and plain during the day. He had loved *and* liked the plain Michelle, but only *liked* the glamorous version. Feeling love for her when she looked like that seemed like some kind of infidelity.

Al said, "There's a nice beach view patio at the Hilton. Let's go there."

♪♪♪

The patio restaurant was perfect: life in a postcard, with a scattering of clouds and the sun turning the ocean into a dance of diamonds. The breeze played with Stephanie's hair, flicking occasional strands across her face, but she didn't seem to notice or care. Al reached over to nudge back the hair from her cheek, saying he didn't want to be cheated of the full view. Against the contrast of her ultra-fair skin and the flash of her smile, the blackness of her hair was stunning, prompting Al to joke that she should change her stage name to Raven. As they squinted seaward, sipping coffee, they talked about music, and people, and lots of nothing important.

As Al was facing away for a rare moment, she reached over and brushed a finger across the scar under his lip. "What happened here," she asked, "sword fight?"

"Cut myself shaving."

"Shaving, huh? Well, maybe if you'd do it more often, you'd be better at it?"

"Ouch. Who are you now? *Donna* Rickles?"

The memory of the real reason behind the scar might normally have begun to erode his mood, but the pain of the past was washed away by the joy of the present.

"Steph, I hope I didn't say anything last night that, you know, bothered you? When I drink, I sometimes get myself in trouble."

"Not to worry, Al. You were a perfect gentleman, even when I practically stripped in front of you. I hope you know I wouldn't be comfortable doing that with just anyone. Did you sleep okay?"

"Not too bad. Got to say though, I thought about you a lot."

"Mmm, that's nice. Must say, you crossed my mind too, once or twice. Guess it was after five by the time I managed to settle down. If I look like shit, it's all your fault."

"Steph, if what you look like is shit, then I'm a fan."

Steph giggled and raised an eyebrow as Al realized his accidental double entendre.

"Man, that came out wrong. I didn't mean as in 'hitting the fan.'"

"Al, I know what you meant. It was sweet, sort of . . . in a shitty way."

"Aw, cut the crap, Steph."

"Oh, my, Al. This is some deep, uh, *stuff.*"

They laughed so loudly, an older couple who had just been seated next to them began to stare.

"Don't mind us," said Al to the people. "We've been here since last night and we're totally enoobriatated."

"Don't listen to him," Stephanie objected. "We're just been making really poopy jokes. But I think we're *dung* now."

Al added, "Sorry, we're just being *feces*-shus." Stephanie snorted into her drink and Al spilled half of his as they both bent over with laughter.

Their patio neighbors moved to another table.

♪♪♪

Stephanie ordered a julienne salad, and Al decided to try the "Ocean Burger", suggesting there might be seaweed in it. They were into their second round of drinks: she, continuing her collection of tiny umbrellas, and Al, switching to Budweiser.

"You think this is real?" he asked, holding her hands across the table.

"It's real. I just don't know exactly what it is, Al. And, I have to talk to you about something before we . . . get in any deeper, I guess."

Talk? There's that awful word again.

"Talk, Steph? About . . . ?"

"This is going to be difficult. Um, don't worry, I'm not married, or a lesbian, or anything like that. But I don't know how to start."

"Take your time. I'm not going anywhere."

Stephanie stared out at the ocean, while seagulls squawked, speedboats roared by, and children splashed in the water. Al hoped she wouldn't be annoyed that he never took his eyes off her.

She asked, "What kind of boat is that way out there?"

"Think it's an oil tanker, one of those Exxon Valdez types."

"Huh, I thought it was like *The Love Boat* or something. What would happen if *The Love Boat* went aground, Al? Would the beach be contaminated with love?" She wasn't laughing, so Al let it go.

♪♪♪

It had been many years since Al had begun to wonder if he'd ever be in love again; now he was questioning if he'd ever been before.

Michelle? It was hard to remember that far back, but he was sure he had been in love with her, at least with her image. But an image can be an illusion—something which can't be trusted.

Nora? He'd grown to love her in a way unlike any other woman in his life, particularly the "second stage" of their relationship, when she had kept him from giving in to his "attention addiction". She, as his methadone gal, had inspired him to make profound changes in behavior; although the permanency of those had died with her. Their relationship never had that magical essence, celebrated in so many poems and songs throughout history—at least, not for him.

Kathleen? She had been a lover and a friend, not proper poem or song fodder either. And Ginny was an ego boost: her youth energizing his body and his mind, but not his heart.

Can a man crawling across a desert toward a mirage be blamed for believing? Perhaps it's the very hope that keeps him alive; but once he's there and sees his dream was folly, does he go on with a fool's faith in his eyes, or simply curl up in the sand and die?

Before Michelle? Some deep stuff way back when. Montreal, New York . . . hell, even farther back. Sue MacDonald? Come on, there has to be a statute of limitations on young love meaning anything. Surely that's too long ago to count. Yeah, and that Al Waters is gone. Rebury those thoughts.

His feelings for Stephanie were a grand mixture of how she looked, how she thought, how she laughed, and how she made him feel; he was Freddy from *My Fair Lady*, as his heart soared high above the world.

"Several stories high," says the song? High? Ha, that's not high. THIS is high. Eat your heart out, Neil Armstrong.

"Steph, I like you a lot. I guess you know that. I won't let it hurt our professional relationship, but you need to know you can trust me. We'll be friends, no matter what. Don't you think?"

She nodded.

He squeezed her hand and said, "Take your time, friend. Talk about it when you're ready."

She arose and came around the table to sit next to him. Pulling the chair as close as possible to his side, she said, "I like you too, Al. That first night when Lou brought me to see you, I knew we'd be friends. Whatever else happens with us, and who knows, you *are* kind of cute. I want to have you as my friend."

God, you can hear the "but" in there.

"There is something I have to talk about, Al. It's important."

"I'm listening," said Al.

Damn, I sound like Frasier Crane. Guess my life is kind of a sitcom. I just hope for once, the joke isn't on me.

CHAPTER 46

ENOUGH IS TOO MUCH

*G*inny knew something was up; although it didn't make a lot of sense. How many men would be cheating on someone they'd just moved in with? One came to mind.

It wasn't difficult for her to locate Stephanie's apartment. As a news reporter, she had plenty of sources, and she prided herself on being a real hound. At 1 p.m. she staked out the building, figuring if Al was out with the singer, they would be returning sometime in the next hour or so. Whatever— she'd wait. This would give her plenty of time to think of the right thing to say.

If Al's appointment was a business meeting, he would have said where he was going, unless he'd been afraid to in lieu of his history. She had been content to share him with Kathleen, with the understanding he was eventually going to get out of the relationship with her. It wasn't too difficult to see how he'd hesitate to leave a nice home, hurt someone he was still fond of as a friend, and give up the financial security in that arrangement. Ginny thought of it as owning a piece of him, fully believing that someday she'd have him all to herself. On Sunday it had looked as if it might have been worth the wait, but now, less than a week later . . . *Could he do this to me . . . again?*

♪♪♪

For a few months in 1994, after she left Al and the studio behind, Ginny buried herself in her studies. No one had ever impressed the journalism profs as much as she did. Her brilliance was instant legend, and it led to a part-time job at the Fort Lauderdale Sun-Times as the first-ever female apprentice to Special Editor Simon Dougherty. The skills she had developed in pleasing Al may have had something to do with her initial success: having quickly passed the "oral exam". But soon she was earning praise for her work *at* the desk, not just under it.

She didn't make a lot of money, but it was inevitable that someday she would. Maybe then Al would be inclined to stick with her? It hurt to think this way, but her gut told her that more than sex was necessary to stave off his wanderlust.

Sure, there were lots of men out there, and Ginny, going on twenty-four now—not a child in anyone's viewpoint—was an "okay-looking" woman, fortunate to live in an era when being less-than-skinny was increasingly more acceptable. During the time she worked at the paper she dated several men, but she couldn't stop thinking about one particular man.

As despicably as Al had treated her—and as unlikely as it was he'd ever change—she nurtured a tiny piece of hope, like a seed which one day might grow and flower.

♪ ♪ ♪

The current manifestation of their relationship had begun a few weeks earlier when Ginny had been collecting information for a story on crime on the Miami Beach strip. During a late-night interview with a hotel-district prostitute, she was startled by a tap on the shoulder, and a voice saying, "So, it's come to this, has it?" She turned, and there was Al with that damned irresistible grin, the one she'd cursed so many times as she lay sleepless.

"You'd think a girl with your brains would come up with a better way to make a living," he said with exaggerated concern. "No offense, ma'am," he offered to the hooker.

"Well," said Ginny, "you taught me so much about pleasing a man that I couldn't stand not to share it with the world."

The hooker looked annoyed. "Hey, I thought you was a reporter. You tryin' to mess in my turf?"

"I'll deal with this," said Al. "I'm a cop, and I have to arrest one of you. How shall I decide?"

"I ain't no hooker," the hooker protested. "Maybe this bitch is, but not me."

Al said, "Okay, lady you better go, while I slap the cuffs on this sorry-ass slut."

The hooker scurried out through the lobby into the night.

"Gee, thanks a lot, Al. I was getting some good local info from my 'professional' friend there. I'm going to have to get another one to trust me now."

"What would you like to know? I've been hanging out in this area since before you had boobs. Oh yeah, I forgot; you still don't."

"Asshole. You didn't talk to me like that when you needed me."

"Hey, sorry, kiddo. Just joking. You know me."

"Goddamn right I do, you big jerk. If you don't buy me a drink, I'll call a real cop and tell him you exposed yourself."

"You buy *me* a drink, and maybe I'll really do that."

Ginny picked up a burning cigarette from an ashtray on the table next to her. Drawing in a long drag, she noticed Al's look of surprise. "What, you got a problem with me smoking? I know you're not a big fan of it, but it's been something I've done since I got into the journalism game. Don't do it a lot at home, but when I'm working I can't seem to get along without it. I've changed a few things about my life since you were in it."

"I guess it makes you look tough. Is that why you do it, little girl? Or should I call you *ma'am* now?"

"Maybe I *am* tough now, Al. Wanna find out?"

"No, what I want is that drink. Let's go."

They headed for the lobby bar, laughing as they threw fake punches at each other.

♪♪♪

When they'd ordered their drinks Ginny said, "Al, I know about Nora. I was very sorry to hear that. From what I've read, she seemed like a great lady. How are *you* doing?"

"Yeah, that's the way the ball bounces, huh? She was great all right. I was with her longer than anyone I've been involved with. You heard how it happened?"

"You got road raged by some schmuck, right?"

"Sometime I'll fill you in. Let's talk about other stuff right now, okay?"

"Sure, Al. So who are you seeing now? Must be someone in your life, huh?"

"I do have a girlfriend, yeah. Her name is Kathleen. We sort of live together at this point, but who knows? I don't think I'm ready to really settle down again yet."

"Al, Al . . . the one and only Al. Why does that not surprise me in the least?"

"I know, little girl. All men are scum, right?"

"So, Mr. Scum, I mean, Waters, what are you doing in this place, looking for some action? How not-committed are you exactly?"

"Nah, I came in to see Frenchy in the lounge. Remember him? He used to do some sessions for me at the studio. Not easy to find any decent music on a Monday night. That's why I brought my horn."

"Yeah, Frenchy used to always treat me really nice, like I was a princess.

He'd say stuff like, 'Bonjour Mam'selle, how is de most belle femme in de world today?' Is he really French, or was that a put-on?"

"Oh, he's the real thing, if you count French Canadian. There's lots of them down here you know. That's partly why this place gets filled up on a Monday, 'cause he's here. Great organ player. Let's go in and see what's going down."

♪♪♪

Seated in a back booth in the lounge, they listened for a while, until Frenchy spotted Al. The organist grabbed his microphone and said, "Mes amis, a treat for you. My old friend Al Waters is here, and I see he has his saxophone with him. Unless dat is a shotgun in dat case. Al, will you join us, s'il vous plaît?"

Al strode to the stage, feeling the surge of adrenaline which comes when playing away from your home turf. It was good to do this occasionally, to feel a little pressure as the unknown quantity, a stranger who had to prove his ability to those who hadn't heard him. Certainly, some of those in the audience were already aware of his reputation, and some were even regular customers at *his* gig; but here in Frenchy's world, he was the guest, not the man in charge. A different degree of scrutiny would measure his chops; tonight, he'd have to live up to the hype.

Frenchy poured it on. "Get ready to listen to the number one tenor man on the strip, a fellow Canadian, formerly of New York City and Las Vegas . . . Mr. Al Waters!"

Frenchy was not only a fine soloist, but an excellent "comper": urging his guest into an inspired level of play through great chord voicing and a feverish rhythmic drive, boosted by strong foot-pedal bass lines. The unmistakable gritty tones from the old Hammond B-3 organ, played with impeccable, stunning technique reminded Al of the times he had jammed with the legendary Jimmy Smith.

His sax was like an old dog: unleashed into a wide-open meadow after too long in a cramped apartment, running joyfully about, sniffing notes and phrases with the energy of a pup.

♪♪♪

Ginny hadn't heard Al play for several months, except for an old tape he'd given her. She found herself wishing she wasn't hearing him now. Old feelings began to reverberate through her system, and her resolve foundered. He had never been far from her mind, but now as he played he invaded her soul. She didn't stand a chance.

When he returned to the table, he asked her to dance. When they'd worked their way to the middle of the dance floor, Al's hand pressed Ginny's head down onto his shoulder as they swayed as one—too slowly for the music. She felt as if he were holding her up off the ground.

Damn it, this is so wrong. Why can't I quit? I'm supposed to hate him.

"Your place . . . or yours?" Al whispered.

♪♪♪

Twenty minutes later, after a reckless ride to Ginny's apartment, they stood facing one another in her bedroom.

"Al," said Ginny, "I don't know your girlfriend, but I feel really bad for her right now. I can relate too well to being cheated on by you. Much as I hate myself for this, I can't stop." She had his pants half off already.

"Damn it," groaned Al, "don't even think about stopping. Oh, yeah . . . ooh, YEAH . . . Uh, you can stop now. Stopping would be good. Guess you knew that."

Ginny didn't mind him climaxing so quickly. In fact, she enjoyed the power she felt in getting him to abandon his control. It was a victory of sorts. She'd achieved satisfaction—an orgasm of her own—without having been touched.

♪♪♪

After that night, they began to see each other once or twice a week. Sometimes they just snuggled and watched TV; sometimes Al would only stay for twenty minutes, with no TV. They talked little about their respective struggles with their feelings about the Kathleen situation, neither Ginny's renewed role as "the other woman", nor his position as unsatisfied life mate: both of them diverging from their professed new ways. Al was resigned to needing more than one woman could give; while Ginny acquiesced to at least temporarily believing she could ever be the only one for him.

Ginny and Al had rekindled their relationship with five-alarm fury, and no amount of guilt or introspection stood a chance to douse it—not with the amount they were able to draw from their limited reservoirs of morality. She accepted from Al that he was getting little or no satisfaction with Kathleen; and, Al *was* getting older. Ginny was certain he couldn't possibly need any more sexual activity than she was providing. But while her newswoman's analysis said those circumstances appeared reasonable, her personal intuition didn't quite buy it.

♪ ♪ ♪

It was 2:30, and no sign of Al and Stephanie. Ginny was stewing.

Where is he? Maybe he isn't with her after all. Maybe he went golfing. I was pretty mad the last time he did that after I'd taken the day off to be with him. That would make him sneak.

♪ ♪ ♪

When Ginny was a little girl, she'd watch at the window every day for her father to come home from work. He would hardly be out of the car when she'd be on him, jumping up into his arms, holding onto his neck so tight he'd always say, "Come on, muffin, not so tight, I won't let you fall." It was love, not fear tightening her grip.

One day a phone call came in place of him, and for the first time in her life, trust became an issue. "Hi, muffin. Have to tell you something . . . I won't be home today. Actually, I won't be there for a while . . . no, not later tonight. It's not just a working-late type of thing. Your mother will talk to you after I hang up. I wanted to tell you myself, before she did . . . I'm not going to be living with you anymore. It's not your fault. Please never think that. Your mother and I are having trouble getting along, and we decided you would be better off if we were apart.

"I know, sweetheart . . . I love you more than anything. I promise I will come to see you every week. We'll get to see each other even more than we do now. You can come and stay sometimes with me at my new place, over-night and everything. This is best for all of us. Trust me."

She wanted to trust him, but could not; she knew he'd meant what he said, but something in a child's simple understanding of life told her it wouldn't be like that at all. She did see him at least once a week for a few months, but gradually the frequency of visits diminished.

The void in her everyday life was never replenished with anything as good. For the rest of her developmental years the loss of precious time with her dad was countered with a multitude of obsessions, from sports, to school studies, to men—usually older men: teachers, coaches, eventually Al. He was the first one she'd allowed to do everything—actual vaginal sex. All the men she had been with, she had managed to keep satisfied with hand jobs and blow jobs. They were never even allowed to see her naked. It was a control thing, and she learned how easy it was to control any man, espe-cially an older, attached man who'd be taking a risk by the very existence of their intimacy.

Al was not only the first person she had allowed to see her nude body, but also to see her gentle, giving side: stirring the feeling she could be a girl again, instead of a man-wannabe. With Al, she recognized that the risks—at least the emotional ones—were mainly hers.

She had tried to trust him—also a first, after what had happened with her father. Having learned so early about the sexual power a woman has, she enthusiastically went about making herself indispensable to him, relishing the chance to be a part of his life in ways both erotic and practical.

She had let down her guard—her need to be in control: for once, relinquishing the helm. Her reward for this gamble? He led her blindfolded to the edge of the world and dropped her off. Heading back to land to seek new ventures, he'd left her floating in a void as vast and desolate as the one her father had dug for her.

Now, she was giving Al something her father never got: a second chance. Here they were, once more heading for that dangerous edge; this time, she wouldn't be so easy to push.

♪ ♪ ♪

Every car, every sound, makes me look. I keep hoping it will be him . . . hoping it won't be. All men are scum.

Ginny wondered how many times Nora—and now Kathleen—had felt like this because of *her*; and a tidal wave of remorse swept over her.

Guess I deserve this.

She decided to wait until at least 3 p.m.

CHAPTER 47

FIVE - SOUTH TOWER [13]

"*H*ave you lost your alleged mind?" said Rosetti as he lowered his weapon. "And you've got the cojones to ask what *I'm* doing? What the hell are *you* doing?"

The man in green glanced toward the patient and said, "You know what I have to do. You said you'd cover me."

"Not this way, you imbecile. You brought the gun? I always knew you were fucked up. Aren't all of your 'kind'?"

The man in green smiled. "If anyone's fucked up around here, it's you. At least I know what I am and I don't deny it. Not like you, and *this* bastard."

Rosetti looked intently at the man in green. This was the first time he'd seen him in his hospital garb, the first time he'd seen his real face. The makeup over and under his right eye mostly covered the bruises from a savage beating of not so long ago, but his appearance was startling in an odd way. More than the cop might have expected, he really looked—like a man.

Rosetti moved closer, eyeing the unhealed facial damage and said, "He messed you up good, didn't he. Maybe you deserved it. Did he *know* about you when you met him, or did you wait until it was too late?"

"He knew soon enough. A bit naive, I guess; not like you."

Through teeth, Rosetti said, "I could blow you away right now, asshole. And maybe I will someday. But I keep my word, and that was to let you do what you have to here with this guy. Just use your fucking head for a change, and be quick and quiet about it."

"Hmm, interesting how you put that, Tony."

Captain Rosetti lifted his weapon back up to point directly at the man's chest. "One shot, one little squeeze of this finger and you'll be out of my life. Don't think that I don't want to do it. Don't dare think I wouldn't. If anyone *ever* knows about you and me, this barrel will be in your mouth, just before it goes in my own."

The cop holstered the pistol and said, "Okay, five minutes. Get it over with, or I *will* be back. And there'll be no more talk."

CHAPTER 48

LA MER ET LA MÈRE

*A*s Al waited for Stephanie to gather courage to continue, he put his arm around her shoulders without saying anything, allowing her the time to be fully ready for whatever it was she needed to say. He was only slightly afraid of her impending revelation. If it was something horrible, like herpes or AIDS, or worse, if she secretly liked country music—then so be it. The feelings growing in him were stronger than any bad news. After the night he'd met her, he hadn't once thought about suicide. And he had been successfully shutting out thoughts about Vickie—until now.

Maybe it's me should be spilling my guts.

♪ ♪ ♪

"Okay, Steph, I'm gonna explode, if you don't tell me what's on your mind. I'm ready for anything. It can't be that bad, can it?"

"Al, it's not really bad. It's more sort of . . . complicated."

"Come ON. I'm gonna throw you in the ocean."

"All right, here goes. I'm, uh, not exactly who you think I am, or rather, I'm more."

"Okay, come on, good start. Keep going."

"It wasn't exactly a coincidence, me showing up here in Florida, and at Lou's and everything."

Al squeezed her hand. "Explain, please."

"I'll do my best, Al. Okay, last Thursday, I was going to come down and see you guys, but Lou's was closed early. So I stopped into Charlie's to check it out, and after I talked with the musicians they asked me to sit in. Lou was there and asked me to meet him on Saturday. That much was coincidence, but I would have been there anyway."

"I'm confused now, Steph. So you mean you had in mind all along to see my band? You came to Florida because of me?"

"Not really you, Al. It was mainly because of . . . Billy."

"Steph, this is getting crazier by the second. What are you talking about?"

Stephanie felt Al's agitation. She drew in a deep breath and took a large swallow of her drink. "Okay, Al, no more sidestepping. Let's start with the easy part; my actual last name is not Leblanc. It's White. Leblanc is only a stage name I thought had more uh, *flare*."

"And this is your big news? Oh, I get it. 'Leblanc'. That's French, sort of for 'white', isn't it? That's where you got your name. That's it? Your ghastly secret is, you changed your name?"

"No, Al. Here, look at this picture. Be careful, it's not in very good shape."

The curled-up photo was of two men and a woman. They were standing in front of a seedy looking nightclub. Al knew the place, *and* the people. He tried to breathe, but he was frozen—as inanimate as the faces in the photo. Only when dizziness from lack of oxygen struck, was he able to suck in enough breath to ask what he already knew. "How . . . ? *Why* do you have this? It's . . ."

"Al, it's my mother. So beautiful, isn't she? You look pretty good too, kind of skinny though," she said, laughing. "Billy looks better *now* I think. Was he strung out all the time back then?"

Charlotte . . . Montreal . . . The room with no windows.

♪♪♪

"My God, your mother is Charlotte? Have you told Billy? He still talks about her sometimes. No woman ever affected him the way she did, or ever got close to him like that. She is one special lady. I was, I mean she and I were friends too. What about Billy? What are you going to say?"

"I haven't talked to Billy about it, because . . . there's more, Al."

"More?"

"My mother told me about Billy, and you too, Al, 'cause you three hung out, and because she wanted me to know . . . that she was certain he was my father."

Al's grip on Stephanie's hand tightened so much she winced.

"Sorry, Steph. This is incredible. This is for real? Like, why does she think that?"

"She was never totally sure. I guess since she and my dad got together so soon after she'd been with Billy, it was easier to believe that her new husband was the father. Mom told me how my dad, Carl, had been in love with her for a long time, but she had thought of him as just a friend. She told me how she went to him just after you guys left Montreal. They were married in less than a month."

"This is wild. You think Billy is your father? You were born nine months after we left Montreal?"

"Thereabouts. It was assumed I was a bit premature, but my mom was pretty sure Billy was really the one. She didn't tell me about it until last year, just before she died."

Al let go of Stephanie's hand and gripped the arm of his chair. "Died? Charlotte is . . . ?"

Something inside him, hanging for years by a single thread, fell into nothingness. He sucked in the escaping rush of feelings before they could taint his feigned air of basic, friendly condolence.

"Oh man, I'm . . . I'm real sorry to hear that, Steph. Your mom was a sweetheart. Billy was crazy about her. I think he always wished that he'd stayed in Montreal and married her. He's never talked about anyone else the same way."

"My father, that I grew up with, Carl White, he always knew, I think. After Mother's funeral, he asked if I knew about it, and when I told him I did, he said he wouldn't be hurt if I looked for Billy. He understood. He knows he'll always be my 'real' dad. I think I love him even more, knowing he stayed with my mother, even while wondering if her child might not be his, and raising me as his own. He's a good man."

"Sounds like it, Steph, especially to have Charlotte marry him, he'd have to be a great guy. She wouldn't have settled for less."

"I don't know what to do next, Al. I came to Florida to work, and to find Billy Crothers. For a 'has-been', he's still pretty well-known. I was in New York for a while and almost anyone I asked in the business had heard of him. Most thought he must be dead, but a couple of guys knew he was down here with you. Your name got me a few strange looks too, Al. Seems you made more than a few enemies back there."

"Geez, Steph, I take it you haven't spoken to Billy about any of this."

"Not a word, Al. I'm kind of afraid to. How do you think he'll take it?"

"Hell, I don't know, Steph. I'm trying to imagine what it would feel like, if it was me. I do know how he feels about Charlotte, and as much as it'll hurt him, he needs to know that she died. Hearing it from you might soften the blow, whether he wants to believe you're his daughter or not. How do you figure you'll ever know? Some kind of blood test or something?"

"Suppose so. But I think I know anyway. My mother wasn't musically gifted. She had a decent voice, but her singing was not exactly uh, pro level.

She always said she sounded—"

"I know, Steph. Like a cat?"

Stephanie laughed. "That *is* what she called it. Wow, and you remember that? Anyway, I don't mean to brag, but you've heard what I can do. I was singing and playing piano without any lessons by the time I was five. When I heard jazz for the first time I knew what I wanted to do. It came easy for me. If I heard a song, I could play it, and I improvised on melodies almost from the start. It was born into me."

"Steph, you've heard of my first wife, Michelle Stirling? She was a dynamite singer, with no training, and her parents weren't musical, not that she ever knew anyway. It could be like that for you."

"I know it happens, Al. But something in the way my mother talked about Billy, I think there was something more to the story. She'd get real sad sometimes. I know she loved Carl, but there was a longing in her heart for 1970. I think if she hadn't died so soon, so unexpected . . . it was a brain aneurysm . . . he might have told me more about that time, and what went on back then. What did Billy do to her? Why didn't they stay together if they cared about each other so much?"

"You could say it was my fault, Steph. It was me who got us a gig back in New York. I talked Billy into coming. I didn't get it then, how much he cared for Charlotte. And that probably wouldn't have stopped me anyway. These things happen when you're on the road. I figured he'd get over it."

"Al, I want to tell him. I need to hear about his time with my mother. If nothing else, maybe I'll learn some stuff about her. Do you think I should do it right away?"

"Yeah, Steph, I think you should tell him tonight, before the gig, even though I can't predict how it might affect his mood or his playing. But at least then we can be pretty sure he'll be sober. And I'd like to be there with you if that's okay?"

"Yes, Al, please. But are you sure about telling him tonight?"

"Billy has been my friend off and on, mostly on, for nearly thirty years. I love the guy, even though he drives me nuts sometimes, and I know him better than you could ever imagine. Trust me on this, I'm a hundred percent sure if you wait, and he suspects I knew ahead of him for any length of time, he'd be mad *and* really hurt. It has to be tonight."

"But, Al, I think we should be kind of discreet about our *relationship*?"

"Don't worry, Steph. We'll play it cool until Billy gets a chance to know you. He likes you a lot already. Got a feeling he wouldn't be too thrilled to think of us as 'more than friends'."

"Thanks, Al, I see why my mother spoke well of you. You really are a good person."

♪♪♪

The room with no windows . . . it's been trying to kill me for all these years. Is it about to have its wish?

CHAPTER 49

REVELATIONS

*I*t was 3:15—well past her deadline. Ginny felt an ache in her gut. There was no sense in staying any longer, but she had to.

Just ten more minutes, that's all.

Al's car pulled in to the front drive of the apartment building.

♪♪♪

"I have to go home for a while, Steph. I'll call Billy and see if he wants to meet us for dinner before the gig."

"Good idea. I feel ready to talk to him, with you there." She kissed him on the cheek. "I'd better go in. I think I need a nap."

"I'll call you in a while, once I get ahold of Billy. Get some sleep. Could be a tense night."

♪♪♪

Ginny waited until Al's dust had settled before she started up her car. After all this time waiting, planning, scripting the play about to unfold—she had frozen. Probably a good thing, considering that one of her options was to shoot them both, and she did have a handgun under the seat. Would spending the rest of her life in prison be worth the pleasure: having him watch the gun rise up to his face; saying the words that would send him from this world; seeing him die at her feet? No, fantasy was fun, but not the way to live.

She pulled out of the driveway into the street, leaving a bigger cloud than Al's. Heading down the first side street, she gunned the engine to maximum and the surge of horsepower was like an aggressive lover, pushing her deeper into the seatback.

"He thinks *he* drives fast," she said out loud.

A car began to emerge from a laneway two blocks down; Ginny kept her foot pressed to the pedal. If the left lane remained clear, she'd have a full block in which to stop, *if* she managed to get by the vehicle in front without killing someone. As she passed it, the car looked as if it were standing still, while the startled driver offered a single-digit salute. As Ginny screeched to a smoky stop at the next main intersection, she glanced in the mirror to see if the man she'd passed was approaching.

She expected at least a verbal confrontation, but all he did was drive up behind her and wait patiently for her to go through or turn. Wasn't he going to mess with her? She almost wished he would as her fingers caressed the gun beneath the seat.

♪ ♪ ♪

The apartment was empty, except for Theo. Al didn't like the cat much, but he let it jump up on his lap as he settled into the couch. When he'd first met the animal, Al asked if its full name was Theophilus; since it was "the awfulest" looking cat he'd ever seen.

"Should have got a beer. Hey, cat, go get me a beer."

Theo closed his eyes and kneaded Al's chest with his disarmed front paws.

"They made a movie about you didn't they, cat? *Clawless*? Sorry, that was *Clueless*, but then, that applies to you too."

Sheesh, am I trying to get a laugh outa the stupid cat now? Guess I've had tougher audiences.

He decided the beer could wait; Theo looked too comfortable. When Ginny came in at four o'clock, Al had slipped into a disquieted sleep, his dreams permeated with images of Stephanie, Billy, Montreal, and full-breasted cat-waitresses bringing him beer.

"Al? Al, come on. Sorry to wake you up, but what are we doing for dinner tonight? I need to know."

"Oh shit, hi . . . What time is it?"

"Sounds like a replay of this morning. Are you going to run out on me again? What was the big deal, you had to leave so quick?"

This was a dangerous moment; to lie well when you are groggy is not for the amateur.

Al said, "Needed to talk with Stephanie, about the gig and stuff. There's more . . . of a personal nature too. Stuff about some people we used to know, sort of . . . a long story."

Al was good at this: using a higher proportion of truth than deceit. It felt something like honesty; it was close enough. Ginny dug into her memories of the day, sorting through a tangle of infuriating impressions to see if this made any sense. What had she seen? The girl had kissed him on the cheek, but that wasn't condemning in itself. He'd been evasive when he left, or was that just his preoccupation with being on time? Damn him, why was it so hard to believe the worst? Did he suspect that she knew where he had been, so he was covering his tracks? Could he be tricked into slipping up? Did she really want him to?

"So, Al, you met with Stephanie? I see. Where did you go . . . Lou's?"

She waited for the lie; she'd catch him in it for sure this time, since she had called Lou's and no one there had seen him or Stephanie.

"Nah," said Al, "I picked her up for lunch. Sorry I didn't tell you. It slipped my mind until this morning, and I didn't realize I hadn't told you where I was going till I was long gone. I'm a goof, as usual."

She had to say it. "Tell me straight, Al. Is there anything going on between you two?"

"Geezes, I can't believe you'd . . . Well, yes I can. Ginny, I haven't been too fair to you in the past. No need to go over that again, but come on. Would I be so stupid as to blow it with you again?"

"Yes you would, Al. Just don't forget, I'm not stupid, not anymore anyway. If you're going to screw around on me, I *will* find out. You better just leave now if that's what's going to happen."

He knew his partial honesty had been the right call. Trying his best to sound offended, he said, "Hey, did you follow me today? Yeah, that's it. Couldn't resist, *could* you?"

"Are you home for dinner tonight?" she asked, in a tone implying the return of normalcy. "Right now, I have to go downtown. Work stuff."

"I have to call Billy," said Al. "Stephanie needs to discuss something with him, right away, and I think I should be there too."

Ginny could feel the lying slithering between his words like a serpent in the branches of a fruit tree. Same old serpent, same old tree.

"I'll be quite late, Al . . . likely later than you. No need to wait up. Go do your thing. I won't ask what you're talking about. Guess that's between you and Billy, and what's-her-name."

"STEPHANIE," he shot back, surprising himself with his own volume. The way he said it, said everything.

Shit, you got me. Ginny, you are dangerous.

That one word—that name—said that *way*, pierced her heart. Love drained from the wound, forming a puddle of Al at her feet. Like a caged gorilla scooping up its own puke, she drank it all back in, knowing it would re-digest as hate.

"I'm heading out," said Ginny. "I'll grab dinner downtown. See ya later."

She was calm. Al wasn't quite sure why he wasn't.

♪♪♪

Al dialed Billy Crothers' number and was pleased to hear the man, not the annoying message.

"Hey, Billy, what's up? Me too. Hey, wanna meet me and Steph for dinner, maybe at Charlie's, then we can scoot down to the gig after? No, no, nothing's wrong . . . Come on, don't be paranoid. Just be nice to get together, right? Yeah, cool. See you about six? Oh, by the way, my friend, I shouldn't have to say this, but please be sober . . . ? Yeah, yeah, yeah . . . see ya at six."

♪♪♪

It was a quiet ride from Stephanie's apartment to Charlie's Place, all possible small talk rendered superfluous by the evening's impending conversation. Billy was waiting at the bar.

Christ, Billy, I hope you haven't been into the sauce yet. You damn well will be after this.

"Hi, guys!" Billy was beaming. "I asked for the table where we used to sit. Remember, Al, when we were on break?"

"Did you have to tip old AJ?" Al spotted the waitress across the room. "I see she hasn't gotten any, uh, *smoother.*"

AJ, Anna Jean, was a lifelong Florida resident who had evidently never heard of sunscreen. She looked like a prune after a long bath. No one knew her age, but she'd been "Old AJ" to them for over ten years.

Billy held Stephanie's hand and whispered, "Hey, beautiful, don't let the sun do that to *you.* Promise?"

"Good advice," said Stephanie. "Don't think I want to be known as 'Old SL.'"

AJ came to escort them to their table. "S'all ready, boys, and girl. Hey, is this that new singer I heard about? Or are they filming a movie on the strip again? You're a doll."

Her voice was as harsh as Lou's, only a bit higher.

Stephanie said, "AJ, you're just as sweet as the boys said."

♪♪♪

When their drinks had arrived, and they'd ordered their meals, Stephanie spoke first. "Billy, I haven't told you before, but I'm from Montreal."

He looked at her for a moment as if waiting for more, then said, "Is this like, a confession, Steph? You're admitting that I have to get used to working with another gol-darned Canuck?"

Billy saw that he was the only one at the table smiling. He said, "Hey, guys, what's up?"

Stephanie reached for Billy's hand and said, "Do you remember a friend of yours from Montreal . . . Charlotte Benoit?"

Billy teared up instantly as he mumbled, "Charlotte? You know Charlotte?"

"I'll get this out quick, Billy. She was my mother."

As important as that sentence had been, and with all the questions it might inspire, only one word rattled around in his head—"was"—a blinding meteor, smashing into and crushing all other thoughts. He wished he could reach inside his skull and rip it out.

"Billy, you okay?" said Al and Stephanie in unison.

Billy held one hand over his eyes, rubbing his forehead. "I'll be okay. Just need a second. Steph, you're telling me Charlotte's your mother?" He sounded like someone who'd just been punched in the stomach.

"Yes," said Stephanie.

"But, you said . . . 'was'?"

"Yes, Billy."

He breathed slowly for a moment, then in a slightly stronger voice said, "So, um, she . . . When?"

"Last year, October second."

"Oh shit," said Billy, covering his eyes again.

"What is it?" asked Stephanie. "Does the date mean something?"

"Steph," said Al, "that's pretty close to the anniversary of when they started seeing each other."

CHAPTER 50

THE CURE

"There's some stuff going on, Doc. Some heavy shit. Don't know how to deal with it."

"Music, or personal matters, Alfred?"

"Guess you could say both, but more personal, with Steph and Ginny. Billy's kinda mixed up in all of it too. Real screwed up situation, Doc."

"Please explain. Take your time."

Al filled in Doctor Davidson on the story of the connection between himself, Billy, Charlotte, and Stephanie. Starting with the pertinent details about the distant past, he went on to describe Friday's dinner meeting.

"Billy was happy to hear that Charlotte had married a nice guy, and had lived a generally happy life. She'd been successful in her career and raised three kids . . . stuff that might not have been so easy if she'd ended up with him. You could see the hurt in him, Doc, every time he said her name. Steph took a long time to get around to the father thing. With him learning about Charlotte's death, I guess she didn't want to hurt him anymore, but it had to come out. We were all drinking, maybe too much. She started to cry and Billy held her hand. Then she just up and blurted out, 'Billy, you have to know, I think you're my father.'

"I'm not a bad judge of people, Doc, and I figure I know Billy as good as anyone can know another human being. But his reaction to this news? Damn, he just blew me away. Didn't freak or anything. Actually, he smiled. Christ, like he already had guessed it? He asked her why she thought that, and she told him the stuff about when she was born and her musical talent and all. He said, 'Did your mother think so too?' Steph told him what she'd already said to me, everything Charlotte had told her. Weird as it sounds, I think they both really felt like they'd *found* each other. And for Billy, maybe like he'd found Charlotte again too? Have to say, I had been second guessing myself over telling him this stuff just before the gig, like maybe should we have waited until after Saturday night? But seeing the way he handled it told me for sure it was the right decision."

"I'm glad it turned out that way, Alfred. Please excuse my digression, but you say this also involved Ginny? I'm confused. Wasn't she the young lady from an affair years ago?"

"Well, yeah, Doc. I haven't really told you all that's been happening."

"Would you mind clearing things up a bit, Alfred?"

"Well, I met up with Ginny a while back, after I'd moved in with Kathleen, and we sort of, you know, fell back into our old arrangement. When Kathleen threw me out, I went to Ginny's place and I've been crashing there since."

"Does Ginny think of you as her 'boyfriend'? Have you given her the impression she's the *one* now?"

"Not exactly, Doc. You see, she's hard to figure. I don't think she really expects to ever, like marry me or anything. Maybe I'm more of a challenge, or a kind of game to her? If I split tomorrow she might be pissed, but she'd forget about me in a day."

"Hmm, Alfred, I believe you are convinced of that. But, if you're wrong, have you considered the consequences for Ginny?"

"Well, sort of, Doc. But it'll work out. Right now there's more important stuff to worry about. I've been hanging out with Steph, more than just to do with music."

"You're dating her?"

"Sort of. Haven't had sex or anything. I'm really falling for her, Doc, but this thing about Billy is a bit of a roadblock."

"Does Billy know about your feelings for Stephanie?"

"I don't think so, but he does know me better than anybody, so he may suspect. Damn, she is gorgeous. He must have figured I'd be interested in her."

"How do you think he'd feel about it?"

"Christ, the way he knows me, he'll likely shoot me."

"Alfred, back to Ginny. Does she know?"

"I'd say she has a pretty good idea. She's too damn smart, even for me. I'm in deep shit, Doc. She'll toss me out for sure, and I took a pay cut last week, so I'm screwed. Don't know how I can afford to keep seeing you. Nora's health plan covered me and I don't think that will be in effect much longer."

"That's something we can look at later. There are ways to accommodate certain circumstances. But listen, Alfred, you talk about this like it's all a matter of what's not convenient, or what problems you may have in regard to finances or accommodation. What about Ginny's emotions? How do you feel about what she is going through?"

"Aw shit, man. It's no biggie for her. She ran away the last time I messed her up, and survived just fine. She's a tough cookie. But as for me, I haven't felt like this in years, Doc. I mean, not this strong. Shit, Michelle got to me, but not the way Steph has."

Before that? Sue MacDonald? Crazy . . . dreamed about her the other night. How can she still hurt me?

"Well, there *was* Montreal. Charlotte could have been the love of my life, but I messed that up so bad, I likely don't deserve to ever find love."

"Alfred, you'll have to go into that in more detail when you're ready. Once again, you've mentioned Nora. And yet, I know little of your time with her, nor how that relationship ended."

"Well, Doc, I was married to Nora for a while. We split up and then got back together again. Real long story. She was a nice, loving supporter, a friend who got me through some tough times. But the 'real thing' never happened with her. Kind of like Kathleen, Nora was a great sarcasm sparring partner, a gentle, giving lover, and one of the few women I've been with who I could actually have a decent interesting discussion about almost anything with. Sometimes I wonder if she's what love is supposed to be, instead of the impossible dream I seem to have. But if it doesn't feel like enough, doesn't that actually mean . . . it *isn't* enough?

"There's been a whole mess of quickies in between. Yeah, between the relationships, and during most of them."

♪♪♪

Godzilla was lying on the couch, curled up in a ball of contentment. As Al scratched the dog's back, a full four-legged stretch resulted, joined by a wide-mouthed yawn with a gurgling, wheezing sound. This was pure, simple, unquestioned ecstasy. Al wondered if a human could ever know that feeling.

Sue doesn't count. We were just kids. Same with Charlotte really. Vickie counts, but in a strictly physical, horrible, impossible, messed up way. Damn, I need to tell Doc about that.

♪♪♪

Al continued. "But nothing's been so amazing overall, like what Steph is doing to me now. I really think I might be able to stick with her; no wandering. I was faithful to Michelle for a couple of years, Doc. And even longer with Nora. Maybe I can do it again."

"So, Alfred, you're living a lie with Ginny? Are you not intimate with her since you started seeing Stephanie?"

"Okay, a couple of times I almost gave in, but I really don't have any inclination to now. I don't want to screw around anymore, period."

"So you're saying that Stephanie's the one you can settle down with? Have you talked with her about your feelings?"

"Too early to get that heavy. Could scare her off. I want this to be right."

"But you still live with Ginny. Does she know what you're thinking?"

"Doc, I know this sounds like wanting to *have* my cake, and . . . Okay, I'm handling this the only way I can. Maybe it's wrong, but it's all I know. I'll try to work it out so Ginny doesn't get hurt again."

"Do you love her?"

"No, Doc, and I don't believe I ever did. You see, she's too much like me."

"Interesting, Alfred. That is certainly a 'theme' with you, to feel a lack of respect for someone who can love you. Your intimacy issues appear to be rooted in your childhood experience with what I would definitely describe as emotional abuse, from parents who withdrew affection and worse. As a 'wounded child', you can be said to suffer from a form of post-traumatic stress disorder, 'PTSD' for short."

"Gee, Doc, sounds nasty. Funny thing is, that sounds like my dad's problem after the war."

"Well, your father certainly exhibited signs of war-induced PTSD. Alfred, before we go further with anything else, I must ask . . . could you explain why you seem to avoid telling me more about Nora?"

"Okay, Doc. After our divorce, we went our separate ways for quite a while. She looked me up again, and I had been nothing but miserable without her. And so was she, so we gave it another shot. I called her my 'methadone gal' because she was like a deterrent to my addiction. I got so I didn't need to run around on her. Is there any scientific basis to that idea, Doc?"

"Well, Alfred, in a strictly clinical sense, no. What methadone does is to mitigate opioid withdrawal symptoms and block the euphoric effects of the addictive drug which, in your case, appears to be an issue of finding love, or more precisely, *attention* from women. At least, that is my assessment thus far. I believe Nora might have been, more accurately, not methadone for you but the 'answer' to what you have always sought. I won't be so dramatic as to call her the 'cure for what ails you', but perhaps as close as one could come?"

♪♪♪

Al knew exactly what the doctor was saying. He'd known it too well, too long. "So, Doc, just like me to blow it."

"And how did you, 'blow it', Alfred?"

"I'm afraid to say the words, Doc. I'm so ashamed of what happened."

"Alfred, guilt and shame are the allies and the fuel of addiction: one slip-up sending the addict to his knees to beg for more of what he craves. Is this what happened to you after your relationship with Nora ended?"

"Guilt and shame, yeah, Doc. They're my buds all right. And after what happened with Nora, the three of us partied regularly . . . guilt, shame, and Al: the three stooges."

"Please tell me about it, Alfred."

"Nora and I were actually planning to get married again last spring. Then, on New Year's Eve, everything changed. She died, and along with her went that 'cure' you mentioned. What ya got in your black bag, Doc? Anything that can replace her?"

"No, Alfred, I don't have the 'cure'. You do, inside you. And as you found it with Nora, you can find it again. Of this, I am confident."

CHAPTER 51

FIVE – SOUTH TOWER [14]

This isn't going to work. I may have to snuff this motherfucker without getting across the message I wanted to. What does it matter anyway? At least it will feel good to hurt him for what he did.

He moved closer to the bed and took a deep breath. Killing, no matter how determined the killer, is seldom easy—not as simple as the innocents of the world would believe for those with black enough hearts to even consider it. The difficulty might ease for someone who has done it before, but not for someone who claims to have—but has not.

♪♪♪

Outside the room, Rosetti clutched Poole's shoulder again. "Everything's okay in there. He'll be done in a minute. You want to go grab a coffee? I can stay here and take your watch till you get back."

"Sure, Captain. Want one too? What do you take?"

"Cream and four sugars, kid. Yeah, don't look at me that way. You heard right . . . *four.*"

As Poole headed for the elevator, Rosetti sat down, but almost immediately stood back up and began to pace in front of the door. This was not going well. How had he let himself get caught up in this? He wanted to go back in and be done with it: to blow that aberration clean to hell. So simple. The man had a gun and was about to kill a patient: the perfect set of circumstances for justifiable, *professional* homicide.

Rosetti knew that someday he'd have to do something. The secret piece of his life was destined to be discovered eventually if this douche bag was still around. There'd been a couple of close calls already. Too close. Maybe tonight might be the time.

CHAPTER 52

LOSERS' – A WINNER

*B*y the third week of Stephanie Leblanc's engagement at Lou's Lounge, business had increased so dramatically, even Lou was convinced. He met with Al in his upstairs office.

"Numbers are pretty good, Al baby. No doubt we got somethin' here."

"I could've told you that last week, Lou. Or the first night actually. Let's talk money. You're making it. I'm not. I need a raise."

"Al baby, let's not get too excited. Guess I can up your cut . . . maybe a touch."

"Lou, you can cut the crap. I want the total for the band to be eighteen hundred. No negotiating. That'll get Steph what she deserves, me back to where I belong, and the guys a decent slice."

"Al, come on, don't break my balls here. Dat's a six hundred smacker increase. I can go two hundred. Okay, maybe three, max."

"Which fucking one of the words 'no' and 'negotiating' did you not understand? It's eighteen hundred, or we walk. I've got people interested."

"You can walk, asshole, but who says da chick wants to go with ya? I can get a new band to back her and save a bundle. Lotsa guys out there looking for a gig, Al."

"That's not an option, Lou. Steph is with us all the way. Yeah, you and I both know she's why the numbers are up. But don't forget, I'm in this business as long as you, pal. You're going be ahead way more than the six hundred extra I'm asking."

"Maybe 'all da way' is what she's doin' with ya, huh . . . for you to think that she won't jump ship?"

Al took a deep breath and held it for a count to three—ten was out of his league. "Lou, right now my fist should be pushing your teeth out the back of your ugly skull. But you know, I'm a new man. Yeah, I'm gonna let that go. Just don't fucking *ever* say anything like that in front of her.

"Screw it, I've got to get to work, Lou. Don't want to keep that roomful of people waiting. And, just to reemphasize, notice I said, room *full* of people."

Wiping the sweat from his face, Lou said, "Al, don't get me wrong, I—"

Al slammed the office door on Lou's words.

♪♪♪

Stephanie was great; the band was great; Al felt great; maybe even life was finally great. As he indulged in a long contented sigh, he noticed Ginny was sitting near the stage. Back to two-out-of-four, just like that.

Al had explained to Stephanie how he was living as a roommate with Ginny; they were old friends, nothing more. The lie hadn't come easily for a change, but he felt it wasn't completely dishonest. Did the past matter, as long as it was true now? For some reason, Ginny had let the whole thing ride, but he knew she was on to him. Was she just going to accept second place status and ultimate rejection again, without a fight? She wasn't a kid anymore and after all, he was living with her now. He didn't get it.

Am I worth all the shit I've put her through? Is she that dumb? Nah, must be a third choice I just can't see.

At the end of the set, Al decided the only thing to do was go with the flow—whatever flow Ginny had in mind, even if it meant down the drain.

I guess I am a piece of shit. Maybe she'll finally flush me away for good?

He beckoned to Stephanie to join him as he sat down next to Ginny.

♪♪♪

"Stephanie," said Ginny, "you're damned good, even better than Al describes you. I wish I'd come down here sooner."

Al was impressed.

Ginny, my dear, you're nearly as good as me at schmoozing.

"Thanks, Ginny," said Stephanie. "It's good to finally meet you. Al says you're the best newshound in Florida."

Ginny turned to Al. "No double meaning implied with that 'hound' thing is there?"

Al smirked and said, "Let me get my two favorite ladies a drink. Brown cow, Ginny?"

Now there's a double meaning you can chew on, sweetie.

"Regular for you, Steph?"

"Stephanie," asked Ginny, "how's it feel to have hooked up with your long-lost father? Must be a trip and a half."

The word "trip" seemed odd for a person of Ginny's age. Stephanie attributed it to having hung out with Al. There was other evidence of his influence: in the way she sat, with her head resting on her outstretched index finger; and her somewhat masculine handshake. This young woman could easily have been taken for Al's daughter. She oozed Al-*isms*, as if his personality, thought processes, and even certain physical characteristics had leaked into her by osmosis. It has oft been said that after time a dog owner starts to resemble his pet; though some contend that's really a case of the pet-buyer having subconsciously sought out his own attributes. In the case of Ginny and Al, a fair degree of assimilation was undeniable.

Stephanie had seemed surprised at Ginny's question about her feelings about finding Billy, but after a moment of introspection she said, "It's really hard to describe: kind of exciting, scary, and a little sad, all at once. The worst part is I don't know for sure if it's true. And maybe I never will."

"I might be able to help," said Ginny. "It's what I do after all: find information. I can even use my sources for stuff like blood samples, DNA and so forth. Want me to look into it?"

"That would be great," said Steph. "What do you need from me?"

"First thing is blood type. I'll ask Billy for his, and if that doesn't tell us anything, we'll go the DNA route. Mind giving me a hair? That's all I need for the test as long as there's a follicle."

"No, here you go," said Stephanie, tugging loose a strand from the top of her head. "I'm excited. Please let me know if you do find anything. It's so cool that you came in tonight."

"A trip," said Ginny, as she waved to her awaited friends who had arrived at the front door. Stephanie used the opportunity to excuse herself. Table-hopping was required.

♪♪♪

It was a typical night at the *new* Losers'. Music, laughter, applause, and booze flowed till last call, like the Niagara River's inevitable plunge into the mist. Sound and emotion plumed skyward, reaching a short-lived, lingering peak—the outside world seemed only a rumored evil—before the mood settled into the placid gorge of closing-time.

♪♪♪

Having bid adieu to her friends, Ginny approached Billy who was still at the piano playing an almost inaudible unfamiliar melody. She listened for a few moments, not wanting to disturb him, but he noticed her and stopped abruptly.

"Aww, don't stop," said Ginny. "That was lovely. What was it?"

Billy scratched his face and neck. "Oh, nothing, really nothing. I'm writing a tune for Steph. Not anywhere near together yet. I want it to be good." A lightbulb clicked on in his eyes and he said, "You're Al's friend . . . Ginny, right?"

"That would be me," said Ginny. "What's up, Billy? You sounded great tonight as usual. Hey, I need some info from you. Got a minute?"

♪♪♪

Al and Stephanie had escaped out the back. The alley wasn't exactly romantic, but they had to be alone.

Al asked, "Does Billy have any idea what's going on with us, Steph? You see him more than I do these days. Has he asked you anything?"

"No, he hasn't, and I don't want him to. Things are too complicated. You know, I sensed my mother was in love with you, Al. I mean, before Billy. And he's told me he always felt like second choice, that she would have gone back to you if you'd asked."

"No, Steph, that's ridiculous. He never got it. Charlotte only pretended to be my friend. She hated my guts."

"Why? What happened that she'd hate you? I don't believe it, with how she talked about you."

"That was nearly thirty years ago. This is what's important now. I'm in love with you, Steph. I need to be with you and I want everyone to know."

"Confession time, Al? Okay, I think I might be in love with you too, but this is so messed up."

"Be honest, Steph, does the age difference bother you? Or is it that I've got kind of a bad record when it comes to sticking with someone?"

"Al, no, especially the age thing doesn't mean anything to me. And if it bothers other people, to hell with them. I see you as 'you', regardless of what some numbers on the calendar say. Funny how my mother seemed old to me in some ways, but like a sister, or an equal, in others. I wonder, if she were here now, if she'd see you as any different from the Al of back then? Other than a few pounds and some cool gray hairs."

"Steph, before I met you, I would have said I hadn't changed much at all.

Now I wish Charlotte could see me and know how I feel about you. I know she'd get it, that I love you sincerely. If anyone could see the changes in me since you came into my life, *she* would."

"And you say you two weren't in love, Al? I can hear it in your words and the way you get when you talk about her. You loved her. Still do. Don't deny it. This is partly why all this is so awkward. If Billy Crothers is really my father, and you're falling for me, and used to be in love with my mother . . . ? Wow, it's a crazy, messed up situation."

"Steph, right now this alley is the whole world. You and me, here, now, is all that matters."

They kissed and held each other, and for a moment their dumpster-world was paradise. Like the original paradise, the bliss was short-lived.

♪ ♪ ♪

"What the *fuck* are you doing?" said Billy, standing at the door with Ginny just behind him.

Stephanie pulled away from Al and ran over to Billy. Putting her hands on his shoulders, she said, "Please don't blame Al. We got into this together, but we didn't know how to tell you."

Al was looking past Billy, his eyes locked with Ginny's. "Hey," he began, "I guess I should have—"

"Save it," said Ginny. "None of my affair. I'm just the roomie." She sounded convincingly apathetic to all but Al, who knew she was boiling inside: her choice of words, far from random. This was the first time she'd had to confront her suspicions face to face, and he could sense her painful resignation to the unsheathed bloodied truth which had excised the final shred of hope from her heart.

Billy pushed his way past Stephanie, trying not to be too rough. He yelled at Al, "I thought maybe for the first time in your sick fucking life, you'd think with your head instead of your dick." With all the grace of a pugilistic penguin, he moved to confront Al, yelling, "You're supposed to be my friend, you prick. You made me lose Charlotte. Now you're going to do it again? I can't let you."

He took a wild swing, but Al avoided the punch easily and caught Billy in his arms. Holding his struggling friend in a bear hug, he said, "Billy, let's cool off, before anybody says too much. I'll go, and you stay with Steph. Ginny, you come with me."

Ginny sneered at him. "I think I'm needed here, Al. You just run along, okay?"

It was easy for him to hate her right now.

What the hell game is she playing?

After being released, Billy didn't try again to fight. He leaned back against the dumpster, slumping downward into a sitting position against it.

He looked up at Al, and in a pain-racked voice said, "Get yourself another piano player. I quit. Steph, you do what you have to. Guess it'll be without me."

CHAPTER 53

REVELATIONS TOO

*L*ate autumn in South Florida—the cooling night air is like a velvet sheet, no longer the draping damp towel of the summer heat, when everyone and everything, even the bugs and time itself seem to slow down, joined reluctantly by the entertainment business. Not counting on meager local support in the off-season, many venues cut entertainment entirely. But now, with the high season approaching, things start to come alive with tourist traffic business, and new gigs are up for grabs.

For the first summer in several years, Lou had faced no decision in that regard. He'd continued the band's run straight through the slow season; since it was atypically *not* slow, with Stephanie's success generating a better cash flow than in normal peak season.

It had been almost a month since Billy had gone; and while his replacement was a talented, experienced pro, Al missed the comfort level his old friend had provided. The new pianist was still sometimes thrown off by Al's accidental excursions away from the form of a song, and endings were always interesting. For the entire quartet, developing synergy was proving to be a slow process.

♪♪♪

Stephanie continued to see Billy, and helped him get a gig playing cocktail piano in a hotel. She reported to the gang at Losers' that he was doing okay, even with having to play "Lady in Red" and "New York, New York" three times or more every night. He told her he could slip in enough good tunes by saying they were requests. He never asked about Al.

♪♪♪

In time, Billy seemed more relaxed talking with Stephanie about Charlotte. One night at dinner at a beach hotel, he really got going after a few drinks.

"She was way too smart for me. Hell, she read more books in a week than I had in my whole life. Didn't seem to matter though. We talked about stuff . . . what life was all about, where you go when you die, stuff I never talked about with anyone before. Music had been my whole life since I was a kid, and books had been hers. But still, we understood each other? Sounds corny I know, but we felt close right away. I know she didn't love me the way I did her. Man, I was so crazy for her. For years I kept her picture tucked in a little secret pocket in my beret. Kind of felt like she was with me wherever I went . . . up until a while ago actually, till some fuckhead swiped it.

"After that happened, Al couldn't figure out why I just didn't buy a new hat of some kind, but that old purple thing had been such a part of me, replacing it would be like trying to buy a new family member who died. And a new one wouldn't have Charlotte in it."

Billy ran his fingers through his hair and sighed. "Whoever took my beret probably just threw it away. Just some stupid prank; they never knew what they'd really stolen from me.

"Anyway, she showed me that life could be interesting away from work. I'd never done anything but play and practice . . . well, if you don't count drugs. With them, I got away; more or less *escaped* from things that were difficult. She hated that about me; wanted to help, but I told her nobody could but me. She got mad and said that it wasn't right to try to solve a big problem like that alone. Too bad I didn't listen to her, huh?

"We only, you know, *slept together* one time. It was just before I went back to New York. I felt in my heart that I was going to go back to her, but I knew she didn't believe it. See what I mean by she was smarter than me?"

Billy scratched his forehead and ran his fingers through his thinning, tonic-laden hair. "She told me Al wasn't going to make it unless I was strong enough to help him, 'cause he wasn't capable of saying no to the distractions that could ruin his potential. How did she know that, Stephanie? It took me months to figure him out, and she saw it in a couple of days. One smart cookie, your mother.

"She had a thing for him ya know. They didn't last very long, 'cause Al was . . . Al. Well, because of that, I got to know her, so I guess I owe him that. She still had special feelings for him though. You could see it when we were all together. Sometimes I'd catch her looking at him, and she looked kind of sad, or thoughtful or something. He never admitted it, but I think he was in love with her. Guess he was too stupid to know she would have had him back if he'd really tried."

Billy motioned for the waitress, and asked for another round. Stephanie declined, but excused herself for a powder room trip. When she returned, Billy slugged back half his beer and continued. "When we got back to New York, we worked together for a year in a great jazz club. Al was at the peak of his career. Papers were calling him the next Chet Baker. He hated that. I bet Chet did too. Jon Faddis and Al Waters were making a name about the same time. Both were young hotshots. Faddis has had quite a career, huh?

"You know, I think it was 'cause of me, partly anyway, that Al never made it really big. I got into the sauce and smack again pretty heavy. That's partly why I never got back to Montreal. Al should have dumped me, but he wouldn't. Lost a couple of gigs 'cause of me, including the one we went back there for in the first place. He wouldn't abandon me though, even when everyone said I was messing up his reputation almost as much as mine. I was bad, showing up late, missing the whole gig sometimes, and playing shitty when I did get there. If I'd been able to see it, I would have fired myself, but the monkey on your back keeps its hands over your eyes, and your ears. Al had his own 'animal' problems. Yeah, *me*, 'cause I think I was like an albatross around the neck of his career."

Billy took a deep breath and stared out the window into the night. Through the open window the invisible ocean waves could be heard slapping and sloshing in and out. He turned back to Stephanie who had been intently watching his face, but now had turned to the same window, as if to discover what he saw in the blackness.

"There was one point, Steph, where it looked like he had it made: our second time in New York in the late seventies, when he was playing great and getting known. And he hooked up with this sort of famous lady music critic. But he blew that all in one shot, messing around with another woman who was married to a bigwig business guy who could make or break you. He'd screwed me around too in that same situation, by not hiring me. But he did stick with me for the rest of the time we were in New York. Too bad for him.

"But before that, in our time in the Apple right after Montreal, things had started off gangbusters. But we kept getting less and less important gigs, 'cause of his reputation *and* mine. As good as Al was, the club owners didn't want to take chances on having a no-show band. He might have been compared talent-wise to Chet and Miles, or Freddie Hubbard, but he wasn't well-known like them, so full houses weren't a guarantee. Jazz is a hard sell unless you got a name guy or two in the band. Al was an almost-name, not famous enough to gamble on to get an audience. After a while, the agents could only get us crappy one-nighters and backup work with singers who Al usually ended up in fights with, 'cause he wouldn't tolerate mediocrity . . . 'cept in me of course.

"We caught a break in the early seventies, when an agent booked us in Florida, yeah, Hollywood, just up the road not that far from here. It sounded like a fun gig, and the money was good. We figured it was a way to get everything back on track. That's when he met Michelle Stirling, and all the tracks we'd ever been on disappeared."

Stephanie turned back toward Billy, having given up on finding what he saw out there in the night. "What does that mean, Billy?" she asked.

"We'd been here only a few weeks and things were going good. If Al was unhappy, I didn't see it; but one night he was Al Waters, jazzman . . . and then bam, the next day he was Al Waters, clown. I know he thought he was in love and everything, but for the first time since we hooked up, he seemed to stop caring about what used to be important: jazz, being his own man, and me.

"He quit the gig we had, without even talking to me about it, and started working with Michelle. Sure, he did try to get me into the band they were in, but the leader wouldn't have anything to do with me. I don't blame him, but for Al to dump me after all those years, it hurt pretty bad."

Billy's skin tightened: an emotionally administered face-lift. "Michelle changed him, Steph. *Show* bands? Give me a break. This was one of the best young jazz guys in the country, and she's got him singing, playing only saxophone, and frigging dancing like a fool. They go off into lounge circuit limbo, and I go back to the Apple, to continue the work on my self-destruction.

"Al called me once from Vegas, more than a year later; said if I came there, he could get me work. I hung up on him. Don't think I even knew who I'd been talking to for a day or so. Later, I did go out there for a while, but it didn't exactly work out. Long story there, honey, for another time.

"Didn't see him again until he came back to New York. When was that, 1978? I was living in a stinking hole, up on 113th Street, worse than the place I'd been in when I first met him. Don't know how he even found me. Well, Al can be, uh, *persuasive*, especially when he's mad."

"Tell me about that, Billy," said Stephanie. "What did Al do when he found you like that?"

Billy's eyes softened to the more recognizable half-closed look of permanent mellow. "He stayed with me for two weeks, keeping me off the drugs.

I should have died, but he wouldn't *let* me. Ever see that old Sinatra movie, *The Man with the Golden Arm?* Well, it was just like that, but worse. No matter how much I told him I hated him, didn't want to live, all the shit a junkie says . . . he stayed. Sometimes he'd hold me like a damned baby. Yeah, in his *arms.* Like he was protecting me . . . from *me.*

"I know I should be able to forgive what he's done—with you, and stuff—but the past doesn't matter. Doesn't excuse him being a thoughtless prick *now.* Steph, I beg you, think twice. No, think a thousand times before you get too mixed up with Al Waters. He'll screw up your life somehow, whether he means to or not. There's a lot of stuff about him you don't know, some of it I'll never even understand, and it's not my place to get into it."

Agitation again began to distort Billy's features, and his voice grew tense. "You saw what he did to that guy at Losers'? That's not the real danger, what he's capable of doing with his fists or his temper. No, the worst thing about Al is that he can't see beyond *now.* Nothing matters except what's in front of him at any particular moment. Like a circus lion that might have gone years being fed by the same trainer; it's like a big puppy dog. Then one day the trainer gets in the way of the raw meat, and becomes just another piece of steak to the beast.

"Doesn't matter if Al loves you. He's capable of tearing you to bits . . . like that lion."

♪ ♪ ♪

Stephanie let some of what Billy had been saying sink in. Then she asked, "That night at Losers' . . . I'm guessing that wasn't the first time you've seen him fight like that?"

"Steph, I wish it was, but no, I've seen Al in that out-of-control mode a few times too many. One of the main reasons we came down to Florida the last time was to get away from the heat over an even worse kerfuffle in New York.

"We were in our last set one night in a Village jazz bar. Musta been about '83, yeah, 'cause that's when . . . Anyways, when an old acquaintance of ours shows up, a guy name of Ed Wilson. That's a long story, but ya see, Al used to live at this guy's place, and Ed was a little on the lighter side of manly; you know, a homo."

Billy gestured with a limp wrist. "Well, anyway, they hadn't seen each other for a few years, and I don't know why they'd been on the outs, but they seemed okay with each other on this particular night. Ed got up and played piano on a tune with Al, and everything was hunky dory. Then this asshole in the audience yells up something about Ed bein' a fag, and Al gets, shall we say, kinda steamed. Ed says he doesn't care, but the guy keeps makin' queer-jokes, and then Al tells the guy to shut the fuck up. 'Course, the guy bein' even stupider than he was drunk, yells, 'What are ya, another queer?' I've never seen him react so fast, Steph. He was off the stage and onto that guy; they looked like a bad tumbling act. This sucker was pretty big and managed to get in a few shots, but unfortunately didn't knock Al out. Only made him madder. The *second* chair Al smashed over that guy's head pretty much ended it.

"But he hadn't noticed the guy's friend comin' up from behind, and he turned just in time to get a bottle right in the face. That was the only lick the second guy got in. As dazed as Al must have been, he grabbed the guy and pulled him to the floor, hands around his throat. He would have killed him, no doubt in my mind, but the cops got there in time. They see the first guy out cold on the floor, and the *other* guy getting choked. Of course, they take Al away in cuffs. Didn't matter who started one like that. It was almost a homicide. He spent a little time in the slammer, about a week was all."

As Billy paused to sip his beer Stephanie said, "Is that how he got that scar then, from being hit with that bottle?"

"Sure is. He's so lucky he was able to play after that. Even so, it put him out for over a month. You know him. He was trying to play his horns way too soon after, and the frustration of not being able to get a single note was devastating to him, way worse than the physical pain. It took him all day *every* day for a few weeks to get his chops back, and eventually his sound was actually even better . . . well, on sax, but not trumpet. I think that bottle basically ended that part of his life forever.

"You know how good he is on sax, baby: no Sonny Rollins or Dexter Gordon, but still nothing to throw tomatoes at. But believe me, on trumpet he might have been one of the best *ever*, if he'd stuck with it."

"Billy, I've heard one recording with you and him from back in the day, and you're right. His sound was incredible, so big and warm. Maybe someday he'll give it another go?"

"I don't think so, Steph. I've seen him when he hears a good trumpet player. He gets on a real downer. And then he drinks too much."

"What happened back in New York, Billy? He got only a week in jail for that fight?"

"Ed Wilson's lawyer eventually got Al off with probation, but word was out on the street that the guy he had messed with was a minor league 'wise guy', you know, organized *grime*?"

Billy smiled as he rubbed his thumb twice across the side of his nose. "Ed's lawyer was kinda *connected* himself, and smoothed it over, but only with the understanding that Al would get out of the Apple for a long time. We've been here in Florida ever since, together and not. Don't know if it's been long enough, but I don't think it matters anymore, in more ways than one. Neither of us cares if we ever go back north."

"Has he been in the same kind of trouble down here?" asked Stephanie.

"Oh yeah, a few times. Remember that cop, the night of the fight at Losers'? Well, that same guy had arrested Al a couple of times. First was back in '92."

"So, Billy, that incident in New York, you think he was fighting for Ed Wilson, like he did for you and Kathleen?"

"You're right, Steph. Does seem like mostly when he loses it, is when someone is getting picked on. Every time it's the same thing. Somebody gets in a pickle of some kind, friend of his or not I guess, and Al has to get involved. Can't help himself if he sees an underdog. I'm not sure if I've ever seen him fight or even really argue with someone just over his own welfare."

Once again Billy turned to watch the nothingness out the window as his fingers gently drummed patterns on the table. He appeared lost in musical musings. Then, without turning back toward Stephanie, he stilled his hands and said quietly, "But that last time, in New York, it was by far the worst. I sensed something a lot heavier was going on inside him. Never could quite figure that out. I wonder if Ed Wilson would have known what exactly."

CHAPTER 54

THE BOOK OF AL

*D*octor Davidson leafed through his notebook, snapping pages back, then forward, then back again. Finally, he flipped the cover over and set the book on the arm of his chair.

"Okay, Alfred, on your personal relationships: please verify if I have all this correct. You're currently living with Ginny, whom you've known for a few years. She was your studio assistant, and you had an affair with her during the end of your second marriage, which was Nora, with whom you later got back together, until her death. And you haven't talked about that at all. I hope you will do so. Bereavement is a pernicious trauma in itself, and along with the rest of the difficulties you've faced, it should not be ignored.

"Then, you began seeing Ginny, sexually again, during your time with Kathleen. Okay so far . . . ? Right, and now you're dating Stephanie, while still living with Ginny. Whew, Alfred, I'm not merely *putting* you in my next book. It's going to have to be an entire book, just about you. Though my colleagues will claim I'm making you up."

The doctor laughed and winked while Al raised an eyebrow in mock concern. "Doc, I assume this is all kidding. You can't really write about real people like that, can you?"

"No, Alfred, at least not with real names and places."

"I've been working on a book, Doc, for a few years now."

"You're writing a book, Alfred?"

"No. *Reading* one."

"Seriously, Alfred, Ginny knows about your feelings for Stephanie, and she accepts it? What's going on? Are you sure she is aware you're involved with another woman? And she doesn't care? No, I'd have to think she cares. She must have some rationalization for not dealing with it, and without talking to her, I can only guess. But she does care . . . guaranteed."

CHAPTER 55

FAIRY TALES CAN COME TRUE

*S*tephanie assured Al that she was cool with the arrangement he had with Ginny. He wondered if her perception of it was predicated on pure unwarranted trust, or naiveté—or if it did in fact bother her—but she wasn't being honest about it, either with him or herself.

As for Ginny, she seemed to have slipped into an illogical, confusing holding pattern. Sometimes Al would look up from his reading and catch her staring at him. Was that a Mona Lisa impression or what? She hadn't said another word about the incident with Stephanie, and the fact that Al never approached her anymore for sex didn't seem to matter. He figured she wasn't interested anyway; and for the first time since Nora, he had no compulsion to be with more than one woman. The problem was that the one he was living with, wasn't that *one*.

Hallelujah, he thought, as the reality of his intention to be a one-woman-man began to sink in. *This ranks up there with healing of lepers and parting of seas. If I can only find an easy way to tell Ginny what's up.*

♪ ♪ ♪

It was a Wednesday night, or more accurately, a Thursday morning, 3 a.m. when Al came in the front door, carefully at first, and then chuckling at himself when he realized Ginny was up. She was in her pajamas on the couch, not reading or watching TV—just sitting.

Al saw the bottle on the coffee table and said, "Hey, what's up with this? You been drinking Scotch?"

She hated Scotch, but the need to numb her mind had overcome her distaste. "If I drink it all up," she spluttered, "won't be any left for poor little Al. Wouldn't that be just the meanest thing?"

Al said, "You'd have to drink a lot, baby. There's a whole other bottle in the cabinet." He hoped there still was.

"You better sit down, Mr. Musician, I have some wudderful news. Did I say 'wudderful'? Geesh. Come on over, next to Miss Ginny, the story lady. You're going to be sooo excited."

Al was too fascinated by her totally out-of-character performance to do anything but play along. He'd never seen her drunk, maybe tipsy a few times, but tonight she was *wasted*.

Ginny crossed her legs and turned to begin her story, holding her hands palms-up, as if reading from a book. "Okay, here we go, here we go . . . Once upon a time there was this cute little girl from a faraway land called Montreal, see? And she came *all* the way to the Land of the Sun to find her long lost papa. Well, a big mean wolf jumped out of the woods. His name was Alfred D. Wolf. And he used his magic powers. Did I tell you he was a magic wolf? Well, he is, and he used his powers to make the little girl love him. Like it so far?"

He saw no reason not to. He was enjoying this fascinating, playful, and creative side of her.

"Go on, story lady."

"Turned out the wolf knew the little girl's lost daddy, and he brought them together so they could be happily ever after. But uh-oh, there was an evil witch in the Land of the Sun. Her name was Virginia . . . just like *my* real name. How cool is that? And she hated to see people get too happy. It was her job to make them sad. Hmm, and she is very good at her job."

This was getting less cute.

"Virginia the Witch loved the bad wolf, 'cause he was the only-est person she ever saw who was meaner than her . . . but she was mad at him for doing a good deed, so she decided to fix *everything*. She went to this sciency medical-type wizard who knows all about everything in the land, and he told her not to worry, for the magic he had was very strong. It was the magic of *knowledge*, and he bestowed it upon Virginia."

Al was not into this anymore. "What the fuck are you getting at, Ginny? If you've got something to say, just fucking say it. I don't have *time* for this."

Ginny grinned and said, "The wolf growled at Virginia, but she was not afraid because her magic was very dangerous. She would use the *knowledge*, to strike him down."

"What goddamn knowledge? Come on, I'm getting pissed *off* here."

Seeing Al's anger approaching red zone, she paused for a long deep breath and then continued. "The wizard had a magic machine that can tell stories about who we are, and who we aren't. It told him a story about the little girl and her father. And guess what? They weren't who they thought! The wizard's machine never lies. The machine knows all about DNA. Does that mean 'Dork Nuts Al'? Whatever . . . Here it is. It turns out that the little girl from Montreal's real father is . . . the wolf."

♪ ♪ ♪

He knew she had wanted to hurt him. Was this a concoction to that end? Pain comes in many forms, and Al had known most, including this kind, but never this devastating: an acid soup, stirred up from your own greed and folly, to be swallowed gulp by searing gulp, until your guts and mind explode. She'd offered him a bowlful of this poison. A howl rose from within, squelched by the single desperate wish that she might be wrong, but hope was crushed by cold logic.

Oddly, this was not truly a surprise, but more an affirmation of a growing suspicion. The tumblers had been rattling around in the rusty lock on his past, falling one by one, until this deft tug by a drunken Ginny had released it.

Now science had blown away the final patches of fog from what he had already begun to surmise. The horror was how he could have allowed this to happen—the ultimate selfishness—to have stayed blind to the evidence; and to have fallen in love with his own daughter.

With all the good in his life seeming forever behind him, Al strove only to make some sense of the moment. "You did tests . . . for DNA? When?"

"The witch doesn't have to—"

"Fuck OFF with that witch crap. More like 'BITCH'. When did you KNOW?"

Ginny was not too drunk to still respect Al's temper, but she still hesitated, only for a second. She had long awaited this moment. No backing down now.

"Guess it's been, um, a few weeks . . . ?"

The implication of those words was so monstrous, so evil. How this one human being could have so much desire for revenge was unimaginable. Had he really done so much to her to deserve this heinous retribution? What about the others involved? Had she considered them? How could he face Billy, and worse . . . Stephanie?

Ginny had intended him to suffer this agony. That had to be it. She must have expected he'd kill himself in a fit of self-pity, maybe throw himself off the balcony? But it wasn't going to work that way—not quite.

Al grabbed Ginny's arms and pulled her up to her feet. "You're going to feel what I feel, you fucking whore bitch."

He dragged her across the apartment to the open balcony. She tried to hook one foot onto the doorframe, but he was unstoppable. As he pulled her inch by inch toward the railing, she said through gritted teeth, "You think I'm gonna make this easy for you, you bastard?"

Kicking at his legs seemed to have no effect; it only made the pain worse in her stretched-back arms. When they reached the edge, she managed to free one hand, and swung at his face, but he caught her by the wrist. Al wrestled both her arms into one of his hands and pulled her head back viciously with the other.

Pushing her roughly against the waist-high railing and forcing her to look down, he asked, "Glad you live on the seventh floor? Huh, are you? Are you maybe thinking right now how much nicer a ground floor place might be?"

He yanked her around to face him. Holding her backward halfway over the railing, he laughed and said, "Where's the wicked witch now, huh? Where's your magic? Can you fly, witch? Shall we find out?"

Ginny was not strong enough to fight him at the best of times, and she could only pray he was bluffing. He wasn't entirely, but he wasn't going to kill her—no matter how much he wanted to. If only he could throw her over the edge; make her body hurt the way his heart did; cripple her physically, to match her dysfunctional morality.

Releasing her hands, he gripped her face with one hand, and caressed her forehead gently with the other. As he drew back his fist and held it up high over Ginny's face, he thought of hitting Vickie, hitting Stupid Stewart Carter, Ed Wilson, Fred Waters—hitting them all, again, and again, and again.

As he reeled between past and present pain, his hand began to tremble. With a deceptive calm he said, "If you were a man, I'd kill you."

Ginny laughed and said, "If *you* were one, I'd be scared."

"I'm still man enough that I don't hit women, not even if they're sick fucks like you."

"Does Vickie count, Al? Huh? How does that whole thing with her fit into your big manly reputation?"

Al lowered his hand. This was beyond belief. "How did you . . . ?"

"Billy told me, Al. He's an easy man to get information out of when you load him up with booze, or whatever."

Anger and anguish erupted from his throat. "No, God DAMN it. NO. I can't be hearing this . . . I can't."

Letting go of Ginny, he turned and slammed his open palm against the wall. He raised his hand to do it once more as Ginny tried to slip by him to the sliding door. Unable to stop himself as she got in the way, he caught the back of her head, driving her face against the wall. She dropped to the balcony floor while Al stood over her, momentarily wondering if he had just accidentally killed someone—again.

When he bent down to check, she pushed him away as she pulled herself into a sitting position. She rubbed her face to inspect the damage. Although there was some blood, it seemed nothing was broken.

Forcing a laugh, she said, "Fuck, that hurt. You've got one wrecking ball of a punch for an old dude."

The pain in her jaw and the look on Al's face told her to shut up.

He whispered, "You know that was an accident. If I'd meant to hit you, I'd be calling an ambulance, or a coroner."

Through the dizziness from the blow and the lingering sedative power of Scotch, she was thinking clearly enough to stay on the balcony floor and remain silent.

Al said nothing more and headed back into the apartment.

♪♪♪

Both Al and the second bottle of Scotch were half-gone by 4:30. Ginny sat at the kitchen table, holding a towel with ice on her face. She was thankful the whiskey had not worn off yet; but knew the pain would increase as the day went on.

Al didn't understand why she hadn't called the police; he could do major time for this. Wasn't that what she wanted?

"Going to see Steph," Al muttered. "Got to tell her. What the fuck am I going to do?"

"Tell her the truth, Al. See what that feels like for a change. You might like it. New things can be exciting. You should know . . . like you and Vickie?" Ginny was not afraid anymore.

"Shut up or I'll put that towel down your throat. Vickie doesn't mean shit, but what you did with that DNA stuff, and holding it back? How could you do this, Ginny? Why'd you let me carry on with Steph, when you knew?"

"How could *you*, Al?"

"But I *didn't* know," said Al. "I had a strange feeling about things maybe, but I thought her assumption about Billy being her father was right. It all made sense."

"Come on, Al, you wanted . . . no, you *needed* it to be that. Even your ego-centric, oversexed fucking mind wouldn't let you screw your own kid. Or would it? I'm confused though, how it all happened. Weren't you too busy chasing every other woman in Montreal to get to Charlotte? And I bet Billy didn't have any idea that you did, right?"

"I was *with* Charlotte, once. You don't need to know any more than that. I'm outa here. I'll pick up my stuff tomorrow . . . today. Hell, it's already tomorrow. Whatever."

♪ ♪ ♪

Al went into the bedroom, shut the door, and called Stephanie. "Hi, sorry to scare you . . . it's only four-something, sorry . . . No, no, nothing's wrong, I'm talking quiet so I don't bother Ginny. But I need to come over right now. Can I . . . ? See ya in a few. Bye."

After Al left, Ginny went to the bathroom mirror.

Not as bad as I thought. Learned a couple of things tonight . . . the hard way, for sure.

She touched her swollen lip.

Ow, the son of a bitch. Only good thing is, I know he's hurting so much more than this.

CHAPTER 56

FIVE - SOUTH TOWER (15)

The orderly tucked the gun into a towel and shoved it in the cleaning cart where he'd hidden it before he'd come to room 510. He knew he had to get it over with. Something in Rosetti's voice had terrified him. Something had changed between them. Maybe what he had surmised about the cop's friendship had never been real. Maybe it had always been a sham. He was used to this. Men were all scum. Pigs, every one of them.

Many times he'd quoted the cliché that after three drinks anyone could be with anyone: man, woman, straight, bi—a hybrid fusion of all?

Is that what I am . . . hybrid, indefinable? Does that make me basically . . . nothing?

He went to the bathroom and stared into the mirror again. The face looking back wasn't his. It was the lie: the always necessary lie that saved him—saved *her*—from being known for who she really was.

Babe, you can pretend to be a man as much as you want, but all you'll get for it is what you already got: nothing. Women need men. We have to. Men want women, but don't need women. They treat us like leftover dinner, then scrape us into the garbage and think about their next meal.

There was no love in her life, nor did it seem there would ever be—only a series of empty, meaningless episodes of sexual activity. If only the man in the bed had been truthful to himself, perhaps this might have been the one time it could have been different.

She went back to the bedside and stared down at the man, whose eyes were closed but tense, as if straining to be aware. It seemed a lifetime of pain was in that notched brow, not just the obvious trauma of the injuries which had put him in this bed.

So sad, and yet, so beautiful.

How could she hate this man so much, when all she wanted to do was love him?

Enough of this crap. Think like a man again. BE a man, and get this done.

CHAPTER 57

ONCE A THIEF

*A*l careened through the empty streets, hoping a cop would see him and stop him so he wouldn't be able to make it to Stephanie's. As he ignored red lights, crossed over medians, and two-wheeled around corners, he mused on how much fun this could be if not for the purpose of the drive. He was trying to think of something to say to Stephanie, at least, how to start.

Her mother would have known. *She* had guts.

♪ ♪ ♪

No heroism from movies or books could outdo the courage of eighteen-year-old Charlotte Benoit, who had come to Al's room on rue MacKay on a chilly Montreal night in 1970. It was nearly two weeks after he'd told Billy and her about the gig offer in New York, and the arrangements had been completed; they'd be leaving Montreal in three days.

Sitting in the room's lone chair, as far from Al as possible, she spoke with passion and eloquence, pointing out all the reasons Billy would be better off staying in Montreal. She knew what would happen to him in New York; and even though she was losing too, her concern was for Billy. Although she didn't love him in the way he loved her, she believed she could be happy being with him, helping him to find his talent again and to stay off drugs.

Al, who had already been drinking heavily before Charlotte arrived, sat quietly on the edge of the bed and listened with feigned consideration—her arguments made sense only to her—but it seemed appropriate to listen, at least for a while.

He had learned early in life how to elude his conscience; guilt was only for those careless enough to get caught. Alcohol mixed with loneliness made it easier yet: a think-with-your-cock cocktail. With half a bottle of cheap Scotch in him, holding back was no longer an option. Arising from the bed, he moved closer, behind the chair where he began to stroke Charlotte's hair and neck. He told her maybe he should stay in Montreal too. Maybe they could all work together to get Billy on track. If she was willing to try, so was he.

He thought about the dollar again, the one his mother was so upset about. *It was a goddamn dollar, and she broke something in me . . . can never be fixed.*

He spoke sweetly to her. "Charlotte, we need to look at what happened with us. I made a mistake. I'm only human. Do you think there's any chance we could, you know, try again?"

The thing about stealing and getting caught is you learn how to steal better next time.

Charlotte pushed his hand away from her neck, but she had hesitated just long enough for him to catch the little bit of "yes" in her "no". He knelt beside her and held her hand, saying, "Don't you know how I feel? I've been nuts about you since the first time I saw you. That thing with that stupid whore, Brigitte? That's just something a man *does* sometimes. Please don't think it means, like, that I don't care for you."

As preposterous as it all seemed, Charlotte was finding it difficult to think rationally. She had loved him: through the hurting; through the lying; even now, as he once again proved his utter egoism.

"Al, you mean you'd stay in Montreal to help Billy, but you want to be . . . my *boyfriend*? That is insane. How does that make any sense? I wish your love for me was real. I wish you loved Billy like you think you do. But the only love you have is for yourself. But no, that's wrong isn't it, Al. I think you don't love yourself or anyone or anything, not even music. I feel sorrow for you. You have nothing. If you could only see beyond whatever it is that makes you so angry with yourself, you could be such a good person, Al, if you'd only let it happen. What is in you that you are so afraid of?"

Al retrieved his bottle from the dresser and sat back down on the bed, looking sullen. He forced down a mouthful of Scotch, then coughed half of it back up onto his shirt. After wiping his hand across his chest, his fingers dripped with booze. He smeared some on his cheeks and said, "There, does it look like I'm crying now? Tears of whiskey. How fitting." He slumped lower.

"You are sulking now." She wished she hadn't said it.

Al sighed. "I don't sulk. I brood. I'm deep, remember? A lonely poet; I have issues. Fucked up in the head I am. Can't love anyone if I can't love myself, eh? Okay tell me, why should I love anything but this?"

He held up the bottle and took another sloppy swig. "Sometimes I stand in front of that stupid broken mirror, and I imagine it's a window. I picture all kinds of cool stuff. Know what I saw today? There was this awesome perfect world out there . . . *in* there. It was like, yeah, the Garden of Eden, with trees, blue sky, with puffy clouds like the kind my dad used to say meant 'good fishing'. Off in the distance there was this man and woman walking hand in hand down a country lane. They looked so happy. Everything was perfect. I wished I could be that guy. Then he turned and looked right at me. He smiled, like he knew something I'd never know."

Charlotte came over, sat next to him, and wiped the lingering Scotch from his mouth and chin with her fingers. "Look at you, you're soaked. Let me get you another shirt."

As she started to get up, he grabbed her arm. She could have escaped easily.

♪ ♪ ♪

Her first time was supposed to be sublime. She had always pictured it as romantic, spiritual, blessed with love and happiness with the man she would spend her life with. But this was what she was dealt. This would have to do.

"Al, please don't. This is wrong, I've never—"

"Shhh, I won't hurt you, Angel Eyes."

He pulled Charlotte down to the bed and under him and dropped the bottle on the floor. As he kissed her and fumbled with the buttons on her blouse, he watched the last drops of whiskey disappearing slowly into the carpet. The room was a thief too.

The smell of whiskey blending with carpet sent a chill through him. It reminded him of something disgusting. A familiar melody drifted from out of the "mirror world", but he refused to listen.

No one else can ever be her first. Dad can't take this from me.

He reached for the string switch, to hide the stinging light of truth from both worlds.

CHAPTER 58

ROOM WITH A DÉJÀ VU

*S*tephanie was standing at her door watching as Al pinballed down the hall toward her. He could see she was agitated. Not surprising: he'd left her only a few hours earlier and everything was fine. Now here he was, coming back, completely intoxicated in the predawn gloom. On the phone, he'd said there was nothing wrong.

Did she really buy that?

She was in her robe, hair tangled, no makeup, still beautiful. She looked so much like Charlotte, so clearly now. How could he have not known right away? After she helped him make his way to the couch, they sat together and he held her hand. The warmth of her skin was a startling contrast to how cold he felt: like a statue, resembling something human; inside, only rock and blackness.

"What is it, Al? Something's up. You don't hide things very well. This is the first time I've seen you this drunk. Come on, let me in on it."

"Steph, I don't know where to begin. Yeah, something has uh, developed. It's not good."

"Tell me, Al. I'm a big girl."

Sounds like something she'd say to her . . . father.

"Got any Scotch?" asked Al.

"Yes, but don't you think you've had enough? I could smell you all the way down the hall."

"Steph, I need some, really. You may want to join me." He got the bottle and drank straight out of it. "Here, have a hit."

"No thanks, Al. You better start talking, while you still can."

He stood up, teetering like a novice high-wire act. "Let's go lie down, in case I can't walk either."

She sighed and helped him maneuver to the bedroom. They barely made it, with Al clutching Stephanie with one hand, and swinging the Scotch bottle to and fro in the other. Al set the bottle on the nightstand and collapsed onto the bed. As he struggled to focus on his surroundings, it seemed there was something odd about the room—it felt smaller. The breast-shaped ceiling light glared down at him.

Like the anger and fear in my mother's eyes when I told her that awful secret about Annie and Dad?

Shielding his face, he reached up for the string switch, but it wasn't there. Somewhere, he could hear someone singing. The melody was from "As Time Goes By", but the words were oddly wrong, or maybe too *right* for Al.

"You can't rewrite the story . . ." Who is that? That's not Steph.

He was standing on a runway in *Casablanca*, watching a plane taxi into the fog of distant memory.

If I'd been in Bogie's spot, I'd never have let her go.

Stephanie snuggled up beside him and ran her fingers over his stubbly face. "Ooh, quite a beard ya got coming in here. My caveman has returned, just like our first date."

"Yeah? Then maybe I'm half a man, at last. Let's call old Snake and Wheelie and tell them."

"Go to sleep, Al. We can talk later."

"Okay, Char . . . I mean, *Steph*. Hey, did you hear that? The window said you're the fairest of them all. Wow, look at it. Oops, can't be. Isn't this the room with no windows? Must be a mirror. What a view. Let's go for a walk there sometime."

"Maybe tomorrow, Al. Right now, please just hold me?"

He flopped his arm across her chest. "I have to tell you something, Steph. And you can't tell Billy. Please?"

"What is it, Al?"

The song continued. *"Too late to say you're sorry . . ."*

Al yelled, "Who the HELL is singing? Where's that coming from?"

"Al, go to sleep," said Stephanie. "No one is singing. Come on, you're scaring me."

"Stephanie, I loved your mother, and I never told her, never showed her. I fucked up everything, everybody. I'm a no-good piece of shit."

"No, Al. You were just a boy. And no matter; that's all so far away now."

As he managed to get his eyes open again, he noticed her robe had slipped open. A searing wave of mortification reddened his face, but he couldn't stop looking. He began to stroke her neck, letting his fingers play a silent lullaby as they slipped slowly down to her breast.

As he leaned in to kiss her, she whispered, "Al, that feels nice, but not now, okay?"

The song's words drifted in again. *"A lie is still a lie . . ."*

Al shouted, "Shut the fuck UP. Whoever's singing, STOP it."

He looked into Stephanie's tear-filled eyes and said," I won't hurt you, baby. I love you, my perfect, beautiful Angel Eyes."

She lay under him, praying he was really talking to *her* while he sang along with the continuing melody in his head. *"Broken hearts, like broken wings, can't fly . . ."*

As he kissed her and began to remove her robe, carnal passion overcame conscience. Sensibility and self-respect were *still* down the hall, and he had no choice but to go there, to the room with no windows—to Charlotte.

The haunting song from nowhere faded away with *"As life slips by . . ."*

He reached out for the Scotch bottle, but it slipped from his shaking fingers and thudded onto the floor. For the second time in his life, he watched morality spill out before him, swallowed greedily by the carpet fibers.

Take my whiskey. Take everything again. Suck me down to hell.

The smell of booze on the floor was working strange tricks on his senses. Something was scaring him from so deep inside, it was as if his soul was being chased out of him, exposing it and all his weakness to the world.

What is that smell? It's only booze. Oh Christ, the smell of the whiskey mixed with self-loathing . . . It's the goddamned stink of my father.

Stephanie managed to reach the wall switch, and now the only light in the room was the first hint of sunrise reflected in the mirror. She thought how lovely it was: a hint of new things to come, perhaps a view into hope and new beginnings.

Al wished he could turn it off—and all the pain it would soon reveal.

CHAPTER 59

DREAMS Я US

*A*l dreamed he was walking with Sue MacDonald; she was still fifteen. They were talking about their new baby. They'd named it Graham. She looked up at him, and in place of eyes were two black, heart-shaped stones. She said, "I'm sorry, Al. I always loved you. Please love me."

She pulled up her shirt and showed him her bra which was overflowing with writhing, hissing snakes. And when she pulled off the bra there was an even more disturbing sight: the smooth, flat, hairless chest of a young boy.

Al screamed and began to run through fields, and down dirt roads, over bridges and rooftops, until falling headfirst into a colossal rotten apple. Emerging from its blackened, rancid skin, he recognized a familiar cityscape. He ran into the Empire State Building, found an elevator and pushed the down button. But it went up, accelerating, moaning, and shaking like a rocket headed for space, until at the top where it burst through the roof up into the sky in an explosion of concrete, glass, and thick egg white-colored liquid. For a precious moment he was flying free, stripped of the bonds of earth and responsibility.

But the dream within a dream ended with a thud as he landed on top of a large propeller-driven airplane made of brass. He climbed in the window and found he was the pilot, sitting at an oversized old '59 Buick steering wheel. The co-pilot was his dad who kept telling him, "Not too fast, Freddy, you're not good at this. Don't get too high, you'll kill us all."

The stewardess brought them milk and cookies. Al gasped, "Mummy?" It was good to see her, but she was crying.

His dad said, "These cookies are stale; the milk is sour; you're hopeless." Her face became Nora's, and Al grabbed her and threw her out the window. Al's dad looked at him and said, "You're no Humphrey Bogart. You'll *never* have Paris."

A new stewardess arrived: Charlotte, wearing a long black coat. She said, "I brought you something really nice, boys." She removed her coat, and she was naked. There was a baby, suckling at her breast. "Want some?" she asked.

Al's dad began sucking at the other breast, and Charlotte slapped him away. "Not that . . . This," she said, as she handed the baby to Al. It was a tiny version of her, a miniature fully formed woman. It was dead.

Charlotte cried, "You don't like what I made for you? Maybe this will help." She pulled out a bottle shaped like a trumpet and poured whiskey over the baby. The baby awoke, and it was now Anne. She smiled at Al and disappeared into the blanket, leaving only a reddish stain which began to grow and become three-dimensional, until it had turned into a cat. The red cat growled at him and ran away, with a tiny gray tail sticking out of the corner of its mouth.

Charlotte looked at Al with disgust. As she reached out to hit him, she became his father, who yelled at his reflection in the cockpit window, "You useless coward. You should have died in 1944." Al looked down, and his father was wearing a dress, a low-cut gown revealing a full sexy décolletage. As Al moved closer, he focused on the breasts which showed several rows of suture scars, with all the jagged surgical subtlety of Doctor Frankenstein.

Suddenly the image dissolved into a ghostly vapor, smelling of whiskey and semen. Al took a deep breath and pulled the apparition completely into his lungs, producing a gurgling, sucking sound which formed a single word . . . "Vickie."

Out the window, Charlotte, baby Anne, and his mother were waving and saying, "Come with us. Forget about him." Sue MacDonald joined them, and they flew away into a cloud. The cloud became an angel, with Stephanie's smiling face bathed in milky white tears.

♪♪♪

When Al awoke, the muted light from the corners of the closed drapes stabbed unmercifully at his half-opened eyes. Although his vision was too foggy to read the clock, he guessed it must be at least late morning or early afternoon. He lowered his left leg carefully to the floor where his toes squished into dampness, and when he moved his foot, there was the Scotch bottle.

That part did happen. Oh God, no! Did I make love to her?

He found his underwear, pulled it on, and went to the living room. Stephanie wasn't there. Heading back to the kitchen, he saw a note on the fridge. With trembling hands he read it slowly, terrified by what each word might reveal.

Went out to get some juice and stuff.
Won't be long.   Don't go anywhere.

You never did say what you had to talk about
last night.   Guess you were just too out of it.

I'm worried about you.

See ya, luv ya,

Steph

CHAPTER 60

FIVE - SOUTH TOWER [16]

*O*fficer Poole returned to find Captain Rosetti in the chair. Even sitting, the man was so big he seemed to be the same height as the standing, six-foot-tall Poole. Still, there was an underlying gentleness about the man, a feeling he'd be someone you could open up to if you had something on your mind.

"Here's your java, Captain," said Poole. "Hope I mixed it okay. *Four* sugars, right?"

"Thanks, kid. Yeah, I get hassled about that all the time. The boys at the precinct like to call me 'sweetie.'"

"Doesn't that piss you off?"

"Nah, don't matter to me. All in fun. And I don't mind if you call me Tony. I like you, kid. You seem all right to me. Just like your dad. Tell you what, I'm heading down to the second floor for two minutes. I'll come back up here after, and you can take a break, maybe grab a walk. You know, stretch your legs a bit?"

"That's okay, Captain, uh, Tony. You don't have to—"

"Wasn't a suggestion, kid. It's an order. See ya in two shakes."

As Rosetti strode away, Poole watched him, and wished his dad could be such a kind and understanding man.

♪♪♪

The orderly's legs were shaking, even though pressed firmly against the edge of the bed. Bending in ever closer, he touched his lips to the patient's ear and whispered, "Time's up. If you don't know me, I guess it doesn't matter. It would've been nice to have you recognize my face as I end you."

He gripped the man's stubbled jaw and squeezed. "Come on, just look at me. Remember these eyes? Remember these hands?"

He touched the patient's cheek and then moved his hand down to his chest. "Mmm, you are so big. Built almost as nice as my friend Tony. He

415

never hated what I am. Actually, I'd say he loves it. I think you do too, but you're too damned ignorant of who you really are. Killing you with the gun was going to be easy, so impersonal. But because I blew that opportunity, I get the chance to be close to you one more time. Maybe I botched it on purpose?"

He brushed his mouth on the patient's cheek like a mother's gentle good-night kiss. It was meant to be "goodbye", but as he lingered there, a memory overtook him and he began to slide his lips toward the man's mouth.

The patient moaned softly and moved his head to the side, as he began to awake.

CHAPTER 61

SHORT NOTICE

*A*l called Doctor Davidson's special number. "Hey, Doc, I know you don't like to hear this phone . . . I know, you said not to hesitate . . . Yeah, I'm driving right now . . . No, not the freeway, not too far from your place actually . . . I know . . . I can wait till three o'clock, sure . . . No, they can't help me there, been through that, they don't know me . . . No, Doc, I'll be okay, don't change anybody for me. I got somewhere to go for a couple hours or so . . . Yeah, I'll be okay. I made you a promise, and for once I intend to keep one. See ya at three. Thanks."

♪♪♪

Al stopped off at Losers'. Big John did a double take at the sight of his uncharacteristically disheveled friend. "Al, you get hit by a truck? You look like, worse than shit, buddy."

"Scotch," said Al. "Any kind, and keep the bottle up."

"You got it, pal. Hey, no clichés intended, but if you need to talk, this old bartender listens pretty good."

"I know you do, John, and I might take you up on that. Lou around?"

"Upstairs."

"Thanks, John." Al tossed back his double and headed for the staircase.

♪♪♪

As each step creaked and groaned under Al's feet, he wondered if the noises were as much from his own joints as from the wood beneath him. He noticed the wide range of pitches almost formed a melody.

Wouldn't this make the perfect blues song: "Singin' Stairway Blues" by Lead-foot Al Waters.

Dank and musty, the dimly lit stairwell seemed perfectly indicative of its destination. *Smells like Lou. In spite of all the cologne he slathers on, it's the true scent of his soul.*

"Who's dat?" grumbled Lou, as Al approached the top steps.

Al said, "Your best friend needs to talk. Let's stay up here where it's private."

"What's up, Waters? Better not want another raise yet."

"No, not a raise. I'm here to tell ya I'm done. Packing it in."

"What? Now come on, dis has got to be a joke. Al, don't fuck around."

"I won't be in tonight. The guys will be fine without me. Nobody will miss me much, not with Steph here."

"So, Al, ya mean you're talking about just you, not the whole band? Steph ain't leavin'?"

"Yeah, I'll miss you too, you slime sucker. Can't talk for her, but she'll probably stay for a while. But she's got nothing to keep her here in Florida anymore. She's going to smarten up and get back to New York or Montreal, pretty certain."

"It's a shame, Al . . . *you*, I mean. Look at ya. Used to be a class act, far as I was concerned anyway. Now what the fuck ya gonna do? Got another gig? Or are ya just tired of shtuppin' the chick already? Ya know, it really is *her* gig now."

Al had turned to go, but Lou's words held him by the shoulders like his father's hands. As he drove his fist into Lou's stomach, he grunted, "Can't talk about my *family* like that." He could feel the air whoosh out of the man like a six-foot, fat bellows. "That felt so good, I may just do it again. Got any more comments about Steph?"

Lou was curled up in the fetal position on the floor, gasping like a wounded walrus. He managed to squeeze out his words, bit by gurgled bit. "Get outa here . . . you fucker . . . Dis time, no cops . . . I'll deal with you . . . you wait!"

♪♪♪

"Where's the bottle, Big John? Told you to leave it."

"Hold on, man, here it is. Hey, what happened up there? You didn't kill him, did ya?"

"Wouldn't hurt the dear man," said Al, slugging back a double. He grabbed the bottle from Big John and guzzled back two shots worth. Blinking back the momentary dizzying punch of the Scotch, he wheezed, "Don't think the ugly dickhead feels quite as warmly towards me though."

John began to wipe up, and then remembered he'd meant to say something before Al had gone to see Lou. "Hey, Al, guess who I saw today sittin' at that sidewalk café patio down on Pine Street? It was Billy, and Stephanie was with him. They didn't see me though. Seemed too busy talkin'. They was with that lady friend of yours. What's-her-name, the youngish one, um, no offense, little on the chunky side? Ginny, is it? It was kinda strange, man. They looked so . . . *serious.*"

"Shit, of course she couldn't wait to . . . Aw, fuck it," mumbled Al as he twice tried to get up from the stool, finally steadying himself by grasping the bar. He held the bottle tightly in his other hand as if John might snatch it away. "Taking this with me, John. Put it on Lou's tab."

Big John frowned and said, "You ain't driving are ya?"

"I drive drunk better than doo, soo . . . you soo . . . doo. SHIT . . . Than you . . . do . . . sober. Holy crap. Don't worry, I can drive; just can't *talk* worth a shit."

He tripped on a chair leg, catching himself just before falling. The door looked a mile away; it was going to be difficult getting that far without looking foolish—too late anyway.

"Got an appointment to get to," said Al as he reached the door. "See ya, Big John . . . well actually I won't. Been nice knowin' ya, Johnny, I'd come back over there and give ya a hug, but I'd never make it."

Big John didn't understand. Wasn't the band playing tonight? As he watched Al stumble out the door, he said, "See ya, my friend. Don't you be drivin', if ya can help it, huh."

Big John reached for the phone. As his finger hovered over the button to speed-dial the police, he thought about the night Nora had died, and how he had failed to act. As much as he hated the thought of making the same mistake on this day, he could not abide turning in his friend, whether for his own good or not. He set the phone back down and reached for a forty of Jack Daniels. He slugged back two shots in one gulp straight from the bottle: his first taste of alcohol in ten years. After only a brief pause to catch his breath, he took another hit, knowing he had to drink as much as he could, short of dying.

Tomorrow would be soon enough to climb back into the ring: a brand new round-one in his never-ending battle with the bottle. Today, he needed to forget everything and everyone as quickly as he could. Temporary oblivion seemed his only chance to ease the guilt.

♩♩♩

The drive to Doc's was not pretty, with Al consciously ignoring stop signs and red lights. As he passed through each one, he looked in the mirror to see how close any cars might have come to colliding with him. This was fun.

Where's a cop when you need one? Not my fault if they're all off somewhere giving parking tickets or eating donuts. Where were all the cops who could have saved Nora?

He narrowly avoided an old woman with a shopping cart. She yelled something, waving her fist.

Stinking lazy cops. If anyone gets hurt, won't be my fault. Why should I care if someone gets in the way? Once you've killed someone, is it easy the next time? Damn it, Nora. Damn it to hell. Why did you let me drive?

A school crossing loomed. Al slowed.

Charlotte got in the way. Loved me, and I ran right over her. Now Stephanie's crossing the same damn road.

He approached a railroad crossing gate.

Damn, no train to beat . . . or not to.

He wondered if the tracks went all the way to Montreal.

Billy's always been in the way, like a big splattered bug on the windshield, blotting my vision of where I should really be going. If I'd left him in New York, he'd be dead, and I'd have had a hell of a lot more chances to make something of my life. He's the only one who ever really needed me. Him and Nora. God damn it, Nora, you were so smart. Why did you let me drive?

Dashing through the sun, in a two-ton loaded gun.

Ginny got in her own way, roadblocked her whole fucking life with me, 'cause she couldn't stand losing. I wish she was walking right there, right now.

A car was in the next intersection, waiting to turn. The accelerator wanted to go for it, begging to be pushed. He slowed again, easing by the stopped car. He saluted the driver and then gave the pedal what it craved.

And Vickie. Fucking Christ, how did she get mixed up in all of this? I wanted her. I can't have wanted her, but I DID. My father must be fucking laughing at me for that one.

He was finding street signs impossible to read through his clouded vision, relying on auto pilot, just as he had for most major life directions. He was the king of losers. Being lost was appropriate.

Michelle didn't give me a chance to fuck it up. She was the only one who was more of a fraud than I was. Maybe she hoped I'd get in HER way, and I couldn't. Guess we knew who the real whore was all along didn't we?

Up ahead, the light was changing to red. He pushed the gas pedal so aggressively his entire leg trembled.

The FEAR was always in MY way, standing there waving a yellow flag . . . fear that I couldn't live up to what they expected me to be, what HE expected. Damn my father. He was less than what he wanted to be and I was afraid to be better than him. Damn it, old man, I'm fucking sorry. I can't HELP it if I AM better than you. It's NOT my fault.

One car choked to a stop as Al roared through the intersection. Another had passed through just before his arrival. They didn't even see what missed 'em.

Stephanie, why didn't you see it? You're as smart as your mother, a lot smarter than your . . . father.

Oh Geezes, God! What have I done? Einstein was right. Time never goes anywhere. You just jump on and then off, like a fucking merry-go-round. If only I could run backwards and jump back on, sort of like what Superman did with the planet to save Lois Lane. I'd go back to New Year's Eve, and let Nora drive.

Or maybe, I'd go all the way back to 1970, and I'd have put Busty in a cab. Wouldn't have touched her. And I'd go to the room with no windows, pull the string switch, and Charlotte would be there, waiting.

But I'm no Superman. Stupidman is more like it.

♪ ♪ ♪

Doctor Davidson's home was now just down the street; he'd made it. Sometimes you just can't win.

Charlotte, you dodged me once, then got right back up smack in the middle of the road. You shouldn't have loved me. No one should. Someone who could love me just isn't worth loving.

What about Annie? If she loved me so much, why'd she leave me behind to deal with Dad on my own. How could she desert me that way? I needed her so much. She protected me from everything when we were little.

The blurry road ahead was suddenly replaced by a crystal clear view of something he hadn't seen in nearly forty-five years. More lucidly than anything in the *now* around him, he saw what Anne had done for him—and why. And he knew why she had died so young.

Oh my God, she got in the way . . . of HIM. Annie was the hero I wanted all along, and I didn't see it. She was what our mother couldn't be. And I buried her in that hole I dug inside me where I buried everything I didn't want to see anymore. Oh, Annie, I'm so sorry. You loved me more than I ever knew, and all I did for you was bury you . . . two different ways.

♪♪♪

The gate guard was not comfortable with Al's arrival: left front wheel up on the curb, the bumper inches from eliminating the booth. He called Doctor Davidson and then raised the gate.

"Next time," said the guard, "if you drive up here like that, I'll call the cops."

"Won't be a next time, buddy," said Al as he screeched into the visitors' lot where he noticed a mint 1964 Ford Mustang parked diagonally, taking up two spaces.

Hate it when people do that, thinking their cars are so fucking special. Ha, always wanted to do this.

Al parked crossways, directly behind the Mustang, so close that its rear bumper creased the passenger door of his Cougar. As he jogged clumsily up the walk to unit 286, he looked back, admiring his efforts. He wished he could be there when the selfish parking-space hog came out to find he was stymied.

♪♪♪

"Alfred," said the doctor, "you've been drinking. You know the rule here. You must be sober to get anything out of a session. But I know this is a different situation and I certainly wouldn't turn you away if you're in need the way it sounds like you are."

Al pulled the bottle from beneath his jacket. "Have a swig, Doc. You should lighten up a bit. Bet you're one funny dude when you've had a nip."

"You're here for a reason, Alfred. Let's get to it. Are you suicidal? I guess if you drove here in this condition, then that's my answer."

"You are the best, Doc. Fucking always right. You know me better than anyone, eh? By the way, did you ever think about how scary your address is?"

"Alfred, I have no idea what that might mean."

"Two-eighty-six . . . get it? To '*eighty-six*' . . . ? You know, gangster talk. To 'eighty-six' someone is to rub 'em out, blow 'em away."

"Alfred, I do know you need far more help than I am able to offer here, and under these circumstances."

"Don't worry, Doc, I'll be fine. A little more of my creative driving and you'll have a nice ending for your book. Some big mother trees down that street, eh? The old Buick won't stand a chance."

Buick? What the . . . ? Don't I drive a Cougar?

"Alfred, I think you have to get to the hospital, I can arrange it right now. We can have you picked up here."

"Ah, the loony bin express, won't *that* be a cool ride. Do they have a siren? Do they blast announcements? I can hear it now: 'INCOMING, incoming nut case'. Okay, Doc, we'll see if you can convince me I should stick around. There's pressure for ya. It's all in your hands. Do your thing. Do they have a betting window in the admitting room? Put your money down. Five hundred to one, Doc will save the sax player. Risky bet, Doc. Hope you feel luckier than I do."

♪ ♪ ♪

Doctor Davidson made the call.

"No fanfare, Alfred. A plain vehicle, and nice people who'll help you. I'll be down to visit you tonight. That's the earliest I can get away, but don't worry, I'll be with you through this."

"Here's my keys, Doc. When you go outside you'll see the second reason you should have 'em. Hey, you don't drive an old Mustang do you?"

"No, Alfred, I don't, but I have a neighbor who does. Don't worry, I'll take care of it, whatever it is you've done."

"Doc, I'm an idiot. I didn't tell you why I came to you in the first place. I never told you that when Nora died on New Year's Eve, it was *my* fault. Doc, why didn't I tell you? How could that not be the first thing I'd say?"

"Thank you for telling me now, Alfred. I think I know why you didn't say it sooner. And that's okay. You've been extremely forthcoming about so much of your life. You can't feel bad about not revealing something you weren't ready to talk about."

"Hey, Doc, you always say the right thing. You're good, ya know. Me and my damn stupid temper killed Nora. And all she did was try to make my life better. Hey, on the way here I had a 'flash' of something from way back. Had to do with my sister, Annie. I'll tell you about it some more when I get sobered up. Maybe we can figure out what it means, okay?"

"Certainly we can do that, Alfred."

"Doc, will you be my father? Can I call you *Dad*? Would that be too weird? Whew, guess I am nuts, right?"

"Alfred, you know you can call me anything you want. Just don't call me after midnight."

Al sang, horribly out of tune, "And you can call meee Al . . ."

The doctor chuckled at Al's attempt at the Paul Simon song, but behind his smile was deep concern.

CHAPTER 62

TEARS FOR GEORGE

*T*hree days in the Broward General psychiatric ward were enough—enough at least for Al to convince himself he was okay to face life again. Despite Doctor Davidson's reservations, with the facility being overcrowded and expensive, practicality came first, and he was released on his own request. Big John, Wesley, and Pete had tried to come to see him, but he'd refused any visitors; he was unaware that Kathleen, during her shifts, had perused his chart and looked in on him more than once as he slept.

As Al was sorting through his bag of belongings, a gentle tapping on the door frame made him turn.

Kathleen peeked in and said, "So you're heading back to the real insanity of the outside world are you?"

"Yeah, babe, although with all the nuts in here, I felt like one of a hundred sidemen in the world's biggest big band. So how are *you*? It's been a while hasn't it."

"I'm doing fine, Al. What about you? I don't know what happened to make you feel so bad that you'd want to . . . Anyway, if you need to talk sometime . . ."

"Kath, you amaze me, as usual. Why the hell did you ever get mixed up with a bum like me anyway?"

"Gee, Al, did they put you on some heavy duty truth pills or something? Maybe they surgically removed a hunk of your personality? Didn't see *that* in your chart."

"A frontal lobotomy? I'd rather have a bottle in front o' me."

"Well," said Kathleen, "if old jokes are a sign of you getting back to normal, I'd say you are doing lots better."

"Kath, let me say this, I'm sorry for everything I did to hurt you. I lied too many times for the truth to catch up."

"Al, haven't you learned yet? *One* lie is too many."

"I know, but my lies started over forty years ago. A hell of a lot of catching up, right?"

Kathleen smiled and said, "Can I walk you to your car?"

"Sure, Kath. Do me a favor when we get to it. I'll lie down and you spin the tires on my head?"

"Al, that's not a particularly healthy request. Should I be reporting that to your doctor?"

"Come on, I'm kidding. Believe it or not, I seem to have awoken with a new lease on life. As mucked up as everything is, I'm promising myself I'm going to fix as much as I can, and maybe even start being a good and honest man. What a concept, huh?"

"Al, it's actually a great concept, and not impossible either. I hope you truly believe it."

"We'll see, Kath. I've screwed up pretty bad. By the way, how'd my car get here?"

Kathleen said, "They told me a very large, bald, black man dropped off the keys and said it was here in the visitors' lot."

♪♪♪

When they arrived at where the car was parked, Al said, "Kathleen, I just don't think I ever realized or understood what love really is until recently. I've kinda figured out that it's not all that complicated. *Falling* in love is like Big John off a high dive board: *kerplunk.* But actual love creeps up on you, slowly, steadily, and without warning: like Big John when you're eating a bag of chips."

"Al, I'm not sure where you're heading with this. Are you trying to—"

"Wait, wait, Kath. Let me finish. Not even Al Waters is selfish enough to try to win you back. You and I could be great friends. But we both know there's no future in anything other than that."

"Al, I . . ."

"Hold on, I'm trying to tell you something, not trying to hit on you. You figured out before anyone what was happening with me and Stephanie. Actually, I think you knew even before I did. They should change that old saying from Murphy's Law to Waters' Law. If something can go wrong, it absolutely will. Anyway, here it is. Ginny got some tests done, and found out that Stephanie's my daughter."

"Oh, Al. Oh my God. And you two have been *seeing* each other?"

"I know, Kath. It's awful, even for me. And I'm almost positive that Ginny told her, and Billy too. I don't know if you've kept tabs, but they didn't even try to come to see me in here. You know what though? As messed up as this might be, I've decided to try to work it out. Somehow we'll get through this. She's one hell of a tough, smart girl. Someday I'll tell you about her mother. You'd have liked her. If Steph can get by this crazy, complicated beginning, maybe we can start fresh."

"Al, if you want it badly enough, you and she can probably get past this, and who knows, maybe develop a healthy relationship."

"Can you and I be friends, Kath?"

"It's possible, Al. But I gotta say not very likely. Lots of people want to try to be friends after they break up, but do you know how many times it actually works? Pretty much zilch. By the way, I'm seeing someone. His name is Dave. He's a great guy, a mechanic, of all things. It's only been a short time, but I think we've got something nice going. Get this, he's teaching me to ride a motorcycle. Can you picture that?"

Al looked at Kathleen and saw a brightness in her eyes he hadn't seen since the times they'd first dated. He smiled and gave her a hug. "Used to call you 'psycho' nurse and now it's 'cycle' nurse? Too wild. Really, babe, I'm happy for you. Tell this *Dave* guy he better treat you right or I'll have Big John sit on him."

"Al, I think Big John is probably the only friend you've got left in this world. Maybe I *could* hang in there and make it two, just so John's not alone with such a burden." She hugged Al and kissed his cheek. "Deal?"

"Deal, friend. John will be very grateful for any assistance in such a thankless job as being my friend. Thanks, babe."

"You're welcome, you big lunkhead."

♪♪♪

Al drove away slowly, looking in the rear view mirror to see if Kathleen was watching him. When he saw that she was, he almost stopped. It was such a rotten time to comprehend how much she could have meant to him. It was too late to stop, too late to go back, too late to be sorry. As honestly happy as he was for her to find a new guy, he knew that being her friend would be impossible. There was too much "baggage". She must have known that too.

Having called to make sure Ginny wasn't home, Al went to her apartment. Theophilus rubbed against his pant leg as he emptied closets and dresser drawers. Al sat on the edge of the bed and let the cat jump up onto his lap.

Scratching behind its ear, he wondered what Ginny would think, to come home and find her pet hanging dead from the ceiling fan in the living room.

"Sorry, Theo, to even think that," said Al softly, while the cat nuzzled up to his face. "You're the closest thing to an offspring Ginny and I will ever have. But that would make you a mix of wolf and witch. Nah, I couldn't hurt you, little guy. I'm not like my dad, except here I am treating a cat better than my *kid.* Christ."

He cleared out everything he owned and headed out, into homelessness. He didn't leave a note. A block away, he pulled into a gas station to get a newspaper and renters' guide. With some creative financing he might be able to get a half-decent place.

Life was crap, but Al felt okay. The road ahead was going to be tough, but for once the challenges involved more than his own agenda. He was filled with hope that somehow he'd find a way to overcome the horrible start with Stephanie. Maybe Doc could see the two of them together? If Stephanie was as much like her mother as it seemed, she'd have the guts to try. This wasn't just one more failed love affair; no, this was a *family* problem. In spite of Al's not-so-healthy history with family complications and outright dysfunction, he felt certain there would be a way to solve everything, no matter how long it might take. This was a challenge he would not quit on. As long as he'd been struggling to find a reason to live, this might just turn out to be a perfect one.

♪ ♪ ♪

The first bullet hit the car roof next to his ear just as he was halfway out the door. It made a dull thud as if someone were hitting a refrigerator with a hammer. He noticed the dime-sized hole next to his face, and only just grasped what it was—when the second shot caught him in the right shoulder.

This is wild. Those were shots? Thought it was backfires or . . . Damn, one got me?

As the third bullet ripped into the side of his chest he was slumping and twisting awkwardly; otherwise it probably would have hit him directly in the heart. This was a trip. Being shot was like nothing he could ever have anticipated. What a rush: not a sharp pain, like stubbing your toe, or a knife cut; but more of a pulling inward of the world into your guts—and there isn't room.

Two more bullets hit the car door, missing his head by inches.

Yeah, shots. Of course they're shots. Fucking idiot, a musician, who can't tell a firearm from a backfire?

In quick succession came the sounds of screeching tires, people yelling, a dog barking, and a car alarm blasting. Al neither saw nor heard any of that as complete darkness and silence enveloped him.

♪ ♪ ♪

Al floated back to Ontario, to the spring of 1978: home from Vegas, ready for a new life. The music scene then was slow for everyone, and seemed especially so for someone who'd spent most of his professional life in hot spots like New York, Montreal, Las Vegas, and South Florida. Gigs weren't happening.

After only a few weeks of struggling in Ontario, Al decided to head back to New York City. He decided to leave little George with his folks. Although it broke his heart to do so, it was unfair to have a pet on the road with him. His parents loved the dog right away and spoiled him mercilessly. His dad, who was retired by then, had never shown so much tenderness for anything. After Anne died, he'd never been quite the same; premature aging seemed to have rusted the armor right off him. He was even expressing interest in Al's music, asking about the switch to saxophone, and what it was like to play with some of the big-name guys he'd encountered.

♪ ♪ ♪

Al's shock-induced dream journey through memory land resurfaced him in New York City in the winter of 1978, when he and Billy were playing in a run-down jazz club on 7th Avenue in the Village. During a break, Al was at the bar when he noticed a man sitting by himself in a corner by the door. There was something both odd *and* familiar about this gloomy looking character, and Al moved closer to see if it was indeed someone he should know. When the man looked up at a passing waiter, Al recognized who it was.

Holy crap, it can't be.

Al waved to Billy who was sitting at the piano, playing quietly for himself. When he had his attention, Al waved for him to come over. "Look, man. That *is* him, isn't it?" asked Al.

"Damn, sure is," said Billy. "Far-fucking-*out.*"

"He's looking pretty wasted, huh?" said Al.

"Birds do flock, don't you think, Al? Maybe the smell of my feathers drew him here."

"You're clean, Billy. And you'll damn well stay that way as long as I'm around."

"Sure, Al, sure. Anyway, I gotta go say hi."

Billy walked over to the table and said, "Whattaya know, Lenny Breau?"

"I'll have another double, pal," said Breau. "Hey, you're not the waiter. But, don't I know you from somewhere?"

"It's me, Lenny. Billy Crothers."

"Billy? Holy shit. Billy the fucking Kid? Sorry, man, it's been a while." Breau laughed until it became a dry cough. "I mean, you sure don't look like a goddamn kid anymore."

"Well, Lenny, you ain't no fucking beauty yourself. What are you, about thirty-six, thirty-seven now? Just a tad older than me anyway, right? Christ, you look like a piece of shit run over by a herd of elephants."

"You working this room, Billy? Was that you I heard playing a minute ago? Shit, thought it sounded familiar. Thought Art Tatum was back from the grave, man."

"Don't shit me, man. I can't play nothing anymore. But you, man, you're still the best guitarist in the fucking world. I first heard you at George's Spaghetti House in '62 in Toronto, when you were potential wrapped in dreams. That's where we jammed the first time, man. Remember? I caught you for part of a set a few weeks ago, Lenny. Gotta say, I don't know how you can play so good, being fucked up as you obviously are."

"Thanks, man. Hey, who's the horn men with you? Sax man sucks, but the guy on trumpet is a bitch, man. Great sound."

"That would be me," said Al, who had approached unnoticed.

"Oh. Like, which one, man?" said Breau, looking mildly embarrassed.

"Both. The sax isn't my main axe as you can tell. I'll always be better on trumpet, but I get more gigs on sax."

Lenny mimicked a spitting sound and said, "Money. Gotta be the focus of everything, eh . . . ? My father died. Did you know that? 'Bout a year ago. Man, fucking seems like yesterday. Did you know he was a guitar player too? A country guy, like my man, Chet Atkins . . . really good, well, if you can handle that shit."

"Yeah, Lenny," said Billy. "I heard that. I'm sorry, man. But you can't let that or any other crap that happens ruin the rest of your life. Fuck, man, you've only just begun to hit your stride. Don't blow it."

Al looked at the clock over the bar and the room manager who was pointing at it. "We gotta get back on. Lenny, can you stay for another set? Don't suppose you have your axe with you . . . or maybe sing a tune with us?"

"Sorry," said Breau, "but I been here too long already, boys."

Al knew from Lenny's eyes that "here" meant much more than just the bar they were in. He could feel the pain radiating from the guitar genius as it soaked through his thin wall of attempted indifference. There is only so much room in a man's heart to help those who struggle with self-destruction, and Al's was full to the brim with Billy and himself.

As he watched Lenny Breau stagger out into the blustery winter night, Al shivered more for the ironic sadness of the scene, than from the sight of the blizzard-like conditions. Was the guitarist heading for a repeat performance of January of that same year, when he'd been found by two New York City policemen, unconscious and near frozen to death in a snowbank?

He was just plain lucky not to have died that time. Or was he? Maybe next time no one will find him in time. Might actually be what he wants.

Al vowed to one day arrange a get-together with this enigmatic compatriot musician and try to get to know him. But that was not in the cards. Only a few years later in 1984, Lenny Breau was found floating in a Los Angeles swimming pool, dead by strangulation, only nine months after moving to the west coast. The crime was never solved.

A new beginning had turned out to be his end. When Al heard about it, he thought, *Lenny and I are the same, except he was a genius: both of us always reaching ends the wrong way, or before we even get started. I wonder . . . if I could trade places with him, would the world be better for it?*

♪♪♪

The doctors looking after Al were confident they could safely extract the bullets, but one lung appeared to be severely damaged.

"What does this guy do? Musician? Ouch. Can that lung ever be back to normal? I hope it isn't a wind instrument he plays."

In Intensive Care, Al's condition was deemed to have become stable, and he was moved to a private room for security reasons, with twenty-four-hour police guard at the door. The doctors were now more concerned about long-term recuperation difficulties.

"His injured lung will never be right again. Someone from Psych will have to talk to this guy as soon as he's strong enough."

♪♪♪

Al dreamed about the phone call in 1987. George had died. It was the only time he could remember hearing his father cry, though there was an eerie familiarity about it. Age tends to make tears come easier, but this was not just an old man's sentimentality. This was a lifetime of pain spilling out, pulled up piece by piece like a magician's chain of handkerchiefs, tied to the earliest, deepest parts of his past. Somewhere along the chain, one piece was Al. He knew it was why his dad had called: a message thirty years late, in those tears for George.

CHAPTER 63

FIVE - SOUTH TOWER [17]

*S*omeone was kissing him. And then a voice was drifting in and out like a bad cell phone connection. "Hey, wake up . . . don't have . . . time . . . you have to . . . back . . . so . . . more I . . . have to say . . ."

Daddy . . . that you? I don't have to pee.

Al managed to whisper, "Who's there? That you, Steph? Doc? Can't tell what you're saying."

A voice above him said, "I'm someone who has a personal interest in your recovery, Al, more or less."

Can't even tell if it's a man or woman.

Al asked, "Are you a doctor? Where am I . . . hospital?"

"Not a doctor. That's a good one. Been called a smooth operator though."

Al tried to open his eyes. The room seemed dark; he could only make out a shadowy figure.

Must be standing back from the foot of the bed. No face.

"I was shot," said Al, "I remember now. Am I okay? Can't move, too damn tired." He could feel his feet, his arms, his fingers.

Move them? Guess so, but not right now. Too weak.

"Who shot me?"

"Cops don't know. First thought was muggers, but you weren't robbed. I know people in the department, and I guess there's no end to the list of who might have wanted to eighty-six you. They've been talking to some of your girlfriends, old *and* new. *That's* a fucking list in itself. And then there's that guy you beat up at Lou's Lounge a few weeks ago, and the club owner there too, and a couple of musicians you screwed around. Yeah, in your case "usual suspects" makes for quite the crowd, huh?"

Al said, "I think I know who did this."

"Don't think so, but I can help. That's what I'm here for: to tell you exactly who."

"You're a cop?" asked Al.

"That's funnier than the doctor suggestion. There's one of them outside the door right now, a cop I mean. But I don't think we need to worry about him since he didn't seem too concerned about me coming in here. He's more interested in some stupid magazine. Isn't that a kick in the head, huh? Maybe he does know who I am, and he just doesn't give a crap? More likely these scrubs and name tag did the trick. Looks good on me, huh? Kind of different from the way *you're* used to seeing me? None of that matters now. By the time anyone checks in here I'll be long gone, and so will you, permanently."

Al was too confused to be frightened. "Who are you? Do I know you? If you're the one, then let me at least know, if you're gonna finish the job. Doesn't really matter, I've been dead for a long time now."

"Well, sax player, you may be right, more than you know. I heard the doctors' chitchat and I can read a medical chart. You ought to know you'll never be playing a horn again, not worth a shit anyway. Maybe you can learn the banjo, huh? Maybe the accordion, and get yourself a dancing monkey?"

The sarcasm was not nearly as painful as it was meant to be. Al had already suspected the worst about his future. Some of the doctors' conversations about his prognosis had filtered through while he was semiconscious, and the horrifying words remained all too clear in his memory.

"Enough about you, *former* sax player. That girl you beat up . . . what was her name?"

Al still couldn't make out the voice, but it was as familiar as it was odd.

"It's your one true love, Al, the one you love to hit. I don't want you to be able to hit anyone anymore. And how could you hit a girl? You aren't a real man, anymore than I am."

The pillow was lowered onto Al's face. "Gonna say nighty-night now. No fuss, okay? Oh, I forgot, you can't move. Not such a tough guy now, *are* you?"

♪♪♪

The voice was getting farther away. It began to sound like distant police motorcycles. Maybe a squadron of Montreal police led by Sergeant Lalonde was about to ride into the room and save him. Maybe Snake and Wheelie would be with him; they'd take care of this murderer. But Montreal was too far—they'd never make it.

Huh. Mike Zabic? He's finally done it. I've been looking over my shoulder for nearly thirty years, and he's finally there waiting for me in the dark.

The pillow's edge was lifted, just enough for a name to be said—softly, but clearly, directly into his ear. The name was whispered once, then again, then a third time, slowly, so close it was more a rush of wind than words. But the vowels and consonants stood out like beacons through a fog, guiding him to the answer.

Now Al knew who was doing this, and why—no real surprise—so simple to understand. But he wasn't about to make it easy.

Reaching up, he found the killer's hand and latched onto it with all the strength he had left, and he knew he'd probably broken one of the fingers on that hand—it felt good. As he began to fade into unconsciousness, he felt his father's hand reaching down to touch his cheek. He thought how nice it would be to break those fingers too.

♪ ♪ ♪

He was lying on the ground, looking up at his dad and Stupid Stewart Carter, who were smiling. His sister, Anne, was there too, singing "Angel Eyes", joined by Charlotte who sang along in perfect counterpoint with an unknown, yet oddly familiar melody. They were accompanied by the most exquisite Lenny Breau guitar chords.

♪ ♪ ♪

Al looked to his side. He was walking hand in hand with someone: a woman. He wasn't sure who she was, but somehow it didn't matter. He smelled wildflowers and felt the fresh spring breeze on his face. He thought he heard someone crying in the distance behind him. He turned and saw himself looking in from the other side of the mirror, and he smiled at the absurdity of it. Charlotte's voice said, "It's okay, Al. Love is not a *quest* here. Love just . . . *is.*"

As enigma began to dissolve in waves of awareness, Al saw it was Anne's hand he was holding. He smiled and turned to see if his "other self" was still looking in from the opposite side. Was that Billy standing there?

He closed his eyes—not more than a blink—for a momentary respite from these impossible visions which, in spite of their inherent tranquility, threatened to overwhelm him. When he dared to look once more, the mirror and all that lay beyond it in the world he'd left behind—were gone.

CHAPTER 64

HANDEL'S LARGO

The funeral service for Al Waters was held at a small nondenominational chapel, three days after his death: arrangements having been made jointly by Kathleen Westland and John Lima. The only immediate family in attendance was his mother, Mrs. Nancy Waters of Ontario, who had arrived from Canada early that same day.

A jazz trio consisting of piano, bass, and drums had been hired to play for the service. Most in attendance were touched by the omission of a horn player in the group: the implication being symbolic absence. To the surprise of all but a few, Stephanie didn't sing. With the blank look of a toll booth attendant, she sat to the right of Billy Crothers in the front row, latched on to his upper arm with both hands, saying nothing.

To Billy's other side was Dixie, who held his left hand. She stroked his cheek and said, "Come on, old man, we'll get through this together. Whether you know it or not . . . *like* it or not, I'm in your corner. Always have been, always will."

Billy appeared not only distraught, but under the influence of something other than emotion. If he'd intended the chemical interference to assuage his emotions, he'd guessed wrong. His feelings were instead heightened—a high which led to a new low. Inevitable embarrassment was anticipated by everyone who knew him. Wesley and Pete spoke to him from their seats in the row behind. But he refused to listen, carrying on ever more loudly in a rapid-fire outburst of epithets about Al. It quickly became evident he was going to ruin the service for those who had come to pay their respects and to mourn.

Pulling free from Stephanie and Dixie, Billy stood up and shouted, "You jerk. I'm glad you're finally outa my hair. God, how I hate your guts. Maybe I can go back home now, without you dragging me down."

Big John moved in to hold him back, as he seemed bent on going up to the casket, while Wesley and Pete scrambled through chairs to help.

"Don't try to stop me, guys," Billy pleaded. "I need to say something to him, before I go. I'll be quiet, and I'll leave if you want . . . if you let me go see him one more time, please?"

Big John said, "Okay, Billy, but I'll be right behind you. Come on, man. His mother is here. Control yourself, for her sake if nobody else's."

Billy turned and bent back down to Stephanie who seemed too shocked to say or do anything. He whispered, "Hey, I'm sorry, sweetheart. Don't hate me for this. I wrote you a song ya know, all about being your daddy, when we still thought I was; and how we were going to be like, together from now on. But no, Al couldn't even let me have you for a little while, *could* he? You made me feel like I was *somebody*, 'cause I'd had a part in making you. Now I'm back to being a nothing, my whole life a waste. All because Al Waters fucking did it again."

Stephanie turned her head, refusing to listen, as Big John pulled him away. "Come on, Billy," said John, "let's get this over with. Go say what you think you have to say to him."

♪♪♪

At the back of the room, Ginny Gerard was taking notes, as part of her self-delegated assignment to cover the funeral for the paper. She wrote: *Billy Crothers, longtime musical associate of the deceased, causes scene . . . touching coffin-side farewell follows angry outburst.*

In front of her, Charlie Smythe, owner of Charlie's Place, and Anna Jean Thurtzen discussed the presence of nightclub regulars and musicians. "I know that guy," said Charlie. "It's Frenchy, the organ player. Hey, I heard his contract was coming up. Maybe I can snag him for our place, huh?"

"Charlie," said AJ, "I thought I'd heard it all. At a funeral, you're thinkin' about stealin' an act from another club? I thought Lou Farina was the worst slimeball of an owner on the strip, but I think you just took top prize."

"Don't know about that, AJ. At least I'm here. I heard Lou took off for New York. Left a couple of days ago. Now that's being a slimeball, don't you think?"

Ginny overheard the comments about Lou and noted them in her report. She'd heard the same rumor—two rumors equal a fact—so down it went: *Lou Farina, owner of Lou's Lounge, and Al Waters' employer for the past five years, leaves town suddenly and mysteriously, shortly after the homicide.*

Scanning the room, she noticed an unfamiliar face in the back row of chairs. The young man held his head in his hands, occasionally looking up toward the coffin. In her reporter mode she was unable to resist investigating. "Excuse me, sir," said Ginny as she sat next to the man, "I'm afraid I don't recognize you. Were you a friend of Al's?"

"More like his worst enemy," said the man in a shaky voice. "I killed him. Well, me and Lenny Breau did." Ginny's instincts and training were smothered by emotion.

"Who are you? And what are you saying exactly? Should I be calling the cops here?"

"No need. I *am* a cop. Or, *was* one anyway. My name is Stanley Poole. It was my fault Al Waters died . . . because I wasn't a very *good* cop."

Recalling the name from police reports, Ginny said, "You're the one who was posted at his door."

"I was supposed to be guarding him, and I got too interested in a damned magazine story about Lenny Breau. I let the bastard who did this into the room."

"You said you aren't a cop anymore?" asked Ginny. "You were fired for what happened?"

"Would have been, maybe, but I quit the same night. There'll be an inquiry of course, and I'll get off with a reprimand for how I handled it. Straight up? Me chasing that guy was a bad decision, plain and simple. I know I should have stayed to help Waters and get help for him, 'cause maybe he'd have made it if the STAT team had got there a minute sooner. Captain Rosetti spoke to me, and he seemed to understand and even *condone* what I did. Seemed real pleased with me actually. I don't get it. I think he knew that guy somehow, but it sure didn't seem to upset him that he was a murderer. I can't figure that one out. As far as the job, I just went home and haven't gone back. The whole thing just made me sick to my gut. Still does. My dad's a career cop, and he took my gun and uniform to the precinct for me. He was mad 'cause I quit. Didn't even try to understand."

Ginny wanted to ask more, but this wasn't the time or place. She'd been asking questions and observing more out of a need to be occupied, than for true professional purposes. She left Poole alone and headed back to her chair. Kathleen caught her eye. Both looked away quickly, giving in to an onrush of mixed emotions. Ginny felt an overwhelming other-woman guilt rise within her like a thermometer in boiling water; while Kathleen fought the inexplicable feeling she should know this girl from somewhere. More than most people in the room, they shared a dark knowledge and understanding of Al Waters; and in Ginny's eyes Kathleen saw it: they'd shared Al in every way.

♪♪♪

Billy was still kneeling at the coffin. Big John was the only one close enough to hear his words.

"Al," whispered Billy, "I don't think it'll be too long before I see you again. We'll work it out . . . we always do. Say hello to Charlotte up there, will ya? That's if *up* is where you're headed. Sorry, I know better'n anyone where you should be, pal. I forgive you, buddy. I only hope you can do the same for me, for screwing up your life, and for quittin' on you.

"And shit, man, you should know better than anyone what happens from doing stuff out of anger. Goodbye, man, my one true friend. Sorry I said I hated you. You know better than that too." He tried to stand and stumbled awkwardly into Big John's arms. "John," said Billy, "I wanna play something. Can we get the guys up here for one tune for Al . . . huh, guys?"

He motioned to Pete and Wesley who hadn't yet retaken their seats. The pair looked toward Stephanie and she was already nodding, anticipating they'd hesitate in deference to her feelings. The musicians who were currently playing readily agreed and moved out of the way.

Pete, a true musical clairvoyant, began to scratch brushes across cymbals, swooshing and tapping the brassy surfaces with a magical touch. Wesley knew instantly what Pete had in mind, and a river of soothing began to flow from the bass. With strength drawn from the others, Billy entered with such delicacy and grace it was impossible for even Nancy Waters not to forgive his earlier rude outburst. Though he didn't recognize the music, Big John thought it sounded—like Al.

Pete and Wesley recalled it as the never-completed improvisation Billy had joined in with on the day of his altercation with Pete: the scuffle Al had broken up. To the listeners, the simple melody had no name, nor did it need one. It was part of Al, the one part which could live forever.

As the eight-bar motif was played, tears appeared in Stephanie's eyes for the first time that day. She knew the melody from her childhood; her mother had hummed it to her countless times as she tucked her into bed. Only Billy was aware of its origin and title: "Charlotte's Song"—begun, but never finished, by Al Waters in 1970.

♪♪♪

The musicians let the music rise to a peak, and instead of winding it down, they nodded with ensemble understanding, and abruptly ended the tune in the middle of a resolving progression; it had no ending. They knew that somewhere, Al would be smiling.

Ginny wrote: *The musicians played a fitting tribute to their friend, in a beautiful, extemporized rendition of what seemed the very essence of Al Waters' style.* A tear dropped onto her notepad, and she realized it wasn't hers.

"Nice thought," whispered Kathleen, who had walked over to see what Ginny was writing. "I guess you must have known him for some time."

"No, not really," said Ginny. "I was a fan."

Kathleen said, "Yes, weren't we all?" and headed back to her chair.

The trio left their borrowed instruments and returned to sit while the pastor read from the scriptures. He then invited those who wished to speak to come to the front and do so. While no musician in the room had more to say than what Pete, Wesley, and Billy had done with their music, one man did rise to say a few words.

♪♪♪

"Al was a friend," said Big John. "I won't try to talk about his music . . . never knew much about that, except that I liked how he sounded. In my line of work, everybody is my friend for an hour or two. But it's what I sell them that makes them really want to know me.

"Not Al. He was my friend, 'cause he liked me as a man, not just as a bartender. And I liked *him* as a man, not just as a musician. He could've been a doctor or a fish cutter; I still would've been his friend, and he would've been mine. This I know. This, I treasure."

♪♪♪

The pastor introduced a trumpet soloist who was to perform Handel's Largo, at the request of Al's friend, Doctor Jason Davidson.

"Doctor Davidson," said the pastor, "who couldn't be here today, mentioned that this unique assembly of fans, friends, and family might not understand why this selection, in particular, played on trumpet was appropriate in saxophonist, Al Waters', honor. The doctor said to trust him. It was something Al would have wanted.

"Mrs. Waters, Mr. Crothers? Doctor Davidson also said both of *you* would understand."

Nancy Waters rose from her chair and shuffled her way toward the casket, brushing away helping hands extended by Big John and the pastor. She leaned in close to kiss her son's face and whispered to him, "Alfred . . . my dear little Freddy, I know I was the worst mother you could have had. I do hope you understood that I loved you, but I failed you so. I don't have long left in this world to live with my misery, but I have something for you that I was supposed to give you long ago. But like always, I let you down. Back then, maybe I thought I was protecting you for once, by not showing you this when I found it. But that was another wrong choice. I know it's too late, but here it is anyway."

She took a small folded page from her purse, slid it into the breast pocket of Al's suit jacket. As she turned away from the casket she looked up into Big John's eyes, and reached up to brush away his tears. She held out her arm, and he gently took her tiny hand to guide her back to her seat.

♪♪♪

There were but a few faded words on the fragile yellowed paper Nancy Waters had left with her son.

Al,

I didn't tell you where I'm going today because
I know you'd try to stop me. But I'm running away
because I'm finally out of strength.
You are stronger than me. You always have been
and always will be.

I love you so much and I'm sorry this has to happen.
I think I helped a bit when you were little, but I
know you don't need me anymore for that.

You will make it.
You'll be a famous musician someday I just know it.

Somewhere I'll be listening and cheering for you.

Love always,

Anne

CHAPTER 65

OFF THE RECORD

"*S*o, Doctor Davidson, I've heard you're the best."

"Well, no one's the *best* in my profession, but if someone is helped by my counseling, then I confess a certain pride in that success, secondarily of course to the satisfaction of having helped. But enough of that; we're not here to talk about me.

"I'm glad you accepted my invitation to come to see me today. I believe Alfred would have approved. I know very well how much he cared about you and worried for your health. Early on in his sessions here, he asked me to help you find an addiction counselor, and with your approval I still intend to do so. Meeting you today will help me to ascertain who amongst my colleagues will be the best match for you. We have an hour. Let's call it 'on Alfred'. I'm offering my services 'off the record', if you just want to talk, about anything at all."

"Sure, that'd be cool, Doc. That's what he said he called you, right? '*Doc*'?"

"Yes, William, that's . . . that *was* I believe, his way of keeping things informal. He tried to trip me up sometimes with his attempts to be 'cool' or in control. But sometimes, he was quite the opposite . . . 'off the wall', to use one of his expressions, and often passionate and emotionally open about many things."

"Yeah, that sounds like Al for sure. He was a strange dude in a lotta ways. Moody, whew, and downright scary if he was pissed off or pissed up. Huh, that's what he called it, 'pissed up' for being drunk? A Canuck expression, *eh*? He'd say those more when he had a few drinks under his belt. Hey, is it okay to talk about Al, even though he was your patient? Thought you guys didn't do that. By the way, call me Billy, okay? And when you call Al 'Alfred', it doesn't sound right. Just 'Al' is better. Cool with you?"

"Certainly. 'Al' it will be. And remember, William . . . I mean, Billy, this meeting is not an official therapy session and any discussion about Al will be treated as you needing to talk about the loss of your friend. If I comment I will be careful not to reveal any privileged information shared by Al."

"Far-fucking . . . sorry, uh, far-out, Doc. You see, there's lots to talk about, and a ton of it has to do with him. And 'off the record' is cool in more ways than one. Huh, sounds like a 'lift', you know, when you listen to a solo on someone's album and you copy it out.

"And funny you mentioned him being 'off the wall'. Al had this oddball habit I've never seen another horn player do. He'd leave his sax sitting on the stand after the gig, usually not even pack it up for the days we were off. Sure, it's an ugly old thing but there are punks would steal anything that isn't tied down, and it's a good horn, even if it is kind of beat and battered. I guess from what I've heard, it's a classic, worth a lot to guys who know about those things. And get this: since he died, that horn is still there on the stage at Losers'. Story is that Big John won't let anyone touch it. He even stood up to Lou who wanted to trash it. John said he'd quit if that happened.

"That's Al though . . . quirky and downright nuts sometimes, but most of the time a good guy. But the times he was at his best was when he was playing good. Stupid part of that was that he never ever played as good as he could have. And he knew it. But it was only because he doubted himself. Was his own worst critic. You know, he could have been a great songwriter too. And I think he wanted to be that, even more than being a great musician. I gotta say though, I wasn't much help to him there. Might have been partly my fault he never finished the songs he started. Way back in Montreal I kind of lied to him about something he'd done . . . long story there, but let's say it was a case of selfish is as selfish does, and I don't think he seriously ever really got back to it. He should have, 'cause as natural as he was at improvising on the spot, he could have written songs by the cart load. I wish I had helped him find a way to do that.

"But he was so dammed negative, about his own abilities anyway. If there was a hundred people in a room thinking he was great, and one schmuck who didn't, Al could only see the schmuck. Even stupider was that he was the opposite when it came to others. Even at my lowest, and we're talkin' *low*, he'd find something positive to say about me. Why couldn't he do that for himself, Doc?"

The doctor surveyed his patient's appearance. From Al's description, he might easily have recognized Billy anywhere, with the slicked back, partially graying hair splitting awkwardly sideways away from its intended role as comb-over. A middle-aged man, he looked far older than his years, with the cracked-desert terrain of a self-abusive lifetime etched into his face.

"Well, Billy, my observation was similar to yours. And frankly, I cannot say why with complete confidence. I don't believe Al was as forthright with certain information about his past which might have shed some light on his behavior."

"I know, Doc. Sometimes when he'd get real wasted, he'd say some heavy shit about his dad and stuff. And as much of a ladies' man as he fancied himself, I think he had some problems there."

"Yes, Billy, that was apparent to me as well."

"Doc, I think he was so good at self-deception, he could have tied his own damned shoelaces together and fell for it. How can you believe anything, *anytime*, from someone who shows they can do that?"

"Well put, Billy. Sadly, to deceive successfully, requires you to be clever enough to stay at least one step ahead of your intended dupe, and to be one very good liar. I'm afraid Al had developed the ability to fool everyone, *including* himself, about what was really in his head or his heart."

"I got an important question, Doc. Does stuff I say here, *stay* here? You know, that privilege thing?"

"Doctor-patient confidentiality? Yes, unless I deem you as an imminent threat to society or to yourself or another individual. Then I'd be obligated to notify the authorities."

"Well, I ain't no threat to no one. But there's some things I need to talk about I wouldn't want anyone to know."

"I will let you know if you are treading on dangerous ground, Billy."

"Okay, Doc. Well, as we were talking about Al, I need to keep going, and what we were just saying could be important. Since he's dead, I don't suppose it'll do any harm to talk about him. And it may help someone else. Ya see, Doc, there's a thing that happened that I wonder if he told you about. Has to do with a sexual situation. Not what you'd expect, either, if he didn't tell you."

"Please go on, Billy."

"Well, a while back, I guess it was just before he started seeing you, there was this incident. As usual after the gig, Al was at the bar, having a Scotch and chatting up a pretty hot looker, a big chick, almost as tall as Al . . . with those high heels anyway. I figured her for a show girl or stripper. She was not shy if you know what I mean, Doc, wrapping her leg around him, and rubbing her body up against him. Well, the two of them headed out the back to the alley and were gone for about ten minutes or so. Meantime, the bartender, Big John, must not have seen 'em go out, 'cause he grabbed up the garbage to take out before I could warn him. He came back in real quick and looked at me with that big grin of his. He came over to me at the piano and said, 'Al's gettin' a blow job, but he ain't gonna be happy.'

"I says, 'Why not, man?' And John says, 'When he finds out who's doin' the blowin', he's gonna flip. I know Vickie . . . and that *ain't* no chick.'

"Yeah, Doc, Al was with a friggin' TV . . . transvestite, she-male, or whatever they are. A 'chick-with-a-dick'. And Al didn't *know* it. When they came back in I didn't know what to do. I was scared for the life of that guy . . . girl, *whatever* it is. I figured if Al found out, he'd go so bananas, he might commit murder. I always knew he had some strange thing about gays, actually kind of protective of 'em, but to have one go down on him? Oh boy. Look out."

Closing his eyes, the doctor said, "What happened then, Billy?"

"Well, call me a coward, and I am, I didn't say anything, and sure as hell neither did Big John. He knew as well as me what could happen. From there I could never have predicted in a million, no, a *billion* years what was gonna happen next. It was a few days later and I'd kinda put the whole thing outa my mind. And then there comes this 'chick' back in the place, with three other 'chicks' who I assume to be of the same messed up variety. Al might have been fooled by the one, 'cause for real, Doc, she was so hot I can't see anyone guessing. Like in that movie a few years ago, you know, where the guy falls in love with one, not knowing what she is? But anyway, two of the others weren't so convincing. They were more what you'd expect of a female impersonator. Pretty as they looked, it would have been fairly easy to tell that they were guys dressed up.

"Al saw them from the stage and it took him only a second to put it together. He dropped his horn in the stand and walked off. I was ready for all hell, but he walked right past their table and out the front door. I couldn't believe it, but I was glad. Not for long though. Vickie got up and went out after him.

"It was over a half-hour before Al came back in. He looked a little rough around the edges and he was out of breath when he tried to blow his horn. I knew enough to say nothing. So did everyone."

"Was that the end of it, Billy?"

"For another couple of days I thought it was. After the gig that Saturday, Al was drinking really heavy. When he left, I went with him, hoping to keep him outa trouble. He waved me off but I wouldn't take no. There was a bench in a spot he liked to go, up near the beach, and we went there, me holding onto the big lug so's he wouldn't fall into the street. Well, when we sat down I couldn't believe it. Al started to cry. Something was way, *way* wrong, man.

"Though it was kinda awkward, I couldn't leave him, so I put my hand on his shoulder and said, 'What's up, pal? Feel like talking?' and boy did he surprise me. Now first of all, I don't think I've ever seen him so wasted. I was surprised he could even sit up. He said he had to tell me something and I was the only one he could talk to.

"What it boiled down to is tough to even picture, let alone put into words, but here goes. Al told me about what happened when that tranny Vickie had followed him out. She caught up with him and tried to stop him, but he pushed her away, saying he wanted nothing to do with any sex with a fag. Well, she wouldn't let up and she was so damned believable-looking, he just couldn't resist. You know some of 'em have boobs, these she-males, and damned real ones sometimes. Although with this one you couldn't really tell whether they were fake or not. I guess Al must have found out though . . . at some point.

"They went to her car to talk about it, but then she started in on him with the rubbing and kissing. As weird as he felt about what was happening, he felt some uncontrollable urge to let her. Maybe it was a case of the old saying, 'if you close your eyes and enjoy, who cares who's blowing you?' Doc, he was crying as he told me this and I tried to say how maybe almost any guy would be tricked by her, being so hot looking and all. But he said there was more, and worse.

"I didn't want to hear it, Doc, but he made me listen. He told me that while she was down on him he started feeling her rear end, not even thinking about it, kind of forgetting who she really was maybe? Anyway, all of a sudden she grabs his hand and pulls it right down onto her, uh, 'man parts'.

"Al said it was like time was suspended or something; that it felt like forever before he reacted. When he realized he didn't pull his hand away as fast as he *should* have, it made him feel so much self-hate he would have blown his own head off if he'd had a gun there. But, instead of getting the hell outa there like he knew he should have, he pushed her head back down and told her to finish him off.

"I didn't know what to say, Doc. Have to admit it made me feel like I was gonna puke as he was telling me this stuff. Shit, almost makes me still feel that right now."

"Have some water, Billy. This must be very difficult for you. Take your time. We have lots. No one is booked in after you today. I always try to arrange things that way with first or special visits."

"Okay, Doc, but seriously, did Al ever tell you any of this?"

"About the Vickie incident? No, he did not, but that said, please remember it would be unethical for me to discuss most details of Al's sessions here."

"Sure, Doc, I get it. You know, it's nuts, but this all reminds me of how I always wondered about a mutual acquaintance of ours, a flaming fag named Ed Wilson back in New York. I always knew he had the hots for Al, but I never thought there'd be any chance anything would happen there. Hell, Al was totally into women. Or was I just blind?"

"Billy, why do I sense such discomfort, and even anger in your use of such derogatory words for a gay man?"

"Sorry, Doc, very un-cool of me. But back to Vickie. This was no typical fag . . . Sorry, *gay* guy. This was a gorgeous chick who happened to come with extra equipment. Still though, if it had been me in that position, and she'd made me touch *that* down there, I couldn't have stayed, not a damned second longer."

"Billy, I can see there's more to this. Please go on."

"Sure, Doc. Well, next it got dangerous. Vickie tried to get Al to go down and suck her, you know, his dick. This *really* pissed Al off, ya know, 'last straw' kind of thing, and then he got rough. She got scared and started to try to fight him. And Al went schizo . . . smacked her pretty hard, and more than once. Knocked her right out. Then he got scared, first because he thought maybe he'd killed her, and second, 'cause he was afraid of being seen in the car in that situation. He split, leaving Vickie heaped in the front seat of her car. I guess she wasn't too busted up though, 'cause he saw her a week later on the street and she looked okay, from a distance anyway.

"His fear, he told me later, was that someone would find out what he'd done and think he was a queer . . . *his* word, Doc. He said he couldn't believe he had let Vickie go down on him after he knew she wasn't really a girl. Man, he was really fucked up over this whole thing.

"Next time he got deep into the Scotch again, he told me that he'd even toyed with the idea of finding her and doing it again. In fact he said he'd fantasized about actually going down on the guy. He'd taken a banana one night and put it in his mouth like it was a cock, and he got a hard-on right away. And he told me more stuff I really didn't want to hear, about how sex had always been a difficult thing for him. Something about not being satisfying, or actually being sad for him? Anyway, the blow job with Vickie had been the best he ever had, none of his usual disappointed feeling. He said it felt like how he always knew it was supposed to? And not the first one in the alley, but the second one in her car . . . when he *knew* she wasn't a girl.

"What the hell did he mean by that, Doc? Al wasn't a . . . he wasn't gay, was he? I just don't get it."

"Billy, I'm afraid the definitions involved in sexual preferences are not black and white. I personally don't believe Al was 'gay', not even bisexual. And by the way, in regard to Vickie, a true transsexual is not by definition a gay man.

"A person's interest in, or perhaps *need* for exploration or questioning of sexual identity is sometimes rooted in some form of emotional damage in their past, with the memories of that time often fully repressed. Al may have suffered in this way, but from his sparse references to early childhood, I can only speculate. In time I may have been able to help him recall early trauma and perhaps deal with it. But, since he is gone, we will most likely never know exactly what happened."

CHAPTER 66

THE HOLE
1955

*W*hen little Freddy Waters saw evil lurking, either in dreams or in the darkest corners of his room, he cried out for Daddy to come and rescue him. Those monsters, even the ones under the bed had no chance against *him*. Just like in the stories his mother read to him, the hero always won, and the endings were always happy.

Then one night things changed forever, as the boy found himself trapped between two kinds of nightmares: one in the sleep world and the other, in reality. Freddy was sucked into a grim story where the hero *was* the monster, with the only possible ending to be written, "and they all lived *un*happily ever after."

♪♪♪

"What is it, little man? Need a drink of water?"

"No, Daddy, gotsa go pee, but I'm scared. They're under there again!"

Freddy's dad came into the room and sat on the edge of the bed. "Look, nothing's grabbing my leg. There's no bed monsters. I got rid of them all. Remember?" He pulled back the covers and hauled the five-year-old up into his arms. "Big hug. Daddy loves your hugs."

Daddy's mouth smelled funny again. Sometimes when he smelled funny, Mummy cried a lot.

"Here's the biggest hug in the world, Daddy. Ooh, come on. I gotsa go bad. Pee pee pee . . . Can't *hold* it."

Freddy's dad hurried to the bathroom, as his wiggling bundle of boy tried to hold off the painful flood ready to burst his tummy. Finally, standing at the toilet, came the ecstasy of release. Alfred Sr. stood behind, reaching around to help guide the needle stream, to avoid getting the floor and walls wet again. Sometimes the little boy's tiny penis would be sticking up like a tiny rocket ready to launch. Without proper redirection, pee would shoot into the air like an unattended fire hose, and the boy was often too tired or inattentive to notice. Both his parents had developed a habit of aim-assist, pushing the little rocket down toward the bowl as he went.

But tonight there was something different in how Daddy was holding Freddy's pee-pee. Instead of just a gentle downward push, his fingers gripped him more like he did his pipe when he used it to send magic smoke rings across the room. But to Freddy this wasn't fun like the smoke rings; it felt *wrong*, even in his sleepy head. But there was no need to worry about it. Daddies knew best. They knew everything, and they'd never hurt you.

Freddy yawned and said, "All done, back to bed now."

♪♪♪

The next time Daddy helped his son with a night pee, it was worse. This time the smell from his mouth was strong. Mummy would be crying for sure. Freddy tried to make his pee-pee go small, go soft, as it was during the day. His dad held it after the pee was done, and began to move his fingers back and forth, just a little bit. It felt nice, but bad at the same time. Something told him his Daddy shouldn't be doing it—but *liking* it, made him a bad boy.

"Wanna go back to bed now," said Freddy, yawning.

His dad snatched his hand away, startled to hear his son was awake enough to speak. "Okay, Freddy, we'll get you back to bed," he said in an odd quivery voice—like a child who was trying to be brave, trying not to cry.

Tucked back in, Freddy said, "Nighty-night," and watched his father close the door behind him. He promised to himself that from now on he'd hold it all night long if he had to. It took forever to get back to sleep, and before he did, he heard the muffled sounds of crying from down the hall—from Annie's room. It reminded him of dreams he'd often had; he'd thought they must be dreams. In defiance of the dangers of the dark, he got up and tiptoed toward her room. The door was open just a crack, and as he peeked in, the dim glow of a nightlight revealed the strangest scene. Was Annie helping Daddy pee? Beside her—in her *bed*?

Freddy ran back to his bed, pulled the covers up tight over his head and closed his eyes so tight it hurt. He promised to be good for the rest of his life if God would make it all a dream. In the morning he stayed in bed until Daddy had gone to work. The frightful image of Annie and Daddy was still in his head, and he knew it wasn't a dream at all. God must not have heard him—or didn't care.

♪♪♪

When Freddy went downstairs for breakfast his mother was sitting alone at the kitchen table. She smiled and said, "Land sakes alive, you'd sleep away the whole day I think, if you had the chance."

"Where's Annie?" he asked timidly.

"Well, she's off to school of course. It's after nine, sweetie. And in the fall you'll be going too. Isn't that exciting? Here, have my toast. I'll make some more. Jam's on the table. Want some orange juice?" She rose and went to the refrigerator.

"Mummy, I saw Annie touch Daddy's pee-pee . . . in her room. Why, Mummy?"

Nancy Waters stood silent for what seemed like hours to the little boy. She held the fridge door partially open the whole time, her fingers gripping ever tighter, until her hand began to shake. The trembling began to reverberate through her body. It reminded Freddy of the time she had let him stand on the washing machine while it chugged away at a load of clothes, and she had held on to him, laughing with him at the strange, scary sensation of having the world shake under his feet. Today, in this terrible frozen moment, there was no chance of laughter from either of them.

When she finally shut the fridge door, she turned to face him, hurriedly pulling up the bottom edge of her apron to wipe her face. He'd seen the tears, but wished he hadn't. The only time he'd ever heard her cry was when Daddy smelled funny, and yelled, and was mean to her. Betrayed by his child's logic, Freddy thought he must have done something bad to make her cry, but he didn't know what.

"Alfred Waters Junior, you mustn't make up nasty stories like that. Only a very bad boy would say such a thing. Don't ever repeat that again. *Never*, to anybody! What might people think? They could take you and Annie away."

"But Mummy, I saw—"

Freddy's mother smacked the rest of the sentence out of his mouth with the palm of her hand which was still wet from her tears. The slap was numbing, not solely by its brutal force which snapped the little boy's head sideways; but more, by its source. His mother had never hit him. That was Daddy's job: to spank, and yell, and threaten with the belt. Mummy wasn't supposed to do that stuff.

He held back his own tears as long as he could, stifling his sobs with painful constrictions of his neck muscles while his abdomen repeatedly heaved against the pressure to push air and angst out of his little body. Facing away from her, he tried to ask what he'd done that was so bad. "Muh . . . Muh . . . Mum . . . mee-eeee . . . Wha, wha, what's wr . . . wrong?" Finally, his wavering strength gave way to the power of fear and shock. He wailed in the way only a child can, releasing a deluge of tortuous gasping sobs.

Nancy Waters held her hand over her own mouth until her fingernails drew blood from her cheek. She turned and ran up to her bedroom and slammed the door, leaving Freddy to figure out why he'd been hurt by the one person in the world he should never have been afraid of.

Freddy sat alone crying for over half an hour, hoping his mother would come back. He tried the piece of toast she'd given him; it had become soggy and cold. He ate it anyway. He didn't want to make her mad again.

Later—it was almost lunchtime—Nancy Waters came back downstairs, her face puffy and red. Freddy was not at the table. She looked around for him where she thought he might normally be playing with his toy cars or soldiers. He wasn't there, and intuition told her to look out the back window. Freddy, still wearing only his pajamas, was kneeling in the tiny garden between the back porch and driveway. In his hand was a toy shovel.

She went out and sat on the bottom step, only a few feet from him. "Freddy, it's too chilly to be out here like that. Land sakes, it's only April, and besides, jammies aren't exactly for wearing outside are they?"

"I'm digging a hole, Mummy. See?" His voice was flat, and he didn't look at her as he spoke.

She wondered if he would ever look at her again—wondered also, if she wanted him to. "What's the hole for, sweetie? You trying to go all the way to China?"

Freddy didn't know what China was, but if it was far away, then it was worth digging for. "No, Mummy, just making a hole. It's for me."

"Can I come in with you when you make it really big?"

"No, Mummy, it's just for me . . . 'kay?"

♪♪♪

Fred Waters headed for the Red Lion Inn, after another day of no sales. A drink or two, or three, might ease the frustration. At the bar he saw three people from the office: Burt, Don, and Judy. He sat next to Judy who had been hired only that Monday as the new receptionist.

Burt said, "Hey, Fred, how was your week? Don and I were just comparing notes, and he's got me by only a couple hundred bucks, total of twenty-five hundred, right Donny?"

"A month ago I did double that," said Fred, "but the last few weeks have been crap since my territory got switched. I'll catch up to you punks soon enough."

"Yeah, Fred, all that experience should make you number-one again, right?" said Don with a weak attempt at sincerity.

Judy said, "Somebody said you play music, Mr. Waters. What kind?"

"Come on, Judy. 'Mister Waters'? Call me Fred, please. You'll make me feel old."

"Sorry, Mister— I mean, *Fred*. So what do you play?"

"I play a few different instruments, honey. Mostly piano though."

"Oh, nice. You play swing or jazz? That's my favorite."

Burt laughed. "Jazz? Fred? Now that's a good one. Our old friend here is a classical music kinda guy. No hep cat here, doll."

Judy sighed and said, "That's too bad, Fred. I was hoping you'd play something on that piano over there, but not if it's stuffy old longhair music. What do you think of this new rock 'n' roll craze that's going on? My folks say it's Negro music, and it's going to ruin society. Pretty dumb, eh? Have you seen the kids dance to that Bill Haley guy? I love it."

Although Fred hadn't even yet heard of rock 'n' roll, if it was indeed "Negro" music, that was okay by him. That would mean it was basically the blues, and would be simple enough to learn. It might be worth a listen if Judy liked it. She had a pretty face and more important, a body like Jane Russell. He whispered into her ear, "What do you say we go somewhere else, honey, just you and me?"

Judy spilled a few drops of her drink on her blouse as she tried to stifle her laugh. "Fred, you're a hoot. The guys said you were funny. As if you'd seriously ask me out. You're an old married man. Get that, Don? Fred's pretending to make a pass at me."

"Come on, Fred," said Don, "you gotta leave one woman for the rest of us, for Christ sakes."

As Fred excused himself to the men's room, Don, Judy, and Burt exploded with laughter. He didn't return to the bar. This last "no-sale" was all he could take.

♪♪♪

"Nancy, where the bloody hell are you," Fred shouted as he dropped heavily into his well-worn leather recliner chair. Gulping back the remainder of the double Scotch he'd poured as soon as he'd entered the house, he yelled, "You better have something ready to heat up for supper, eh?"

Trying to make a cheery voice to mask her fear, Nancy called down from the bathroom, "Supper's in the oven, honey. Macaroni and cheese; shouldn't be too bad. Been waiting on 'warm' for you a couple of hours."

"Damn it, Nancy, what're ya doing up there? Aren't the kids in bed? Christ, it's after nine!"

"Annie's in bed, reading, I think. And I'm giving Freddy his bath. It's Friday night, remember, dear?"

"Guess that means I gotta get my own goddamn supper then? Shit. Hurry the hell up and get done there, Nancy. Don't forget, you got me to look after too, speaking of goddamn remembering things."

He went to the kitchen to get more ice for his next Scotch, and to check on his still-warming supper.

♩♩♩

Freddy was splashing about, lying on his back in the bath, while he played with his favorite boat. "Watch, Mummy, the boat's going to crash into the beach!"

He pushed the toy against his tummy and said, "Gooosh . . . bam . . . blub, blub, blub. Poor boat gots to sink now."

"Poor boat," said his mother. "Bye bye, boat."

Freddy let the boat slip away under the water and reached for the wash-cloth his mother had left on the edge of the tub while she went to get the shampoo. He began to scrub himself all over with the warm soapy water.

"Ooh, look at my big boy, washing himself just like a grown-up. Pretty soon you won't need me to bath you anymore then, *will* you?"

"No, Mummy. I'm going to be a big boy really really soon. Watch this."

He rubbed the cloth back and forth over his genitals and then abandoned the rag to concentrate with just his hands. "Lookit, Mummy. I can make it change." He giggled as he pulled back his foreskin, exposing the head of his penis. "It feels good to do this Mummy. It's fun to wash my pee-pee."

"Good Lord, Alfred. Don't *do* that. It's bad. You just wash it, but don't *play* with it. It'll give you dirty thoughts. Your pee-pee is . . . to *pee* with. ONLY. Don't let me ever catch you doing that again. You should be ashamed of yourself, very, very ashamed."

Freddy pulled his hands up over his eyes. He thought he'd seen the same look on her face as when she had slapped him. For a few minutes, thoughts of that morning's incident had been washed away by the fun of the bath, but the vivid memory had flashed back into his mind as soon as she began to speak loudly. He would forever associate that tone of voice with pain—from his tingling cheek, to his broken trust.

♪♪♪

When Freddy was tucked into bed, he looked up into his mother's face and felt sad for her. She wasn't crying, but he knew she felt bad. He'd heard his father's voice with that nasty edge it had when he came home smelling funny. He knew tonight would probably be a night when Annie would cry. He now understood—that his mother knew it too.

♪♪♪

Freddy woke up in the middle of a dream. In it, he was peeing into a bucket, and the water was flowing over the edges. It was making a mess, and he'd be in big trouble. Waking up was a confusing mixture of relief and fear. The need to pee was real, and he had to do something about it fast.

He was afraid of the bed monsters and of his father, and now too, of his mother. He couldn't call on anyone for help, but he had to go. He leaned over the edge of the bed, peeking carefully to see if anything was there at the side. Nothing. He pulled back the covers and crawled to the end of the bed. There, he jumped as far as he could toward the door, and fell on his rear end as his feet slipped out from under him on the hardwood floor.

It was too dark and scary to worry about whether anyone had heard the noise. He pulled open the door and scurried to the bathroom down the hall. As he passed his parents' room, he noticed the door was open, but no light was on. Next to that door was Annie's room, closed up tight. A sliver of dim light crept through the crack at the bottom of the door. No time to pay attention to that; he had to go so bad. Freddy got to the toilet just in time and peed just like in the dream, pouring an endless wonderful stream into the toilet. It was the happiest he'd felt all day.

His father's voice at the door ruined the joy. "What's going on, little man? You in there going all by yourself, in the middle of the night? Don't need me to help anymore? What about those monsters? Did you kill 'em all?" He laughed with a hideous witch's voice. The smell was strong: the smell which made him a bad daddy.

"All done, Daddy. Gotsa get back to bed."

"So you don't need your old dad anymore, eh? Big boy and all independent now? Well, good luck when you go back to your room. I hear that bed monsters get mad when they hear about little boys who try to grow up too fast. Makes 'em real hungry."

Freddy couldn't stop the tears. "Daddy, please go with me then. Please? I promise I'll never grow up. Don't let them get me."

"Okay, little guy. I'm your hero, as always, eh? Let's get you back to bed." Fred Waters picked up his son, carried him to his room, and gently laid him down on the bed. He said, "I have a new game for you to try . . . a good bedtime game, okay?"

The bad-daddy smell—the smell of sadness—made it far from okay. Freddy said nothing.

"Look, Freddy. My pee-pee is just like yours when you pee at night . . . all big and sticking out. Come on, look."

Freddy would rather have looked at the monsters from his worst nightmares than do what he was being asked, but his father's strong hands lifted him up and closer. He'd seen his daddy pee a few times, through the partly open bathroom door. But this was different; this was scary; this was—*wrong*.

"Want to touch it?" said his father, slowly stroking himself. "Just do what I'm doing. Daddy would like that."

"No, Daddy. I don't wanna."

"Shhh. Don't talk loud, and *don't* say no to me."

His father's penis looked like a monster to Freddy. He'd never thought much about what his own looked like. It was just—*there*. But his father's looked ugly, evil, and terrifying.

"Daddy, I'm scared. Don't make me, please."

"Keep your voice down, Freddy. We don't want to bother anyone."

Defenses against extraordinary danger must come from extraordinary depths, and even a child can sometimes reach into surprising resources of resilience.

"Daddy, Mummy got real mad at me today."

"Why? What'd ya do this time?"

"I told her I saw you and Annie, and she was helping you pee, in her bed."

"When did you . . . ? God damn it Freddy, you never saw that. You must be a sick little bugger to make up something like that. I—"

"Don't yell at him, Daddy," said a small voice from the doorway. "Leave him alone. He doesn't understand. He's too little."

Fred hurriedly pushed his penis back into his pants, then turned and stood up. "Anne, go back to your room. *Now*. I'll be there in a minute and we'll talk about this. Don't you be going and getting mouthy with me, little girl."

He grabbed her by the arm and pushed her out the door. When she said, "Ow," from the force of her father's grip, Freddy cried, "Daddy, no! Don't hurt her."

The little boy punched his father's leg as hard as he could. Fred Sr. laughed and said, "Wow, what a brave little fart you are." He pushed him down onto the bed and added, "If you ever mess with me again, I'll give you something more than monsters to deal with. Now go to sleep."

When his father left the room with Annie, Freddy knew right where they were headed. In a few minutes, he heard the sounds of his sister crying; and from downstairs, the sobs of his mother mixed in between the notes of her odd little "La dee da dee da" song.

In fairytales, the heroes always win and everyone is safe. In life, some are paid in pain for their efforts. Annie had protected her little brother from the one who was supposed to be the hero to both of them. And in return, all Freddy could do was listen, as she suffered.

♪♪♪

Fred Waters Sr. knew what he was doing was wrong, knew he was destined for damnation, knew the world would be better if he had died with his buddies on Normandy Beach. Each time after he'd let this happen with Annie, he hated himself more. But on this night, he knew he had gone one more step closer to hell, perhaps one more step beyond what could be forgiven by a God who could forgive thieves, and murderers, and soldiers who cowered behind the bodies of the fallen, while their comrades obeyed orders which sent them to be blown apart.

Every time he had given in to the "need", guilt and shame became the hands of the puppeteer, controlling his body and his conscience; with the main string wrapped tight around his neck, as if to prevent this puppet from looking down upon what this demonic dance really was.

Anne and Freddy would survive. Their bodies weren't being destroyed; although most certainly their love for him *was*. But that was undeserved anyway. If you can't trust God, how can you ask your children to trust their earthly father?

Fred Waters could make himself think this way only when the booze and the memories of Normandy allowed his anger to cloud all reason. Afterward, he would go to the garage where he'd load his hunting rifle and sit in the car, and cry in solitude, wondering if this would be the time he'd finally find the courage to do it: to put the gun in his mouth, and join those with whom he should have been all along.

♪♪♪

Daddy never helped Freddy with night pees again. Out of the boy's sheer will to be left alone, the bed monsters disappeared too. He sometimes wished they hadn't. During the times when his father was alone with Annie, he often prayed the monsters would suddenly reappear, become his friends and come with him to rescue her, as she had done for him. But eventually he stopped praying for anything from anyone.

Denial protects the soul as long as it can, and for a child it's often the only defense he has. As Freddy got older, certain memories faded, but not the feelings—they would be forever—even though on a conscious level he became unaware of what happened in the spring of 1955.

Fred Waters began to drink less at home, preferring to spend time with people he had no love for. His extramarital affairs brought nowhere near the remorse caused by his in-home activities, neither for him nor for his wife. What he had done to his children never left him, never faded. Instead, it became a tumor in his soul, eventually crowding out not just the memories he wanted to erase, but all hope of ever again knowing true joy.

There were times as Annie got older when her father's "need" recurred beyond his restraint. To his surprise, Annie never protested, as if she too had developed a need of her own. Other than their music together, this was the only intimacy her dad had ever offered. Her denial was of a different nature from her brother's.

♪♪♪

Freddy never finished that hole in the garden. He didn't need it. Deep inside the wound in his heart, he buried the memories of that time—where he thought they couldn't hurt him anymore.

CHAPTER 67

OFF THE RECORD
(continued)

"Well anyways, I guess we're supposed to be talking about *me*, aren't we, Doc? I know you're trying to set me up with another shrink. I really wish it could be *you* though."

"Some of my colleagues are specialists in drug and alcohol problems, Billy. And I'm sure with my recommendation one of them may offer his services pro bono, at least for a while. But under the circumstances, I felt it appropriate to see you myself, this one time anyway."

"Doc, you have no idea just how appropriate."

The tears had filled Billy's eyes so suddenly, he was unable to stop them before he could rip half a tissue from the box at his side.

"It's okay, Billy," said the doctor, "perfectly okay for any emotion to surface here. You may wait until you're composed before you try to talk."

"You gotta understand, man. I'm not crying for fucking Al Waters," Billy croaked in the loudest voice his worn-out throat could handle. "I'm here for *me*. For a fucking change, maybe Al won't be the center of everything?"

As Billy clutched more tissues and slapped away tears, the doctor looked downward at his book and jotted notes before saying, "Take your time, Billy. You're absolutely right. From what I know of you, there have been times in your life when Al was your best friend, *and* times when his decisions may have hurt you. But you are a talented and accomplished man. I must tell you, I have several recordings of you with different groups from your early career. In the world of music, you take second chair to no one. And not to bring attention to Al again, but he knew that better than anyone. His respect for you was immense."

"Yeah, Doc, I always knew he felt that way. But in spite of the good stuff there were so many times he fucked me over too. Kind of like a brother who loves you, but can still beat the crap out of you the next minute?"

"Do you have any brothers or sisters, Billy?"

"Nahh. My folks were pissed off enough just gettin' stuck with me. Guess I proved 'em right too, huh? Shoulda never had me."

"What makes you think they felt that way, Billy?"

"Ha, no secret there at all. Guess what? They were both doctors. That's a hoot, huh? Think maybe that's how I ended up so interested in drugs?" Billy cackled and cleared his throat. "My dad was a hot shot surgeon and my mother was a shrink. Wrote some books. Doctor Martha Crothers. Heard of her?"

"Why, yes I have, Billy. Her books on early childhood behavior and emotional development were required material in my university studies. She is a well-known and respected researcher and author."

"Yeah, and you'd think she'd be the world's greatest mother, huh? Wrote books on how to make your kid happy and develop into a perfect human being. Trouble was, she and my dad had no real interest in me. The only thing I can thank them for is getting me some piano lessons when I was only three. They at least saw that in me, that I showed some talent. But it also gave them an out, from having to look after me when the nanny wasn't there. All I ever did was play and practice. Kept me outa their hair, didn't it?"

"Unfortunately, that scenario is not as uncommon as one might think, Billy. Being an 'expert' in an area doesn't always mean one practices what one teaches. Do you think they are proud of your musical achievements?"

"You kiddin', Doc? I have no idea what they think about anything I've done, good or bad."

"Do you have any contact with them at all now?"

"Doc, I left home when I was fifteen and never looked back. Haven't seen or spoken to either of them since. Huh, I wonder if they even noticed I was gone."

He closed his eyes and settled back, his frail body almost disappearing amongst the couch pillows. Godzilla hopped up beside him and lay his little head down on his lap, looking up as he licked at one of the pianist's gnarled hands. After a moment Billy sat up straighter, wiping roughly at his face and said, "Okay, Doc, I gotta get down to it. There's more to why I'm here than you can guess. Hafta tell you some shit. It's gonna be a bitch, but here goes . . .

"That chick-with-a-dick, Vickie, well she was fucked up pretty bad by Al.

Nothing was broken, but she was hurting for days after. And this affected her work and almost could've cost her job. He/she's an orderly, Doc. Yeah, at Broward General; works there as a man, not in the 'role' he plays in his private life. And yeah, I bet you're wondering how I know all this."

"Go on, Billy."

Billy's voice had strengthened remarkably and the tears had ceased.

"You know who Ginny is, right, Doc? Al's *big* little girlfriend? Here's where this all gets fucked up, *really* fucked up. She, Ginny I mean, comes to me the day after I'd quit the gig at Losers'. It was a rough time for me, having seen him kissing Stephanie in the alley, and then me walking out on them like that. Ginny was as pissed off at Al as I was, and we sort of had this 'bond' on account of that. Do you know what he did to her, Doc, how bad he treated her over the years? Her and me, we kind of had an Al-bashing party, sharing the crap we'd both been through with him. I shouldn't have, but since I was higher than high I told her all about Vickie. As if I could make him look any worse in her eyes, huh?"

The doctor rubbed his forehead. "Billy, do you think Al ever found out that Ginny knew about Vickie?"

"Well, Doc, I had thought maybe that was part of why he freaked out the way he did. But more likely it was just 'cause of her telling him about her DNA test results and that Steph was *his* daughter instead of mine. That was the same day Al went nuts and punched out Lou and ended up in the loony bin."

"I was involved with that, Billy," said Doc. "He came here, clearly in a state of mind to do harm to himself."

"Sure he went off the deep end," said Billy. "No surprise. Well, what about me, Doc? When I heard that he'd had sex with Charlotte, and when she was supposedly *my* girl, it hurt just as much after all these years as if we were still there in Montreal. And as much as Al has done for me over the years, he sure has caused me misery too. But nothing he ever did was as bad as what he stole from me by taking away what I thought was a part of the only woman I ever loved. Steph is Charlotte's daughter, man. And here I was thinking she was mine too? For the first time in my life I thought I had a family."

"And how did this make you feel, Billy?"

"Angry for sure, but that's not a strong enough word, Doc. I went schizo. This was too much . . . too much for even Al to have pulled off. I called Ginny and she and I met Steph at a café patio and we told her too. She was really freaked; didn't know what to say, and when Ginny made it clear that Al *knew* from the night before, then she lost it big time. She called Al the world's most incredible, unbelievable asshole, and then she got up and ran . . . literally *ran* down the street. I couldn't follow her, not on these old legs. Ginny said to let her go; she knew how she felt. She said maybe if we're all lucky, Steph would be mad enough to go get a gun and blow the bastard away. I knew that wouldn't happen, but it made me think. And I made a sick, crazy, unavoidable decision.

"I tracked Vickie down. It was easy with Ginny's help. We got her real name, Vick Griffin, and I went to see her . . . *him*. It was fucked up, Doc, I mean the guy and how he lived. It was the first time I saw him *not* dolled up and it really blew my mind. Thought maybe I was on a bad trip. He was a fairly big guy, not as big as Al, but sure not short, and not muscular. But not really what you'd call skinny either. Tell you what, there was nothing obvious about his looks as a man that would give away what he could look like when he dressed up as a woman. Nothing visual anyway, but there was a creepy thing in the air around him, like a cloud of *weirdness*. And his apartment looked like a couple lived there, with *guy* stuff lyin' around, like golf clubs and sports mags . . . but girl stuff too. The furniture was frilly and flowery, and the main room walls were sort of pinkish colored. And there was a blond wig hanging on the top edge of the open bathroom door. I got the creeps just being there.

"But, my instincts were right on. He was into revenge on Al, *big* time. Since Al had been so fucking dishonest with me, I figured it was fair game to do the same. I told Vick that Al had been laughing about busting him up and was telling everyone. And it was going to get back to the hospital pretty soon that they had a female impersonator on their staff. I don't know what this might have meant for real, but it seemed to do the trick. He looked pissed off and scared at the same time."

Billy paused for a drink of water. Both hands trembled as he drew the glass to his lips. "Vick told me he was going to stop Al from fucking up everyone around him. I didn't want to know what he meant, but it should have been clear when he took a gun out of a drawer. He said something about it being 'stripped', meaning no serial, no registration. Got it from someone he knew . . . someone he had something *on*.

"Guess I didn't think it through, huh? Could have been he was just going to scare Al or rough him up at gunpoint or something. How could I have been so stupid? I didn't really think he'd shoot him. Or did I? Can you read minds, Doc . . . or at least what's left of mine?"

CHAPTER 68

FIVE - SOUTH TOWER [18]

The pain in Vick Griffin's hand was a searing, blinding destroyer of common sense. As in all best laid plans, the unexpected—getting his finger broken—had occurred. The idea had been to make sure that Waters knew who was killing him, and of course, to make sure he was dead this time. Then the final task, to push the cart out the door as if everything was normal. But the plan required a new ending: getting out now and leaving the cart behind.

It was done. No critically injured man could last that long under a pillow; Al Waters was history. Griffin knew he needed medical attention before he passed out. If he could just get to the ER, someone could get him something strong for the pain. He went to the cart and pulled out the towel-wrapped gun.

Can't leave this here. And the damn cart will slow me down.

He stuck the towel and gun under his left arm and headed out.

Officer Poole was standing, stretching, only a few feet from the door. "Hey, buddy, what's up?" he said, as the sweat-bathed man in green came out the door.

"Nothing," he mumbled. "Need to . . . to get, uh . . ."

"Hey, hold up there, pal," said Poole as Griffin headed down the hall. "What's the hurry?"

Griffin turned and pushed through the exit door to his right, screaming in pain as his broken finger smashed against metal.

Poole rushed to the door, gun in hand. "Stop. Stop. NOW," he yelled with all the power of his training arising in his voice. Griffin, almost down to the fourth-floor landing, slipped and reeled backward on the last stair as he turned to face the cop. As he instinctively raised his hand to shield himself from the policeman's pointed gun, the towel fell from under his arm and the gun clattered to the floor. Spontaneously, he reached down to retrieve it, and lifted the weapon upward.

Oh God, I'm an idiot.

For the first time away from the target range, Stanley Poole fired his weapon, twice, with no hesitation. His guitarist's hands were strong and steady, and fear had no effect on his accuracy, as each bullet ripped through Vick Griffin's heart.

CHAPTER 69

FINAL CHORD

Billy Crothers sat quietly for a few moments, awash in a flood of flashbacks. As he submerged into memories of a life filled with more pain than joy, he was briefly able to allow the happier times to sooth his tormented heart. A single thought rudely pulled the plug on his peace, draining the warmth, leaving him naked and shivering against the cold reality of what had to be said.

"Yeah, Doc. Vick, Vickie . . . whatever. Turns out he wanted revenge on Al real bad."

The doctor nodded and said, "And a police officer killed Vick Griffin after he'd finished the murder with a pillow in the hospital room, correct? It was never understood why this person would have killed Al Waters. But now, with what you've explained, the motive is clear."

"Doc, that stinking she-male was as phony a killer as he was a woman. After he didn't get it done with the gun . . . son of a bitch was about as accurate as spit in a hurricane . . . he had the idea of finishing it when Al was sent to Broward General where he figured he could get at him because he worked there. Sort of seemed like it was *meant* to be. Then he actually screwed up the deal for the second time . . . when he tried to smother a man who's spent his life developing breath control.

"But here's the saddest, stupidest, most fucked up part of the whole thing: I knew what Vick was planning that night, 'cause he called and told me. And I tried to argue him out of it, but he hung up on me, and wouldn't answer when I tried to call him back.

"Yeah, I know I had set the wheels in motion for the whole thing to happen. It was on me. When I first set up the deal with Vick I was in a real confused state after what Al had done, and I was drinking and drugging a ton again because of it all. My head was exploding with hate, and what's left

465

of my busted old heart just fucking *had* to have revenge. But after Vick failed with the gun, I realized how crazy the whole thing was. Al was my friend, my only real friend ever, I guess. Maybe the only reason I'm even alive is 'cause of him.

"After Vick messed up his first attempt I knew I had to do something. It was going to be kind of a second chance, like all the second chances Al had given me over the years. So I went there, Doc, to the hospital, and sat in the visitors' lounge across the hall from Al's room. Was waiting for Vick to show up, and I was going to do something to stop him; either talk to him if I could, or just give him up to the fuzz. I actually rapped with that guard cop for a sec, when he came over looking for something to read. Been no sign of Vick yet, so I couldn't very well say anything then, right? I'd be in a pickle if I'd said anything, and then Vick didn't show.

"Anyway, what I didn't plan on, was fucking falling asleep while I was waiting. Yeah, I had a small hit of smack and a few shots of booze to keep me calm. Shouldn't have been enough to . . ."

Billy stopped and held his hands over his face, rubbing his eyes with his palms as if trying to erase the pain. "Doc, in the worst way ever, I let Al down again. I woke up to the hubbub when Vick ran out of the room and got chased by the cop. I hobbled in there and I could see that Al was breathing . . . not well, but he was still alive. When I got to the bed I tried to get the oxygen thing back on him, but he just pushed my hand away, Doc. His eyes were open, and he looked right at me. Didn't say anything, just looked at me and sort of smiled. I could tell he was in real bad shape, more than just physical. From what I'd heard, it looked like his playing days were over and I could see Al knew that too. Music was all he ever really had that he could love and trust, and now it was taken from him. I knew what he wanted, what he needed. Just like the way we played together all those years, we always knew what each other was thinking. I held his hand just for a minute. His breathing was getting real weak and raspy. And I told him I'd see him on stage at Carnegie Hall. Then I hummed a bit of 'Angel Eyes' as he slipped away. He loved that song . . ."

Billy began to cry again, uncontrollable sobs shaking him like a twig in an earthquake. Godzilla, startled by the outburst, scurried to his master's side. For one of the few times in his life Doctor Jason Davidson had no clear thoughts, no advice, no words at all. At the image of Billy's last moments with Al, he felt tears sneak into his own eyes, as he thought of the first admonition he'd given Al Waters about suicidal thoughts. This was a moment all therapists dread: when in spite of all apparent progress, a patient is lost. Although the doctor's professional mind-set would not—*could* not—allow him to accept blame, he was still a human being. All the certificates on his wall were no protection against the sorrow of this moment.

After a slow deep breath, the doctor said, "Billy, I assume you left before the STAT team arrived. Wouldn't they have been able to resuscitate Al?"

Billy spoke slowly, between deep breaths and continuing sobs. "Sure, they musta tried, Doc, but you should know, man, better than most. If someone really wants to die . . . they die."

"Yes, Billy, sometimes a heart breaks in more than one way."

♪ ♪ ♪

A calm settled over Billy once more as he said, "But hey, there's more yet. You are going to flip, man. There's even fucking more."

The doctor said nothing. How could there be more? Billy Crothers had engineered the death of his best friend, albeit regretfully, and had to live with that knowledge forever. With his frail constitution and lifetime of drug use, could he survive this physically, let alone emotionally?

"Doc, a few days ago Ginny looked me up again. She had something she had to tell me."

"Ginny . . . ? Again?"

"Yeah, Doc, she sat me down and we sucked back a bunch of wine, and then she broke me into so many pieces you could never find 'em all, let alone put 'em back. She told me that it had *all* been a lie."

"What was . . . ? Oh no, Billy, you mean—"

"Yeah, Doc. She'd made it all up about the DNA testing and stuff, just to punish Al. He had hurt her, and she was blind with revenge. Didn't care who she took along for that joy ride into hell. The only reason she told me and Stephanie that *Al* was her father was so Steph would hate him, and so would I. She had no idea how much that would have hurt me, 'cause she didn't know the details of all that history with Charlotte. And she hadn't factored in that one of us might go as far as I did, or what Vick Griffin would really do. She also didn't know how much she loved him herself, until it was too late. But . . . there was one other reason she had to tell me this."

"Billy, there cannot be anything else you can add to this 'now that could shock me."

"No, this ain't a shock at all. She actually did finally get real tests done, and they showed the truth all along was what we first thought. Steph is *my* kid."

"Oh my. Billy, have you told her yet?"

"I don't know how to tell her, Doc. It wouldn't make her feel any different about Al, would it? Because if you think about it, he slept with her even though he believed she was his daughter. I could never forgive him for that, but I *can* for what he did to me and Charlotte. I figured out after all these years that I can't blame Al for me losing her. I didn't have to go with him to New York. I chose to leave Montreal and I could have gone back.

"Al always knew I was a better musician than him, but one thing he always had over me was that Charlotte would have picked him in a flash if he'd tried to get her back. I guess I let him win that one by having us both lose her. Not so smart, *was* it?"

"Billy," said the doctor, "are you certain about this? If I may be so forward, I believe you should tell her, for the sake of her own healing."

"I'm thinking Stephanie can forgive him, Doc . . . *only* if she thinks of him as her father. Is that stupid? She sure needs to find peace in all this, and all I know for sure is, with this beautiful person I helped create, that I *have* made a difference in this stinking world after all. And for me, there's no better peace than that."

"I understand, Billy, but I still would beg you to reconsider, so that Stephanie knows you as her father. You say she wouldn't feel any different about Al either way, but is that really your decision to make? Don't you think she needs to know the truth? I don't mean about your part in Al's death. That's an entirely different issue. But I do believe she needs to know who her father is and has a chance to have a relationship with you with that perspective.

"Billy, you speak of her 'finding peace'. Well, I can assure you that she will have a difficult time with this if it is left unexplained. Right now she is under the terrible notion she has had a love affair with her biological father. Even though she might well rationalize her 'peace' by considering she was unaware of that fact at the time, this could be a devastating thing to live with. That's primarily why children who have been parentally abused, so often involuntarily completely repress the memories, to avoid the pain and guilt associated with them. In my professional opinion, your choices are to either tell her that you are her father, or at the very least, that Al wasn't."

"Sure, Doc, you're as right as righteous. But what's the rush? Plenty of time left for getting to it. After all, I know I'm destined to live a lotta years yet. Maybe as punishment, huh?" Billy's subdued attempt to cackle could not hide the real story told by his weary eyes.

As the doctor closed his notebook, he smiled and said, "Remember, you need to be honest with me. Let me put it this way, Billy. You feel you let Al down countless times and perhaps you did, but his love and respect for you allowed him to keep giving you more chances. Can you perhaps this time do that for yourself, and for Stephanie? Forgive me, but as *officially* wrong as it is for me to ask, would you please do that?"

Billy relaxed back into the cool leather of the couch, and almost immediately Godzilla was there next to him, plopping his head down onto his lap. The dog's heavy sigh seemed to embody Billy's emotions.

"Doc, I can sure see why Al liked you. And no offense, but you kinda remind me of him, the good part of him that is. Wish you could be there with me when I tell her."

"In a way, Billy, I will be. As will Al . . . as he always will, the *good* part of him. And, no offense taken, none whatsoever."

CODA

*T*here were the usual conflicts of sounds and purpose, as gentle jazz struggled through the clinking of glasses, scattered conversation, and occasional laughter from the sparse audience. Surviving this gauntlet of indifference, ragged remnants of melody arrived at the front door and escaped into the night—from orchestrated darkness to nature's own. Street noises, seagull squawks, and the moonless sky's infinite solitude swallowed up what remained of the notes—born, and gone so soon. There was no time to mourn them; the musicians had moved on. And no one else had noticed they'd lived at all.

The battered upright piano was "desafinado", slightly out of tune—had been for years—not quite "broke" enough to fix. Equally decrepit and less than upright, was the man playing it, his gnarled fingers coaxing notes from yellowed ivory, like a gentle lover trying hard to please. As the drummer brushed cymbals and snare with delicate swishing strokes, the bass player slumped over his instrument, holding its slender neck close to his cheek. He was the spine binding a book from scattered notes and rhythm, pulling simple patterns from the strings, and meaning from the madness.

Like portraits painted in smoke and sickly blue light, the faces of the musicians revealed nothing. The music was their story: new thoughts mixed with old, innovation born of habit—disappearing inexorably into the ether of spent ideas. Wasted on apathetic ears, it wove an ancient tale of love, fear, ecstasy, and despair into a tapestry: the fabric of their souls.

Barely visible in the shadows to the side of the stage sat a tenor saxophone, collared in its rusty stand like a dog, waiting with infinite patience. The funereal lighting hid the true face of the beast: dents, scant pitted remains of darkened lacquer, discolored mouthpiece, and pads in various degrees of decrepitude. Ugly to most, it might still be beautiful to someone who needed it to be—like a last-chance pickup at closing time, if tired eyes and whiskey's lies could work their magic once again.

From its solitude, you could almost hear the cold silent metal begging for someone to hold it, love it, and let it sing.

♪ ♪ ♪

"Isn't somebody gonna play that saxophone?" asked the man at the table nearest the stage.

The waitress grumbled, "Nope. I ain't even sure why it's here. Hell, as if I could ever understand these damned *musicians*." Surprising herself with the snap of resentment in that last word, she allowed a tiny smile to betray her stony demeanor. She glanced toward the stage and said, "Ask the old bugger up there."

The piano player, who had overheard the exchange, looked up from the keys through half-closed eyes and said, "You know, Dixie my darlin', you're always growlin' at me, but I can read between the lines. You ain't foolin' anyone. You love me . . . and that's *most* copacetic."

As sweet music continued to flow from his hands, he shut his eyes completely and sighed. Then, he lifted his head skyward and said, "Yeah, between the lines, between the years, careers, beers, tears . . . sometimes, you can find somethin' where you thought there was nothin'. Like that ol' horn there. It *is* bein' played, man . . . by someone who understood the silence in the melody . . . a true swingman. Him and Lenny are jamming with us, in the spaces between the notes. Can't you hear it . . . ?"

As he bowed his head back down to the piano, his cackle segued into a feeble cough which soon disappeared, like the world around him, into the music.

— END —

APPENDIX

A CD entitled *Swingman* was produced, composed, arranged, and performed by Joe Edmonds to complement this novel. Each song title is either a direct reference to a chapter, or character, or scene in the book. The idea was to capture the atmosphere and moods of the golden age of bebop and post-bop jazz, with most of the songs being composed as "contrafacts" based on popular standards. This form of composition has the writer taking the chord progression from a published song and writing a new melody on those chords, with some additions or amendments to better fit the new melody. This writing technique was a common practice with many jazz greats such as Charlie Parker, Dizzy Gillespie, Sonny Rollins, et al. To see what each of Joe's songs was inspired by, see the contrafact details list below.

For excerpts of the following songs, if you are reading *Swingman* in an e-reader, please click on this link: *Swingman* CD Page for entire list . . . or click on the individual links below.

Groovin' at the Vanguard

Losers' Lounge

Charlotte's Song

Blues for Joe B.

Simply Copacetic

Waltz for Wendy

Tears for George

Rhythmajig

Paseo en la Playa

Nora

Swingman

Print edition readers: please go to www.joeedmonds.ca
for excerpts and information on how to acquire CDs.

CONTRAFACT DETAILS

Original material from the "Swingman" CD, and the
songs from which Joe Edmonds' tunes are "built".

Groovin' at the Vanguard
(Autumn Leaves - Joseph Kosma)

Losers' Lounge
(Basic minor blues form, popular with John Coltrane and many others)

Charlotte's Song
(Angel Eyes - Matt Dennis)

Blues for Joe B.
(Basic blues similar to Charlie Parker's writing style)

Simply Copacetic
(Modal, mostly Dorian, mix of bebop and post-bop style licks)

Waltz for Wendy
(Moon River - Henry Mancini)

Tears for George
(Song for my Father - Horace Silver)

Rhythmajig
(I've Got Rhythm - George Gershwin)

Paseo en la Playa
(Caravan - Juan Tizol)

Nora
(Blue Moon - Richard Rodgers)

Swingman
(Mr. PC - John Coltrane)

CPSIA information can be obtained at www.ICGtesting.com
Printed in the USA
LVOW07s2136260116

471926LV00002B/67/P